JOHN SANDFORD

THREE
COMPLETE
NOVELS

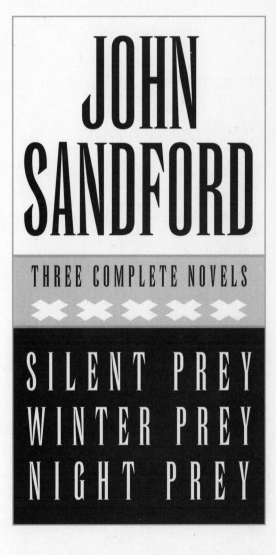

JOHN SANDFORD

THREE COMPLETE NOVELS

SILENT PREY
WINTER PREY
NIGHT PREY

G. P. PUTNAM'S SONS   NEW YORK

G. P. Putnam's Sons
Publishers Since 1838
a member of
Penguin Putnam Inc.
375 Hudson Street
New York, NY 10014

Library of Congress Cataloging-in-Publication Data

Sandford, John, date.
   [Novels. Selections]
      p.   cm.
      Contents: Silent prey — Winter prey — Night prey.
      ISBN 0-399-14191-X
      1. Davenport, Lucas (Fictitious character)—Fiction.   2. Private
   investigators—Minnesota—Minneapolis—Fiction.   3. Detective and
   mystery stories, American.   4. Minneapolis (Minn.)—Fiction.
   I. Title.
   PS3569.A516A6   1996   96-7278   CIP
   813'.54—dc20

Printed in the United States of America
10   9   8   7   6   5   4   3   2

Book design by M.J. DiMassi

CONTENTS

A THOUGHT SPARKED in the chaos of Bekker's mind.
The jury.

He caught it, mentally, like a quick hand snatching a fly from midair.

Bekker slumped at the defense table, the center of the circus. His vacant blue eyes rolled back, pale and wide as a plastic baby-doll's, wandering around the interior of the courtroom, snagging on a light fixture, catching on an electrical outlet, sliding past the staring faces. His hair had been cut jailhouse short, but they had let him keep the wild blond beard. An act of mercy: the beard disguised the tangled mass of pink scar tissue that crisscrossed his face. In the middle of the beard, his pink rosebud lips opened and closed, like an eel's, damp and glistening.

Bekker looked at the thought he'd caught: *The jury.* Housewives, retirees, welfare trash. His *peers*, they called them. A ridiculous concept: he was a doctor of medicine. He stood at the top of his profession. He was *respected.* Bekker shook his head.

Understand . . . ?

The word tumbled from the judge-crow's mouth and echoed in his mind. "Do you understand, Mr. Bekker?"

What . . . ?

The idiot flat-faced attorney pulled at Bekker's sleeve: "Stand up."

What . . . ?

The prosecutor turned to stare at him, hate in her eyes. The hate touched him, reached him, and he opened his mind and let it flow back. *I'd like to have you for five minutes, good sharp scalpel would open you up like a goddamn oyster: zip, zip. Like a goddamn clam.*

The prosecutor felt Bekker's interest. She was a hard woman; she'd put six hundred men and women behind bars. Their petty threats and silly pleas no longer interested her. But she flinched and turned away from Bekker.

What? Standing? Time now?

Bekker struggled back. It was so hard. He'd let himself go during the trial.

He had no interest in it. Refused to testify. The outcome was fixed, and he had more serious problems to deal with. Like survival in the cages of the Hennepin County Jail, survival without his medicine.

But now the time had come.

His blood still moved too slowly, oozing through his arteries like strawberry jam. He fought, and simultaneously fought to hide his struggle.

Focus.

And he started, so slowly it was like walking through paste, trudging back to the courtroom. The trial had lasted for twenty-one days, had dominated the papers and the television newscasts. The cameras had ambushed him, morning and night, hitting him in the face with their intolerable lights, the cameramen scuttling backward as they transferred him, in chains, between the jail and the courtroom.

The courtroom was done in blond laminated wood, with the elevated judge's bench at the head of the room, the jury box to the right, tables for the prosecution and defense in front of the judge. Behind the tables, a long rail divided the room in two. Forty uncomfortable spectator's chairs were screwed to the floor behind the rail. The chairs were occupied an hour before arguments began, half of them allotted to the press, the other half given out on a first-come basis. All during the trial, he could hear his name passing through the ranks of spectators: *Bekker Bekker Bekker.*

The jury filed out. None of them looked at him. They'd be secluded, his *peers,* and after chatting for a decent interval, they'd come back and report him guilty of multiple counts of first-degree murder. The verdict was inevitable. When it was in, the crow would put him away.

The black asshole in the next cell had said it, in his phony street dialect: "They gon slam yo' nasty ass into Oak Park, m'man. You live in a motherfuckin' cage the size of a motherfuckin' refrigerator wit a TV watching you every move. You wanta take a shit, they watchin' every move, they makin' movies of it. Nobody ever git outa Oak Park. It is a true motherfucker."

But Bekker wasn't going. The thought set him off again, and he shook, fought to control it.

Focus . . .

He focused on the small parts: The gym shorts biting into the flesh at his waist. The razor head pressed against the back of his balls. The Sox cap, obtained in a trade for cigarettes, tucked under his belt. His feet sweating in the ridiculous running shoes. Running shoes and white socks with his doctor's pinstripes— he looked a fool and he knew it, hated it. Only a moron would wear white socks with pinstripes, but white socks *and* running shoes . . . no. People would be laughing at him.

He could have worn his wing tips, one last time—a man is innocent until proven guilty—but he refused. They didn't understand that. They thought it was another eccentricity, the plastic shoes with the seven-hundred-dollar suit. They didn't know.

Focus.

Everyone was standing now, the crow-suit staring, the attorney pulling at his sleeve. And here was Raymond Shaltie . . .

"On your feet," Shaltie said sharply, leaning over him. Shaltie was a sheriff's deputy, an overweight time-server in an ill-fitting gray uniform.

"How long?" Bekker asked the attorney, looking up, struggling to get the words out, his tongue thick in his mouth.

"Shhh . . ."

The judge was talking, looking at them: ". . . standing by, and if you leave your numbers with my office, we'll get in touch as soon as we get word from the jury . . ."

The attorney nodded, looking straight ahead. He wouldn't meet Bekker's eyes. Bekker had no chance. In his heart, the attorney didn't want him to have a chance. Bekker was nuts. Bekker *needed* prison. Prison forever and several days more.

"How long?" Bekker asked again. The judge had disappeared into her chambers. *Like to get her, too.*

"Can't tell. They'll have to consider the separate counts," the attorney said. He was court-appointed, needed the money. "We'll come get you . . ."

Pig's eye, they would.

"Let's go," said Shaltie. He took Bekker's elbow, dug his fingertips into the nexus of nerves above Bekker's elbow, an old jailer's trick to establish dominance. Unknowingly, Shaltie did Bekker a favor. With the sudden sharp pulse of pain, Bekker snapped all the way back, quick and hard, like a handclap.

His eyes flicked once around the room, his mind cold, its usual chaos squeezed into a high-pressure corner, wild thoughts raging like rats in a cage. Calculating. He put pain in his voice, a childlike plea: "I need to go. . . ."

"Okay." Shaltie nodded. Ray Shaltie wasn't a bad man. He'd worked the courts for two decades, and the experience had mellowed him—allowed him to see the human side of even the worst of men. And Bekker was the worst of men.

But Bekker was nevertheless human, Shaltie believed: *He that is without sin among you, let him cast the first stone.* . . . Bekker was a man gone wrong, but still a man. And in words that bubbled from his mouth in a whiny singsong, Bekker told Shaltie about his hemorrhoids. Jail food was bad for them, Bekker said. All cheese and bread and pasta. Not enough roughage. He had to go. . . .

He always used the bathroom at noon, all through the ten days of the trial. Raymond Shaltie sympathized: he'd had them himself. Shaltie took Bekker by the arm and led him past the now empty jury box, Bekker shuffling, childlike, eyes unfocused. At the door, Shaltie turned him—docile, quiet, apparently gone to another world—and put on the handcuffs and then the leg chains. Another deputy watched the process, and when Bekker was locked up, drifted away, thinking of lunch.

"Gotta go," Bekker said. His eyes turned up to Ray Shaltie.

"You'll be okay, you'll be okay," Shaltie said. Shaltie's tie had soup stains on it, and flakes of dandruff spotted his shoulders: an oaf, Bekker thought. Shaltie led Bekker out of the courtroom, Bekker doing the jailhouse shuffle, his legs restricted to a thirty-inch stride. Behind the courtroom, a narrow hallway led to an internal stairway, and from there, to a holding cell. But to the left, through a service door, was a tiny employees-only men's room, with a sink, a urinal, a single stall.

Shaltie followed Bekker into the men's room. "Now, you're okay . . ." A warning in his voice. Ray Shaltie was too old to fight.

"Yes," Bekker said, his pale-blue eyes wandering in their sockets. Behind the wandering eyes, his mind was moving easily now, the adrenaline acting on his brain like a dose of the purest amphetamine. He turned, lifted his arms up and back, thrusting his wrists at Shaltie. Shaltie fitted the key, uncuffed the prisoner: Shaltie was breaking the rules, but a man can't wipe himself if he's wearing handcuffs. Besides, where would Bekker go, high up here in the government building, with the leg chains? He couldn't run. And his wildly bearded face was, for the moment at least, the most recognizable face in the Cities.

Bekker shuffled into the stall, shut the door, dropped his trousers, sat down. Eyes sharp now, focused. They used disposable safety razors in the jail, Bics. He'd broken the handle off one, leaving only the head and a stub, easy to hide during the shakedowns. When he'd had a chance, he'd burned the stub with a match, rounding the edges, to make it more comfortable to wear. This morning he'd taped it under his balls, fixed with the end of a Band-Aid. Now he peeled the razor off himself, pulled the remaining tape off the razor, and began hacking at his beard.

He'd grown the beard to cover his furrowed face. Bekker, once so beautiful, the possessor of a classic Nordic face, a pale, uninflected oval with rose lips, had been beaten into a grotesque gnome, torn to pieces and only poorly repaired. *Davenport. Get Davenport.* The fantasy seized him: opening Davenport, using the knife to peel the face, lifting the skin off inch by inch. . . .

He fought it: fantasies were for the lockup. He forced Davenport out of his mind and continued shaving, quickly, raggedly, the razor scraping over his dry skin. The pain prompted a groan. Outside the stall, Shaltie winced.

" 'Bout done in there?" Shaltie called. The bathroom smelled of ammonia, chlorine, urine, and wet mops.

"Yes, Ray." Bekker dropped the razor in his jacket pocket, then worked on the toilet-paper holder. Originally, it had been held in place with four screws. He'd removed and flushed two of them during the first three days of the trial, and had worked the other two loose. He'd actually had them out the day before, to make sure the holder would pull free. It had. Now he removed the screws one last time, dropped them in the toilet and eased the paper-holder free from the wall. When he grasped it by the roller, it fit his hand like a steel boxing glove.

"Okay now, Ray." Bekker stood, pulled his pants up, pulled off his jacket, dropped the coat over the iron fist, flushed the toilet. Took a breath. Put his head down, as though he were looking at his fly. Opened the door. Shuffled forward.

Shaltie was waiting with the cuffs: jowly, freckled, slow on the uptake. "Turn around. . . ."

Seeing Bekker's face, realizing: "Hey . . ."

Bekker was half-turned, wound up. He dropped the jacket, his right hand whipping like a lash, his mouth open, his white teeth flashing in the fluorescence. Shaltie lurched back, tried to cover with a hand. Too late, too late. The stainless-steel club hit him above the ear: Shaltie went down, cracking the back of his head on the porcelain sink as he fell.

And then Bekker was on him, lifting the steel fist, smashing it down, lifting it, feeling Shaltie's skull crack, the blood spatter.

Hit hit hit hit . . .

The synapses of Bekker's brain lit with the static sparks. He fought it, fought for control, but it was hard, the smell of fresh blood in his nose. He stopped swinging, found his left hand on Shaltie's throat. Pulled the hand away, half stood, brain not quite right: He said aloud, shushing himself, "Shhh. Shhhhhh," finger to his lips.

He straightened. His blood was running like water now, like steam, filling him. Now what? Door. He hobbled to the door, flipped the catch. Locked. Good. He went back to Shaltie, who was supine on the tile floor, blowing blood bubbles through his torn nose. Bekker had watched the deputy handle his keys, and the keys had gone in Shaltie's right pocket. . . . He found them, popped the locks on the leg chains. Free. *Free.*

Stop. He brought himself back, looked in the mirror. His face was a mess. He retrieved the razor from his jacket pocket, splashed water and liquid soap on his face and raked the razor across it. Listened to Shaltie, breathing, a gargling moan. Shaltie's head lay in a puddle of blood, and Bekker could smell it.

Bekker threw the razor in a trash basket, turned, stooped, caught Shaltie under the shoulders, dragged him to the toilet stall, sat him on the toilet and propped him against the wall. Shaltie made a snoring sound and more blood bubbled from his nose. Bekker ignored him. Not much time.

He stripped off his suit pants, put the Sox hat on his head, and used the pants to wipe up the blood on the floor. When he finished, he threw the pants, jacket, shirt and tie over Shaltie's body. Checked himself in the mirror: green tank top, red shorts, gym shoes, hat. A jogger. The face was bad, but nobody had seen him close up, without a beard, for weeks. A few of the cops would know him, a couple of lawyers. But with any luck, they wouldn't be looking at joggers.

Davenport. The thought stopped him. If Davenport was out there, had come to see the verdict, Bekker was a dead man.

No help for that. He threw off the thought, took a breath. Ready. He stepped inside the stall with Shaltie, locked it, dropped to his back, slid under the door, stood up again.

"Motherfucker." He said it out loud, had learned it in jail: the standard, all-purpose curse. He dropped back on the floor, slid halfway under the stall, groped for Shaltie's wallet. Found it, checked it. Twelve dollars. One credit card, a Visa. Not good. Money could be a problem. . . . He slipped the wallet into his underpants, went to the door, listened.

Could hear Shaltie breathing, bubbling. Bekker thought about going back into the stall, strangling him with his belt. All the humiliations of the past week, the torture when they took away his chemicals . . . Not enough time. Time was hurting him now. Had to move.

He left Shaltie, living, turned the lock knob, peered into the hallway. The internal corridor was empty. Went to the next door—public hall. Half-dozen people, all down at the public end, near the elevators, talking. He wouldn't have to walk past them. The stairs were the other way: he could see the exit sign, just beyond the fire hose.

Another breath. And move. He stepped out into the hall, head down. A lunchtime bureaucrat-jogger on his way outside. He walked confidently down the hall to the stairs, away from the elevators. Waiting for a shout. For someone to point a finger. For running feet.

He was in the stairway. Nobody took the stairs, not from this high up. . . .

He ran down, counting the floors. As he passed six, a door slammed somewhere below and he heard somebody walking down ahead of him. He padded softly behind, heard another door open and shut, and stepped up the pace again. At the main level, he stopped and looked out. Dozens of people milled through the reception area. Okay. This was the second floor. He needed one more. He went down another level, and found an unmarked steel door. He pushed it open. He was outside, standing on the plaza. The summer sun was brilliant, the breeze smelled of popcorn and pigeons. A woman sitting on a bench, a kid next to her. She was cutting an apple with a penknife, her kid waiting for the apple.

Head down, Bekker jogged past her. Just another lunchtime fitness freak, weaving through the traffic, knees up, sweating in the sunshine.

Running like a maniac.

LUCAS WHIPPED DOWN the asphalt backroads of Wisconsin, one hand on the wheel, one on the shifter, heel-and-toe on the corners, sunlight bouncing off the Porsche's dusty windshield. He slow-footed across the St. Croix bridge at Taylor's Falls into Minnesota, looking for cops, then dropped the hammer again, headed south into the sun and the Cities.

He caught Highway 36 west of Stillwater, the midday traffic sparse and torpid, pickups and station wagons clunking past the cow pastures, barns and cattail sloughs. Eight miles east of Interstate 694, he blew the doors off a red Taurus SHO. Clear road, except for the occasional crows picking at roadkill.

His eyes dropped to the speedometer. One hundred and seven.

What the fuck are you doing?

He wasn't quite sure. The day before, he'd rolled out of his lake cabin late in the afternoon and driven eighty miles north to Duluth. To buy books, he thought: there were no real bookstores in his corner of Wisconsin. He'd bought books, all right, but he'd wound up drinking beer in a place called the Wee Blue Inn at eight o'clock in the evening. He'd been wearing a dark-blue dress shirt under a silk jacket, khaki slacks, and brown loafers, no socks. A laid-off ore-boatman, drunk, had taken exception to the bare feet, and for one happy instant, before the barkeeps arrived, it had looked like the boatman would take a swing.

He needed a bar fight, Lucas thought. But he didn't need what would come afterward, the cops. He took his books back to the cabin, tried to fish the next day, then gave it up and headed back to the Cities, driving as fast as he knew how.

A few miles after blowing off the SHO, he passed the first of the exurban ramblers, outriders for the 'burbs. He groped in the glove box, found the radar detector, clipped it to the visor and plugged it into the cigarette-lighter socket as the Porsche screamed down the cracked pavement. He let his foot settle further; punched up the radio, Cities-97. Little Feat was playing hard hot boogie, "Shake Me Up," the perfect sound to accompany a gross violation of the speed limit.

The interstate overpass flicked past and the traffic got thicker. A hundred and eighteen. Hundred and nineteen. A stoplight he'd forgotten about, looming suddenly, with a blue sedan edging into a right-on-red turn. Lucas went left, right, left, heel-and-toe, blowing past the sedan; and past a station wagon, for a split second catching at the periphery of his vision the surprised and frightened face of a blonde matron with a car full of blond kids.

The image fixed in his mind. Scared. He sighed and eased off the gas pedal, coasting. Dropped through a hundred, ninety, eighty. Across the northern sub-urbs of St. Paul, onto the exit to Highway 280. When he'd been a cop, he'd always been sneaking off to the lake. Now that he wasn't, now that he had time sitting on him like an endless pile of computer printout, he found the solace of the lake less compelling. . . .

The day was warm, sunshine dappling the roadway, playing games with cloud-shadows on the glass towers of Minneapolis to the west. And then the cop car.

He caught it in the rearview mirror, nosing out of Broadway. No siren. His eyes dropped to the speedometer again. Sixty. The limit was fifty-five, so sixty should be fine. Still, cops picked on Porsches. He eased off a bit more. The cop car closed until it was on his bumper, and in the rearview mirror he could see the cop talking into his microphone: running the Porsche's tags. Then the light bar came up and the cop tapped his siren.

Lucas groaned and rolled to the side, the cop fifteen feet off his bumper. He recognized him, a St. Paul cop, once worked with the Southwest Team. He used to come into the deli near Lucas' house. What was his name? Lucas dug through his memory. Kelly . . . Larsen? Larsen was out of the car, heavy face, sunglasses, empty-handed. No ticket, then. And he was jogging. . . .

Lucas shifted into neutral, pulled the brake, popped the door and swiveled in the seat, letting his feet fall on the shoulder of the road.

"Davenport, God damn it, I *thought* this was your piece of shit," Larsen said, thumping the Porsche's roof. "Everybody's looking for your ass. . . ."

"What . . . ?"

"Fuckin' Bekker blew out of the government center. He's knocked down two people so far."

"What?" Lucas Davenport: deep summer tan, jagged white scar crossing his eyebrow, khaki short-sleeved shirt, jeans, gym shoes. A surge of adrenaline almost took his breath away.

"Two of your buddies are laying up at your place. They think he might be coming for you," Larsen said. He was a large man who kept hitching up his belt, and peering around, as though he might spot Bekker sneaking through a roadside ditch.

Lucas: "I better get my ass down there. . . ."

"Go." Larsen thumped the top of the car again.

Back on the highway, Lucas picked up the car phone and poked in the direct-dial number for the Minneapolis cops. He was vaguely pleased with himself: he didn't need the phone, rarely used it. He'd installed it the week after he'd bought the gold-and-steel Rolex that circled his wrist—two useless symbols of his freedom from the Minneapolis Police Department. Symbols that he was doing what every cop supposedly wanted to do, to go out on his own, to *make* it. And now the business was snaking off in new directions, away from games, into computer simulations of police tactical problems. Davenport Games & Simulations. With the growing sales, he might have to rent an office.

The switchboard operator said, "Minneapolis."

"Gimme Harmon Anderson," Lucas said.

"Is that you, Lucas?" the operator asked. Melissa Yellow Bear.

"Yeah." He grinned. Somebody remembered.

"Harmon's been waiting. Are you at home?"

"No, I'm in my car."

"You heard what happened?" Yellow Bear was breathless.

"Yes."

"You take care, honey. I'll switch you over. . . ."

A moment later, Anderson came on, and said without preamble, "Del and Sloan are at your place. Sloan got the key from your neighbor, but they're wasting their time. He won't be coming after this long. It's been three hours."

"How about Del's place? He and Bekker are relatives of some kind."

"We've got a couple of guys there, too, but he's hiding somewhere. He won't be out, not now."

"How did he—"

"Go on home and Sloan can fill you in," Anderson said, interrupting. "I gotta go. This goddamn place is a madhouse."

And he was gone. *Police work to do, no time for civilians.* Lucas got off at University Avenue, took it to Vandalia, across I-94 and down Cretin, then over to the tree-shaded river road. Brooding. *No time for Davenport.*

Feeling sorry for himself, knowing it.

Two blocks before he got to the house, he slowed, watching, then turned a block early. The neighborhood offered few places to hide, other than inside the houses. The yards were open, tree-filled, burning with color: crabapple blossoms and lines of tulips, banks of iris, pink peonies and brilliant yellow daffodils, and the odd patch of buttery dandelions that had somehow escaped the yard-service sprayers. The day was warm, and people were working in their yards or on their houses; a couple of kids in shorts shot baskets at a garage-mounted hoop. Bekker couldn't hide in the open yards, and breaking into a house would be tough. Too many people around. He turned a corner and idled down toward his house.

Lucas lived in what a real estate woman had once called a soft rambler: stone and clapboard, a fireplace, big trees, two-car garage. At the end of the asphalt drive, he slowed, punched the garage-door opener, and waited at the end of the driveway until the door was all the way up. A curtain moved in the front room.

When Lucas pulled into the garage, Sloan was waiting in the door between the house and the garage, hand in his jacket pocket. He was a thin man with high cheekbones and deep-set eyes. As Lucas got out of the car, Del drifted up behind Sloan, the butt of a compact 9mm pistol sticking out of his waistband. Del was older, with a face like sandpaper, a street burnout.

"What the hell happened?" Lucas asked as the garage door rolled down.

"An old-fuck deputy uncuffed him so he could take a shit," Sloan said. "Bekker'd been telling everybody that he had hemorrhoids and he always went to the can at the noon recess."

"Setting them up," Lucas said.

Del nodded. "Looks like it."

"Anyway, the jury went out and the deputy took him to the bathroom before hauling him down to the holding cell," Sloan continued. "Bekker unscrewed a steel toilet-paper holder from the wall of the stall. Came out of the stall and beat the shit out of the old guy."

"Dead?"

"Not yet, but he's leaking brains. He's probably paralyzed."

"I heard he hit two guys?"

"Yeah, but the other was later . . ." Del said, and explained. Witnesses waiting outside a courtroom had seen Bekker leave, without knowing until later who he was. Others saw him cross the government-center plaza, running past the lunchtime brown-baggers, through the rafts of pigeons, heading down the street in his shorts. "He went about ten blocks, to a warehouse by the tracks, picked up a piece of concrete-reinforcement rod, went in the warehouse and whacked a guy working at the dispatch desk. A clerk. Took his clothes and his wallet. That's where we lost him."

"The clerk?"

"He's fucked up."

"I'm surprised Bekker didn't kill him."

"I don't think he had time," Del said. "He's in a hurry, like he knows where he's going. That's why we came here. But it don't feel right anymore, the longer I think about it. You scare the shit out of him. I don't think he'd take you on."

"He's nuts," said Lucas. "Maybe he would."

"Whatever, you got a carry permit?" asked Sloan.

"No."

"We'll have to fix you up if we don't get him. . . ."

THEY DIDN'T GET HIM.

Lucas spent the next forty-eight hours checking old sources, but nobody seemed much inclined to talk to him, not even the cops. Too busy.

He brought a Colt Gold Cup .45 up from the basement gun safe, cleaned it, loaded it, kept it under the bed on a book. During the day, he carried it hidden in the Porsche. He enjoyed the weight of the gun in his hand and the headache-making smell of the gun-cleaning solvent. He spent an hour in a Wisconsin gravel pit, shooting two boxes of semi-wadcutters into man-sized silhouettes.

Then, two days after Bekker broke out of the courthouse, neighbors found the body of Katherine McCain. She'd been an antiques dealer and a friend of Bekker's wife, and she'd had the Bekkers to a party six or eight weeks before Bekker's wife had been murdered. Bekker knew the house and knew she lived alone. He'd been waiting when she came home, and killed her with a hammer. Before he left in her car, he'd used a knife to slash her eyes, so her ghost couldn't watch him from the other world.

And then he disappeared.

McCain's car was eventually found in an airport parking lot in Cleveland, Bekker long gone. On the day the car was found, Lucas put the .45 back in the gun safe. He never got the carry permit. Sloan forgot, and then after a while, it didn't seem important.

Lucas had temporarily gone off women, and found it hard to focus on the idea of a date. He tried fishing, played golf every day for a week. No good. His life, he thought with little amusement, was like his refrigerator—and his refrigerator contained a six-pack of light beer, three cans of diet caffeine-free Coke, and a slowly fossilizing jar of mustard.

At night, unable to sleep, he couldn't get Bekker out of his head. Couldn't forget the taste of the hunt, of closing in, of cornering him . . .

He missed it. He didn't miss the police department, with its meetings and its brutal politics. Just the hunt. And the pressure.

Sloan called twice from Minneapolis, said it looked like Bekker was gone. Del called once, said they'd have to get a beer sometime.

Lucas said *yeah*.

And waited.

Bekker was a bad penny.

Bekker would turn up.

3

L OUIS CORTESE WAS DYING.
A brilliant floodlight lit his waxy face and the blood on his cheeks, and emphasized the yellow tint in his eyes. His lips were twisted, like those of an imp in a medieval painting.

Bekker watched. Touched a switch, heard the camera shutter fire. He could feel death swooping down on them, in the little room, in the lights, as Louis Cortese's life drained into a plastic jug.

BEKKER'S BRAIN WAS a calculator, an empty vessel, a tangle of energy, a word processor, and an expert anatomist. But never more than one thing at a time.

Three months in the Hennepin County Jail had changed him forever. The jailers had taken away his chemicals, boiled his brain, and broken forever the thin electrochemical bonds that held his mind together.

In jail, lying in his cell in his rational-planner mode, he'd visualized his brain as an old-fashioned Lions Club gumball machine. When he put in a penny, he got back a gumball—but he never knew in advance what color he'd get.

The memory of Ray Shaltie, of the escape, was one color, a favorite flavor, rattling down the payoff chute of his psyche. When he got it, it was like a wide-screen movie with overpowering stereo sound, a movie that froze him in his tracks, wherever he was. He was *back there* with Ray Shaltie, with the steel fist, smashing. . . .

BEKKER, REAL TIME.
He sat in a chromed-steel chair and watched Cortese's death throes, his eyes moving between the monitor screens and the dying subject's face. A clear plastic tube was sewn into Cortese's neck, piping the blood from his carotid artery to an oversized water jug on the floor. The blood was purple, the color of cooked beets, and Bekker could smell it, his fine nostrils twitching with the scent. On the EKG, Cortese's heart rate soared. Bekker trembled. Cortese's consciousness was moving outward, expanding, joining with . . . what?

Well. Nothing, maybe.

Cortese's . . . essence . . . might be nothing more than a bubble reaching the top of a cosmic glass of soda water, expanding only to burst into oblivion. The pressure of the thought made Bekker's eyebrow jump uncontrollably, twitching, until he put a hand to his forehead to stop it.

There *had to be* something beyond. That he himself might just blink out . . . No. The thought was insupportable.

Cortese convulsed, a full-body rictus throwing him against the nylon restraining straps, his head cranking forward, his eyes bulging. Air squeezed from his lungs, past the elaborate gag, a hoarse bubbling release. He was looking at nothing: nothing at all. He was beyond vision. . . .

The alarm tone sounded on the blood-pressure monitor, then on the EKG, twin tones merging into one. With his left hand still clapped to his forehead, restraining the unruly eyebrow, Bekker turned toward the monitors. Cortese's heart had stopped, blood pressure was plummeting toward zero. Bekker felt the large muscles of his own back and buttocks tighten with the anticipation.

He looked at the EEG, the brain-wave monitor. A jagged, jangled line just seconds before, it began flattening, flattening . . .

He felt Cortese go: could feel the *essence* go. He couldn't measure it—not yet—but he could feel it. He bathed in the feeling, clutched at it; fired a half-dozen photos, the motor drives going *bzz-whit, bzz-whit* behind his head. And finally the magic *something* slipped away. Bekker jumped to his feet, frantic to hold on. He leaned over Cortese, his eyes four inches from the other's. There was something about death and the eyes. . . .

And then Cortese was gone, beyond Bekker's reach. His body, the shell of his personality, went slack beneath Bekker's hands.

The power of the moment spun Bekker around. Breathing hard, he stared at a reflection of himself in a polished stainless-steel cabinet. He saw himself there a dozen times a day, as he worked: the raw face, the sin face, he called it, the cornrows of reddened flesh where the gunsights had ripped through him. He said in a small, high voice: "Gone."

But not quite. Bekker felt the pressure on his back; his spine stiffened, and a finger of fear touched him. He turned, and the dead man's eyes caught him and held him. They were open, of course. Bekker had carefully trimmed away the eyelids to ensure they would remain that way.

"Don't," he said sharply. Cortese was mute, but the eyes were watching.

"Don't," Bekker said again, louder, his voice cracking. Cortese was watching him.

Bekker snatched a scalpel from a stainless-steel tray, stepped to the head of the table, leaned over the body and slashed at the eyes. He was expert: it only took a second. He carved the eyes like boiled eggs, and the vitreous aqua leaked down Cortese's dead cheeks like jellied tears.

"Good-bye," Bekker said dreamily. The ruined eyes were no longer threatening. A gumball dropped, and Bekker went away. . . .

THICK STOPPED at the curb, rocking on his heels, waiting patiently for the light. Thin snapped a cigarette into the street, where it exploded in a shower of sparks. The cars went by in a torrent, battered Toyotas and clunking Fords, fender-bent Dodges, pickups and vans blocking the view ahead, trucks covered with graffiti, buses stinking up the streets with noxious diesel fumes, all rolling past like iron salmon headed upstream to spawn. Through all of it, the taxis jock-eyed for position, signaling their moves with quick taps on their horns, an amber warp to the woof of the street. New York was noise: an underground rum-ble of trains and steam pipes, a street-level clash of gears and motors and bad mufflers, a million people talking at once, uncounted air conditioners buzzing above it all.

All of it congealed in the heat.

"Too fuckin' hot," Thick said. And it was; he could feel it on his neck, in his armpits, on the soles of his feet. He glanced at Thin, who'd stopped at the curb beside him. Thin nodded but didn't answer. They were both wearing long-sleeved shirts with the sleeves rolled down to their wrists. Thin was a problem, and Thick didn't quite know what to do about it. Hadn't really known, he thought wryly, for almost forty years now. . . .

The walk sign flashed on and he and Thin crossed the street. A traffic-light pole, splattered with pigeon shit and encrusted with the grime of decades, sat on the corner. At the bottom, and up as high as a hand could reach, it was cov-ered with fading posters. Above that, two street signs were mounted at right an-gles to each other, a bus-stop sign faced the street, and a temporary traffic-diversion sign pointed an arrow to the left. Above all that, a spar went out to the traffic signal, and another supported a streetlight.

Oughta put one in a fuckin' museum someplace, just like that. Our own fuckin' totem poles . . .

"Dollar . . ." The woman on the sidewalk reached up at him, holding a dirty hand-lettered card: "Help me feed my children." Thick walked past, thinking that it was impossible that the woman had children. In her forties, perhaps, she was withered as a week-old carrot, her emaciated legs sprawled beneath her, her bare feet covered with open sores. Her eyes had a foggy-white glaze, not cataracts, but something else. She had no teeth at all, only dimples in gray gums, like the va-cant spots left by corn kernels popped from a cob.

"I read this book about Shanghai once, the way it was before World War Two," Thick said as they passed on. Thin looked straight ahead, not respond-ing. "The thing was, begging was a profession, you know? But an ordinary guy couldn't get any alms. You needed to be special. So they'd take kids and burn their eyes out or smash their arms and legs with hammers. They had to make them pitiful enough to get money in a whole city full of beggars. . . ."

Thin looked up at him, still saying nothing.

"So we're getting there, too," Thick said, looking back at the woman on the street. "Who's gonna give money to your average panhandler when you walk by something like that every day?" He half turned to look back at the woman.

"Dollar," the woman wailed, "Dollar . . ."

Thick was worried. Thin was talking about running out. He glanced at his partner. Thin's eyes were angry, fixed straight ahead. Thinking . . .

Thick was carrying a large, flat, cardboard box. It wasn't particularly heavy, but the shape was awkward, and he slowed to hitch it up under his arm.

"I wouldn't mind . . ." Thick started, then let it go. He reached up to scratch his face, but he was wearing thin, flesh-colored surgeon's gloves, and he couldn't effectively scratch. They moved along, quickly, to an apartment building across the street from the steak house. Thick had the key in his free hand and opened the door.

Thin said, "I can't do it."

"We gotta. Jesus Christ, if we don't we're fuckin' dead, all of us. . . ."

"Listen . . ."

"Off the street, off the street . . ."

Inside the door, the hall and landing were dimly lit by a yellow sixty-watt bulb. The stairs were immediately to the right, and Thick started up. Thin, undecided, looked back out at the street, then, reluctantly, because Thick was already moving, followed. At the top of the stairs, they stopped in the hallway for a moment and listened, then went to the front apartment and opened the door with a key. The only light in the apartment came through the yellowed shades on the front windows, from the street. The place smelled of dead air, old coffee grounds, and dry plants. The owners had been in Rome for a week, to see the Pope. They'd go to the Holy Land afterward. The Holy Land in July. They'd burn their brains out, if they had any, which they probably didn't, if they were going to the Holy Land in July.

Thin shut the door behind them and said, "Listen . . ."

"If you weren't going to do it, why'd you come this far?"

"Because you got us into it. I don't want you to get fucked up."

"Jesus . . ." Thick shook his head and stepped carefully through the dark room to the windows and lifted a shade. "Get the rifle."

"I'm not . . ."

"All right, I'll do it. Jesus, if that's the way you feel about it, go. Get the fuck out," Thick said, anger riding his voice. He was older than Thin by twenty-three years and two days, his face stamped with the cuts and gullies of a life on the street. He picked up the box he'd carried in. "Go."

Thin hesitated, watching. The box was five feet long by three wide, but only eight inches deep. It might have held a mirror, or even a painting, but it didn't— it held a Colt AR-15 with a flash suppressor, a twenty-shot magazine, a two-power light-gathering scope, and a laser sight. The weapon, manufactured as a semiautomatic, had been converted to selectible fire, semiauto or full auto, by a machinist in Providence.

Thick had spent an afternoon in the Adirondacks shooting plastic milk jugs from a perch high on the bank of a gully. The gallon-sized jugs closely simulated the kill zone of a man's chest from any angle. Thick used hand-loaded cartridges, and he was a very good shot. When hit by one of Thick's hot loads, the milk jugs literally exploded.

Thick used a penknife to cut the twine that held the box shut, stripped off a couple of pieces of tape, opened it, and took the weapon out of the sponge-rubber packing. New scope mounts weren't as delicate as those he'd grown up with, but there was no point in taking chances. He hadn't. A fully loaded magazine was packed with the weapon. Each cartridge had been polished with a chamois to eliminate fingerprints. Thick slapped the magazine home with his rubber-gloved hands.

"Get the couch," Thick said. "Hurry it up."

"No: he's a cop. If he wasn't a cop . . ."

"Bullshit." Thick went to the windows, looked out on the empty street, then unlocked one of them and carefully raised it until it was fully open. Then he turned, glanced at Thin, and picked up the rifle.

"You never had this problem before. . . ."

"The guy hasn't done anything. The others were scumbags. . . . This is a cop. . . ."

"He's a goddamn computer asshole cockroach and he's gonna put good guys in jail for doing what had to be done. And you know what happens if we get sent up? We're fuckin' dead, that's what. I personally doubt that I'd last a fuckin' week; if they come for me, I'm stickin' my goddamn pistol in my mouth, because I ain't goin'. . . ."

"Jesus . . ."

Thick, standing well back from the window, looked at the restaurant across the street through the low-powered scope. A Visa emblem was stuck to the window on the door, under the script of the restaurant's name and logo. Looking at the logo, the theme song from an old television show trickled through his head: *"Have gun, will travel" is the card of a man* . . .

He picked up the Visa sign in the scope, touched the laser switch with his thumb. A red dot bloomed on the sign. Thick had a head the size of a gasoline can, with small ears that in the semidark looked like dried apricots. "He's worse than the shooflies."

"He . . ." Thin's eyes went to the street, and Thick followed them. The restaurant door was opening.

"Wrong guy," Thin blurted.

"I know. . . ."

A man in a white tennis shirt and white shoes stood there, probing his gums with a plastic toothpick. The toothpicks were shaped like swords, Thin knew. They'd made a recon trip to the steak house the night before, to figure times and placements. The target always came in for the Friday special, New York strip with sour-cream baked potato and choice of draft beer. The man in the tennis shirt ambled down the street.

"Fuckin' faggot," said Thick. He flicked the switch on the laser sight and the red dot bloomed on the Visa sign.

BEKKER SIGHED.

All done.

He turned away from Cortese's body, his mind like a coil of concertina wire, tense, sharp, dangerous. He touched his shirt pocket: the pocket was empty. He stepped out of his room, with a touch of anxiety, and went to the old dresser where he kept his clothes. A half-handful of pills were scattered across the top of it, and he relaxed. Enough. He picked up several, developing a combo rush as he went, popped them into his mouth, savored the acrid bite, and swallowed. So good; but so few. He looked at the top of the dresser, at the pills there. Enough for another day, no more. He'd have to think about it—but later.

He went back into the workroom, killed the monitors, their green screens blanking out. Nothing to see anyway, just horizontal lines. Bekker ignored the body. Cortese was simply garbage, a matter of disposal.

But before the death . . . A new gumball dropped, and Bekker froze beside the worktable, his mind sliding away.

Louis Cortese had been dark-haired, seventy-one and one-half inches tall, one hundred and eighty-six pounds, and thirty-seven years old—all of it carefully recorded in Bekker's notebooks. He'd been a graduate in electrical engineering from Purdue University. Before Bekker'd cut off his eyelids, when Cortese had still been trying to ingratiate himself, still fending off the idea that he was about to die, he'd told Bekker that he was a Pisces. Bekker had only a vague idea what that meant, and he wasn't interested.

Cortese's body lay on a stainless-steel countertop, which had cost six hundred and fifty dollars at a restaurant-supply shop in Queens. The countertop, in turn, was fixed to an old wooden library table; Bekker'd had to cut down the legs to get the proper working height. Overhead, a rank of three shop lamps threw a flat, cold light on the table.

Because his research subjects would be alive, Bekker had fixed restraining rings to the table. A brown nylon strap was clipped to a ring just below Cortese's right armpit, and ran diagonally from the armpit across the chest between the nipple and the shoulder, to another ring behind the neck, then from behind the neck, back across the opposite side of the chest to another ring below the left armpit; it held Cortese like a full nelson. Additional straps crossed the body at the waist and knees and bound the wrists and ankles.

One of the hands was taped as well as bound: Bekker monitored blood pressure through a catheter placed in the radial artery, and the wrist had to be totally immobilized. Cortese's jaws were spread wide, held open by a hard-rubber cone: the subject could breathe through the nose, but not through the mouth. His screams, when he tried to scream, sounded like a species of humming, though not quite humming.

Mostly, he'd been as silent as a book.

At the head of the table, Bekker had stacked his monitoring equipment in what a discount stereo store had called a home entertainment center. The arrangement was pleasingly professional. The monitors measured body temperature, blood pressure, heartbeat, and brain-wave activity. He also had a neuro-intracranial pressure monitor, but hadn't used it.

The room around the equipment was also carefully finished: he'd worked on it for a week before he was satisfied. Scrubbed it with disinfectant. Installed an acoustic-tile ceiling and Formica wall panels in a smooth oyster-white finish. Put down the royal-blue carpet. Brought in the equipment. The monitors had been the hard part. He'd finally gotten them from Whitechurch, a dealer at

Bellevue. For two thousand in cash, Whitechurch had taken them out of a repair shop, first making sure they'd been fixed. . . .

Sigh.

One of the monitors was telling him something.

What was it? Hard to concentrate . . .

Body temperature, eighty-four degrees.

Eighty-four?

That was too low. He glanced at the clock. 9:07 . . .

He'd been gone again.

Bekker rubbed the back of his neck, disturbed. He would go away, sometimes for an hour. It never seemed to happen at critical times, but still: he should have recognized it, the sigh when he came back. When he went away, he always came back with a sigh. . . .

He stepped to the tape recorders, looked at the counters. They were slightly out of sync, one of them at 504, the other at 509. He rewound them to 200 and listened to the first.

"*. . . direct stimulus brings only a slight reaction, no more than one millimeter . . .*"

His own voice, hoarse with excitement. He turned off the first recorder, turned on the second. "*. . . no more than one-millimeter reflex in the iris followed by immediate release of . . .*"

He turned off the second one. The recorders were working fine. Identical Sonys, with battery backup in case of power failure, they were better than the ones he'd used at the University of Minnesota.

Bekker sighed, caught himself, looked quickly at the clock, afraid that he'd been away again. No. 9:09. He had to clean up, had to get rid of Cortese's body, had to process the Polaroid color-slide film in the cameras. And he had some ideas about the taking of the specimens, and those ideas should be noted. Many things to do. But he couldn't, not at just this moment. The PCP hadn't arrived, and he felt . . . serene. The session had been a good one.

Sigh.

He glanced at the clock, felt a tiny thrill of fear. Nine twenty-five. He'd been gone again, frozen in one place; his knees ached from the unmoving stance. It was happening too much. He needed more medication. Street cocaine was good, but not precise enough. . . .

Then: *Dink.*

Bekker turned his head. The intrusive sound came from a corner of his basement apartment. Almost a bell, but not quite. Instead of ringing, it simply struck once each time the old woman pushed the button.

Dink.

Bekker frowned, walked to the intercom, cleared his throat, and pressed the talk button. "Mrs. Lacey?"

"My hands hurt." Her voice was shrill and ragged. Old. She was eighty-three, hard of hearing, nearly blind in one eye. Her arthritis was bad and growing worse. "My hands hurt so much," she complained.

"I'll bring a pill . . . in a few minutes," Bekker said. "But there are only three left. I'll have to go out again tomorrow. . . ."

"How much?" she asked.

"Three hundred dollars . . ."

"My golly . . ." She seemed taken aback.

"It's very difficult to find these days, Mrs. Lacey," Bekker said. And it had been for decades. She knew that. Morphine had never been street-legal in her lifetime. Neither had her marijuana.

A FEW DAYS AFTER he'd taken the job as a live-in helper—the old woman's word, she didn't need bathroom assistance—he'd shown her a *Wall Street Journal* story about bank failures. She'd read it, nearly whimpering. She had her Social Security, she had her savings, some $370,000, and she had her building. If any of them broke down . . .

Edith Lacey had watched the old street women as they went by, pushing their shopping carts along the broken pavement, guarding their bundles of rags. She knew them, she said, although Bekker didn't believe her. She'd look out and make up stories about them. "Now that one, *she* once owned a grocery on Greenwich . . ."

Bekker suggested that she spread her cash among three or four unrelated banks, so more would be insured by the Federal Deposit Insurance Corporation.

"Uncertain times," he told her in his careful voice.

She'd talked to her only ambulatory friend about it. Bridget Land, who didn't like Bekker, had thought that spreading the money among banks would be a good idea. And she'd volunteered to go with them: "To make sure everything is on the up-and-up," she'd said, her eyes moving almost involuntarily toward Bekker. "At the banks, I mean."

They'd moved the money in a single day, the two old women nervously guarding the cashier's checks like mother hens. Edith Lacey carrying one inside her blouse, Bridget Land the other in a buttoned pocket, *just in case*. They'd focused so closely on the checks that neither had paid much attention to Bekker as he reviewed Edith's applications for new accounts. Bekker had simply checked the "yes" box that asked if the applicants wanted automatic-teller cards. He picked up the mail each afternoon; a week after they'd moved the money to the banks, he'd intercepted the automatic-teller codes, and a week after that, the cards themselves. The cards were each good for five hundred dollars a day. During the first month, Bekker worked the accounts almost daily, until he had twenty thousand in cash.

"Get fruit," the old woman ordered.

"I'll stop at MacGuire's," he said on the intercom.

"Apricots."

"Okay." He started to turn away.

"Be sure to get apricots. . . ."

"Yes," he snapped.

"You didn't get them last time. . . ."

He was seized by a sudden urge to go up and choke her: not the urge that took him to his subjects, but an almost human desire to choke the shit out of a common nag. "I'm sorry," he said, abjectly, hiding the sudden fury. "And I'll *try* to get your pills."

That would shut her up. . . .

BEKKER TURNED AWAY from the intercom and, through the dark living quarters, saw Cortese's body in the bright light flowing from the operating room. *Might as well do it now.*

From the kitchen, he brought a long roll of black polyethylene, sold as painter's dropcloth. He unrolled it beside the dissection table, used a scalpel to cut it to the right length, then unfolded it. Unstrapped the body. Pulled the catheter from the wrist, pulled the temperature probe. The temperature was down to seventy-nine. Cooling quickly.

Bodies are hard to manipulate, and Bekker, with much experience, didn't even try. He simply walked to the far side of the table and pushed. The body rolled out of the tray and fell on the plastic sheet with a meaty thwack. He walked back around the table, wrapped it, folded the extra length, tied it with clothesline. He took two extra loops at the waist, to use as a handle. He hauled the body through the living quarters and up the steps to the building's reinforced back door, struggling with it. Even when you didn't care if they were damaged, bodies were difficult. And Cortese had been hefty. He should go after smaller people. . . .

THE BACK DOOR of the Lacey building was hidden from the street by a lean-to structure, designed as a car shelter. He popped open the door, chain still on, and checked the lean-to. In the past, bums had sheltered there. Nothing but the Volkswagen, undisturbed. He dragged the body outside, and, with some difficulty, stuffed it into the passenger seat. When it was in, he stepped to the edge of the lean-to and peeked toward the street. Nobody. He went back inside, closed the door, and hurried down the stairs.

Bekker showered, shaved carefully, dressed, and put on his makeup. The process was intricate: The heavy base makeup covered his ruined face, but had to be carefully shaded into the clear skin at his temples without obvious lines. He took half an hour, working at it. He'd just finished when Mrs. Lacey rang again.

"What?" *Old hag* . . .

"My hands," she whined.

"I'm coming now," he said. Maybe he should kill her, he thought. He allowed himself to feel the pleasure of the idea. But then he'd have to explain her absence to Bridget Land. Though he *could* eliminate Land . . . But that led into a maze of unresolvable questions and dangers: Did Land have other friends, and did they know she came to see Edith Lacey? If Land disappeared, would others come looking for her?

Killing her would be dangerous. . . . No, he would kill neither of them. Not yet. Lacey was the perfect front and Land was, so far, only a modest inconvenience. Bekker, thinking about them, got a bottle of pills from his bureau, shook one into the palm of his hand, went to the bottom of the stairs, flicked a light switch, and went up.

The stairs emerged into the back part of the first floor, then curled and went up to the second and third floors. The first floor had once been a plumbing-parts supply business, but had been vacant for years. During the day, a murky green light filtered through from the street. At night, the grille-covered windows were simply dark panels on either side of the street door.

The old woman huddled on the second floor, where she'd lived with her two cats since her husband's death. The second floor reeked of the three of them: cooked carrots, dope, and cat piss. Bekker hated the cats. They knew what he was and watched him from shelves, their eyes glittering in the gloom, as the old woman huddled in front of the television, wrapped in her tie-dyed shawl.

The third floor had once been part of the living quarters, when Mrs. Lacey's husband was living, but now, like the first, was vacant.

Bekker climbed to the second floor, the smell of carrots and marijuana closing around him. "Mrs. Lacey?"

"In here." She was a small woman, with thick glasses that enlarged her rheumy blue eyes. Her hair, wiry and gray, clung close to her head. She had a small button nose and tiny round lips. She was wrapped in a housecoat. She had four of them, quilted, in different pastel colors. She was waiting in the big chair in the living room, facing the television. Bekker went to the kitchen, ran a glass of water and carried the pill out to her. A cat ran from under her chair and hid in the next room, looking back at Bekker with cruel eyes.

"This'll help. I'll get more tomorrow."

"Thank you." She took the pill and drank greedily from the glass.

"You have your pipe and lighter?"

"Yes."

"You have enough of your tea?"

"Yes, thank you kindly." She cackled. She'd washed out of the bohemian life of the forties, but she still had her tea.

"I'm going out for a while," he said.

"Be careful, it's dangerous this late. . . ."

Bekker left her in her chair and went back down the stairs and carefully checked the lean-to again. Nobody.

The Lacey building fronted on Greene Street. The buildings on either side ran all the way back to Mercer, but the Lacey building filled only half the lot. The back lot, overgrown weeds and volunteer sumac, was closed off with a ten-foot chain-link fence. Before Bekker had arrived, vandals and bums had been over and through it and had broken the lock on the gate. After Bekker had bought the Volkswagen, he'd had the fence fixed and a long twisty strand of razor wire laid along the top.

Now he backed the Volkswagen out of the lean-to, wheeled it to the fence, hopped out, opened the gate, drove through, stopped once more, and locked the gate again.

New York, he thought.

Bagels and lox / Razor wire and locks.

Bekker giggled.

"DOOR," SAID THICK. He was standing by the window, the M-15 at his shoulder.

On the street below, an old-fashioned Volkswagen, a Bug, zipped past. Thick, looking through the scope, ignored it. A man had stepped out on the street and paused. He had light hair, slightly mussed, and gold-rimmed glasses. Narrow shoulders. He was smiling, his lips moving, talking to himself. He was wearing a blue short-sleeved shirt, and jeans that were too long for his legs. He used his index fingers to push his glasses up on his nose.

"Yes," Thick grunted, his finger tightening on the trigger.

"No . . ." said Thin, taking two steps toward the window.

But a red dot bloomed on the target's chest. He may have had an instant to think about it; again, maybe not. The blast of the gun was deafening, the muzzle flash brighter than Thin had expected. The target seemed to jump back, and then began a herky-jerky dance. Thin had once seen a film showing Hitler dancing a jig after the fall of France. The man on the street looked like that for just a second or two: as though he were dancing a jig. The thunder rolled on, six shots, eight, twelve, quick, evenly spaced, the lightning flickering off their faces.

A little more than halfway through the magazine, Thick flicked the selector switch and unloaded the remaining cartridges in a single burst. The target was now flat on the sidewalk, and the burst of bullets splattered about his head like copper-jacketed raindrops.

Thin stood by the window, unspeaking.

"Go," said Thick. He dropped the rifle on the floor. "Hands."

With their gloved hands pressed to their faces, they walked down the hall to the back of the building, ran down a flight of stairs, along another hallway, then out a side door into an alley. The alley led away from the shooting.

"Don't run," said Thick as they emerged onto the street.

"Watch it," said Thin.

A Volkswagen lurched past, a Bug, catching them in its lights, their pale faces like street lamps in the night. It was the same car that had driven past the restaurant just before the computer fag came out on the sidewalk. . . .

WITH THE BODY beside him, Bekker was tense, cranked, watching for cop cars, watching everything that went by. He had a small pistol by his side, a double-barreled derringer .38 Special, but if he had to use it, he'd probably be finished.

But so far, so good.

SoHo streets were quiet at night. Once out of the neighborhood, things would get more complicated. He didn't want anything high beside him, a van or a truck. He didn't want a driver looking down into the Volkswagen, even though he probably wouldn't see much. The body, wrapped in dark plastic, looked more like a butterfly's chrysalis than anything, a cocoon. What you might expect from a Bug.

Bekker almost laughed. Not quite; he was too crazy to have a genuine sense of humor. Instead he said, "Motherfucker."

He needed a wall, or an unguarded building with a niche in the wall. Some place where nobody would look out and see him unloading the body. He hadn't thought much about disposal: he'd have to think more. He'd need a random dispersal pattern, nothing they could use to focus on his particular block. He'd have to decide the optimum distance—far enough not to point at SoHo, but not so far that the drive itself became risky.

He drove past the Manhattan Caballero, a Village steak house, a couple of bright beer signs in the small barred windows. The door opened as he went by and he saw a slender man come out, caught just for a moment by the light inside the doorway; and behind him, a cigarette machine.

The gunshots sounded like popcorn. Or like a woman ripping a piece of dress material. Bekker looked in the mirror, saw the lightning. Bekker had been in Vietnam; he'd heard this noise from a distance, this snickering popcorn thunder. He'd seen this flickering light. The man he'd seen in the doorway was flopping on the sidewalk as the bullets tore through him.

"Motherfucker . . ." Teeth bared, mouth wide, Bekker screamed the word: he was innocent, he had nothing to do with it, and he could get caught, right here. Half panicked, afraid that neighbors would take the number of every car they saw, Bekker floored the accelerator and raced to the end of the long block. The gunfire lasted for only two or three seconds. It took another five before he could turn left, out of sight, onto a one-way street. The adrenaline surged through him, the PCP panic. And up ahead, yellow lights flashed in the street.

What?

The panic jumped him. He jammed on the brake, forgetting the clutch, and the Volkswagen stalled. The body crinkled its plastic coat as it swayed in the seat toward him. He pushed it back with one hand, fighting the fist in his throat, trying to breathe, trying to get some air, and stabbed at the gas pedal. Finally realizing what had happened, he dropped the clutch and turned the key again, got started, shifting into second.

He jerked the car to the left, still dazzled, before he realized that the yellow lights were road-construction warnings. No reason to turn—but he already had, and he sped on. Near the end of the block, two figures stepped out of an alley. His headlights swept them, and he saw their hands come up. They were hiding their faces, but before they'd covered them, they'd been as clear as the face of the moon.

Bekker swerved, kept going.

Had they seen his plates? No way to tell. He peered into the rearview mirror, but they were already lost in the dark. He was okay. He tried to choke down the fear. The back plates were old and dirty.

But the gunfire.

Had to think. Jesus, he needed help. He felt for the matchbox. No, that wouldn't be right. He needed speed. Uppers, to help him think.

Sirens.

Somewhere behind him. He wasn't sure quite where he was anymore, took a left, moving away, coming up to a major intersection. He looked up at the street signs. Broadway. What was the other? He rolled forward a few feet. Bleecker. Okay. Good. Straight ahead, along Bleecker. Had to get the body out. A darker block, a deep-red building with niches, but no place to pull over. Another fifty feet . . . there.

He pulled to the curb, hopped out, and looked around. Nobody. He could hear somebody talking, loud, but it sounded like a drunk. He hurried around the car, shifted the body out and dropped it in a doorway. Looked up: the ceiling in the deep doorway was decorated with intricate designs in white terra-cotta; the designs caught his mind, dragged it into the maze of curves. . . .

Another siren brought him back. It was somewhere down Bleecker, but he couldn't see the lights. He hurried back to the car, sweating, climbed inside, and looked back through the open door at the mortal remains of Louis Cortese. From any more than a few feet, the body looked like a bum sleeping on the sidewalk. And there were hundreds of bums in the area.

He risked a last look at the terra-cotta, felt the pull, then tore his eyes away and slammed the door. Hunched over the steering wheel, he headed for home.

THICK PICKED UP the pay phone and dialed the number scrawled on a scrap of paper. He let the phone ring twice, hung up, waited a few seconds, dialed again, let it ring twice more, hung up again.

Thin was waiting in the car, didn't speak.

"It'll be okay," Thick said.

After a very long time, Thin said, "No, it won't."

"It's fine," the big man said. "You did good."

WHEN BEKKER GOT TO the Lacey building, he parked the car, went down into the basement, stripped off his clothes, scrubbed his face, changed into a sweat suit. And thought about the killing he'd seen. New York was a dangerous place—someone really ought to do something about it. . . . There was some cleanup to do in the operating theater. He worked at it for ten minutes, with a sponge and paper towels and a can of universal cleaner. When he was done, he wrapped all the paper and put it in the garbage. He remembered the blood just as he was about to turn out the lights. He picked up the bottle and tipped it into a drain, the blood as purple and thick as antifreeze.

Again he reached for the lights, and saw the four small nubbins of skin sitting on top of an anesthetic tank. Of course, he'd put them there, just a convenient place at the time.

He picked them up. Shriveled, with the long shiny lashes, they looked like a new species of arachnid, a new one-sided spider. They were, of course, something much more mundane: Cortese's eyelids. He peered at them in the palm of his hand. He'd never seen them like this, so separate, so disembodied.

Ha. Another one. Another joke. He looked in the stainless-steel cabinet, laughed and held his belly, and pointed a finger at himself. *Disembodied . . .*

He went back to them, the eyelids. Fascinating.

L UCAS WAS LYING on the roof of his house, the shingles warm against his shoulder blades, eyes closed, not quite snoozing. He'd put down one full flat of green fiberglass shingles and didn't feel like starting another. A breeze ruffled the fine black hair on his forearms; the humid air was pregnant with an afternoon storm and pink-and-gray thunderheads were popping up to the west.

With his eyes closed, Lucas could hear the after-work joggers padding along the sidewalk across the street, the rattle of roller blades, radios from passing cars. If he opened his eyes and looked straight up, he might see an eagle soaring on the thermals above the river bluffs. If he looked down, the Mississippi was there, across the street and below the bluff, like a fat brown snake curling in the sunshine. A catsup-colored buoy bobbed in the muddy water, directing boat traffic into the Ford lock.

It all felt fine, like it could go on forever, up on the roof.

When the taxi pulled into the driveway, he thought about it instead of looking to see who it was. Nobody he knew was likely to come calling unexpectedly. His life had come to that: no surprises.

The car door slammed, and her high heels rapped down the sidewalk.

Lily.

Her name popped into his head.

Something about the way she walked. Like a cop, maybe, or maybe just a New Yorker. Somebody who knew about dog shit and cracked sidewalks, who watched where she put her feet. He lay unmoving, with his eyes closed.

"What are you doing up there?" Her voice was exactly as he remembered, deep for a woman, with a carefully suppressed touch of Brooklyn.

"Maintaining my property." A smile crept across his face.

"You could have fooled me," she said. "You look like you're asleep."

"Resting between bouts of vigorous activity," he said. He sat up, opened his eyes and looked down at her. She'd lost weight, he thought. Her face was narrower, with more bone. And she'd cut her hair: it had been full, to the shoulders. Now it was short, not punk, but asymmetrical, with the hair above her ears cut almost to the skin. Strangely sexy.

Her hair had changed, but her smile had not: her teeth were white as pearls against her olive skin. "You're absolutely gorgeous," he said.

"Don't start, Lucas, I'm already up to my knees in bullshit," she answered. But she smiled, and one of her upper incisors caught on her lower lip. His heart jumped. "This is a business trip."

"Mmmm." Bekker. The papers were full of it. Six already dead. Bodies without eyelids. Cut up, in various ways—not mutilated. Bekker did very professional work, as befitted a certified pathologist. And he wrote papers on the killings: strange, contorted, quasiscientific ramblings about the dying subjects and their predeath experiences, which he sent off to scientific journals. "Are you running the case?"

"No, but I'm . . . involved," she said. She was peering up at him with the comic helplessness with which people on the ground regard people on roofs. "I'm getting a crick in my neck. Come down."

"Who'll maintain my property?" he teased.

"Fuck your property," she said.

He took his time coming down the ladder, aware of the special care: *Five years ago, I'd of run down . . . hell, three years ago . . . getting older. Forty-five coming up. Fifty still below the horizon, but you could see the shadow of it . . .*

He'd been stretching, doing roadwork, hitting a heavy bag until he hurt. He worked on the Nautilus machines three nights a week at the Athletic Club, and tried to swim on the nights he didn't do Nautilus. Forty-four, coming onto forty-five. Hair shot through with gray, and the vertical lines between his eyes weren't gone in the mornings.

He could see the two extra years in Lily as well. She looked tougher, as though she'd been through hard weather. And she looked hurt, her eyes wary.

"Let's go inside," he said as he bent to let her kiss him on the cheek. He didn't have to bend very far; she was nearly as tall as he was. Chanel No. 5, like a whiff of distant farm flowers. He caught her by the arm. "Jesus, you look good. Smell good. Why don't you call?"

"Why don't you?"

"Yeah, yeah . . ." He led the way through the front door to the kitchen. The kitchen had been scorched in a gunfight and fire two years past, a case he'd worked with Lily. He'd repainted and put in a new floor.

"You've lost some weight," he said as they went, groping for something personal.

"Twelve pounds, as of this morning," she said. She dropped her purse on the breakfast bar, looked around, said, "Looks nice," pulled out a stool and sat down. "I'm starving to death."

"I've got two cold beers," Lucas said. He stuck his head in the refrigerator. "And I'm willing to split a deli roast beef sandwich, heavy on the salad, no mayonnaise."

"Just a minute," Lily said, waving him off. He shut the refrigerator door and leaned against it as she took a small brown spiral notebook from her purse. She did a series of quick calculations, her lips moving. "Airline food can't be much," she said, more to herself than Lucas.

"Not much," he agreed.

"Is it light beer?"

"No . . . but hell, it's a celebration."

"Right." She was very serious, noting the calories in the brown notebook. Lucas tried not to laugh.

"You're trying not to laugh," she said, looking up suddenly, catching him at it. She was wearing gold hoop earrings, and when she tipped her head to the side, the gold stroked her olive skin with a butterfly's touch.

"And succeeding," he said. He tried to grin, but his breathing had gone wrong; the dangling earring was hypnotic, like something out of a magician's show.

"Christ, I hate people with fast metabolisms," she said. She went back to the notebook, unaware of his breathing problems. *Maybe.*

"That's all bullshit, the fast-metabolism excuse," Lucas said. "I read it in the *Times.*"

"Another sign of decline, the *Times* printing obvious bullshit," Lily said. She stuffed the notebook back in her purse, put the purse aside and crossed her legs, clasping her hands on her knees. "Okay, a beer and half a sandwich."

THEY ATE at the breakfast bar, facing each other, making small talk, checking each other. Lucas was off the police force and missed the action. Lily had moved up, off the street, and was doing political work with a deputy commissioner. Lily asked, "How's Jennifer? And Sarah?"

Lucas shook his head, finishing the sandwich. "Jen and I—we're all done. We tried, and it didn't work. Too much bad history. We're still friends. She's seeing a guy from the station. They'll probably get married."

"He's okay?"

"Yeah, I guess," Lucas said.

But he was unconsciously shaking his head as he said it.

Lily considered the tone: "So you think he's an asshole?"

"Hell . . . No. Not really." Lucas, finished with his half of the sandwich, stepped over to the sink, squirted Ivory Liquid into the palm of one hand, turned on the water and washed off the traces of the sandwich's olive oil. His hands were large and square, boxer's hands. "And he likes Sarah and he's got a kid of his own, about seven months older than Sarah. They get along. . . ."

"Like a family . . ." Lily said. Lucas turned away and shook the water off his hands and she quickly said, "Sorry."

"Yeah, well, what the fuck," Lucas said. He went back to the refrigerator, took out another bottle of Leinenkugel's and twisted the top off. "Actually, I've been feeling pretty good. Ending it. I'm making some money and I've been out on the road, looking at the world. I was at Little Bighorn a couple of weeks ago. Freaked me out. You can stand by Custer's stone and see the whole fucking fight. . . ."

"Yeah?"

He was marking time, waiting for her to tell him why she'd come to the Cities. But she was better at waiting than he was, and finally he asked, "What're you here for?"

She licked a chip of roast beef from the corner of her mouth, her long tongue catching it expertly. Then: "I want you to come to New York."

"For Bekker?" he asked skeptically. "Bullshit. You guys can handle Bekker. And if I was a New York cop, I'd get pissed off if somebody came in from the outside. A small-town guy."

She was nodding. "Yeah, we can handle Bekker. We've got guys saying all kinds of things: that we'll have him in a week, in ten days. . . . It's been six weeks, Lucas. We'll get him, but the politics are getting ugly."

"Still . . ."

"We want you to jawbone the media. You're good at that, talking to reporters. We want to tell them that we're doing everything we can, that we're even importing the guy who caught him the first time. We want to emphasize that we're pulling out all the stops. Our guys'll understand that, they'll appreciate it—they'll know we're trying to take the heat off."

"That's it? A public-relations trick?" He grimaced, began to shake his head. He didn't want to talk to reporters. He wanted to get somebody by the throat. . . .

"No, no. You'll work the case, all right," she said. She finished the sandwich and held her hands out, fingers spread, looking for a napkin, and he handed her a paper towel. "Right down on the street with the rest of them. And high priority, too. I *do* value your abilities."

Lucas caught something in her voice. "But?"

"But . . . all of that aside, there's something else."

He laughed. "A third layer? A Lily Rothenburg layer? What're you doing?"

"The thing is, we've got serious trouble. Even bigger than Bekker, if you can imagine it." She hesitated, searching his eyes, intent, then balled up the paper napkin and did a sitting jump shot into a wastebasket before continuing. "This can't come out anywhere."

Irritated, he wordlessly backhanded the comment away, like a bothersome gnat. She nodded, slipped off the stool, took a quick turn around the kitchen, picked up an enamel coffee cup, turned it in her hands, put it down.

"We're looking at thirteen murders," she said finally. "Not Bekker's. Someone else's. These are all . . . hits. Maybe. Of the thirteen—those are the ones we're sure of, we think there are more, as many as forty—ten were out-and-out assholes. Two of them were pretty big: a wholesaler for the Cali cartel and an up-and-coming Mafia guy. The other eight were miscellaneous small-timers."

"Number eleven?"

"A lawyer," Lily said. "A criminal defense lawyer who represented a lot of big dopers. He was good. He put a lot of people back on the street that shouldn't have been there. But most people thought he was straight."

"Hard to be straight, with that job," Lucas said.

"But we think he was. The investigation hasn't turned up anything that'd change our mind. We've been combing his bank records, along with the IRS and the state tax people. There's not a goddamned thing. In fact, there wouldn't have been any point in his being crooked: he was pulling in so much money he didn't need any more. Three million bucks was a slow year."

"Okay. Who was twelve?"

"Number twelve was a professional black . . . spokesman," she said. "A community leader, a loudmouth, a rabble-rouser, whatever you want to call him. But he wasn't a crook. He was a neighborhood politician trying to climb the pole. He was shot in a drive-by, supposedly a couple of gang-bangers. But it was very slick for gang-bangers, good weapons, a stolen car."

"Thirteen?"

"Thirteen was a cop."

"Crooked?"

"Straight. He was investigating the possibility that we've got a rogue group inside the police department, inside intelligence, systematically killing people."

There was a moment of silence as Lucas digested it. "Sonofabitch," he said finally. "They've killed thirteen people for sure, and maybe forty?"

"The cop who was killed—his name was Walter Petty—claimed there were twelve, for sure. He's the thirteenth. We think. He said there could be thirty or forty more."

"Jesus Christ." Lucas pulled at his lip, turned away from her, blankly staring at the microwave. Forty? "You should've picked it up. . . ."

"Not necessarily," Lily said, shaking her head. The short hair whipped around her ears, like a television advertisement, and he caught a smile and suppressed it. This was *business*, she said. "For one thing, they were killed over a long time. Five years, anyway. And most of them died like you'd have expected, knowing their records. Except more efficiently. That's what you notice when you decide you've got a pattern: the efficiency of it. Bang, bang, they're dead. Never any cops close by—once or twice, they were actually decoyed out. There are never any good witnesses. The getaways are preplanned. No collateral damage, no mushrooms getting knocked down."

"So you've got a pattern of small-time assholes killed by big-time shooters," Lucas said.

"Right. Like this one guy, I met him myself, years ago, when I was just coming off patrol. Arvin Davies." She lifted her eyes to the ceiling and wet her lips, remembering the file. "He was forty-two when he was killed. He was a doper, a drunk. A brawler. He had twenty priors going back to age twelve, and he'd been picked up for one thing or another maybe twenty more times. All small stuff. Street muggings, burglaries, car thefts, rip-offs, possession. He'd get his nose clogged up with angel dust and beat his victims. He killed one five or six years ago, but we could never prove it. He spent twenty years inside, all short time. The last time he got out, he did a couple of muggings and then somebody put him on a wall. Shot him twice in the heart and once in the head. The head shot came when he was already down, a coup de grace. The shooter walked away," she said, hopping back up on the breakfast-bar stool across from him.

"A pro," Lucas said.

"Yeah. And there just wasn't any reason a pro would go after Arvin Davies. He was small-time, chickenshit. But whoever killed him took a real asshole off the streets for good. Maybe forty or fifty nasty crimes a year."

"All the miscellaneous hits are like that?"

"Yup. I mean the techniques are different, but they're all cold, efficient, re-searched."

Lucas nodded, studying her. "All very enlightening—but where do I come in?"

She looked straight into him, fixing him. "A couple of guys in intelligence spotted the pattern. They got nervous about it. All of the victims, or whatever you'd call them, were heavy in intelligence files. Like the files had been used to choose them. Once they made the report, a secret working group of six ranking officers was set up to monitor it. Petty was eventually brought in to do the dog work."

Lucas interrupted. "He was a shoofly, or whatever you guys call them?"

She shook her head. "He was a crime-scene guy for most of his career, and later on a computer specialist. He was officially a detective second. In this case, he was reporting to the working group under the direct supervision of my boss, John O'Dell. John chairs the working group."

"So there was no past internal-affairs work that might have left a grudge," Lucas said.

"No. And just before he was shot, there was an odd break on the case. . . ." Lily put a hand on top of her head as if she were patting herself, a gesture of thought. "The black guy who was killed, the loudmouth, was named Waites. The file is still open, we still have people digging into it. As a matter of routine, Walt got all the reports coming out of the active cases. He found a report that said a supposed witness to the Waites killing had recognized one of the shooters as a cop. The witness was named Cornell, last name probably Reed. The trouble is, when Walt went looking for him, Cornell Reed had disappeared. Maybe left town. But Walt found him, somehow. He tried to get in touch with us that af-ternoon, he came by the offices, and when he couldn't, he left a note on voice mail. He said he knew where Reed went."

"Where?"

"We don't know. And Walt was killed that night."

"Jesus—somebody got the voice mail?"

"Unlikely; it's coded," Lily said. "And the shooting was too well set up. They'd planned it ahead of time. If finding the witness had anything to do with it, it was just the trigger that made them go ahead with the shooting."

"Huh. How about Petty's records? Notes?"

"Nothing in his office, but he wasn't keeping anything there, anyway, because of the sensitivity," she said. "He was working out of his apartment, mostly. And that's another thing: somebody got to his apartment before we did. All of his computer disks were gone, and the internal drive—hard drive, is that it?—had been wiped somehow. I don't know how you do it, but there was nothing recoverable."

"Another computer freak?"

"Not necessarily. Whatever they did wasn't fancy. A couple of short commands apparently took care of it. Something like a reformat with a write-over? Does that make sense?"

"Yeah, yeah. Petty must've talked to somebody. It's hard to believe he'd get a break and coincidentally be hit that same night. . . . Who'd he tell about the witness?" Lucas asked.

"We don't know," Lily said. "We *do* know he came up to our office, after hours, looking for us. O'Dell and I spend a lot of time in a car, going around, putting out political brush fires. We were talking to some people in one of the projects that night. Walt didn't try the car—our driver was waiting in it, and nobody called. The thing is, when Walt came up to the office, he might've bumped into somebody from the working group, there in the hallway. He really wouldn't talk to anybody else, not on this topic."

"So he accidentally bumps into another member of the working group and that guy leaks?"

Lily frowned. "Well . . . the shooting was too quick for a careless leak. Whoever tipped the rogue group did it directly. A phone call. In other words, whoever leaked knows the killers. Maybe he even runs them."

"Sonofabitch. But if you know it's one of the six working-group guys . . ."

Lily shook her head and smiled. "Nothing's ever that easy. For one thing, every one of those six reports to somebody, and they did. And every one of the six has assistants, and some of the assistants know what the working group is doing."

"Doesn't sound very secret," Lucas said.

"Maybe fifteen people know details, and twenty-five know about the problem," Lily said. "That's pretty secret for the department . . . but you see where that leaves us. If one of the working group tipped the killers, he's in a position to know everything. So we're paralyzed. The working group appointed a new lead investigator, an unassigned captain, but he's not doing anything. He's just there to cover our asses, in case something leaks. You know, so we can say we've got an active case under investigation by a ranking officer."

"And you want *me* to look into it," Lucas said.

Lily nodded. "My boss and I talked it over. We need the work done off the books. Nobody will know but the two of us. It's the only way. And because of Bekker, you're a perfect fit. The goddamn media's going nuts about Bekker, of course, the TV and the *Post* and *News*, Doctor Death and all that. You can't get in a cab without hearing a radio talk show about him. So we bring you in, the guy who caught him last time. A consultant. But while you're looking, we're going to put you close to a couple of people Walt was looking at."

"Huh." Lucas sat and thought for a long moment, then he looked up. "This guy who got shot," he said. "You called him Walt, like . . . he wasn't just another guy. Is there something I should know?"

She looked at his face, but not into his eyes: her eyes seemed suddenly blank, as though she were seeing another face. "Walt was my oldest friend," she said.

And she told him about the dream. . . .

The dream had started the night Petty was killed; it began not with a vision, but with an odor, the smell of ozone, as if electrical circuits were burning somewhere. Then she saw herself, through a haze, but with increasing clarity, seated on a simple marble bench, the kind found in cemeteries, with Petty's bleeding, shattered body stretched across her lap. A pietà. She did nothing at all, but simply sat there, looking into his face. In the dream, the point-of-view closed on the face, like a camera creeping forward, and at the last moment, focused not on an image of Christ-like peace, but on a face that had been shredded by high-velocity slugs, at yellow molars slick with drying blood. . . .

A ludicrous image, but one that came, night after night.

But that wasn't the way it had been, the night Petty was killed.

Petty's seventy-one-year-old mother had called, confused, incoherent. Her only child had been killed, she said, her voice an ancient moan. Walt was dead, dead . . . Lily could see the old woman in her mind's eye, the narrow gray face bent over the black telephone, body shaking, twitching, the withered hand with the handkerchief, the doilies on the TV behind her, the Sacred Heart on the wall. Lily could even smell it, cabbage and bread dough. . . .

The old woman said that Lily had to go to Bellevue to identify Walter. Was there a cop there, Lily asked? Yes, right here, and Father Gomez. And the mayor was coming.

Lily spoke to the cop. Take care of Gloria Petty, she said, the wife of a cop, the mother of a cop. The last one alive in this family. Then, trembling with fear and grief, she'd gone to Bellevue.

No pietà at Bellevue.

Just a body, waxlike, dead, sprawled on a blood-soaked gurney, raw from the pickup. The body was wrapped in layers of plastic, like beef being moved. She noted professionally that one of the slugs had ripped off Petty's cheek, exposing his molars; a preview of Petty as a naked skull, a reminder of Petty's naive, happy smile. The smile that flashed every time he saw her, delighted with her presence.

She recalled a day from their Brooklyn childhood, when the two of them were seven or eight. Late fall, blue skies, crisp weather, a hint of Halloween. There were maple trees on the block, turning red. She'd been sick and had been kept home from school, but her mother let her out in the afternoon to sit on the stoop.

And here was Walter, running down the street, a paper held overhead, flapping, joy in his eyes. Her spelling test from the day before. A perfect score. Common enough for Lily, but Walter, so generously pleased for her, that smile, that young blond hair slicked down with Vaseline . . .

Come to this, the bloody teeth.

"That's Walter Petty," she told a tired assistant M.E.

At home again, changing clothes, preparing herself to see Petty's mother, she thought of her school yearbook. She went into the living room, pulled a box from a built-in cupboard, and found three of them. And his senior picture: his hair never quite right, his face too slender, the slightly dazed smile.

Lily broke and began to weep. The spasm was uncontrollable, unlike anything she'd experienced before, a storm that ended with dumb exhaustion. Wearily, she finished dressing, started for the door.

And smelled Petty: Petty in the morgue, the stink of the blood and the body in her nose. She ran back to the bathroom, washed her face and her hands, over and over.

Early the next morning, after the nightmare interlude with Gloria Petty, as she fought for an hour or two of sleep, she dreamed and saw herself on the marble bench, Walter Petty draped on her lap, broken, torn, his bloody teeth leering from the side of his face. . . .

Petty was gone.

"JESUS." LUCAS WAS STARING at her. "I didn't know you had . . ."

"What?" She tried to smile. "That kind of depth?"

"That kind of old-time relationship. You know about me and Elle Kruger . . ."

"The nun, yes. What would you do if somebody murdered her?" Lily asked.

"Find whoever did it and kill him," Lucas said quietly.

"Yes," Lily said, nodding, looking straight at him. "That's what I want."

The late-afternoon sun had gone red, then a sullen orange. A heavy atmospheric hush, accompanied by a distant rumbling, announced the line of thunderstorms that Lucas had seen from the roof. When Lily first arrived, Lucas, sitting on the roof, had said, "You're absolutely gorgeous." She'd cooled the sense of contact with a quick, "Don't start, Davenport." But there was an underlying tension between them, and now it sprang up again, riding with them as they moved out of the kitchen, into the living room.

Lily perched on a couch, knees together, fumbled through her purse, found a roll of Certs, tipped a couple of them into her hand, then popped them into her mouth. "You've changed things," she said, looking around the house.

"After Shadow Love, the place was pretty shot up," Lucas said. He dropped onto a leather recliner, sitting on the edge of it, leaning toward her. "Some wiring got wrecked and I needed a new floor. Plaster work. He was shooting that goddamn M-15, it was a mess."

Lily looked away: "That's what they used on Walt. An M-15. A full clip: they emptied a full clip into him. They found pieces of him all over the block."

"Jesus . . ." Lucas groped for something else to say, but all he could find was, "How about you? Are you okay?"

"Oh, sure," she said, and fell silent.

"The last time I saw you, you were on a guilt trip about your old man and the kids. . . ."

"That's not over. The guilt trip. Sometimes I feel so bad I get nauseous," she said.

"Do you see the kids?"

"Not so much," she said sadly, looking away from him. "I tried, but it was wrecking all of us. David was always . . . peering at me. And the boys blame me for leaving."

"Do you want to go back?"

"I don't love him," she said, shaking her head. "I don't even like him very much. I look at him now, and it all seems like bullshit, the stuff that comes out of his mouth. And that's weird, because it used to seem so smart. We'd go to parties and he'd spin up these post-Jungian theories of racism and class strug- gle, and these phonies would stand around with their heads going up and down like they were bobbing for apples. Then I'd go to work and see a report on some twelve-year-old who shot his mom because he wanted to sell the TV to buy crack, and she wouldn't let him. Then I'd go back home and . . . shit. I couldn't stand listening to him anymore. How can you live with somebody you can't stand lis- tening to?"

"It's hard," he said. "Being a cop makes it worse. I think that's why I spent so much time with Jennifer. She was a professional bullshit artist, but basically, she knew what was what. She spent the time on the streets."

"Yeah . . ."

"So where're you at?" he asked again.

She looked at him unsteadily, not quite nervous, but apprehensive some- how. "I didn't want to get into that right away—I wanted to get you committed first. Will you come?"

"Somebody new?" he asked, his voice light.

"Will you come?"

"Maybe . . . so you've got someone."

"Sort of."

"Sort of? What's that?" He hopped off the chair and took a turn around the room. He wasn't angry, he thought, but he looked angry. He reached down and turned on the TV and a tinny, distant voice instantly cried, "Kirrrbeee Puck-it." He snapped it off again. "What does 'sort of' mean? One foot on the floor at all times? Nothing below the waist?"

Lily laughed and said, "You cheer me up, Davenport. You're so fucking crass. . . ."

"So . . . ?" He went to the window and looked out; the thunderheads were gray, with soaring pink tops, and were bearing down on the line of the river.

She shrugged, looked out the window past him. "So, I was seeing a guy. I still am. We hadn't started looking for an apartment together, but the possibil- ity was out there."

"What happened?"

"He had a heart attack."

Lucas looked at her for a minute, then said, "Why does that make perfect sense?"

She forced a smile. "It's really not very funny, I'm afraid. He's in terrible shape."

"He's a cop?"

"Yeah." The smile faded. "He's like you, in some ways. Not physically—he's tall and thin and white-haired. But he is—was—in intelligence and he loves the streets. He writes articles for the Times op-ed page about the street life. He has the best network of spies in the city. And he has a taste for, mmm . . ." She groped for the right phrase.

"Dark-eyed married women?" Lucas suggested, moving closer.

"Well, that," she said, the tentative smile returning. "But the thing is, he likes to fight . . . did like to fight. Like you. Now he can't walk two dozen steps without stopping for a breath."

"Jesus." Lucas ran a hand through his hair. He'd had nightmares of being crippled. "What's the prognosis?"

"Not so good." Tears glistened at the corners of her dark eyes. At the same moment, she smiled and said, "Shit. I wish I didn't do this." She wiped the tears away with the heel and knuckles of her hand. "This was his third attack. The first one was five years ago. That was bad. The second one was a couple months after the first, and wasn't so bad. Then he was coming back. He'd almost forgotten about them, he was working. . . . Then this third one, this was the worst of all. He's got extensive damage to the heart muscle. And he won't stop working. The doctors tell him to spend a year doing graded exercise, to stay away from work, from the stress. He won't do it. And he's still smoking, I think. He's sneaking them. I can smell them on his clothes . . . in his hair."

"So he's going to die," Lucas said.

"Probably."

"That's not so bad," Lucas said, leaning back, looking at her, his voice flat. "You just say fuck it. You do what you want, and if you go, you go."

"That's what you'd do, isn't it?"

"I hope so," he said.

"Men are such goddamn assholes," Lily said.

After another long silence, Lucas asked, "So what are you doing for sex?"

She started to laugh, but it caught in her throat, and she stood up and picked up her purse. "I better get going. Tell me you'll come to New York."

"Answer the question," Lucas said. Without thinking about it, he moved closer. She noticed it, felt the pressure.

"We're . . . very careful," she said. "He can't get too carried away."

Lucas' chest felt curiously thick, a combination of anger and expectation. The electricity between them crackled, and his voice was suddenly husky. "You never really liked being careful."

"Ah, Jesus, Lucas," she said.

He stepped up to her until he was only inches away. "Push me away," he whispered.

"Lucas . . ."

"Push me away," he said, "I'll go."

She stepped back, dropped her purse. Outside, the first heavy drops of rain careened off the sidewalk, and a woman with a dog on a leash dashed past the house.

She rocked back on her heels, looked down at her purse, then grabbed his shirt sleeve to balance herself, lifted one foot, then the other, pulled off her shoes, and stepped into the hallway that led to the bedroom. Lucas, standing in the living room, watched her go, until halfway down the hallway she turned her head, her dark eyes looking at him, and began to unbutton her blouse.

THEIR LOVEMAKING, she said later, sometimes resembled a fight, had an edge of violence, a tone of aggression. They might begin with an effort at tenderness, but that would slip and they would be bucking, wrenching, twisting. . . .

That night, as the last of the storm cells rumbled off into Wisconsin, with the room smelling of sweat and sex, she sat on the edge of the bed. She seemed weary, but there was a smile at the corner of her lips.

"I'm such a goddammned slut," she said.

"Oh, God . . ." He laughed.

"Well, it's true," she said, "I can't believe it. I was such a nice girl for so long. But I just *need*. It's not intimacy. You're about as intimate as a fuckin' bear. I need the *sex*. I need to get *jammed*. I really can't believe it."

"Did you know you were going to sleep with me?" Lucas asked. "When you got here?"

She sat unmoving for a moment, then said, "I thought it might happen. So I went to the hotel first, and checked in. In case anyone called."

He ran a fingernail down the bumps of her spine, and she shivered. She was going back to the hotel in case "anyone" called. . . .

"This guy you're sleeping with? 'Anyone'?" Lucas said.

"Yes?"

"What are you going to tell him?"

"Nothing. He doesn't need to know." She turned toward him. "And don't you tell him anything, either, Davenport."

"Why?" Lucas said. "Why would I ever see him?"

"His name's Dick Kennett." In the half-light of the bedroom he could see a tiny, rueful smile lift the corner of her mouth again. "He's running the Bekker case," she said.

EARLY MORNING.

Lucas strolled along Thirty-fifth Street, sucking on half of an orange, taking in the city: looking at faces and display windows, at sleeping bums wrapped in blankets like thrown-away cigars, at the men hustling racks of new-made clothing through the streets.

The citric acid was sharp on his tongue, an antidote for the staleness of a poor night's sleep. Halfway down the block, he stopped in front of a parking garage, stripped out the last of the pulp with his teeth, and dropped the rind into a battered trash barrel.

Midtown South squatted across the street, looking vaguely like a midwestern schoolhouse from the 1950s: blocky, functional, a little tired. Six squad cars were parked diagonally in front of the building, along with a Cushman scooter. Four more squads were double-parked farther up the street. As Lucas paused at the trash basket, disposing of the orange, a gray Plymouth stopped in the street. A lanky white-haired man climbed out of the passenger side, said something to the driver, laughed and pushed the door shut.

He didn't slam the door, Lucas noticed: he gave it a careful push. His eyes came up, checked Lucas, checked him again, and then he turned carefully toward the station. The fingers of his left hand slipped under a brilliant-colored tie, and he unconsciously scratched himself over his heart.

Lucas, dodging traffic, crossed the street and followed the man toward the front doors. Lily had said Kennett was tall and white-haired, and the hand over the heart, the unconscious gesture. . . .

"Are you Dick Kennett?" Lucas asked.

The man turned, eyes cool and watchful. "Yes?" He looked more closely. "Davenport? I thought it might be you. . . . Yeah, Kennett," he said, sticking out his hand.

Kennett was two inches taller than Lucas, but twenty pounds lighter. His hair was slightly long for a cop's, and his beige cotton summer suit fit too well. With his blue eyes, brilliant white teeth against what looked like a lifetime tan, crisp blue-striped oxford-cloth shirt and the outrageous necktie, he looked like a doctor who played scratch golf or good club tennis: thin, intent, serious. But a gray pallor lay beneath the tan, and his eye sockets, normally deep, showed bony knife ridges under paper-thin skin. There were scars below the eyes, the remnants

of the short painful cuts a boxer gets in the ring, or a cop picks up in the street—
a cop who likes to fight.

"Lily's been telling me about you," Lucas said, as they shook hands.

"All lies," Kennett said, grinning.

"Christ, I hope so," Lucas said. Lucas took in Kennett's tie, a bare-breasted
Polynesian woman with another woman in the background. "Nice tie."

"Gauguin," Kennett said, looking down at it, pleased.

"What?"

"Paul Gauguin, the French painter?"

"I didn't know he did neckties," Lucas said uncertainly.

"Yeah, him and Christian Dior, they're like brothers," Kennett said, flashing the grin. Lucas nodded and they went on toward the door, Lucas holding it
open. "I fuckin' hate this, people holding doors," Kennett grumbled as he went
through.

"Yeah, but when you croak, how'd you like it to say on the stone, 'Died opening a door'?" Lucas asked. Kennett laughed, an easy extroverted laugh, and Lucas
liked him for it, and thought: *Watch* it. Some people could *make* you like them.
It was a talent.

"I could die pulling the tab on a beer can, if they let me drink beer, which
they don't," Kennett was saying, suddenly sober. "Hope the fuck it never happens to you. Eat aspirin. Stop eating steak and eggs. Pray for a brain hemorrhage.
This heart shit—it turns you into a coward. You walk around listening to it tick,
waiting for it to stop. And you're weak. If some asshole mugged me, I'd have to
take it."

"I don't want to hear about it," Lucas said.

"I don't want to talk about it, but I do, all the time," Kennett said. "Ready
to meet the group?"

"Yeah, yeah . . ."

Lucas followed Kennett through the entrance lobby, waited with him until
the reception sergeant buzzed them through to the back. Kennett led the way to
a conference room with a piece of notebook paper Scotch-taped to the door:
"Kennett Group." The room had four corkboards hung from the walls, covered
with notes and call slips, maps of Manhattan, telephones, a couple of long tables and a dozen plastic chairs. In the center of it, a burly, sunburned cop in a
white shirt and a thin dog-faced detective in a sport coat were facing each other,
both with Styrofoam coffee cups in their hands, voices raised.

". . . your people'd get off their fuckin' asses, we could get somewhere. That's
what's fuckin' us up, nobody wants to go outside because it's too goddamn hot.
We know he's using the shit and he's got to get it somewhere."

"Yeah, well I'm not the asshole who told everybody we'd have him in a week,
am I? That was fuckin' crazy, Jack. As far as we know, he's buying whatever shit
he's using in Jersey, or down in fuckin' Philly. So don't give me no shit. . . ."

A half-dozen more plainclothes cops, in thin short-sleeved shirts and wash
pants, weapons clipped to their belts, watched the argument from the plastic

chairs spread around the institutional carpet. Four of the six held Styrofoam coffee cups, and two or three were smoking cigarettes, snubbing them out in shallow aluminum ashtrays. One unattended cigarette continued to burn, the foul odor like a fingernail scratch on a blackboard.

"What's going on?" Kennett asked quietly, moving to the front of the room. The argument stopped.

"Discussing strategy," the sunburned cop said shortly.

"Any conclusions?" Kennett asked. He was polite, but pushing. Taking over. The cop shook his head and turned away. "No."

Lucas found a seat halfway back, the other cops looking at him, openly, carefully, with some distance.

"That's Lucas Davenport, the guy from Minneapolis," Kennett said, almost absently, as Lucas sat down. He'd picked up a manila file with his name on it, and was flipping through memos and call slips. "He's gonna talk to the press this morning, then go out on the street this afternoon. With Fell."

"How come you let this motherfucker Bekker get out?" the sunburned cop asked.

"Wasn't me," Lucas said mildly.

"Should of killed him when you could," dog-face said. Dog-face's two top-middle teeth pointed in slightly different directions and were notably orange.

"I thought about it," Lucas said, staring lazily at dog-face until the other broke his eyes away.

Somebody laughed, and somebody else said, "Shoulda."

Kennett said, "You won't remember this, Davenport, but let me introduce Lieutenants Kuhn, Huerta, White, Diaz, Blake, and Carter, and detectives Annelli and Case, our serial-killer specialists. You can get the first names sorted out later. . . ."

The cops lifted hands or nodded at him as their names were called out. They looked like Minneapolis cops, Lucas thought. Different names, but the attitude was the same, like a gathering of paranoid shoe salesmen: too little pay, too many years of burgers and fries and Butterfingers, too many people with big feet trying to get into small shoes.

A red-haired woman walked into the room carrying a stack of files, and Kennett added, "And this is Barb Fell. . . . Barb, that's Lucas Davenport in what appears to be a five-hundred-dollar silk-blend jacket and two-hundred-dollar shoes. . . ."

Fell was in her mid-thirties, slender, her red hair just touched with gray. An old scar, shaped like a new moon, cupped one side of her long mouth, a deadwhite punctuation mark on a pale oval Welsh face. She sat next to him, perching, shook hands quickly and turned back to the front of the room.

"John O'Dell's coming over, he's going to sit in," one of the cops was telling Kennett. Kennett nodded, dragged a chair around to face the others and said, "Somebody tell me we've got something new."

After a moment of silence, Diaz, a tall, gaunt detective, one of the lieutenants, said, "About the time Bekker would've got here, a cab disappeared. Three months old. One of them new, round Caprices. Poof. Gone. Stolen while the driver was taking a leak. Supposedly."

Kennett's eyebrows went up. "Never seen again?"

"Not as far as we can tell. But, ah . . ."

"What?"

"One of the guys checked around. The driver doesn't know anything from anything. Went into a bar to take a leak, comes out, and it's gone. But the thing had been in two accidents, and the driver says it was a piece of shit. Says the transmission was shot, there was something wrong with the suspension, the front passenger-side door was so tight you could barely open it. I'd bet the sonofabitch is in a river someplace. For the insurance."

Kennett nodded but said, "Push it. We've got nothing else, right?" He looked around. "Nothing from the Laski surveillance . . . ?"

"No. Not a thing," said another of the lieutenants.

"Um . . ." Lucas lifted a finger, and Kennett nodded at him.

"Lily told me about the Laski scam, and I've been thinking about it."

The cops at the front of the room turned in their chairs to look at him. "Like what?" asked Kennett.

"I don't think Bekker'll go for it. He'd think of Laski as a wrong-headed colleague, not somebody he'd hit. Maybe somebody he'd debate. He's an equal, not a subject."

"We got nothing else going for us," snapped Carter, the sunburned cop. "And it's cheap."

"Hey, it's a smart idea," Lucas said. Laski was a Columbia pathologist who had agreed to analyze Bekker's medical papers for the media. He had condemned them, attacked their morality and science, attacked Bekker as a sadist and a psychotic and a scientific moron—all of it calculated to bring Bekker in. Laski, his apartment and his office were covered by a web of plainclothes cops. So far, Bekker hadn't touched any of the trip wires. "That's why I was thinking about it. About variations."

"Like what?" prompted Kennett.

"Back in the Cities, Bekker subscribed to the *Times*, and I bet he reads it here. If we could set somebody up to give a lecture, some kind of professional speech that would pull him in . . ."

"Don't tease me, darlin'," Kennett said.

"We have some guy lecture on the medical experiments done by Dr. Mengele," Lucas said. "You know, the Nazi dude . . ."

"We know . . ."

"So he lectures on the ethics of using Mengele's studies in research and the ethics of using Bekker's stuff," Lucas said. "And what might come out of their so-called research that's valuable. And we make an announcement in the *Times*."

The cops all looked at each other, and then Huerta said, "Jesus Christ, man, half the fuckin' town is Jewish. They'd go batshit. . . ."

"Hey, I don't mean any goddamn anti-Semite fruitcake lecture," Lucas said.

"I mean some kind of, you know, soft, intellectual, theory thing. I read about this Mengele ethics debate somewhere, so there's something to talk about. I mean, legit. Maybe we get somebody Jewish to front it, so nobody gets pissed off. Somebody with credentials."

"You think that'd do it?" Kennett said. He was interested.

"Bekker couldn't resist, if he heard about it. He's nuts about the topic. Maybe we could arrange for this guy, whoever we get, to have a controversy with Laski. Something that would get in the papers."

Kennett looked at the others. "What do you think?"

Carter tipped his head, grudgingly nodded. "Could you fix it?"

Kennett nodded. "Somebody could. O'Dell, maybe. We could get somebody at the New School. We know Bekker's around there."

"Sounds okay," said Huerta. "But it'll take a while to set up."

"Two or three days," said Kennett. "A week."

"We oughta have him by then. . . ."

"So we cancel. It's like Laski: I don't see any downside, frankly, and it's cheap," Kennett said. He nodded at Lucas. "I'll get it started."

"Quick."

"Yeah," Kennett said. He looked around the room. "All right, so let's go over it. John, what'd we have from Narcotics?"

"We're hassling everybody, but nothing sounds good," said Blake. "Lotsa bullshit, we're chasing it . . ."

As they reviewed the status of the case, and routine assignments, Fell whispered to Lucas, "Your interviews are all set up. A couple of reporters are already here, and three or four more are coming."

Lucas nodded, but as she was about to add something, her eyes shifted away from him toward the door. A fat man walked in, his body swaying side to side, bumping the door frame, small dark eyes poking into the corners of the room, checking off the detectives, pausing at Lucas, pausing at Fell. He looked like H. L. Mencken in the later years. Spidery veins crisscrossed the gray cheeks; his thinning reddish hair was combed straight back with some kind of oil. His jowls were emphasized by a brooding, liverish underlip that seemed fixed in a permanent pout. He wore a three-piece suit in a color that might have been called oxblood, if anyone made oxblood suits.

"O'Dell," Fell said under her breath, at his ear. "Deputy commissioner in charge of cutting throats."

Lily followed O'Dell into the room, picked out Lucas, tipped her head and lifted her eyebrows. She wore a tailored navy-blue suit and a long, mannish red necktie knotted with a loose Windsor. She carried a heavy leather cop's purse over her shoulder, her hand lying casually on the strap at the back of the purse. If she moved her hand four inches, she'd be gripping the butt of a .45. Lucas had seen her use it once, had seen her shove the .45 in a man's face and pull the trigger, the man's face smearing as though he'd been struck with a hammer, all in the space of a tenth of a second. . . .

Lily touched O'Dell's elbow, guided him toward a chair, then moved around where she could sit next to Lucas. "Get a chance to talk to Dick?" she whispered.

"Yeah. He seems like a pretty good guy. . . ."

She looked at him, as though checking to see if he was serious, then nodded and looked away.

O'Dell was up-to-date on the case's progress, and had no particular ideas about what to do next, he told the cops. He just wanted to sit in, to get a feel for the movement. "What about decoys?" he asked. "Somebody downtown suggested that we might put a few people on the street. . . ."

They argued about decoys for a while, a last-resort effort, but Kennett shook his head. "The area's too big," he said. He wandered over to a bulletin board–sized map of Manhattan, ran a finger from Central Park to the financial district. "If he was hitting a specific group, like hookers or gays, then maybe. But there's no connection between the victims. Except some negatives. He doesn't take street people, who'd probably be the easiest. . . ."

"He may specifically pick victims who look healthy," said Case, one of the serial-killer specialists. "This science thing he has—Danny and I think he rules out anybody who's too odd, or diseased or infirm. They'd mess up his findings. The medical examiner reports are all pretty much the same: these people are healthy."

"All right," said Kennett. "So he takes seven people, five female, two male, one black, six white. Two of the whites are Hispanic, but that doesn't seem to mean anything."

"They're all noticeably small, except the first one," Kuhn said. "The second guy was only five-six and skinny."

"Disposal," Huerta grunted.

They all nodded, and there was another long moment of silence, everybody in the room staring at the map of Manhattan.

"It's gotta be a cab," somebody said. "If he can't let anybody see him, and he's gotta have money for drugs, and he's gotta have someplace to gas these people. . . ." One of the cops looked at Lucas: "What are the chances that he had some money stashed? He was pretty well-off, right? Could he have ditched . . . ?"

Lucas was shaking his head. "When we took him, we blindsided him. He thought he was home free. When his wife's estate got into court, all their money was accounted for."

"Okay, that was pretty thin."

"It seems to me that somebody's protecting him," Lucas said. "An old friend or a new friend, but somebody."

Kennett was nodding. "I've worried about that, but if that's right, there isn't much we can do about it."

"We can try pushing his friend, using the media again," Lucas said. "If he depends on somebody else . . ."

O'Dell, seated heavily on a shaky folding chair, interrupted. "Wait, wait. You guys are getting ahead of me. How do we think this, that he has a friend?"

"We've papered the goddamn town with his picture and with simulations of what he'd look like if he dyed his hair or grew a beard or if he shaved his head," said Kennett. "These aren't identikit mock-ups, these are based on good-quality photographs. . . ."

"Yeah, yeah . . ." O'Dell said impatiently.

"So unless he's invisible or living in the sewers, he's probably being protected," Lucas said, picking up the thread from Kennett. "He can't be a regular tenant somewhere. He'd have to pay rent and people'd see him on a regular basis. He can't risk landlords or nosy neighbors."

"And that means he's living with somebody or he's on the street," Kennett said.

"He's not on the street," Lucas said positively. "I can't see him living like that. He just wouldn't do it. He's . . . fastidious. Besides, he's got to have a vehicle. He didn't call a cab to haul these bodies around."

"Unless he drives a cab himself," said Huerta.

"Not much there," said Diaz, shaking his head. "We'll push the stolen one. . . ."

"And it'd still be pretty risky," Lucas said.

"Yeah, but it answers a lot of questions: how he gets transportation, how he makes money and still keeps his face hidden," Kennett said. "If he worked a couple of hours a night, late, and picked his spots . . . maybe concentrated on the tourist and convention areas, you know, the Javits Center, places like that. He'd mostly be dealing with out-of-towners, which would explain Cortese. People trust cabbies. Like if he pretended he had a parcel, gets out and asks somebody where an address was . . ."

"I don't know," said Lucas.

They all stared at the map some more. Too much city; single buildings that would hold the populations of two or three small towns.

"But I still think you might be right, that he's living with somebody," Kennett said finally. "How he gets his money . . ."

"He's got skills," Lucas said. "He's got an M.D., he knows chemistry. A good chemist on the run . . ."

"Methedrine," said White, a bald man in gray knit slacks. "Ecstasy. LSD. It's all back, almost like the old days."

"Be a good reason to protect him, too," said Kuhn. "He'd be a cash cow."

"Assuming this isn't just bullshit, what does it get us?" O'Dell asked impatiently.

"We start looking for ways to put pressure on whoever he's living with or who's covering for him," Lucas said. "We need some heavy-duty contact with the media."

"Why?" said O'Dell.

"Because we have to move them around. Get them to do a little propaganda for us. We need to talk about how anybody who's hiding Bekker is an accessory to mass murder. We need some headlines to that effect. That their only hope is to roll over on him, plead ignorance, get immunity. We've got to chase him out in the open."

"I could call somebody," O'Dell said.

"We need the right emphasis . . ."

"We can figure something out," O'Dell said. "Are you still talking to the reporters this morning?"

"Yeah."

"Throw something in, then. . . ."

When the meeting broke up, O'Dell lurched ponderously out of his chair, leaned toward Lucas, and said, "We'd like to sit in on the press thing. Me and Lily."

Lucas nodded. "Sure." O'Dell nodded and headed toward the front of the room, and Lucas turned to Fell. "We're going out this afternoon?"

"Yeah. They've got us looking for fences," she said. She had gray eyes that matched the touch of gray in her hair; she was five-six or so, with a slightly injured smile and nicotine-stained fingers.

"Could I get copies or printouts of all the Bekker files, or borrow what I can't copy?"

"Right here," she said, patting the stack of manila folders in her lap.

From the front of the room, where he was talking to Kennett, O'Dell called, "Davenport." Lucas stood up and walked over, and O'Dell said, "Dick has been telling me about your idea, the lecture thing, the Mengele. I'll call around this afternoon and set it up. Like for next week. We'll play it like it's been set for a while."

Lucas nodded. "Good."

"I'll see you in the hall," O'Dell said, breaking away. Out of the corner of his eye, as O'Dell spoke to him, Lucas could see Kennett's mouth tic. Disgust? "I've gotta pee."

When he was gone, Lucas looked at Kennett and asked, "Why don't you like him?"

The distaste that had flicked across Kennett's face had been covered in an instant. He looked at Davenport for a long, measured beat and then said, "Because he never does anything but words. Maneuvers. Manipulations. He looks like a pig, but he's not. He's a goddamn spider. If he had a choice between lying and telling the truth, he'd lie because it'd be more interesting. That's why."

"Sounds like a good reason," Lucas said, looking after O'Dell. "Lily seems to like him."

"I can't figure that," Kennett said. They both glanced down the room at Lily, who was talking with Fell. "That pig-spider business, by the way . . . I put my ass in your hands. If he knew I thought that, my next job'd be directing traffic out of a parking garage."

"Not really," said Lucas. Power equations weren't that simple.

Kennett looked at him, amused. "No. Not really. But the asshole could be trouble."

They were both looking toward Lily, and when she tipped her head toward the hall, Lucas started for the door. "You coming?" he asked Fell.

She looked up from one of her files. "Am I invited?"

"Sure. Gotta be careful, though. . . ."

Reporters from three papers and two television stations were waiting, along with two TV cameras. The reporters were in a good mood, joking with him, chatting with each other about problems at the papers. They didn't think much of the story: the interviews were easy and loose, focused on a trap that Lucas had built for Bekker in Minneapolis, and on Bekker himself.

"Really quick," one of the television reporters said to Lucas as the talk was wrapping up, " 'cause we're not going to have much time. . . . You know Michael Bekker. You even visited with him in his home. How would you characterize him? From your personal acquaintance? He's been called an animal . . ."

"To call Bekker an animal is an insult to animals," Lucas said. "Bekker's a monster. That's the only word I can think of that's even close to what he is. He's a real, live horror-show freak."

"Far out," said the reporter, a harried blonde in a uniform blue blazer. She asked her cameraman, "How'd that look?"

"Looked good, that's what they'll use. Let's get a reverse shot on you, reacting . . ."

When the reporters were gone, O'Dell, sitting spread-legged on a folding chair, the way fat men do, nodded approvingly. "That was good. You say Bekker's smart and hard to catch and that everything is being done." His heavy lips moved in and out a couple of times. "Like the blonde broad said, 'Far out.' "

THE TROPIC OF SIXTH AVENUE.

The sky was pink from the pollution haze boiling off the asphalt, and heat mirages made the light poles shimmy like belly dancers. Fell pushed the beat-up Plymouth through the cab traffic, one arm out the window, an unfiltered cigarette between her fingers, old-gold rock 'n' roll playing from a personal boombox in the backseat. The Doors, "Light My Fire."

". . . don't have enough money to fix the air conditioner," she was saying, "but we get three computer terminals so we can do more paperwork, and they're not even new terminals, they're rehabs . . ."

Black and brown arms hung from the driver's windows of the amber taxis beside them, while the paler passengers slumped in back, simmering in their own juices.

"Why fences?" Lucas asked. They were looking for fences. Fell, he'd been told, specialized in burglary and industrial theft, down through the manufacturing district of Manhattan.

"Because Kennett was reading one of these nut-case medical papers Bekker is writing, and figured out that Bekker was taking measurements that you can only take with medical monitoring gear. One of the papers mentions blood pressure taken from a catheter at the radial artery. You gotta have the right stuff. . . ."

"Check the medical-supply houses?"

"Yup, everywhere in North America and the major Japanese and European suppliers. Nothing. Checked the hospitals for stolen stuff and came up empty, but he had to get it somewhere. . . . There are a couple of other guys checking secondary sources. . . ."

They stopped at a traffic light. On the sidewalk, a fruit vendor sat in a plastic lawn chair with a wet rag on his forehead and took a continuous long peel off a red apple, using a thin-bladed stiletto with a pearl handle. A slow-moving, ratty-furred tiger-striped cat walked past him, stopped to look at the dangling peel, then hopped down into the gutter, took a last look around at the daylight world, and dropped into the sewer. Anything to get out of the heat.

". . . some kind of heat inversion and the temperature never goes down at night, see. That's when things get weird," Fell said, gunning the car through the intersection. "I got a call once where this PR stuck his old lady's head . . ."

"A what?"

"Puerto Rican. Where this Puerto Rican dude stuffed his old lady's head in the toilet and she drowned, and he said he did it because it was so fuckin' hot and she wouldn't shut up. . . ."

They rolled past the Checks Cashed and the Mexican and Indian restaurants, past the delis and the stink of a dog-'n'-kraut stand, past people with red dots on their foreheads and yarmulkes and witty T-shirts that said "No Farting," past bums and sunglassed Mafia wannabees in nine-hundred-dollar loose-kneed suits with shiny lapels.

Past a large woman wearing a T-shirt with a silhouette of a .45 on the front. A newspaper-style map arrow pointed at the gun's muzzle and said, "Official Map of New York City: You Are Here."

"There's Lonnie," Fell said, easing the car to the curb. A taxi behind them honked, but Fell ignored it and got out.

"Hey, whaddafuck . . ."

Fell made a pistol of her thumb and index finger and pointed it at the cabby and pulled the trigger and continued on around the car. Lonnie was sitting on an upturned plastic bottle crate, a Walkman plugged into his ear, head bobbing to whatever sound he was getting. He was looking the other way when Fell walked up and tapped the crate with her toe. Lonnie reared back and looked up, then pulled the plug out of his ear.

"Hey . . ." Lucas turned in front of him, on the other side. Nowhere to run.

"You sold three hundred hypodermic syringes to Al Kunsler on Monday," Fell said. "We want to know where you got them and what else you got. Medical stuff."

"I don't know nothing about that," Lonnie said. He had scars around his eyebrows, and his nose didn't quite line up with the center of his mouth.

"Come on, Lonnie. We know about it, and I don't much give a shit," Fell said impatiently. Her forehead was damp with the heat. "You fuck with us, we take you down. You tell us, we drive away. And believe me, this is something you don't want to get involved in."

"Yeah? What's going on?" He looked like he was about to stand up, but Lucas put his hand on his shoulder, and he settled back on the crate.

"We're looking for this fruitcake Bekker, okay? He's getting medical gear. We're looking for suppliers. You know at least one. . . ."

"I don't know from this Bekker dude," Lonnie said.

"So just tell us where you got them," Lucas said.

Lonnie looked around, as if to see who was watching. "Atlantic City. From some guy in a motel."

"Where'd he get them?" Lucas asked.

"How the fuck would I know? Maybe off the beach."

"Lonnie, Lonnie . . ." said Fell.

"Look, I went to Atlantic City for a little straight action. You know you can't get straight action around here anymore. . . ."

"Yeah, yeah . . ."

". . . And I meet this guy at the motel and he says he's got some merchandise, and I say, 'Whatcha got?' And he says, 'All sortsa shit.' And he did. He had, like, a million sets of Snap-On tools and some computer TV things and leather flight bags and belts and suits and shit, and these needles."

"What was he driving?" Lucas asked.

"Cadillac."

"New?"

"Naw. Old. Great big fuckin' green one, color of Key Lime pie, with the white roof."

"Think he's still there?"

Lonnie shrugged. "Could be. Looked like he'd been there awhile. I know there was some girls down the way, he was partying with them, they acted like they knew him. . . ."

THEY TOUCHED a half-dozen other fences, small-time hustlers. At half-hour intervals, Fell would find a pay phone and make a call.

"Nobody home?"

"Nobody home," she said, and they went looking for more fences.

Fell was a cowgirl, Lucas thought, watching her drive. She'd been born out of place, out of time, in the Bronx. She'd fit in the Dakotas or Montana: bony, with wide shoulders and high cheekbones, that frizzy red hair held back from her face with bobby pins. With the scar at the end of her mouth . . .

She'd been jabbed with the broken neck of a beer bottle, she said, back when she was on patrol. "That's what you get when you try to keep assholes from killing each other."

Babe Zalacki might have been a babe once, before her teeth fell out. She shook her head and smiled her toothless pink smile at Lucas: "I don't know from medical shit," she said. "The closest I got to it was, I got three hundred cases of Huggies a couple of weeks ago. Now Huggies, you can sell Huggies. You take them up to Harlem and sell them on the street corners like that. . . ." She snapped her fingers. "But medical shit . . . who knows?"

Back on the street, Fell said, "Sun's going down."

Lucas looked up at the sky, where a dusty sun hung over the west side. "Still hot."

"Wait'll August. August is hot. This is nothin'. . . . Better make a call."

Up the street, a bald man in a jean jacket turned to face a building, braced a hand against it, and began urinating. Lucas watched as he finished, got himself together, and continued down the street. No problem.

Fell came back and said, "He's home. Phone's busy."

They took a half hour, cutting crosstown as the light began to fail, through a warehouse section not far from the water. Fell finally slowed, did a U-turn, and bumped the right-side wheels over the curb. She killed the engine, put her radio on the floor in the backseat, fished a sign out from under the seat and tossed it on the dashboard: "No radio inside."

"Even a cop car?"

"Especially a cop car—cop cars got all kinds of goodies. At least, that's what they think."

Lucas climbed out, stretched, yawned, and ran his thumb along his beltline, under his jacket, until it hit the leather of the Bianchi holster. The street was in deep shadow, with doorway niches and shuttered carports in brick walls. A red brick cube, unmarked by any visible sign or number, loomed overhead like a Looney Tune. Rows of dark windows started three stories up; they were tall and narrow, and from the third to the eleventh floor, dark as onyx. Half of the top floor was lit.

"Lights are on," Fell said.

"Weird place to live," Lucas said, looking around. Scrap paper sidled lazily down the street, borne on a hot humid river breeze. The breeze smelled like the breath of an old man with bad teeth. They were close to the Hudson, somewhere in the twenties.

"Jackie Smith is a weird guy," Fell said. Lucas stepped toward the door, but she caught his arm. "Slow down. Give me a minute." She dug into her purse and came up with a pack of Luckys.

"You've got it bad," Lucas said, watching her. "The habit."

"Yeah, but at least I don't need an alarm clock."

"What?" He stepped into it.

"Every morning at seven o'clock sharp, I wake myself up coughing." When Lucas didn't smile, she peered at him and said, "That was a joke, Davenport."

"Yeah. Inside, I'm laughing myself sick," he said. Then he smiled.

Fell tapped a Lucky on the back of a pack of matches, stuck it in her mouth with a two-finger flipping motion, cupped it with her hands and lit it.

"You're not going to fuck me up, are you?" she asked, her eyes flicking up at him.

"I don't know what that means," Lucas said. He stuck a finger between his collar and his neck. His neck felt like sandpaper. If ring around the collar were a terminal disease, they'd be burying him.

"I saw the pictures of Bekker, after the arrest," Fell said. "He looked like somebody stuck his face in a blender. If you do that in New York, with somebody connected downtown, like Jackie is, your fuckin' *career* goes in the blender."

"I don't have a career," Lucas said.

"I do," said Fell. "Four more years and I'm out. I'd like to make it."

"What're you going to do when you get out?" Lucas asked, making talk while she smoked. He tipped his head back and looked up again. He seemed to do that in New York, even with buildings only twelve stories tall.

"I'm gonna move to Hollywood, Florida, and get a job as a topless waitress," Fell said.

"What?" She brought him down, startled him.

"Joke, Davenport," she said.

"Right." He looked back up, turning in the street. "Who is this guy?"

She took a drag, coughed, covered her mouth with a rolled fist. "Jackie? He's fairly big. The others we've talked to, they were middle-sized or small-timers. Jackie's a wholesaler. There are three or four of them here in midtown. When somebody hijacks a truck full of Sonys, one of the wholesalers'll get it and parcel it out to the small-timers. If Jackie feels like it, he could put out the word on Bekker to fifty or sixty or a hundred guys. If he feels like it. And those guys could probably talk to a million junkies and thieves. *If* they feel like it."

"If you know all this . . . ?" He looked at her with a cool curiosity. A man turned the corner behind them, saw them standing on the sidewalk, and went back around the corner out of sight.

"He's got his own business, remaindering stuff," Fell continued. "If somebody has six zillion nuts and no bolts to go with them, he calls up Jackie. Jackie buys them and finds somebody who needs them. That's all legal. If you tag him, you'll find him going in and out of warehouses all day, ten or twenty a day, different ones every day of the week. Talks to all kinds of people. Hundreds of them. Somewhere in the mess, he's got eight or ten people working for him, running the fencing business out the back door of these legit warehouses. . . . It's tough, man. I know he's doing it, but I can't find his dumps."

"He knows you?"

"He knows who I am," she said. "I once sat outside this place for three days, watching who came and went. Running license numbers. It was colder than shit. You know how it gets when it's too cold to snow?"

"Yeah. I'm from . . ."

"Minnesota. Like that," she said, looking down the street, remembering. "So the third night, this guy comes out of the building, knocks on our window, my partner and me, and hands us a Thermos of hot coffee and a couple of turkey sandwiches, courtesy of Jackie Smith."

"Hmph." He looked at her. "You take it?"

"I poured the coffee on the guy's shoes," Fell said. She was talking through her teeth. She took a last drag, grinned at him and flicked the cigarette into the street, where it bounced in a shower of sparks. "The silly shit thought he could buy me with a fuckin' turkey sandwich. . . . C'mon, let's do it."

The warehouse door was built of inch-thick glass poured around stainless-steel rods, with an identical second door six feet farther in. A video camera was mounted on the wall between the two doors. Fell pushed a doorbell marked "Top." A moment later, an electronic voice said, "Yes?"

Fell leaned close to the speaker plate. "Detectives Fell and Davenport to see Jackie Smith."

After a short pause, the voice said, "Step inside and hold your badges in front of the camera."

The door lock buzzed and Fell pulled the door open, and they went inside. Now between the two doors, they held their badges in front of the camera. A second later, the lock on the second door buzzed. "Take the elevator to twelve. It's on the way down," the voice said.

A sterile lobby of yellow-painted concrete block waited behind the second door. There were no windows, only the elevator doors and a steel fire door at the far end of the lobby. The elevators were to the left, and another video camera, mounted in a wire cage near the ceiling, watched them.

"Interesting," Lucas said. "We're in a vault."

"Yeah. You'd have a hell of a time getting this far if Jackie didn't want you in. You'd probably need plastique to do it in a hurry. Then you'd have to get through the fire door, to find the stairs, assuming that the elevator was up and locked. By that time, Jackie'd be gone, of course. I'm sure he's got a bolthole somewhere. . . ."

"And he's probably recording all of this," Lucas said.

Fell shrugged. "I'd like to get him, and I've thought about it—that ain't no secret." Halfway up, she said, "You got a thing with Rothenburg?"

He looked down at her. "Why?"

"Just curious," she said. They watched numbers flickering off the floor counter, and then she said, "When she came in, the way she looked at you, I thought you had a thing."

"Nah . . ."

She shook her head; she didn't believe him. Then the elevator doors opened and they stepped into a lobby identical to the one on the bottom floor: yellow-painted concrete block with a gray steel door set in one wall. Another video camera was mounted in a corner.

"Come in," the disembodied voice said.

The steel door opened on Wonderland.

Lucas followed Fell onto a raised hardwood deck, shaped like a half-moon, overlooking an enormous room. Ten or twelve thousand square feet, Lucas thought, most of it open. Different activity areas were defined by furniture, lights and carpet, instead of walls. The kitchen was to the right; a blond man was peering into a stove, and the odor of fresh hot bread suffused the room. To the left, halfway back, a dark-haired man stood on a square of artificial turf with a golf club.

"Over here," said the voice from the hallway, and the man with the golf club waved at them. Fell led the way, a weaving route through what seemed like an acre of furniture.

A jumble of furniture, with no specific style, Lucas thought: it looked as though it had fallen off the back of a truck. Or trucks—different trucks, from different factories. A king-sized English four-poster bed sat on a huge Oriental carpet, and was covered with an American crazy quilt. A six-foot projection TV faced the bed, and three tripod-mounted video cameras pointed at it.

Behind the TV, a semicircular wall of shoulder-high speakers flanked a conversation pit; a marble-topped table in the center held an array of CD and tape equipment, along with a library of a thousand or more compact discs. The floor beneath the stereo area was hardwood, covered with animal skins: tiger and jaguar, stitched beaver, a buffalo robe, a sleek dark square of what might have been mink. Erroll Garner bubbled out of the speakers, working through "Mambo Carmel."

Beyond the bed, and between the bed and the sports area, a glass shower stall stood out of the floor like an oversized phone booth. Two toilets sat next to it, facing each other, and on the other side, a huge tub.

Smith waited in the sports area, two thirds of the way to the back wall. The wall was pierced by three or four doors. So there were more rooms, Lucas thought. . . .

Smith, his back to them, waggled a driver, drove a golf ball into a net, shook his head, and put the club in a bag that hung from a wall peg. Behind him, a rank of unlit lights waited over what appeared to be a real grass putting green, built on a raised surface. Beyond the green, a stained-glass lamp hung over an antique pool table; and at the back of the room, a basketball net hung from a wall. Below it, a court was complete out to the top of the free-throw circle.

"Can't keep my head down," Smith said. He strode toward them, his golf shoes scuffing over the artificial turf. Smith was a short, barrel-chested, barrel-gutted man with a fuzzy mustache and kinky black hair. He wore a black golf shirt tucked into black pleated slacks, with a woven leather belt circling his waist. A gold chain dangled from his neck, with what looked like a St. Christopher medal. He smiled at Fell and stuck his hand out. "You're the cop who was watching me last year . . ."

Fell ignored the hand. "We need to talk to you about this Bekker guy," she said bluntly. "The guy who's chopping up these people . . ."

"The freak," Smith said. He took his hand back, couldn't find a place for it, and finally stuck it in his slacks pocket. He was puzzled, his mustache quivering. "Why talk to me?"

"He needs money and drugs, and he can't get them legitimately," Lucas said. He'd drifted past the driving area to the putting green. The green's surface was knee high, but dished, to provide a variety of contours. He reached down and pressed his fingers against it. Real grass, carefully groomed, cool and slightly damp to the touch.

"Now that's a hell of a project, right there," Smith said enthusiastically. He picked up a remote control, touched a series of buttons, and the lights over the putting green flickered and came on. "Those are special grow lights," he said, pointing up at the lighting fixture. "Same spectrum as the sun. Joe over there, he knows all about different grasses, he set it up. This is genuine bent grass. It took him a year to get it right."

Smith stepped up and onto the green, walked lightly across it, then turned to look at Lucas. Back to business: "So this guy needs money and drugs?"

"Yeah. And we want you to put the word out on your network. Somebody is dealing with him, and we want him. Now."

Smith picked up a putter that was leaning against the far end. Three balls waited in a rack, and he popped them out, lined up the first one, stroked and missed. The ball rolled past the cup and stopped two feet away.

"Twenty-two feet. Not bad," he said. "When you've got a long lag like that, you just try to get it within two feet of the cup. You pretend you're shooting for a manhole cover. That's the secret to single-bogey golf. Do cops play golf?"

"We need you to put out the word," Fell said.

"Talk into my belly button, said Little Red Riding Hood," Smith said. He lined up another putt, let it go. The ball rolled four feet past the cup. "Fuck it," he said. "Nerves. You guys are putting pressure on me."

"There's no wire," Lucas said quietly. "Neither one of us is wired. We're looking for a little help."

"What do I get out of it?" Smith asked.

"Civic pride," Lucas said. The pitch of his voice had dropped a bit, but Smith pretended not to notice, and lined up the last ball.

"Civic pride? In fuckin' New York?" He snorted, looked up and said, "Excuse the language, Dr. Fell. . . . Anyway, I really don't know what you're talking about, this network."

He walked around the green, squinting at the short putt. The blond man approached with a china platter covered with steaming slices of bread. "Anybody for fresh bread? We've got straight and garlic butter. . . ."

"Fuck the bread," said Fell. She looked at Lucas. "We're not getting to him. Maybe we ought to have the fire department check his . . ."

"Nah, political shit doesn't work with a guy who's really connected," Lucas said. "Mr. Smith sounds like he's connected."

Smith squinted at him. "Who're you? I don't remember you. . . ."

"I've been hired as a consultant here," Lucas said. He wandered back to the driving net, speaking so softly that the others could barely pick up the words. He pulled a three iron out of the golf bag and looked at it. "I used to work in Minneapolis, until I got thrown off the force. I caught Bekker the first time, but not before he killed a good friend of mine. Cut her throat. He let her see it coming. Made her wait for it. Then he sawed right through her neck. . . . She was tied up, couldn't fight back. So later, when I caught Bekker . . ."

"His face got all fucked up," Smith said suddenly.

"That's right," said Lucas. He'd come back, carrying the iron. "His face got all fucked up."

"Wait a minute," said Fell.

Lucas ignored her, hopped up on the putting green, and walked toward Smith. Out of the corner of his eye, he saw Fell's hand sliding into the fold of her shoulder bag. "And I didn't worry about fucking him up. You know why? Because I've got a lot of money of my own and I didn't need the job. I don't need any job."

"What the fuck are you talking . . ." Smith backed away, looked quickly at the blond.

". . . And Bekker got me really pissed," Lucas said to Smith, his voice riding over the other man's. His eyes were wide, the tendons in his neck straining at his shirt collar. "I mean *really fuckin' pissed*. And I had this pistol, with this big sharp front sight on it, and when I caught him, I pounded his face with the sight until you couldn't tell it was a face. Before that, Bekker'd been really pretty, just like this fuckin' green. . . ."

Lucas pivoted and swung the three iron, a long sweeping swing into the perfect turf. A two-pound divot of dirt and grass sprayed off the platform across the pool table.

"Wait, wait . . ." Smith was waving his hands, trying to stop it.

The blond had set the china tray aside and his hand went toward the small of his back and Fell had a pistol out, pointed at his head, and she was yelling, "No, no, no . . ."

Lucas rolled on, swinging the club like a scythe, screaming, walking around Smith, saliva spraying on Smith's black shirt. "Pounded his face, pounded his motherfuckin' face, you believe the way we pounded his fuckin' face."

When he stopped, breathing hard, a dozen ragged furrows slashed the surface of the green. Lucas turned and looked at the blond man. Hopped down off the platform, walked toward him.

"You were going to pull out a gun," he said.

The blond man shrugged. He had heavy shoulders, like a weight lifter, and he shifted, setting his feet.

"That really pisses me off," Lucas shouted at him.

"Hold it, for Christ's sake," said Fell, her voice low and urgent.

Lucas swung the iron again, quickly, violently, overhead, then down. The blond flinched, but the iron smashed through the freshly baked bread and the platter beneath it. Pieces of china skittered across the floor, and he shouted, "And tried to fuckin' bribe us . . ."

Then he ran down, staggered, turned back to Smith and pointed the club like a saber.

"I don't want to be your friend. I don't want to deal. You're a goddamned dirtbag, and it makes me feel nasty to be here. What I'm telling you is, I want you to put the word out on your network. And I want you to call me. Lucas Davenport. Midtown South. If you don't, I will fuck you up six different ways. I'll talk to the *New York Times* and I'll talk to the *News* and I'll talk to *EyeWitness News* and I'll give them pictures of you and tell them you're working with Bekker. How'd that help business? And I might just come back and fuck you up personally, because this is a serious matter with me, this Bekker thing."

He turned in a half-circle, his breath slowing, took a step toward the door, then suddenly whipped the club into the kitchen like a helicopter blade. It knocked a copper tureen off a wall peg, bounced off the stove, and clattered to the floor with the tureen. "Never was any fucking good with the long irons," he said.

ON THE WAY OUT of the building, Fell watched him until Lucas began to grin.

"Nuttier'n shit, huh?" he said, glancing at her.

"I believed it," she said seriously.

"Thanks for the backup. I don't think blondie would've done much. . . ."

She shook her head. "That was funny; I mean, funny-strange. I didn't know Jackie Smith was gay until I saw this guy. That's like dealing with spouses, only worse. You whack one and the other's liable to come after you with a knife. . . ."

"Are you sure they're gay?"

"Does Raggedy Ann have a cotton crotch?"

"I don't know what that means," Lucas said, laughing.

"It means yes, I'm sure they're gay," she said.

"How come he called you Dr. Fell?" Lucas asked. "Are you a doctor?"

"No. It's from the nursery rhyme: 'I do not love thee, Dr. Fell; the reason why I cannot tell; but this I know, and know full well: I do not love thee, Dr. Fell.' "

"Huh. I'm impressed," Lucas said.

"I know several nursery rhymes," Fell said, digging in her purse for the pack of Luckys. "Want to hear 'Old King Cole' ?"

"I mean with Smith. Knowing the rhyme."

"I don't impress you, huh?" She flipped the cigarette into her mouth, her eyes slanting up at him.

"Don't know yet," he said. "Maybe . . ."

· · ·

BARBARA FELL LIVED ON the Upper West Side. They dropped her city car at Midtown South, found a cab, and she said, "I've got a decent neighborhood bar. Why don't you come up and get a drink, chill out, and you can catch a cab from there."

"All right." He nodded. He needed some more time with her.

They went north on Sixth, the sidewalk traffic picking up as they got closer to Central Park, tourists walking arm in arm along the sidewalks.

"It's too big," Lucas said, finally, watching through the window as the city went by. "In the Twin Cities, you can pretty much get a line on every asshole in town. Here . . ." He looked out and shook his head. "Here, you'd never know where it was coming from. You got assholes like other places got raindrops. This is the armpit of the universe."

"Yeah, but it can be pretty nice," she said. "Got the theaters, the art museums . . ."

"When was the last time you went to a theater?"

"I don't know—I really can't afford it. But I mean, if I could."

"Right."

In the front seat, the taxi driver was humming to himself. There was no tune, only variations in volume and intensity as the driver stared blank-eyed through the windshield, bobbing his head to some unheard rhythm. His hands gripped the wheel so tightly that his knuckles were white. Lucas looked at the driver, looked at Fell and shook his head. She laughed, and he grinned and went back to the window.

THE BAR WAS SMALL, carefully lit, convivial. The bartender called Fell by her first name, pointed her at a back booth. Lucas took the seat facing the entrance. A waitress came over, looked at him, looked at Fell, said, "Ooo."

Fell said, "Strictly business."

"Ain't it always," the waitress said. "Didja hear Louise had her kid, baby girl, six pounds four ounces?"

Lucas watched Fell as she chatted with the waitress. She looked a little tired, a little lonesome, with that uncertain smile.

"So," she said, coming back to Lucas. "Do you really freeze your ass off in Minnesota? Or is that just . . ."

Small talk, bar talk. A second drink. Lucas waiting for a break, waiting. . . .

Getting it. A slender man walked in, touched a woman on the cheek, got a quick peck in return. He was blond, carefully dressed, and after a moment, looked at the back of Fell's head, said something to the woman he'd touched, then looked carefully at Lucas.

"There's a guy," Lucas said, leaning across the table, talking in a low voice. "And I think he's looking at you. By the bar . . ."

She turned her head and lit up. "Mica," she called. To Lucas she said, "He used to be my hairdresser. He's, like, moved downtown." She slid out of the booth, walked up to the bar. "When did you get back . . . ?"

"I thought that was you . . ." Mica said.

Mica had been to Europe; he started a story. Lucas sipped the beer, lifted his feet to the opposite seat, caught Fell's purse between his ankles, pulled it in. Fumbled with it, out of sight, watching. The waitress glanced his way, lifted her eyebrows. He shook his head. If she came over, if Mica's story ended too soon, if Fell hurried back to get a cigarette . . .

There. Keys. He'd been waiting all day for a shot at them. . . .

He glanced at the key ring in his hand, six keys. Three good candidates. He had a flat plastic box in his pocket that had once held push pins. He'd dumped the pins and filled both the bottom and the lid with a thin layer of modeling clay. He pressed the first key in the clay, turned it, pressed again. Then the second key. The third key he did in the lid; if he made the impressions too close together, the clay tended to distort. . . . He glanced into the box. Good, clean, impressions, six of them.

Fell was still talking. He slipped the keys back into her purse, gripped it with his ankles, lifted it back to her seat. . . .

Pulse pounding like an amateur shoplifter's.

Jesus.

Got them.

LILY CALLED THE NEXT morning, "Got them," she said. "We're going to breakfast. . . ."

Lucas called Fell, catching her just before she left her apartment.

"O'Dell called," he said. "He wants me to have breakfast with him. I probably won't make it down until ten o'clock or so."

"All right. I'll run the guy Lonnie told us about, the guy with the Cadillac in Atlantic City. It won't be much. . . ."

"Unless the guy's into medical supplies. Maybe the syringes weren't his only item."

"Yeah . . ." She knew that was bullshit, and Lucas grinned at the telephone.

"Hey, we're driving nails. I'll buy you lunch later on."

The Lakota Hotel was old, but well-kept for New York. It was close to the publishing company that produced Lucas' board games, convenient to restaurants, and had beds that his feet didn't hang off of. From this particular room, he had a view over the roof below into the windows of a glass-sided office building. Not wonderful, but not bad, either. He had two nightstands, a writing table, a chest of drawers, a window seat, a color television with a working remote, and a closet with a light that came on automatically when he opened it.

He went to the closet, pulled out a briefcase and opened it on the bed. Inside was a monocular, a cassette recorder with a phone clip, and a Polaroid Spectra camera with a half-dozen rolls of film. Excellent. He closed the briefcase, made a quick trip to the bathroom, and rode back down to the street. A bellhop, loitering in the phone-booth-sized lobby, said "Cab, Mr. Davenport?"

"No. I've got a car coming," he said. Outside, he hurried down the street to a breakfast bar, got a pint of orange juice in a wax carton, and went back outside.

After leaving Fell the night before, he'd gone to Lily's apartment and given her the key impressions. Lily knew an intelligence officer who could get them made overnight, discreetly.

"Old friend?" Lucas asked.

"Go home, Lucas," she'd said, pushing him out the door.

And now she called his name again: a black town car slid to the curb, a cluster of antennas sticking out of the trunk lid, and when the back window slid down, he saw her face. "Lucas . . ."

O'DELL'S DRIVER WAS a broad man with a Korean War crew cut, his hair the color of rolled steel. A hatchet nose split basalt eyes, and his lips were dry and thick; a Gila monster's. Lucas got in the passenger seat.

"Avery's?" the driver asked. The front seat was separated from the back by an electric window, which had been run down.

"Yeah," O'Dell said. He was reading the *Times* editorial page. A pristine copy of the *Wall Street Journal* lay between his right leg and Lily's left. As he looked over the paper, he asked Lucas, "Did you eat yet?"

"A carton of orange juice."

"We'll get you something solid," O'Dell said. He'd not stopped reading the paper, and the question and comment were perfunctory. After a moment, he muttered, "Morons."

Lily said to the driver, "This is Lucas Davenport next to you, Aaron—Lucas, that's Aaron Copland driving."

"Not the fuckin' piano player, either," Copland said. His eyes went to Lucas. "How are ya?"

"Nice to meet you," Lucas said.

At Avery's, Copland got out first and held the door for O'Dell. Copland had a wide, solid gut, but the easy moves of an athlete. He wore a pistol clipped to his belt, just to the left of his navel, and though his golf shirt covered it, he made no particular attempt to conceal it.

A heavy automatic, Lucas thought. Most of the New York cops he'd seen were carrying ancient .38 Specials, revolvers that looked as though they'd been issued at the turn of the century. Copland, whatever else he might be, was living in the present. He never looked directly at Lucas or Lily or O'Dell as they were getting out of the car, but around them, into the corners and doorways and window wells.

In the closest doorway was a solid oak door with a narrow window at eye height, and below that, a gleaming brass plaque that said AVERY's. Behind the door was a restaurant full of politicians: they had places like this in Minneapolis and St. Paul, but Lucas had never seen one in New York. It was twenty feet wide, a hundred feet deep, with a long dark mahogany bar to the right side of the entrance. Overhead, wooden racks held hundreds of baseball bats, lying side by side, all of them autographed. A dozen flat Plexiglas cases marched down the left-hand wall opposite the bar, like stations of the cross, and each case held a half-dozen more bats, autographed. Lucas knew most of the names—Ruth, Gehrig, DiMaggio, Maris, Mays, Snider, Mantle. Others, like Nick Etten, Bill Terry, George Stirnweiss, Monte Irvin, rang only faint bells in his memory. At the end of the bar, a double row of booths extended to the back of the restaurant; almost all of the booths were occupied.

"I'll be at the bar," Copland said. He'd looked over the occupants of the restaurant, decided that none of them was a candidate for shooting.

O'Dell led the way back: he was an actor, Lucas realized, rolling slowly down the restaurant like a German tank, nodding into some booths, pointedly ignoring others, the rolled copy of the *Wall Street Journal* whacking his leg.

"Goddamn town," O'Dell said when he was seated at the booth. He dropped the papers on the seat by his leg. Lily sat opposite him, with Lucas. He peered at Lucas across the table and said, "You know what's happening out there, Davenport? People are stringing razor wire—you see it everywhere now. And broken glass on the tops of walls. Like some goddamned Third World city. New York. Like fuckin' Bangkok." He lowered his voice: "Like these cops, if they're out there. A death squad, like Brazil or Argentina."

A balding waiter with a pickle face came to the table. He wore a neck-to-knees white apron that seemed too neatly blotched with mustard.

"Usual," O'Dell grunted.

Lily glanced at Lucas and said, "Two coffees, two Danish."

The waiter nodded sourly and left.

"You got a reputation as a shooter," O'Dell said.

"I've shot some people," Lucas said. "So has Lily."

"We don't want you to shoot anybody," O'Dell said.

"I'm not an assassin."

"I just wanted you to know," O'Dell said. He groped in his pocket and pulled out a strip of paper and unfolded it. The *Times* story. "You did a good job yesterday. Modest, you give credit to everyone, you stress how smart Bekker can be. Not bad. They bought it. Have you read the files? On this other thing?"

"I'm starting tonight, at Lily's."

"Any thoughts so far? From what you've seen?" O'Dell pressed.

"I don't see Fell in it."

"Oh?" O'Dell's eyebrows went up. "I can assure you that she is, somehow. Why would you think otherwise?"

"She's just not right. How did you find her?"

"Computer. We ran the dead guys against the cops who busted them. She came up several times. Repeatedly, in a couple of cases. Too many times for it to be a coincidence," O'Dell said.

"Okay. I can see her nominating somebody. I just can't see her setting up a hit. She's not real devious."

"Do you like her?" asked Lily.

"Yeah."

"Will that get in the way?" O'Dell asked.

"No."

O'Dell glanced at Lily and she said, "I don't think it will. Lucas fucks over both men and women impartially."

"Hey, you know I get a little tired . . ." Lucas said irritably.

"Fell looks like another Davenport kill," Lily said. She tried for humor, but there was an edge to it.

"Hey, hey . . ." O'Dell said.

"Look, Lily, you know goddamned well . . ." Lucas said.

"Stop, stop, not in a restaurant," O'Dell said. "Jesus . . ."

"Okay," said Lily. She and Lucas had locked up, and now she broke her eyes away.

The waiter returned with a plate piled with French toast and a small tureen of hot maple syrup. A pat of butter floated on the syrup. He unloaded the French toast in front of O'Dell, and coffee cups in front of Lucas and Lily. O'Dell tucked a napkin into his collar and started on the toast.

"There's something more going on here," O'Dell said, when the waiter had gone. "These three hits we're most worried about, the lawyer, the activist, and Petty himself—I believe these guys may be coming out. The shooters."

"What?" Lucas glanced at Lily, who stared impassively at O'Dell.

"That's my sense, my political sense," O'Dell said. He popped a dripping square of toast into his mouth, chewed, leaned back and watched Lucas with his small eyes. "They're deliberately letting us know that they're out there and that they aren't to be fooled with. The word is getting around. Has been for a couple of months. You hear this shit, 'Robin Hood and his Merry Men,' or 'Batman Strikes Again,' whenever some asshole is taken off. There are a lot of people who'd like the idea that they're out there. Doing what's necessary. Half the people in town would be cheering them on, if they knew."

"And the other half would be in the streets, tearing the place apart," Lily said to Lucas. She turned her head to O'Dell. "There's the other thing, too, with Bekker."

"What?" asked Lucas, looking between them.

"We're told that this is real," she said. She fished in her purse, took out a folded square of paper and handed it to him. A Xerox copy of a letter, addressed to the editor of the *New York Times*.

Lucas glanced down at the signature: Bekker. One word, an aristocratic conceit and scrawl.

. . . taken to task for what I consider absolutely essential experiments
into the transcendental nature of Man, and accused of crimes; so be it.
I will stand on my intellectual record, and though accused of crimes,
as Galileo was, I will, like him, be vindicated by a future generation.

Though accused of crimes, I am innocent, and I will have no truck
with criminals. It is in that spirit that I write. On Friday night last, I witnessed an apparent gangland shooting. . . .

"Jesus Christ," Lucas said, looking at Lily. "Was this one of the killings you
were talking about?"

"Walt," she said.

Lucas went back to the letter. Bekker had seen the two killers clearly.

. . . would describe him as white, thick, square-faced with a gray, well-
trimmed mustache extending the full length of his upper lip, weighing two hundred and twenty pounds, six feet, two inches tall, sixty-one
years old. As a trained forensic pathologist, I would wager that I am
not wrong by more than five pounds either way, or by more than an
inch in height, or two years in age.

The description of the other one, the one I have called Thin, I will
hold to myself, for my own reasons. . . .

"This never ran in the paper?" Lucas asked, looking at O'Dell.

"No. They've agreed to hold it at our request, but they've reserved the right
to print it if it seems relevant."

"Do you have any idea who it is? This Thick guy?"

He shook his head: "One of four or five hundred cops—if it's a cop at all."

"You could probably narrow it more than that," Lucas said.

"Not without going public," Lily said. "If we started checking out five hundred cops . . . Christ, the papers would be all over us. But the main thing is, you
see . . ."

Lucas picked up her thought: "Bekker can identify two cop killers and he's
willing to do it. . . ."

"And for that reason, we think these guys'll make a run at Bekker."

"To shut him up."

"Among other things."

"If they are coming out, they're more likely to go for Bekker," O'Dell said.
"They might have to go for him anyway, if they think he can identify two of them.
But there's more than that: Killing Bekker would be one way to make their
point, that some people have to be killed. Bekker's a nightmare. Who can object to killing him? He's made to order for them, if they can find him."

"This is getting complicated," Lucas said. "I worry about Lily. She's close to
this thing, funneling stuff around. What happens if they come after her?"

"They won't," O'Dell said confidently. "Two dead cops would be unacceptable. . . ."

"I'd think one dead cop would be unacceptable."

"One dead cop can be finessed. Denied. Two is a pattern," O'Dell said.

"Besides, I'm not exactly a pushover," Lily said, patting the purse where she kept her .45.

"That'll get your ass killed," Lucas said, anger in his voice. They locked up again. "Anyone's a pushover when the shooters are using a fuckin' machine gun from ambush. You're good, but you ain't bulletproof."

"All right, all right . . ." She rolled her eyes away.

"And there's always Copland," O'Dell said. "When Lily's outside working, she's usually with me in the car. Copland's more than a driver. He's tough as a nail and he knows how to use his gun. I'll have him take her home at night."

"Okay." Lucas looked at Lily again, just for a second, then shifted back to O'Dell. "How'd you get onto Fell? Exactly?"

"Exactly." O'Dell mopped up a river of syrup with a crust of the toast, looked at it for a minute, then popped it in his mouth and chewed, his small eyes nearly closing with the pleasure of it. He swallowed, opened his eyes. Like a frog, Lucas thought. "This is it, exactly. Once or twice a semester I go up to Columbia and lecture on Real Politics, for a friend of mine. Professor. This goes way back. So a few years ago—hell, what am I saying, it was fifteen years ago— he introduced me to a graduate student who was using computerized statistical techniques to analyze voting patterns. Fascinating stuff. I wound up taking classes in statistics, and a couple in computers. I don't look like it"—he spread his arms, as if to display his entire corpulent body—"but I'm a computer jock. When these guys in intelligence found what they thought was a problem, I sorted the killings. There *was* a pattern. No mistake about it. I called in Petty, who specialized in computer searches and relational work. We turned up almost two hundred possibles. For one reason or another, we eliminated a lot of them and got it down to maybe forty. And twelve of those, we were just about sure of. I think Lily told you that . . ."

"Yeah. Forty. That's a pretty unbelievable number."

O'Dell shrugged. "Some of the killings are probably just what they seem to be—thugs getting killed on the street by other thugs. But not all of them. And I'm sure we missed some. So balancing everything out, I think forty, fifty aren't bad numbers."

"How does Fell fit in?" Lucas asked.

"Petty ran the bad guys against cops who'd know them—a lot of complicated name sorts here, but I've got total access."

"And Fell's name came up. . . ."

"Way too much."

"I hate statistics," Lucas said. "The newspapers were always fuckin' with them back in Minneapolis, drawing stupid conclusions from bad data."

"That's a problem, the data," O'Dell agreed. "We'd certainly never get Fell in court, based on my numbers."

"Mmmph." Lucas looked at Lily and then O'Dell. "I need some heavy time to dig through this. . . ."

"Don't," said O'Dell. He pointed a fork at Lucas' nose. "Your first priority is to find Bekker and to provide a diversion for the media. We need a little air. You've got to do that for real. If this gang is out there, these killers, they won't be easily fooled. Bringing you to New York was supposed to be like bringing in a psychic from Boise: to keep the Boises in the newsroom happy. Everybody's buying it so far. They've got to keep buying it. This other thing has to be way, way in the background."

"What happens if we catch Bekker too soon?" Lucas asked. "Before we identify these guys?"

Lily shrugged. "Then you go home and we find some other way to do it."

"Mmm."

"So. We're in a position where we're hopin' a goddamn psycho holds out for another few weeks and maybe butchers somebody else's kid, so we can run down our own guys," O'Dell mumbled, half talking to himself, staring into the half-eaten sludge pile of toast and syrup. He turned to Lily. "We're really fucked, you know that, Lily? We're really and truly fucked."

"Hey, this is New York," Lucas said.

O'Dell slogged through the rest of the French toast, filling in background on Petty's computer search for the killers.

"Is there any possibility that he turned up something unexpected with the computer?" Lucas asked.

"Not really. Things don't work that way—with a computer, you grind things out, you inch forward. You don't get a printout that says 'Joe Blow Did It.' I think something must have happened with this witness."

WHEN THEY LEFT the restaurant, O'Dell walked ahead, again nodding into some booths, pointedly ignoring others. Lily grabbed Lucas' sleeve and held him back a step.

"Here." She handed him three keys on a ring.

"That was quick," Lucas said.

"This is New York," she said.

LUCAS TOOK A CAB from Avery's to Fell's apartment building. The cab-driver was a small man with a white beard, and as soon as Lucas settled in the backseat, he asked, "See *Misérables*?"

"What?"

"Let me tell you, you're missing something," the driver said. He smelled like a raw onion and was soaked with sweat. "Where're you going? Okay—Listen, you gotta see *Misérables*, I mean why d'ya come to New York if you ain't gonna see a show, you know what I mean? Look at the crazy motherfucker over there, you should excuse the language, you think they should let a jerk like that on the streets? Jesus Christ, where'd he learn to drive?" The driver stuck his head out the window, leaning on the horn. "Hey, buddy, where'd you learn to drive, huh? Iowa? Huh? Hey, buddy." Back inside, he said, "I tell you, if the mayor wasn't black . . ."

. . .

LUCAS CALLED FELL at the office from a pay phone mounted on the outside wall of a parking garage. The garage paint, covered with indecipherable graffiti, was peeling off, to reveal another layer of graffiti. "Barb? Lucas. I gotta run back to my place, just for a minute. Are we still on for lunch?"

"Sure."

"Great. See you in a few minutes," Lucas said. He hung up and looked across the street at Fell's apartment building. A thousand apartments, he thought. Maybe more. Ranks of identical balconies, each with a couple of plants, most with bicycles. Yuppie-cycles, the mountain bikes, in case the riders encountered an off-trail situation in Central Park. Some of them, as high as he could see, were chained to the balcony railings.

The lobby of her building was a glass cage surrounding a guard. At the back were two ranks of stainless-steel mailboxes. The guard, in an ill-fitting gray uniform, was stupidly watchful.

"Where's the sales office?" Lucas asked. A light flickered in the guard's eyes. This situation was specifically covered in his orders. "Second floor, sir, take a right."

"Thanks." Apartment security; it was wonderful, if you had it. Lucas walked back to the elevators, punched two. The second floor had several offices, all down to the right. Lucas ignored them, took a left. Found the stairs, walked up a floor, went back to the elevators and punched sixteen.

The telephone call assured him that Fell was still at Midtown; he didn't have to worry that she'd slipped back home for a snack or to pay bills, or whatever. She lived alone, she'd said. He'd gotten her apartment and home phone numbers from an office roster sheet.

He rode up alone, got out in an empty corridor, took a left, got lost, retraced his steps past the elevators. Her door was green; the others were blue, a tomato-red and beige. Other than that, they were identical. He knocked. No answer. Looked around, knocked again. No answer. He tried a key, hit it the first time, popped the door. The silence inside seemed laced with tension.

Gotta move, move, move . . .

The apartment smelled lightly, inoffensively, of tobacco. The living room had a sliding glass door that led out to the balcony; the doors were covered by off-white curtains, half-drawn. She had a view of a similar building, but if he looked sideways, across the street, Lucas could see another rank of buildings across a gap. The gap was probably the Hudson, with Jersey on the other side.

The apartment was neat, but not compulsively so. Most of the furniture was good, purchased as matched sets. Two green overstuffed La-Z-Boy chairs faced a big color television. A low table sat between the chairs, stacked with magazines. *Elle, Vogue, Guns & Ammo.* More magazines lay on the table, and under it he found a pile of novels. Beside the television was a cabinet with a CD player, a tuner, a tape deck and a VCR. A second table held more magazines, four remote controls, an oversize brandy snifter full of matchbooks—Windows on the World, the Russian Tea Room, the Oak Room, The Four Seasons. They were pristine, and looked as though they'd come from a souvenir packet. Other matchbooks were more worn, half-used—several from the bar they'd visited the night before, one with a crown, one with a chess knight, one with an artist's palette. An ashtray held four cigarette butts.

On the walls around the television were photo portraits: a woman standing on a pier with two older people who might have been her parents, and another picture of the same woman in a wedding veil; a square-shouldered young man on a hillside with a collie and a .22, and another of the young man, grown older, dressed in an army uniform, standing under a sign that said, "I know I'm going to heaven, because I served my time in Hell: Korea, 1952." Something wrong with the young man . . . Lucas looked closer. His upper lip was twisted slightly, as though he'd had a harelip surgically repaired.

Her parents? Almost certainly.

A hallway broke to the left out of the living room. He checked it, found a bathroom and two bedrooms. One bedroom was used as an office and for storage; a small wooden desk and two file cabinets were pushed against one wall, while most of the rest of the space was occupied by cardboard boxes, some open, some taped shut. The other bedroom had a queen-sized bed, unmade, with a sheet tangled by its foot, and two chests of drawers, one with a mirror. An oval braided rug lay underfoot, just at the side of the bed, and a pair of underpants lay in the middle of the rug. A thigh-high woven-bamboo basket with a lid half-hid behind one of the chests. He opened it. Soiled clothes: a hamper.

He could see it. *She sleeps in her underpants, sits up, still tired, yawns, gets out of beds, drops her pants for a shower, figures to toss them in the hamper when she gets back, forgets. . . .*

He went back through the living room to the kitchen, which looked almost unused—a half-dozen water glasses sat in a drying rack in the sink, along with a couple of forks, but no dishes. A Weight Watchers lasagna package lay inside a wastebasket. A bottle of Tanqueray gin sat on the cupboard, two-thirds full. He looked in the refrigerator, found bottles of lime-flavored Perrier and Diet Pepsi, a six-pack of Coors, a bottle of reconstituted lime juice and four bottles of Schweppe's Diet Tonic Water. A sack of nectarines lay on top of the fruit drawer. He touched the stove-top. Dust. A freestanding microwave took up half the counter space. No dust. She didn't cook much.

He did the kitchen first: women hide things in the kitchen or the bedroom. He found a set of dishes, inexpensive, functional. Rudimentary cooking equipment. A drawer full of paper, warranties for all the appliances and electronics in the place. He pulled the drawers out, looked under and behind them. Looked in tins: nothing, not even the flour and sugar that was supposed to be there.

In the bedroom, he looked under the bed and found a rowing machine and dust bunnies the size of wolverines; and in the bedstand drawer, where he found a Colt Lawman with a two-inch barrel, chambered for .38 Specials. Swung out the cylinder: six loaded chambers. He snapped the cylinder back, replaced the weapon as he'd found it.

Looked through the chest of drawers. Bundles of letters and postcards in the top drawer, with cheap jewelry and a sealed box of lubricated Trojans. He looked through the letters, hurrying.

Dear Barb, Just back from New Hampshire, and you should have come! We had the best time!

Dear Barb: Quick note. I'll be back the 23rd, if everything goes right. Tried to call, but couldn't get you, they said you were out, and I was afraid to wake you during the day. I really need to see you. I think about you all the time. I can't stop. Anyway, see you on the 23rd. Jack.

The letter was in an envelope, and he checked the postmark: four years old. He made a mental note: Jack.

Not much else. He pulled out the drawers. Ah. More paper. Polaroid photos. Barbara Fell, sitting on a man's lap, both holding up bottles of beer. They were naked. She was thin, with small breasts and dark nipples.

He was as thin as she, but muscular, dark-haired, and looked at the camera with a practiced lack of self-consciousness. Another shot: the two of them sitting on what looked like a zebra-skin rug, both nude, their eyes red pinpoints. In the background, a mirror, with a brilliant flash reflecting back at the camera. The camera in the mirror was on a tripod, unattended. No third person. The expression on her face . . . Fear? Excitement? Trepidation?

Another photo, the two of them clothed, standing outside what looked like a police station. A cop? He went back to his briefcase, got the Polaroid out, clipped on the close-up attachment, knelt, and duplicated the photos.

There was nothing else in the bedroom. The bathroom was odorless, freshly scrubbed, but the vanity countertop was a jumble of lipsticks, shampoos, soap, deodorant, a box of something called YeastGard, panty shields, a pack of needles, tweezers, a huge box of Band-Aids and a bottle of sesame body oil. The medicine cabinet held a small selection of over-the-counter items: aspirin, Mycitracin, Nuprin.

He headed for the office.

She was meticulous about her accounts, and everything seemed about right: she had one bank account, a safety-deposit box, and an account with Fidelity Investments, which turned out to be an IRA.

And where was her book? He shuffled through the desk drawers. She must have a personal phone book. She probably carried an annual one with her, but she should have some sort of book she kept at home, that she wouldn't be changing every year. He frowned. Nothing in the desk. He walked out to the front room and looked around the telephone. Nothing there. The phone had a long cord, and he walked over to the pile of magazines on the television table, stirred through them. The book was there, and he flipped it open. Names. Dozens of them. He got the Polaroid and began shooting. When he finished, he'd used all but two shots.

Enough. He looked around, checked the lights and backtracked out of the apartment. The guard was staring stoically at a blank marble wall when Lucas left, and never looked up. The guard's job was to keep people out, not keep people in.

KENNETT AND ANOTHER detective were looking at paper, while a third cop talked on a telephone.

"Barbara's down the hall," Kennett said, looking up when Lucas walked in. "We got you an empty office so you can have a little peace. . . ."

"Thanks," Lucas said.

Fell was sorting through a stack of manila files. He stopped in the doorway, watched her for a moment. She was focused, intent. Attractive. The nude photos popped up in his mind's eye: she looked smaller in the photos, more vulnerable, less vivid. She began paging through a file. After a moment, she felt him in the door, looked up, startled: "Jesus, I didn't hear you," she said.

He stepped inside, walked around the table. Picked up a file: "Robert Garber, 7/12." "Is this everything?"

"Yeah. I've been reading through it. A zillion details," she said. She brushed a lock of hair out of her eyes. "The problem is, we don't need any of it. We know who Bekker is and what he looks like, and he admits in these crazy medical papers that he did the killings. All we have to do is find him; we don't need all the usual shit."

"There must be something. . . ."

"I'll be goddamned if I can see it," Fell said. "The other guys made a list, like the stuff you were talking about at the meeting this morning. He needs an income. He needs a place to hide. He needs a vehicle. He needs to change his face. So they've put out the publicity to employers: watch who you're paying. They've contacted all the hotels and flophouses and anyplace else he might stay. They're talking with the taxi companies, thinking maybe he's moving around in the cab—that would explain how he gases them, using the back seat as a gas chamber. They've gone to all the stores that sell cover-up makeup for people who are disfigured, and every place that sells theatrical makeup. The narcotics guys are talking to dealers, and we're chasing fences. What else is there?"

"I don't know, but it's not enough," Lucas said. He flipped his hand at the stack of paper. "Let's look at the victims first. . . ."

They spent an hour at it. Bekker had killed six people in Manhattan, their bodies found scattered around Midtown, the Village, SoHo and Little Italy. Working on the theory he wouldn't take them far, he was probably south of Central Park, north of the financial district. The zip codes on the envelopes he'd mailed to the medical journals suggested the same thing: three papers, three different zips: 10002, 10003 and 10013.

"He uses halothane?"

"That's what they assume," Fell said, nodding. "They found traces in all three people when they were doing the blood chemistry. And that supposedly accounts for the lack of any sign of a struggle. The stuff is quick. Like one-two-three-gone."

"Where did he get it?"

"Don't know yet—we've run all the hospitals in Manhattan, northern Jersey, Connecticut. Nothing yet, but you know, nobody tracks exact amounts of the stuff. You could transfer some from one tank to another. If the tank wasn't gone, how can you tell?"

"Nnn. Okay. But how does he get close enough to whip it on them?" Lucas got up and went out into the hallway, came back with a cone-shaped throwaway water cup. "Stand up."

She stood up. "What?"

He thrust the cup at her face. "If I come at you like this, from the front, I can't get the leverage."

Fell stepped back and the cup came free.

"Even if they got some gas, they could get far enough back to scream," he said.

"We don't know that they didn't scream," said Fell.

"Nobody heard anything."

She nodded. "So if he hits them on the street, he must come up from the back."

"Yeah. He grabs them, pulls them in, claps it over their mouth . . ." He turned her around, clapped the cup over her mouth, his elbow in her spine, his hand hooked over her shoulder. "One, two, three . . . Gone."

"Do it again," she said.

He did it again, but this time, she grabbed his wrist and twisted. The paper cup crumbled and her mouth was open. "Scream," she said. He let go and she said, "That doesn't work too well, either."

"This woman . . . Ellen Foen." Lucas picked up the file, flipped it open. "Statements from her friends say she was very cautious. She'd had some trouble with street people—they hang out in the alley behind the place she worked, going through the dumpsters. She could look out through the glass port in the door while it was still locked, and she always checked before she went out. So if Bekker was there, she must have seen him."

"It was late."

"Nine o'clock. Not quite dark."

"Maybe he was dressed okay. He's not a real big guy—maybe she just wasn't worried."

"But with his face?"

"Makeup. Or . . . I don't know. It makes more sense to me that he's driving a cab. She gets in, he's got one of the security windows between himself and the backseat. He's got it sealed up somehow, and when she shuts the door, he turns on the gas. She passes out. I mean, I just can't see a woman, somebody supposedly cautious, letting a guy get that close to her. And even if he comes up from behind, she'd fight it. You're a hell of a lot bigger than Bekker, but you'd have a hard time holding a mask over my mouth, even from behind."

"Maybe that's why he picks small people, women," Lucas suggested.

"Even so, you just twist away. Even if he gets you, there'd be bruises—but the M.E. hasn't found any bruises. It's gotta be a cab, or something like it."

"But why did Foen take a cab? She was running across the street to get Cokes for everybody. Her boyfriend was supposed to pick her up at nine-thirty, when she got off."

"Maybe . . . fuck, I don't know."

"And look at Cortese. Cortese walks out of this club and across Sixth Avenue, down Fifty-ninth Street toward the Plaza. His friends saw him go in at the Sixth Avenue end. He apparently never arrived at the other end, because there was a phone message for him at the Plaza from nine o'clock on, and he never got it. So he gets picked up on Fifty-ninth between Fifth and Sixth. What happened in there? Why would he flag a cab? He only had to go a few hundred feet."

She shrugged. "I don't know. And it's dark in there, so maybe he got jumped. But you gotta be careful when you start looking for logic, man. . . ."

"I know, I know. . . ."

"It could be anything. Maybe Cortese left his friends because he was looking for a little action."

Lucas shook his head. "He sounds awful straight."

"So does Garber . . . I don't know."

"Keep reading," said Lucas.

She was watching him, he thought. Odd glances, wary. "Is there something wrong?" he asked finally.

After a moment, she asked, "Are you really here working on Bekker?"

"Well . . ." He spread his arms to the stack of paper on the table. "Yeah. Why?"

"Oh, the more I think about it, the odder it seems. We'll catch him, you know."

"Sure, I know," Lucas said. "I'm mostly here for the publicity thing. Take some heat off."

"That doesn't seem quite right either," Fell said. She studied him. "I don't know about you. You hang out with O'Dell. You're not Internal Affairs?"

"What?" He pulled back, surprised. "Jesus, Barbara. No. I'm not Internal Affairs."

"You're sure?"

"Hey. You know what happened to me in Minneapolis?"

"You supposedly beat up somebody. A kid."

"A pimp. He'd cut up a woman with a church key, one of my snitches. Everybody on the street knew about it and I had to do something. So I did. He turned out to be a juvenile—I guess I knew that—and I got hammered by Internal Affairs. There was nothing particularly fair about it. I was just doing what I had to do, and everybody knew it, I got fucked because fucking me was safer than not fucking me. But I'm not Internal Affairs. You can check, easy enough."

"No, no."

She went back to her papers, and Lucas to his, but a minute later he said, "Jesus, Internal Affairs."

"I'm sorry."

"Well . . ."

. . .

THEY TOOK A BREAK, walked two blocks down, bumping hips, and got a booth in a Slice-o'-Pie pizza joint, with gallon-sized paper cups of Diet Pepsi. She liked him: Lucas knew it and let the talk drift toward the personal. He told her about his onetime long-distance relationship with Lily; about the ambiguity now. About his kid.

"I wouldn't mind having a kid," Fell said. "My fuckin' biological alarm clock is banging like Big Ben."

"How old are you?" he asked.

"Thirty-six."

"Any fatherhood prospects on the horizon?"

"Not at the moment," she said. "All I meet are cops and crooks, and I don't want a cop or a crook."

"Hard to meet people?"

"Meeting them isn't the problem. The problem is, the guys I like, don't like me. Eventually. Like five years ago, I was going out with this lawyer dude. Not a big-time lawyer, just a guy. Divorced. Long hair, did a lot of pro bono. And pretty hip. You know."

"Yeah. Exactly. Nice neckties."

"Yeah. He was looking around to get remarried. I mighta. But then one day I was out decoying and this big asshole comes onto me really hard, gets me on a wall, whacks me—he's getting off on whacking me. And I go down and I've got this little hideout piece on my leg, this .25 auto, and he's just bending over to pick me up and I stick the piece in his teeth and his eyes get about the size of dishpans and I back him off, he's saying, 'Hold it, hold it . . .' "

"Where's your backup?"

"They're just running up. They put the guy on the wall and one of them says, 'Jesus, Fell, you're gonna have a mouse bigger'n Mickey'—the asshole'd whacked me right under the eye, right on the eye-socket bone, you know?" She rubbed her eye socket, and Lucas nodded. "Hurt like hell. And I say, 'Yeah?' And they got the guy leaning on the wall with his legs apart, and I say, 'Say good-bye to your nuts, shitbag,' and I punted the sonofabitch so hard his balls had to take a train back from Ohio."

"Yeah?" Lucas laughed. Cop stories were the best stories, and Fell looked positively merry.

"So I tell this story to my lawyer friend and he freaks out. And he's not worried about my eye," she said wryly.

"He's worried about the guy on the wall?"

"No, no. He knew that happened. He didn't mind if *somebody* did it, he just didn't want me to do it. And I think what really bothered him was my quote: 'Say good-bye to your nuts, shitbag.' I shouldn't have told him that. It really bothered him. I think he wanted to join a country club somewhere, and he could see me sitting out on the flagstone terrace with a mint julep or some fuckin' thing, telling the other country club ladies this, 'Say good-bye to your nuts, shitbag.' "

Lucas shrugged. "You ever tried a cop?"

"Yeah, yeah." She nodded, with a small smile, eyes unfocusing. "A trouser snake. We were hot for a while, but . . . You want a little peace and quiet when you're home. He wanted to go out cruising for dopers."

Lucas took a bite out of a slice of pepperoni, chewed a minute and then said, "A couple of years ago, Lily and I were involved. This is between you and me?"

"Sure." The curiosity was wide on her face, unhidden.

"We were getting intense, this was back in Minneapolis, her marriage was falling apart," Lucas said. "Then this Indian dude shot her right in the chest. God-damn near killed her."

"I know about that."

"I freaked out. Man. So then we saw each other a few times, but I'm afraid to fly, and she was busy. . . ."

"Yeah, yeah . . ."

"Then last year . . ."

"The actress," Fell said. "The one that Bekker killed."

"I'm like a curse," Lucas said, staring past Fell's head, eyes and voice gone dark. "If I'd been a little smarter, a little quicker . . . Shit."

After lunch, they went back to the paper, working through it, finding noth-ing. Fell, restless, wandered down to the team room as Lucas continued to read. Kennett brought her back a half-hour later.

"Bellevue," she said, plopping down in the chair across from Lucas.

"What?" Lucas looked at Kennett, leaning in the door.

"Bellevue lost some monitoring equipment from one of its repair shops. We never found out because it wasn't too obvious—everything was accounted for, on paper. But when the stuff didn't come back from repair, somebody checked, and it was gone. The repair people have receipts, they thought it was back on the floor. Anyway, it's been gone for more than a month, and probably more like six or seven weeks. From before the time Bekker killed the first one," Ken-nett said.

"They lost exactly what Bekker's been using in his papers," Fell said.

"He could've gotten the halothane there, too, and probably any amount of drugs," Lucas said. "All from one source, if it's a staffer."

"Sounds like him," Fell said.

"I'd bet on it," Kennett said. He ran a hand through his hair, straightened his tie. Pissed. "God damn it, we were slow pulling this in."

"What're you going to do?"

"Move very quietly: we don't want to scare anybody off," Kennett said. "We'll start processing Bellevue staffers against criminal records. And we'll touch all the dopers we know, see who knows who on the inside. Then we do inter-views. It'll take a few days. Maybe you guys could get back to your fences? See if you could find somebody who handles Bellevue."

"Yeah." Lucas looked at his watch. Almost three. "Let's get back to Jackie Smith," he said to Fell.

. . .

SMITH MET THEM in Washington Square. The afternoon was oppressively hot, but Smith was cool: he arrived in a gray Mercedes, which he parked by a hydrant.

"I don't want to talk to you. You want to talk to somebody, talk to my lawyer," Smith said as Lucas and Fell walked up. They stood just off the boccie ball courts, under a gingko tree, hiding from the sun.

"Come on, Jackie," Lucas said. "I'm sorry about the goddamn putting green. I got a little overheated."

"Overheated, my ass," Smith snarled. "You know how long it'll take to fix it?"

"Jackie, we really need to make an arrangement, okay?" Lucas said. "Something new came up on this Bekker guy, and you're in a position to help. Like I said last night, it's personal with me. No bullshit. I just need a little information."

"I don't know fuckin' Bekker from any other asshole," Smith said impatiently.

"Hey, we believe you," Lucas said. "And I had to do the green. I had to get your attention—you were blowing us off. Isn't that right?"

Smith stared at him for a long beat, then said, "So what do you want? Exactly?"

"We need the names of guys who can get stuff out of Bellevue."

"That's all you want? Then you'll get off my back?"

"We can't promise," Lucas said. "I can't talk for Barbara—but I'd be a hell of a lot friendlier."

"Jesus Christ, I'm dealing with a fuckin' fruitcake," Smith said. Then: "I don't handle deals at that level. That's small-time."

"I know, I know, but we need a guy who does handle that kind of action. A couple of names, that's all."

"You gonna fuck them over?"

"Not if they talk to me. But if they fuck me over, I'll be back to you."

Fell jumped in with a sales pitch: "Jesus, Jackie, this'd be so easy if you just ride along. It's no skin off your ass. You're actually not helping the cops. You're helping some poor woman who's gonna get her heart cut out, or something."

"Yeah, you're the one who poured my coffee on the street," Smith said, apropos of nothing at all. He looked across the plaza, where a group of black kids were working through a dance routine to rap music from a boombox. "All right," he said. "Two guys. Well: a guy and a woman. They're not actually inside the hospital, but they can put you onto guys who are inside."

"That's all we were asking for. . . ."

"Yeah, yeah. Jesus, you're both full of shit. . . ." Then he started toward his car and said, "I'll be a minute."

"Making a call," Fell said as Smith disappeared into the Mercedes.

He was back in two minutes, with two names and addresses. Lucas wrote the names in his notebook. Smith, with a snort of disgust, turned back to his car, shaking his head.

"Angela Arnold and Thomas Leese," Lucas said to Fell. "Where're these addresses?"

Fell looked and said, "Lower East Side. Never heard of them, though. Want me to run them?"

"Yes. Or just drop them off, get them run overnight," Lucas said, looking at his watch. "Kennett wants to be careful, and I don't want to step on him. Let's not worry about talking to them until tomorrow."

FELL DROPPED HIM AT the hotel, then went on to Midtown South. Lucas cleaned up, ate dinner in the hotel restaurant, went back to his room and watched the Twins and Yankees through the seventh inning, then caught a cab for Lily's apartment. She buzzed him up and came to the door in her bare feet.

"You're late," she said.

"Got hung up," Lucas said, stepping inside. He'd stayed in her apartment almost two years earlier, when she'd just moved in: the furniture then had a temporary, scrounged look. Boxes had been stacked in the living room, a television had sat on two short metal file cabinets. The kitchen wallpaper had been a bizarre bamboo design, with monkeys; the countertops a well-chipped plastic. Now the place had a careful, colored look: warm rugs over a beige carpet; bright hand-printed graphics on the walls; sparse, but carefully chosen chairs and a broad leather couch. The kitchen was a subtle gold with hardwood counters. He'd stopped by the night before to drop off the key impressions, but hadn't stayed long enough to look around. Now he took a few minutes. "The place looks good," he said finally. He felt a pressure: when he'd been there two years before, they'd spent a lot of time in bed, Lily intent on exploring, feeling, desperate for the intensity of the sex. Now they were polite.

"That's what happens when your marriage splits up. You work on the apartment," she said. She stood close to him, but not too close, one hand just touching the other at her waist, like a hostess. Polite and something else. Wary?

"Yeah, I know."

"I made the back bedroom into an office, everything's stacked up in there. Go on back. Want a beer?"

"Sure." He wandered back to the office, yawned, sat down at the desk, pushed the chair back far enough that he could get his heels on a half-open drawer, picked up the first file. He'd been reading files all day; a million facts floating around free-form.

"Kays, Martin." He flipped the file open. Kays had been arrested twice for rape. Served two years the first time, acquitted the second time. He was suspected in as many as thirty attacks on the Upper West Side. He had had it down to a science, attacking women at night in locked parking garages. He apparently entered when a car exited, ducking under the descending door, then waited until he caught a woman alone in the dark. Half-dozen busts on drug-possession charges, assault, theft, drunkenness.

"Kays," Lily said, looking over his shoulder. "He should've gotten it five years earlier."

"Wrong thinking, *mon capitaine,*" Lucas said, looking up at her. She handed him a Special Export.

"Yeah, but it's part of the problem: with the exception of the three killings I told you about, and Walt, which they can deny, most people in town would be rootin' for these guys if they knew about them. Especially when they're doing guys like Kays. I doubt we could find a jury that'd convict them."

"You mean it was all right, as long as they were hitting dirtbags?"

"No. Just that if you kill somebody who deserves to die, and will anyway, someday, but maybe fuck up a hundred people's lives before then . . . hurrying the due date along doesn't seem that terrible. Compared to killing innocent people. But these guys aren't hitting criminals anymore, they're attacking . . . freedom."

"I can't operate at that kind of rarefied theoretical level," Lucas said, grinning at her.

"It does sound like wimpy-ass bullshit, doesn't it?" she said.

"It does."

"But it isn't," she said.

"All right."

"If you don't feel it . . . why'd you sign on?" she asked.

He shrugged. " 'Cause you're a good friend of mine."

"Is that enough?"

"Sure. As far as I'm concerned, it's one of the few good reasons for doing anything. I'd hate to kill somebody out of patriotism or duty; I could never be a warden and throw the switch on somebody. But in hot blood, to protect family or friends . . . that's all right."

"Revenge?"

He thought for a minute, then nodded. "Yeah, revenge is in there. I like hunting Bekker. I'm gonna get him."

"You and Barb Fell."

"Yup. Speaking of whom . . ." He dug in his jacket shirt pocket. "Look at these. The guy looks like a cop and she's tight with him, or was." He handed her two of the Polaroids he'd taken at Fell's.

"Oh, Barbara," Lily muttered, looking at them, shaking her head. "I know this guy. Vaguely. He's a lieutenant in Traffic. We'll run him against the killings and see what we get."

"And I've got some names for you. Friends of hers. I don't know how many are cops, but if you could run them . . ."

"Sure."

LUCAS STAYED UNTIL two o'clock, taking notes on a yellow legal pad, when Lily came in and asked, "Find anything?"

"No. And you were right. These guys were the scum of the scum. How many people could put together a list like this?"

"Hundreds," she said. "But Barb Fell was at the intersection of a lot of possibilities."

Lucas nodded, ripped the sheets off the legal pad, folded them and stuck them in his jacket pocket. "I'll keep working her."

LILY'S APARTMENT WAS on the second floor of a converted townhouse. Lucas left at ten after two, the night just beginning to find the soft coolness that lay between the tropical days. He was a little tired, but still awake; at home he might have gone for a walk along the river, smoothing down for bedtime. In New York . . .

The street was reasonably well lit; a taxi loitered in the next block. He turned that way and started walking, hands in his pockets.

There were two of them.

They were big, quick, like professional linebackers.

The cars along the street were parked bumper-to-bumper. The guy behind the Citation got Lucas to turn toward him by dragging something metallic across the bumper, a chilling, ripping sound, like a knife dragged down a washboard.

Lucas instinctively stepped away and half-turned, pivoting toward the sound. Something was happening: a sound like that had to be intentional. His hand dropped to the small of his back, toward the weight of his .45.

And as he turned, the second guy, the guy who'd hidden behind the stoop, charged onto the walk, slashed at Lucas' elbow with a sap, hit him in the spine with a shoulder, and drove him into the Citation.

The pain from the sap was like an explosion, as clear as a star on a cold night, separate from the impact, standing by itself: a skillful, debilitating cop-pain. It began at his elbow and exploded up his arm to his shoulder, and Lucas screamed, thinking he might have been shot, his arm flopping uselessly as he was smashed into the car. He tried to swing the arm back, to clear out to the right, but it wouldn't move.

He saw the other man's hand coming down, and partially blocked it with his left, then was hit in the cheekbone with a fist and rocked back against the car.

The second man, coming over the car's fender, hit him, leather gloves, the second punch in a quick one-two-three combo, and Lucas, back hunched, tried to cover.

Thought: *Clear out, clear out . . .*

He was hit again, across the ear, but this time it didn't hurt: it was stunning and he started down, rolling. A gloved hand struck at him and he grabbed it with his good left hand, pulled it under him, pinned it against his chest, let his weight fall on it. He heard what seemed to be a faraway screaming as they hit the concrete walk, felt a snap; he'd broken something. He felt a dim, distant satisfaction, because he was losing this, they were killing him. . . .

Heard glass breaking, registered it, didn't know what it was, but felt the pressure change.

Thought: *Clear out, clear out.* Let go of the gloved hand, felt it wrench away, and the other man screaming . . . Tried to roll under the car, but it was too close to the curb. Tried to cover his head with his good arm . . .

The .45 was like a thunderbolt.

The muzzle-flash broke over them like lightning, freezing everything in a strobe effect. The attackers wore nylon ski masks and gloves, long-sleeved shirts. The one who'd hit him from behind was pivoting, already running. A sap dangled from his hand, long, leather-bound, with a rounded bulge at the business end. The one whose arm Lucas had broken scrabbled to his feet and screamed, "Jesus . . ." and ran.

The .45 struck down again as Lucas sat down on the curb, his legs gone, trying to roll under the car and away from the lightning, not knowing where it came from, groping in the small of his back with his good arm, but the holster was too far around, trying to free his pistol as the attackers faded like ghosts, without a word, down the sidewalk. . . .

Then silence.

And Lily was there in a cotton nightgown, the .45 in her fist, a ludicrous combination, the soft white human cotton and the dark steel killer Colt.

"Lucas . . ." She maneuvered toward him, controlling the .45, not really looking at him, her eyes searching for targets. "Are you okay?"

"Fuck no," he said.

BEKKER WAS FIRST ASTONISHED, then swept away. When he returned to the bookstore, he glanced at the counterman with a sigh.

"Are you okay?" The counterman was concerned. He had a long neck and a narrow head with small features, like an oversized thumb sticking out of his shoulders. His face was cocked to one side and the store lights glittered off the right lens of his spectacles, lending him a Strangelovian menace.

"I'm fine, I'm fine," Bekker squeaked. He shuffled his feet and looked away, down the store.

The store was fifteen feet wide and forty deep. Vinyl paneling sagged away from the walls behind rough shelving; the linoleum floor was cracked and holed. The narrow aisles smelled of moldy paper, disintegrating bookcovers and the traffic of the unwashed. An obese man stood at a sale table halfway back, under a round antishoplifting mirror, a hardcover Spiderman anthology propped on his gut, feeding a nut-covered ice cream bar into his face. Bekker hadn't even seen him come in.

He looked down at the book in his hands, the book that had taken him away. He'd dug it out of a pile of crap in the Medicine/Anthropology section. . . .

"You didn't move for so long, I thought maybe, I don't know . . ." thumb-face said, his Adam's apple bobbing like a toy boat.

He's trying to pick me up, Bekker thought. The notion was flattering, but unwanted. Nobody was allowed too close. Before the Minneapolis cops had beaten him with their pistols, Bekker had been beautiful, but now Beauty was dead. And though he wore heavy Cover Mark makeup to hide the scars, they were visible in bright light. The *Post* had carried the pictures, with every cut and scar for the world to see. . . .

Bekker nodded, polite, not speaking, glanced at his watch. He'd been gone five minutes; he must have been an odd sight, a reader frozen, absolutely unmoving, unblinking, for five minutes or more.

Better leave. Bekker walked to the counter, head down, and pushed the book across. He'd trained himself to speak as little as possible. Speech could give him away.

"Sixteen-fifteen, with tax," the counterman said. He glanced at the book's cover. "Pretty rough stuff."

Bekker nodded, pushed seventeen dollars across the counter, accepted the change.

"Come back again," thumb-face called, as Bekker went out into the street. The bell above the door tinkled cheerily as he left.

Bekker hurried home, saw his name on the front of a newspaper, and slowed. A picture, a familiar face. What?

He picked up a half-brick that held the newspapers flat. Davenport? Christ, it *was* Davenport. He snatched up the paper, threw a dollar at the kiosk man and hurried away.

"Want yer change?" The dealer leaned out of the kiosk.

No. He had no time for change. Bekker scuttled down the street, his heels scratching and rapping, trying to read the paper in the dim ambient light. Finally, he stopped in the brilliantly lit doorway of an electronics store, the windows full of cameras, fax machines, tape recorders, calculators, disc players, portable telephones, miniature televisions and Japanese telescopes. He held the paper close to his nose.

. . . controversial former detective from Minneapolis who is generally credited with solving Bekker's first series of murders and identifying Bekker as the killer. In a fight at the time of the arrest, Bekker's face was badly torn . . .

. . . could have shot him," Davenport said, "but we were trying to take him alive. We knew he had an accomplice, and we believed that the accomplice was dead—but unless we took Bekker alive, we'd never know for sure . . .

Liar. Looking up from the paper, Bekker wanted to scream it: *Liar.* Bekker touched his face, hidden beneath the layers of special cosmetic. Davenport had ripped it. Davenport had destroyed Beauty. Bekker froze, was gone. . . .

A bum came up, saw him in the doorway.

"Hey," the bum said, blocking the sidewalk, and Bekker came back. The bum was not particularly large, but he looked as though he'd been hit often and wasn't afraid to be hit again. Bekker wasn't buying it.

"Fuck off," he bawled, his teeth showing. The bum stepped aside, suddenly afraid, and Bekker went by like a draft of Arctic air. Cursing to himself, Bekker turned the corner, waited for a moment, then stepped back to see if the bum was coming after him. He wasn't. Bekker went on to the Lacey building, muttering, growling, crying. He let himself in the front door, hurried down to the basement, dropped into his reading chair.

Davenport in town. The fear gripped him for a moment and he flashed back to the trial, Davenport's testimony, the detective staring at him the whole time, challenging him. . . . Bekker lived through the testimony, mind caught, tangled in the random sparking of his mind. . . . And he came back, with a sigh.

What? He had a package on his lap. He looked at it in puzzlement, dumped it. The book. He'd forgotten. *Final Cuts: Torture Through the Ages.* The book was filled with illustrations of racks and stakes, of gibbets and iron maidens. Bekker wasn't interested. Torture was for freaks and perverts and clowns. But near the end of it . . .

Yes. A photo taken in the 1880s. A Chinese man, the caption said, had assassinated a prince, and had been condemned to the death of a thousand cuts. The executioners had been slicing him to pieces as the photo was taken.

The dying man's face was radiant.

This was what he'd sought in his own work, and here it was, in a century-old photo. This was the light, the luminance of death, pouring from the face of the Chinese man. It wasn't pain—pain was disfiguring: he knew that from his work. He'd been doing his own photography, but had never achieved anything like this. Perhaps it was the old black-and-white film, something special about it.

Bekker sat and gnawed his thumb, Davenport forgotten, obliterated by the importance of this discovery. Where did the aura come from? The knowledge of death? Of the imminence of it? Was that why old people, at the edge, were often described as radiant? Because they knew the end was there, they could see it, and understood there was no eluding it? Was the knowledge of impending death a critical point? Could that be it? An intellectual function, somehow, or an emotional release, rather than an autonomic one?

Too excited to sit, he dropped the book and took a turn around the room. The matchbox was there, in his pocket; three pills. He gobbled them, then looked at the now empty box. *Here* was a crisis. He'd have to go back out. He'd been putting it off, but now . . .

He glanced at his watch. Yes. Whitechurch would be working.

He stopped in the bathroom, clumsily fished himself out of the pants, peed, flushed, rearranged himself, then went to the telephone. He knew the number by heart and punched it in. A woman's voice answered.

"Dr. West, please," Bekker said.

"Just a moment, please, I'll page."

A moment later: "West." The voice was cool, New Jersey, and corroded. The voice of a fixer.

"I need some angels," Bekker breathed; he used a breathy voice with Whitechurch.

"Mmm, that's a problem. I'm short. I've got plenty of white, though, and I've got crosses. Almost none of the other," Whitechurch said. He sounded anxious. Bekker was an exceptional customer, white, careful, and paid in cash. A Connecticut schoolteacher maybe, peddling to the kids.

"That's difficult," Bekker said. "How much of the white?"

"I could give you three."

"Three would be good. How many crosses?"

"Thirty? I could do thirty."

"Good. When? Must be soon."

"Make it a half-hour."

"Excellent, half an hour," Bekker breathed, and hung up.

When he'd cleaned out the basement, he'd found a pile of discarded sports equipment—a couple of dried-out leather first baseman's mitts with spiderwebs in the pockets; a half-dozen bats, all badly marred, and one split; a deflated basketball; mold- and dirt-covered baseball shoes with rusted metal spikes; two pairs of sadly abused sneakers; and even a pair of shorts, a tank top and a jock. He'd thrown it all in a long box with a Frisbee, a croquet set and a couple of broken badminton racquets. He'd pushed the box into a dark corner. Anybody looking into it could see all the junk with a glance; nothing good; nothing you'd even want to touch.

Bekker had sliced a C-shaped hatch in the bottom of the basketball and stashed his cash inside. Now he picked up the ball, took out three thousand dollars and carefully put the ball back.

After a quick check in the mirror, he climbed the stairs to the ground floor and padded to the back. Just as he reached the back door, the old woman's voice floated down the stairs. "Alex . . . ?"

Bekker stopped, thought about it, then exhaled in exasperation and walked back across the darkened floor to the staircase. "Yes?"

"I need the special pills." Her voice was shadowy, tentative.

"I'll get them," Bekker said.

He went back down to his apartment, found the brown bottle of morphine, shook two into his hand, and climbed back up the stairs, talking to himself. Images of the deathly radiance played through his mind, and, preoccupied, he nearly stumbled into Bridget Land. Land was standing at the base of the stairs that led up to Edith Lacey's apartment.

"Ah," she said, "I was just leaving, Alex. . . . You have Edie's medicine?"

"Yes, yes . . ." Bekker kept his face turned away, head down, tried to brush past.

"Are the pills illegal? Are they illegal drugs?" Land asked. She had squared herself up to him, her chin lifted, tight, catching his shirt sleeve as he passed her. She had smart, dark eyes that picked at him.

Bekker, his voice straining, nodded and said, "I think so. . . . I get them from a friend of hers. I'm afraid to ask what they are."

"What are you . . ." Land began, but Bekker was climbing the stairs away from her. At the top of the stairs, he glanced back, and Land was turning away, toward the door.

"Please don't tell," Bekker said. "She's in pain. . . ."

"DID YOU SEE BRIDGET?" Mrs. Lacey asked.

"Yes, down below. . . ." He got a glass of water and carried the pills to Mrs. Lacey. She gulped them greedily, hands trembling, smacking her lips in the water.

"Bridget asked me if these were illegal drugs. I'm afraid she might call the police," Bekker said.

Mrs. Lacey was horrified. "You mean . . ."

"They *are* illegal," Bekker said. "You could never get these in a nursing home."

"Oh no, oh no . . ." The old woman rocked, twisting her gnarled, knobby fingers.

"You should call her. Give her time to get home, and talk to her," Bekker said.

"Yes, yes, I'll call her. . . ."

"Her number's on the emergency pad, by the telephone," Bekker said.

"Yes, yes . . ." She looked up at him, her thin skin papery and creased in the moody light.

"Don't forget . . ."

"No . . ." And then: "I can't find my glasses."

He found them near the kitchen sink; handed them to her without a word. She bobbed her head in thanks and said, "My glasses, my glasses," and shuffled toward the TV. "Have you seen . . . No, you don't watch. I saw Arnold on the news."

Arnold Schwarzenegger. She expected him any day to clean the crooks out of New York.

"I've got to go."

"Yes, yes . . ." She waved him away.

"Call Bridget," Bekker said.

"Yes . . ." From the side, her face glowed blue in the light from the television screen, like a black-light painting. Like the face of the dying Chinese . . .

Ultraviolet.

The idea came from nowhere, but with a force that stopped him at the head of the stairs. Could the illumination of the dying man be related to a shifted spectrum? A light phenomenon that occurred in infrared or ultraviolet, that occasionally strayed into visible light? Was that why some people glowed and others didn't? Was that how an old camera caught it, with the poor, wide-spectrum film of the nineteenth century? He'd seen both ultraviolet and infrared photography as a medical student. Ultraviolet could actually increase the resolution of a microscope, and highlight aspects of a specimen not visible in ordinary light. And infrared could pick up temperature variations, even from dark objects.

But that was all he knew. Could he use his ordinary cameras? How to check?

Excited, excited, the science pounded in his brain. He hurried down the stairs, remembering Bridget Land only at the last minute. He slowed, looked ahead apprehensively, but she was gone.

He hurried out the back, got in the Volkswagen, drove it to the fence, hopped out, unlocked the fence, drove through, checked for intruders, climbed back out, locked the gate behind him. He was flapping, frantic, eager to get on his way, to sustain the insights of the evening.

North across Prince, east across Broadway, keeping to the side streets, the buildings pressing against him, working his way north and east. There. First Avenue. And Bellevue, an aging pile of brick.

Bekker looked at his watch. He was a minute or so early; no problem. He took it slowly, slowly. . . . And there he was, walking toward the bus stop. Bekker leaned across the car and rolled the passenger-side window halfway down, pulled to the curb.

Whitechurch saw him, looked once around, stepped to the window. "Three of the white, thirty crosses, all commercial. Two of the angels, good stuff . . ."

"Only two?" Bekker felt the control slipping, fought to retain it. "Okay. But I'll be calling you in a couple of days."

"I'll have more by then. How many could you handle?"

"Thirty? Could you get me thirty? And thirty more of the crosses?"

"Yeah, I think so," Whitechurch said. "My guy's bringing out a new line. Call me . . . and I'll need twenty-one hundred for tonight."

Bekker nodded, peeled twenty-one one-hundred-dollar bills from the roll in his pocket and handed them to Whitechurch. Whitechurch knew Bekker carried a pistol; in fact, he had sold it to him. Bekker wasn't worried about a rip-off. Whitechurch stuffed the bills in his pocket and dropped a bag onto the front seat.

"Come again," he said, and turned toward the hospital.

Bekker rolled the window up and started back, the sack shoved under the seat; but he knew he wouldn't make it without a sample. He *deserved* a sample. He'd had a revolutionary idea this night, the recording of the human aura. . . .

He stopped at a traffic light, checked the streets, turned on the dome light and opened the bag. Three fat twists of coke and two small Zip-Loc bags. Thirty small commercial tabs in one, two larger tabs in the other. His hands shook as he kept watch and unrolled one of the twists. Just enough to get home.

The coke jumped him and his head rolled backward with the force of it roaring through his brain like a freight train. After a moment, he started out again, slowly, everything preternaturally clear. If he could hold this . . . His hand groped for the PCP bag, found it; only two. But the coke had him, and he popped them both: the angels would hold the coke in place, build on it. . . . He could see for miles now, through the dark. No problem. His mouth worked, fathering a wad of saliva, and he popped a hit of speed, crunched it in his teeth. Only one, just a sample, a treat . . .

A red light. The light made him angry, and he cursed, drove through it. Another. Even more angry, but he held it this time, rolled to a stop. One more pinch of the white: sure. He *deserved* one more. One more hit . . .

He hadn't taken an experimental subject in more than a week. Instead, he'd huddled in the basement, typing his papers. He had a backlog now, data that had to be collated, rationalized. But tonight, with the angels in his blood . . . And Davenport in town, looking for him.

In taking the other subjects, he worked out a system: hit them with the stun gun, use the anesthetic. And more important, he'd begun looking for safe hunting grounds. Bellevue was one. There were women around Bellevue all the time, day and night, small enough to handle, healthy, good subjects. And the parking ramp there was virtually open. . . . But Bellevue wasn't for tonight, not after he'd just come from there.

In fact, he shouldn't even think of taking one tonight. He hadn't planned it, hadn't done the reconnaissance that provided his margin of safety. But with the angels in his blood, anything was possible.

A picture popped into his head. Another parking ramp, not Bellevue. A ramp attached to a city government building of some kind.

Parking ramps were good, because they were easy to hide in, people came and went at all hours, many of them were alone. Transportation was easily at hand. . . .

And this one was particularly good: each level of the parking ramp had an entrance into the government building, the doors guarded by combination lockpad. A person entering the ramp in a car would not necessarily walk out past the attendants in the ticket booth. So Bekker could go in, and wait. . . .

The ramp itself had a single elevator that would take patrons to the street. In his mind's eye, he could see himself in the elevator with the selected subject, getting off at the same floor, hitting her with the stun gun as they came out of the elevator, using the gas, hiding her body between a couple of cars, then simply driving around to make the pickup. . . . Simple.

And the ramp was close by, on the edge of Chinatown. . . .

The rational Bekker, trapped in the back of his mind, warned him: *no no no no* . . .

But Gumball-Bekker cranked the wheel around and headed south, the PCP angels burning in his blood.

Chinatown.

There were people in the street, more than Bekker would have thought likely. He ignored them, the PCP-cocaine cocktail gripping his mind, focusing it: he drove straight into the parking garage, hunched over the wheel, got his ticket, and started around the sequence of up-slanting ramps. Each floor was lit, but he saw no cameras. The sequence had him now, his heart beating like a hammer, his face hot. . . .

He went all the way to the top, parked, opened the cocaine twist, cupped some in his hand, snorted it, licked up the remnant.

And went away . . .

When he came back, he climbed out of the car, taking his collection bag from the backseat. A stairwell wrapped around the elevator shaft and he took the stairs down, quietly, the stairs darker than the main ramp area. Bekker was on his toes, his collecting bag around his shoulder, hand on the stun gun. . . .

At the second floor, he stopped, checked the anesthetic tank and mask. Okay. He rehearsed the sequence in his mind: get behind her, hit her with the stun gun, cover her mouth against screams, ride her down, get the gas. He stepped out of the stairwell, glanced into the tiny elevator lobby. Excellent.

Back to the stairwell.

He waited.

And waited.

Twenty minutes, tension rising. Fished in his pocket, did another cross, chewing it, relishing the bite. He heard a steel door close somewhere overhead, echoing through the ramp, and a few minutes later, a car went down. Then silence again. Five more minutes, ten.

A car came in, stopped on the second floor, high heels on concrete . . . Bekker tensed, his hand going quickly to the tank, flicking the switch once on the stun gun.

Then . . . nothing. The sound of high heels receding. The woman, whoever it was, was walking down the ramp to get out, rather than entering the stairwell or going to the elevator.

Damn. It wasn't working. He glanced at his watch: another ten minutes. No more . . . His mind flashed back to the Twin Cities, to an actress. He'd fooled her by dressing as a gas company employee looking for leaks, had killed her with a hammer. He remembered the impact and the flush. . . . Bekker went away.

And came back, sometime later, with the telltale sigh. At the sound of feet below, and a woman's voice.

The elevator doors opening, one floor below . . .

He picked up his bag, hurried around, went into the lobby, pushed the up button: the Bekker at the back of his mind saying *no no no no*, the foreground Bekker hot with anticipation . . .

The elevator came up, lurched to a stop, and the doors opened. Inside was a dark-haired woman with an oversized purse, eyes large, one hand in her purse. She hadn't expected the stop at the second floor. She saw Bekker, relaxed. Bekker nodded, stepped inside, waited for the doors to close. The woman had punched six, and Bekker reached for it, then stopped, as if he were also going to six. He stepped against the back of the elevator, looking up at the numbers flashing down at them. . . .

She had a gun in her purse, Bekker thought, a gun or tear gas. He thought about that, thought about that . . . got caught in a loop, thinking about thinking about it . . . and when he came back, groping in his collection bag for the stun gun, they were already at six.

He glanced sideways at the woman, caught her staring at him; he looked away. Eye contact might tell her too much. . . . He glanced again, and the woman seemed to be shrinking away, had her hand in her purse again. A tone sounded, a sharp *bing,* and the doors slid open. For a moment, neither of them moved, then the woman was out. Bekker followed a few feet behind, turned toward her, slipping his shoes off, expecting to pad after her, catch her unexpectedly. . . .

But the woman suddenly stepped out of her own shoes and began running, and at the same time, looking back at him, screaming, a long, shrill, piercing cry.

She knew. . . .

Bekker, frozen for an instant by the scream, went after her, the woman screaming, her purse skidding across the floor, spilling out lipsticks and date books and a bottle of some kind, rolling on the rough concrete. . . . She dodged between two cars, backing toward the outer wall, a can in her hand, screaming. . . .

Tear gas.

Bekker was right behind her, losing his bag, going after her bare-handed, the urgency gripping him, the need to shut her up: *She knows knows knows* . . .

The woman had braced herself between the cars, her hand extended with the tear gas, her mouth open, her nostrils flexing. No way to get her but straight ahead . . .

Bekker charged, stooping at the last moment, one hand up to block the tear-gas spray. She pressed the can toward him, but nothing happened, just a hiss and the faint smell of apple blossoms. . . .

She'd backed all the way to the ramp wall, the lights of the city behind her, the wall waist-high, her shrill scream in his ears, piercing, wailing.

He went straight in, hit her in the throat with one hand, caught her between the legs with the other, heaved, flipped . . .

And the woman went over the waist-high wall.

Simply went over, as though he'd flipped a sack of fertilizer over the wall.

She dropped, without a sound.

Bekker, astonished at what he'd done, panting like a dog, looked down over the wall as she went. She fell faceup, arms reaching up, and hit on the back of her head and neck.

And she died, like that: like a match going out. From six floors up, Bekker could see she was dead. He turned, looking for someone coming after her, a response to the scream.

Heard nothing but a faraway police siren. Panicked, he ran back to the stairs, up two flights, climbed in the Volkswagen, started it, and rolled down through the ramp. Where were they? On the stairs?

Nobody.

At the exit booth, the woman ticket-taker was standing on the street, looking down at the corner. She came back and entered the booth. She was chewing gum, a frown on her face.

"One-fifty," she said.

He paid. "What's going on?"

"Fight, maybe," she said laconically. "A couple of guys were running . . ."

TWELVE HOURS LATER, Bekker hunched over an IBM typewriter, a dark figure, intent, humming to himself "You Light Up My Life," poking the keys with rigid fingers. Overhead, a flock of his spiders floated through the air, dangling from black thread attached to a wire grill. A mobile of spiders . . .

The PCP made the world perfectly clear, and he marveled over the crystal quality of the prose as it poured forth from the machine onto the white paper.

. . . refuted claims that cerebral-spinal pressure obfuscated reliable intercranial measurements during terminal brain activity as per Delano in TRS Notes [Sept. 86]; Delano overlooked the manifest and indisputable evidence of . . .

It simply sang—and that cockroach Delano would undoubtedly lose his job at Stanford when the world saw his professional negligence. . . .

Bekker leaned back, looking up at his spiders, and cackled at the thought. A gumball dropped, and he leaned forward, thoughtful now, Bekker the Thinker. He'd made a mistake this night. The worst he'd made yet. His time was probably coming to an end: he needed more work, he needed another specimen, but he had to be very, very careful.

Mmmm. He turned off the typewriter and laid his manuscript aside, carefully squaring the corners of the paper. Went to the bathroom, washed his face again, stared at the scars. The drugs were still with him, but he was also running down. Might even catch some sleep. When had he last slept? Couldn't remember.

He dropped his clothing on the floor, looked at the clock. Midmorning. Maybe a couple of hours, though . . .

He lay down, listened to his heart.

Closed his eyes.

Almost slept.

But then, just on the edge of oblivion, something stirred. Bekker knew what it was. He felt his heart accelerate, felt the adrenaline spurting into his blood.

He hadn't done her eyes. It had been impossible, of course, but that made no difference. She could see him, the dark-haired woman.

She was coming.

Bekker stuffed a handful of sheet in his mouth, and screamed.

9

THE CAR SLOWED and the window between the front seat and the backseat dropped an inch. The early-morning traffic was light, and they were
moving quickly, but O'Dell was grumpy about the early hour. Lily hadn't slept
at all.

"You want a *Times*?" Copland asked over his shoulder.

"Yes." O'Dell nodded, and Copland eased the car toward the curb, where a
vendor waved newspapers at passing cars. A talk show babbled from the front-
seat radio: Bekker and more Bekker. When Copland rolled his window down,
they could hear the same show from the vendor's radio. The vendor handed Copland a paper, took a five-dollar bill, and dug for change.

"I'm worried," Lily said. "They could try again."

"Won't happen. They didn't mean to kill him, and coming after him again,
that way, would be too risky. Especially if he's this tough guy you keep telling
me about. . . ."

"We thought they wouldn't go after him the first time. . . ."

"We never thought they'd try to mug him. . . ."

Copland handed a copy of the *Times* into the backseat. A headline just
below the fold said, "Army Suspects Bekker of Vietnam Murders."

"This has gotta be bullshit," O'Dell grumbled, scanning the story. "Anything
from Minneapolis?"

"No."

"Dammit. Why don't these assholes check on him? For all they know, the
Minneapolis story could be a cover for an Internal Affairs geek."

"Not a thing, so far. And the people in Minneapolis are looking for it."

Silence, the car rolling like an armored ghost through Manhattan.

Then: "It must be Fell. It has to be."

Lily shook her head: "Nothing on her line. She got one call, from an automated computer place saying that she'd won a prize if she'd go out to some Jersey condominium complex to pick it up. Nothing on the office phone."

"Dammit. She must be calling from a public phone. We might need some
surveillance here."

"I'd wait on that. She's been on the street for a while. She'd pick it up, sooner
or later."

"Had to be Fell, though. Unless it really was muggers."

"It wasn't muggers. Lucas thinks they were cops. He says one of them was carrying a black leather-wrapped keychain sap; about the only place you can buy them is a commercial police-supply house. And he says they never went for his billfold."

"But they weren't trying to kill him."

"No. But he thinks they were trying to put him out of commission. Maybe break a few bones . . ."

"Huh." O'Dell grunted through a thin smile. "You know, there was once a gang on the Lower East Side, they'd contract to bite a guy's ear off for ten bucks?"

"I didn't know that," said Lily.

"It's true, though. . . . All right. Well. With Davenport. String him along. . . ."

"I still feel like I'm betraying him," Lily said, looking away from O'Dell, out the window. A kid was pushing a bike with a flat tire down the sidewalk. He turned as the big black car passed, and looked straight at Lily with the flat gray serpent's eyes of a ten-year-old psychopath.

"He knew what he was getting into."

"Not really," she said, turning away from the kid's trailing eyes. She looked at O'Dell. "He thought he did, but he's basically from a small town. He's not from here. He really doesn't know, not the way we do. . . ."

"What'd you tell Kennett, about why Davenport was at your place?"

"I . . . prevaricated," Lily said. "And I could use a little backup from you."

"Ah."

LUCAS HADN'T BEEN badly hurt, so Lily flagged a cab, took him to Beth Israel, then reported the attack. Because she'd fired her weapon, there had been forms to fill out. She'd started that night, and called Kennett to tell him about it.

"Should I ask why he was at your place at two in the morning?" Kennett had asked. He'd sounded amused, but he wasn't.

"Um, you don't want to know," Lily had said. "But it was strictly business, not pleasure."

"And I don't want to know."

"That's right."

After a moment: "Okay. Are you all right? I mean, really all right."

"Sure. I've got a busted window I've gotta get fixed. . . ."

"Good. Get some sleep. I'll talk to you tonight."

"That's all? I mean . . . ?"

"Do I trust you? Of course. See you tonight."

LILY LOOKED OUT the car window, at the city rolling past. Maybe she was betraying Lucas. Maybe she was betraying Kennett. She wasn't sure anymore.

O'Dell said, "Cretins," and his paper shook with anger.

10

THE REPORTERS CAME AND WENT, the naive ones swallowing Lucas' story that he had been mugged, others not so sure. A reporter from *Newsday* said flatly that something else was going on: that Bekker had a gang, or that somebody else was trying to stop Lucas' investigation.

"I don't know about muggers in Minneapolis, but in New York they don't work in professional tag teams. Unless you're lying, you were done by professionals. . . ."

After they were gone, Lucas took a few more Tylenol, wandered down to the bathroom and got back in time to see Lily coming down the hall.

"You look . . . pretty rough," she said.

"It's my cheek. My cheek hurts like hell," he said. He touched a swollen magenta bruise with his middle finger. "At least the headache's going away. They're letting me out after lunch."

"I heard," Lily said.

"Thanks for sending the jeans over. The other pants . . ."

"Are shot." Lily said.

"Yeah."

"O'Dell's fixed the Mengele speech—there'll be a notice in all the papers this afternoon, the *Times* tomorrow morning, and we're asking everybody to do a note about it. TV, too. We found a guy, a legit guy, who already lectures on Mengele."

"Terrific," Lucas said. "When?"

"Monday."

"Jesus, that quick?"

"We gotta do everything quick. Maybe we can get him before he does another one. . . ." Lily backed into a hospital chair, dropped her purse by her foot. "Listen, about last night. Are you absolutely sure they were cops?"

"Fairly sure. They could have been professional bone-breakers, but it didn't feel that way. They felt like cops. Why?"

"I was thinking about another possibility."

"Smith?"

"Yeah. After you chopped up his putting green . . ."

Lucas pulled his lip. "Maybe," he said. "But I doubt it. One thing you learn as a sleazoid businessman is to roll with the punches."

"Have you talked to Fell this morning?"

"She's on her way over. We have a line on a couple of people who might know something about Bellevue. She's been talking to Kennett, to make sure we don't step on any toes. . . ."

"Okay. I've got Bobby Rich coming over. He's the guy who took the tip about the witness."

"The witness Petty found . . ."

"Yeah, the day he got killed. And there's still some more paper to look at."

"That's pointless, I think," Lucas said. "With these guys, the dead guys, we won't find anything in their lives that'll point to the killers. It has to be bureaucratic: who pulled their files, and when . . ."

"That's impossible."

"Yeah, I know."

"So we're stuck?"

"Not quite, but it's getting sparse. Maybe Rich'll have something. We've still got Fell. I want to take a look at Petty's apartment, his personal stuff. And I wouldn't mind seeing the place where he was shot."

"That's about a half-mile from my apartment—we could walk. His apartment's sealed. I'll get some new seals and take you over. When?"

"Tonight? After we talk to Rich?"

"Fine."

"What'd you tell Kennett . . . ?"

"About you being at my apartment? I said you came over to visit. I told him that sex was not a consideration, last night or in the future. I told him that you weren't making any moves on me and I wasn't making any moves on you, but that we had things to talk about."

"Sounds pretty awful," Lucas said, grinning.

"It could have been, but I just came out with it. I also told him O'Dell was there part of the time. John will back that up."

A FEW MINUTES LATER, Kennett and Fell arrived together, and Lily blew up: "For Christ's sakes, Dick, what're you doing here? Did you walk all the way in?" Hands on hips, she turned to Fell, angry. "Barbara, did you let him . . . ?"

"Shut up, Lily," Kennett said. He touched her cheek with an index finger. To Lucas, he said, "Well, you look like shit."

"What do you think, Barb?" Lucas asked.

Fell had taken cover behind Kennett, and she peered out and said, "He's right. You look like shit."

"Then it's unanimous," Lucas said. "That's what Lily said when she came in. The only one who didn't was a twenty-four-year-old *Times* reporter with a great ass, who thought I looked pretty good and would probably like to hear more about this case from the hero of it. . . ."

"Gotta be a concussion," Fell said to Lily.

"He's always been like this," Lily said. "I think it's native stupidity."

Kennett, shaking his head, said, "Goddamn women, they're always impressed by a beat-up face. I used to get beat up whenever I needed to get laid.

Worked like a charm . . ." He stopped, and frowned at Lucas: "Are you trying to get laid?" and his eyes flicked sideways at Lily.

Fell said, "Not very hard."

Lucas and Kennett laughed; Lily didn't.

Kennett said, "Listen, I wanted to tell you. Go ahead with those names you got. Barb's run them down. . . ."

"One good address and one probable," Fell said.

"Junkies?"

"Nope. Neither one of them. Not the last anybody heard, anyway."

"All right." Lucas eased down from the hospital bed. "Let's go down to the nursing station. Maybe I can talk my way out before lunch."

The charge nurse said the attending physician wanted another look at him: she'd send him down as soon as he arrived, which should be within the next few minutes. "We'll see you first," she said.

"All right, but pretty quick?"

"Soon as he gets here."

Lily said, "I've gotta go. Take it easy today."

"Yeah."

He walked gingerly back to the room with Fell, trying not to move his head too quickly. At the door, he looked back toward the elevators. Kennett and Lily were waiting, looking up at the numbers above the door, then Kennett leaned toward Lily, and she went up on her toes, a kiss that wasn't taken lightly by either of them. Lucas turned away, and caught Fell watching him watch Lily and Kennett.

"True love," he said wryly.

THE HOT, HAZY SUN left him feeling faintly nauseous, and the headache lurked at the back of his skull.

"You look pale and wan," Fell said.

"I'm all right." He looked up at the storefront: Arnold's TV and Appliance, Parts & Repair. "C'mon, let's do her."

A bell tingled when they went through the door; a heavyset woman looked up from a ledger, slapped it shut, and moved ponderously to the counter. "Can I help ya?" She had a cheerfully yellow smile and an improbable West Virginia hills accent. To Lucas: "Whoa, you look like you've been in a dustup."

"We're police officers," Fell said. She lifted the flap of her purse, flashed the badge. "Are you Rose Arnold?"

The woman's smile sagged into a frown. "Yeah. What'd you want?"

"We're looking for a guy," Lucas said. "We thought you could help."

"I ain't been here all that long. . . ."

Lucas dug in his pocket, took out his money clip, freed his driver's license and handed it to Arnold. "Barbara here"—he nodded at Fell—"is a New York cop. I'm not. I'm from Minneapolis. They brought me in to help look for this Bekker dude who's chopping people up."

"Yeh?" Arnold was giving nothing away, watching him with her small wandering eyes like a pullet who suspects the axe.

"Yeah. He killed my woman out there. Maybe you read about it. I'm gonna catch him and I'm gonna do him."

Arnold nodded and asked, "So what's that got to do with me?"

"We think he's getting stuff—drugs and medical equipment—from Bellevue. We know that you handle stuff out of Bellevue."

"That's bullshit, I never touch nothing. . . ."

"You moved five hundred cases of white Hammermill Bond copy paper out of there two weeks ago, paid a dollar a case, and sold it to a computer supply place for three dollars a case," Fell said. "We could bust you if we wanted to, but we don't want to. We just want some help."

She looked at them, quietly, a gleam of strong intelligence in her eyes. Calculating. Lucas had a quick vision of her jerking some crappy piece of hillbilly iron out of a drawer, something like a rusty Iver Johnson .32, and popping him in the chest. But nothing happened, except the sound of flies bumping against the front window.

"Killed your woman?" she asked. She tipped her head, looking at him from the corner of her eyes.

"Yeah," he said. "It's real personal."

She mulled it over for another few seconds, then asked, "What do you want?"

"I need the name of a guy who rips stuff out of there on a regular basis."

"Will this come back on me?"

"No way."

She thought about it, then mumbled: "Lew Whitechurch."

"Lew . . ."

"Whitechurch," she said.

"Who else?"

"He's the only one, right out of Bellevue. . . ."

"Any chance he might be peddling pills, too?"

"I think he might. I never touch them, but Lew . . . he's got a problem. He takes a little nose."

"Thanks," Lucas said. He took a personal business card from his pocket, turned it over, wrote his hotel phone number on it. "Have you handled, or know anybody who has handled, a load of emergency-room monitoring equipment?"

"No." Her voice was positive.

"Ask around. If you find somebody, have them call me. It'll never get past us, I swear it on a Bible. I'm only in this because Bekker cut my woman's throat."

"Cut her throat?" The fat woman touched her neck.

"With a bread knife," Lucas said. He let the bitterness flow into his voice. "Listen: anybody dealing with Bekker is liable to find himself strapped to an operating table, eyelids cut off, getting his heart sliced out while he's still alive. . . . You read the papers."

"Watch TV." She nodded.

"Then you know."

"Fuckin' lunatic, is what he is," Arnold said.

"So ask around. Call me."

OUTSIDE, FELL SAID, "You're a scary sonofabitch sometimes. You sorta used your friend . . ."

"My friend's dead, she doesn't care," he said. And he shrugged. "But hill-billies understand that revenge shit."

"What's the name?"

"Lew Whitechurch. And she thinks he might deal pills."

"Let's get him," Fell said. As they were flagging the cab, she said, "If I bust Bekker myself, I'll make detective first before I get out."

"That'd be nice." A cab zigged through the traffic toward them.

"More pension. I could probably afford a straight waitress job. I wouldn't have to dance topless," Fell said.

"Aw," he said. "I was planning to come down for your first night."

"Maybe we could work something out," she said, and climbed into the cab before he could think of a comeback.

THEY CAUGHT Lewis Whitechurch pushing a tool cart through a basement hallway at Bellevue. His supervisor pointed him out, the hospital's assistant ad-ministrator hovering anxiously in the background. Kennett's people had been there earlier, had talked to two employees, she said, but not Whitechurch.

"What?" Whitechurch said.

Fell flashed her badge, while Lucas blocked the hall. "We need to talk to you, privately."

Whitechurch shook his head. "I don't want to talk to anyone."

"We can talk here or I can call a squad and we can go over to Midtown South."

"Talk about what?" Whitechurch shot a glance at the supervisor.

"Let's find a place," Lucas suggested.

They found a place in the hospital workshop, sitting on battered office chairs, Whitechurch spinning himself in quarter-turns with the heel of one foot. "I honest to God don't know. . . ."

Five hundred cases of paper, they said.

"I ain't gonna talk about nothing like that," he said, his Jersey accent as thick as mayonnaise. "You want to talk about this other guy, Bekker, I'd help you any way I can. But I don't know nothing about him, or any medical gear. I wouldn't touch that shit. . . ." He caught himself. "Listen, I don't take nothing out of here, but if I did, I wouldn't take that stuff. I mean, people might die because of it."

"If we catch the guy who's helping Bekker . . . that guy's going down as an accessory. Attica, and I'll tell you what, man: there'd be no fuckin' parole, not for somebody who helped this asshole. . . ."

"Jesus Christ, I'd tell you," Whitechurch said. He was sweating. "Listen, I know a couple of people who might know something about this. . . ."

"**What do you think?**" Fell asked.

"He covered himself pretty well. I don't know. We got names, anyway. We'll come back to him. Let him stew. . . ." Whitechurch had given them two more names. Both men were working.

"Jakes is an orderly—he oughta be around," the assistant administrator said. She was getting into the hunt, falling into Fell's laconic speech pattern. "Williams—I'll have to look him up."

They found Harvey Jakes moving sheets out of the laundry.

"I don't know about this shit," he said. He was worried. "Listen, I don't know why you'd come looking to me. I never been up on anything, never took anything, where'd you get my name . . ."

Williams was worse. Williams worked in the laundry, and was stupid. "Said what?"

"Said you boosted stuff out of here and . . ."

"Said what?"

Lucas looked at him closely, then at Fell, and shook his head. "He's not faking."

"What?" Williams looked slowly from one to the other, and they sent him back to his laundry.

"**We're into a** black market—pretty casual, hard to pin down, picking up the occasional opportunity," Fell said as they ambled down the hall. Like the rest of New York, the Bellevue interior was mostly a patch, painted white with black trim. "Doesn't feel like a real tight ring. Whitechurch might be bigger, if he really organized a truck to haul that paper out of there. Jakes and Williams are small-time, if they're stealing anything at all."

"That's about right," Lucas said. "Whitechurch might be something, though."

"Want to go back on him?"

"We should," he said, sticking his hands in his pockets. "But I fuckin' hurt. . . ."

"You keep poking at your cheek," she said. She reached out and touched the bruise, and her light hand didn't hurt at all. "So what are we doing?"

"I'm going back to the hotel. I need a nap, I feel like shit," Lucas said.

"We're stuck?"

"Except for Whitechurch, I don't know where we go," Lucas said. "Let's think about it. I'll call you tomorrow."

11

A T THE LAKOTA, Lucas examined his swollen cheek in the mirror. The color of the bruise was deepening, a purple blotch that dominated the side of his face, shiny in the middle, rougher toward the edges. He touched the abraded skin and winced. He'd been hit before, and knew what would happen: the abrasions would scab over while the skin around them turned yellow-green, and in a week, he'd look even worse; he'd look like Frankenstein. He shook his head at himself, tried a tentative grin, ate a half-dozen aspirin and slept for two hours. When he woke, the headache had faded, but his stomach was queasy. He gobbled four more aspirin, showered, brushed his teeth, fished an oversize Bienfang art pad from under the bed and got a wide-tipped Magic Marker from his briefcase. He wrote:

> *Bekker.*
> Needs money.
> Needs drugs.
> Lives Midtown w/friend?
> Has vehicle.
> Hasn't been seen. Disguise?
> Chemist skills.
> Medical skills.
> Contact at Bellevue.
> Night.

He tacked the chart to a wall and lay on his bed, studying it. Bekker needed money if he was buying drugs, and he almost certainly would be. In the Hennepin County Jail he'd begged for them, for chemical relief.

Therefore: he had to be talking to dealers, or at least one dealer. Could he be working for one? Not likely as a salesman: even the dumbest of the dumb would recognize him as a time bomb, if they knew who he was. But if he was working as a chemist—methedrine was simple to synthesize, with the right training and access to the raw materials. If he were running a crank line, that would explain where he'd get money, and drugs, and maybe even a place to stay.

The car was another problem. He was dumping the bodies, obviously from a vehicle. How would he get access? How would he license it? Everything pointed to an accomplice. . . .

He stood, wandered into the bathroom and looked in the mirror. The abrasion was stiffening. He probed it with a fingernail, lifting a flake of skin, and blood trickled down his cheek. Damn. He knew better. He got a wad of toilet paper, held it to his cheek, and went back to the bed.

He looked at the chart again, but his mind drifted away from Bekker, toward the other case. Why had they jumped him? And had they really gone after him, or was something else happening? They could have taken him with guns: they had him cold. If they hadn't wanted to kill him, they still could have gotten to him more quickly, with baseball bats. Why had they risked resistance? If he'd had a gun in his hand, he would have killed them. . . .

Why had Lily looked out the window when she did?

But the major puzzle was more subtle. He wasn't getting anywhere, and Lily and O'Dell must see that. All he could do was look at paper, and listen to people talk. He had none of the insider information, the history, that could point him in the right direction. And yet . . . he was surrounded by people who might be involved: Fell, Kennett, O'Dell himself, even Lily. And not coincidentally.

At eight-thirty he got up; he dressed, went out to the street, flagged a cab, and rode ten minutes to Lily's apartment. She was waiting.

"You still look rough," she said as she opened the door. She touched his cheek. "Feels hot. Are you sure you want to do this? It's a lot of running around."

"Yeah," he said, nodding. "Rich is set for nine?"

"Yes. He's nervous, but he's coming."

"I don't want him to see me," Lucas said.

"Okay. You can sit in the kitchen with the lights out, talk to him down the hall."

"Fine." Lucas, hands in his pockets, wandered down toward the kitchen.

"Anything new on Bekker?" she asked, trailing behind.

"No. I was thinking, though, he must be out only at night." Lucas perched on a tall oak stool and leaned on the breakfast bar. A handicraft ceramic bowl full of apples sat on the bar, and he picked one of them up and turned it in his fingers. "Even with stage makeup, his face would be too noticeable in daylight."

"So?"

"Would it be possible to make random stops of single men driving inexpensive cars, after midnight, Midtown?"

"Jesus, Lucas. The chance of picking him up that way would be nil—and we'd probably get three cops shot by freaks in the meantime."

"I'm trying to figure out ways to press him," Lucas said. He dropped the apple back in the bowl.

"Do we really want to chase him out of here? He'd just go somewhere else, start again. . . ."

"I don't know if he can. Somehow, I don't know how, he's got a unique situation here. He can hide, somehow," Lucas said. "If he travels, he loses that—I mean, look, right now Bekker's one of the most famous people in the country. He can't go to motels or gas stations, he can't take any kind of public transportation. He can't really ride in a car without a lot of tension—if he gets pulled over by a cop, he's done. And he needs his dope, he needs his money. If we pushed him out, if he tried to run, he'd be finished."

She thought about it, then nodded. "I suppose we could do something. I wouldn't want to make a lot of stops, but we could *announce* that we are, and ask for cooperation from the public. Maybe make a couple of stops for the TV crews . . ."

"That'd be good."

"I'll talk to Kennett tomorrow," she said. She perched on a stool opposite from him, crossed her legs and wrapped her hands around the top knee.

"How'd he get on this case? Kennett?" Lucas asked.

"O'Dell pulled some strings. Kennett's one of the best we've got on this kind of thing, organizing and running it."

"He and O'Dell don't like each other."

"No. No, they don't. I don't know why O'Dell pulled him, exactly, but I can tell you one thing: he wouldn't have done it unless he thought Kennett would find Bekker. Back in Minneapolis, you can control the bureaucratic fall-out, because the department's small and everybody knows everybody else. But here . . . We've got to find Bekker, or heads'll start rolling. People are pissed off."

Lucas nodded, thought about it for a second, and said, "Kennett's an intelligence guy: are you sure he's not involved with Robin Hood?"

Lily looked down at her hands. "In my heart, I'm sure. I couldn't prove it, though. Whoever's running this thing must have a fair amount of charisma, to hold it together, and good organizational skills . . . and certain political opinions. Kennett fits."

"But . . . ?"

"He has too much sense," Lily said. "He's a believer in, what? Goodness, maybe. That's what I feel about him, anyway. We talk about things."

"Okay."

"That's not exactly proof," Lily said. She was tight, unhappy with the question, chewing at it.

"I wasn't asking for proof, I was asking for an opinion," Lucas said. "What about O'Dell? He seems to be running everything. He runs you, he runs Kennett. He's running me, or thinks he is. He picked Fell out of the hat. . . ."

"I don't know, I just don't know. Even the way he picked Fell, it seems more like magic than anything. We may be on a complete wild-goose chase." She was about to go on, but chimes sounded from the door. She hopped off her stool and walked down the hall and pushed her intercom button. A man's voice said, "Bobby Rich, Lieutenant."

"I'll buzz you in," Lily said. To Lucas, she said, "Get the lights."

Lucas turned off the lights and sat on the floor, legs crossed. Sitting in the dark, he watched Lily as she waited by the door, a tall woman, less heavy than she once was, with a long, aristocratic neck. *Charisma. Good organizational skills. Certain political opinions.*

"How did you talk O'Dell into bringing me here?" he asked abruptly. "Was he reluctant? How hard did you have to press?"

"Bringing you here was more his idea than mine," Lily said. "I'd told him about you and he said you sounded perfect."

Rich knocked on the door as Lucas thought, *Really?*

RICH WAS A TALL black man, balding, athletic, hair cropped so closely that his head looked shaven. He wore a green athletic jacket with tan sleeves, and blue jeans. He said, "Hello," and edged inside the apartment. Lily pointed him at a chair where Lucas could see his face, and then said, "There's another guy in the apartment, in the kitchen."

"What?" Rich, just settling on the chair, half rose and looked down the hall.

"Don't get up," Lily snapped. She pointed him back into the chair.

"What's going on here?" Rich asked, still peering toward the kitchen.

"We have a guy who's getting close to Robin Hood. Maybe. He doesn't want you to see his face. He doesn't know who to trust. . . . If you don't want to talk about it, with him back there, we can cut it off right here. You can go back into the bedroom while he leaves. Then it'll be just you and me . . . but I wanted you to know."

Rich's tongue slid over his lower lip, his hands gripping the arms of the chair. After a minute, he relaxed. "I don't see how he can hurt me," he said.

"He can't," Lily said. "He's mostly going to listen, maybe ask a couple of questions. Why don't you just tell me what you told Walt? If either of us has questions, we'll break in."

Rich thought about it for another moment, looked into the dark, trying to penetrate it, then nodded. "Okay," he said.

He'd been at home when he got a call from an ex-burglar he'd busted a couple of times, a man named Lowell Jackson. Jackson was trying to go straight, as a sign painter, and was doing okay.

"He said an acquaintance of his had called, a kid named Cornell, nicknamed Red. Cornell had said he'd seen Jimmy King go down and that it wasn't no gangbangers—that one of the guys in the car was an old white guy and Cornell thought he was a cop. Jackson gave me an address."

Old white guy?

"Did you go after Cornell?" asked Lily.

"Yeah. Couldn't find him. So I went and talked to Jackson."

"What he say?"

"He said right after he talked to me, that same day, he saw Cornell at this playground on 118th—this is all in my report. . . ."

"Go ahead," Lily said.

"Cornell came down to a playground on 118th and said he was going home. Getting out of town. Nobody knew where he went. His last name is Reed. Cornell Reed. He's got a sheet. He's a doper, into crack. But he used to be some kind of college kid. Not a regular asshole."

"How old is he?" Lily asked.

"Middle twenties, like that."

"New York guy?"

"No. Supposedly he came from down south somewhere, Atlanta maybe. Been here a few years, though—Jackson said he didn't talk about where he came from. There was something . . . wrong. He just wouldn't talk about it. Used to cry about it, though, when he was drunk."

"How many times was he busted?"

"Half-dozen, nothing big. Theft, shoplifting, minor possession. We looked for background on him, NCIC, but there's nothing—his first busts were here in New York, addresses up in Harlem."

"And he's gone."

"Nowhere to be found. We checked Atlanta, but they don't know him."

"Dead?"

Rich frowned. "Don't think so. When he took off from the playground, he had some new shoes and a big nylon suitcase. That's what the guys at the playground say. He came up to 118th to say good-bye, they were sitting around. Then he jumped a cab and that's the last they saw of him."

"You wrote a report on all of this?"

"Yeah. And we're still looking for him. To tell you the truth, he's about the only thing we ever got on the case."

"What were you doing for Petty?" Lucas asked.

"Just looking at guys, mostly," Rich said. "Made me a little nervous, tell you the truth. I tried to get off it. I don't like looking at our own people."

"How'd you get assigned to the case?" Lucas asked.

"I don't know. Someone downtown, I guess," Rich said, his forehead wrinkling as he thought about it. "My lieutenant just said to report down to City Hall for a special assignment. He didn't know what was going on either."

"All right," said Lucas. Then, "How did Cornell know the white guy was old?"

"Don't know; if I find him, I'll ask him. Maybe just because he knows him from somewhere . . ."

They talked for another half hour, but Rich had almost nothing that wasn't in the reports. Lily thanked him and let him go.

"Waste of time," Lily said to Lucas.

"Had to try. What do you know about him? Rich?"

"Not much, really," she said.

"Good detective?"

"He's okay. Competent. Nothing spectacular."

"Hmp." Lucas touched the sore cheek, head down, considering.

"Why?"

"Just wondering," he said, looking back up. "You ready to go?"

"Want to walk? Down to the restaurant?"

"How far?" Lucas asked.

"Ten, fifteen minutes, taking it easy."

"Are we gonna get shot, going out the door?"

"No. O'Dell had a couple of people talk to the supers all along the block," Lily said. "They're looking for strange people wandering around their apartments."

The street outside the apartment was clear, but before they went out through the lobby door, Lucas scanned the windows across the street.

"Nervous?"

"No. I'm trying to figure it," he said.

She studied his face. "What?"

"Nothing." He shook his head. Rich had seemed straight enough.

"C'mon . . ."

"Nothing, really . . ."

"All right," Lily said, annoyed, still watching him.

THE VILLAGE WAS PRETTY, quiet, well-tended brick townhouses with flowers in window boxes, touches of wrought iron, the image wounded here and there by a curl of concertina, a touch of razor wire. And the people looked different, Lucas thought, from the people farther uptown; a deliberate touch of the Bohemian: sandals and canvas shorts, beards and waist-length hair, old-fashioned bikes and wooden necklaces.

The Manhattan Caballero was buried in a street of red stone buildings, a small place, its name and logo painted on one window, a beer sign in the other.

"They shot from up there, the third window in, second floor," Lily said, standing on the sidewalk outside the Caballero door, pointing across the street.

"Couldn't miss with a laser sight," Lucas said, looking up at the window, then down at the sidewalk. "He must've been about right here, you see the chip marks."

Caught by the geometry and technicalities of the killing, he'd paid no attention to her. Now he looked up and she had one hand on the restaurant window, as if for support, her face pale, waxen.

"Jesus, I'm sorry. . . ."

"I'm okay," she said.

"I thought you were gonna faint."

"It's anger now," she said. "When I think about Walt, I want to kill somebody."

"That bad?"

"So bad I can't believe it. It's like I lost a kid."

They flagged a cab to go to Petty's apartment. Crossing the Brooklyn Bridge, Lily asked, "Have you ever been here? Brooklyn Heights?"

"No."

"Great place for an apartment. I thought about it, I would've come, except, you know, once you live in the Village, you don't want to leave."

"This looks okay . . ." Lucas said, peering out the window as they rolled off the end of the bridge. "The woman at Petty's apartment building . . ."

"Logan."

"She says somebody was in his apartment when he was already dead, and before the cops arrived?"

"Yes. Absolutely. She remembers that she thought he'd come home and then gone out again. She was watching television, remembered the show, and what part of the show. We checked—he'd been dead for ten minutes."

"Somebody was moving fast."

"Very fast. Had to know the minute Walt went down. Had to be *waiting* for it. There's a question about how he got into Walt's apartment. Whoever it was must have had a key."

"That's simple enough, if you're talking about an intelligence operation."

"You should know," she said.

PETTY'S APARTMENT WAS in a brown brick building stuck on the side of a low hill, in a cul-de-sac, the area long faded but pleasant. Marcy Logan's door was the first one to the left, inside the tiny lobby.

"Very late," Logan said, peering over the door chain at Lily's badge. She was an older woman, in her middle sixties, gray hair and matching eyes. "You said ten o'clock."

"I'm sorry, but something else came up," Lily said. "We just need to talk for a minute."

"Well, come in." Her tone was severe, but Lucas got the impression that Logan was happy for the company. "I'll have to warm up the coffee. . . ."

She had made cookies and coffee, the cookies laid out on a silver tray. She stuck a carafe of coffee in a microwave, fussed with cups and saucers.

"Such a nice apartment," Lily said.

"Thank you. They filmed *Moonstruck* just down the way, you know. Cher was right down by the Promenade, I saw her . . ."

When the coffee was hot, Logan poked the tray of cookies in Lucas' face. Lucas tried one: oatmeal. He took another, with a cup of coffee.

"It wasn't a woman," Logan said, positively, when Lily asked. "The footsteps were too heavy. I didn't see him, but it was a man."

"You're sure?"

"I hear people come and go all day," Logan said. "That's something I'd know. I thought it was Walter coming back—I wouldn't have thought that if it was a woman."

"He went up, was there for a few minutes, then came right back down?" Lily asked.

"That's right. Couldn't have been more than a half-hour, because my show was a half-hour, and he came after the show started and left before it ended."

"You told the investigators that it occurred to you that it wasn't Petty," Lily said. "But not seriously enough that you actually looked. Why did you think it might not be him?"

"Whoever it was, stopped in the lobby. Like he was looking at my apartment door or maybe listening for anybody inside. Then he went up. Walter was always very forthright. Walked right in, went right up. Especially on his Fridays.

He'd always have two or three beers, and he couldn't hold it at all, and by the time he got here, he'd . . . you know: he had to go. You could hear the water running from the toilet, right after he went up. That night, though, whoever it was stopped inside. He did the same thing on the way back out. Stopped in the lobby. It gives me the shivers. Maybe he was thinking about rubbing out witnesses."

"I don't think that's much of a threat," Lily said, smiling at the "rubbing out."

"Why don't you say something, young man?" Logan asked Lucas, who was eating his sixth cookie. He couldn't seem to stop.

"Too busy eating cookies," he said. "These things are great. You could make a fortune selling them."

"Oh, that's nice," she said, smiling. "What happened to your face?"

"I was mugged."

"Isn't that just like New York? Even the cops . . ."

"How do you know this guy went to Petty's apartment?" Lucas asked.

"Well, I heard him come in, and then the elevator dinged, so he was going up. Then just a second later, I heard another ding, like it was coming from the kitchen. That's the second floor. If it goes to the third floor, I can barely hear it. If it goes to the fourth, I can't hear it at all."

"Okay," Lucas said, nodding. "So you heard it ding on the second floor."

"Yes. And the Lynns and Golds were already in and the Schumachers were at Fire Island that whole weekend. So it had to be Walter, and it was about the time he always came in. I didn't hear him flush, though. Then I heard the elevator ding on the second floor again, and it came down. Then whoever it was, I thought was looking at apartments again, because it was a minute before the outside door opened. . . . I should have looked, but I was watching my show."

"That's fine," said Lucas, nodding. "And it wasn't a visitor to one of the other apartments?"

"No," Logan said, shaking her head. "When the cops got here and I found out what happened, I told them about somebody coming, and they talked to everybody up there. Nobody came in at that time, and nobody had any visitors."

When they finished with Logan, they rode up in the elevator and Lily cut the seals off Petty's door. The apartment had been neatly kept but had been pulled apart by investigators. The refrigerator had been unplugged, and the door stood open. Cupboard doors were open and paper was stacked everywhere. Lucas went to Petty's desk, which was set in a tiny alcove, and thumbed through financial records. . . . No personal phone book.

"No phone book."

"The Homicide guys probably have it. I'll ask."

Ten minutes later, Lily said, "This is like the interview with Rich. There isn't anything here."

On the way out, Mrs. Logan met them in the hallway with a brown paper bag, which she handed to Lucas. "More cookies," she said.

"Thanks," he said, and then, "When I finish them, I may come back for more."

The old lady giggled, and Lucas and Lily went looking for a cab.

. . .

CORNELL REED. Cornell Reed had seen the killer, an old white guy, and recognized him as a cop.

Lucas lay on the hotel bed and thought about it, sighed, rolled off the bed, found his pocket address book, and picked out Harmon Anderson's home phone number. As he dialed the number, he glanced at his watch. It would be midnight, Minneapolis time.

Anderson was in bed.

"Jesus, Lucas, what's going on?"

"I'm in New York. . . ."

"I know, I heard. I wish I was there. . . ." Lucas heard him turn away from the phone and say to someone in the background, "Lucas." Then to Lucas, he said, "My wife's here, she says hello."

"Look, I'm sorry I woke you up . . ."

"No, no . . ."

"And I don't want to cause you any problems, but would you be available to do a little computer work? I'd pay you a consultant's fee."

"Ah, fuck that, what do you need?"

"I'm in a snakepit, man. Could you find out what airlines fly out of New York, all the big airports, including Newark, and check from the beginning of the month, see if there's a ticket for a Cornell Reed? Or any first name Cornell, if you can do that? Or Red Reed? I don't think it'd be overseas, except maybe the Caribbean. Check domestic first, like Atlanta, L.A. or Chicago. I need to know where he went and I need to know who paid for the ticket, if we can find that out."

"Could take a couple of days."

"Get back to me—and I'm serious about a fee, man. A few bucks."

"We can work that out. . . ."

"Get back to me, man."

When he hung up, Lucas dropped back on the bed, thinking back to the interview with Rich. Rich didn't know why he'd been picked for Petty's team. Neither did Lily. His only qualification seemed to be that he'd later get a call from a burglar he knew, producing the only lead in the case. Good luck of a rare and peculiar variety.

Rich said that Cornell Reed was heavy into the crack. If that was right, Reed shouldn't be flying out of town. If he had enough cash to fly, he'd buy dope with the cash and take the bus. Or hitchhike. Or just not go. With enough crack, you didn't have to go anywhere. . . . He certainly wouldn't take several hundred dollars out to La Guardia and push it across the ticket counter.

On the other hand, a doper doesn't take a cab to the bus depot, not when the A train would have him there quicker and leave him enough change for a rock or two. La Guardia was another story. There was no easy way to get there, except by cab. . . .

So maybe he was flying. And maybe he was flying on an unrefundable ticket. And that sounded like a ticket issued by a government.

Or a police department.

And then there was Mrs. Logan's story.

That was very interesting; interesting and disturbing. Had Lily not understood it? Or had she hoped that Lucas hadn't?

THIRTY HITS OF SPEED, two days; Bekker hadn't slept forever. He was carried along on the chemicals like a leaf in a river, the flow of time and thought rolling about him. And he was avoiding the woman with the eyes, the woman watching him. She terrified him: but the chemicals had defeated her after two days, and she was losing her grip.

But other things were happening.

Late in the afternoon of the second day, the bugs came. He could feel them, lines of them, inching through his veins. All of his veins, but in particular, a vein on the forearm; he could feel them, little bumps, rattling along, doing their filthy work. Eating him.

Eating the blood cells. He could remember, as a child, kicking open ant nests and seeing the ants running for cover, their mealy white eggs in their jaws. And this was the image that came to him: ants running, but with blood cells caught in their pincers. Thousands of them, running through his veins. If he could let them out . . .

A voice in his head: *No no no, hallucination, no no no . . .*

He stood up, his knees and feet aching. He'd walked for miles in the basement, back and forth, back and forth. How far? A few errant brain cells wandered away and did the calculation . . . say five thousand round trips, twenty feet each way . . . thirty-seven point eight seven eight miles. Thirty-seven point eight seven eight seven eight seven eight seven eight seven . . .

He was snared in the eight-seven loop, captivated by the sheer infinity of it, a loop that would last longer than the sun, would last longer than the universe, would go on for . . . what?

He shook himself out of the loop, felt the bugs raging through his veins, took his forearm to the bathroom, turned on the light, looked for bumps, where the bugs scuttled along. . . .

A voice: *formication . . .*

He pushed it away. Had to let them out, squeeze them out somehow. He walked into the operating theater, went to the instruments pan, found a scalpel, let them out. . . .

He began to walk, the bugs draining away, began to pace again—what was that smell? So clean and coppery, like the sea. Blood?

He looked down at himself. Blood was running from his arm. Not heavily, now slowing, but his hand and forearm looked as though they had been flayed. Where he'd been pacing, blood splattered the floor, an oval line marking his pattern, as though someone had been swinging a decapitated chicken.

The voice: *stereotypy.*

What? He stared at the arm and a bug zipped down the vein. Like Charlie Victor on the Ho Chi Minh Trail, like Charlie Victor at the Hotel Oscar, Charlie Hotel India Mike November Lima Tango Romeo . . .

Another loop—where had that come from? 'Nam? He shook himself out. The bugs were waiting, in all their ranks.

Medication. He went to his medicine table, found a half-dozen pills. That was all. He popped one, then another. And a third.

He picked up the phone, struggled with himself, put it back down. No telephone from here, not to a dealer. Cops bugged dealers, bugged . . . He looked down at his arm, at the sticky blood. . . .

Calmed himself. Washed. Dressed. Put a bandage on the cut on his forearm. Cut? How did that . . .

He lost the thought and fixed himself in the mirror, preparing for his public, the *need* always there, looking over his shoulder. The *need* brought up the street personality. Changed his voice. Changed his manner. When he finished dressing, he went out to the corner, to a pay phone.

"Yes?" Woman's voice.

"May I speak to Dr. West?"

Whitechurch was there a second later. "Jesus Christ, we gotta talk. Like now. The cops have been here and they're looking for your buddy—or whoever you sold that shit to, the monitoring gear."

"What?"

"The guy you sold it to," Whitechurch said insistently. "He's this fruitcake killer, Bekker. Jesus Christ, the cops were all over me."

"New York cops?"

"Yeah, some cooze and this mean-looking asshole from Minneapolis."

"Are they on your phone?"

"This is not my phone. Don't worry about that. Just worry about the dude who bought that shit. . . ."

"I can handle that," Bekker squeaked. The effort hurt. "But I need some product."

"Jesus Christ . . ."

"A lot of it."

"How much?"

"How much do you have?"

There was a moment's silence, then Whitechurch said, "You're not with this Bekker dude, are you?"

"It wasn't Bekker. I sold it to a high school kid out on Staten Island. He's using it for his science project."

That clicked with Whitechurch: Schoolteacher . . .

Whitechurch had decided to take a vacation to Miami, could use the extra cash. "I could get you two hundred of the crosses, thirty of the angels and ten of the white, if you can handle it."

"I can handle it."

"Twenty minutes?"

"No . . . I've got to come over. . . ." Let him think Bekker lived on Staten Island. "I need a couple of hours."

"Two hours? All right. Two hours. See you at nine. Usual place."

BEKKER LEFT THE Volkswagen in a staff parking ramp off First Avenue; the ramp was open to the public from six until midnight. He nodded to the guard in the booth and rolled all the way up to the top floor. He'd watched Whitechurch before. He believed in taking care and knew that drug dealers routinely sold friends and customers to the cops. He'd learned a lot in jail; another side of life.

Whitechurch insisted on punctuality. "That way, I only have the stuff on me, on the street, for a minute. Safer that way, you know?"

Usually, Whitechurch would be walking out of the hospital, or down the sidewalk toward a bus bench, when Bekker came by. Once Bekker, arriving early, had watched him from the ramp. Whitechurch had come out, walked down the sidewalk toward the bus bench, had waited for two or three minutes, then had gone back inside, using the same door he'd used on the way out. Bekker had called to apologize, and made the pickup a few minutes later.

Bekker walked down to the first floor, past the pay booth, and down the street to an alleylike passage to the emergency room. Night was settling in, the streetlights coming on. He was early, slowed down. Several people around. Not good. He turned down the alley to the emergency room, walked up to the door that Whitechurch usually came through. Pulled on the handle. Locked. Glanced at his watch. Still two minutes early. Whitechurch should be coming, just any moment. . . .

He'd done an angel before he came, part of his emergency stash. Strong stuff; it freed his power. . . .

The derringer was in his hand.

The door opened and Whitechurch stepped out, and jumped, startled, when he saw Bekker.

"What . . ."

"We've got to talk," Bekker whispered. "There's more to this than I thought. . . ."

He looked past Whitechurch to an empty tile-walled corridor. "Back inside, just a few minutes. I feel obligated to tell you about this."

Whitechurch nodded and turned, leading the way. "Did you bring the cash?"

"Yes." He held out the cash envelope and Whitechurch took it. "Have you got the product?"

"Yeah." Whitechurch turned as the metal fire door closed behind them. The corridor lights weren't strong, but they were unforgiving blue fluorescents.

Whitechurch had a plastic baggie in his hand and half stepped toward Bekker when he said, "You're . . ." He stopped, catching his tongue, and began to back away.

"The fruitcake killer," Bekker said, smiling. "Just like on *I've Got a Secret*. You remember that show? Garry Moore, I think."

Whitechurch's head snapped around, looking for room, then turned back to Bekker, but already his body was moving, trying to run.

"Listen," he said, half over his shoulder.

"No." Bekker leveled the gun at Whitechurch's broad back and Whitechurch shouted, "No way," and Bekker shot him in the spine between the shoulder blades. The muzzle blast was deafening, and Whitechurch pitched forward, tried to catch himself on the slick tile walls, bounced and turned. Bekker pointed the pistol at him, from two feet.

"No way . . ."

Bekker pulled the trigger again, firing into Whitechurch's forehead. Then he pushed the gun into his pocket, hurrying, took out a scalpel, stooped, and ruined Whitechurch's dead eyes. Good.

Down the hall, a door banged open. "Hey." Somebody yelling.

Bekker looked down the corridor: empty. He grabbed the baggie full of pills, stood, remembered the money, saw it half trapped under Whitechurch. Down the hall, the door banged open again and Bekker jerked at the money envelope. The envelope ripped, but he got most of it, just a bill or two still trapped under the body.

"Hey . . ." He looked back as he went through the door, but there was nothing in the corridor but the voice. Outside, he gathered himself and hurried, but didn't run, down the alley, turning left on the sidewalk to the parking ramp. He went inside to the stairs, heard footsteps behind, and half turned.

A young woman was hurrying after him. He started up the steps and she caught up with him, a few steps behind. "Wait up . . ." Breathless. "I hate to go up here alone. If there were somebody . . . You know."

"Yes." The woman was worried about being attacked. There was only one open entrance to the ramp, but anyone could get in over the low walls. Judging from the graffiti spray-painted on the concrete walls, several people had.

"God, what a day," the woman said. "I hate to work when it's so nice outside, I never see anything but computer terminals."

Bekker nodded again, not trusting his voice. If he'd had the time, he could have taken her. She'd have been perfect: young, apparently intelligent. A natural observer. Might possibly understand the privilege she was being given. He could take her, he thought. Right now. Hit her in the head . . .

Behind her, he balled his hand into a fist, and he thought, *Or the gun. I could use the gun.* He felt the weight of the gun in his pocket. Empty now, but a threat . . .

But if he hurt her, struck her, had to fight, if she was less than a perfect specimen . . . his results would be impeachable. People were watching him, people who hated him, who would do anything to impeach his results. He fell back a step, his heart beating like a drum.

"See you," she said, one half-level below his car. She looked out on the open floor before she went through the door. "Nobody here . . . makes you feel a little stupid, doesn't it?"

He could, but . . . wait. No improvisation. *Remember the last time . . . Easy, easy, there are plenty of them.*

Bekker lifted a hand and risked it: "Good-bye," he said, in his careful voice.

He had to get one. Had to. He didn't realize, until he saw the woman get in the car and lock the doors, how strong the need was now.

He rolled out of the ramp, straight down the street; there was some commotion in the emergency entrance alley, but he didn't stop to look. Instead, he went straight back to his apartment, almost frantic now, and got out his collector's bag: the stun gun and the anesthetic tank and mask. He flicked the stun gun once, checked the discharge level. Fine. And dug through the bag he'd taken from Whitechurch: just a taste. He snapped one of the angels between his teeth, thinking to take a half, but a half wouldn't do, and he took a whole, waiting for the power to come.

Cruising, thinking: *Infrared. Ultraviolet. Breakthrough.*

He knew this bar. . . .

Later. He saw the woman slouch out of the back of the bar, lean against the brick exterior, and light a cigarette with what looked like an old-fashioned Zippo. Not many men around, lots of women coming and going, many of them alone. Easy targets.

The woman was leaning against the outside wall, wearing jeans and a sleeveless T-shirt, with a wide leather belt. She had short black hair, with gold hoop earrings.

Bekker came up, stepping carefully around the Volkswagen as though he didn't own it. Not too aggressive. Stun gun in his hand, tank under his arm, hand on mask.

"Terrific night," he said to the woman.

She smiled. "You're looking pretty good," she said.

Bekker smiled back and stopped next to the nose of the Volkswagen.

Come to the gingerbread house, little girl . . .

WHAT'S WRONG?" Lily asked.

Kennett rolled toward her and put an arm under her head. "I feel like an invalid when we do that. I mean, nothing *but* that."

The forward double berth was wedge-shaped, shoved into the bow of the boat. Kennett was lying on his side. He reached toward her face in the near-darkness, touched her at the hairline with the pad of his index finger, drew it down her nose, gently over her lips, between her breasts, then up to gently tap each nipple, then down around her navel, over her hipbone and down the inside of her thigh to her knee. She was still warm, sweating.

"We're not . . . compelled . . . to do it," Lily said.

"Maybe you're not, but I am," Kennett grumbled. "If I couldn't make love anymore, I'd feel like a goddamn vegetable."

"You just wanna be on top," she said, trying to make a joke out of it. When he didn't respond, she said, "You've got to listen to Fermut."

"Fuckin' doctors . . ." Fermut, the cardiologist, had reluctantly agreed that Kennett could resume his sex life "as long as your partner does the hard work."

"Listen to him," Lily said, gently but urgently. "He's trying to save your life, you dope."

"Yeah." Kennett turned his head away from her, his hand scratching at his chest."

"You want a cigarette, right?"

"No, that's not it. I was just thinking . . . it's not the doctors. It's me. When I get turned on and my heart starts thumping, I start listening to it. . . ."

"Then we oughta quit. Maybe only for a few weeks . . ." Lily said.

"No. That'd be worse. It's just . . . Christ, I wish one thing—just one goddamn thing in this world—was simple. Just one thing. I gotta get laid, but if I get laid, I can't help thinking about my heart, and that can mess up getting laid. Then with you on top all the time, and me just laying there like a dead man with a hard-on, I start thinking, what's it like for her? It must be like necrophilia, screwing me."

"Richard, you idiot . . ."

"Christ, I'm glad I met you," he said after a while. "I couldn't believe you were in there, working for O'Dell. I kept thinking, she can't be just working for him, a woman like that, there's gotta be something else going on here."

"Oh, God . . ." Lily giggled, an odd, pleasant sound with her husky voice.

"Sorry 'bout that," Kennett said, touching her again. "I wonder what O'Dell does for sex? Fly out to Vegas and get a couple-three fat ones in the sack? I wonder how long it's been since he's seen his dick? He's so fat I don't think he can even reach it anymore. . . ."

"C'mon . . ." Lily said, but she giggled again, a big woman giggling, and that set Kennett off, laughing.

And then: " 'Course, things must've been different with Davenport."

Lily cut him off: "Shut up. I don't want to hear it."

"Probably hung like a Shetland pony . . ."

"You wanna get bit?"

"Is that a clear offer?"

"Dick . . ."

"Hey. I'm not jealous. Well, maybe a little. But I really like the guy. This whole business of bringing him to dance with the media, that's pretty bizarre, and it's working. You think he'll get in the sack with Barbara Fell?"

"I don't know," she said, crisply.

"He seems like the kind of guy who'd be looking around," he offered.

"Pot and kettle."

"Hey—I didn't say it was bad. I just wondered about him and Fell. That's a match made in hell."

"She's very attractive."

"I guess, if you like the type," Kennett said. "She looks like a biker chick who fell off the Harley one too many times. Why'd you put him with her? Some kind of psychological compulsion to bury your sexual history?"

"No, no, no. We just needed somebody who knew Midtown fences. . . ."

"Yeah, but Davenport's supposed to be a talking head."

"He's never a talking head. Even when he's talking. The guy has more moves than you do, and you're the sneakiest, shiftiest . . ."

". . . crookedest . . ."

". . . most underhanded asshole on the force. Besides, he had to do something to get the media to talk to him."

"I suppose." Kennett's fingertips slipped along her thigh again, her skin soft and slightly cool from evaporating sweat. "We'll either have to get a sheet to cover up or figure out some way to warm up the place again."

Lily groped for his groin and said, "Oh, Jesus. Are you sure? Dick . . ."

He rolled into her, his arm around her, pulling her tight. "That's the word, all right. Dick."

"Be serious."

"All right. How's this: I really do need you; it's the thing that keeps my heart going. . . ."

Much later, when he was sleeping, she thought: *They can all make you feel guilty; it's what they do best. . . .*

THE PHONE RANG EARLY and Lucas rolled out of the blankets, dropped his feet to the floor and sat a moment before he picked up the receiver. "Yeah?"

"How's your head?" Kennett sounded wide awake and almost chipper.

"Better," Lucas said. He couldn't seem to focus and noticed that the window shade was bright with low-angle sunshine. "What time is it?"

"Seven o'clock."

"Ah, Jesus, man, I don't get up at seven. . . ." His face hurt again, and when he turned toward the bed, he noticed a spot of blood on the pillowcase.

"Hey, it's a great day, but it's gonna be hot," Kennett said cheerfully.

"Thanks. If you hadn't called, I woulda had to look out the window. . . ." *What's going on?*

"I understand that you and Fell talked to a guy named Whitechurch yesterday, at Bellevue?"

"Yeah?"

"Bekker took him off last night."

"What?" Lucas stood up, trying to understand.

"Shot him in a hallway. Cut his eyes," Kennett said. "The morgue guys said it's gotta be Bekker, 'cause it was done too well to be a copycat. And with you talking to him about Bekker, there's no way it's a coincidence. When they called me, a couple of hours ago now, I shipped Carter over to the hospital. Somebody there finally figured out that cops were talking to Whitechurch yesterday. . . ."

"Ah, Jesus," Lucas said. "Whitechurch was wrong, too. We knew it. We knew he was bullshitting us."

"How'd you get onto him?"

"A fence," Lucas said. "Down on the Lower East Side."

"Smith?"

"No, a small-timer, a woman named Arnold. We'll go back and talk to her, but I don't think she has any connection with Whitechurch except to handle occasional shipments from him. But why was Bekker talking to Whitechurch again? More equipment?"

"Whitechurch was dealing dope," Kennett said.

"Ah. For sure?"

"Yeah, we got it from a couple of places. And I'd bet that's where the halothane is from."

"Telephones?"

"We sent a subpoena over, and the phone company's mopping up their computers right now. They'll run back all the calls that came into Whitechurch's apartment and his office phone, both, and where they came from, for the last two months."

"That should do it," Lucas said. "Fell's got a beeper: if you find him, call us. I'd like to see the end of it."

"Mmm. It doesn't feel that easy," Kennett said.

"All right. Well: I'll get Fell and get back to the fence. Goddammit, why'd Whitechurch cover for him? That'd be something to figure out."

LUCAS CALLED FELL and told her.

"Did we mess it up?" she asked anxiously.

"No. We barely touched the guy—there was no way to know. But Kennett's people are all over him now. Everybody who knew him. We've got to talk to what's-her-name, the fence."

"Arnold. Rose."

"Yeah . . . So what's your status? Are you ready?" Lucas asked.

"Hey, I'm just sitting here on my bed, buck naked, half asleep."

"Jesus, if you had a warm croissant and a cup of coffee, I'd come right over," Lucas said. The nude photo of Fell and the other cop popped up in his head.

"Fuck you, Davenport," Fell said, laughing. "If you're ready, why don't you get a cab? I'll be out front by the time you get here."

"You come get me," Lucas said. "I'm barely awake, and I gotta shave." He touched his raw cheek.

"Be ready," she said.

Fell, when she arrived, was wearing a black tailored cotton dress with small flowers—the kind of dress women wore in Moline, Illinois—black low heels and nylons.

"Jesus, you look terrific," Lucas said, climbing into the cab behind her.

She blushed and said, "We just gonna walk in on Arnold?"

"You don't want to talk about how terrific you look?"

"Hey, just shut the fuck up, okay, Davenport?" she said.

"Anything you want . . ." Under his breath, he added, "Toots."

"What? What'd you just say?"

"Nothing," Lucas said innocently.

She closed one eye and said, "You're walking on the edge, buddy."

ARNOLD WAS SCARED. "He maybe got done because he talked to you," she said, sucking her heavy lips in and out.

"No. He got done because he called this asshole Bekker, who he was protecting, and told him that we'd interviewed him," Lucas said. "Bekker knows me. He didn't want to take any chances."

"So what do you want from me? I gave you everything."

"How'd you get in touch with Whitechurch when you needed to?" Lucas asked.

"I never needed to. When he had something good, he'd bring it over. Otherwise—shit, I don't handle hospital stuff. I handle shit you can sell, cheap. Suits. Neckties. Telephones. I wouldn't know what to do with no hospital stuff."

Fell pointed a finger at her: "You took down Simpson-McCall, what, two months ago . . . ?"

Arnold looked away. "No. I don't know nothing about that."

Fell studied her for a moment, then looked at Lucas. "Brokerage moves to a new building, one of those over-the-weekend moves. Trucks coming and going all night with files, computers, telephones, furniture, putting it in. The only thing is, not all of the trucks were hired by the brokerage. Some assholes rented trucks, drove them up to the loading docks, and disappeared over the horizon. . . . One of them took off six hundred brand-new beige two-button phones. Somebody else got fifty Northgate IBM compatibles, still in the boxes."

"Really?" said Arnold, faintly distressed. "Computers?"

Fell nodded, and Lucas looked back at Arnold. "If you *had* to get to Whitechurch, what'd you do?"

Arnold shrugged. "Call him at the hospital. Wasn't no big secret where he worked. Nights only, though."

"Did he have a special number?"

"I don't know, man, I never called him."

"Did . . ."

Fell's beeper went off. She took it out of her purse, glanced at the readout. "Where's the phone?" she asked Arnold. To Lucas, she said, "I bet they got him."

"Over there, at the end of the counter, underneath . . ." Arnold said, pointing.

As Fell punched the number into the telephone, Lucas went back to Arnold. "Did he work with anybody?"

"Man, I bought telephones from him, four dollars apiece," Arnold said impatiently. "Boxes of pens and pencils. Notepads. Cartons of Xerox paper. Cleaning supplies. He once came in with two hundred bottles of ERA, you know, the laundry soap. I don't know where he got it, I didn't ask any questions. And that's all I know about him."

"Yeah, this is Fell, you beeped?" Fell said into the phone. And then, voice hushed, "Jesus. What's the address. Huh? Okay." She hung up and looked at Lucas. "Bekker did another one, another woman. Ten minutes from here, walking."

Lucas pointed a finger at Arnold: "Did you hear that? Think about Whitechurch. Anything you think of, call us. Anything."

"Man, there's nothin' . . ."

But Lucas and Fell were out the door.

THE BODY WAS in a dead-end alley off Prince. Uniforms blocked the mouth of the alley, kept back the curious. Fell and Lucas flashed their badges and went through. Kennett and two other plainclothesmen were there, staring into a window well. Kennett's hands, gripping the rail around the well, were white with tension.

"Goddamn maniac," he said as Lucas and Fell walked up. The crime-scene techs had dropped a ladder into the well. Lucas looked over the railing and saw a small woman's body at the bottom of the well, nude, crumpled like a doll, the techs working over her.

"No question it was Bekker?" Lucas asked.

"No, but it's different. This doesn't look so scientific. She's pretty slashed up, like he . . . I don't know. It looks like he was having fun."

"Eyes?"

"Yeah, the eyes are cut and the doc says it looks like his work. The eyelids gone, very neat and surgical. The sonofabitch has a signature."

"How long has she been down there?" Fell asked.

"Not long. A few hours at the most. Probably went in before dawn, this morning."

"Got an ID?" asked Lucas.

"No." Kennett looked at Fell, who was lighting a Lucky. "Could I bum one, I . . ."

"No." Fell shook her head, carefully not looking at him.

"God damn it," Kennett said. He stuck one hand in his jacket pocket, put two fingers of the other between his shirt buttons, over his heart. He caught himself, pulled them out, looked at his hand and finally stuck it in the other jacket pocket. "Fuckin' do-gooders."

"Anything on the Bellevue phones?" Lucas asked, watching the techs get ready to roll the woman's body.

Kennett's forehead wrinkled. "Think about this, Davenport: We got a guy who deals drugs, but he gets no phone calls. I mean, like, almost none. He got six calls at his apartment last month. There was a phone in the maintenance office he could use, but he didn't, much. At least, that's what his supervisor says."

"Did he carry a beeper? Maybe a cellular?" Fell asked.

"Not that we can find," said Kennett.

"That's bullshit," Lucas said flatly. "He was dealing, right? We know that for sure?"

"Yeah."

"Then he's got a phone. We've just got to find it. . . ."

"Carter's guys are interviewing people over there right now, at Bellevue. Maybe you could listen in for a while?" Kennett said. He looked at Fell. "You're the only guys who've come up with anything."

At the bottom of the window well, the crime-scene techs rolled the body. The woman's head flopped over, and her wide white eyes suddenly looked up at them.

"Aw, shit," Fell gagged. She turned away, hunched over the alley cobblestones, and a stream of saliva poured from her mouth.

"You okay?" Lucas asked, his hand on her back.

"Yes," she said, straightening. "Sorry. That just caught me, the eyes . . ."

Five minutes later, the body was out of the window well. The removal crew had wrapped it in a blanket, but Kennett ordered the wrapper peeled away. "I want to look," he said evenly. "I wish the fuck I could have gotten down there. . . ."

Kennett and Lucas squatted next to the collapsible gurney as the blanket was lifted. The woman's face was like marble, white, solid, her dying pain and fear still graven on her face. The gag was like the earlier ones, carved from hard rubber, held in place with a wire that had been twisted tight behind her ear.

"Pliers," Kennett said absently.

"Treats them like . . . lumber," Lucas said, groping for the right concept.

"Or lab animals," Kennett said.

"Sonofabitch." Lucas leaned to one side, almost toppled, caught himself with his hand, then knelt over the body until his face was only inches from the body's left ear. He looked up at one of the techs and said, "Roll her a little to the left, will you?" He took a pen from his shirt pocket and, to Kennett, said, "Look at this."

Kennett knelt beside him and Fell squatted behind the two of them, the other detectives crowding in. Lucas used the pen to point at two oval marks on the dead woman's neck muscle.

"Have you ever seen anything like that?" Lucas asked.

Kennett shook his head. "Looks like a burn," he said. "Looks like a fuckin' snakebite."

"Not exactly. It looks like a discharge wound from one of those electroshock self-defense gizmos, stun guns. The St. Paul cops carry them. I went over to see a demonstration. If you keep the discharge points on bare skin for more than a second or two, you can get this kind of injury."

"That's why there's no fight," Fell said, looking at him.

Lucas nodded. "He hits them with the shocker. When you get hit, you go down, like right now. Then he comes with the gas."

"Couldn't be too many places around that sell those things," Kennett said.

"Police-supply places, but I've seen them in gun magazines, too, mail order," Lucas said.

Kennett stood and rubbed alley sand from his hands and tipped his head back, as though looking up to heaven. "Please, God, let me find a Midtown address on an order form."

LUCAS AND FELL TOOK a cab to Bellevue, windows open, the hot popcorn smell of the city roaring in as they dodged through traffic, and got trapped for five minutes in a narrow one-lane crosstown street. Fell's jaw was working with anger.

"Thinking about Bekker?"

"About the body . . . Jesus. I hope Robin Hood gets him," she said. "Bekker."

"What? Robin Hood?" He looked at her curiously.

"Nothing," she said, looking away.

"No, c'mon, who's Robin Hood?"

"Ah, it's bullshit," she said, digging in her purse for a cigarette. "Supposedly somebody is knocking off assholes."

"You mean, a vigilante?"

She grinned. "How else you gonna run this place?" she asked, gesturing out the window. "It's supposed to be cops, but I think it's just bullshit. Wishful thinking."

"Huh."

She lit the cigarette, coughed, and looked out the window.

WHITECHURCH HAD BEEN a maintenance foreman. A changing roll of a dozen people worked under his loose supervision, doing minor repairs all over the hospital on the three-to-eleven shift.

"A great goddamn job if you're stealing stuff," Fell said as they joined Carter in an employees' lounge. Three detectives were interviewing hospital employees, with Carter supervising.

"Or if you're dealing," said Carter. He looked at his list. "Next one is Jimmy Beale. Goddamn, I got little faith in this."

"I know what you mean," Lucas said, watching the scared employees trooping through the lounge.

Beale knew nothing. Neither did any of the rest. Fell burned through a pack of Luckys, left to get another, came back and leaned in the door.

"God damn it, Mark . . . it's Mark?" Carter was saying. "God damn it, Mark, we're not getting anywhere and it's hard to believe that a guy could be stealing the place blind and nobody'd know about it. Or dealing dope, and nobody'd know. . . ."

Mark, tall, narrow, acned, nodded nervously, his Adam's apple working convulsively, sliding up and down his thin neck. "Man, you never seen the dude, you know? I mean, I'd come in and he'd say, Mark, g'wan up to 441D and put on a new doorknob and then see if there's a leak on the drinking fountain up on six, and that's what I'd do. He'd come by, but like, I never hung out with him or nothing."

When he was gone, Lucas said, "Nobody knew. How many do you believe?"

"Most of them," Carter said. "I don't think he was dealing here. And if you're stealing stuff, you don't talk about it. Somebody'll try to cut in—or somebody'll try to do the same thing, then feed you to the cops on plea bargain."

"Somebody must've known," Fell objected. "That was the last of them?"

"That was the last . . ." said Carter.

A woman knocked on the edge of the door and stuck her face in. She had curly white hair and held her hands in front of her as though she were knitting.

"Are you the police?" she asked timorously.

"Yeah. C'mon in," Lucas said. He yawned and stretched. "What can we do for you?"

She stepped inside the room and looked nervously around. "Some of the others were saying you were asking if Lew had a beeper or a walkie-talkie?"

"Yes. Who are you?"

"My name is Dotty, um, Bedrick, I work in housekeeping?" She made her sentences into questions. "Last week, Lew split out his pants, right down by housekeeping? There was some kind of pipe thing he was working on and he bent over and they went, split, right up the back?"

"Uh-huh," Lucas said.

"Anyway, I was right there? And everybody knows I sew, so he came in and asked if I could do anything? He slipped right out of his pants—he was wearing boxer shorts, of course—he slipped right out and I sewed them up. He was just wearing a T-shirt on top, and the boxer shorts, and I had his pants. There was nothing in there but his wallet and his keys and his pocket change. There wasn't any beeper or anything like that."

"Hey. Thank you," Lucas said, nodding. "That was a problem for us."

"Why did you have to know?" Bedrick asked. Lucas thought, *Miss Marple.*

"We think that—I'm sure you've heard this from the others—we think he was dealing drugs. If he was, he needed access to a telephone."

"Well, there was something odd about the man. . . ."

She wanted to be led: Lucas put his hands on his waist, pushing his sport coat back on both sides, like a cop on television, let a hip pop out and said, "Yeah?"

She approved: "Sometimes when the calls came over the speakers for doctors, I've seen him look up at the speakers. And the next thing, *he'd* be calling in. I saw him do it two or three times. Like he was a *doctor.*"

"Sonofagun," Carter said. "There'd be a call for a doctor?"

"That's right."

"Jesus," he said, turning to Lucas and Fell, dumbfounded. "That's it."

"That's it?" chirped Bedrick.

"That's it," Carter said. He smiled at the old lady and shook his head. "I never had a civilian do that before."

FELL DECIDED TO STAY at Bellevue and work the lead. Lucas, shaking his head, decided to head back to Midtown South.

"You don't think it'll be anything?" Fell asked.

"It might be—but with Whitechurch dead, I don't know how you'd find out," he said.

"I want to stay anyway," she said. "It's all we've got."

All we've got, Lucas thought. *Yeah. We find Bekker's supplier, the best damned lead all week, and Bekker kills him right under our noses.* Some hotshot cops they were. There had to be another way to approach this situation, to find a way in. . . .

At Midtown South, Lucas could hear Kennett all the way out to the reception desk.

". . . know it's hot, but I don't give a shit," he was saying. "I don't want people around here reading the goddamn reports, I want everybody out on the street. I want the fuckin' junkies to know there's a war going on. Instead of coming in here, I want you out on the street with your people, rousting these assholes. Somebody knows where he's at. . . ."

Lucas leaned in the door. Seven or eight detectives were sitting uncomfortably around the conference room, while Kennett sat on a folding chair at the front, his fingers over his heart, an angry flush on his face. He looked over the cops to Lucas and snapped, "Tell me something good."

"Did you talk to Carter?"

"I'm supposed to call him back," Kennett said, looking at a phone slip. "What happened?"

"An old lady maybe told us how Whitechurch got his calls."

"Well, goddamn," somebody said.

Lucas shook his head: "But it might not be good. He may have had doctor code names for his clients. When a buyer needed to call in, the switchboard—or somebody—would page the doctor. Whitechurch would pick up a phone and answer the page. There are thousands of doctors in there every day, thousands of phone calls. Hundreds of pages."

"Sonofabitch," Kennett said. He ran his hand through his hair, and a swatch of it stood up straight, in a peak. "Carter's pushing it?"

"Yeah. Six guys and Fell stayed to help."

Kennett thought about it for a second, then exhaled in exasperation and asked, "Anything else?"

"No. I'm still reading paper on him, but I think . . . Look, I had an idea on the way over. Entirely different direction. Carter's taking the phone angle, you got guys on everything else. I was thinking again about how hard Bekker is to find, about where he's getting his money, about all the things we don't know about him. So I was thinking, maybe I should talk to the guys who *did* know Bekker."

"Like who?"

"Like the guys who were in jail with him. Maybe I ought to go back to the Cities. I could run down the people who were in the next cells to his. Maybe he said something to somebody, or somebody gave him an idea of how to hole up. . . ."

"That's not bad," said Kennett, scratching his breastbone. "Kind of a long shot, though, and it takes you out of the action here." He thought about it some more. "I'll tell you what. Read paper for the rest of the day, think about the phones. Day after tomorrow's the lecture. If we've got nothing by then, let's talk about it. . . . You see the art?"

"Art?"

Kennett said, "Jim . . ."

One of the detectives handed Lucas a brown envelope. Lucas opened it and found a sheath of eight-by-ten color photos. Fell stood at his elbow as he flipped through them. Whitechurch, dead in the hallway, flat on his back. Blood on the tile behind his head, and on the wall. A twenty-dollar bill half pinned under the body.

"What's the money?" Lucas said.

"They must have been hassling over the cash when Bekker shot him," said the cop named Jim. "One of the janitors heard the shots. Not being stupid, he hollered before he went to look. Then he kind of carefully stuck his head through a fire door and saw Whitechurch on the ground. The outside door was just closing. Bekker must've grabbed what he could and run for it."

"He didn't take the eyelids," Lucas said. Except for the blood, Whitechurch might have been a sleeping drunk.

"Nope. Just poked him in the eyes and grabbed the dope, if there was any. They got a print, by the way, off a bill. It was Bekker."

"All right, let's get out there," Kennett said to the cops. There was an unhappy silence, all of them on their feet and moving through the door, shaking heads. "Hey. Everybody. Tell your people to put on the vests, huh? They're gonna be talking to some pissed-off people."

Huerta, bumping past Kennett, stopped to pat him on the head, pushing his hair down.

Kennett said, "What?" and Huerta, grinning, said, "Just knocking down your mohawk. With all that white hair stickin' up you looked like Steve Martin in *The Jerk*, except skinny and old."

"Yeah, old, kiss my ass, Huerta," Kennett said, laughing, straightening his hair.

Lucas, astonished, watched Huerta walk away, then looked back at Kennett.

"What?" Kennett asked, puzzled, raking at his hair again.

"Steve Martin?" Lucas asked.

"Asshole," Kennett grumbled.

"They're probably calling you the same thing, you putting them on the street like that," Lucas said. Switching the topic away from Steve Martin, covering, covering . . .

"I know," Kennett said soberly, looking after the detectives. "Jesus, roustin' junkies in this heat . . . it's gonna stink and the junkies'll be pissed and the cops are gonna be pissed and somebody's gonna get hurt."

"Not a hell of a lot of choice," Lucas said. "Keep pushing everywhere. With Whitechurch dead, Bekker's gotta find a new source."

AN HOUR LATER, Lucas lay on his bed at the Lakota and thought about what Huerta had said. That he looked like Steve Martin, with all that white hair . . .

All right. You're on the street. There's been a killing. A car speeds by and inside is an old white guy. That's what Cornell Reed told Bobby Rich's snitch. An old white guy. How would you know he was old, when he was in a moving car? If he had white hair . . .

And then there was Mrs. Logan, and what she'd said, in the apartment beneath Petty's. . . .

Kennett fit. He was a longtime intelligence operative. He was high up, with good access to inside information. He was tough but apparently well liked; he had charisma. He had white hair.

Kennett was sleeping with Lily. How did that cut across it? How did she wind up in the sack with a guy who might be a suspect? And the biggest question: with several hundred possible suspects, how did Kennett wind up in Lucas' lap, available for daily inspection?

O'Dell was one answer. Lily was another. Or both together.

He lay on the bed with the Magic Marker and his art pad, trying to put together a list. Finally he came up with:

1. Cornell Reed.

LUCAS WAS FLAT ON his back, half asleep, when Fell called. The room was semidark; he'd turned out all the lights but the one in the bathroom, and then half closed the door.

"I'm downstairs," she said. "If you're awake, let's get something to eat."

"Anything at Bellevue?" Lucas asked.

"I'll tell you about it."

"Ten minutes," he said.

He was fifteen minutes. He shaved, going easy over the bruises, brushed his teeth and took a quick shower, put on a fresh shirt, dabbed on after-shave. When he got down to the lobby, Fell looked him over and said, "Great. You make me feel like a rag."

"You look fine," he said, but she didn't. She looked worn, dirty around the eyes. The dress that had been crisp that morning hung slackly from her shoulders. "There's an Italian place a couple of blocks down that's friendly."

"Good. I couldn't handle anything complicated." As they were going out the door, she said, "I'm sorry about ditching you and going with Kennett, but this case really could mean a lot for me. And Mrs. Bedrick, she was mine . . . ours . . . and I wanted to be there to get the credit."

Lucas nodded and said, "No problem." On the sidewalk, he added, "You don't sound happy."

"I'm not. Bellevue's a rat's nest. They have a dial-in paging system, so now we're trying to figure out if we can match up the calls. And we're looking for people who might have been paging doctors who shouldn't have, that somebody else might have noticed. There are about two thousand suspects."

"Can you thin them out?"

"Maybe. We're trying extortion. Kennett worked out a routine with an assistant D.A. Everybody we talk to, we tell them the same thing: if we find out who Whitechurch's phone contact is before she comes forward, we'll charge her as an accomplice in the Bekker murders. If she comes forward and cooperates, we'll give her immunity on Bekker. And she can bring a lawyer and refuse to cooperate on anything else. . . . So there's a chance. If we can scare her enough."

"How do you know it's a *her*?"

Fell grinned up at him: "That's Kennett. He said, 'Have you ever heard a male voice on a hospital intercom?' We all thought about it, and decided, Not very often. If a male voice kept calling out the names of nonexistent doctors—that's what we think she was doing, whoever she is, calling out code names—he'd be noticed. So we're pretty sure it's a her."

"What if it's just the switchboard?"

"Then we're fucked . . . although Carter thinks it probably isn't. A switchboard might start recognizing names and voices. . . ."

THE WHETSTONE HAD an old-fashioned knife-grinding wheel in the window, a dozen tables in front, a few booths in back. Between the booths was a wooden floor, worn smooth and soft by a century of sliding feet. A couple turned slowly in the middle of it, dancing to a slow, sleepy jazz tune from an aging jukebox.

"Booth?" asked Lucas.

"Sure," said the waitress. "One left, in the no-smoking area."

Fell smiled ruefully at Lucas, and said, "We'll take it."

They ate spaghetti and garlic bread around a bottle of rosé, talking about Bekker. Lucas recounted the Minneapolis killings:

". . . started killing them to establish their alibis. They apparently picked out the woman at the shopping mall at random. She was killed to confuse things."

"Like a bug. Stepped on," Fell said.

"Yeah. I once dealt with a sexual psychopath who killed a series of women, and I could understand him, in a way. He was nuts. He was *made* nuts. If he'd had a choice, I'd bet that he'd have chosen not to be nuts. It was like, it wasn't his fault, his wires were bad. But with Bekker . . ."

"Still nuts," Fell said. "They might look cold and rational, but to be that cold, you've got to be goofy. And look what he's doing now. If we take him alive, there's a good chance that he'll be sent to a mental hospital, instead of a prison."

"I'd rather go to prison," Lucas said.

"Me, too, but there are people who don't think that way. Like doctors."

A heavyset man in work pants and a gray Charlie Chaplin mustache stepped across to the jukebox and stared into it. The waitress came by and said, "More wine?"

Lucas looked at Fell and then up at the waitress and said, "Mmmm," and the waitress took the glasses.

Behind her, the heavy man in work pants dropped a single quarter in the jukebox, carefully pressed two buttons, went back to his table and bent over the woman he had been sitting with. As she got up, the "Blue Skirt Waltz" began bubbling from the jukebox speakers.

"Jesus. *Blue Skirt.* And it's Frankie Yankovich, too," Lucas said. "C'mon, let's dance."

"You gotta be kidding. . . ."

"You don't want . . . ?"

"Of course I want," she said. "I just can't believe that you do."

They began turning around the floor, Fell light and delicate, a good dancer, Lucas denser, unskilled. They turned around the heavy man and his partner, the two couples caught by the same rhythm, weaving around the dance floor. The waitress, who'd taken menus to another table, lingered to watch them dance.

"One more time," the heavy man said to Lucas, in a heavy German accent, as the song ended. He bowed, gestured to the jukebox. Lucas dropped a quarter, punched "Blue Skirt," and they started again, turning around the tiny dance floor. Fell fit nicely just below his jaw, and her soft hair stroked his cheek. When the song ended, they both sighed and wandered back to the booth, holding hands.

"Sooner or later, I'd like to spend some time in your shorts, as we say around the Ninth," Fell said across the table as she sat down. "But not tonight. I'm too fuckin' dirty and miserable and tired and I've got too many bad movies in my head."

"Well," he said.

"Well, what? You don't want to?"

"I was thinking, well, I've got a shower."

She cocked her head, looking at him steadily, unsmiling. "You think it'll wash away that woman rolling over this morning, with those eyes?" she asked somberly.

After a moment, he said, "No. I guess not. But listen . . . you interest me. I think you knew that."

"I didn't really," she said, almost shyly. "I've got no self-confidence."

"Well." He laughed.

"You keep saying that. Well."

"Well. Have some more wine," he said.

HALFWAY THROUGH THE second bottle of wine, Fell made Lucas play it again and they turned around the room, close, her face tipped up this time, breathing against his neck, warm, steamy. He began to react and was relieved to get her back to the booth.

She was drunk, laughing, and Lucas asked about the cop she used to date.

"Ah, God," she said, staring up at the ceiling, where a large wooden fan slowly turned its endless circles. "He was *so* good-looking, and he was *such* a snake. He used to be like this *Pope of Greenwich Village* guy with these great suits and great shoes, and he hung out, you know? I mean, he was cool. His socks had clocks on them."

"How cool can a Traffic guy be?" Lucas cracked.

She frowned. "Were we talking about him? I don't . . ."

"Sure, at your place," he said, thinking, *As a matter of fact, you didn't, Lily did, Davenport, you asshole.* "I remember, mm, important details. . . ."

"Why's that important?" she asked, but she knew, and she was flattered.

"You're the fuckin' detective," Lucas said, grinning at her. "Have another drop of wine."

"Trying to get me drunk?"

"Maybe."

Fell put her wineglass on the table and poked a finger at him. "What the fuck are you doing, Davenport? *Are* you Internal Affairs?"

"Jesus Christ—I told you, I'm not. Look, if you're really serious, my goddamn publisher's not far from here and my face is on the game boxes. There's a biography and everything, we could go over . . ."

"Okay. But why are you pumping me?"

"I'm not pumping you. . . ."

"Bullshit," she said. Her voice rose. "You're a goddamn trouser snake just like he was, and just like Kennett. I knew that as soon as you asked me to dance. I mean, I could feel myself *melting.* Now, what the fuck are you doing?"

Lucas leaned forward and said, trying to quiet her, trying not to laugh, "I'm not . . ."

"Jesus," she said, pulling back. She went back to the table and picked up her purse. "I'm really loaded."

"Where're we going?"

"Up to your room. I've changed my mind."

"Barbara . . ." Lucas threw three twenties at the tabletop, and hurried after her. "You're a little drunk . . ."

"Fuckin' trouser snake," Fell said as she led the way through the door.

HE WOKE IN the half-lit room, a thin arrow of light from the bathroom falling across the bed. He was confused, a feeling of déjà vu. Didn't Fell just call, didn't she say . . . ? He stopped, feeling the weight. She'd fallen asleep cradled beneath his arm, head on his chest, her leg across his right. He tried to ease out from beneath her, and she woke and said, "Hmmm?"

"Just trying to rearrange," he said, whispering, catching up with the night. She'd been almost timid. Not passive, but . . . wary.

"Um . . ." She propped herself up, her small breast peeking at him over the top of the blanket. "What time is it?"

Lucas found his travel clock, peered at it. "Ten minutes of three," he said.

"Oh, God." She pushed herself up, her back to him, and the sheet fell off. She had a wonderful back, he decided, smooth, slender, but with nice muscles. He drew a finger down her spine and she arched away from him. "Oooo. Stop that," she said over her shoulder.

"Come lay down," he said.

"Time to go."

"What?"

She turned to look at him, but her eyes were in shadow and he couldn't see them. "I really . . ."

"Bullshit. Come on and sleep with me."

"I really need some *sleep*."

"So do I. Fuckin' Bekker."

"Forget Bekker for a few hours," she said.

"All right. But lay down."

She dropped back on the bed, beside him. "You're not still with Rothenburg?"

"No."

"It's over?"

"It's weird, is what it is," he said.

"You're not saying the right thing," said Fell. She propped herself up again, and he drew three fingers across the soft skin on the bottom of her breast.

"That's because Lily and I are seriously tangled up," Lucas said. "You know she's sleeping with Kennett."

"I figured. The first time I saw them together, she was dropping him off at Midtown South, and she kissed him good-bye and I had to go inside and put a cool wet rag on my forehead. I mean, hot. But then I saw you two talking to each other, you and Rothenburg, and it looked like unfinished business."

"Nah. But I was there when her marriage came apart and she helped kill off the last of my relationship with a woman I had a kid with. We were kind of . . . pivotal . . . for each other," Lucas said.

"All right," Fell said.

"Lily was driving?"

"What?"

"You said she dropped off Kennett."

"Well, yeah, Kennett can't drive. That'd kill him, the Manhattan traffic would." She sat up again, half turned, and this time he could see her eyes. "Davenport, what the *fuck* are you up to?"

"Jesus . . ." He laughed, and caught her around the waist, and she let him pull her down.

"The one thing I want to know—if you're up to something, you're not screwing me to get it, are you?"

"Barbara . . ." Lucas rolled his eyes.

"All right. You'd lie to me anyway, so why do I ask?" Then she frowned and answered her own question: "I'll tell you why. Because I'm an idiot and I always ask. And the guys always lie to me. Jesus, I need a shrink. A shrink and a cigarette."

"So smoke, I don't mind," Lucas said. "Just don't dribble ashes on my chest."

"Really?" She scratched him on the breastbone.

"I mean, it's killing you, slowly but surely, but if you need one . . ."

"Thanks." She got out of bed—a wonderful back—found her purse, got her cigarettes, an ashtray and the TV remote. "I gotta get some nicotine into my bloodstream," she said. Ingenuously, genuinely, she added, "I didn't have a cigarette because I was afraid my mouth would taste like an ashtray."

"I thought you'd decided not to sleep with me, and changed your mind."

She shook her head. "Dummy," she said. She lit the cigarette and pointed the remote control at the TV, popped it on, thumbed through the channels until she got to the weather. "Hot and more hot," she said, after a minute.

"It's like Los Angeles, 'cept more humid," Lucas said.

"Shoulda been here last year. . . ."

They talked and she smoked, finished the cigarette, and then lit up another and went around the room and stole all his hotel matches. "I never have enough matches. I always steal them," she said. "When I'm working I've got two rules: pee whenever you can, and steal matches. No. Three rules . . ."

"Never eat at a place called Mom's?"

"No, but that's a good one," she said. "Nope: it's never sleep with a goddamn cop. Cops are so goddamn treacherous. . . ."

SUNDAY MORNING.

Sunlight poured like milk through the venetian blinds. Fell woke at nine o'clock, stirred, then half-sat, looking down at Lucas' dark head on the pillow. After a moment, she got up and stumbled around, picking up clothes. Lucas opened an eye and said, "Have I mentioned your ass?"

"Several times, and I appreciate all of them," she said. She offered a smile, but weakly. "My head . . . that goddamn cheap wine."

"That wine wasn't cheap." Lucas sat up, still sleepy, dropped his feet to the floor, rubbed the back of his neck. "I'll call Kennett, see if we can figure something out."

She nodded, still groggy. "I gotta go home to change clothes, then back to Bellevue. There'll be people around we wouldn't see during the week."

Lucas said, "This is really important to you, isn't it?"

"It's the biggest case I've ever been on," she said. "God, I'd love to get him. I mean, me, personally."

"You won't get him at Bellevue," Lucas said. "Even if you find Whitechurch's helper, and she talks, I wouldn't be surprised if Bekker's using a pay phone. Then where are you?"

"So if we find the phone, we can stake it out. Or maybe he uses one on the block where he lives, we can look at the apartments."

"Mmm."

"Maybe we'll get him tomorrow night, at the speech."

"Maybe . . . C'mon. I'll make sure you get clean in the shower."

"That's something I've always needed," she said. "Help in the shower."

"Well, you said your head feels weird. What you need is a hot shower and a neck massage. Really. I say this in a spirit of fraternity and sorority."

"Good, I don't think I could handle another sexual impulse," Fell said. But the shower took them back to the bed, and that took them back to the shower, and Fell was leaning against the wall, Lucas standing between her legs, drying her back with a rough terry-cloth towel, when Anderson called from Minneapolis.

"Cornell Reed. United to Atlanta out of La Guardia, transfer to Southeast to Charleston. No return. Paid for by the City of New York."

"No shit . . . Charleston?"

"Charleston."

"I owe you some bucks, Harmon," Lucas said. "I'll get back to you."

"No problem . . ."

Lucas hung up, turning it over in his head.

"What's Charleston?" Fell asked from the bathroom doorway.

"It's both a dance and a city. . . . Sorry, that was a personal call. I was trying to get through to my kid's mother. She's gone to Charleston with the Probe Team."

"Oh." Fell tossed the towel back into the bathroom. "You're still pretty tight with her?"

"No. We're done. Completely. But Sarah's my kid. I call her."

Fell shrugged and grinned. "Just checking the oil level," she said. "Are you going to call Kennett?"

"Yeah."

THEY ATE A QUICK breakfast in the hotel coffee shop, then Lucas put Fell in a cab back to her apartment. He called Kennett from his room and got switched from Midtown South to a second phone. Kennett picked it up on the first ring.

"If we don't get him tomorrow, at the speech, I'm heading back to the Twin Cities, see what I can find," Lucas said.

"Good. I think we've got all the routine stuff pinned down here," Kennett said. "Lily's here, and we were about to call you. We're thinking about a boat ride."

"Where's here?" Lucas asked.

"Her place."

"So come and get me," Lucas said.

After talking to Kennett, Lucas sat with his hand on the phone, thinking about it, then picked it up again, dialed the operator, and got the area code for

Charleston. He had no idea how big the city was, but had the impression that it was fairly small. If they knew assholes in Charleston the way they knew them in the Twin Cities . . .

The information service got him the phone number for the Charleston police headquarters, and two minutes later, he had the weekend duty officer on the line.

"My name is Lucas Davenport. I'm a cop working out of Midtown South in Manhattan. I'm looking for a guy down your way, and I was wondering about the prospects of finding him."

"What's the problem?" A dry southern drawl, closer to Texan than the mush-mouth of Alabama.

"He saw a guy get shot. He didn't do it, just saw it. I need to talk to him."

"What's his name?"

"Cornell Reed, nickname Red. About twenty-two, twenty-three . . ."

"Black guy." It was barely a question.

"Yeah."

"And you're from Midtown South."

"Yeah."

"Hang on . . ."

Lucas was put on hold, waited for a minute, then two. Always like this with cops. Always. Then a couple of clicks, and the line was live again. "I got Darius Pike on the line, he's one of our detectives. . . . Darius, go ahead . . ."

"Yeah?" Pike's voice was deep, cool. Children were laughing in the background. Lucas identified himself again.

"Am I getting you at home? I'm sorry about that. . . ."

" 'S okay. You're looking for Red Reed?"

"Yeah. He supposedly witnessed a killing up here, and I'm pretty hot to talk to him."

"He came back to town a month ago, the sorry-ass fool. You need to bust him?"

"No, just talk."

"Want to come down, or on the phone?"

"Face-to-face, if I can."

"Give me a call a day ahead. I can put my hands on him about any time."

Now he had to make a decision: Minneapolis, Charleston. Two different cases, two different leads. Which first? He thought about it. He wouldn't be able to get down to Charleston and back in time. The New School trap was the next night; if they didn't get Bekker, then the trip to Minneapolis was critical. Bekker was killing people, after all. Charleston might shed some light on Robin Hood, and Robin Hood was killing people, too—but those were mostly *bad* people, weren't they? He shook his head wryly. It wasn't supposed to matter, was it? But it did.

Lucas made one more call, to Northwest Airlines, and got a seat to

Minneapolis–St. Paul, then a triple play, Minneapolis–St. Paul to Charleston to New York. There, that was all he could do for now. It all hinged on tomorrow night.

When Lily called from the front desk, he'd changed to jeans and blue T-shirt. He went down, found her waiting, eyes tired but relaxed. She was wearing jeans and a horizontally-striped French fisherman's shirt that might have cost two hundred dollars on Fifth Avenue, and an aqua-colored billed hat.

"You look like a model," he said.

"Maybe I oughta call *Cruising World.*"

"Yeah, you look kinda gay," he said.

"That's a sailboat magazine, you dope," she said, taking a mock swipe at him.

Kennett was waiting in the passenger seat of a double-parked Mazda Navaho, wearing comfortable old khakis and a SoHo Surplus T-shirt.

"Nice truck," Lucas said to Lily as he crawled in back.

"Kennett's. Four-wheel drive must help testosterone production," Lily said, walking around to the driver's side and climbing in. "You've got one, don't you?"

"Not like this: this is sort of a *Manhattan* four-wheel drive," he said, tongue in cheek. To Kennett he said, "I didn't think you could drive."

"Got it before the last attack," Kennett said. "I think the price is what brought the attack on. And don't give me any shit about Manhattan four-by-fours, this is a fuckin' workhorse. . . ."

"Yeah, yeah . . ."

They left Manhattan through the Lincoln Tunnel, emerging in Jersey, took a right and then followed a bewildering zigzag path back to the waterfront. The marina was a modest affair, filling a dent in the riverbank, a few dozen boats separated from a parking lot by a ten-foot chain-link fence topped with razor wire. Most of the boats were in concrete slips, halyards clinking softly against the aluminum masts like a forest of one-note wind chimes; a few more boats were anchored just offshore.

"Look at this guy, putting up his 'chute," Kennett said, climbing down from the truck. Lucas squeezed out behind him as Lily climbed out of the driver's seat. Kennett pointed out toward the river, where two sailboats were tacking side-by-side down the Hudson, running in front of a steady northwest breeze, their sails tight with the wind. A man was standing on the foredeck of one of them, freeing a garish crimson-and-yellow sail. It filled like a parachute, and the boat leapt ahead.

"You ever sailed?" Kennett asked.

"A couple times, on Superior," Lucas said, shading his eyes. "You feel like you're on a runaway locomotive. It's hard to believe they're barely going as fast as a man can jog."

"A man doesn't weigh twenty thousand pounds like that thing," Kennett said, watching the lead boat. "That *is* a locomotive. . . ."

They unloaded a cooler from the back of the truck and Lucas carried it across the parking lot, past a suntanned woman in a string bikini with a string of little girls behind her, like ducklings. The smallest of the kids, a tiny redheaded girl with a sandy butt and bare feet, squealed and danced on the hot tarmac while carrying a pair of flip-flops in her hands.

Lily led the way through a narrow gate in the chain-link fence, Lucas right behind her, Kennett taking it slow, down to the water. Here and there, people were working on their boats, listening to radios as they worked. Most of the radios were tuned to rock stations, but not the same ones, and an aural rock-'n'-roll fest played pleasantly through the marina. Few of the boats actually seemed ready to go out, and the work was slow and social.

"There she blows, so to speak," Kennett said. The *Lestrade* was fat and graceful at the same time, like an overweight ballerina.

"Nice," Lucas said, uncertainly. He knew open fishing boats, but almost nothing about sailboats.

"Island Packet 28—it *is* a nice boat," Kennett said. "I got it instead of kids."

"Not too late for kids," Lucas said. "I just had one myself."

"Wait, wait, wait." Lily laughed. "I should have a say in this."

"Not necessarily," Lucas said. He stepped carefully into the cockpit, balancing the cooler. "The goddamned town is overrun with nubile prospects. Find somebody with a nice set of knockers, you know, not too smart so you wouldn't have to worry about the competition. Maybe with a fetish for housework . . ."

"Fuck the sailing, let's go back into town," Kennett said.

"God, I'm looking forward to this," Lily said. "The flashing wit, the literary talk . . ."

LILY AND LUCAS RIGGED the sails, with Kennett impatiently supervising. When he was bringing the sails up, Lucas took a moment to look through the boat: a big berth at the bow, a tidy, efficient galley, a lot of obviously custom-built bookshelves jammed with books. Even a portable phone.

"You could live here," Lucas said to Kennett.

"I do, a lot of the time," Kennett said. "I probably spend a hundred nights a year on the boat. Even when I can't sail it, I just come over here and sit and read and sleep. Sleep like a baby."

Kennett took the boat out on the motor, his fine white hair standing up like a sail, his eyes shaded by dark oval sunglasses. A smile grew on his tanned face as he maneuvered out along the jetty, then swung into the open river. "Jesus, I love it," he said.

"You gotta be careful," Lily said anxiously, watching him.

"Yeah, yeah, this takes two fingers. . . ." To Lucas he said, "Don't have a heart attack—it just unbelievably fucks you up. I can run the engine and steer, but I can't do anything with the sails, or the anchor. I can't go out alone."

"I don't want to talk about it," Lucas said.

"Yeah, fuck it," Kennett agreed.

"What does it feel like?" Lucas asked.

"You weren't gonna talk about it," Lily protested.

"It feels like a pro wrestler is trying to crush your chest. It hurts, but I don't remember that so much. I just remember feeling like I was stuck in a car-crusher and my chest was caving in. And I was sweating, I remember being down on the ground, on the floor, sweating like a sonofabitch. . . ." He said it quietly, calmly enough, but with a measure of hate in his voice, like a man swearing revenge. After another second, he said, "Let's get the sails up."

"Yeah," Lucas said, slightly shaken. "I gotta pull on a rope, right?"

Kennett looked at the sky. "God, if you heard the man, forgive him, the poor fucker's from Minnesota or Missouri or Montana, some dry-ass place like that."

Lucas got the mainsail up. The jib was on a roller, with the lines led back to the cockpit. Lily worked it from there, sometimes on her own, sometimes with prodding from Kennett.

"How long have you been sailing?" Lucas asked her.

"I did it when I was a kid, at summer camp. And then Dick's been teaching me the big boat."

"She learns quick," Kennett said. "She's got a natural sense for the wind."

They slid lazily back and forth across the river, water rushing beneath the bow, wind in their faces. A hatch of flies was coming off the water, their lacy wings delicately floating around them. "Now what?" Lucas asked.

Kennett laughed. "Now we sail up and then we turn around, and sail back."

"That's what I thought," Lucas said. "You're not even trolling anything."

"You're obviously not into the great roundness of the universe," Kennett said. "You need a beer."

KENNETT AND LILY GAVE him a sailing lesson, taught him the names of the lines and the wire rigging, pointed out the buoys marking the channel.

"You've got a cabin on a lake, right? Don't you have buoys?"

"On my lake? If I peed off the end of the dock, I'd hit the other side. If we put in a buoy, we wouldn't have room for a boat."

"I thought the great North Woods . . ." Kennett prompted, seriously.

"There's some big water," Lucas admitted. "Superior: Superior'll show you things the Atlantic can't. . . ."

"I *seriously* doubt that," Lily said skeptically.

"Yeah? Well, once every few years it freezes over—and you look out there, a horizon like a knife and it's ice all the way out. You can walk out to the horizon and never get there. . . ."

"All right," she said.

They talked about ice-boating and para-skiing, and always came back to sailing. "I was planning to take a year off and single-hand around the world, maybe . . . unless I got stuck in the Islands," Kennett said. "Maybe I would have got stuck, maybe not. I took Spanish lessons, took some French . . ."

"French?"

"Yeah . . . you run down the Atlantic, see, to the Islands, then across to the

Canaries, maybe zip into the Med for a look at the Riviera—that's French—then come back out and down along the African coast to Cape Town, then Australia, then Polynesia. Tahiti: they speak French. Then back up to the Galápagos, Colombia and Panama, and the Islands again . . ."

"Islands—I like the idea," Lucas said.

"You like it?" asked Kennett, seriously.

"Yeah, I do," Lucas said, looking out across the water. His cheekbones and lips were tingling from the sun, and he could feel the muscles relax in his neck and back. "I had a bad time a year ago, a depression. The medical kind. I'm out now, but I never want to do that again. I'd rather . . . run. Like to the Islands. I don't think you'd get depressed in the Islands."

"Exactly what islands are we talking about?" Lily asked.

"I don't know," Kennett said vaguely. "The Windwards, or the Leewards, or some shit . . ."

"What difference would it make?" Lucas asked Lily.

She shrugged: "Don't ask me, they're your islands."

After a moment of silence, Kennett said, "A unipolar depression. Did you hear your guns calling you?"

Lucas, startled, looked at him. "You've had one?"

"Right after the second heart attack," Kennett said. "The second heart attack wasn't so bad. The depression goddamned near killed me."

They turned and started back downriver. Kennett fished in his pocket and pulled out a pack of cigarettes.

"Dick. Throw those fuckin' cigarettes . . ."

"Lily . . . I'm smoking one. Just one. That's all for today."

"God damn it, Dick . . ." Lily looked as though she were going to cry.

"Lily . . . aw, fuck it," Kennett said, and he flipped the pack of Marlboros over the side, where they floated away on the river.

"That's better," Lily said, but tears ran down her cheeks.

"I tried to bum one from Fell the other day, but she wouldn't give it to me," Kennett said.

"Good for her," said Lily, still teary-eyed.

"Look at the city," Lucas said, embarrassed. Kennett and Lily both turned to look at the sunlight breaking over the towers in Midtown. The stone buildings glowed like butter, the modern glass towers flickering like knives.

"What a place," Kennett said. Lily wiped her cheeks with the heels of her hands and tried to smile.

"Can't see the patches from here," Lucas said. "That's what New York is, you know. About a billion patches. Patches on patches. I was walking to Midtown South from the hotel, crossing Broadway there at Thirty-fifth, and there was a pothole, and in the bottom of the pothole was another pothole, but somebody had patched the bottom pothole. Not the big one, just the little one in the bottom."

"Fuckin' rube," Kennett muttered.

They brought the boat back late in the afternoon, their faces flushed with the sun. And after Lucas dropped the mainsail, Lily ran it into the marina with a soft, skillful touch.

"This has been the best day of my month," Kennett said. He looked at Lucas. "I'd like to do it again before you go."

"So would I," Lucas said. "We oughta go down to the Islands sometime. . . ."

Lucas hauled the cooler back to the truck and Lily brought along an arm-load of bedding that Kennett wanted to wash at home.

"Shame that he can't drive the truck," Lucas said as Lily popped up the back lid.

"He does," she said in a confidential voice. "He tells me he doesn't, but I know goddamn well that he sneaks out at night and drives. A couple of months ago I drove back to his place, and when we parked I noticed that the mileage was something like 1-2-3-4-4, and I was thinking that if I only drove one more mile, I'd have a straight line of numbers: 1-2-3-4-5. When I came over the next day, the mileage was like 1-2-4-1-0, or something like that. So he'd been out driving. I check it now, and lots of times the mileage is up. He doesn't know. . . . I haven't mentioned it, because he gets so pissed. I'm afraid he'll get so pissed he'll have another attack. As long as it has power steering and brakes . . ."

"It'll drive a guy nuts, being penned up," Lucas said. "You oughta stay off his case."

"I try," she said. "But sometimes I just can't help it. Men can be so fucking stupid, it gives me a headache."

They went back to the boat and found Kennett below, digging around. "Hey, Lucas, a little help? I need to pull this marine battery, but it's too heavy for Lily."

"Dick, are you messing around with that wrench again . . . ?" Lily started, but Lucas put an index finger over his lips and she stopped.

"I'll be down," Lucas said.

Ten minutes later, while Kennett and Lily did the last of the buttoning-up, Lucas humped the battery back to the car. In the parking lot, he propped one end of it on the truck bumper while he sorted out the keys, then turned and looked back through the fence. Lily and Kennett were on the dock, Lily leaning into him, his arms around her waist. She was talking to him, then leaned forward and kissed him on the mouth. Lucas felt a pang, but only a small one.

Kennett was okay.

17

THE NEW SCHOOL AUDITORIUM was compact, with a narrow lobby between the interior auditorium doors and the doors to the street.

"Perfect," Lucas told Fell. They'd taken the tour with a half-dozen other cops, and now, waiting, wandered outside to Twelfth Street. Fell lit a cigarette. "Once he comes around the corner, he'll be inside the net. And the lobby's small enough that we can check everyone coming through before they realize there are cops all over the place."

"You still think he'll show?" Fell asked skeptically.

"Hope so."

"It'd be too easy," she said.

"He's a nut case," Lucas said. "If he's seen the announcement, he'll be here."

A car dropped Kennett at the curb. "Opening night," he said as he climbed out. He looked up and down the fashionable residential street, bikes chained to wrought-iron fences, well-kept brick townhouses climbing up from the street. "It feels like something's gonna happen."

They followed him inside, and Carter came by with radios. They each took one, fitting the earpieces, checking them out. "Stay off unless it's critical," Carter said. "There are twelve guys here, and if all twelve start yelling at the same time . . ."

"Where do you want me?" Lucas asked.

"Where do you think?" Carter asked. "Ticket booth?"

"Mmm, I'd be looking at too many people's backs," Lucas said. He glanced around. A short hall led from the auditorium lobby to the main entrance lobby of the New School. "How about if I stood back there in the hall?"

"All right," Carter said. To Fell, he said, "We've got you handing out programs. You'll be right there in the lobby."

"Terrific . . ."

"What's the setup?" Kennett asked.

"Well, we're supposed to start in twenty minutes. We've got you just inside the auditorium entrance, where you can see everyone, or get back out to the lobby in a hurry," Carter said. "It's right down here. . . ."

BEKKER TOTTERED DOWN Twelfth Street ten minutes before the lecture was scheduled to begin, past a guy working on a car in the failing daylight. Bekker was nervous as a cat, excited, checking the scattering of people walking along the street with him, and toward him, converging on the auditorium. This was dangerous. He could feel it. They'd be talking about him. There might be cops in the crowd. But still: worth it. Worth some risk.

Most of the people were going through a series of theater-style doors farther up the street. That would be the auditorium. There was another door, closer. On impulse he entered there, turned toward the auditorium.

Almost stumbled.

Davenport.

Trap.

The fear almost choked him, and he caught at his throat. Davenport and another man, their backs to Bekker, were in the hallway between the separate entries. Not ten feet away. Watching the crowd come through the other door.

Davenport was to the left, half turned toward the second man, his back directly to Bekker. The second man, half turned toward Davenport, glanced toward Bekker as simple momentum took Bekker inside. Couldn't stop. He went straight through the school lobby, past the entrance to the auditorium. An empty guard desk was to the right, with a phone behind it. Ahead of him, another hallway that seemed to lead back outside.

Bekker unconsciously touched his face, felt the hard scars under the special makeup. That night in the funeral home, Davenport hacking at him . . .

Bekker wrenched himself back, forced himself to walk down the stairs, through the next door, outside. He was sweating, almost gasping for breath.

He found himself in a sculpture garden, facing another door like the one he'd come through. On the other side of the door was a hallway, and beyond that, maybe a hundred feet away, another set of doors and the next street. Nobody ahead. He strode quickly across the courtyard, caught the door, pulled.

Locked. Stricken, he gave it a tug. It didn't budge. The glass was too thick to break, even if he had something to break it with. He turned and looked back, toward the way he'd come. If he tried to get out that way, he'd be face to face with Davenport for several seconds, just as he'd been with the cop Davenport had been talking to.

He stood, frozen, unable to sort the possibilities. He had to get out of sight. He went to his left, found a short hallway with a door marked with a B and the word "Stair." He jerked at the door, hoping . . .

Locked. Damn. He huddled in the doorway, temporarily out of sight. But he couldn't stay: if anybody saw him like this, hiding, they'd know.

Another goddamned Davenport trap, pulling him in . . .

Bekker lost it for a moment, his mind going away, dwindling, imploding. . . . He came back with a gasp, found himself pulling at the door, fighting the door handle.

No. There must be something else. He let go of the door, turned back to the courtyard. He needed help, needed to think. He groped for his pillbox, found it, gulped a half-dozen crosses. The acrid taste on his tongue helped cool him, get him thinking again.

If they caught him—and if they didn't kill him—they'd put him back inside, they'd pull him off his chemicals. Bekker shuddered, a full-body spasm. Take him off: he couldn't live through that again, he couldn't even think about it.

He thought of the funeral home again. Davenport's face, inches from his, screaming, the words unintelligible, then the pistol coming up, the gunsight coming around like a nail on a club, the nail ripping through his face . . .

Had to think. Had to think.

Had to move. But where? Davenport was right there, watching. Had to get past him. Only half aware of what he was doing, he fetched the pill box and gulped the rest of the speed and a single tab of PCP. Think.

"THEY GOTTA START pretty soon," Carter said.

"Give him another five minutes," Davenport said. "Fuck around with the slide projector or something."

"The crowd's gonna be pissed when Yonel makes the announcement."

"Maybe not," said Kennett, who'd gotten tired of waiting in the auditorium. "Maybe they'll get a kick out of it."

"Yonel says he'll do a half-hour on Mengele and Bekker anyway, before he says anything," Lucas said. He stood and stepped to the door: "I'm going to take a quick turn through the crowd. There're not many people coming in."

"Fuck it, he's not coming," Carter said.

"Maybe not, but he should have," Lucas said.

BEKKER, DESPERATELY exploring the courtyard, followed a short flight of steps into an alcove and found another door. Behind the stage? Would there be cops back there? He took the handle in his hand, pulled . . . and the door moved. He eased it open until just a crack of light was visible and pressed his eye to the opening. Yes. Backstage. A man was there, wearing slacks and a sport coat, peering out at the audience from a dark corner on the opposite side of the stage. As Bekker watched, he lifted a rectangular object to his face. A radio? Must be. Cop.

Just inside the door, in front of Bekker, was a scarred table, and on the table an empty peanut butter jar, a black telephone and what looked like a collapsible umbrella in a nylon case. Bekker let the door close, turned back toward the steps. A finger of despair touched him: no way out. No way. And they'd be checking the building before they left. He knew that. He had to get out. Or hide.

Wait. A radio? The cop had a *radio*.

Bekker turned, went back to the door, peeked inside again. The cop was still in the corner, peering out from behind the curtain, checking the crowd. And on the table, not an umbrella, but a folding music stand, apparently left behind after a concert.

He flashed on Ray Shaltie, and the blood splashing from his head. . . .

The PCP was coming up now, warming him, bringing him confidence. He needed that radio. He let the door close, took a quick, silent turn around the alcove outside the door, thinking. A paper? He dug in his bag, found an envelope, folded it. Thought again for a moment, but there was no other way: he *would not* be beaten. Bekker took a breath, posed for a moment, then stepped to the door, pulled it open, and stepped inside.

The cop saw him immediately and frowned, took a step toward him. Bekker held up the envelope, and in a whisper, called, "Officer. Officer."

The cop glanced out at the crowd, then started across the stage behind the curtain. Radio in his hand. Bekker took a step forward, touched the music stand. It would be flimsy when opened, but when closed, and wrapped in its plastic sheath, a perfect club.

"You're not . . ." the cop started. Deep voice.

"The man out there . . ." Bekker whispered, and thrust the envelope at the cop, dropping it at the same time. The envelope fell to the cop's feet. Without thinking, the cop bent to catch it.

And Bekker hit him.

Hit him behind the ear with the music stand, swinging it like a hatchet. The impact sounded like a hammer striking an overripe cantaloupe, and the cop went down, the radio hitting the floor beside him. There'd been little noise, and that was muffled by the curtains, Bekker thought, but he hooked the man by the collar and dragged him into the corner by the door. And waited. Waited for the call, for the shout, that would end it. Nothing.

The cop couldn't be allowed to talk about how he was ambushed. Bekker stood over him for a moment, waiting, waiting, then pushed open the exterior door, dragged the body through it. The courtyard was still empty. Bekker lifted the music stand and hit the unconscious cop again and again, until the head resembled a bloody bag of rice.

Stop . . . no time. But the eyes . . .

Hurrying now, he used his penknife to cut the eyes, then patted down the body and found an identification card: Francis Sowith. The radio. Shit. The radio was still inside. He went to the door, peeked through, saw the radio, stepped quickly inside and retrieved it.

Back out on the porch again, stepping over the dead man. He noticed he had blood on his hands, and wiped them on the cop's coat. Still sticky: he lifted them to his face and sniffed. The smell of the blood was familiar, comforting.

He looked at the radio. Basic thumb switch. Calmed himself, checked his clothing, straightened it, and walked up the steps to the door back inside.

He took a breath, tensing, opened the door, and walked straight ahead. A staff member, he thought. That's what he was: a teacher who worked here. He heard a voice, a man, from around the corner. He slipped up to the guard desk, where he'd seen the telephone, and stepped around behind the desk, the phone to his ear. He could see the shoulder and sleeve of Davenport's jacket now, if that was in fact Davenport, in the same place. He leaned over the desk, head down, put the radio to his mouth, and thumbed the switch.

"This is Frank," he blurted. "He's here, backstage, backstage. . . ."

He dropped the radio hand, and pressed the phone receiver to his ear, his shoulder turned away: the body language said *making a date*. At the same time, there was a shout, then another. Davenport's shoulder disappeared from the doorway, but another man came through it, running, right past the desk and down into the courtyard.

Moving quickly, Bekker walked from behind the desk, looking straight ahead, out through the school doors into the street. A woman screamed from the auditorium. Bekker kept walking. The man who'd been working on the car hurried past him, heading toward the doors, a pistol in his hand.

And then the night closed around him. Bekker was gone.

T HEY WOUND UP in the courtyard, a half-dozen senior police officers shouting at each other. Lights burned in every room of the building and uniformed cops crawled through it inch by inch, but the people in the court-yard knew the search was pointless.

"Silly motherfucker . . . How many got out? How many?"

"I was trying to save his ass. Where the fuck were your guys, huh? Where the fuck . . ." A square guy pushed a tall guy, and for a moment it looked like a fight; but then other cops got between them.

"Jesus Christ, you gotta go out the back, the fuckin' TV is sweeping the streets. . . ."

"Who had the watch on the stairs? Where was . . ."

"Shut up." Kennett had been sitting on a bench, talking to Lily and O'Dell. Now he shouldered through the ring of cops, his voice cutting through the bab-ble like an icicle going through a sponge cake. "Shut the fuck up."

He stood on the sidewalk, pale, two fingers hovering over his heart. He turned to one of the cops: "How many got out?"

"Listen, it wasn't my . . ."

"I don't give a shit whose fault it was," Kennett snarled. "We all fuckin' blew it. What I want to know is, how many got out?"

"I don't know," the cop said. "Twenty or thirty. When everybody stam-peded backstage, a bunch of people in the lobby and near the doors just went outside. Nobody was there to stop them. When I came back . . . most of them were gone."

"There were only about fifty people in the auditorium," Kennett said. "So maybe half of them got out."

"But that's not the thing," the cop said.

"What's the thing?" Kennett asked. His voice was like a hangnail, sharp, ragged, painful.

"The thing is, I looked into every one of those faces. Bekker wasn't there. I don't care if you hang me up by my nuts, you ain't gonna get me to say he was, 'cause he wasn't. He wasn't there."

"He had to be somewhere," Carter snapped.

"Nobody came across the stage. Nobody went out through the courtyard. There was only one other door, and that doesn't go anywhere, it just comes back to the lobby. . . ."

There was a long moment of silence, compounded of anger and fear. Heads would roll for this one. Heads would roll. A couple of cops glanced furtively at O'Dell and Lily, deep in private talk. After a moment, Huerta said, "He must've been here all the time. He must've hid out before we got here, saw that he couldn't get out, figured we'd sweep the place before we left, and nailed Frank to get his radio."

Kennett was nodding. "That couldn't have been Frank who called. . . ."

"Sounded like Frank. . . ."

"So Bekker's got a deep voice, big fuckin' deal. We had people back there in five seconds, and Frank was gone. It took a while to mess him up like that."

"Then why'd he call? Bekker? If he was already gone?" Kuhn asked.

"To get us running back there," Lucas said. "Say he goes back there, nails Frank, takes the radio, goes off through the side door around the corner from the lobby, makes the call, then pushes through the door and goes right through the lobby and out."

"Billy said nobody came through the door," Kuhn said.

A young plainclothes cop with his hands in his pockets shook his head. "I swear to God, I don't see how anybody could've got through there. Lieutenant Carter told me to stay there, and even when Frank called, I stayed there. I saw everybody running . . ."

"But your back was to the door?" Kennett asked.

"Yeah, but I was right *there*," the young cop said. He could feel the goat horns being fitted for his head.

Kennett turned to Lucas: "You're sure he didn't come past you?"

"I don't see how. It's like this guy said . . ." Lucas pointed at the cop who looked at the faces. "I looked at every goddamn face coming through the door; he just wasn't there."

"All right, so he was inside," Kennett said. "We assume he made the radio call as a diversion to get out. . . ."

"Or to hide," somebody said. "If he had a bolthole during the day . . ."

"We'll find out," Kennett said, peering up at the brightly lighted windows. He glanced sideways at Lucas, who shook his head. Bekker was gone. "The other possibility is that he went out a window somewhere and made the radio call to pull the guys off the street. . . ."

"What if he had keys and was already outside, and was just taunting us?" one of the cops asked.

They talked for twenty minutes before drifting away to specific assignments, or simply drifting away, afraid that their names and faces might become associated with the disaster. In the alcove outside the stage door, a crime-scene crew worked under heavy lights, picking up what they could. But there was no real question: it was Bekker. But Bekker, how?

"Okay, now we're out of cop work: now we're down to politics," Kennett said to Lucas as they stood together in the courtyard.

"You gonna hang?" Lucas asked.

"I could," Kennett nodded. "I gotta start calling people, gotta get some spin on the thing, fuzz it up."

"Gonna be tough, with you right here," Lucas said.

"So what would you do?" Kennett asked.

"Lie," Lucas said.

Kennett was interested. "How?"

"Blame Frank. Unlock the back door," Lucas said, nodding to the opposite side of the courtyard. "Tell them that Bekker hid in the building during the day and that he must've stolen keys from somewhere. That when he came out and got down here, cutting through the courtyard, using his keys—where we only had one man, because we'd secured the place ahead of time—and he ran head-on into Frank. There was a fight, but Bekker's a PCP freak and he killed Frank and escaped back out the other side of the building. If anybody gets blamed, the blame goes on Frank. But nobody'll say anything, because Frank's dead. You could even do a little off-the-record action. *Tell* them that Frank fucked up, but we can't say it publicly. He was a good guy and now he's dead. . . ."

"Hmph." Kennett pulled at his lip. "What about the radio call?"

"Somebody's already suggested that he was taunting us: go with that," Lucas suggested. "That he was already outside. That fits Bekker's character, as far as the media's concerned."

"Do you think . . . ?"

"No, I think he suckered us."

"So do I." Kennett stared at his feet for a moment, then glanced at Lily and O'Dell. "The story might not hold up for long."

"If we get him before it breaks, nobody'll care."

Kennett nodded. "I better go talk to O'Dell. We'll need a ferocious off-the-record media massage."

"You think he'll help?"

Kennett permitted himself a very thin grin. "He was here too," Kennett said. "They'd just pulled up outside . . ."

Kennett started toward Lily and O'Dell, then stopped and turned, hands in his pockets, no longer grinning. "Get your ass back to Minneapolis. Find something for us, God damn it."

LUCAS SAT ALONE IN the worst row of seats on the plane, in tourist class behind the bulkhead, no good place to put his feet except in the aisle. The stewardess was watching him before they crossed Niagara Falls.

"Are you all right?" she asked finally, touching his shoulder. He'd dropped the seat all the way back, tense, his eyes closed, like a patient waiting for a root canal.

"Are the wheels off the ground?" he grated.

"Uh-oh," she said, fighting a smile. "How about a scotch? Double scotch?"

"Doesn't work," Lucas said. "Unless you've got about nine phenobarbitals to put in it."

"Sorry," she said. Her face was professionally straight, but she was amused. "It's only two more hours. . . ."

"Wonderful . . ."

He could see it so clearly in his mind's eye: ripped chunks of aluminum skin and pieces of engine nacelle scattered around a Canadian cornfield, heads and arms and fingers like bits of trash, fires guttering just out of sight, putting out gouts of oily black smoke; women in stretch pants wandering through the wreckage, picking up money. A Raggedy Ann doll, cut in half, smiling senselessly; all images from movies, he thought. He'd never actually seen a plane crash, but you had to be a complete idiot not to be able to imagine it.

He sat and sweated, sat and sweated, until the stewardess came back and said, "Almost there."

"How long?" he croaked.

"Less than an hour . . ."

"Sweet bleedin' Jesus . . ." He'd been praying that it was only a minute or two; he'd been sure of it.

The plane came in over the grid of orange sodium-vapor lights and blue mercury lights, banking, Lucas holding on to the seat. The window was filled with the streaming cars, the black holes of the lakes stretching down from just west of the Minneapolis Loop. He looked at the floor. Jumped when the wheels came down. Made the mistake of glancing across the empty seat next to him and out the window, and saw the ground coming and closed his eyes again, braced for the impact.

The landing was routine. The bored pilot said the usual good-byes, the voice of a Tennessee hay-shaker, which he undoubtedly was, not qualified to fly a '52 Chevy much less a jetliner. . . .

Lucas stunk with fear, he thought as he bolted from the plane, carrying his overnight bag. *My God, that ride was the worst.* He'd read that La Guardia was over-crowded, that in a plane you could get cut in half in an instant, right on the ground. And he'd have to do it again in a day or two.

He caught a cab, gave directions, collapsed in the backseat. The driver took his time, loafing along the river, north past the Ford plant. Lucas' house had a light in the window. The timer.

"Nice to get home, huh?" the cabdriver asked, making a notation in a trip log.

"You don't know how good," Lucas said. He thrust a ten at the driver and hopped out. A couple strolled by on the river walk, across the street.

"Hey, Lucas," the man called.

"Hey, Rick, Stephanie." Neighbors: he could see her blond hair, his chrome-rimmed glasses.

"You left your backyard sprinkler on. We turned it off and put the hose be-hind the garage."

"Thanks . . ."

He picked up the mail inside the door, sorted out the ads and catalogs and dumped them in a wastebasket, showered to get the fear-stink off his body and fell into bed. In thirty seconds, he was gone.

"LUCAS?" QUENTIN DANIEL stuck his head out of his office. He had dark circles under his eyes and he'd lost weight. He'd been the Minneapolis chief of police for two terms, but that wasn't what was eating him. Innocent people had died because of Quentin Daniel: Daniel was a criminal, but nobody knew except Daniel and Lucas. Lucas had resolved it in his mind, had forgiven him. Daniel never could. . . . "C'mon in. What happened to your face?"

"Got mugged, more or less . . . I need some help," Lucas said briefly, set-tling into the visitor's chair. "You know I'm working in New York."

"Yeah, they called me. I told them you were Mr. Wunnerful."

"I need to find the guys who were in the jail cells next to Bekker—or any-body he talked to while he was in there."

"Sounds like you're scraping the bottom of the bucket," Daniel said, play-ing with a humidor on his desk.

"That's why I'm here," Lucas said. "The cocksucker's dug in, and we can't get him out."

"All right." Daniel picked up his phone, punched a number. "Is Sloan there? Get him down to my office, will you? Thanks."

There was a moment of awkward silence, then Lucas said, "You look like shit."

"I feel like shit," Daniel said. He turned the humidor around, squared it with the edge of the desk.

"Your wife . . . ?"

"Gone. Thought it'd be a lift, seeing her go, but it wasn't. I'd get up every morning and look down at her and wish she was gone, and now I get up and look at the bed and there's a hole in it."

"Want her back?"

"No. But I want something, and I can't have it. I'll tell you one thing, between you and me and the wall—I'm getting out of here. Two months and I hit a crick in the retirement scale. Maybe go up north, get a place on a lake. I've got the bucks."

There was a knock on the door, and Daniel's secretary stuck her head in and said, "Sloan . . ."

Lucas stood up. "I do wish you luck," he said. "I'm serious."

"Thanks, but I'm cursed," Daniel said.

SLOAN WAS LOUNGING in the outer office, a cotton sport coat over a tennis shirt, chinos, walking shoes. He saw Lucas and a grin spread across his thin face.

"Are you back?" he asked, sticking out his hand.

Lucas, laughing: "Just for the day. I gotta find some assholes and I need somebody with a badge."

"You're working in the Big Apple. . . ."

"Yeah. I'll tell you about it, but we gotta go talk to the sheriff."

Three names, a deputy sheriff said. He'd looked at the records, checked with the other guards. They all agreed.

Bekker had been next to Clyde Payton, who was now at Stillwater, doing twenty-four months on a drugstore burglary, third offense. A doper.

"Motherfucker's gonna come out and kill people," the deputy said. "He thought Bekker was like some rock idol, or something. You could see Payton thinking: *Killing people. Far out.*"

Tommy Krey, car theft, had been on the other side. He was still out on bail; Krey's attorney was dragging his feet on the trial. "The car owner's gonna move to California, I hear. Tommy's lawyer's looking for a plea," the deputy said.

Burrell Thomas had been across the aisle, and pled to simple assault, paid a fine. He was gone.

"I know Tommy, but I don't know the other two," Lucas said. Out of touch.

"Payton's from St. Paul, Rice Street. Basically a doper, sells real estate when he's straight," Sloan said. "I don't know Thomas either."

"Burrell's a head case," the deputy said. "They call him Rayon. Y'all know Becky Ann, the cardplayer with the huge hooters, see her down on Lake sometimes?"

"Sure." Lucas nodded.

"She was going with this super-tall black dude. . . ."

"Manny," said Sloan, and Lucas added, "Manfred Johnson."

"Yeah, that's him—he's a friend of Burrell's. Like from high school and maybe even when they were kids . . ."

. . .

"HOW'S NEW YORK?" Sloan asked. They were in Sloan's unmarked car, poking into the south side of Minneapolis.

"Hot. Like Alabama."

"Mmm. I never been there. I mean New York. I understand it's a dump."

"It's different," Lucas said, watching the beat-up houses slide by. Kids on bikes, rolling through the summer. They'd called Krey's attorney, a guy who worked out of a neighborhood storefront. He could have Krey there in a half-hour, he said.

"How different? I mean, like, Fort Apache?"

"Nah, not that," Lucas said. "The main thing is, there's an infinite number of assholes. You never know where the shit is coming from. You can't get an edge on anything. You can't know about the place. Here, if somebody hijacks a god-damn Best Buy truck and takes off fifty Sonys, we got an idea where they're going. Out there . . . Shit, you could make a list of suspects longer than your dick, and that'd only be the guys that you personally *know* might handle it. And then there are probably a hundred times that many guys that you don't know. I mean, a list longer than *my* dick."

"We're talking long lists here," Sloan said.

"It's strange," said Lucas. "It's like being up at the top of the IDS Building and looking out a window where you can't see the ground. You get disoriented and you feel like you're falling."

"How 'bout that Bekker, though?" Sloan said enthusiastically. "He's a fuckin' star, and we knew him back when."

TOMMY KREY WAS SITTING on a wooden chair in his attorney's office. His attorney wore a yellow-brown double-knit suit and a heavily waxed hairdo the precise shade of the suit. He shook hands with Sloan and Lucas; his hands were damp, and Lucas smothered a grin when he saw Sloan surreptitiously wipe his hand on his pant leg.

"What can Tommy do for yuz?" the lawyer asked, folding his hands on his desk, trying to look bright and businesslike. Krey looked half bored, skeptical, picked his teeth.

"He can tell us what he and Michael Bekker talked about in jail," Lucas said.

"What are the chances of knocking down this car-theft , . ."

"You're gonna have to do that on your own," Lucas said, looking from the lawyer to Krey and back again. "Maybe Sloan goes in and tells the judge you helped on a big case, but there's no guarantees."

The lawyer looked at Krey and lifted his eyebrows. "What d'you think?"

"Yeah, fuck, I don't care," Krey said. He flipped his toothpick at the basket, rimmed it out, and it fell on the carpet. The lawyer frowned at it. "We talked about every fuckin' thing," Krey said. "And I'll tell you what: I been beatin' my brains out ever since he went out to New York, trying to figure out if he gave me, like, any *clues*. And he didn't. All we did was bullshit."

"Nothing about friends in New York, about disguises . . . ?"

"Naw, nothing. I mean, if I knew something, I'd a been downtown trying to deal. I know that his buddy, the guy who did the other kills, was an actor . . . so maybe it is disguises."

"What was he like in there? I mean, was he freaked out . . . ?"

"He cried all the time. He couldn't live without his shit, you know? It hurt him. I thought it was bullshit when I first went in, but it wasn't bullshit. He used to cry for hours, sometimes. He's totally fuckin' nuts, man."

"How about this Clyde Payton? He was in for some kind of dope deal, he was around Bekker."

"Yeah, he came in the day before I made bail. I don't know; I think he was a wacko like Bekker. Square, but wacko, you know? Kind of scary. He was some kind of businessman, and he gets onto the dope. The next thing he knows, he's busting into drugstores trying to steal prescription shit. He mostly sat around and cursed people out while I was there, but sometimes he'd get like a stone. He figured he was going to Stillwater."

"He did," said Sloan.

"Dumb fuck," said Krey.

"How about Burrell Thomas?"

"Now, there's something," Krey said, brightening. "Bekker and Burrell talked a lot. Rayon's one smart nigger."

BURRELL'S ADDRESS WAS a vacant house, the doors pulled down, the floor littered with Zip-Loc plastic bags. They crunched across broken glass up an open stairway, found a burned mattress in one room, nothing in the other, and a bathtub that'd been used as a toilet. Flies swarmed in an open window as Sloan reeled back from the bathroom door.

"We gotta find Manny Johnson," Sloan said.

"He used to work at Dos Auto Glass," Lucas said. "Not a bad guy. I don't think he's got a sheet, but that woman of his . . ."

"Yeah." Manny's girlfriend called herself Rock Hudson. "She took twenty-five grand out of a high-stakes game down at the Loin last month. That's going around."

"She's a piece of work," Lucas agreed.

They found both Manny and Rock at the auto glass. The woman was sitting in a plastic chair with a box full of scratch-off lottery tickets, scratching off the silver with a jackknife blade, dropping the bad ones on the floor.

"Cops," she said, barely looking up when they came in.

"How are you?" Lucas asked. "Doing any good?"

"What d'ya want?"

"We need to talk to Manny," Lucas said. She started to heave herself to her feet, but Lucas put a hand in front of her head. "Go ahead with the tickets. We can get him."

Sloan had moved to the door between the waiting area and the workroom. "He's here," he said to Lucas.

They went back together. Johnson saw them, picked up a rag, wiped his hands. He was at least seven feet tall, Lucas thought. "Manny? We need to talk to you about Burrell Thomas."

"What's he done?" Johnson's voice was deep and roiled, like oil drums rolling off a truck.

"Nothing, far as we know. But he was bunked down at the jail next to Michael Bekker, the nut case."

"Yeah, Rayon told me," the tall man said.

"You know where we can reach him?"

"No, I don't know where he's living, but I could probably find him, tonight, if I walked around the neighborhood for a while. He usually goes down to Hennepin after nine."

"Bekker's chopping people up," Sloan said. "I mean chopping them up. I don't know if Burrell's got trouble with the cops, but if there's any way he could help us . . ."

"What?"

Sloan shrugged, picked up a can of WD-40, turned it in his hand, and shrugged. "We might be able to take a little pressure off, if he has another run-in with the cops. Or if your friend out there, if she . . ."

Johnson looked them over for a minute, then said, "You got a phone number?"

"Yeah," Sloan said. He fished a card out of his pocket. "Call me there."

"Like tonight," Lucas said. "This guy Bekker . . ."

"Yeah, I know," Johnson said. He slipped Sloan's card in his shirt pocket. "I'll call you, one way or another."

THE DRIVE TO STILLWATER cut another hour out of the day; the interview took ten minutes. Payton looked like an ex–college lineman, square, running to fat. He wasn't interested in talking. "What the fuck'd the cops ever do for me? I'm a sick man, and here I am in this cage. You guys can fuck yourselves."

They left him talking to himself, muttering curses at the floor.

"How're you gonna threaten him? Tell him you're gonna put him in jail?" Sloan asked as they walked back through the parking lot.

Lucas glanced back at the penitentiary. It looked like an old Catholic high school, he decided, inside and out, until you heard the steel doors open and shut. Then you knew it couldn't be anything but the joint. . . .

Johnson called Sloan's number a little after six o'clock. Burrell would talk and he'd meet Lucas at Penn's Bar, on Hennepin. Johnson would come down, to introduce them.

"Um, I got some shit to do at home," Sloan said.

"Hey, take off," Lucas said. "And thanks."

They shook hands, and Sloan said, "Don't take no wooden women."

PENN'S BAR HAD a sagging wooden floor and a thin mustachioed bartender who poured drinks, washed glasses, ran the cash register and kept one eye on the door. A solitary black hooker leaned on the bar, smoking a cigarette and reading a comic book, ignoring a half-drunk, pale-green daiquiri. The hooker picked up Lucas' eyes for a second, saw something she didn't like, and went back to her comic.

Farther toward the back, four men and two women stood around a coin-op pool table. Layers of cigarette smoke floated around them like the ghosts of autumn leaves. Lucas walked past the bar to the back, past the pool table, past a beat-up pay phone hung in an alcove next to a cigarette machine. He looked in the men's john, came back, walked around the crowd at the pool table. The men wore jeans and vests, with big wallets chained to their belts, and looked at him sideways as he went through. Johnson wasn't there. Neither was anyone who might be Burrell.

"What can I do you for?" the bartender asked, drying his hands on a mustard-stained towel.

"Bottle of Leinie's," Lucas said.

The bartender fished it out of a cooler and dropped it wet on the bar: "Two bucks." And then, tipping his head toward the back, "Looking for someone?"

"Yeah." Lucas paid and sat on a stool. The back-bar mirror ended before it got that far down, and Lucas stared into the fake walnut paneling opposite his stool, hitting on the beer, trying to straighten his schedule out.

If he didn't find Burrell quick, he'd have to stay over a day. Then he'd miss the early flight to Atlanta. Instead of getting into Charleston in the morning, he wouldn't make it until the afternoon and probably wouldn't get out until the next day. Then he'd have to think of an excuse for the New York people.

The hooker rapped on the bar with her knuckles, nodded at the daiquiri, got a new one. She wore a pale-green party dress, almost the color of the drink. She caught his eyes again, let her gaze linger this time. Lucas didn't remember her. He'd known most of the regulars when he was working, but he'd been off the streets for months now. A week is forever, on the streets. A whole new class of thirteen-year-old girls would be giving doorway blow jobs to suburban insurance agents who would later be described in court documents as good fathers. . . .

Lucas was halfway through the beer when Johnson walked in, out of breath, as though he'd been running.

"Jesus, Davenport," he said. "Missed the bus." He looked down the bar at the hooker as Lucas swiveled on the stool.

"Where is he?" Lucas said.

Johnson's face lit up. "What'd you mean, where is he? He's right there."

Lucas looked past the hooker to the back of the bar; all the pool players were white.

"Where?"

Johnson started to laugh, lifted a leg and slapped a thigh. "You sittin' next to him, man."

The hooker looked at Lucas and said, in a voice an octave too low, "Hi, there."

Lucas looked at the hooker for a second, rereading the features, and closed his eyes. Transvestite. In a half-second, it all fell into place. Goddamn Bekker. This was how he got close to the women and the tourist males. As a woman. With the right makeup, at night, with his small, narrow-shouldered body. That was how he got out of the New School. . . .

God damn it.

"Did you tell Bekker how to . . . do this?" Lucas asked, gesturing at the dress. "The dress, the makeup."

"We talked about it," Thomas said. "But he was a sick motherfucker and I didn't like talking to him."

"But when you talked about it . . . was he real interested, or did you just talk?"

Thomas tipped his head back, looked up at the ceiling, remembering. "Well . . . he tried it. A couple of things." He hopped off the bar stool and walked away from Lucas and Johnson, moving his hips, turned and posed. "It ain't that easy to get just the right walk. If you forget halfway through the block, it ruins your whole image."

The bartender, watching, said, "Are you guys gay?"

"Cop," said Lucas. "This is official."

"Forget I asked . . ."

"I won't forget, honey," Thomas said, licking his lower lip.

"You fuckin' . . ."

"Shut up," Lucas snapped, poking a finger at the bartender. He looked back at Thomas. "But did he do it? The walk?"

"Couple times, a few times, I guess. You know, we *did* talk about it, when I think back. Not so much about how good it feels, but how to do it. You know, gettin' the prosthetic bras and like that. He'd make a good-lookin' girl, too, 'cept for the scars."

"You think so?" Lucas asked. "Is that a professional opinion?"

"Don't dick me around, man," Thomas said, flaring.

"I'm not. That's a real question. Would he make a good woman?"

Thomas stared at him for a minute, decided the question was real: "Yeah, he would. He'd be real good at it. 'Cept for the scars."

Lucas hopped off the bar stool, said thanks, and nodded to Johnson: "We owe you. You need something, talk to Sloan."

"That's all?" asked Thomas.

"That's all," Lucas said.

LUCAS CALLED FELL FROM the pay phone at the back of the bar. When she answered, he could hear the television going in the background, a baseball game. "Can you get to Kennett? Right now?"

"Sure."

"Tell him we've figured out how Bekker is doing it," Lucas said. "How he's staying out of sight on the streets, getting out of the New School."

"We have?"

"Yeah. I just talked to his former next-door neighbor at the Hennepin

County Jail, name of Rayon Thomas. Nice-looking guy. Good makeup. Great legs. He's wearing a daiquiri-green party dress. He gave Bekker lessons. . . ."

After a moment of silence, she breathed, "Sonofabitch, Bekker's a woman. We're so fuckin' stupid."

"Call Kennett," Lucas said.

"You haven't talked to anyone?" she asked.

"I thought you'd like to break it."

"Thanks, man," Fell said. "I . . . thanks."

BEKKER COULD COUNT THE DROPS, each and every one, as the shower played off his body. The ecstasy did that: two tiny pills. Gave him the power to imagine and count, to multiply outrageous feelings by ineffable emotions and come up with numbers. . . .

He turned in the shower, letting jets of water burn into him. He no longer used the cold water at all, and the stall was choked with heat and steam, his body turning cherry red as the old skin scalded away. And as he turned, his eyes closed, his head tipped back, his hands beneath his chin, his elbows close together, on his belly, he could count all the drops, each and every one. . . .

He stayed in the shower until the water ran cold, then, shivering, blue, annoyed, he leaped out. What time was it? He walked to the end of the room where he'd fitted a black plastic garbage bag over a barred basement window, and peeled back a corner of the plastic. Dark. Midnight. That was good. He needed the night.

Bekker walked back toward the bed, felt the stickiness on the soles of his feet and looked down. He needed to wash the floor. The sight of the dried blood on the floor reminded him of the cut. He looked at his arm, rolled it between his thumb and forefinger. The cut was painful, but the ants were gone.

He caught sight of himself in a wall mirror, his furrowed face. He went into the bathroom and washed his face, grimacing at the sight of the scars. They were in long jagged rows, raised above the soft skin around them. The gunsight cuts had been sewn closed by an emergency-room butcher, instead of a qualified plastic surgeon.

He thought of Davenport, Davenport's teeth, the eyeteeth showing, his eyes, the gun swinging, battering . . .

He sighed, came back, shaken, staring at his face in the mirror. He put the makeup on mechanically, but carefully. Cover Mark to hide the scars, then straight, civilian makeup. Max Factor New Definition. Cover Girl nail polish. Suave styling spritz, to pull his blond hair down to cover his jawline, which was a bit too masculine.

The lipstick was last. Lipstick the color of a prairie rose. Just a touch. He didn't want to be mistaken for a harlot. . . . He made kisses at the mirror, smoothed the lipstick with his tongue, blotted it with toilet paper. Just right.

Satisfied, finally, he went to the chest, picked out underwear, got the prosthetic bra and sat on the bed. He'd shaved his legs the night before, and they were just getting prickly. Bekker was fair-haired, fine-haired: even if he hadn't shaved, his legs wouldn't have been a problem. But he did shave, to capture the feel. Rayon had said that was important, and Bekker understood—or he'd understood at the time. You had to live the part, feel the part. He flashed. A woman hurrying behind him, afraid of the dark parking ramp. Live the part . . .

The panty hose slid smoothly up his leg; he'd discovered the technique of gathering them, slipping them up piece by bit-bit-bit. When the hose were on, he stood and looked at himself in the dressing mirror; he looked like a fencer, he thought, bare chest and tights. He posed, turning sideways. A little full in the front. He reached into the panty hose and arranged his penis, pushing it down and under, tight, pulling the hose up to hold it in place. Posed again. Good.

The bra was next. He disliked it: it was cold and awkward, and cut into the muscles of his shoulders. But it gave him the right look and even the right feel. He snapped it in back, and again checked the mirror. With his soft blond hair, falling naturally now to his shoulders—no more wigs—he *was* a woman. Whitechurch had certainly been convinced. Bekker flashed: the look on Whitechurch's face as the *realization* came to him, and the gun came up . . .

He picked out a medium-blue blouse with a high collar and the remnants of shoulder padding, a conservative, midcalf-length pleated skirt, and dark gym shoes with thick walking soles. With the breast prosthetics and his narrow shoulders, he had the figure of a woman, but his hands and feet might yet give him away.

They were simply too big, too square: he wore size ten men's shoe. But when he wore dark women's gym shoes, the size was not so obvious. As a woman he was taller than average, but not awkwardly so. And people expected blondes to be tall. Hiding his hands was a bigger problem. . . .

When he'd finished dressing, he looked in the mirror. Fine. Excellent. The big shoulder bag was something he might keep dressier shoes in, wearing the gym shoes to walk back and forth to the parking ramp. Yuppie. He added a necklace of synthetic pearls, picked up a bottle of Poison by Christian Dior, dabbed it along his throat, on the inside of his wrists. The perfume was too flowery, and he deliberately used too much. Perfume, Rayon told him, was a feminine, psychological thing. The odor of perfume alone might subliminally convince, in close quarters. . . .

There. Ready. He touched himself at the pit of his throat, and remembered that he'd seen his late wife do that, touch herself there, a sort of completion. He stepped to the mirror again, to take in the whole ensemble, and spontaneously laughed with the joy of it.

Beauty was back.

BEAUTY STEPPED CAREFULLY through the weeds to the lean-to garage, careful to not to snag the hose. He left the car lights out, drove it to the gate, looked up and down the street, unlocked the gate, drove through, relocked it behind himself. He sat in the car for a moment, trying to think.

The parking garage at Bellevue was locked in his brain. Bellevue. He reached across the floor to his purse, found the bag, shook out a greenie: PCP. Popped one, two. Folded the bag and dropped it back in the purse, turned left. Careful. Bellevue? The hands on the steering wheel took him there, rolling through the dimly lit streets, precisely, evenly. A woman? Yes. Women were smaller and handled more easily, after they'd been taken. He recalled the struggle with Cortese, wedging the deadweight into the backseat of the Bug.

And women, he thought with sudden clarity and some curiosity, lasted longer. . . .

The guard nodded. He recognized the attractive blonde in the old Volkswagen Bug. She'd been there before. . . .

Bekker took the car to the top floor, which was virtually deserted. A red Volvo sat in a corner and looked like it might have been there for a couple of days. Two other cars were widely spaced. The garage was silent. He got his bag from the passenger-side floor, with the tank of anesthetic and the stun gun.

Bekker flashed: Cortese, the first one. Bekker'd hit him with the stun gun, had ridden him like a . . . No image came for a moment, then a hog. A heavy, midwestern boar, a mean brute. Bekker had ridden him down in the alley behind the Plaza, then used the mask. The power . . .

A car door slammed somewhere else in the garage; a hollow, booming sound. An engine started. Bekker went to the elevator, pushed the down button, waited. A sign on the wall said: "REMOVE VALUABLES FROM CAR: Although this ramp is patrolled, even locked cars are easily entered. Remove all valuables."

The first hit of PCP was coming on, controlling, toughening him, giving his brain the edge of craft it needed. He glanced around. No camera. He walked slowly down the stairs past the cashier, around the corner toward the main entrance of the hospital. The sidewalk that led to the entrance was actually built as a ramp, slanting down between the parking ramp and a small hospital park. Bekker walked down the ramp, paused, then went left into the park, sat at a bench under a light.

Outside, the night was warm and humid, the smell of dirty rain and cooling bubble gum. A couple on the street were walking away from him, the man wearing a straw hat; the hat looked like an angel's halo at that distance, a golden-white oval encircling his head.

Then: A main hospital door opened and a woman walked out. Headed toward the ramp, digging in a purse for keys. Bekker got up, started after her. She paused, still digging. Bekker closed. The woman was big, he realized. As he got closer, he saw she was too big. A hundred and eighty or two hundred pounds, he thought. Moving her would be difficult.

He stopped, turned, lifted a foot so he could look at the sole of his left shoe. Watch women, Rayon had told him. Watch what they do. Bekker had seen this, the stop, the check, the look of anger or disgust, depending on whether a heel was broken or she'd simply stepped in something, and then a turn. . . .

He turned, as though he might be going somewhere to fix whatever he was looking at, walked away from the heavy woman, back down into the park. He might be waiting for someone inside, might even be grieving. There were cops around, nobody would bother him. . . .

SHELLEY CARSON WAS a graduate nurse. She ran an operating suite, took no crap from anyone.

And she was just the right size.

Bite-size, Bekker's brain said when he saw her.

At five-two, she barely reached a hundred pounds when she was fully dressed. Aware of her inviting size, she was careful about the ramp. Tonight she walked out with Michaela Clemson, tall, rangy, blonde and tough; a lifelong tennis player, both a nurse and a surgical tech. They were still in uniform, tired from the day.

"Then you heard what he said? He said 'Pick it up and put it where I told you to in the first place,' like I was some kind of child. I am definitely going to complain . . ." Clemson was saying.

Bite-sized Shelley Carson encouraged her: nurses were not less than doctors, they were members of a different profession. They should take no shit. "I'd certainly go in. . . ."

"I just can't ignore it this time," the blonde said, building her courage. "The asshole is a bad surgeon, and if he'd spend more time working on his surgery and less time trying to pull rank . . ."

Bekker slid in behind them. They saw him, peripherally, but neither really looked at him until they started into the ramp together, and then up the stairs.

"I definitely would," the small one was saying. Her dark hair was cut close to the head, like a helmet, with little elfin points over her ears.

"Tomorrow afternoon at three o'clock I'm going to march in . . ." The blonde looked down at Bekker, then back up at her friend. Bekker climbed behind them, one hand on the stun gun.

Halfway up, the blonde said, "Tomorrow, I go for it."

"Do it," said the elf. "See you tomorrow."

The blonde broke away, stepping into the main part of the ramp, peering out. "All clear," she said. The blonde started toward a Toyota. Bekker and the dark-haired woman continued up, Bekker's heels rapping on the stairs.

"We have an arrangement," the elf said, looking down at Bekker. "If one of us has to go out alone, we watch each other."

"Good idea," Bekker squeaked. The voice was the hard part. Rayon had said it would be. Bekker put a hand to his mouth and faked a cough, as though his voice might be roughed by a cold, rather than forty years of testosterone.

"This parking garage, somebody's going to get attacked here someday," the woman said. "It really isn't safe. . . ."

Bekker nodded and went back to the purse. The elf looked at him, a puzzled look, something not quite right. But what? She turned away. Turn away from trouble. Bekker followed her out at the top floor, heard the Toyota's engine start below. Brought the stun gun out, got the tank ready in the bag. Heard the hiss. Felt the action in his feet . . .

The woman saw him moving. A fraction of a second before he was on her, she took in the violence of his motion and started to turn, her eyes widening in reflex.

Then he had her. One hand over her mouth, the other pressing the stun gun against her neck. She went down, trying to scream, and he rode her, pressing the stun gun home, holding it. . . .

She flapped her arms like the wings of a tethered bird. He dropped the stun gun, groped for the tank, found it, flipped the valve and clapped the mask over her face. He had her now, his hair a bush around his head, his eyes wide, feral, like a jackal over a rabbit, breathing hard, mouth open, saliva gleaming on his teeth.

He heard the sound of the Toyota going down the ramp as the bite-sized woman's struggles weakened and finally stopped. He stood up, listening. Nothing. Then a voice, far away. The little woman was curled at his feet. So sweet, the power . . .

Bekker worked all night. Preparing the specimen—wiring the gag, immobilizing her. Taking her eyelids; he held them in the palms of his hands, marveling; they were so . . . interesting. Fragile. He carried them to a metal tray, where he'd collected the others. The others were drying now, but kept their form, the lashes still shiny and strong . . .

Shelley Carson died just before seven o'clock, as silently as all the rest, the gag wired around her skull, her eyes permanently open. Bekker had crouched over her with the camera as she died, shooting straight into her eyes.

And now he sat in his stainless-steel chair and gazed at the proof of his passion, eight ultraviolet photos that clearly showed something—a radiance, a presence—flowing from Carson as she died. No question, he exulted. No question at all.

Dink.

The intercom bell. It cut through the sense of jubilation, brought him down. Old bitch. Mrs. Lacey got up early, but habitually slumped in front of the television until noon, watching her morning shows.

Dink.

He went to the intercom: "Yes?"

"Come quick," she squawked. "You have to see, you're on the television."

What? Bekker stared at the intercom, then went quickly to the bed, picked up his robe, wrapped himself, put fluffy slippers on his feet. The old lady didn't see very well, didn't hear very well, he could pass . . . and he still had on his makeup. On television? As he passed the dresser he slipped two tabs off the tray, popped them, as brighteners. What could she mean?

The first floor was dark, musty, a thin orangish morning light filtering through the parchmentlike window shades. The second floor was worse, the odor of marijuana hanging in the curtains, a stench of decaying cat shit, the smell of old vegetables and carpet mold. And it was dark, except for the phosphorescent glow of the tube.

Mrs. Lacey was standing, staring at the television, a remote control in her hand. Bekker was there on the screen, all right. One of the photos that had plagued him, had kept him off the street. But in this photo, he was a woman and a blonde. The details were perfect:

". . . credited to Detective Barbara Fell and former Minneapolis detective lieutenant Lucas Davenport, who had been brought to New York as a consultant . . ."

Davenport. Bekker was struck by a sudden dizziness, a wave of nausea. Davenport was coming; Davenport would kill him.

"But . . ." said Mrs. Lacey, looking from the screen to Bekker.

Bekker steadied himself, nodded. "That's right, it is me," he said. He sighed. He hadn't expected the old woman to last this long. He stepped carefully across the carpet to her.

She turned and tried to run, a shuffling struggle against age and infirmity, gargling in terror. Bekker giggled, and the cats, hissing, bounded across the over-stuffed furniture to the highest shelves. Bekker caught the old woman at the edge of the parlor. He put the heel of his left hand against the back of her skull, the cup of his right under her chin.

"But . . ." she said again.

A quick snap. Her spine was like a stick of rotten wood, cracked, and she collapsed. Bekker stared down at her, swaying, the brightener tab coming on.

"It is me," he said again.

21

MOST VISITORS CAME THROUGH O'Dell's office; when the knock came at Lily's unmarked office door, she looked over the top of her *Wall Street Journal* and frowned.

There was another light knock and she took off her half-moon reading glasses—she hadn't let anyone see them yet—and said, "Yes?"

Kennett stuck his head in. "Got a minute?"

"What're you doing down here?" she asked, folding the paper and putting it aside.

"Talking to you," he said. He stepped inside the door, peeked through a half-open side door into O'Dell's office, and saw an empty desk.

"He's at staff," Lily said. "What's going on?"

"We've papered the town with the female Bekker picture," Kennett said, dropping into her visitor's chair. Small talk. He tried a smile, but it didn't work. "You know Lucas got it, the cross-dressing thing. It wasn't Fell."

"I thought maybe he did," Lily said. "He wants Fell to do well."

"Nice," he said, his voice trailing off. He was looking at her as though he were trying to see inside her head.

"Let's have it," she said finally.

"All right," he said. "What do you know about this Robin Hood shit that O'Dell is peddling?"

Lily was surprised—and a small voice at the back of her head said, that was good, that look of surprise. "What? What's he peddling?"

Kennett looked at her, eyes blinking skeptically, as though he were reevaluating something. Then he said, "He's been putting out shit about Robin Hood, the so-called vigilantes. I've got the feeling that the fickle finger is pointed at my ass."

"Well, Jesus," Lily said.

"Exactly. There aren't any vigilantes. It's all bullshit, this Robin Hood business. But that doesn't mean he can't fuck me up. If they think they've got a problem . . ." He pointed a thumb at the ceiling, meaning the people upstairs, "And they can't find anybody, they might just want to hang somebody anyway, to cover their asses."

"Boy . . ." Lily shook her head. "I've got a pretty good line on what O'Dell's doing, but I don't know anything like that. And I'm not holding out on you, Richard. I'm really not."

"And I'm telling you, he's behind it."

Lily leaned forward. "Give me a few days. I'll find out. Let me ask some questions. If he's doing it, I'll tell you."

"You will?"

"Of course I will."

"All right." He grinned at her. "It's, like, when you're a lieutenant and down, you've got friends and lovers. When you're a captain or above, you've got allies. You're my first ally-lover."

She didn't smile back. She said: "Richard."

The smile died on his face. "Mmm?"

"Before I risk my ass—you're not Robin Hood?"

"No."

"Swear it," she said, looking into his eyes.

"I swear it," he said, without flinching, looking straight back at her. "I don't believe there is such a guy. Robin Hood is a goddamn computer artifact."

"How?"

He shrugged. "Flip a nickel five hundred times. The events are random, but you'll find patterns. Flip it another five hundred times, you'll still find patterns. Different ones. But the pattern doesn't mean anything. Same thing with these computer searches—you can always find patterns if you look at enough numbers. But the pattern's in your head; it's not real. Robin Hood is a figment of O'Dell's little tiny imagination."

Her eyes narrowed: "How'd you find out so much about what he's doing?"

"Hey, I'm in intelligence," he said, mildly insulted by the question. "The word gets around. I thought his little game was pretty harmless until my name started popping up."

She thought about it a minute, then nodded. "All right. Let me do some sneaking around."

22

L UCAS CALLED DARIUS PIKE in Charleston and gave him the plane's arrival time, then met Sloan and Del downtown. They hit a sports bar, talking, remembering. Lucas was long out of the departmental gossip—who was kissing whose ass, who was shagging who. Sloan went home at one o'clock and Lucas and Del wound up in an all-night diner on West Seventh in St. Paul.

". . . shit, I said, gettin' married was okay," Del said. "But then she started talking about a kid. She's, like, forty."

"Ain't the end of the world," Lucas said.

"Do I look like *Life with Father*?" Del asked. He spread his arms: he was wearing a jeans jacket with a black sleeveless tank top. An orange and black insignia on the sleeve of the jacket said, *"Harley-Davidson*—Live to Ride, Ride to Live." He had a five-day beard, but his eyes were as relaxed and clear as Lucas had ever seen them.

"You're looking pretty good, actually," Lucas said. "A year ago, man, you were ready for the junk heap."

"Yeah, yeah . . ."

"So why not have a kid?"

"Jesus." Del looked out the window. "I kinda been asking myself that."

Del peeled off at three o'clock and Lucas went home, opened all the windows in the house, and began writing checks to cover the bills that had arrived with the mail. At five, finished with the bills, and tired, he closed and locked all the windows, went back to the bedroom and repacked his overnight bag. He called a cab, had the driver stop at a SuperAmerica all-night store, bought two jelly doughnuts and a cup of coffee, and rode out to the airport.

The plane taxied away from the terminal at six-thirty. The stewardess asked if he wanted juice and eggs.

"I'm gonna try to go to sleep," he said. "Please, please don't wake me up. . . ."

The fear got him as the takeoff run began, the sense of helplessness, the lack of control. He closed his eyes, fists clenched. Got off the ground with body English. Held his breath until the engine noise changed and the climb rate slowed. Cranked back the seat. Tried to sleep. A while later, he didn't know how long, he realized that his mouth tasted like chicken feathers, and his neck hurt. The stewardess was shaking his shoulder: "Could you bring your seat upright, please?"

He opened his eyes, disoriented. "I was sleeping," he groaned.

"Yes," she said in her most neutral voice. "But we're approaching Atlanta, and your seat . . ."

"Atlanta?" He couldn't believe it. He never slept on airplanes. The plane's left wing dipped, and they turned on it, and, looking down, he could see the city of Atlanta, like a gritty gray rug. Ten minutes later, they were down.

The Atlanta airport was straight from *RoboCop*, with feminine machine voices issuing a variety of warnings just below the level of consciousness, and steel escalators dropping into sterile tile hallways. He was glad to get out, though the flight to Charleston was bad. He fought the fear and managed to compose himself by the time the plane was on the ground.

Pike was waiting inside the small terminal, a stolid black man wearing a green cotton jacket over a white shirt and khaki pants. When his jacket moved, Lucas could see a half-dozen ballpoint pens clipped to his shirt pocket and a small revolver on his belt.

"Lucas Davenport," Lucas said, shaking hands.

"I gotta car," Pike said, leading the way. "How's New York?"

"Hotter'n here," Lucas said.

"This is nothin'," Pike said. "You ought to be here in August."

"That's what they say in New York. . . ."

They left the airport at speed. Lucas, disoriented, asked, "Where's the ocean?"

"Straight ahead, but the city's not really on the ocean. It's kind of like . . . Manhattan, actually," Pike said. "There's a river coming in on both sides, and they meet, and that's the harbor, and then you gotta go on out past the Fort to get into the ocean."

"Fort Sumter?"

"That's it," Pike said.

"I'd like to see it sometime. I've been going to battlefields. Tell me about Reed."

Pike whipped past a gray Maxima, took an off-ramp, then turned left at the bottom. The street was cracked, the borders overgrown with weeds and scrub.

"Reed is a stupid motherfucker," he said matter-of-factly. "I get mad talking about it. His old man has lived here all his life, runs a garage and gas station, does the best body work in town, and makes a ton of money. And Red did good in high school. Did good on his tests and got into Columbia University on a scholarship. The silly fuck goes up to New York and starts putting junk up his nose, the cocaine. Hanging out in Harlem, coming back here and talking shit. Then he didn't come back anymore. The word was, he was putting it up his nose full-time."

"Huh. How long's he been back?"

"Few weeks," Pike said. "I feel bad for his folks."

"Is he staying?"

"I don't know. When he first got back, there were a couple of rumbles from Narcotics that he was hanging out with the wrong people. But I haven't heard that lately. Maybe something changed."

Lucas hadn't thought about what Charleston might look like, but as they drove through, he decided it was just right: Old South. Clapboard houses with peeling paint, and weird trees; bushes with plants that had leaves like leather, and spikes. A few palms. A lot of dirt. Hot.

The Reed garage was a gray concrete-block building sitting side by side with a Mobil gas station and convenience store. All but one set of the gas pumps had a car parked next to them, and uniformed attendants moved around cleaning windshields and checking oil. "You come in here, they wipe your windshield, check your oil, put air in your tires. The only place you'll find it," Pike said. "That's why Don Reed makes the money he does."

He killed the engine in the body shop's parking lot and Lucas followed him into the shop office. The office smelled of motor oil, but was neatly kept, with plastic customer chairs facing a round table stacked with magazines. Behind a counter, a large man was hunched over a yellow-screen computer, poking at a keyboard one finger at a time. He looked up when they came in and said, "Hey, Darius."

"Hey, Don. Is Red around?"

Reed straightened up, his smile slipping off his face. "He done somethin'?"

Pike shook his head and Lucas said, "No. I'm from New York. Your son witnessed a shooting. He was a passerby. I just need to talk to him for a couple of minutes."

"You sure?" Reed asked, a hostile tone scratching through. "I got a lawyer . . ."

"Look: You don't know me, so . . . But I'm telling you, with a witness standing here, that all I want to do is talk. There's no warrant, no anything. He's not a suspect."

Reed regarded Lucas coolly, then finally nodded. "All right, come on. He's out back."

Red Reed was coming out of a paint room when they found him, a plastic mask and hat covering his head. When he saw his father and the two cops, he pulled off the protective gear and waited uncertainly by the paint room door. He was tall, too thin, with prominent white teeth.

"Police to talk to you. One from New York," his father said. "I'm gonna listen." Red Reed looked apprehensive, but nodded.

"Can we find a place to sit?" Lucas asked.

The elder Reed nodded: "Nobody in the waiting room. . . ."

LUCAS TOOK BOBBY RICH'S report from his pocket, unfolded it, and led Red Reed through it, confirming it bit by bit.

"White-haired guy," Lucas said. "Thin, fat?"

"Yeah. Skinny, like."

"Dark? Pale? What?"

"Tan. He was, like, tan."

"What was the scene like, when Fred Waites was shot?"

"Well, man, I wasn't right there. I saw the car go by and I thought I saw a gun and I headed the other way. I heard the shooting, saw the car."

"What kind of car?"

"I don't know, man, I wasn't paying attention to that," Reed said. He was looking at his hands. Pike moved impatiently, and Reed's father looked out the door but didn't say anything. Reed's eyes wandered to his father, then back to Lucas.

"What time was it?" Lucas asked.

"I didn't have a watch. . . ."

"I mean, afternoon, evening, night?"

Reed nervously licked his lips, then seemed to pick one: "Evening."

"It was three o'clock in the afternoon, Red," Lucas said. "Bright daylight."

"Man, I was fucked up . . ."

"You don't know what kind of car it was, but you could see inside that the guy was white-haired, skinny and tanned? But you didn't see anything about the other guys? Red . . ." Lucas glanced at Don Reed. "Red, you're lying to us. This is an important case. We think the same guys shot a cop and, before that, a lawyer."

"I don't know nothing about that," Reed said, now avoiding everyone's eyes.

"Okay, I don't think you do. But you're lying to me . . ."

"I'm not lying," Reed said.

Don Reed turned to face his son and in a harsh, cutting voice said, "You remember what I told you? No bullshit, no lies, no dope, no stealing, and we'll try to keep you alive. And you're lying, boy. There never was a time, from when you were a little baby, that you didn't know what kind of car was what—and you see a man and know he's got white hair and a tan, and you don't know what car he was in? Horseshit. You're lying. You stop, now."

Lucas said, "I want to know how much John O'Dell had to do with it."

Reed had been staring miserably at his feet, but now his head popped up.

"You know Mr. O'Dell?"

"Aw, shit," Lucas said. He stood up, walked once around the tiny room, whacked the spherical Lions Club gum machine with the palm of his hand, then pinched the bridge of his nose, closing his eyes. "You're fuckin' working for O'Dell."

"Man . . ." said Reed.

"O'Dell a dope pusher?" Don Reed asked, voice dark, angry.

"No," Lucas said. "He's about the fifth most important cop in New York."

The two Reeds exchanged glances, and Pike asked, "What's going on?"

"A goddamned game, pin the tail on the donkey," Lucas said. "And I'm the jackass."

He said to Reed, "So now I know. I need some detail. Where'd you meet him, how'd you get pulled in on this . . ."

Reed blurted it out. He'd met O'Dell at a Columbia seminar. O'Dell spoke three times, and each time, Reed talked to him after class. Harlem was different than an Irish cop could know, Reed said. The fat cop and skinny southerner argued about life on the streets; went with a few other students and the professor to a coffee shop, talked late. He saw O'Dell again, in the spring, but he was into the dope by then. Busted in a sweep of a crack house, called O'Dell. The arrest disappeared, but he was warned: never again. But there *was* another time. He was arrested twice more for possession, went to court. Then a third time, and this time he had a little too much crack on him. The cops were talking about charging him as a dealer, and he called O'Dell. He got simple possession, and was out again.

Then O'Dell called. Did he know anybody, a crook, with a connection to a cop? To a detective? Well, yes . . .

"Sonofabitch. It was too neat, it had to be," Lucas said.

"What the fuck is going on?" Pike asked again.

"I don't know, man," Lucas said. To Reed, he said, "Don't call O'Dell. You're out of this and you want to stay out. Whatever's going on here, and it's pretty rough, doesn't have anything to do with you. You'd best lay low."

"He's out," Don Reed said, looking at his son.

Reed's head bobbed. "I don't want nothing more to do with New York."

ON THE WAY BACK to the airport, Pike said, "I don't think I'd like New York."

"It's got some low points," Lucas said. He took a card from his pocket diary, scribbled his home phone number on the back of it. "Listen, thanks for the help. If you ever need anything from New York or Minneapolis, call me."

The flight to Atlanta was bad, but on the way to New York, the fear seemed to slip away. Lucas had reached a tolerance level: his fifth flight in three days. He'd never flown that much in his life. More or less relaxed, he found a notepad in his overnight case and doodled on it, working it out.

Bobby Rich hadn't been assigned to work the case because he had the best qualifications—he'd been assigned simply because he knew a guy who knew Red

Reed. So that Red Reed could call his friend and insist that the friend pass information to the cops about the shooting of Fred Waites.

Except that Reed hadn't been there at all. The man with white hair and the deep tan was an O'Dell invention. Lucas grinned despite himself. In a crooked way, it was very nice: lots of layers.

He closed his eyes, avoiding the next question: Did Lily know?

At La Guardia he saw a copy of the *Times* with Bekker as a blonde woman. He bought a copy, queued for a cab, got a buck-toothed driver who wanted to talk.

"Bekker, huh?" buck-tooth said, his eyes on the rearview mirror. He could see the picture on the front of the paper as Lucas read the copy inside. "There's a goofball for ya. Dressed up like a woman."

"Yeah."

"This last one, man, took her right out of a parking garage. Girlfriend says Bekker was right there with them, could've took them both."

Lucas folded the paper down and looked at the back of the driver's head. "There's another one? Today?"

"Yeah, this morning. They found her in a parking lot with the wire gag and the cut-off eyelids and the whole works. I say, when they get him, they ought to hang him off a street sign by his nuts. Be an example."

Lucas nodded and said, "Listen, forget about the hotel. Take me to Midtown South."

CARTER, HUERTA AND JAMES were huddled together over a tabloid newspaper in the coordinating office, all three of them with Styrofoam coffee cups in their hands. Lucas looked in and James said, "Kennett's down in the corner office, he wants to see you."

"Have you seen Barbara Fell?" Lucas asked.

"Gone home." There was a rapid-fire exchange of glances among the three cops, a vein of thin amusement. They knew he was sleeping with Fell.

"Anything happening?"

"About a thousand sightings on Bekker, including three good ones," Carter said. "He's driving a Volkswagen Bug. . . ."

"Jesus, that's terrific," Lucas said. "Who saw him? How'd you get the car?"

"Two witnesses last night at the parking ramp. The Carson woman's girl-friend and the cashier. The girlfriend is a sure thing—she even told us he was wearing too much Poison. That's a perfume . . ."

"Yeah."

". . . And the cashier remembers the blonde part, and says she—he—was driving an old Volkswagen. He remembers because it looked like it was in pretty good shape and he wondered if Bekker was an artist or something. He thinks it was dark green or dark blue. We're running it through the License Bureau right now, but the Volkswagen part isn't public yet. If he goes outside now, he's gonna have to go in a car. And we're stopping every Bug in Midtown."

"You said three people. . . ."

"The third's a maybe, but pretty definite. The night clerk in a bookstore down in the Village says he remembers the face very clearly, says it was Bekker. He says he was buying some weird book about torture."

"Huh."

"We're getting close," Carter said. "We'll have him in two or three days, at the outside."

"I hope," Lucas said. "Any returns on that stun-gun business?"

"Three. Nothing."

"Phones?"

"Nope. Goddamn rat's nest."

"Okay . . ."

Lucas started to turn away, and Carter said, "You've seen the papers?"

"With Bekker? Yeah . . ."

"No, that was this morning; the afternoon paper . . ." Huerta picked up the paper they'd been looking at, closed it, and handed it to Lucas. On the cover was a woman's face, eyes staring; before the headlines reached the brain, the terror of the face came through, then the words: *Kill #8—Bekker Death Pix.*

"This legit?" Lucas asked.

"That's Carson," Carter said grimly. "He sent notes and photos to three news-papers and two TV stations. They're using them."

"Jesus . . ."

FROM DOWN THE HALL, he heard a woman's voice.

Lily.

He walked down to the corner, found the room in semidarkness, the door open. He knocked, standing back, and Kennett said, "Yeah?"

Lucas stuck his head in. "Davenport," he said.

"Come on in. We were just talking about you," Kennett said. He was sitting in a visitor's chair in front of a standard-issue metal desk, his feet up. His shirt collar was open, and his bright Polynesian Gauguin tie was draped across a stack of phone books at the front edge of the desk. Lily sat in another chair at the side of the desk, facing him.

"Fuckin' photographs," Lucas said.

"The shit is hitting the fan," Kennett said grimly. "First the New School thing and now the pictures. The mayor had the commissioner on the carpet. You could hear the screaming in Jersey."

Lucas dragged a third chair around, bumped Kennett. "Move your ass over so I can get my feet up."

"And me with a fuckin' bad heart," Kennett mumbled as he moved.

"You told Fell about the transvestite thing," Lily said. She pushed the phone books out of the way, picked up the necktie.

Lucas shrugged, sat down, put his feet up. "We talked it over and decided it was likely."

"That came at a good time. We told everybody that Carson'll probably be the last, that we've pretty much got him pinned down," she said.

"Should have thought of it sooner, the cross-dressing," Kennett said glumly. "The one before was a lesbian, we knew that. We should have seen that she wouldn't let a strange guy get too close, not outside a lesbian bar."

"Hell, you did everything right . . ." Lily began.

Kennett interrupted: "Everything but catch him . . ."

"He's pinned."

"We fuckin' hope," Kennett said.

Lily had been rolling the tie in her fingers, and now she looked down at the bare-breasted Polynesian woman, shook her head and said, "This is the craziest tie."

"Don't knocker it," said Kennett, then slapped his leg and laughed at the pun, while Lily rolled her eyes.

"You were jerking me around, Gauguin and Christian Dior," Lucas said to Kennett. He looked at Lily. "He told me this Gauguin dude was Christian Dior's necktie partner."

Lily laughed again, and Kennett said, "How do you know he wasn't?"

"Looked him up," Lucas said. "He died in 1903. He was associated with the symbolists."

"Now if you knew what a symbolist was, you'd be in fat city," Lily said.

"It was the use of color specifically for its symbolic impact, the emotional and intellectual impact," Lucas said. "Which makes sense. Some holding cells are painted bubble-gum pink for the same reason. The color cools people out."

Kennett, staring, said, "I never fuckin' thought of that."

"Carter tells me you'll have Bekker in three days at the outside," Lucas said.

"That fuckhead. That's the kind of talk that gets us in trouble," Kennett grumbled. "We'll get him soon, but I wouldn't bet on the three days. If he's got food and water, he could hole up."

"Still . . ."

"I figure no more than a week," Kennett said. "He'll break. I just hope I'm still working for the goddamn police department when it happens. I mean, people are *pissed*. These fuckin' pictures, man: the mess at the New School was nothing, compared to this."

"People think cops . . ." Lucas started.

But Lily was shaking her head. "It's not the people, it's the politicians. People understand you can't always catch a guy immediately; most of them do, anyway. But the politicians think *they've* got to do something, so what they do is run around and scream and threaten to fire people."

"Mmmm. A week," Lucas said. "That's a long time, in ward-heeler years."

"Anxious to get home?" Kennett asked.

"Nah. I'm enjoying myself. I want be there for the bust."

"Or the kill," said Kennett.

"Whatever . . ."

Lily pushed herself out of the chair, stretched, and tousled Kennett's hair. "Let's go look at the river," she said.

"Jesus Christ, the woman's indefatigable, and me with this heart," Kennett complained.

Lucas, vaguely embarrassed, stood and drifted toward the door. "See you guys tomorrow. . . ."

A MESSAGE FROM FELL was waiting at the hotel: "Call when you get in, until one o'clock." He held the slip in his hand as he rode the elevator to his floor, dropped it on the bedstand, went into the bathroom, doused his face with hot water, and looked up in the mirror, the water trickling down his face.

He'd had a long relationship with a woman, the mother of his daughter, that now, when he looked back, seemed to have been based on a shared cynicism. Jennifer was a reporter, with too much time on the street, edging toward burnout. A baby, for her, had been a run at salvation.

He'd had a shorter, intense relationship with Lily, who had been struggling with the end of her own marriage; that might have been something, if they'd been in the same town, from the same emotional places. But they hadn't been, and some of the guilt of their affair still stuck to their relationship.

He'd had any number of other relationships, long and short, happy and unhappy. Most of the women he'd gone with still liked him well enough, in a wary, once-burned way; but he tended to think of them as *others*, not Jennifer, not Lily.

Fell was one of the others. A wistful, lovely, finally lonely woman. In a permanent relationship, they would drive each other crazy. He wiped his face with one of the rough hotel towels and wandered back to the bed. He sat down, picked up the phone, looked at the receiver for a moment, then smiled. He'd felt for a year as though he were under water: quiet, placid, out of it. The New York cops were bringing him up, and Fell was fixing him in other ways. He tapped out her number. She picked it up on the second ring.

"This is Lucas," he said.

"Kennett knew it was you, but I got good mileage out of the cross-dressing thing," Fell said, without preamble. "My name was on the TV news, and it's in the *Times* and the *Post*. That never hurts."

"I saw it. . . ."

"I'd like to find a way to thank you. Oral sex comes to mind, if I get my share," Fell said.

"Women are so *forward* these days," Lucas said. "How quick can you get here?"

. . .

FELL BROUGHT A CHANGE of clothes with her, and they spent the evening laughing and making love. The next morning, when they were dressed, Lucas asked, "How would we find Jackie Smith?"

"Call his office," she said.

"That easy?"

"He's a hustler," Fell said. "Getting found is part of his business."

"So call him."

Smith called back in five minutes. "Aren't you guys ever going away? Can't you find out anything on your own?" he complained. "I've done everything you wanted. . . ."

"All we want to do is talk," Lucas said.

"I gave you what you wanted," Smith said again. He was angry.

"Jackie . . . ten minutes, please? Have breakfast with us or something. We'll buy."

Smith would meet them at a café outside the St. Moritz hotel, he said. They caught a cab, struggling north through the midmorning traffic, the driver with his arm out the window, whistling. The day would be hot again; already the sky was showing a whitish haze, and when they got out of the cab across from Central Park, Lucas could see the leaves on the park trees were curling against the heat.

Smith was sitting at a metal table, eating a cream cheese croissant and drinking coffee. He didn't get up when they arrived.

"Now what?" he asked, a sullen look on his face.

"We wanted to thank you—those names you gave us started a chain reaction. We've maybe got the asshole pinned down."

"No shit?" Smith looked surprised. "When'll you get him?"

"Some of the guys are betting a couple-three days. Nobody gives him more than a week," Lucas said. "But we do have something we need from you. All the small-time fences who buy from the junkies—they need to tell the dopers that Bekker'll be out looking for angel dust, ecstasy, speed. Maybe acid. And he'll kill. The guy we got to, with your help, was boosting stuff out of Bellevue, but he was also dealing dope. Bekker killed him. Cold blood. Walked up and *bam*. Killed him."

"I saw that on TV. I wondered . . ."

"That was him," said Lucas.

Smith nodded. "Okay. No skin off my butt. I'll tell everybody I know and ask them to pass the word."

"He's probably around the Village, but could be anywhere between the civic center and Central Park. That's about all we know. That's where the word's got to be," Lucas said.

"That's my territory," Smith said. "Is that all?"

Lucas glanced at Fell, then said, "No. I gotta ask you something else. You might not want to talk about it with another witness here." He tipped his head at Fell. "But if you don't mind if she stayed . . ."

Fell frowned at him, and Smith said, "What's the deal?"

"Back when I first got here, I banged up your place. Tried to get your attention . . ."

"Well, that worked," Smith said ruefully.

"Yeah. A couple of days later, I got the snot beat out of me when I was coming out of a friend's place. I need to know if that was you. Off the record. If it was, it's no problem, I swear it."

Smith dropped his croissant on the plate and laughed. "Jesus Christ, it wasn't me. I read about it, though—but it wasn't me."

"Yeah?"

"Yeah. And if you don't mind me saying so, you're the kind of guy that shit happens to, getting beat up," Smith said.

Lucas looked at Fell. "Could you hike down to the end of the block for a minute?"

"I don't know," she said, studying him.

"C'mon," Lucas said.

"Are you Internal Affairs?"

"Fuck no, I told you," Lucas said impatiently. "C'mon, take a hike."

Fell pushed back her chair, picked up her purse and stalked away.

"She's pissed," Smith said, looking from Fell to Lucas and back to Fell. "Are you screwing her?"

Lucas ignored the question: "There's a big-dog shoot-out going on. Inside the department. And I'm tangled up in it. Now. The people who jumped me might be one set of those big dogs. That's why I really need to know."

"Listen . . ."

"Just a minute," Lucas said, putting up a hand. "I want to put it to you as simple as I can. If you tell me no, it wasn't you, and I find out that it was, I'll come back and hurt you. All right? I really will, because I've gotta know the truth of this. Not knowing the truth could get me killed. On the other hand, if you say yes, it was you, there's no problem. I'll take the lumps."

Smith shook his head in disbelief, a half-smile fixed on his face. "The answer is still no. I didn't do it. I wasn't even particularly happy to see the story in the paper, because I thought you might come back on me."

Lucas nodded, and Smith spread his hands, lifted his shoulders: "I'm a businessman. I don't want any shit. I don't want any muscle around. I hate people with guns. Everybody's got a fuckin' gun." He stared off across Sixth Avenue, the traffic waiting for the light at Central Park South, then looked back at Lucas. "No. Wasn't me."

"All right," Lucas said. "So get the word out to the junkies on Bekker. You might also point out that there's a twenty-five-thousand-dollar crime-stoppers award for his capture."

Lucas turned away from Smith and walked down the street to Fell. "I wish I could read lips," she said. "I'd give a lot to know what you just told him."

"I told him why I wanted to know if those were his guys who came after me," Lucas said.

"Tell me," she said.

"No. And I'm not Internal Affairs."

THEY SPENT THE DAY walking through the Village and SoHo, drifting in and out of shops, talking to Fell's contacts on the street, chatting with uniform cops in Washington Square, watching the street action on Broadway. They found the bookstore where Bekker had been spotted, a long, narrow shop with a narrow front window and a weathered, paint-peeled door three steps up. A sign in the door said "Open All Night, 365 Nights a Year."

The clerk who had talked to Bekker wasn't working, but happened by on his bike a few seconds after they asked for him. A thin man with a goatee and a book of poetry, he looked like a latter-day Beat, his face animated as he told them about the encounter.

"He's a good-looking woman, I'll tell you that," the clerk said. "But you can look at somebody and know what kind of book they're going to buy, and I never picked her—him—out for the one he found. Torture and shit. I thought maybe he was, like, an NYU professor or something, and that's why he bought it. . . ."

Down the sidewalk, Fell said, "I think he's real."

"So do I," said Lucas. "He saw him." He looked up at the red-brick buildings around him, with their iron stoops and window boxes full of petunias. "And he's somewhere close, Bekker is. He didn't drive any distance to get to a small bookstore. I can smell the sonofabitch."

He took her to the restaurant where Petty had been killed, sat and had Cokes, and almost told her about it.

"Not too bad a place," he said, looking around.

"It's all right," she said.

"You ever been here? Your regular precinct is around here, right?"

"Ten blocks," Fell said, poking a straw in her Coke. "Too far. Besides, this is sort of a sit-down place, not the kind of place you come to for lunch if you're a cop."

"Yeah, I know what you mean."

Late in the afternoon, while Fell browsed a magazine rack, Lucas stopped at a pay phone, dropped a quarter, and got Lily in O'Dell's car.

"Where are you?"

"Morningside Heights."

"Where's that?"

"Up by Columbia."

"I need to see you. Tonight. By yourself. Won't take too long."

"All right. How about nine, at my place?"

"Good."

When he hung up, Fell looked up from a copy of *Country Home* and said, "So. Are you up for dinner?"

"I'm talking to Lily tonight," he said. "I'd like to come around later, though."

"I hate to see you hanging around with that woman," Fell said, dropping the magazine back on the rack.

"This is purely business," Lucas said. "And look, could you stop by Midtown and pick up those file summaries? We've been floating around all day, listening to bullshit . . . maybe something'll come out of the files."

"All right. I'll haul them over to my place. . . ."

LILY WAS SITTING in a living room chair, her high heels in the middle of the carpet, her bare feet up on a hassock. The hassock was covered with a bro-caded throw that seemed to Lucas to be vaguely Russian, or Old World. She was sipping a Diet Coke, tired smudges under her eyes.

"Sit down. You sounded tense," she said. "What happened?" Her head was back, her dark hair a perfect frame around her pale oval face.

"Nothing happened, not today, anyway. I just need to talk to you," he said. He perched on the edge of her other overstuffed chair. "I need to know about you and Walter Petty—your relationship."

She leaned farther back in the chair, wiggled once to settle in, laid her head back, and closed her eyes. "Can I ask why you need to know?"

"Not yet."

She opened her eyes and looked at him carefully and said, "Robin Hood?"

"I'm not sure. What about Petty?"

"Walt and I went back as far as you can go," Lily said, her eyes unfocusing. "We were born on the same block in Brooklyn, sort of middle-class brownstones. I was exactly one month older, to the day. June first and July first. His mother and mine were friends, so I suppose I first laid eyes on him when I was five or six weeks old. We grew up together. Went to kindergarten together. We were both in the smart group. Someplace along the way, sixth or seventh grade, he got in-terested in math and science and ham radio in that geeky way boys do, and I got interested in social things. After that we didn't talk so much."

"Still friends, though . . ."

She nodded. "Sure. I'd talk to him when I saw him around the block, but not at school. He was in love with me for most of his life. And I guess I loved him, you know, but not sexually. Like a handicapped brother, or something."

"Handicapped?"

She carefully set the glass on the table and said, "Yeah, he was socially hand-icapped. Walked around with a slide rule on his belt, his table manners went from bad to worse, he got weird around girls. You know the type. Sort of inef-fectual, nonphysical. Really nice, though. Eager . . . too eager."

"Yeah. A dork. A nerd. The kind of kid that gets shredded by girls."

"Yes. Exactly. The kind that gets shredded," she said. "But we were friends. . . . And whenever I needed something done—you know, get an apartment painted, or help fixing something—I could call him up and he'd drop everything and be there. I took him for granted. He was always there, and I assumed he always would be."

"Why'd he become a cop?"

" 'Cause he could. It was a job you could get with a test and with family con-nections. He was brilliant on tests and had the connections."

"Was he a good cop?"

"He was terrible in uniform," she said. "He didn't have that . . . that . . . cold spot. Or hot spot. Or whatever it is. He couldn't get on top of people—you ought to know about that."

"Yeah." Lucas grinned. "I don't know if it's hot or cold, though. Anyway, Petty . . ."

"So he was terrible on the street and they moved him inside. He was working guard details and so on. Then they tried him on dope. And Jesus, he was something else. I mean nobody, *nobody* would believe he was a cop. He'd make a buy and the backup would drop on the dealer, and they still wouldn't believe it. This *dork* couldn't be an undercover cop. Sometimes even the judges didn't believe it. Anyway, that's about the first job he ever did really well at; he was a bit of an actor. Then he got interested in investigation, in crime-scene processing. He was good at that, too. The best. He'd go into a crime scene and he'd see *everything*. And he could put it together, too. Then computers came along, and he was great with computers." She laughed, remembering. "Suddenly, the guy who fucked up everything, the nerd as big as the moon, was a hot item. And he was still good old Walt. When you needed your apartment painted, there he was. He had this great open smile, completely . . . geeky, but honest. When he looked happy to see you, he was happy to see you; he'd just light up. And if he got angry, he'd go off and start yelling, and then he'd maybe start crying or something; or you thought he would. . . ."

Lily's lip was trembling, and she dropped her feet off the hassock and dropped her head.

"How'd he get the job looking for Robin Hood?"

"He knew computers and he'd worked with O'Dell, and we swung it for him. He could help us, and it was a chance for him to break out. And maybe I had something to do with it—he'd be working with me. Like I said . . ."

"Yeah. I know exactly what you mean."

"Sounds like arrogance, or vanity."

Lucas shook his head. "Not really. Just life . . . You think he got close to Robin Hood?"

"He must have. Jesus, when he was killed, I couldn't stop crying for a week. I really . . . I don't know. There was no sexual impulse at all, but when I thought of him over all those years, that puppy-dog quality, that he loved me . . . It was like . . . I don't know. I loved him. That's what it came to."

"Huh." He was watching her, his elbow on the arm of the chair, one finger at his chin.

"So what's this all about?" she asked. The weariness had slipped from her voice, and she looked up, intent.

"You and O'Dell are running me as some kind of lure," Lucas said. "You're dragging me out in front of whoever your targets are. I need to know who you think they are."

After a long moment of silence, she said, "Fell. As far as I know, that's it."

"Bullshit."

"It's not bullshit," she said. "She's all we've got."

"That can't be right."

"It is."

"You know everything that O'Dell is doing?"

"Well, yes, I mean I schedule for him . . . I suppose he could run something on the side. . . ."

There was another moment of silence, then Lucas said, "I'm afraid you're betraying me."

She was offended, angry. "God damn it."

"I know you are—or somebody is. O'Dell for sure, and you're with O'Dell. . . ."

"Tell me about it," she said, sitting back again.

Lucas looked her over and said, "First of all, Fell's not involved."

"Why not?"

"I just know, and I'm not wrong," Lucas said.

"Lucas, instincts or no instincts, the goddamn records aren't lying about this," Lily said. "She's all over the place."

"I know. She's an alarm."

"What?"

"She's a trip wire," Lucas said. "Working the jobs she has, in Burglary, and as a decoy, she knows half the assholes in Midtown. So Robin Hood used her as a reference and picked on assholes that she knew. Then they watched her. If anybody got close, they'd get close to her first. . . ."

"I don't know." Lily was shaking her head. She didn't believe it.

"It'd have to be a tough sonofabitch to set that up," Lucas continued. "As soon as you pulled her off her regular job and put me next to her, the alarm went off. Petty's been killed, the official investigation seems to be dead in the water—and here comes Lily Rothenburg and the department's Svengali, towing me along behind. And you stick me next to Fell. They never bought the Bekker thing: they've been reading us like a book."

"Who?"

Lucas hesitated. "I'm tempted to say Kennett."

"Bullshit." Lily shook her head. "I'd know. In fact, I asked him. He doesn't even think there is such a group."

"But we know there is. And I'm still tempted to say Kennett. O'Dell put me right up against Fell and he put me right up against Kennett. It's possible that O'Dell *knows* it's Kennett, but doesn't have the proof."

Lily thought it over, staring at him. "That's . . ."

"Bizarre. I agree. And of course, there're other possibilities, too."

"That it's me?" She smiled a small and frosty smile.

"Yeah." Lucas nodded. "That's one of them."

"And what do you think?"

He shook his head. "It's not you, so . . ."

"How do you know it's not me?" she asked.

"Same way I know it's not Fell—I've seen you operate."

"Thanks for that," Lily said.

"Yeah . . . which brings us to the last possibility."

"O'Dell?"

"O'Dell. He has access to everything he needs to organize the group. He knows everybody on the force, and he probably could pick out likely candidates for his hit teams. He has the computer files to pick out the assholes, and to set up Fell as an alarm. . . ."

"There's a hole," Lily said quickly. "He's so high up he wouldn't need an alarm. . . ."

"Internal Affairs—he might not know about Internal Affairs investigations."

She bit her lip. "Okay. Go ahead."

"Since Petty was a computer maven too, maybe computers led him to O'Dell. Whatever it was, for whatever reason Petty got hit, O'Dell was right there to manage the investigation. Kept it out of Internal Affairs . . ."

"Said it was too political," Lily said thoughtfully.

"Yeah. Then he pulls me into it, produces Fell, and he puts me up against Kennett. And you know what? Fell and Kennett are all I've got—all that paper you gave me, the regular investigation, the reports. It's all bullshit. It's all a stone wall. It looks impressive, but there's nothing in it."

"Why would O'Dell pick on Kennett?"

"Because Kennett's going to die," Lucas said bluntly. "Suppose he gets everything pointed at Kennett, and then Kennett . . . dies. Natural causes, a heart attack. If there was an agreement that Kennett was it, the investigation would die and the real organizer would be clear."

Lily, pale as notebook paper: "He couldn't have . . . I don't think."

"Why not?"

"I don't think . . . I don't think he's brave enough. Physically. He'd be thinking about prison."

"That all depends on how he's set it up. Maybe his shooters don't know him."

"Yeah, but remember—if O'Dell is it, he wouldn't have to give you Fell. If Fell's an alarm, I mean, he'd know what you were here for."

"Yeah. And he'd know that Fell would get me exactly where she has: nowhere. And at the same time, lend a touch of truth to the whole business. Fell did know all those dead guys. Besides, with Petty talking to both of you, and Fell popping out of the computer, there was no way to get her back inside. . . ."

"Maybe," she said.

"How'd you meet Kennett?" Lucas asked abruptly.

"In the intraconference meetings."

"As O'Dell's assistant?"

"Yes."

"Did O'Dell feed you to him?" Lucas asked.

"Jesus, Lucas," she said.

"Did he? I mean, he knows both of you. Could he have figured . . ."

"I don't know. They don't like each other, you know." Lily stood and turned in place, like a dog trying to make a bed more comfortable. "You know, you've put this whole tissue together without a single goddamned fact. . . ."

"I've got one interesting, surprising, generally unknown fact," he said; and it was his turn to produce a wintry smile.

"What?"

"I know that O'Dell's trying to frame Kennett. I know *that* for sure. The question is, is he doing it because Kennett's guilty and it's the only way to get him? Or because he's looking for a scapegoat?"

"Bullshit," she said, but he could see the shock in her eyes.

"I found Red Reed in Charleston, South Carolina," he said. "He's a friend of O'Dell's, from Columbia. . . ."

And then he told her most of the rest of it, except for the curious thing Mrs. Logan had said, when they interviewed her in the apartment below Petty's.

L ILY LISTENED AS LUCAS called Fell, watched his face, watched him smiling, turning away, setting up a date. Lucas left, hurrying, and she stood at the window with her purse, watching him. He flagged a cab, and just before he got in, looked up and saw, pointed at her purse, waved.

Then he was gone.

She walked through the apartment, touching things, with the sense of something ending, with a sense of dread.

Kennett? No. But O'Dell was unthinkable too. Could O'Dell have coldly executed his own man . . .

Finally, she picked up the phone and punched in the number for Kennett's boat. He picked it up and said, "Lily."

Pleased, she said, "How'd you know it was me?"

"I think it might be love," he said. "Are you feeling lonely?"

"You're reading my mind."

"The river's beautiful tonight. . . ."

The river was quiet, smelling of mud and oil and salt. Halyard hardware tinkled against the aluminum masts. A late-night squall was rolling off the coast far to the northeast, and they could see the lightning in the sky far beyond the lights of Manhattan.

As Lily and Kennett made love, she had a moment of absolute clarity, could hear the Crash Test Dummies' song "Superman" roll mournfully out of a nearby boat, muted by the ten thousand unidentifiable cheeps and knocks of the marina.

Later, in the cockpit . . .

"Jesus, I'm sitting here bullshitting and you're sitting there crying," Kennett said quietly. He reached across and thumbed a tear off her cheek. "What's all this about?"

"I was just looking across the river, thinking how pretty it was, how good it feels. Then I thought about Walt, about how he'd never see it again."

"Petty?"

"Yeah. God damn it."

"The guy has a strange hold on you, m'dear," Kennett said, trying to keep his voice light: an invitation to talk.

"You know why?" she asked, taking up the invitation.

"Why?"

"Because we were so goddamn mean to him, that's why. Us girls, in school. Lucas got me thinking about it. . . ."

"It's hard to see you as mean," Kennett said.

"I didn't think about it at the time. The thing about Walt was, he'd do anything for you. He was always so *eager*. And when we were in school—and even after that, on the force—we paid him back by laughing about the way he dressed, and the way he acted, and all those pens he used to carry around. We made him be a clown and he wasn't a clown; but whenever he tried to be serious, we wouldn't let him. We hurt him. That's what I was thinking about, the times I know we hurt him—girls, in high school—that hurt look on his face when he'd try to do something, try an approach and we'd laugh in his face. He never really understood. . . . Oh, God."

Suddenly, she was sobbing and Kennett patted her on the back, helplessly. "Jesus, Lily . . ."

A moment later she said, her voice clearing, "You're a Catholic. Do you believe in visions? You know, like the Virgin Mary and all of that, talking to shepherds?"

"I'd want to see it myself," Kennett said wryly.

"The thing is, I keep seeing Petty. . . ." She laughed, a short, sad laugh, and poked him. "No, no, no, I don't see him floating around my room, I see him in my mind. . . ."

"Whew."

"But the thing is, it's so clear. Walt running down the street, and his hair plastered down and his ears sticking out . . . Jesus Christ. Walt was the only guy who ever loved me and didn't want anything from me. No sex, no kids, no favors, just me being there and he was happy."

Kennett found nothing to say, and they sat there, their feet up, watching the dark river. After a while, Lily began to cry again.

L UCAS CALLED FELL FROM LILY'S, apologizing for the late hour.
"I was going down to the tavern," she said. "Why don't you meet
me...."

He flagged a cab, Lily watching from her window, smiling down at him. He
waved, and she lifted her purse in her left hand, slipped her right inside the gun
tote. *Remember the last time?*

At the tavern, Lucas pulled a twenty out of his Muskies Inc. money clip and
tipped the driver two dollars for the eight-dollar ride. Fell was in the back booth,
a beer on the table with a bowl of peanuts. She was reading a free newspaper.

"Hey," he said, slipping into the booth.

"Hi. Any developments at Rothenburg's?"

"No . . ."

"Good," she said.

Lucas shook his head. "Jesus." And then: "I gotta get a beer." He waved at a
waitress, pointed at Fell's glass and gave her a victory/two sign. While they
waited, a swarthy man in a light-blue sport coat and khaki slacks, a glass of dark
beer in his hand, wandered up to the table and said to Fell in a bad imitation
Bogart, "Howdy, shweet-heart. Sheen your name in the public prints."

"Hey, Tommy. Sit down." Fell patted the seat beside her, then pointed her
trigger finger at Lucas. "That's Lucas Davenport, who's a cop."

"I know who he is," Kantor said, dropping into the booth. "But somehow
I got left off the invitation list for the Welcome to New York interviews."

"And Lucas," Fell continued, "this is Tommy Kantor, who's a columnist for
the *Village Voice*. . . ."

They talked about the case for a while, and Kantor attracted the attention
of a free-lance magazine writer and his girlfriend. They pulled up a chair and ordered a pitcher of beer. Then a TV producer stopped by and began talking to Fell.

"You'd make a good piece," she told Fell.

"I'd certainly agree with that," Lucas said, straight-faced.

"Fuckin' Davenport . . ." Fell said.

They got back to Fell's apartment at two o'clock, spent ten soapy minutes
in the shower, dropped into her bed.

"That was fun, talking to those people," Lucas said. "As long as your friend
Kantor doesn't get us in trouble."

"He takes care of sources," Fell said. "It'll be okay. I'm surprised you get along so well with media people. . . ."

"I like them, mostly," he said. "Some are a little stupid and half of them would kill for two dollars, but the good ones I like."

"You like *this?*" she asked.

"Ooo, I think I do," he said. Then: "I'm sure of it."

HE CAME OUT OF the shower the next morning, rubbing his hair dry with a terry-cloth towel, and heard Fell's voice from the living room. She came down the hall to the bedroom as he was pulling on his underwear. She was still naked and stood on her tiptoes to kiss him.

"I just talked to Carter. Not a thing, nada."

"All right. Did you bring those files?"

"In the front room, on the floor," she said.

"I'd like to sit around and read for a while, then maybe go back and change clothes. I don't know, I'd like to be there when they get him. . . ."

"Bullshit. You'd give your left nut to get him yourself. So would I."

"You'd give my left nut?" he asked, appalled.

"Well . . . you want a bagel with chive cream cheese and some juice?"

"Yeah, as a matter of fact."

They read the files and talked, and sometime after one o'clock Lucas chased her back into the bedroom, and they didn't make it back out until two.

"I'm going back to the hotel to change," he said, pulling on his jacket. "Why don't we get together at Midtown. Like four-thirty, for the daily roundup."

"All right . . ."

He looked at the floor by his feet, at a Xerox copy of the crime-scene photograph of Whitechurch, dead in the hospital. The few pitiful twenties stuck out from under his body like a comment on greed.

"Change oxen in midstream and you'll come to a bad end," he said.

"What?"

"An old English proverb my mom used to tell me," Lucas said.

"Bullshit," she said.

"You're calling my mom a liar?"

"Get out of here, Davenport. See you at four-thirty."

He took the elevator to the lobby, nodded at a guard who knew a one-night stand when he saw one, spotted a cab pulling up to the curb to drop a passenger, stopped and slapped his coat pocket where his wallet was.

"Dammit," he said.

"Huh?" The guard looked up from his desk.

"Sorry. Not you . . . I forgot something upstairs."

He went back up, knocked on the door. Fell, wrapped in a robe, let him in. "You got twenty bucks you can loan me?" he asked. "I got like two dollars left after last night. All the traveler's checks are at the hotel."

"Oh, jeez . . ." She went to her purse, opened it, took out a billfold. "I've got six bucks," she announced. Then she brightened and dug further. "And a cash card. There's a machine down the block. I'll trust you with my code and change it when you skip on me."

He looked at the cash card, looked down past it to the floor, at the Xerox of Whitechurch, the twenties under his body. The money, the money. Bekker.

"Get dressed," Lucas snapped. "Hurry the fuck up."

THREE TWENTY-DOLLAR BILLS had been found around and under Whitechurch's body. They drew the money from the evidence locker, under the watchful eye of the custodian.

"Consecutive?" Fell whispered. She was excited, barely controlled.

Lucas scanned the numbers, rearranged the bills on the countertop. "Two of them," he said. He took the numbers down on a notepad. "Let's go talk to the feds."

TERRELL SCOPES OF THE Federal Reserve had a procedure for everything, including the dispensing of information about serial numbers. "I can't just have people come in here . . ." He waved, a wave that seemed to suggest that they didn't quite meet a standard. Lucas was rumpled. Fell's hair was beginning to go haywire, standing around her head in a halo.

"If we take several hours to get the data and Bekker cuts the heart out of somebody, your picture'll be on the front page of the *New York Times* right along with his," Fell snarled, leaning across his desk.

Scopes, naturally pale, went a shade paler. "Just a minute," he said. "I'll have to make some inquiries."

After a while he came back and said, "Citibank . . ."

CITIBANK WAS MORE cooperative, but the process was a long one. "The money came out of a machine on Prince, all right, but exactly when, or where it went, that'll take a while to figure out," said a round-faced banker named Alice Buonocare.

"We need it in a hurry," said Lucas.

"We're running it as fast as we can," Buonocare said cheerfully. "There's a lot of subtraction to do—we have to go back to a known number and then start working through the returns, and there's a lot of stuff we have to do by hand. We're not set up for this kind of sorting . . . and there are something like twenty thousand items. . . ."

"How about the pictures?"

"They're not really very good," Buonocare confessed. "If all you know is that he's got blond hair, there are probably a thousand blondes on the tape. . . . It'd be easier to do the numbers, then confirm with the pictures."

"All right," Lucas said. "How long?"

"I don't know: an hour, or maybe two. Of course, that's almost quitting time."

"Hey . . ." Lucas, ready to get angry.

"Just kidding," Buonocare said, winking at Fell.

Three hours. A mistake was found halfway through the first run, a question of which numbers went where, and another machine on Houston Street.

"All right," one of the computer operators said at six o'clock. "Give us another twenty minutes and we'll have it down to one person. If you want to look right now, I can give you a group of eight or ten and it's ninety percent that he's in that group."

"How about the photos?"

"We'll get the tape up now."

"Let's see the ten accounts," Buonocare said.

The programmer's fingers danced across the keyboard and an account came up on the green screen. Then another, and another and more. Ten altogether, six men, four women. Two accounts, one man, one woman, showed non-Manhattan addresses, and they eliminated them.

"Can we get account activity on the other eight? For the last two months?" Buonocare asked over the shoulder of the computer operator.

"No problemo," he said. He rattled through some keys, and the first account came up.

"Looks routine . . ." Buonocare said after a minute. "Get the next one."

"Better find it in a hurry," Fell said. "I'm about to pee my pants."

Edith Lacey's account was the fifth one they looked at. "Oh-oh," Buonocare said. To the computer operator: "Get the rest of this up, go back as far as you can."

"No problemo . . ."

When the full account came up, Buonocare reached past the computer operator and pressed a series of keys, then paged down through an extensive account listing. After a moment, she ran it back to the top and turned to Lucas and Fell.

"Look at this: she started with a balance of $100,000 six weeks ago, and then started pulling out the max on her bankcard, five hundred a day, just about every day for a while. Even now, it's three or four times a week."

"That could be him," Lucas said, nodding, excited. "Let's get a picture up. You've got a name and address?"

"Edith Lacey . . ."

"In SoHo. That's good, that's right," Fell said, tapping the screen.

"How about the video . . . ?"

"Let's get the reference numbers on those withdrawals . . ." Buonocare said. She wrote the number on a scratch pad and they carried it to the storage. The right cassette was already in the machine, and Buonocare ran it through, looking at the numbers. . . .

"Here," she said.

The screen showed a blonde, her face down.

"Can't tell," Fell said. "I swear to God, I'm gonna pee my pants."

"Let's try another withdrawal in that sequence," Buonocare said.

She ran the tape, stopped, started, searched. Found another blonde.

"Motherfucker," Lucas said, looking at the screen. "Nice to see you again, Mike."

"That's him?" Fell asked, peering at the screen. "He's so pretty."

"That's him," Lucas said.

Bekker was smiling at the lens, his blond hair pulled demurely away from his forehead.

BEKKER AWOKE AT NOON. He wandered about the apartment, went to the bathroom, and stared at himself. Pretty. Pretty blonde. Too late for pretty blonde.

He cried, sitting on the edge of the tub, but he had to do it. He shaved his head. Hacked his fine silken hair to stubble with a pair of orange-handled scissors from Mrs. Lacey's sewing box, lathered it with shampoo, scraped off the stubble with a safety razor. Cut himself twice, the blood pink in the lather . . .

Sigh.

He found himself in front of the mirror, dried soap around his ears, hair. Gone. The tears came again, in a rush. His head was far too small, and sickly white, like a marble. Where was Beauty?

He examined himself with the eye of an overseer, the Simon Legree of inspections. Bald. Pale. No good. Even in the Village, the scalp pallor would attract the eye, and the facial makeup would be obvious.

The scars—the scars would give him away. He touched his face, felt the furrowed, marbled flesh. A new role, that's what he needed. He'd thought to cut his hair, shift back to a male role, but that wouldn't work. Besides, women were allowed a greater latitude of disguise. He'd go back to the wigs he'd worn before his own hair grew out.

Bekker strode through the apartment, headed for the stairs, stopped to touch the cloud of spiders that hung over his desk in the outer apartment. So fine, so pretty . . .

Go. Get the wig, get dressed—he hadn't bothered to dress. Clothes seemed inconvenient and restrictive. He marched now, directed by the PCP, upright and dignified, then he was suddenly aware of his penis, bobbling along like an inconveniently large and flaccid nose, doing a color commentary on his dignity. Bekker pressed his penis to his thigh, but the rhythm of the march was broken. . . .

A new gumball dropped. From when? The fifties? A comedian on *The Ed*

Sullivan Show? Yes. A small man looking into a cigar box, talking to a voice inside . . . *Okay? Okay.* Was that the line? Yes.

Bekker, passing the kitchen, swerved, went in. Opened the refrigerator and peeked inside: Have a Coke, Mr. Bekker. Thank you. I will. *Okay? Okay.* He slammed the refrigerator door like the comedian and howled with laughter. *Okay? Okay.*

Really funny . . . He howled. . . .

Coke in hand, he staggered back to the television, turned to CNN, and watched for a few minutes. He'd been on one of the news shows in the morning, with the pictures of the Carson woman; they'd ridiculed him, said the halos from Carson had been finger-press points on the photo paper. What did that mean? Was that methodology? He had a hard time remembering anymore. . . .

He watched, hoping to see the report again, but they'd cut him out of the news cycle.

He went downstairs, naked and barefoot, stepped carefully through the shambles of the first-floor shop, and down into the basement. Found the dark wig, with the pixie cut. Carried it back up, to the bathroom, put it on. It was warm on his head, like a fur piece, and scratchy. But it looked good. He'd have to do something about his eyebrows, shade them, and his lashes. Maybe something to tone his face . . .

Mrs. Lacey had been too old for sophisticated makeup, had been satisfied with a pinkish mascara to make two little pink spots on her cheeks, like Ronald Reagan's. But she had an eyebrow pencil. He found the pencil, came back to the mirror, wet it with his tongue and began feathering it through the lashes. A new face began to form in the mirror. . . .

He ventured out at five-thirty, tentative, wary, the day still bright, and turned toward Washington Square. He was unused to the sunlight, and squinted against it, his speed-hyped vision dazzled by the color and intensity. He carried his handbag and an old newsprint drawing pad he had found in one of Mrs. Lacey's cupboards.

Not much foot traffic, not north and south. He stayed on the shadier side of the narrower streets, head down. Dark hair, dark eyebrows, dark blouse, jeans, gym shoes. A little dykey. A little too tough for a woman. An attitude.

During his early reconnaissance of the city, he'd seen some action around the square. Dealers drifting through. Baggies and cash. He felt the plastic box in his jeans pocket, the tabs rattling inside. Six left, six between himself and . . . He couldn't think about it. He had five thousand in cash in his purse, and the pistol, just in case.

He needed some luck.

OLIVEO DIAZ HAD TEN hits of ex and another ten of speed, and maybe a couple of hours to sell it. Party that night; he could use the cash to pick up some coke for himself. Coke was a mellower high than the speed. With enough speed, Oliveo felt that he could go anywhere. With cocaine, he'd already arrived.

Oliveo crossed the south side of the square, saw Bekker sitting on a concrete retaining wall, sketching. Looked nice, from a distance, with the inky black hair, like maybe a PR. Closer, and he thought, maybe Irish, black Irish with the pale skin.

Bekker paid no attention to him, his face down in the sketch pad, a pencil busy in his hand. But watching . . .

"Hey, Oliveo, doood . . ."

Oliveo turned, flashed the automatic smile. Some guy named Shell. Young white guy with a battered forehead, hazy blue eyes and a Mets hat with the bill turned backward. Oliveo had a theory that a guy's intelligence could be determined by how far around his head the bill was turned. Backward was a complete fool, unless he was a baseball catcher. Shell's hat was backward, and he said again, "Hey, doood," and he lifted a hand for a cool five.

"Shell, my man, what's happenin' . . . ?" Oliveo said. Shell worked in a tire-recap place, had cash sometimes.

"You servin'?" A quick look left and right.

"Man, what you need?" The smile clickin' on again. Oliveo thought of himself as a pro, a street Mick Jagger, smile every ten seconds, part of the act.

"Gotta get up, man . . ."

"I got ten hits of really smooth shit straight from Miami, man. . . ."

BEKKER SAT ON THE WALL and drew the fire hydrant; drew it well, he thought. He'd learned drawing techniques in medical school, found them useful as a pathologist. They made structure clear, simple. He struggled to keep the drawing going as he watched Oliveo chatting with the white kid, watched them circle each other, checking for cops, and finally a flash of plastic.

Bekker looked around. There *were* cops in the square, but on the other side, near the arch. Three blue Plymouths parked side by side, the cops sitting on the hoods or leaning on the fenders, talking. Bekker picked up his purse and, as the white guy peeled away from Oliveo, sauntered over.

"Servin'?" he squeaked.

Oliveo jumped. The woman with the art pad, her head down. He couldn't see her face very well, but he knew he'd never dealt to her. She was wrong, something wrong. A cop?

"Get the fuck off me, man," he said.

"I've got a lot of cash," Bekker said, still squeaking. He sounded like a mouse in his own ears. "And I'm desperate. I'm not a cop. . . ."

The word "cash" stopped Oliveo. He *knew* he should walk away. He knew it, had told himself, don't sell to no strangers. But he said, "How much?"

"A lot. I'm looking for speed or angels or both. . . ."

"Fuckin' cop . . ."

"Not a cop . . ." Bekker glanced up the street, over at the cop cars, then put his hand in the bag and lifted out an envelope full of cash. "I can pay. Right here."

Oliveo looked around, licked his lips, then said, "What you look like, mama?" He reached out, grabbed Bekker under the chin and tried to lift his face. Bekker grabbed his arm at the wrist and twisted. There was muscle there, testosterone muscle. As he pushed Oliveo away, his head came up, his teeth bared, eyes wide.

"Motherfucker . . ." Oliveo said, backing away, sputtering. "You're that dude."

Bekker turned away, started across the street, half running, mind twisting, searching for help, for an answer, for anything.

Behind him, Oliveo had turned toward the cop cars across the square. "Hey," he screamed. He looked from the cops to Bekker, then at the cops again, then dashed toward them, yelling, waving his arms. "Hey, hey, that's him, that's him. . . ."

Bekker ran. He could run in the gym shoes, but there were a lot of cops, and if they came quickly enough, and if they asked about a woman running . . .

A bum stood at the mouth of an alley, picking through a garbage can. He wore a crumbled hat and a stained army coat, ankle length.

A half-brick sat on the sidewalk, a remnant of concrete lapped over it like frosting on a piece of carrot cake.

It was a narrow street, the closest people a block away, not looking.

Bekker snatched the brick off the street, still running. The bum looked up, straightened, leaned away, astonished when Bekker hit him squarely in the chest. The bum pitched over the garbage can and went down into the alley, on his back. "Hey," he groaned.

Bekker hit him between the eyes with the brick, then hit him again. Hovered over him, growling like a pit bull, feeling his blood rising . . .

A siren, and another.

He stripped the hat and trench coat from the bum, pulled the trench coat over the purse, stripped off the wig, pulled the hat down low on his head. The bum blew a bubble of blood. Still alive. Bekker lurched back to the mouth of the alley, trying on the new persona, the mask of beggary. . . .

Behind him, a gargling sound. He half turned; the bum was looking at him, one good eye peering brightly out of a ruined face. The bum was dying. Bekker recognized the gargle. Something cold, distant and academic spoke into his mind: cerebral hemorrhage, massive parietal fracture. And that eye, looking at him. The bum would die, and then he'd be back, watching. . . . Bekker looked both ways, then hurried back to the bum. Pocketknife out, quick jabs; eyes gone. The bum moaned, but he was going anyway.

The brick was by the bum's head, and Bekker picked it up and jammed it in his pocket. Good weapon. A gun was too noisy. But he groped for the gun inside the bag and transferred it to the pocket.

Into the street. Six blocks. He saw a cop car go by, screech to a stop at the intersection, the cops looking both ways out the windows, then go on. The coat stunk: dried urine. The smell clogged his throat, and he imagined fleas crawling onto him. More sirens, cops flooding the neighborhood. Bekker hurried . . .

Turned onto Greene, tottering, a drunk, his shabby coat dragging on the pavement. A woman coming. Closer, same side. Bekker changed to the other side of the street. His vision wavered, changed tenses: Approaching Lacey building. Sirens in the distance, but fading. Woman goes to Lacey building door . . .

What . . .

The panic gripped him for a moment. Confused. What did she want? Blank-faced buildings looking down. Gumball drops. Red one, loading anger. They would do this to him, a man of talent. The woman was half turned toward him, head cocked.

A distant voice, in the back of his head: Bridget. Bridget Land. Come to visit . . .

He straightened, walked back across the street, away from her, and she put a key in the front-door lock and turned it, pushing the door open. Bridget Land, he'd forgotten about her. . . . She must not know.

She pushed the door open, her shoulders rounded, aged, straining with the effort, then stepped up and inside. Bekker, caught by anger and opportunity, began moving. There was no space or time, it seemed, and he hit the door, smashed inside, and hit her.

He was fast, angel-dust fast, quicker than a linebacker, smacking her with the brick full in the face. She went down with a strange, harsh croak, like a wing-shot raven.

Bekker, indiscreet, beyond caring, slammed the door, grabbed her by the hair and dragged her to the stairs, and down.

He forgot the bum's clothes, and paid no attention to the woman, yipping like a chihuahua with a bone in its throat. He dragged her to the room, strapped her down. Her legs started to work now, twitching. He wired the silencer into her mouth, working like a dervish, hovering. . . .

B UONOCARE, THE BANKER, ran the photo tape through two more withdrawals. Bekker posed in all three, a startling feminine beauty coming through despite the rough quality of the tape.

"Jesus, I wish I looked that good," Buonocare said. "I wonder who does his hair."

"Gotta call Kennett," Fell said, reaching across the desk to pick up a phone.

"No." Lucas looked into her eyes, shook his head. "No."

"We've gotta . . ."

"Talk to me outside," Lucas said, voice low.

"What?"

"Outside." Lucas looked at Buonocare and said, "There's a security thing here, I'm sorry I can't tell you. . . ."

Fell got her purse, Lucas his coat, and they half ran to the door. "Will I see it on the news?" Buonocare asked as she escorted them past a security guard to the front door.

"You'll probably be *on* the news, if this is him," Fell said as the guard let them out.

"Good luck, then. And see you on TV," Buonocare said. "I wish I could come . . ."

Outside, it had begun to rain, a warm, nasty mist. Lucas waved at a taxi, but it rolled by. Another ignored him.

Fell grabbed his elbow and said urgently, "What're you doing, Lucas? We've gotta call now. . . ."

"No."

"Look: I want to be there too, but we don't have time. With this traffic . . ."

"What? Fifteen minutes? Fuck it, I want him," Lucas said.

"Lucas . . ." she wailed.

A cab pulled to the curb and Lucas hurried over, three seconds ahead of a woman who sprinted from a door farther up the street. He hopped in, leaving the door open. Fell was behind him, still in the street. "Get in."

"We gotta call . . ."

"There's more going on here than you know about," Lucas said. "I'm *not* Internal Affairs, but there's more going on."

Fell looked at him for a long beat, then said, "I knew it," and climbed in the cab. As the cab pulled away, the woman who'd run for it, back in the doorway, gave them the finger.

They inched silently uptown through the nightmare traffic, the rain growing heavier. Fell was tight-lipped, agitated. The cab dropped them on Houston, Lucas paid. A squad car rolled by, the cops looking carefully at Lucas before going on. They dodged into a convenience store, damp from the misty summer rain.

"All right," said Fell, fists on her hips. "Let's have it."

"I don't know what's going to happen, but it could be weird," he said. "I'm trying to catch Robin Hood. That's why they brought me here, from Minneapolis."

Her mouth dropped open. "Are you nuts?"

"No. You can either come along or you can take a hike, but I don't want you fuckin' this up," Lucas said.

"Well, I'll come," she said. "But Robin Hood? Tell me."

"Some other time. I gotta make a call of my own. . . ."

Lily was with O'Dell, just coming off the Brooklyn Bridge into Manhattan, ten minutes from Police Plaza.

"Have you heard?" she asked.

"What?"

"Bekker was spotted at Washington Square, but took off. This was around three o'clock. We've got people all over the place, but nothing since. . . ."

"That sounds right, because I think we know where he is. Fell and me. And it's up in SoHo."

"What?" And he heard her say, "Lucas says he's got Bekker."

O'Dell's voice replaced Lily's. "Where are you?"

"We're at Citibank and we're stuck here. I think Bekker's holed up with an old lady in SoHo, but I'm not sure. I'm going up there to take a quick informal look around before I call in the troops. I just wanted Lily to know, in case something misfires. . . ."

"Besides, if you called now and you're stuck downtown, Kennett would get all the credit for the bust," O'Dell said with his wet chuckle. "Is there any possibility that what you've done, whatever it is, has tipped off Bekker?"

"No. But it'll take us a while to get up there; it's raining here, and cabs are impossible."

"Yeah, it's raining here, too. . . . Okay, go ahead. But take care. Just in case there's a problem, why don't you give me the address, and I'll get Lily to start a search warrant. That'll help explain the delay, why you didn't call it in."

"All right . . ." Lucas gave him the address, and Lily came on the line. "Careful," she said. "After your . . . look around . . . give us a ring. We'll have the backup waiting."

Lucas hung up, and Fell asked, "All right—what's going on?"

"We're gonna surveil for a while. . . ."

"Surveil what?" Another cop car rolled by, and again they got the look.

"This Lacey woman's building, for a start. Bekker knows me, I don't want to go right up front . . ."

"I know where we can get a hat," Fell said. "And it's on the way. . . ."

THEY DODGED FROM doorway to canopy, staying out of the rain as much as they could. Fell finally led Lucas into a clothing store that apparently hadn't changed either stock or customers since '69. Every male customer other than Lucas was bearded, and three of the four women customers wore tie-dye. Lucas bought an ill-fitting leather porkpie hat. In the mirror, he looked like a hippie designer's idea of an Amazon explorer.

"Quit grumbling, you'd look cute in the right light," Fell said, hurrying him along.

"I look like an asshole," Lucas said. "In any light."

"What can I tell you?" she said. "You ain't posing for *Esquire.*"

The rain had slowed further, but the streets were wet and slick, stinking of two centuries of grime emulsified by the quick shower. They found Lacey's building, cruised it front and back. The back wall was windowless brick. A weathered shed, or lean-to, folded against the lower wall. The gate in the chain-link fence had been recently opened, and car tracks cut through the low spotty weeds to the shed.

Lucas walked to the edge of the lot, where he had the sharpest angle on the shed. "Look at this," he said.

Fell peered through the fence. The back end of a rounded chrome bumper was just visible inside the shed. "Sonofabitch, it's a Bug," she breathed. She grabbed his arm. "Lucas, we gotta call."

"Lily and O'Dell are taking care of it," he said.

"I mean Kennett. He's our supervisor. Christ, we're cutting out the boss. . . ."

"Soon," Lucas promised. "I want to sit and watch for a few more minutes."

They walked around front, and Lucas picked out a store a hundred feet up the street from Lacey's, on the opposite side, an African rug-and-artifact gallery. The owner was a deep-breasted Lebanese woman in a black turtlenecked silk dress. She nodded, nervous, and said, "Of course," when they showed their badges. She brought chairs and they sat at an angle to the window, among draperies and wicker bookcases, watching the street.

"What if he goes out the back?" asked Fell.

"He won't. There're cops all over the place. He's holed up."

"Then what are we waiting for?"

"For some guys. Robin Hood and his merry men. If nothing happens in a half-hour, we go in. . . ."

"Would you like some cookies?" the Lebanese store owner asked, a touch of anxiety in her voice. She was twisting her hands, and looked, Lucas thought, remarkably like the wicked-witch stepmother in *Snow White*, if he had his Disney movies right. "Baklava, maybe . . . ?"

"No, thanks, really," Lucas said. "We're fine. We might want to use your phone."

"Yes, surely . . ." The woman gestured at a black telephone next to the cash register and retired to the rear of the shop, where she perched on a high stool and continued to rub her hands.

"Eat her goddamn baklava and your nuts'd probably wind up sealed in a bottle with a genie," Lucas muttered.

Fell glanced back and said, "Shh," but smiled and shook her head. "Fuckin' midwestern white guys, it must be something out there, wall-to-wall Wasps. . . ."

"Look," Lucas said.

Two men in sport coats and slacks were walking up the street, not looking at Lacey's building. One was beefy, the other rail-thin. Their sport coats were too heavy for a New York summer, the kind of coat called "year-round" by the department stores, too hot in summer, not warm enough in winter. The beefy one walked stiffly, as though something were wrong with his back; the thin one showed a cast on his left arm.

"Cops," Fell said. She stood up. "They look like cops."

"The sonofabitch with the cast is the guy who whacked me, I think," Lucas said. Fell took a step toward the door, but Lucas caught her by the arm and said, "Wait, wait, wait . . ." and backed toward the counter and picked up the phone, still watching the two cops. They passed Lacey's building, strolling, talking too animatedly, phony, walked on until they were in front of the next building, then stopped.

Lucas punched Lily's office number into the telephone. She picked it up on the second ring. "I'm at Lacey's place. . . ."

"How'd you get . . . ?"

"I lied. And the Robin Hoods just walked in, we're watching them across the street. So it's O'Dell. . . ."

"Can't be. He hasn't touched a phone."

"What?"

"I'm with him now. In his office."

"Shit . . ."

Across the street, the Robin Hoods had turned and had started back toward Lacey's. One drew a pistol while the other dropped a long-handled sledge from beneath his jacket.

"Get me backup . . ." Lucas said. "Jesus—they're going in. Get me backup *now*."

Lucas dropped the phone back on the hook. "Let's go," he said. "Get on my arm, really drag on it, like we had a few too many."

They went out the door and Lucas, hat tipped down, wrapped an arm around Fell's shoulder and put his face close to hers. The two cops paused just before they passed the windows in front of Lacey's, looked around one more time, saw Lucas and Fell fifty feet away. Lucas pushed Fell into a building front with one hip, groped at a breast with his free hand. She pushed him away, and the two cops went to the door.

They were running now.

The cop with the hammer stopped, pivoted, swinging his hip like a golfer. Backswing and drive, the hammer flashing overhead.

The hammerhead hit the door just at the handle and it exploded inward, glass breaking, wood splintering.

The cop with the gun and the cast went through; the other dropped the hammer and drew his pistol. Then he went in, crouched, focused, straight ahead.

"Go," said Lucas. His .45 was in his hand, and he was at the door in three seconds. Through the door. The two cops were inside, their pistols pointing up an open stairway, and Lucas dropped in the doorway, screaming, "Police, freeze."

"We're cops, we're cops. . . ." The cop nearest Lucas kept his gun pointed at the stairs.

"Drop the piece, drop, drop it, God damn it, or I'll blow your fuckin' ass off, drop it. . . ."

"We're cops, you asshole. . . ." The heavyset cop was half turned toward him, his gun still pointed up the stairs. The pistol was black with a smooth, plastic look about it, a high-capacity Glock 9mm. This guy wasn't using the issue crap from the department.

"Drop it . . ."

Fell came in behind, her gun out, searching for a target, Lucas feeling the black barrel of the cut-off Colt .38 next to his ear.

"Drop it," Lucas screamed again.

The slat-thin cop, who was closest to the door, dropped his weapon, and Lucas focused on the other, who was still looking uncertainly up the stairs. The disarmed cop said, "Jesus, you asshole, we're plainclothes for Bekker. . . ."

Lucas ignored him, focused on the other gun: "Said drop the fuckin' weapon, jerkweed; you assholes beat the shit out of me, and I'm not in the mood to argue. I'll fuckin' pull the trigger on you right now. . . ."

The cop stooped and laid his gun on the floor, glanced at his partner. "Listen . . ."

"Shut up." Lucas looked at Fell. "Keep your gun up, Bekker's here somewhere."

"Lucas, Jesus . . ." Fell said, but she kept the gun up.

Lucas motioned the two cops to a steam radiator, tossed them a set of handcuffs. "I want to hear them click," he said.

"You motherfucker, I oughta fuckin' pull your face off," the heavy one said.

"I'd kill you if you tried," Lucas said simply. "Cuffs."

"Motherfucker . . ." But the two cuffed themselves to the radiator pipe. Lucas looked up the stairs.

"Now what?" asked Fell.

"Backup's on the way, should be here." He kept the .45 pointed at the chained cops.

"You're fuckin' up," said the thick cop.

"Tell that to O'Dell," Lucas said.

"What?" the cop said. He frowned, puzzled.

Lucas shifted around behind him, his .45 pointed at the guy's ear. "I'm going for your ID, don't fuckin' move. . . ." He slipped his hand inside the cop's coat pocket and came out with a badge case. "Now you," he said to the other one.

When he had both IDs, he stepped back and flipped them open. "Clemson," he said. "A sergeant, and Jeese . . ." Lucas looked at the man with the cast, Clemson, and said, "That's what you yelled—you yelled 'Jeese.' You thought he left you behind, running off like that. I thought you yelled 'Jesus'. . ."

"Here comes the cavalry," Fell said. A blue Plymouth jerked to a stop at the door, and they heard screeching tires from up the block. A uniform came through the door, his gun out.

"Davenport and Fell," Lucas said to them, holding up his badge case. "Working for Kennett with the Bekker team. These guys are cops too, but they're cuffed for a good reason. I want them left like that, okay?"

"What's going on?" the uniform asked. He was a sergeant, older, a little too heavy, uneasy about what he'd walked into. Another car screeched to a stop outside.

"Politics," Lucas said. "Somebody's got their tit in a wringer and the top guys are going to have to sort it out later. But these guys will shoot you if they have a chance. They already shot one cop . . ."

"Bullshit, motherfucker," said one of the cuffed cops.

". . . So stay cool. Their weapons are on the floor, but I haven't checked them for backup pieces, which they've probably got."

"I don't know . . ."

Two more uniforms squeezed in, their pistols in their hands.

"Look, half the goddamn department will be here in five minutes," Lucas said. "If we're fucked up, we can always apologize to each other later. For now, just freeze the place."

"What about you guys . . . ?" the uniform asked.

"We're going upstairs. You stay here, don't let anybody or anything in or out. Just freeze the scene and be careful. Bekker might be down below, for all we know, and he's armed."

"This is Bekker?"

"This is Bekker," Lucas confirmed. To Fell, he said, "Come on. Let's get him."

LILY CALLED THE PATROL LIEUTENANT at the Fifth Precinct and or-dered backup squads to Lacey's building: "It's Bekker," she said. "Get them there *now*."

She dropped the phone back on its cradle and sat down, heavily, in O'Dell's visitor's chair, sorting it out.

They were in the car . . .

O'Dell peered at her across his expansive desk. "What was that all about?" he asked. "The call from Davenport? I believe I was mentioned." His voice was ugly, peremptory. Cold.

Lily shook her head.

"I want to know what he said, Lieutenant," O'Dell barked.

"Shut up, I'm thinking," she said.

O'Dell's eyes narrowed and he sat back. He'd been a politician for five decades, and he instinctively reacted to the warning tone in her voice. Balances had changed somewhere, and he didn't know exactly where. He tried a probe.

"I won't be maneuvered, Lieutenant," he said, emphasizing the rank. "Per-haps a precinct-level job would be more your style after all."

Lily had been peering at the wall above his head, her lips moving slightly. Now she dropped her eyes to his face: "You should have wiped out the ticket requisition for Red Reed before you sent him to South Carolina, John. I've got the ticket vouchers with your signature, I've got the reports on his alleged state-ments, I've even got the Columbia University transcripts showing that he took classes you lectured at. I also know you fixed at least one drug arrest for him. So don't give me any shit about precinct-level jobs, okay?"

O'Dell nodded and settled in his chair. This could be handled. Everything can be handled by he who waits. He sat silently as she stared at the wall above his head. Finally, a tear trickled down her cheek and she said, "I need your help with the computer."

"What about the Red Reed stuff?" O'Dell asked.

"I'm not going to *use* it, for Christ's sakes. I mean, I can't conceive of any circumstances that I'd use it. It was just something . . . I found out."

O'Dell grinned in spite of himself. This could be handled, all right. The question now was, who would do the handling? "Davenport," he said. "You *told* me not to underestimate him. But he looks like a fuckin' brawler with that scar on his face, and what he did to Bekker . . ."

"Two Robin Hoods just showed up at Bekker's hideout. Lucas is going to take them."

"What?" Now O'Dell was confused.

"The computer?"

"Tell me what's going on. . . ."

"I want you to run Copland against Kennett."

O'Dell stared, his thick lips going in and out as he did the calculations, a nursing motion, wet and unpleasant. "Oh, no," he said. He turned, pulled himself across to the computer terminal, flicked a switch, waited until the computer booted up, entered a user name and password, and began the process.

The matching run took ten minutes. A double column of dates and times marched down the screen.

"All so many years ago," O'Dell said tonelessly, reading down the list. "They must've been like father and son. Copland broke him in on the beat. Copland was a tough old bird. He busted more than a few heads in his day."

"Kennett planted him on you. How long ago?"

O'Dell shrugged. "Five years now. He's been driving me for five years. He must have a microphone arrangement in the car, or a bug—or maybe he just pulled out some sound insulation, so he could hear us talk. Every damn thing we said." He looked at Lily. "How?"

"Lucas looked at everything, figured that Robin Hood was either you or Kennett. . . . He trusted my judgment that it wasn't Kennett. At least, he said he trusted my judgment. And he likes Kennett."

"I'm mildly flattered that he thought I could do it," O'Dell said. "So you and Davenport set me up?"

"He suggested that I cover your phones, then plant some information with you and see what happened. Watch where it went. We hadn't agreed on exactly what to do, we were going to talk about it tonight. Then this came up. When he called us with the Bekker thing, he wasn't at Citibank. He was already watching Bekker's place. He expected you to call somebody and maybe send somebody down, some Robin Hoods. And some showed up. But I've been with you. . . ."

O'Dell said, "Now what?"

The tears had started down her face again, but she seemed unaware of them. "What do you mean?"

He made a questioning gesture with his hands, palms up. At the same time, an oddly satisfied expression had settled on his face. "You seem to be running things for the time being. So what do we do?"

She looked at him for a moment, then said, "Call Carter, with Kennett's group."

"Yeah?"

"Tell him what's happening with Bekker, but tell him to cut Kennett out of the loop."

"What about you?"

"Don't ask," she said. She stood and wobbled toward the door of her own office. "Don't fuckin' ask, 'cause I don't know."

29

BEKKER CROUCHED OVER Bridget Land, his scalpel in hand, frozen, humming. . . .

When the front door came down, he snapped back, looked down at himself, as though to make sure he was still there, and then at the woman on the table, the scalpel, the monitoring equipment. He heard the footsteps, then the shouts.

Too soon, they'd come too soon, when he was so close.

A tear ran down his cheek. His life had been like this, misunderstood, tormented, unappreciated. Bridget Land, still alive, but hurt, strained away from him, silently. . . .

To do one more would only take minutes, he thought. If he could hold himself together, if they didn't come down too soon.

But Davenport was coming. The gun. He turned, the scalpel in front of his face. The gun was in the other room.

Two impulses fought for control. One propelled him toward the gun, for Davenport; the other told him to finish with Land. Maybe Land would be the transcendent one. . . .

"DON'T SHOOT ME in the ass," Lucas said.

He edged up the stairs, Fell two steps behind. Her face was pale, determined, her pistol at Lucas' waist and to the left.

"Just don't roll left," she said.

"Uh-uh . . ."

The smell of marijuana was steeping from the walls, and something else. Lucas sniffed, frowned. Cat urine? And the marijuana odor was years old, not Bekker. In any case, Bekker wasn't much interested in the weed.

At the corner, the first landing, Lucas could see the second-floor door standing partly open, hear Fell breathing below and beside him, smell her faint scent under the odors of the grass and cat piss. . . .

He moved up slowly, across a landing, back against the wall. With the tip of his .45, he pushed the door open. A hall led away, past a closet door, into a living room; he could see the left edge of a television screen. There was no movement, no sound. And the room lacked the peculiar spatial tension of a person in hiding. It *felt* clear.

"Going in," he whispered.

He stepped past the open doorway to another flight of stairs, the second flight stacked with cardboard cartons, the cartons grimy with years of dust and flaking paint.

"Move," he whispered to Fell. She nodded and eased past him, leveled her gun through the door.

"Go," she whispered back. Lucas crouched, took a breath, then scuttled through the open door on his hands and knees, one hand pushing, his gun extended toward the living room arch, searching for movement, for an anomaly. . . . Nothing.

He stood, held up a hand cautioning her, did a quick head-juke to scan the living room again, then went in. When he was sure it was clear, he waved her in. They checked a sitting room and a dining room; found a pair of glasses lying beside the couch, thick lenses, bifocals. Old-lady glasses. Checked the closets, groped through them. Nothing.

The kitchen was small, smelled of boiled beets, boiled cabbage, boiled carrots, porridge. A pool of water shimmered below the refrigerator. Fell squatted next to it, then looked up at the refrigerator. The main door wasn't quite closed, and water dripped from the bottom of it. She pointed, then put her finger to her lips.

Lucas, standing beside her, reached out, took the door handle. Nodded. Jerked it open.

"Aw, shit," Fell said, lurching away from the refrigerator.

Mrs. Lacey hadn't fit that well, but Bekker had managed to crush her into the limited space. Her head lay at right angles across her shoulders, and the light behind her head glowed like a perverse advertisement. Her eyes were bloody holes. A dozen cans of Coke were carefully stacked around her body, one jammed between her twisted arms and her chest. Two dead cats were stuffed in a plastic meat compartment, their tails trailing out.

"Jesus. Jesus." Lucas backed away. "Let's go up the next one, but make it quick."

"You think he's up there?" Fell asked doubtfully. She was staring at the refrigerator, her throat working.

"No. If he's in the building, he's down—I don't feel anything up here."

"Air's too quiet," Fell said. "C'mon, you cover me. . . ."

She went ahead for the next flight, climbing past the cartons, through the dust. At the top, they found three bedrooms and an old-fashioned bath. They checked the closets, the shower, under the beds. Nobody home.

"Down," Lucas said.

"How about the roof?"

"We'll send a couple of guys up—but Bekker would look for a hole, not a perch."

Six cops were spread through the first floor, all looking up apprehensively when Lucas and Fell hurried down the stairs.

"He killed an old woman and stuffed her body in the refrigerator," Lucas told the partrol sergeant, flicking a thumb at the stairs. The two Robin Hoods watched silently from the radiator, their hands still looped through the cuffs. "We went through both floors, nobody home. Send a couple of good people up, see if they can find the roof access. We didn't check that. Tell them to be careful. He's got a gun."

"I'll go myself. . . ."

"No. You stay here. You've got enough rank to keep these assholes cuffed up," Lucas said, nodding at Clemson and Jeese. "There'll be more people coming soon, just hang on. We're gonna do the basement. . . ."

"Take it easy, then," the sergeant said, still uneasy, looking at the two sullen cops chained to the radiator.

THE STAIRS WERE CLEAN; they looked used. Lucas edged down, taking it easy, leading with the .45, while Fell crouched at the top, focused on the corner at the bottom. If Bekker came around, she would see him before Lucas. But as Lucas reached the corner, her firing line was cut off and he held up a hand to caution her.

Crouching on the bottom step, he did a head-juke around the corner, a one-eyed peek at waist level. A short concrete-floored hallway ended at a green wooden door. A bare bulb hung in the hall above the door. He groped around the corner for the switch, found it, flicked it on.

He stood and crooked two fingers at Fell and she padded down the stairs. "Get that sledgehammer and bring back somebody who knows how to throw it."

Fell nodded. "Be right back," she whispered.

Lucas waited by the door, the gun pointed at the knob. If Bekker was in the basement, and alive, he'd know the cops had arrived. But if he was waiting with a gun, it was critical that he not know the instant that the door would come down. . . .

Fell came back down the stairs with the sergeant and the sledge.

"We got an entry team coming," the sergeant whispered urgently. "They got the armor. . . ."

Lucas shook his head. "Fuck it. I'm taking him. . . ."

"Listen, these guys can take him, no problem. . . ."

"I'm going," Lucas said. He looked at Fell. "What about you?"

"I'll cover, or go in, whatever. . . ."

"God damn it, you're gonna get our asses shot," the sergeant whispered.

"Give me the sledge," Lucas said.

"Listen to me."

"Give me the fuckin' sledge. . . ."

"Ahhh, shit . . ." The sergeant shook his head and hefted the hammer. "I'll swing it, you assholes back me up. I'm going to hit that fucker once, and then I'm on the floor."

"Let's do it," said Fell.

BEKKER WANDERED THROUGH the murky basement, trying to remember why he was going to the couch. A song went through his head:

Jesus loves me this I know, for the Bible tells me so. . . .

Sung at a funeral, sometime, way back, he could remember a bronze coffin that sat higher than his head and the choir singing. It was all very sharp, as though he'd just stepped into the picture. . . .

A spider brushed his cheek, tickling, and Bekker snapped out of the funeral picture. Something thumped overhead. That was it. The noise. He had to go to the couch because of the noise overhead.

The couch had been pushed out from the wall, and he stepped behind it and sat down on the rug. The gun was waiting, cheap chrome steel. Loaded. Two shots. He picked it up. Said, Hello, put it in his mouth, sat, like a man with his pipe, then took it out and looked down the barrel.

Hello . . .

His finger tightened, he felt the pressure of the trigger, took up the slack . . . and his mind cleared. Clear as a lake. He saw himself, huddled in the corner of the basement. Saw Davenport come in. Saw himself, hands crossed over his chest, shoulders pulled in, head down.

Saw Davenport coming closer, screaming at him; saw himself rocking back and forth on his heels. Felt the pistol in the bottom hand on his chest, concealed. Saw Davenport reaching out to him, ordering him to turn; Davenport unaware, unknowing, unthinking. Saw himself reach out with the derringer, press it to Davenport's heart, and the explosion and Davenport's face . . .

THE SERGEANT LOOKED AT Lucas, raised an eyebrow. Ready? Lucas nodded. The sergeant took a breath, raised the hammer overhead, paused, then brought it crashing down. The door flew inward, and the sergeant hit the ground. There was no immediate fire from the dark room, and he scrambled back past Fell to the stairs, groping for his gun.

"Too fuckin' old for this shit," he said.

Lucas, focused on the room, said, "Flashlights."

"What?"

"Get some flashlights. . . ."

With quick peeks around the corner, they established that the interior of the basement wasn't quite dark. A light was on somewhere, but seemed to be partially blocked, as though the thin illumination were seeping through a crack in the door, or coming from a child's night-light. Lucas and Fell, looking over the sights of their weapons, could see the blocky shapes of furniture, a rectangle that might be a bookcase.

"Got 'em," the sergeant said.

"Poke them around the corner, hit the interior, about head high. Keep your hand back if you can. Tell me when you're going, I'll shoot at a muzzle flash," Lucas said. He looked at Fell, saw that she was sweating, and grinned at her. "Life in the big city."

The cop nodded. "Ready?"

"Anytime."

"Now."

The cop thrust the light around the corner, and Lucas, four feet below, followed with the muzzle of his gun, and his arm, and one eye. No movement. The sergeant leaned a bit into the hallway, played the light around the interior.

"I'm going," said Lucas.

"Go," said Fell.

Lucas scrambled across the floor to the apartment door, then, flat on the floor, eased his head and shoulders through the door, reached up, flicked a light switch. A single bulb came on. Nothing moving. He crouched, and Fell eased down the hall.

"What's that?" she whispered.

Lucas listened.

Jesus loves me . . .

Not a child's voice. But not an adult's, either—nothing human, he thought. Something from a movie, a special effect, weird, chilling.

For the Bible tells me so. . . .

"Bekker," Lucas whispered. "Over there, I think . . ."

He was inside the apartment, duckwalking, the .45 in a double-handed grip, following his eye-track around the apartment. Fell, behind him, said, "Covered to the right."

"I got the right, you watch that dark door. . . ." The sergeant's voice. Lucas glanced back, quickly, saw the older man easing inside with his piece-of-shit .38.

"Got it," Fell agreed.

"He's in the corner," Lucas said. He half stood, looking at a velour couch. The couch was pushed away from the wall, and the unearthly voice was coming from behind it.

"Bekker," he called.

Jesus loves me . . .

"Stand up, Bekker. . . ."

This I know . . .

Lucas focused on the couch, crept up on it, the gun fully extended. Up close, he could see the top of Bekker's head, shaven, smooth, bobbing up and down with the simple rhythms of the song.

"Up, motherfucker," he yelled. And to Fell and the cop: "He's here, got him . . ."

"Watch a gun, watch a gun . . ."

Lucas, pointing his weapon at the top of Bekker's head, slid around the side of the couch and looked down at him. Bekker looked up, then stood, hands across his chest, rocking, humming. . . .

"Turn around," Lucas shouted.

Fell moved up beside him. . . .

"Nuttier 'n shit," she whispered.

"Watch him, watch him . . ."

She stepped around to get a better angle, then batted at her face and batted again, then waved her hand overhead.

Lucas, glancing sideways: "What?"

"I'm tangled . . ."

Bekker's head turned, like a ball bearing rotating in a socket. "Spiders . . ." he said.

The sergeant, near the kitchen door, coming up slowly, punched a light switch, and Fell groaned, weakly, thrashing at the objects that hung around her head.

"Get away," she choked. "Get away from me. . . ."

They hung on individual black threads from a bundle of crossed wire coat hangers, floating in their separate orbits around Fell's head, wrinkled now, drying, the varicolored lashes as sleek as the day the eyelids were cut from their owners. . . .

Fell staggered away from them, appalled, her mouth open.

"Get him," Lucas said, his pistol three feet from Bekker's vacant eyes. The sergeant took a step forward. Behind Fell, a thin shaft of light cut through a crack in a door. The light was hard, sharp, blue, professional. As the sergeant stepped forward, Fell pushed the door open.

Bekker took a step toward Lucas, his hands crossed on his chest. "Spi . . ."

An old woman lay there, bound and wired silent, her eyes permanently open now, staring, white eyeballs, the skin removed from her chest. . . .

Alive . . .

"Aw, fuck," Fell screamed. She pivoted, the gun coming up, her mouth open, working, her hands clutching.

Lucas had time to say "No."

Bekker said, ". . . ders." And one hand dropped and the other swung up, a glint of steel. He thrust the derringer at Lucas' chest . . .

. . . and Fell fired a single .357 round through the bridge of Michael's Bekker's nose and blew out the back of Michael Bekker's sleek, shaven head.

30

THE WALLS OF LILY'S OFFICE seemed to melt, and Petty was there, the adult face superimposed on the child's face, both of them together. And then Kennett's face.

Kennett's face in the dark, in Lily's bedroom. Must've been in winter: she'd bought a Christmas tree, shipped into a lot on Sixth Avenue from somewhere in Maine, and she could remember the scent of pine needles in the apartment as they talked.

No sex, just sleeping together. Kennett laughing about it, but unhappy, too. His heart attack not that far past . . .

"Hanging out with a geek," he said. "I can't believe it. I'm not enough, she's got a geek on the side."

"Not a geek," she said.

"All right. A dork. A nerd. Revenge of the Nerds, visited on Richard X. Kennett personally. A nerd may be dorking my woman. Or wait, maybe it's a dork is nerding my woman. Or wait . . ."

"Shut up," she said, mock-severely. "Or I will fondle your delicate parts and then leave you hanging—in good health, of course."

"Lily . . ." A change of tone. Sex on the mind.

"No. I'm sorry I said it. Kennett . . ."

"All right. Back to the dork . . ."

"He's not a dork. He's really a nice guy, and if he cracks this thing, he could go somewhere. . . ."

She'd talked, Lily had, about the Robin Hood case. She'd talked in bed. She'd talked about the intelligence guys who'd stumbled over it, she'd talked about Petty being assigned to it, she'd talked about computers.

Not all at once. Not formally. But bits and pieces. Pillow talk. But Kennett got most of it. With what Copland overheard, and what Kennett got in bed, they must've known it all.

Petty's image floated in her mind's eye, his hair slicked down, his red ears sticking out, running down the Brooklyn sidewalk with the paper overhead, so happy to see her. . . .

"I killed you," she said to his image, speaking aloud. Her voice was stark as a winter crow. "I killed you, Walt."

THE RIVER WAS BLACK as ink, but thick, oily, roiled, as it pushed the last few miles toward the sea. A full moon had come up in the east, red, huge, shrouded by smog over the city. Lily waited until the elderly night guard and his dog were at the far end of the marina, then used her key at the member's gate.

The docks were cluttered, as always, badly lit by widely spaced yellow bug lights. Out in the water, anchor lights shone off the masts of a half-dozen anchored boats. Here and there, lights showed at portholes, and a light breeze banged halyards against aluminum masts, a pleasant whipping tinkle like wind chimes. The smell of marijuana hovered around a small Capri daysailer and a man was giggling inside the tiny cabin. She walked out of the marijuana stink into the river smell, compounded of mud and decaying fish.

"Lily." Kennett's voice came out of the dark as she approached the *Lestrade*. He was sitting behind the wheel, smoking a cigarette. "I was wondering if you'd come."

"You know about Bekker?"

"Yeah. And that I've been cut out of the loop."

Lily stepped into the cockpit, sat down, staring at him. His face was flat, solemn; he was looking steadily back. "You're Robin Hood," she said.

"Robin Hood, bullshit," he said wearily. He flicked the cigarette into the water.

"I'm not wearing a wire," she said.

"Stand up, turn around." She stood up and Kennett ran his hands down her, between her legs. "Gimme the purse."

He opened the purse, clicked on an electric light that hung from the backstay, looked inside. After poking inside, he took the .45 out of its holder, dropped the magazine and shucked the shells out into the water. Then he jacked the slide, to eject the shell in the chamber. The chamber was empty, and he shook his head. "You oughta carry one under the hammer."

"I'm not here to talk about guns," she said. "I'm here to talk about you being Robin Hood. About using me as a dummy to spy on O'Dell. About killing Walt Petty."

"I didn't use you as a dummy," he said flatly. "I got with you because I liked you and I'm falling in love with you. You're beautiful and you're smart and you're a cop, and there aren't many women around I can talk to."

"I don't doubt that you like me," she said, squaring off with him. "But that didn't keep you from running me. On the way up here, I was remembering when we'd lie down below there, in the berth, and you running those goddamn fantasies about what O'Dell did for sex. Do you remember that? You must've scripted those things, to get me talking about O'Dell. And before that, talking about Walt. When I think of the things I told you, because I felt secure. Because you were a lover and a brother cop. Jesus Christ, every time we got into bed, you were pumping me for information."

"Christ, Lily . . . Lily, if you told me anything about O'Dell or Petty . . . it was by-product. I wasn't sleeping with you to get information. Jesus, Lily . . ."

"Shut up," Lily said. She reached overhead and pulled the chain on the backstay light and they were plunged into the dark again. "I want to know some shit. We've got Jeese and Clemson, Davenport got them, and we know about Copland. . . ."

"I knew Davenport was dangerous," Kennett said quietly. "I really didn't underestimate him. I knew he was a *really* dangerous sonofabitch when he looked up Gauguin, about the necktie. And I couldn't help liking him."

"Is that why your guys tried to beat him up, instead of just whacking him?"

Kennett grinned: she could see his teeth. Not a happy smile, a rueful one. "Another mistake," he said. "You start feeling that everything in New York is *more*. That a small-town guy could never hold off a couple of real New York pros. So we were just gonna break a few ribs, maybe. Something that'd take him off the street for a month. They said he was quick as a pro fighter. They were pissed, said that if they'd been a half-inch slower, he'd of blown them up, he'd of had his .45 out. . . ."

"They were lucky," Lily said. "Why didn't you try again?"

Kennett shrugged. "At that point, we figured it was either kill him or forget him. He didn't seem . . . close enough . . . to kill. And I don't know if the guys would've done it anyway. Petty was already hard to stomach. Davenport's message to O'Dell, the one Copland picked up. That was fake?"

"Not completely. It was Davenport who found Bekker, all right. He was feeding the message to O'Dell to see if any hitters showed up. They did, but I was with O'Dell the whole time. He didn't make any calls. So I started thinking about it."

"God damn it. I thought about skipping Bekker."

"You should have."

"Couldn't. Didn't know what he'd say about . . ." He stopped, remembering.

"About the guys he saw hit Walt. Jeese and Clemson. Thick and Thin."

"No," Kennett said evenly. "It wasn't them."

"Bullshit," she flared. "They fit."

"No. It wasn't."

"Who, then?"

"I won't tell you, but Jeese and Clemson, no." He pulled at his lip. "Old Copland. A good guy. What happens to him?"

"O'Dell will think of something. . . . How many of you are there? And how many people have you done?"

Kennett shook his head. "There are . . . several. Some singles, some two-man teams. None of them knows the others, and I won't tell you who they are."

"We can put Jeese and Clemson in Attica if we want—assault on a police officer with a firearm. And if O'Dell wants to fix it, I'm sure we can find a problem with Copland's pension. He'll spend his last twenty years sitting on a park bench. Or rolled in an army blanket on a sidewalk."

"Don't fuckin' do that," Kennett whispered.

"That's what happens when you lose," Lily said, her voice like ice.

"We were doing right," Kennett said. "I'll call it off. Walk away, and I'll call it off. I'll quit the force, if you want."

"What, so you can write for the *Times*? You'd be a bigger danger there than where you are now," Lily said.

"So what do you want from me?"

"I want the goddamned names."

Kennett shook his head. "No. Never happen. If I gave you the names, only two things could happen: a lot of good guys would get ripped off, or O'Dell would set up his *own* little force of stormtroopers. I'm not going to let any fat, puling, alcoholic fixer do that, I won't. . . ." His voice grew cold as he said it. He bared his teeth and added, "I really like you. But the worst thing you do is, the worst thing about you, is that you associate with that . . . that . . . cunt O'Dell."

"I'm the cunt," Lily said. "I'm the one you rolled for information."

"Fuck you, then," Kennett said, and turned away. "You want to make something out of it, make it in court. I'll tear you up. Now take your ass off my boat."

"I've got another question before I go."

"What?"

"Why Walt?"

Kennett stared at her a moment, then dug in his shirt, found a pack of cigarettes, shook one out, lit it with a match. Tossed the match overboard: they heard it hit, the hiss hanging in the damp air.

"Had to," he said. "Him and his fucking computers. When I started this, nobody really knew about computers and what they could do. They were like electric filing cabinets. Looking in a computer was like snooping through papers on somebody's desk. We didn't know that every time we went into a file, we left tracks. Petty nailed us down. We had to have time to get into the machines, to fix things. We did that. The information's gone now." He looked downriver, at the Manhattan glittering along the river, the arcs of the bridges. "Listen, Lily. If you could take five hundred or a thousand people out of Manhattan, you could make it eighty percent safer. You could make it a paradise."

"Not a thousand," she said. "Maybe ten thousand."

"No. No, not really. A thousand would do it. We couldn't take down a thousand people, probably, but we could make a difference. Arvin Davies. You look at him? Was he one of the people . . ."

"Yes."

"We think . . . intelligence estimates . . . that he committed up to a hundred crimes, all sorts: assaults, burglaries, rapes, murder. He could have done a hundred more. Now he won't."

"You can't make that decision."

"Sure I can. And somebody has to," Kennett said, looking at her. "Your average junkie does fifty or a hundred burglaries for every time he gets caught, and for small burglaries, chances are he'll be right back out on the street. Plea-bargains out, or he'll do thirty days or six months or something. Not enough. If we let all the one-time passion killers out of prison and put all the junkies inside, Manhattan would be a garden spot. Even the ones we took off . . . Christ, we knocked down a thousand violent crimes a year, just the ones we took down."

"How many were there?"

He shook his head. "You don't need to know. But that's why."

"That's why you shot Petty? So we'd have a garden spot?"

Kennett turned away. "We didn't like doing that. But we had no choice. . . . O'Dell is trying to frame me, by the way. Supposedly had a witness who saw me when Waites was gunned down."

"I know."

His eyebrows went up. "You know?"

"Davenport found the kid who supposedly saw you. Found him in Charleston and broke him down. He knows it was phony."

Kennett smiled. "When he went to Minneapolis, he went to Charleston the next day. I thought it was weird that he took the day off—weird for a guy like Davenport."

"How about the others? Waites was a loudmouth, but . . ."

"They nurtured it, the festering. My God, look over there, look at that city, think what it could be. . . ."

She looked across the water at the twinkling lights, like the lights of the Milky Way, seen large. "And you sold it out. And used me like a fucking Kleenex."

"Bullshit," he said. His face was getting red.

"When Walt was killed, I came over here and cried on your shoulder, and you took care of all the arrangements and patted me on the head and took me down below and made love to me, comforting me. I can't believe I did it."

"Yeah, well . . ."

"Well, what?"

"That's life." His teeth were clenched. "Now, go on, Lily, get the hell out of here."

Lily stood, took a step toward the dock. Then another step, toward Kennett.

"What . . ." Kennett began.

She hit him, open-handed, hard: a slap that almost knocked him down. He took a step toward her, hand on his face, and caught her arm. "Lily, dammit!"

"Let go of me," she said. She tried to pull away, but he held on, and for a moment, they struggled together, his face getting redder; then suddenly, he pinched his shoulders and let his hand drop away.

He turned, seeming to crouch, then went to his knees. "Oh, Jesus," he gasped. "Lily . . . in my bag, down below . . ."

His pills. His pills were in the bag. She started to turn toward the cabin.

A spasm hit him and he went flat in the cockpit, his face straining, the tendons standing out in his neck. "Lily . . ."

She stopped. Looked at the cabin and then back at him. And then carefully, as if in slow motion, she climbed out of the boat, stood on the dock a second, looked at the city and then back down at Kennett. His face was chalky, his mouth open, straining, his eyes large and staring. His hand scrabbled along the deck, as though he were trying to get hold of it. "Lily . . ."

"Say hello to Bekker," she said.

O'DELL SAT IN HIS semidarkened office, an air of satisfaction about him, like a bullfrog who'd snapped up a particularly tasty fly. "I really don't give a fuck what you think," he told Lucas.

"Which makes me want to come across the desk and slap the shit out of you," Lucas snarled.

"The New York jails aren't pretty," O'Dell said, mildly. "I could guarantee you a tour. . . ."

Lucas shook his head. "Nah. You wouldn't do that. I spent too much time with Red Reed. We had witnesses. So I slap the shit out of you, you put me in jail, and I tell the papers about Reed, and tell them that you hid a key witness in the murder of a well-known black politician. You'd be right in there with me."

O'Dell seemed to think about it for a minute, then sighed and half closed his heavy-lidded eyes. "All right. But look, if you're gonna slap the shit out me, why don't we get it over with? I need some sleep."

They sat quietly for a minute, then Lucas said, "You know I won't. But you owe me, God damn it. You got me whacked by Kennett's hoods. What I want to know is, how much was set up? Did you know it was Kennett? Is Lily in it? How about Fell? And who else?"

"Lily's okay—she never had anything to do with it. And Lily says you believe Fell was an alarm. I don't know if I believe it, but I can see the possibility. . . ."

"Kennett?"

"Yeah, I knew about Kennett and a couple more—and frankly, you and Lily should have known that," O'Dell said. "Petty's investigation wasn't a TV show. He didn't sneak off and do all the work and keep all of his conclusions to himself. He came up and sat here every day and told me what he thought. We had Kennett and a couple more people spotted—not Copland, unfortunately. We *didn't* know that Kennett had his own computer people. We figured we could go into the system anytime, print out our evidence. Then Petty got killed and his printouts were lifted. When I went back into the system, the files had been trashed. All I had were a few names and no way to push."

"So you set us up."

O'Dell smiled, still pleased with himself. "Yes. Lily had talked about you. Said you were smart. And I saw one of your simulations. So I put Kennett on Bekker, and you on Kennett, and brought Fell to work with you, and had Lily running you on the side. With all that pressure, something had to blow. Anyway, I had nothing to lose."

Lucas thought about it, stood, stretched, yawned, wandered to O'Dell's window, pulled back the heavy plush drapes and looked out at the twinkling city. "This goddamn place is one big patch, you know? Have I given you my rap on how the place is one big patch?"

"Yeah."

"And I was another one."

"Yeah."

Lucas stretched again, then wandered across the room toward the door. "Nice game," he said.

O'Dell looked at him, then laughed, low and long, genuinely delighted. "It was, wasn't it?"

LUCAS SAT BEHIND a round, simulated-wood table the size of a manhole cover, in a plastic bar full of plastic pictures of old airplanes. Through the clear Plexiglas walls, he could watch the people streaming out toward the departure gates. He glanced at his watch: three twenty-seven in the afternoon, more or less. With a Rolex, he'd discovered, more or less had to be good enough. He sipped at his Budweiser, not interested, just holding his seat.

Fell showed up at three-thirty, thin, bird-gawky, tough. And maybe angry or something else. She stopped near the end of a long queue for the security gates, looked both ways, and spotted the bar. She paused again at the door, and Lucas raised a hand. She saw him and threaded her way through the tables. When she saw his suitcase by his leg, she looked from the case to Lucas and said, "So I was a three-night stand, or whatever it was."

"Not exactly," Lucas said. "Sit down."

She didn't sit down. Instead she said, "I thought we might go someplace for a while." Tears rimmed her eyes.

"Sit down," Lucas said.

"You fuck," she said, but she sat down, dropping heavily into the chair across from him, hands dangling dispiritedly between her legs. "You said we . . ."

"I thought about asking you to come down to the Islands with me," Lucas said. "I even called out to Kennedy, out to United, to find out what islands we could go to."

She looked down at the tabletop. "Tell me," she said.

"Well, I . . . couldn't." He dug in his pocket and tossed a red matchbook on the table in front of her. The matchbook had a horsehead on it. She picked it up and put it in her purse.

"So you were in the restaurant where Walter Petty got killed," he said. "You told me you weren't."

"Yeah?"

"Yeah. I saw the matches in your apartment."

"When?"

"Well, when we were up there. . . ."

"Bullshit, I got rid of them. When I thought you might be coming over, I saw them, and I thought, 'I got to get rid of these.' I threw them out. So when did you see them?"

He looked levelly across the table at her. "The first day we worked together, I copped your purse, made molds of your keys. The next day I went in."

"You sonofabitch," she said. Then a realization came to her eyes. "You're wearing a wire?"

"No. I like you too much. But the thing is, I can't trust you. Not completely. I thought about going down to the Islands with you and decided I couldn't. I'd eventually talk to you about this, and then . . ." He let the thought dangle, and so did she. He went on: "I tried to think up a lie that would get me back to Minnesota. But I couldn't think of one. And I wanted to tell you why."

"Well. I appreciate it. But you'd have been safe enough. A matchbook is pretty thin . . ."

"There was more than a matchbook. This whole goddamned episode was a game set up by O'Dell. It was so beautiful it makes me laugh. He used every one of us. But anyway—he did a computer run on the victims. You come up way too often. That was a big piece."

She frowned. "Will they get me?"

"No, I don't think so. They think you're an alarm." He explained, and she listened quietly, staring at the floor.

"And you won't tell them different?" she asked, when he finished.

"No. I'm the one who sold them the alarm idea."

"Why?"

He shrugged. "You're a friend."

She looked him over for a moment and then nodded. "Okay."

"If Lily ever found out, though, she very well might kill you. That's another reason I wanted to talk. . . ."

"Did she kill Kennett?" Fell blurted.

"Kennett? No, no, she was downtown with O'Dell all evening."

"Goddamn," Fell said, gnawing a thumbnail. "When I shot Bekker . . ."

"Bekker knew you," Lucas said. "And that's why, in his letter, he wouldn't say anything about Thin. He didn't want people thinking about women killers. . . ."

"Yeah," Fell said. "But that's not why I shot him. I shot him because of their eyelashes, and that woman . . . and everything."

"I know. I mean, I believe it. But why Petty?"

"I didn't want to do Petty," Fell said, voice low, out of gas. "I was there, but I tried to stop it."

"You didn't have to be there. . . ."

"Well . . . I was. If I'd had a couple of more minutes, I think I would've talked . . . the other guy out of it. But Petty came through the door a minute too soon. A minute later and nothing would've happened. At least, not then. Petty had something on us. . . . I'll burn in hell for Petty."

"I doubt it," Lucas said wryly.

"Well, so do I," she said. Then: "I would've liked the Islands, though. Going down with you."

"Yeah, it would have been nice. But I'm the only one who knows about you. You're quick with that gun . . . and you might start thinking about it, if I'm there, laying around."

"I wouldn't," she said, but she couldn't suppress a small grin. "It's interesting that you're scared of me, though."

"Yeah, well . . ."

She sighed. "Fucking trouser-snake cops. So goddamned treacherous."

"And I wanted to tell you about Lily," he said.

"What?"

"She's got a line on a half-dozen of Kennett's shooters. She's gonna be tough, one way or another. But I want you to know two things: they've got no proof of anything. They just want it to stop."

"What's the other thing?"

"The other thing is, if anybody takes Lily, I'll be coming back to town," he said. He'd been watching her, and his eyes had gone hard as granite.

"You oughta be one of us," she said.

"Pass the word on," he said.

"I don't know anybody, except my . . . pal . . . and one other guy. But I'll tell them. Maybe they know more. We don't talk about it. That was one of Kennett's rules. Nobody talks about nothin', he'd say."

"Good rule," Lucas said. He looked at his watch again. "Lily's coming pretty soon."

"Here?"

"Yeah, I've got to talk to her too."

"Then I better get going," Fell said, picking up her purse. She stood and stepped away from the table, then turned back. "Remember when you said something like, 'This place is the armpit of the universe,' the first day we were together?"

"Yeah?"

"Kennett's people . . . we were just trying to make it something else."

"Okay."

"Were we wrong?"

He thought about it for a while. "I don't know," he said finally.

. . .

FELL WENT AWAY AND Lucas stared at his beer bottle, making wet O's on the table. After the shooting in the basement, after the dictated statements and interrogations, after the press conference, he'd gone back to the team office. Most of the office staff had gone, but he'd found a computer adept, and said that he needed to look up some information on a couple of cops: Jeese and Clemson.

The computer operator had put him at a vacant terminal, showed him how to call up the files. He'd done it, read through them quickly, then punched in Fell's name. When he'd gotten the file, he'd scanned through to the bottom, found the next of kin: Roy Fell, at an address in Brooklyn. He'd punched in Roy Fell. A file had come up. *Retired*, it said. Then: *Retrieve Retired File? (Y/N)*.

Lucas had pushed the Y key. A photoscan was a simple matter of selecting the right option on a short menu, and Fell's father's face had come up. Heavy face, gray hair, gray mustache, a smile that looked almost painful. Six feet, two inches tall. Born 1930. Bekker had had him pegged almost exactly.

"Thick," Lucas had said aloud.

The computer operator said, "What?"

"Nothing," said Lucas, and he'd shut the terminal down.

Sitting at the airport now, drawing circles with the bottom of his beer bottle, Lucas thought, *You can't walk away from family. . . .*

LILY ARRIVED TEN minutes later. Like Fell, she stopped by the security queue, looking for the bar. She saw him as she came in, her face ashen, tired, but controlled.

"You talked to O'Dell," she said as she sat down.

"Yeah."

"He fixed the whole thing."

"Yup."

"When did you know?" she asked.

"In Charleston. I suspected before that—everybody was too close together, everything was too convenient. But I didn't know for sure that he wasn't Robin Hood."

"Do you still think Fell was an alarm?"

"Yeah, I'm pretty sure. Not positive. But I think she was simply set up by Kennett. I mean, she *took* those Robin Hoods at Bekker's place. She didn't have to: her piece was right in my ear."

"The word is going around that Robin Hood *did* get Bekker."

"What'd you expect? He got shot to death."

Lily sat for a moment, staring at the fake grain on the tabletop. "When did you know about Dick?" she asked.

"O'Dell tried to set him up—that thing about a white-haired guy killing the politician. I didn't know it was a setup, so even then, I was thinking about him."

"But when . . . ?"

"When we went to Petty's apartment and that Logan woman said whoever came to Petty's apartment seemed to stop before he got to the elevator, and after he got off the elevator, and to take a long time getting to the door. . . ."

"Sure," she said, avoiding his eyes. "Dick."

"Yeah, but I couldn't figure it. I assumed he couldn't drive—that's what everybody assumed—and saw a driver dropping him off at Midtown South. And if he couldn't drive, it wasn't him. If he'd been driven, by Copland or one of his other buddies, he wouldn't have had to walk up all those steps himself. He could have sent the driver in for the stuff. So that pushed me off him for a while. Until the day on the river and you told me that he *could* drive. That he sometimes drove the four-by-four, and it pissed you off . . ."

"So," she said. "I not only betrayed Petty, I betrayed Dick."

"Ah, come on, Lily, stop sniveling. You were doing the best you could in a goddamned rat's nest," Lucas said.

"And everybody winds up dead," she said.

"Hey." There wasn't much else to say. Lucas looked at his Rolex. "I gotta go. They're probably boarding the plane now," he said.

AT THE END OF the security queue, Lucas faced her, hands in his pockets, and said, "If this was a movie, there'd be a big hot kiss right here and everything'd be all right."

She had eyes that Rembrandt would have painted. "But there's never anything after a movie," she said. "It ends with a hot kiss and you never see the going-back-to-work part."

"The getting-to-be-important part . . ."

"Yeah. And to tell you the truth, if there was going to be a big hot kiss, I thought Fell'd be getting it. I thought you'd be going out to the Islands with her."

"Nah. She's New York, I'm not. Besides . . ."

"What?"

"There really aren't any Islands, are there?"

She looked away from him, thinking of Petty and Kennett. "No," she said after a minute, "I guess not."

There was another moment, and she stuck out her hand.

"Give me a fuckin' break, Rothenburg," Lucas said, and leaned into her and kissed her on the lips, almost, but not quite, chastely. He turned and started through the security check. "If you get another Bekker, give me a whistle. You know . . . ?"

"Yeah, yeah. Jesus," she said, not quite believing him. A tiny smile crinkled the corner of her mouth. "I do know how to whistle."

1

A ND WHISTLED DOWN the frozen run of Shasta Creek, between the blacker-than-black walls of pine. The thin naked swamp alders and slight new birches bent before it. Needle-point ice crystals rode it, like sandpaper grit, carving arabesque whorls in the drifting snow.

The Iceman followed the creek down to the lake, navigating as much by feel, and by time, as by sight. At six minutes on the luminous dial of his dive watch, he began to look for the dead pine. Twenty seconds later, its weather-bleached trunk appeared in the snowmobile headlights, hung there for a moment, then slipped away like a hitchhiking ghost.

Now. Six hundred yards, compass bearing 270 . . .

Time time time . . .

He almost hit the lake's west bank as it came down from the house, white-on-white, rising in front of him. He swerved, slowed, followed it. The artificial blue of a yard-light burrowed through the falling snow, and he eased the sled up onto the bank and cut the engine.

The Iceman pushed his faceplate up, sat and listened. He heard nothing but the pat of the snow off his suit and helmet, the ticking of the cooling engine, his own breathing, and the wind. He was wearing a full-face woolen ski mask with holes for his eyes and mouth. The snow caught on the soft wool, and after a moment, melt-water began trickling from the eye holes down his face beside his nose. He was dressed for the weather and the ride: the snowmobile suit was windproof and insulated, the legs fitting into his heavyweight pac boots, the wrists overlapped by expedition ski mitts. A heavyweight polypropylene turtleneck overlapped the face mask, and the collar of the suit snapped directly to the black helmet. He was virtually encapsulated in nylon and wool, and still the cold pried at the cracks and thinner spots, took away his breath . . .

A set of bear-paw snowshoes was strapped behind the seat, on the sled's carry-rack, along with a corn-knife wrapped in newspaper. He swiveled to a sidesaddle position, keeping his weight on the machine, fumbled a miniature milled-aluminum flashlight out of his parka pocket, and pointed it at the carry-rack. His mittens were too thick to work with, and he pulled them off, letting them dangle from his cuff-clips.

The wind was an ice pick, hacking at his exposed fingers as he pulled the snowshoes free. He dropped them onto the snow, stepped into the quick-release bindings, snapped the bindings and thrust his hands back into the mittens. They'd been exposed for less than a minute, and already felt stiff.

With his mittens on, he stood up, testing the snow. The latest fall was soft, but the bitter cold had solidified the layers beneath it. He sank no more than two or three inches. Good.

The chimes sounded in his mind again: Time.

He paused, calmed himself. The whole intricate clockwork of his existence was in danger. He'd killed once already, but that had been almost accidental. He'd had to improvise a suicide scene around the corpse.

And it had almost worked.

Had worked well enough to eliminate any chance that they might catch him. That experience changed him, gave him a taste of blood, a taste of *real* power.

The Iceman tipped his head back like a dog testing for scent. The house was a hundred feet further along the lake shore. He couldn't see it; except for the distant glow of the yard-light, he was in a bowl of darkness. He pulled the corn-knife free of the carry-rack and started up the slope. The corn-knife was a simple instrument, but perfect for an ambush on a snowy night, if the chance should present itself.

IN A STORM, AND especially at night, Claudia LaCourt's house seemed to slide out to the edge of the world. As the snow grew heavier, the lights across the frozen lake slowly faded and then, one by one, blinked out.

At the same time, the forest pressed in: the pine and spruce tiptoed closer, to bend over the house with an unbearable weight. The arbor vitae would paw at the windows, the bare birch branches would scratch at the eaves. All together they sounded like the maundering approach of something wicked, a beast with claws and fangs that rattled on the clapboard siding, searching for a grip. A beast that might pry the house apart.

When she was home alone, or alone with Lisa, Claudia played her old Tammy Wynette albums or listened to the television game shows. But the storm would always come through, with a thump or a screech. Or a line would go down somewhere: the lights would stutter and go out, the music would stop, everybody would hold their breath . . . and the storm would be there, clawing. Candlelight made it worse; hurricane lanterns didn't help much. For the kinds of wickedness created by the imagination during a nighttime blizzard, only modern science could fight: satellite-dish television, radio, compact disks, telephones, computer games. Power drills. Things that made machine noise. Things that banished the dark-age claws that pried at the house.

Claudia stood at the sink, rinsing coffee cups and stacking them to dry. Her image was reflected in the window over the sink, as in a mirror, but darker in the eyes, darker in the lines that framed her face, like an old daguerreotype.

From outside, she'd be a madonna in a painting, the only sign of light and life in the blizzard; but she never thought of herself as a madonna. She was a Mom with a still-shapely butt and hair done with a red rinse, an easy sense of humor, and a taste for beer. She could run a fishing boat and swing a softball bat and once or twice a winter, with Lisa staying over at a friend's, she and Frank would drive into Grant and check into the Holiday Inn. The rooms had floor-to-ceiling mirrors on the closet doors next to the bed. She *did* like to sit on his hips and watch herself fuck, her head thrown back and her breasts a burning pink.

Claudia scraped the last of the burnt crust from the cupcake tin, rinsed it and dumped it in the dish rack to air-dry.

A branch scraped against the window. She looked out, but without the chill: she was humming to herself, something old, something high school. Tonight, at least, she and Lisa weren't alone. Frank was here. In fact, he was on the stairs, coming up, and *he* was humming to *himself*. They did that frequently, the same things at the same time.

"Um," he said, and she turned. His thinning black hair fell over his dark eyes. He looked like a cowboy, she thought, with his high cheekbones and the battered Tony Lamas poking out of his boot-cut jeans. He was wearing a tattered denim shop apron over a t-shirt and held a paintbrush slashed with blood-red lacquer.

"Um, what?" Claudia asked. This was the second marriage for each of them. They were both a little beat-up and they liked each other a lot.

"I just got started on the bookcase and I remembered that I let the wood-stove go," he said ruefully. He waggled the paintbrush at her. "It's gonna take me another hour to finish the bookcase. I really can't stop with this lacquer."

"Goddammit, Frank . . ." She rolled her eyes.

"I'm sorry." Moderately penitent, in a charming cowboy way.

"How about the sheriff?" she asked. New topic. "Are you still gonna do it?"

"I'll see him tomorrow," he said. He turned his head, refusing to meet her eyes.

"It's nothing but trouble," she said. The argument had been simmering between them. She stepped away from the sink and bent backwards, to look down the hall toward Lisa's room. The girl's door was closed and the faint sounds of "Guns 'N Roses" leaked out around the edges. Claudia's voice grew sharper, worried. "If you'd just shut up . . . It's *not* your responsibility, Frank. You *told* Harper about it. Jim was *his* boy. *If* it's Jim."

"It's Jim, all right. And I told you how Harper acted." Frank's mouth closed in a narrow, tight line. Claudia recognized the expression, knew he wouldn't change his mind. Like what's-his-name, in *High Noon*. Gary Cooper.

"I wish I'd never seen the picture," she said, dropping her head. Her right hand went to her temple, rubbing it. Lisa had taken her back to her bedroom to give it to her. Didn't want Frank to see it.

"We can't just let it lay," Frank insisted. "I told Harper that."

"There'll be trouble, Frank," Claudia said.

"And the law can handle it. It don't have nothing to do with us," he said. After a moment he asked, "Will you get the stove?"

"Yeah, yeah. I'll get the stove."

Claudia looked out the window toward the mercury-vapor yard-light down by the garage. The snow seemed to come from a point just below the light, as though it were being poured through a funnel, straight into the window, straight into her eyes. Small pellets, like birdshot. "It looks like it might be slowing down."

"Wasn't supposed to snow at all," Frank said. "Assholes."

He meant television weathermen. The weathermen said it would be clear and cold in Ojibway County, and here they were, snowing to beat the band.

"Think about letting it go." She was pleading now. "Just think about it."

"I'll think about it," he said, and he turned and went back down to the basement.

He might think about it, but he wouldn't change his mind. Claudia, turning the picture in her mind, put on a sweatshirt and walked out to the mudroom. Frank had gotten his driving gloves wet and had draped them over the furnace vent; the room smelled of heat-dried wool. She pulled on her parka and a stocking cap, picked up her gloves, turned on the porch lights from the switch inside the mudroom and stepped out into the storm.

The picture. The people might have been anybody, from Los Angeles or Miami, where they did these things. They weren't.

They were from Lincoln County. The printing was bad and the paper was so cheap it almost crumbled in your fingers. But it was the Harper boy, all right. If you looked close, you could see the stub of the finger on the left hand, the one he'd caught in a log splitter; and you could see the loop earring. He was naked on a couch, his hips toward the camera, a dulled, wondering look on his face. He had the thickening face of an adolescent, but she could still see the shadow of a little boy she'd known, working at his father's gas station.

In the foreground of the picture was the torso of an adult man, hairy-chested, gross. The image came too quickly to Claudia's mind; she was familiar enough with men and their physical mechanisms, but there was something about this, something so bad . . . the boy's eyes, caught in a flash, were black points. When she'd looked closely, it seemed that somebody at the magazine had put the pupils in with a felt-tipped pen.

SHE SHIVERED, NOT FROM the cold, and hurried down the snow-blown trench that led out to the garage and woodshed. There were four inches of new snow in the trench: she'd have to blow it out again in the morning.

The trench ended at the garage door. She shoved the door open, stepped inside, snapped on the lights and stomped her feet without thinking. The garage was insulated and heated with a woodstove. Four good chunks of oak would burn slowly enough, and throw off enough heat, to keep the inside temperature above the freezing point on even the coldest nights. Warm enough to start the cars, anyway. Out here, in the Chequamegon, getting the cars to start could be a matter of life and death.

The stove was still hot. Down to coals, but Frank had cleaned it out the night before—she wouldn't have to do that, anyway. She looked back toward the door, at the woodpile. Enough for the night, but no more. She tossed a few wrist-thin splits of sap-heavy pine onto the fire, to get some flame going, then four solid chunks of oak. That would do it.

She looked at the space where the woodpile should have been, sighed, and decided she might as well bring in a few chunks now—give it a chance to thaw before morning. She went back outside, pulling the door shut, but not latched, walked along the side of the garage to the lean-to that covered the woodpile. She picked up four more chunks of oak, staggered back to the garage door, pushed the door open with her foot and dropped the oak next to the stove. One more trip, she thought; Frank could do his share tomorrow.

She went back out to the side of the garage, into the dark of the woodshed, picked up two more pieces of oak.

And felt the short hairs rise on the back of her neck.

Somebody was here with her . . .

Claudia dropped the oak splits, one gloved hand going to her throat. The woodlot was dark beyond the back of the garage. She could feel it, but not see it, could hear her heart pounding in her ears, and the snow hitting her hood with a delicate pit-put-pit. Nothing else: but still . . .

She backed away. Nothing but the snow and the blue circle of the yard-light. At the snow-blown trench, she paused, straining into the dark . . . and ran.

Up to the house, still with the sense of someone behind her, his hand almost there, reaching for her. She pawed at the door handle, smashed it down, hit the door with the heel of her hand, followed it into the heat and light of the mudroom.

"Claudia?"

She screamed.

FRANK STOOD THERE, with a paint rag, eyes wide, startled. "What?"

"My God," she said. She pulled down the zip on the snowmobile suit, struggled with the hood snaps, her mouth working, nothing coming out until: "My God, Frank, there's somebody out there by the garage."

"What?" He frowned and went to the kitchen window, looked out. "Did you see him?"

"No, but I swear to God, Frank, there's somebody out there. I could *feel* him," she said, catching his arm, looking past him through the window. "Call nine-one-one."

"I don't see anything," Frank said. He went through the kitchen, bent over the sink, looked out toward the yard-light.

"You *can't* see anything," Claudia said. She flipped the lock on the door, then stepped into the kitchen. "Frank, I swear to God there's somebody . . ."

"All right," he said. He took her seriously: "I'll go look."

"Why don't we call . . . ?"

"I'll take a look," he said again. Then: "They wouldn't send a cop out here, in this storm. Not if you didn't even see anybody."

He was right. Claudia followed him into the mudroom, heard herself babbling: "I loaded up the stove, then I went around to the side to bring some wood in for tomorrow morning . . ." and she thought, *I'm not like this.*

Frank sat on the mudroom bench and pulled off the Tony Lamas, stepped into his snowmobile suit, sat down, pulled on his pacs, laced them, then zipped the suit and picked up his gloves. "Back in a minute," he said. He sounded exasperated; but he knew her. She wasn't one to panic.

"I'll come," she blurted.

"Nah, you wait," he said.

"Frank: take the gun." She hurried over to the service island, jerked open the drawer. Way at the back, a fully loaded Smith and Wesson .357 Magnum snuggled behind a divider. "Maybe it's Harper. Maybe . . ."

"Jesus," he said, shaking his head. He grinned at her ruefully, and he was out the door, pulling on his ski gloves.

On the stoop, the snow pecked his face, mean little hard pellets. He half-turned against it. As long as he wasn't looking directly into the wind, the snowmobile suit kept him comfortable. But he couldn't see much, or hear anything but the sound of the wind whistling over the nylon hood. With his head averted, he walked down the steps onto the snow-blown path to the garage.

THE ICEMAN WAS THERE, next to the woodpile, his shoulder just at the corner of the shed, his back to the wind. He'd been in the woodlot when Claudia came out. He'd tried to get to her, but he hadn't dared use the flashlight and in the dark, had gotten tangled in brush and had to stop. When she ran back inside, he'd almost turned away, headed back to the snowmobile. The opportunity was lost, he thought. Somehow, she'd been warned. And time was pressing. He looked at his watch. He had a half hour, no more.

But after a moment of thought, he'd methodically untangled his snowshoes and continued toward the dark hulk of the garage. He had to catch the LaCourts together, in the kitchen, where he could take care of both of them at once. They'd have guns, so he'd have to be quick.

The Iceman carried a Colt Anaconda under his arm. He'd stolen it from a man who never knew it was stolen. He'd done that a lot, in the old days. Got a lot of good stuff. The Anaconda was a treasure, every curve and notch with a function.

The corn-knife, on the other hand, was almost elegant in its crudeness. Homemade, with a rough wooden handle, it looked something like a machete, but with a thinner blade and a squared end. In the old days it had been used to chop cornstalks. The blade was covered with a patina of surface rust, but he'd put the edge on a shop grinder and the new edge was silvery and fine and sharp enough to shave with.

The corn-knife might kill, but that wasn't why he'd brought it. The corn-knife was simply horrifying. If he needed a threat to get the picture, if he needed to hurt the girl bad but not kill her, then the corn-knife was exactly right.

Standing atop the snow, the Iceman felt like a giant, his head reaching nearly to the eaves of the garage as he worked his way down its length. He saw Frank come to the window and peer out, and he stopped. Had Claudia seen him after all? Impossible. She'd turned away, and she'd run, but he could hardly see her, even with the garage and yard-lights on her. He'd been back in the dark, wearing black. Impossible.

The Iceman was sweating from the short climb up the bank, and the struggle with the brush. He snapped the releases and pulled the bindings loose, but stayed balanced on the shoes. He'd have to be careful climbing down into the trench. He glanced at his watch. *Time time time . . .*

He unzipped his parka, pulled his glove and reached inside to touch the wooden stock of the Anaconda. Ready. He was turning to step into the trench when the back door opened and a shaft of light played out across the porch. The Iceman rocked back, dragging the snowshoes with his boots, into the darkness beside the woodshed, his back to the corrugated metal garage wall.

Frank was a dark silhouette in the light of the open door, then a three-dimensional figure shuffling down the snow trench out toward the garage. He had a flashlight in one hand, and played it off the side of the garage. The Iceman eased back as the light crossed the side wall of the garage, gave Frank a few seconds to get further down the path, then peeked around the corner. Frank had gotten to the garage door, opened it. The Iceman shuffled up to the corner of the garage, the gun in his left hand, the corn-knife in his right, the cold burning his bare hands.

Frank snapped on the garage lights, stepped inside. A moment later, the lights went out again. Frank stepped out, pulled it tight behind him, rattled the knob. Stepped up the path. Shone the flashlight across the yard at the propane tank.

Took another step.

The Iceman was there. The corn-knife whipped down, *chunked.* Frank saw it coming, just soon enough to flinch, not soon enough to avoid it. The knife chocked through Frank's parka and into his skull, the shock jolted through the Iceman's arm. A familiar shock, as though he'd chopped the blade into a fence post.

The blade popped free as Frank pitched over. He was dead as he fell, but his body made a sound like a stepped-on snake, a tight exhalation, a ccccuuuhh-hhh, and blood ran into the snow.

For just a second then, the wind stopped, as though nature were holding her breath. The snow seemed to pause with the wind, and something flicked across the edge of the woods, at the corner of the Iceman's vision. Something out there . . . he was touched by an uneasiness. He watched, but there was no further movement, and the wind and snow were back as quickly as they'd gone.

The Iceman stepped down into the trench, started toward the house. Claudia's face appeared in the window, floating out there in the storm. He stopped, sure he'd been seen: but she pressed her face closer to the window, peering out, and he realized that he was still invisible. After a moment, her face moved back away from the window. The Iceman started for the house again, climbed the porch as quietly as he could, turned the knob, pushed the door open.

"Frank?" Claudia was there, in the doorway to the kitchen. Her hand popped out of her sleeve and the Iceman saw the flash of chrome, knew the flash, reacted, brought up the big .44 Mag.

"Frank?" Claudia screamed. The .357 hung in her hand, by her side, unready, unthought-of, a worthless icon of self-defense. Then the V of the back sight and the i of the front sight crossed the plane of her head and the .44 bucked in the Iceman's hand. He'd spent hours in the quarry doing this, swinging on targets, and he knew he had her, felt the accuracy in his bones, one with the target.

The slug hit Claudia in the forehead and the world stopped. No more Lisa, no more Frank, no more nights in the Holiday Inn with the mirrors, no memories, no regrets. Nothing. She didn't fly back, like in the movies. She wasn't hammered down. She simply dropped, her mouth open. The Iceman, bringing the Colt back to bear, felt a thin sense of disappointment. The big gun should batter them down, blow them up; the big gun was a Universal Force.

From the back room, then, in the silence after the shot, a young girl's voice, not yet afraid: "Mom? Mom? What was that?"

The Iceman grabbed Claudia's parka hood, dragged her into the kitchen and dropped her. She lay on the floor like a puppet with the strings cut. Her eyes were open, sightless. He ignored her. He was focused now on the back room. He needed the picture. He hefted the corn-knife and started back.

The girl's voice again. A little fear this time: "Mom?"

LUCAS DAVENPORT CLIMBED down from his truck. The light on the LaCourt house was brilliant. In the absolutely clear air, every crack, every hole, every splinter of glass was as sharp as a hair under a microscope. The smell of death—the smell of pork roast—slipped up to him, and he turned his face toward it, looking for it, like a stone-age hunter.

The house looked oddly like a skull, with its glassless windows gaping out at the snowscape. The front door was splintered by fire axes, while the side door, hanging from the house by a single hinge, was twisted and blackened by the fire. Vinyl siding had melted, charred, burned. Half of the roof was gone, leaving the center of the ruin open to the sky. Pink fiberglass insulation was everywhere, sticking out of the house, blowing across the snow, hung up in the bare birch branches like obscene fleshy hair. Firehose ice, mixed with soot and ash, flowed around and out of the house like a miniature glacier.

On the land side of the house, three banks of portable stadium-style lights, run off an ancient gas-powered Army generator, poured a hundred million candlepower of blue-white light onto the scene. The generator underlined the shouting of the firemen and the thrumming of the fire truck pumps with a ferocious jackhammer pounding.

All of it stank.

Of gasoline and burning insulation, of water-soaked plaster and barbecued bodies, diesel fumes. The fire had moved fast, burned fiercely, and had been smothered in a hurry. The dead had been charred rather than cremated.

Twenty men swarmed over the house. Some were firemen, others were cops; three or four were civilians. The snow had eased, at least temporarily, but the wind was like a razor, slashing at exposed skin.

LUCAS WAS TALL, dark-complected, with startling blue eyes set deep under a strong brow. His hair was dark, but touched with gray, and a bit long; a sheath of it fell over his forehead, and he pushed it out of his eyes as he stood looking at the house.

Quivering, almost—like an expensive pointer.

His face should have been square, and normally was, when he was ten pounds heavier. A square face fit with the rest of him, with his heavy shoulders and hands. But now he was gaunt, the skin stretched around his cheekbones: the face of a boxer in hard training. Every day for a month he'd put on either skis or snowshoes, and had run up through the hills around his North Woods cabin. In the afternoon he worked in the woodlot, splitting oak with a mall and wedge.

Lucas stepped toward the burnt house as though hypnotized. He remembered another house, in Minneapolis, just south of the loop, a frozen night in February. A gang leader lived in the downstairs apartment; a rival group of 'bangers decided to take him out. The top floor was occupied by a woman— Shirleen something—who ran an illegal overnight child-care center for neighborhood mothers. There were six children sleeping upstairs when the Molotov cocktails came through the windows downstairs. Shirleen dropped all six screaming kids out the window, breaking legs on two of them, ribs on two more, and an arm on a neighbor who was trying to stop their fall. The woman was too big to jump herself and burned to death trying to get down the single stairway. Same deal: the house like a skull, the firehose ice, the smell of roast pork. . . .

Lucas unconsciously shook his head and smiled: he'd had good lines into the crack community and gave homicide the 'bangers' names. They were locked in Stillwater, and would be for another eight years. In two days he'd done a number on them they still didn't believe.

Now this. He stepped back to the open door of his truck, leaned inside, took a black cashmere watch cap off the passenger seat and pulled it over his head. He wore a blue parka over jeans and a cable-knit sweater, pac boots, and expedition-weight polypropylene long underwear. A deputy walked around the Chevy Suburban that had pulled into the yard just ahead of Davenport's Ford. Henry Lacey wore the standard tan sheriff's department parka and insulated pants.

"Shelly's over here," Lacey said, jerking a thumb toward the house. "C'mon—I'll introduce you . . . what're you looking at, the house? What's funny?"

"Nothing."

"Thought you were smiling," Lacey said, looking vaguely disturbed.

"Nah . . . just cold," Lucas said, groping for an excuse. Goddamn, he loved this.

"Well . . . Shelly . . ."

"Yeah." Lucas followed, pulling on his thick ski gloves, still focused on the house. The place might have been snatched from a frozen suburb of hell. He felt at home.

SHELDON CARR STOOD ON a slab of ice in the driveway, behind the volunteer tanker and pumper trucks. He wore the same sheriff's cold-weather gear as Lacey, but black instead of khaki, with the sheriff's gold star instead of the silver deputy's badge. A frozen black hose snaked past his feet down to the lake, where the firefighters had augered through three feet of ice to get at the lake water. Now they were using a torch to free the hose, and the blue flame flickered at the edge of Carr's vision.

Carr was stunned. He'd done what he could, and then he stopped functioning: he simply stood in the driveway and watched the firemen work. And he froze. His cold-weather gear wasn't enough for this weather. His legs were stiff and his feet numb, but he couldn't go into the garage, couldn't tear himself away. He stood like a dark snowman, slightly fat, unmoving, hands away from his side, staring up at the house.

"Piece a . . ." A fireman slipped and fell, cursing. Carr had to turn his whole body to look at him. The fireman was smeared with ash and half-covered with ice. When they'd tried to spray the house, the wind had whipped the water back on them as sleet. Some of the firemen looked like small mobile icebergs, the powerful lights glistening off them as they worked across the yard. This one was on his back, looking up at Carr, his mustache white with frost from his own breath, face red from the wind and exertion. Carr moved to help him, hand out, but the fireman waved him away. "I'd just pull you down," he said. He clambered awkwardly to his feet, struggling with a frozen firehose. He was trying to load it into a pickup truck and it fought back like an anaconda on speed. "Piece a shit . . ."

Carr turned back to the house. A rubber-encased fireman was helping the doctor climb through the shattered front door. Carr watched as they began to pick their way toward the back bedroom. The little girl was there, so burnt that

God only knew what had happened to her. What had happened to her parents was clear enough. Claudia's face had been partly protected by a fireproof curtain that had fallen over her. A fat bullet hole stared out of her forehead like a blank third eye. And Frank . . .

"Heard anything from Madison?" Carr called to a deputy in a Jeep. The deputy had the engine turning over, heater on high, window down just far enough to communicate.

"Nope. It's still snowin' down there. I guess they're waitin' it out."

"Waitin' it out? Waitin' it out?" Sheldon Carr was suddenly shouting, eyes wild. "Call the fuckers back and tell them to get their asses up here. They've heard of four-by-fours, haven't they? Call them back."

"Right now," the deputy said, shocked. He'd never heard Sheldon Carr say anything stronger than *gol-darn*.

Carr turned away, his jaw working, the cold forgotten. *Waiting it out?* Henry Lacey was walking toward him, carefully flatfooted on the treacherous slab of ice that had run down into the yard. He was trailed by a man in a parka. Lacey came up, nodded, said, "This is Davenport."

Carr nodded: "Th–th–thanks f–f–f coming." He suddenly couldn't get the words out.

Lacey took his elbow. "Have you been out here all the time?"

Carr nodded numbly and Lacey tugged him toward the garage, said, "My God, Shelly, you'll kill yourself."

"I'm okay," Carr ground out. He pulled his arm free, turned to Lucas. "When I heard you were up here from the Cities, I figured you'd know more about this kind of thing than I do. Thought it was worth a try. Hope you can help us."

"Henry tells me it's a mess," Lucas said.

He grinned as he said it, a slightly nasty smile, Carr thought. Davenport had a chipped tooth, never capped, the kind of thing you might have gotten in a fight, and a scar bisected one eyebrow. "It's a . . ." Carr shook his head, groping for a word. "It's a gol-darn *tragedy*," he said finally.

Lucas glanced at him: he'd never heard a cop call a crime a tragedy. He'd never heard a cop say gol-darn. He couldn't see much of Carr's face, but the sheriff was a large man with an ample belly. In the black snowmobile suit, he looked like the Michelin tire man in mourning.

"Where's LES?" Lucas asked. The Division of Law Enforcement Services did mobile crime-scene work on major crimes.

"They're having trouble getting out of Madison," Carr said grimly. He waved at the sky. "The storm . . ."

"Don't they have four-by-fours? It's all highway."

"We're finding that out right now," Carr snapped. He apologized: "Sorry, that's a tender subject. They shoulda been halfway here by now." He looked back at the house, as if helpless to resist it: "Lord help us."

"Three dead?" Lucas asked.

"Three dead," Carr said. "Shot, chopped with some kind of ax or something, and the other one . . . shoot, there's no way to tell. Just a kid."

"Still in the house?"

"Come on," Carr said grimly. He suddenly began to shake uncontrollably, then, with an effort, relaxed. "We got tarps on 'em. And there's something else . . . heck, let's look at the bodies, then we'll get to that."

"Shelly, are you okay?" Lacey asked again.

"Yeah, yeah . . . I'll show Davenport—Lucas?—I'll show Lucas around, then I'll get inside. Gosh, I can't believe this cold."

FRANK LACOURT LAY FACEUP on a sidewalk that led from the house to the garage. Carr had one of the deputies lift the plastic tarp that covered the body and Lucas squatted beside it.

"Jesus," he said. He looked up at Carr, who'd turned away. "What happened to his face?"

"Dog, maybe," Carr said, looking sideways down at the mutilated face. "Coyotes . . . I don't know."

"Could have been a wolf," Lacey said from behind him. "We've had some reports, I think there are a few moving down."

"Messed him up," Lucas said.

Carr looked out at the forest that pressed around the house: "It's the winter," he said. "Everything's starving out there. We're feedin' some deer, but most of them are gonna die. Shoot, most of them are already dead. There're coyotes hanging around the dumpsters in town, at the pizza place."

Lucas pulled off a glove, fumbled a hand-flash from his parka pocket and shone it on what was left of the man's face. LaCourt was an Indian, maybe forty-five. His hair was stiff with frozen blood. An animal had torn the flesh off much of the left side of his face. The left eye was gone and the nose was chewed away.

"He got it from the side, half-split his head in two, right through the hood," Carr said. Lucas nodded, touched the hood with his gloved finger, looking at the cut fabric. "The doc said it was some kind of knife or cleaver," Carr said.

Lucas stood up. "Henry said snowshoes . . ."

"Right there," Lacey said, pointing.

Lucas turned the flashlight into the shadows along the shed. Broad indentations were still visible in the snow. The indentations were half drifted-in.

"Where do they go?" Lucas asked, staring into the dark trees.

"They come up from the lake, through the woods, and they go back down," Carr said, pointing at an angle through the jumble of forest. "There's a snowmobile trail down there, machines coming and going all the time. Frank had a couple sleds himself, so it could have been him that made the tracks. We don't know."

"The tracks come right up to where he was chopped," Lucas said.

"Yeah—but we don't know if he walked down to the lake on snowshoes to look at something, and then came back up and was killed, or if the killer came in and went out."

"If they were his snowshoes, where are they now?"

"There's a set of shoes in the mudroom, but they were so messed up by the firehoses that we don't know if they'd just been used or what . . . no way to tell," Lacey said. "They're the right kind, though. Bearpaws. No tails."

"Okay."

"But we still got a problem," Carr said, looking reluctantly down at the body. "Look at the snow on him. The firemen threw the tarps over them as soon as they got here, but it looks to me like there's maybe a half-inch of snow on him."

"So what?"

Carr stared down at the body for a moment, then dropped his voice. "Listen, I'm freezing and there's some strange stuff to talk about. A problem. So do you want to see the other bodies now? Woman was shot in the forehead, the girl's burned. Or we could just go talk."

"A quick look," Lucas said.

"Come on, then," Carr said.

Lacey broke away. "I gotta check that commo gear, Shelly."

Lucas and Carr trudged across a layer of discolored ice to the house, squeezed past the front door. Inside, sheetrock walls and ceiling panels had buckled and folded, falling across burned furniture and carpet. Dishes, pots and pans, glassware littered the floor, along with a set of ceramic collector's dolls. Picture frames were everywhere. Some were burned, but every step or two, a clear, happy face would look up at him, wide-eyed, well-lit. Better days.

Two deputies were working through the house with cameras: one with a video camera, the power wire running down his collar under his parka, the other with a 35mm Nikon.

"My hands are freezing," the video man stuttered.

"Go on down to the garage," Carr said. "Don't get yourself hurt."

"There're a couple gallon jugs of hot coffee and some paper cups in my truck. The white Explorer in the parking lot," Lucas said. "Doors are open."

"Th–thanks."

"Save some for me," Carr said. And to Lucas: "Where'd you get the coffee?"

"Stopped at Dow's Corners on the way over and emptied out their coffeemaker. I did six years on patrol and I must've froze my ass off at a hundred of these things."

"Huh. Dow's." Carr squinted, digging in a mental file. "That's still Phil and Vickie?"

"Yeah. You know them?"

"I know everybody on Highway 77, from Hayward in Sawyer County to Highway 13 in Ashland County," Carr said matter-of-factly. "This way."

He led the way down a charred hall past a bathroom door to a small bedroom. The lakeside wall was gone and blowing snow sifted through the debris. The body was under a burnt-out bedframe, the coil springs resting on the girl's chest. One of the portable lights was just outside the window, and cast flat, prying light on the scorched wreckage, but left the girl's face in almost total darkness: but not quite total. Lucas could see her improbably white teeth smiling from the char.

Lucas squatted, snapped on the flash, grunted, turned it off and stood up again.

"Made me sick," said Carr. "I was with the highway patrol before I got elected sheriff. I saw some car wrecks you wouldn't believe. They didn't make me sick. This did."

"Accidents are different," Lucas agreed. He looked around the room. "Where's the other one?"

"Kitchen," Carr said. They started down the hall again. "Why'd he burn the place?" Carr asked, his voice pitching up. "It couldn't have been to hide the killings. He left Frank's body right out in the yard. If he'd just taken off, it might have been a day or two before anybody came out. Was he bragging about it?"

"Maybe he was thinking about fingerprints. What'd LaCourt do?"

"He worked down at the res, at the Eagle Casino. He was a security guy."

"Lots of money in casinos," Lucas said. "Was he in trouble down there?"

"I don't know," Carr said simply.

"How about his wife?"

"She was a teacher's aide."

"Any marital problems or ex-husbands wandering around?" Lucas asked.

"Well, they were both married before. I'll check Frank's ex-wife, but I know her, Jean Hansen, and she wouldn't hurt a fly. And Claudia's ex is Jimmy Wilson and Jimmy moved out to Phoenix three or four winters back, but he wouldn't do this, either. I'll check on him, but neither one of the divorces was really nasty. The people just didn't like each other anymore. You know?"

"Yeah, I know. How about the girl? Did she have any boyfriends?"

"I'll check that too," Carr said. "But, uh, I don't know. I'll check. She's pretty young."

"There's been a rash of teenagers killing their families and friends."

"Yeah. A generation of weasels."

"And teenage boys sometimes mix up fire and sex. You get a lot of teenage firebugs. If there was somebody hot for the girl, it'd be something to look into."

"You could talk to Bob Jones at the junior high. He's the principal and he does the counseling, so he might know."

"Um." Lucas said. His sleeve touched a burnt wall, and he brushed it off.

"I'm hoping you'll stay around a while," Carr blurted. Before Lucas could answer, he said, "Come on down this way."

They picked their way toward the other end of the house, through the living room, into the kitchen by the back door. Two heavily wrapped figures were crouched over a third body.

The larger of the two people stood up, nodded at Carr. He wore a Russian-style hat with the flaps pulled down and a deputy sheriff's patch on the front. The other, with the bag, was using a metal tool to turn the victim's head.

"Can't believe this weather," the deputy said. "I'm so fuck—uh, cold I can't believe it."

"Fucking cold is what you meant to say," said the figure still crouched over the body. Her voice was low and uninflected, almost scholarly. "I really don't mind the word, especially when it's so fucking cold."

"It wasn't you he was worried about, it was me," Carr said bluntly. "You see anything down there, Weather, or are you just fooling around?"

The woman looked up and said, "We've got to get them down to Milwaukee and let the pros take a look. No amateur nights at the funeral home."

"Can you see anything at all?" Lucas asked.

The doctor looked down at the woman under her hands. "Claudia was shot, obviously, and with a pretty powerful weapon. Could be a rifle. The whole back of her head was shattered and a good part of her brain is gone. The slug went straight through. We'll have to hope the crime lab people can recover it. It's not inside her."

"How about the girl?" Lucas asked.

"Yeah. It'll take an autopsy to tell you anything definitive. There are signs of charred cloth around her waist and between her legs, so I'd say she was wearing underpants and maybe even, um, what do you call those fleece pants, like uh . . ."

"Sweat pants," Carr said.

"Yes, like that. And Claudia was definitely dressed, jeans and long underwear."

"You're saying they weren't raped," Lucas said.

The woman stood and nodded. Her parka hood was tight around her face, and nothing showed but an oval patch of skin around her eyes and nose. "I can't say it for sure, but just up front, it doesn't look like it. But what happened to her might have been worse."

"Worse?" Carr recoiled.

"Yes." She stooped, opened her bag, and the deputy said, "I don't want to look at this." She stood up again and handed Carr a Ziploc bag. Inside was something that looked like a dried apricot that had been left on a charcoal grill. Carr peered at it and then gave it to Lucas.

"What is it?" Carr asked the woman.

"Ear," she and Lucas said simultaneously. Lucas handed it back to her.

"Ear? You can't be serious," Carr said.

"Taken off before or after she was killed?" Lucas asked, his voice mild, interested. Carr looked at him in horror.

"You'd need a lab to tell you that," Weather said in her professional voice, matching Lucas. "There are some crusts that look like blood. I'm not sure, but I'd say she was alive when it was taken off."

The sheriff looked at the bag in the doctor's hand and turned and walked two steps away, bent over and retched, a stream of saliva pouring from his mouth. After a moment, he straightened, wiped his mouth on the back of a glove, and said, "I gotta get out of here."

"And Frank was done with an ax," Lucas said.

"No, I don't think so. Not an ax," the woman said, shaking her head. Lucas peered at her, but could see almost nothing of her face. "A machete, a very sharp machete. Or maybe something even thinner. Maybe a something like, um, a scimitar."

"A what?" The sheriff goggled at her.

"I don't know," she said defensively. "Whatever it was, the blade was very thin and sharp. Like a five-pound razor. It *cut* through the bone, rather than smashing through like a wedge-shaped weapon would. But it had weight, too."

"Don't go telling that to anybody at the *Register*," Carr said. "They'd go crazy."

"They're gonna go crazy anyway," she said.

"Well, don't make them any crazier."

"What about the guy's face?" Lucas asked. "The bites?"

"Dog," she said. "Coyote. God knows I see enough dog bites around here and it looks like a dog did it."

"You can hear them howling at night, bunches of them," the deputy said. "Coyotes."

"Yeah, I've got them up around my place," Lucas said.

"Are you with the state?" the woman asked.

"No. I used to be a Minneapolis cop. I've got a cabin over in Sawyer County and the sheriff asked me to run over and take a look."

"Lucas Davenport," the sheriff said, nodding at him. "I'm sorry, Lucas, this is Weather Karkinnen."

"I've heard about you," the woman said, nodding.

"Weather was a surgeon down in the Cities before she came back home," the sheriff said to Lucas.

"Is that Weather, like 'Stormy Weather'?" Lucas asked.

"Exactly," the doctor said.

"I hope what you heard about Davenport was good," Carr said to her.

The doctor looked up at Lucas and tilted her head. The light on her changed and he could see that her eyes were blue. Her nose seemed to be slightly crooked. "I remember that he killed an awful lot of people," she said.

THE DOCTOR WAS FREEZING, she said, and she led the way toward the front door, the deputy following, Carr stumbling behind. Lucas lingered, looking down at the dead woman. As he turned to leave, he saw a slice of nickeled metal under a piece of crumbled and blackened wallboard. From the curve of it, he knew what it was: the forepart of a trigger guard.

"Hey," he called after the others. "Is that camera guy still in the house?"

Carr called back, "The video guy's in the garage, but the other guy's here."

"Send him back here, we got a weapon."

Carr, Weather, and the photographer came back. Lucas pointed out the trigger guard, and the photographer took two shots of the area. Moving carefully, Lucas lifted the wallboard. A revolver. A nickel-finish Smith and Wesson on a heavy frame, walnut grips. He pushed the board back out of the way, then stood back as the photographer shot the gun in relation to the body.

"You got a chalk or a grease pencil?" Lucas asked.

"Yeah, and a tape measure." The photographer groped in his pocket, came up with a grease pencil.

"Shouldn't you leave it for the lab guys?" Carr asked nervously.

"Big frame, could be the murder weapon," Lucas said. He drew a quick outline around the weapon, then measured the distance of the gun from the wall and the dead woman's head and one hand, while the photographer noted them. With the measurements done, Lucas handed the grease pencil back to the photographer, looked around, picked up a splinter of wood, pushed it through the fingerguard, behind the trigger, and lifted the pistol from the floor. He looked at the doctor. "Do you have another one of those Ziplocs?"

"Yes." She opened her bag, supported it against her leg, dug around, and opened a freezer bag for him. He dropped the gun into it, pointed the barrel at the floor, and through the plastic he pushed the ejection level and swung the cylinder.

"Six shells, unfired," he said. "Shit."

"Unfired?" Carr asked.

"Yeah. I don't think it's the murder weapon. The killer wouldn't reload and then drop it on the floor . . . at least I can't think why he would."

"So?" Weather looked up at him.

"So maybe the woman had it out. I found it about a foot from her hand. She might have seen the guy coming. That means there might have been a feud going on; she knew she was in trouble," Lucas said. He read the serial number to the photographer, who noted it: "You could try to run it tonight. Check the local gun stores, anyway."

"I'll get it going," Carr said. Then: "I n–n–need some coffee."

"I think you're fairly hypothermic, Shelly," Weather said. "What you need is to sit in a tub of hot water."

"Yeah, yeah."

As they climbed down from the front door, Lucas carrying the pistol, another deputy was walking up the driveway. "I got those tarps, Sheriff. They're right behind me in a Guard truck."

"Good. Get some help and cover up the whole works," Carr said, waving at the house. "There'll be guys in the garage." To Lucas he said, "I got some canvas sheets from the National Guard guys and we're gonna cover the whole house until the guys from Madison get here."

"Good." Lucas nodded. "You really need the lab guys for this. Don't let anybody touch anything. Not even the bodies."

THE GARAGE WAS WARM, with deputies and firemen standing around an old-fashioned iron stove stoked with oak splits. The deputy who'd been doing the filming spotted them and came over with one of Lucas' Thermos jugs.

"I saved some," he said.

"Thanks, Tommy." The sheriff nodded, took a cup, hand shaking, passed it to Lucas, then took a cup for himself. "Let's get over in the corner where we can talk," he said. Carr walked around the nose of LaCourt's old Chevy station wagon, away from the gathering of deputies and firemen, turned, took a sip of coffee. He said, "We've got a problem." He stopped, then asked, "You're not a Catholic, are you?"

"Dominus vobiscum," Lucas said. "So what?"

"You are? I haven't been in the Church long enough to remember the Latin business," Carr said. He seemed to think about that for a moment, sipped coffee, then said, "I converted a few years back. I was a Lutheran until I met Father Phil. He's the parish priest in Grant."

"Yeah? I don't have much interest in the Church anymore."

"Hmph. You should consider . . ."

"Tell me about the problem," Lucas said impatiently.

"I'm trying to, but it's complicated," Carr said. "Okay. We figure whoever killed these folks must've started the fire. It was snowing all afternoon—we had about four inches of new snow. When the firemen got here, though, the snow'd just about quit. But Frank's body had maybe a half-inch of snow on it. That's why I had them put the tarp over it, I thought we could fix an exact time. It wasn't long between the time he was killed and the fire. But it was *some* time. That's important. *Some* time. And now you tell me the girl might have been tortured . . . *more* time."

"Okay." Lucas nodded, nodding at the emphasis.

"Whoever started the fire did it with gasoline," Carr said. "You can still smell it, and the house went up like a torch. Maybe the killer brought the gas with him or maybe he used Frank's. There're a couple boats and a snowmobile out in the back shed but there aren't any gas cans with them, and no cans in here. The cans'd most likely have some gas in them."

"Anyway, the house went up fast," Lucas said.

"Yeah. The folks across the lake were watching television. They say that one minute there was nothing out the window but the snow. The next minute there was a fireball. They called the firehouse."

"The one I came by? Down at the corner?"

"Yeah. There were two guys down there. They were making a snack and one of them saw a black Jeep go by. Just a few seconds later, the alarm came in. They thought the Jeep belonged to Phil . . . the priest. Father Philip Bergen, the pastor at All Souls."

"Did it?" Lucas asked.

"Yes. They said it looked like Phil was coming out of the lake road. So I called him and asked him if he'd seen anything unusual. A fire or somebody in the road. And he said no. Then, before I could say anything else, he said he was here, at the LaCourts'."

"Here?" Lucas eyebrows went up.

"Yeah. Here. He said everything was all right when he left."

"Huh." Lucas thought about it. "Are we sure the time is right?"

"It's right. One of the firemen was standing at the microwave with one of those prefab ham sandwiches. They take two minutes to cook and it was about ready. The other one said, 'There goes Father Phil, hell of a night to be out.' Then the microwave alarm went off, the guy got his sandwich out, and before he could unwrap it, the alarm came in."

"That's tight."

"Yeah. There wasn't enough time for Frank to have that snow pile up on him. Not if Phil's telling the truth."

"Time is weird," Lucas said. "Especially in an emergency. If it *wasn't* just a minute, if it was five minutes, then this Father Phil *could* have . . ."

"That's what I figured . . . but doesn't look that way." Carr shook his head, swirled coffee around the coffee cup, then set it on the hood of the Chevy and flexed his fingers, trying to work some warmth back in them. "I got the firemen and went over it a couple of times. There just isn't time."

"So the priest . . ."

"He said he left the house and drove straight out to the highway and then into town. I asked him how long it took him to get from the house, here, to the highway, and he said three or four minutes. It's about a mile, so that's about right, with the snow and everything."

"Hmp."

"But if he had something to do with it, why'd he admit being here? That doesn't make any gol-darned sense," the sheriff said.

"Have you hit him with this? Sat him down, gone over it?"

"No. I'm not real experienced with interrogation. I can take some kid who's stolen a car or ripped off a beer sign and sit him down by one of the holding cells and scare the devil out of him, but this would be . . . different. I don't know about this kind of stuff. Killers."

"Did you tell him about the time bind?" Lucas asked.

"Not yet."

"Good."

"I was stumped," Carr said, turning to stare blankly at the garage wall, remembering. "When he said he was here, I couldn't think what to say. So I said, 'Okay, we'll get back to you.' He wanted to come out when we told him the family was dead, do the last rites, but we told him to stay put, in town. We didn't want him to . . ."

". . . Contaminate his memory."

"Yeah." Carr nodded, picked up the coffee he'd set on the car hood, and finished it.

"How about the firemen? Would they have any reason to lie about it?"

Carr shook his head. "I know them both, and they're not particular friends. So it wouldn't be like a conspiracy."

"Okay."

Two firemen came through the door. The first was encased in rubber and canvas, and on top of that, an inch-thick layer of ice.

"You look like you fell in the lake," Carr said. "You must be freezing to death."

"It was the spray. I'm not cold, but I can't move," the fireman said. The second fireman said, "Stand still." The fireman stood like a fat rubber scarecrow and began chipping the ice away with a wooden mallet and a cold chisel.

They watched the ice chips fly for a moment, then Carr said, "Something else. When he went by the fire station, he was towing a snowmobile trailer. He's big in one of the snowmobile clubs—he's the president, in fact, or was last year. They'd had a run today, out of a bar across the lake. So he was out on the lake with his sled."

"And those tracks came up from the lake."

"Where nobody'd be without a sled."

"Huh. So you think the priest had something to do with it?"

Carr looked worried. "No. Absolutely not. I know him: he's a friend of mine. But I can't figure it out. He doesn't lie, about anything. He's a moral man."

"If a guy's under pressure . . ."

Carr shook his head. Once they'd been playing golf, he said, both of them fierce competitors. And they were dead even after seventeen. Bergen put his tee shot into a group of pines on the right side of the fairway, made a great recovery and was on the green in two. He two-putted for par, while Carr bogied the hole, and lost.

"I was bragging about his recovery to the other guys in the locker room, and he just looked sadder and sadder. When we were walking down to the bar he grabbed me, and he looked like he was about to cry. His second shot had gone under one of the evergreens, he said, and he'd kicked it out. He wanted to win so bad. But cheating, it wrecked him. He couldn't handle it. That's the kind of guy he is. He wouldn't steal a dime, he wouldn't steal a golf stroke. He's absolutely straight, and incapable of being anything else."

The fireman with the chisel and mallet laid the tools on the floor, grabbed the front of the other fireman's rubber coat, and ripped it open.

"That's got it," said the second man. "I can take it from here." He looked at Carr: "Fun in the great outdoors, huh?"

THE DOCTOR WAS EDGING between the wall and the nose of the station wagon, followed by a tall man wrapped in a heavy arctic parka. The doctor had light hair spiked with strands of white, cut efficiently short. She was small, but athletic with wide shoulders, a nose that was a bit too big and a little crooked, bent to the left. She had high cheekbones and dark-blue eyes, a mouth that was wide and mobile. She had just a bit of the brawler about her, Lucas thought, with the vaguely Oriental cast that Slavs often carry. She was not pretty, but she was strikingly attractive. "Is this a secret conversation?" she asked. She was carrying a cup of coffee.

"No, not really," Carr said, glancing at Lucas. He gave a tiny backwards wag of his head that meant, *Don't say anything about the priest.*

The tall man said, "Shelly, I hit every place on the road. Nobody saw anything connected, but we've got three people missing yet. I'm trying to track them down now."

"Thanks, Gene," Carr said, and the tall man headed toward the door. To Lucas, he said, "My lead investigator."

Lucas nodded, and looked at Weather. "I don't suppose there was any reason to do body temps."

The doctor shook her head, took another sip of coffee. Lucas noticed that she wore no rings. "Not on the two women. The fire and the water and the ice and snow would mess everything up. Frank was pretty bundled up, though, and I did take a temp on him. Sixty-four degrees. He hadn't been dead that long."

"Huh," said Carr, glancing at Lucas.

The doctor caught it and looked from Lucas to Carr and asked, "Is that critical?"

"You might want to write it down somewhere," Carr said.

"There's a question about how long they were dead before the fire started," Lucas said.

Weather was looking at him oddly. "Maddog, right?"

"What?"

"You were the guy who killed the Maddog after he sliced up all those women. And you were in that fight with those Indian guys."

Lucas nodded. "Yeah." *The Crows coming out of that house in the dark, .45s in their hands. . . . Why'd she have to bring that up?*

"I had a friend who did that New York cop, the woman who was shot in the chest? I can't remember her name, but at the time she was pretty famous."

"Lily Rothenburg." *Damn. Sloan on the steps of Hennepin General, white-faced, saying, "Got your shit together? . . . Lily's been shot." Sweet Lily.*

"Oh, yes," Weather said, nodding. "I knew it was a flower name. She's back in New York?"

"Yeah. She's a captain now. Your friend was a redheaded surgeon? I remember."

"Yup. That's her. And she was there when the big shoot-out happened. She says it was the most exciting night of her career. She was doing two ops at the same time, going back and forth between rooms."

"My God, and now it's here," Carr said, appalled. He looked at Lucas. "Listen, I spent five years on the patrol before I got elected up here, and that was twenty years ago. Most of my boys are off the patrol or local police forces. We really don't know nothin' about multiple murder. What I'm askin' is, are you gonna help us out?"

"What do you want me to do?" Lucas asked, shaking away the memories.

"Run the investigation. I'll give you everything I can. Eight or ten guys, help with the county attorney, whatever."

"What authority would I have?"

Carr dipped one hand in his coat pocket and at the same time said, "Do you swear to uphold the laws of the state of Wisconsin and so forth and so on, so help you God?"

"Sure." Lucas nodded.

Carr tossed him a star. "You're a deputy," he said. "We can work out the small stuff later."

Lucas looked at the star in the palm of his hand.

"Try not to shoot anybody," Weather said.

THE ICEMAN'S HANDS WERE FREEZING. He fumbled the can opener twice, then put the soup can aside and turned on the hot water in the kitchen sink. As he let the water run over his fingers, his mind drifted. . . .

He hadn't found the photograph. The girl didn't know where it was, and she'd told the truth: he'd nearly cut her head off before she'd died, cut away her nose and her ears. She said her mother had taken it, and finally, he believed her. But by that time Claudia was dead. Too late to ask where she'd put it.

So he'd killed the girl, chopping her with the corn-knife, and burned the house. The police didn't know there was a photo, and the photo itself was on flimsy newsprint. With the fire, with all the water, it'd be a miracle if it had survived.

Still. He hadn't *seen* it destroyed. The photo, if it were found, would kill him.

Now he stood with his fingers under the hot water. They slowly shaded from white to pink, losing the putty-like consistency they'd had from the brutal cold. For just a moment he closed his eyes, overwhelmed by the sense of things undone. And time was trickling away. A voice at the back of his head said, *Run now. Time is trickling away.*

But he had never run away. Not when his parents had beaten him. Not when kids had singled him out at school. Instead, he had learned to strike first, but slyly, disguising his aggression: even then, cold as ice. Extortion was his style: *I didn't take it, he gave it to me. We were just playing, he fell down, he's just a crybaby, I didn't mean anything.*

In tenth grade he'd learned an important lesson. There were other students as willing to use violence as he was, and violence in tenth grade involved larger bodies, stronger muscles: people got hurt. Noses were broken, shoulders were dislocated in the weekly afternoon fights. Most importantly, you couldn't hide the violence. No way to deny you were in a fight if somebody got hurt.

And somebody got hurt. Darrell Wynan was his name. Tough kid. Picked out the Iceman for one of those reasons known only to people who pick fights: in fact, he had seen it coming. Carried a rock in his pocket, a smooth sandstone pebble the size of a golf ball, for the day the fight came.

Wynan caught him next to the football field, three or four of his remora fish running along behind, carrying their books, delight on their faces. A fight, a fight . . .

The fight lasted five seconds. Wynan came at him in the stance of an experienced barehanded fighter, elbows in. The Iceman threw the rock at Wynan's forehead. Since his hand was only a foot away when he let go, there was almost no way to miss.

Wynan went down with a depressive fracture of the skull. He almost died.

And the Iceman to the cops: I was scared, he was coming with his whole gang, that's all he does is beat up kids, I just picked up the rock and threw it.

His mother had picked him up at the police station (his father was gone by then, never to be seen again). In the car, his mother started in on him: *Wait till I get you home,* she said. *Just wait.*

And the Iceman, in the car, lifted a finger to her face and said, *You ever fuckin' touch me again I'll wait until you're asleep and I'll get a hammer and I'll beat your head in. You ever touch me again, you better never go to sleep.*

She believed him. A good thing, too. She was still alive.

HE TURNED OFF THE hot water, dried his hands on a dish towel. *Need to think. So much to do.* He forgot about the soup, went and sat in his television chair, stared at the blank screen.

He had never seen the photograph as it had been reproduced, although he'd seen the original Polaroid. He had been stupid to let the boy keep it. And when the boy had sent it away . . .

"WE'RE GONNA BE FAMOUS," *the kid said.*

"What?" They were smoking cigarettes in the trailer's back bedroom, the boy relaxing against a stack of pillows; the Iceman had both feet on the floor, his elbows on his knees.

The boy rolled over, looked under the bed, came up with what looked like a newspaper. He flipped it at the Iceman. There were dozens of pictures, boys and men.

"What'd you do?" the Iceman asked; but in his heart he knew, and the anger swelled in his chest.

"Sent in the picture. You know, the one with you and me on the couch."

"You fuck."

The Iceman lurched at him; the boy giggled, barely struggling, not understanding. The Iceman was on his chest, straddling him, got his thumbs on the boy's throat . . . and then Jim Harper knew. His eyes rolled up and his mouth opened and the Iceman . . .

Did what? Remembered backing away, looking at the body. Christ. He'd killed him.

THE ICEMAN JUMPED TO his feet, reliving it and the search for a place to dump the body. He thought about throwing it in a swamp. He thought about shooting him with a shotgun, leaving the gun, so it might look like a hunting accident. But Jim didn't hunt. And his father would know, and his father was nuts. Then he remembered the kid talking about something he'd read about in some magazine, about people using towel racks, the rush you got, better than cocaine . . .

The Iceman, safe at home, growled: thinking. Everything so difficult. He'd tried to track the photo, but the magazine gave no clue to where it might be. Nothing but a Milwaukee post office box. He didn't know how to trace it without showing his face. After a while he'd calmed down. The chances of the photo being printed were small, and even if it was printed, the chances of anyone local seeing it were even smaller.

And then, when he'd almost forgotten about it, he'd gotten the call from Jim Harper's insane father. The LaCourts had a photo.

Remember the doctor.

Yes. Weather . . .

If the photo turned up, no one would immediately recognize him except the doctor. Without the doctor, they might eventually identify him, but he'd know they were looking, and that would give him time.

He got to his feet, went to wall pegs where he'd hung his snowmobile suit over a radiator vent. The suit was just barely enough on a night like this. Even with the suit, he wouldn't want to be out too long. He pulled it on, slipped his feet into his pac boots, laced them tight, then dug into his footlocker for the .44. It was there, wrapped in an oily rag, nestled in the bottom with his other guns. He lifted it out, the second time he'd use it today. The gun was heavy in his hand, solid, intricate, efficient.

He worked it out, slowly, piece by piece:

Weather Karkinnen drove a red Jeep, the only red Jeep at the LaCourt home. She'd have to take the lake road out to Highway 77, and then negotiate the narrow, windblown road back to town. She'd be moving slow . . . if she was still at the LaCourt house.

WEATHER'S WORK WAS FINISHED. The bodies were covered and would be left in place until the crime lab people arrived from Madison. She'd performed all her legal duties: this was her year to be county coroner, an unpleasant job rotated between the doctors in town. She'd made all the necessary notes for a finding of homicide by persons unknown. She'd write the notes into a formal report to the county attorney and let the Milwaukee medical examiner do the rest.

There was nothing holding her. But standing in the shed, drinking coffee, listening to the cops—even the cops coming over to hit on her, in their mild-mannered Scandinavian way—was something she didn't want to give up right away.

And she wouldn't mind talking to Davenport again, either, she thought. Where'd he go to? She craned her neck, looking around. He must be outside.

She flipped up her hood, pulled it tight, put on her gloves. Outside, things were more orderly. Most of the fire equipment was gone, and the few neighbors who'd walked to the house had been shooed away. It still stank. She wrinkled her nose, looked around. A deputy was hauling a coil of inch-thick rope up toward the house, and she asked, "Have you seen, uh, Shelly, or that guy from Minneapolis?"

"I think Shelly's up to the house, and the other guy went with a bunch of people down to the lake to look at the snowmobile trail, and they're talking to snowmobile guys."

"Thanks."

She looked down toward the lake, thought about walking down. The snow was deep, and she was already cold again. Besides, what'd she have to contribute?

She went back to the garage for another cup of coffee, and found that it was gone, Davenport's Thermoses empty.

Davenport. God, she was acting like a teenager all of a sudden. Not that she couldn't use a little . . . friendship. She thought back to her last involvement: how long, a year? She counted back. Wait, jeez. More than two years. God, it was nearly three. He'd been married, although, as he said charmingly, *not very*, and the whole thing was doomed from the start. He'd had a nice touch in bed, but was a little too fond of network television: it became very easy to see him as a slowly composting lump on a couch somewhere.

Weather sighed. No coffee. She put on her gloves, went back out and trudged toward her Jeep, still reluctant to go. In the whole county, this was the place to be this night. This was the center of things.

But she was increasingly feeling the cold. Even with her pacs, her toes were feeling brittle. Out on the lake, the lights from a pod of snowmobiles shone toward the house. They'd been attracted by the fire and the cops and by now, undoubtedly, the whole story of the LaCourt murders. Grant was a small town, where nothing much happened.

THE ICEMAN SLICED ACROSS the lake. A half-dozen sleds were gathered on the ice near the LaCourt house, watching the cops work. Two more were cruising down the lakeshore, heading for the house. If the temperature had been warmer, a few degrees either side of zero, there'd have been a hundred snowmobiles on the lake, and more coming in.

Halfway across, he left the trail, carved a new cut in the soft snow and stopped. The LaCourt house was a half mile away, but everything around it was bathed in brilliant light. Through a pair of pocket binoculars he could see Weather's Jeep, still parked in the drive.

He grunted, put the glasses in a side pocket where they'd stay cold, gingerly climbed off the sled and tested the snow. He sank in a foot before the harder crust supported his weight. Good. He trampled out a hole and settled into it, in the lee of the sled. Even a five-mile-an-hour wind was a killer on a night like this.

From his hole he could hear the beating of a generator and the occasional shouts of men working, spreading what appeared to be a canvas tent over the house. Their distant voices were like pieces of audible confetti, sharp isolated calls and shouts in the night. Then his focus shifted, and for the first time, he heard the other voices. They'd been there, all along, like a Greek chorus. He turned, slowly, until he was facing the darkness back along the creek. The sound was unearthly, the sound of starvation. Not a scream, like a cat, but almost like the girl, when he'd cut her, a high, quavering, wailing, note.

Coyotes.

Singing together, blood songs after the storm. He shivered, not from the cold.

BUT THE COLD HAD NEARLY gotten to him twenty minutes later when he saw the small figure walking alone toward the red Jeep. Yes. Weather.

When she climbed inside her truck, he brushed the snow off his suit, threw a leg over the sled and cranked it up. He watched as she turned on the head-lights, backed out of her parking space. She had further to go than he did, so he sat and watched until he was sure she was turning left, heading out. She might still stop at the fire station, but there wasn't much going on there except equipment maintenance.

He turned back toward the trail, followed it for a quarter mile, then moved to his right again, into new snow. Stackpole's Resort was over there, closed for the season, but marked with a yard-light. He could get off the lake on the resort's beach, follow the driveway up to the highway, and wait for her there.

He'd had an image of the ambush in his mind. She'd be driving slowly on the snowpacked highway, and he'd come alongside the Jeep with the sled. From six or ten feet away, he could hardly miss: the .44 Magnum would punch through the window like it was toilet paper. She'd go straight off the road, and he'd pull up beside her, empty the pistol into her. Even if somebody saw him, the sled was the perfect escape vehicle, out here in the deep snow. Nothing could follow him, not unless it had skis on the front end. Out here, the sled was virtually anonymous.

THE SNOW-COVERED BEACH CAME UP fast, and he braked, felt the machine buck up, took it slowly across the resort's lakeside lawn and through the drifts between two log cabins. The driveway had been plowed after the last storm, but not yet after this one, and he eased over the throw-piles down into it. He stopped just off the highway, where a blue fir windbreak would hide the sled. He felt like a motorcycle cop waiting behind a billboard.

Waiting. Where was she?

There was a movement to his left, at the corner of his eye, sudden but furtive, and his head snapped around. Nothing. *But there had been something . . .*

There. A dog, a small German shepherd, caught in the thin illumination of the yard-light. No. Not a shepherd, but a coyote. Looking at him from the brush. Then another. There was a snap, and a growl. They never did this, never. Coyotes were invisible.

He pulled down the zip on his suit, took the .44 out of the inside pocket, looked nervously into the brush. They were gone, he thought. Somewhere.

Headlights turned the corner down at the lake road. Had to be Weather. He shifted the pistol to his other hand, his brake hand. And, for the first time, tried to figure out the details of the attack. With one hand on the accelerator and the other on the brake. . . . He was one hand short. Nothing to shoot with. He'd have to improvise. He'd have to use his brake hand. But . . .

He put the gun in his outside leg pocket as the headlights closed on him. The Jeep flashed by and he registered a quick flickering image of Weather in the window, parka hood down, hat off.

He gunned the sled, started after her, rolling down the shallow ditch on the left side of the road. The Jeep gained on him, gained some more. Its tires threw up a cloud of ice and salt pellets, which popped off his suit and helmet like B-Bs.

She was traveling faster than he'd expected. Other snowmobiles had been down the ditch, so there was the semblance of a trail, obscured by the day's snow; still, it wasn't an official trail. He hit a heavy hummock of swamp grass and suddenly found himself up in the air, holding on.

The flight might have been exhilarating on another day, when he could see, but this time he almost lost it. He landed with a jarring impact and the sled bucked under him, swaying. He fought it, got it straight. He was fifty yards behind her. He rolled the accelerator grip forward, picking up speed, rattling over broken snow, the tops of small bushes, invisible bumps . . . his teeth chattered with the rough ride.

A snowplow had been down the highway earlier in the evening, and the irregular waves of plowed snow flashed by on his right. He moved further left, away from the plowed stuff: it'd be hard and irregular, it'd throw him for sure. Weather's taillights were right *there*. He inched closer. He was moving so fast that he would not be able to brake inside his headlight's reach: if there was a tree down across the ditch, he'd hit it.

He'd just thought of that when he saw the hump coming; he knew what it was as soon as he picked it up, a bale of hay pegged to the bottom of the ditch to slow spring erosion. The deep snow made it into a perfect snowmobile jump, but he didn't want to jump. But he had no time to go around it. He had no time to do anything but brace himself, and he was in the air again.

He came down like a bomb, hard, bounced, the sled skidding through the softer snow up the left bank. He wrestled it to the right, lost it, climbed the right bank toward the plowed snow, wrestled it left, carved a long curve back to the bottom.

Got it.

The Iceman was shaken, thought for an instant about giving it up; but she was right *there*, so close. He gritted his teeth and pushed harder, closing. Thirty yards. Twenty . . .

WEATHER GLANCED IN her side mirror, saw the sled's headlight. He was coming fast. Too fast. Idiot. She smiled, remembering last year's countywide outrage. Intersections of snowmobile trails and ordinary roads were marked with diamond-shaped signs painted with the silhouette of a snowmobile. Like deer-crossing signs, but wordless. The year before, someone had used black spray paint to stencil IDIOT CROSSING on half the snowmobile signs in Ojibway County. Had done the job neatly, with a stencil, a few signs every night for a week. The paper had been full of it.

Davenport.

An image of his face, shoulders, and hands popped into her mind. He was beat-up, wary, like he'd been hurt and needed help; at the same time, he looked tough as a railroad spike. She'd felt almost tongue-tied with him, found herself trying to interest him. Instead, half the things she'd said sounded like border-line insults. *Try not to shoot anyone.*

God, had she said that? She bit her tongue. Why? Trying to impress him. When he'd focused on her, he seemed to be looking right into her. And she liked it.

The bobbing light in her side mirror caught her eye again. The fool on the snowmobile was still in the ditch, but had drawn almost up beside her. She glanced back over her shoulder. If she remembered right, Forest Drive was coming up. There'd be a culvert, and the guy would catapult into Price County if he tried to ride over the embankment at this speed. Was he racing her? Maybe she should slow down.

THE ICEMAN WAS BEFUDDLED by the mechanics of the assassination; if he'd had a sense of humor, he might have laughed. He couldn't let go of the accelerator and keep up with her. If he let go of the brake . . . he just didn't feel safe without some connection with the brake. But he had no choice: he took his hand off the brake lever, pulled open the Velcro-sealed pocket flap, got a good grip on the pistol, slid it out of his pocket. He was fifteen feet back, ten feet. Saw her glance back at him . . .

Five feet back, fifteen feet to the left of her, slightly lower . . . the snow thrown up by the Jeep was still pelting him, rattling off his helmet. Her brake lights flashed, once, twice, three times. Pumping the brakes. Why? Something coming? He could see nothing up ahead. He lifted the gun, found he couldn't keep it on the window, or even the truck's cab, much less her head. He saw the edge of her face as she looked back, her brake lights still flashing . . . What? What was she doing?

He pushed closer, his left hand jumped wildly as he held it awkwardly across his body; the ride was getting rougher. He tried to hold it, the two vehicles ripping along at fifty miles an hour, forty-five, forty, her brakes flashing . . .

Finally, hissing to himself like a flattening tire, he dropped the gun to his leg and rolled back the accelerator. The whole thing was a bad idea. As he slowed, he slipped the pistol back into his pocket, got his hand back on the brake. If he'd had a shotgun, and he'd been in daylight, then it might have worked.

He looked up at the truck and saw her profile, the blonde hair. So close.

He slowed, slowed some more. She'd stopped pumping her brakes. He turned to look back, to check traffic. And suddenly the wall was there, in front of him. He jerked the sled to the right, squeezed the brake, leaned hard right, wrenched the machine up the side of the ditch. A block of frozen snow caught him, and the machine spun out into the road and stalled.

He sat in the sudden silence, out of breath, heart pounding. The Forest Road intersection: he'd forgotten all about it. If he'd kept moving on her, he'd have hit the ends of the steel culvert pipes. He'd be dead. He looked at the embankment, the cold moving into his stomach. Too close. He shook his head, cranked the sled and turned toward home. He looked back before he started out, saw her taillights disappear around a curve. He'd have to go back for her. And soon. Plan it this time. Think it out.

WEATHER SAW THE SNOWMOBILE slow and fall back. Forest Road flashed past and she came up on the highway. He must have read her taillights. She'd seen the road-crossing sign in her headlights, realized she wouldn't have time to stop, to warn him, and had frantically pumped her brakes, hoping he'd catch on.

And he had.

Okay. She saw his taillight come up, just a pinprick of red in the darkness, and touched the preset channel selector on her radio. Duluth public radio was playing Mozart's *Eine kleine Nachtmusik*.

Now about Davenport.

They really needed to talk again. And that might take some planning.

She smiled to herself. She hadn't felt like *this* for a while.

LUCAS FOLLOWED CARR down the dark, snow-packed highway. A logging truck, six huge logs chained to the trailer, pelted past them and enveloped them in a hurricane of loose snow. Carr got his right wheels in the deep snow on the shoulder, nearly didn't make it out. A minute later, a snowplow pushed glumly past them, then a pod of snowmobiles.

He leaned over the steering wheel, tense, peering into the dark. The night seemed to eat up their headlights. They got past the snowplow and the highway opened up for a moment. He groped in the storage bin under the arm rest, found a tape, shoved it in the tape player. Joe Cocker came up, singing "Black-Eyed Blues."

LUCAS FELT LIKE he was waking from an opium dream, spiderwebs and dust blowing off his brain. He'd come back from New York and a brutal manhunt. In Minneapolis, he'd found . . . nothing. Nothing to do but work for money and amuse himself.

In September he'd left the Cities for two weeks of muskie fishing at his Wisconsin cabin east of Hayward. He'd never gone back. He'd called, kept in touch with his programmers, but could never quite get back to the new office. The latest in desktop computers waited for him, a six-hundred-dollar swivel chair, an art print on the wall beside the mounted muskie.

He'd stayed in the north and fought the winter. October had been cold. On Halloween, a winter storm had blown in from the southern Rockies. Before it was done, there were twenty inches of snow on the ground, with drifts five and six feet high.

The cold continued through November, with little flurries and the occasional nasty squall. Two or three inches of new snow accumulated almost every week. Then, on the Friday after Thanksgiving, another major storm swept through, dumping a foot of additional snow. The local papers called it Halloween II and reported that half the winter snowplow budget had been used. Winter was still four weeks away.

December was cold, with off-and-on snow. Then, on January second and third, a blizzard swept the North Woods. Halloween III. When it ended, thirty-four more inches of snow had been piled on the rest. The drifts lapped around the eaves of lakeside cabins.

People said, "Well you shoulda been here back in . . ." But nobody had seen anything like it, ever.

And after the blizzard departed, the cold rang down.

On the night of the third, the thermometer on his cabin deck fell to minus twenty-nine. The following day, the temperature struggled up to minus twenty: schools were closed everywhere, the radio warned against anything but critical travel. On this night, the temperature in Ojibway County would plunge to minus thirty-two.

Almost nothing moved. A rogue logging truck, a despondent snowplow, a few snowmobile freaks. Cop cars. The outdoors was dangerous; so cold as to be weird.

He'd been napping on the couch in front of the fireplace when he first heard the pounding. He'd sat up, instantly alert, afraid that it might be the furnace. But the pounding stopped. He frowned, wondered if he might have imagined it. Rolled to his feet, walked to the basement stairs, listened. Nothing.

Stepped to the kitchen window. He saw the truck in the driveway and a second later the front doorbell rang. Ah. Whoever it was had been pounding on the garage door.

He went to the door, curious. The temperature was well into the minus twenties. He looked through the window inset in the door. A cop, wearing a Russian hat with the ear flaps down.

"Yeah?" Lucas didn't recognize the uniform parka.

"Man, we gotta big problem over in Ojibway County. The sheriff sent me over to see if you could come back and take a look at it. At least three people murdered."

"C'mon in. How'd you know about me?"

Lacey stepped inside, looked around. Books, a few wildlife watercolors on the walls, a television and stereo, pile of embers in the fireplace, the smell of clean-burning pine. "Sheriff read that story in the Milwaukee *Journal* 'bout you in New York, and about living up here. He called around down to Minneapolis and they said you were up here, so he called the Sawyer County sheriff and found out where you live. And here I am."

"Bad night," Lucas said.

"You don't know the half of it," said Lacey. "So cold."

CARR'S TAILLIGHTS BLINKED, then came up, and he slowed and then stopped, turned on his blinkers. Lucas closed up behind, stopped. Carr was on the highway, walking around to the front of his truck.

Lucas opened his door and stepped out: "You okay?"

"Got a tree down," Carr yelled back.

Lucas let the engine run, shut the door, hustled around Carr's truck. The cold had split a limb off a maple tree and it had fallen across the roadside ditch and halfway across the right traffic lane. Carr grabbed the thickest part of it, gave it a tug, moved it a foot. Lucas joined him, and together they dragged it off the road.

"Cold," Carr said, and they hurried back to their trucks.

Weather, Lucas thought. Her image popped up in his mind as he started after Carr again. Now *that* might be an efficient way to warm up, he thought. He'd been off women for a while, and was beginning to feel the loss.

GRANT APPEARED AS a collection of orange sodium-vapor streetlights, followed by a Pines Motel sign, then a Hardee's and a Unocal station, an LP gas company and a video-rental store with a yellow-light marquee. The sheriff turned right at the only traffic light, led him through the three-block-long business district, took a left at a half-buried stop sign and headed up a low hill. On the left was a patch of pines that might have been a park.

A white clapboard church stood at the top of the hill, surrounded by a grove of red pine, with a small cemetery in back. The sheriff drove past the church and stopped in the street in front of a small brick house with lighted windows.

Lucas caught a sign in his headlights: RECTORY. Below that, in cursive letters, REV. PHILIP BERGEN. He pulled in behind Carr, killed the engine, and stepped down from the truck. The air was so cold and dry that he felt as though his skin were being sandpapered. When he breathed, he could feel ice crystals forming on his chin and under his nose.

"That logging truck almost did us," Lucas said as Carr walked back from his Suburban. Gouts of steam poured from their mouths and noses.

"Gol-darned fool. I called back and told somebody to pull him over," Carr said. "Give him a breath test, slow him down." And as they started across the street, he added, "I'm not looking forward to this."

They scuffed through the snow on the rectory walk, up to the covered porch. Carr pushed the doorbell, then dropped his head and bounced on his toes. A man came to the door, peered out the window, then opened it.

"Shelly, what happened out there?" Bergen held the door open, glanced curiously at Lucas, and said, "They're dead?"

"Yeah, um . . . let's get our boots off, we gotta talk," Carr said. "This is our new deputy, Lucas Davenport."

Bergen nodded, peered at Lucas, a wrinkle forming on his forehead, between his eyes. "Pleased to meet you."

The priest was close to fifty, a square, fleshy Scandinavian with blond hair and a permanently doubtful look on his pale face. He wore a wool Icelandic sweater and black slacks, and was in his stocking feet. His words, when he spoke, had a softness to them, a roundness, and Lucas thought that Bergen would not be a fire-and-brimstone preacher, but a mother's-milk sort.

Lucas and Carr dumped their pac boots in the front hallway and walked in stocking feet down a short hall, past a severe Italianate crucifix with a bronze Jesus, to the living room. Carr peeled off his snowmobile suit and Lucas dumped his parka next to a plain wood chair, and sat down.

"So what happened?" Bergen said. He leaned on the mantel over a stone fireplace, where the remnants of three birch logs smoldered behind a glass door. A Sacred Heart print of the Virgin Mary peered over his shoulder.

"There was an odd thing out there." Carr dropped the suit on the floor, then settled on the edge of an overstuffed chair. He put his elbows on his knees, laced his fingers, leaning toward the priest.

"Yes?" Bergen frowned.

"When I called, you said the LaCourts were okay when you left."

"Yes, they were fine," Bergen said, his head bobbing. He was assured, innocent. "They didn't seem nervous. How were they killed, anyway? Is it possible that one of them . . ." He answered his own question, shaking his head. "No, not them."

"A fireman saw your Jeep passing the station," Carr continued. "A few seconds later the fire call came in. When the firemen got there, maybe five or six minutes later, it appeared that the LaCourts had been dead for some time. A half hour, maybe more."

"That's not possible," Bergen said promptly. He straightened, looked from Lucas to Carr, a shadow in his eyes. Suspicion. "Shelly . . . you don't think *I* was involved?"

"No, no, we're just trying to straighten this out."

"So what were they doing when you left?" Lucas asked.

Bergen stared at him, then said, "You're the homicide fellow who lives over in Sawyer County. The man who was fired from Minneapolis."

"What were you doing?" Lucas repeated.

"Shelly?" The priest looked at the sheriff, who looked away.

"We've got to figure this out, Phil."

"Mr. Davenport is a mercenary, isn't he?" Bergen asked, looking again at Lucas.

"We need him, Phil," Carr said, almost pleading now. "We've got nobody else who can do it. And he's a good Catholic boy."

"What were you doing?" Lucas asked a third time. He put glass in his voice, a cutting edge.

The priest pursed his lips, moving them in and out, considering both Lucas and the question, then sighed and said, "When I left, they were fine. There was not a hint of a problem. I came right back here, and I was still here when Shelly called."

"The firemen say there's no mistaking the time," Lucas said. "They're certain."

"I'm certain, too," Bergen snapped.

Lucas: "How long were you there at the house?"

"Fifteen minutes, something like that," Bergen said. He'd turned himself to face Lucas more directly.

"Did you eat anything?"

"Cupcakes. A glass of milk," Bergen said.

"Were the cupcakes hot?"

"No, but as a matter of fact, she was frosting them while we talked."

"When you left, did you stop anywhere on the way out? Even pause?"

"No."

"So you went right out to your Jeep, got in, drove as fast as seemed reasonable to get out of the road."

"Well . . . I probably fiddled around in the Jeep for a minute before I left, a minute or two," Bergen said. He knew where they were going, and began to stretch the time. "But I didn't see any sign of trouble before I left."

"Was the television on?" Lucas asked.

"Mmm, no, I don't think so."

"How about the radio?"

"No. We were talking," Bergen said.

"Was there a newspaper on the table?"

"I just can't remember," Bergen said, his voice rising. "What are these questions?"

"Can you remember anything that would be peculiar to this day, that you saw inside the LaCourt house, that might still be there, that might have survived the fire? A book sitting on a table? Anything?"

"Well . . ." The priest scratched the side of his nose. "No, not particularly. I'll think about it. There must be something."

"Did you look at the clock when you got home?"

"No. But I hadn't been here long when Shelly called."

Lucas looked at Carr. "Shelly, could you call in and have somebody patch you through to the LaCourt house, and tell somebody to go into the kitchen and check to see if there was a bowl of frosting."

He turned his head back to Bergen: "Was the frosting in a bowl or out of one of those cans?"

"Bowl."

To Carr: ". . . check and see if there was a frosting bowl or a cupcake tin in the sink or around the table."

"Sure."

"She might have washed the dishes," Bergen suggested.

"There couldn't have been too much time," Lucas said.

"Use the office phone, Shelly," the priest said to Carr.

He and Lucas watched the sheriff pad down the hall, then Lucas asked, "Did Frank LaCourt come outside when you left?"

"No. He said good-bye at the door. At the kitchen table, actually. Claudia came to the door. Did you go to Catholic schools?"

"Through high school," Lucas said.

"Is this what they taught you? To interrogate priests?"

"Your being a priest doesn't cut any ice with me," Lucas said. "You've seen all the scandals these last few years. That stuff was out there for years and you guys hid it. There were a half a dozen gay brothers at my school and everybody knew it. And they affected more than a few kids."

Bergen stared at him for a moment, then half-turned and shook his head.

"Was Frank LaCourt wearing outdoor clothing or look like he was getting ready to go outside?" Lucas asked, returning to the questions.

"No." Bergen was subdued now, his voice gone dark.

"Did you see anyone else there?"

"No."

"Did Frank have a pair of snowshoes around?" Lucas asked.

"Not that I saw."

"Did you see any snowshoe tracks outside the door?"

"No." Bergen shook his head. "I didn't. But it was snowing."

"Did you pass any cars on the way out?"

"No. How far is it from the corner by the firehouse back to LaCourts'?"

"One-point-one miles," Lucas said.

Bergen shook his head. "I'm a careful driver. I said it took a minute or two to get out to the corner, but two minutes would be thirty miles an hour. I wasn't doing thirty. I was probably going a lot slower than that. And I was pulling my trailer."

"Snowmobile?"

"Yes, I'd been out with the club, the Grant Scramblers, you can check with them."

Carr came back: "They're looking," he said. "They'll call back."

Lucas looked at Carr. "If we have somebody waiting for Father Bergen to leave, and if he lures Frank LaCourt outside somehow, right away, kills him, then kills the other two, burns the place immediately and gets out, in a frenzy, and if you build a little extra time in between the firemen's arrival at the place and finding the bodies—we could almost make it."

Carr looked at Bergen, who seemed to ponder what Lucas had said. He'd chosen Lucas as the enemy, but now Lucas had changed direction.

"Okay," Carr said, nodding. To Bergen: "I hated to hit you with it, Phil, but there did seem to be a problem. We can probably figure it out. When you were there, what were you talking about? I mean, it's not confessional stuff, is it? I . . ."

"Actually, we were talking about the Tuesday services and the concept of an exchange with Home Baptist. I wanted to get some ground rules straight."

"Oh." Now Carr looked uncomfortable. "Well, we can figure that out later."

"What's all this about?" Lucas asked.

"Church stuff, an argument that's going around," Carr said.

"Could somebody get killed over it?"

Bergen was startled. "Good grief, no! You might not get invited to a party, but you wouldn't get killed."

Carr glanced at him, frowned. The phone rang down the hallway, and the priest said, "Let me get that." A moment later he returned with a portable handset and passed it to Carr. "For you."

Carr took it, said, "This is the sheriff," then, "Yeah." He listened for a moment, said, "Okay, okay, and I'll see you out there in a bit . . . okay." He pushed the clear button and turned to Lucas: "There was a bowl in the sink that could have been used to make frosting. No frosting in it, but it was the right kind of bowl."

"Like I told you," said Bergen.

"Okay," Lucas said.

"If we're done here, I'm going back out to the LaCourt place," Carr said. He picked up his snowmobile suit and began pulling it over his feet. "I'm sorry we bothered you, Phil, but we had to ask."

"These killings are . . . grotesque," the priest said, shaking his head. "Obscene. I'll start thinking about a funeral service, something to say to the town."

"That'll be a while yet. We'll have to send them down to Milwaukee for autopsies," Carr said. "I'll stay in touch."

WHEN THEY WERE OUTSIDE again, Carr asked, "Are you coming back out to LaCourts'?"

Lucas shook his head. "Nah. There's nothing there for me. I'd suggest you button the place up. Post some deputies to keep out the curiosity-seekers and coyotes, and wait for the Madison guys."

"I'll do that. Actually, I could do it from here, but . . . politics." He was apologetic. "I gotta be out there a lot the next couple of days."

Lucas nodded. "Same way in the Cities."

"How about Phil? What do you think?"

"I don't know," Lucas said. Far away, somebody started a chain saw. They both turned to look up the street toward the sound, but there was nothing visible but garage and yard lights. The sound was an abrasive underline to the conversation. "We still don't have enough time. Not really. The bowl thing hardly clears him. But who knows? Maybe a big gust of wind scoured off the roof and put that snow on LaCourt in two minutes."

"Could be," Carr said.

"This Baptist thing—that's no big deal?" Lucas asked.

"It's a bigger deal than he was making it," Carr said. "What do you know about Pentecostals?"

"Nothing."

"Pentecostals believe in direct contact with God. The Catholic Church has taught that only the Church is a reliable interpreter of God's word. The Church doesn't trust the idea of direct access. Too many bad things have come of it in the past. But some Catholics—more and more all the time—believe you can have a valid experience."

"Yeah?" Lucas had been out of touch.

"Baptists rely on direct access. Some of the local Pentecostal Catholics, like Claudia, were talking about getting together with some of the Baptists to share the Spirit."

"That sounds pretty serious," Lucas said. The cold was beginning to filter through the edges of the parka, and he flexed his shoulders.

"But nobody would kill because of it. Not unless there's a nut that I don't know about," Carr said. "Phil was upset about Claudia talking to Home Baptist, but they were friends."

"How about Frank? Was he a friend of Bergen's?"

"Frank was Chippewa," said Carr. He stamped his feet, and looked back in the direction of the irritating chain saw. "He thought Christianity was amusing. But he and Phil were friendly enough."

"Okay."

"So what are you gonna do now?" Carr asked.

"Bag out in a motel. I brought clothes for a couple of days. We can get organized tomorrow morning. You can pick some people, and I'll get them started. We'll need four or five. We'll want to talk to the LaCourts' friends, kids at school, some people out at the Res. And I'll want to talk to these fire guys."

"Okay. See you in the morning, then," Carr said. The sheriff headed for his Suburban and muttered, mostly to himself, "Lord, what a mess."

"Hey, Sheriff?"

"Yeah?" Carr turned back.

"Pentecostal. I don't mean to sound impolite, but really—isn't that something like Holy Rollers?"

After a moment Carr, looking over his shoulder, nodded and said, "Something like that."

"How come you know so much about them?"

"I am one," Carr said.

THE MORNING BROKE bitterly cold. The clouds had cleared and a low-angle, razor-sharp sunshine cut through the red pines that sheltered the motel. Lucas, stiff from a too-short bed and a too-fat pillow, zipped his parka, pulled on his gloves and stepped outside. His face was soft and warm from shaving; the air was an icy slap.

The oldest part of Grant was built on a hill across the highway from the motel, small gray houses with backyard clotheslines awash in the snow. Wavering spires of gray woodsmoke curled up from two hundred tin chimneys, and the corrosive smell of burning oak bark shifted through town like a dirty tramp.

Lucas had grown up in Minneapolis, had learned to fish along the urban Mississippi, in the shadow of smokestacks and powerlines and six-lane bridges, with oil cans, worn-out tires and dead carp sharing space on the mud flats. When he began making serious money as an adult, he'd bought a cabin on a quiet lake in the Wisconsin's North Woods. And started learning about small towns.

About the odd comforts and discomforts of knowing everyone; of talking to people who had roads, lakes, and entire townships named after their families. People who made their living in the woods, guiding tourists, growing Christmas trees, netting suckers and trapping crawdads for bait.

Not Minneapolis, but he liked it.

He yawned and walked down to his truck, squinting against the sun, the new snow crunching underfoot. A friendly, familiar weight pulled at his left side. The parka made a waist holster impractical, so he'd hung his .45 in a shoulder rig. The pistol simply felt *right*. It had been a while since he'd carried one. He touched the coat's zipper tag with his left hand, pulled it down an inch, then grinned to himself. Rehearsing. Not that he'd need it.

Ojibway County *wasn't* Minneapolis. If someone came after him in Ojibway County, he'd bring a deer rifle or a shotgun, not some bullshit .22 hideout piece. And if somebody came with a scoped .30-06, the .45 would be about as useful as a rock. Still, it felt good. He touched the zipper tag again with his left hand and mentally slipped the right hand into the coat.

The truck had been sitting in the brutal cold overnight, but the motel provided post outlets for oil-pan heaters. Lucas unplugged the extension cord from both the post and the truck, tossed the cord in the back seat, cranked up the engine and let it run while he went down to the motel office for a cup of free coffee.

"Cold," he said to the hotel owner.

"Any colder, I'd have to bring my brass monkey inside," the man said. He'd been honing the line all morning. "Have a sweet roll, too, we got a deal on them."

"Thanks."

Cold air was still pouring from the truck's heater vents when Lucas returned to it, balancing the coffee and sweet roll. He shut the fan off and headed into town.

There were only two real possibilities with the LaCourt killings, he thought. They were done by a stranger, a traveling killer, as part of a robbery, picked out because the house was isolated. Or they were done for a reason. The fire suggested a reason. A traveler would have hauled Frank LaCourt's body inside, locked the doors, turned off the lights, and left. He might be days away before the murders were uncovered. With the fire, he couldn't have been more than fifteen or twenty minutes away.

A local guy who set a fire meant either a psychotic arsonist—unlikely—or that something was being covered. Something that pointed at the killer. Fingerprints. Semen. Personal records. Or might the fire have been set to distract the investigation?

The gun he'd found with Claudia LaCourt, unfired, suggested that the LaCourts knew something was happening, but they hadn't called 9-1-1. The situation may have been somewhat ambiguous . . . Huh.

And the girl with the missing ear might have been interrogated. Another suggestion that something was going on.

The image of the ear in the Ziploc bag popped into his mind. Carr had bent and retched because he was human, as the LaCourt girl had once been. She'd been alive at this time yesterday, chatting with her friends on the telephone, watching television, trying on clothes. Making plans. Now she was a charred husk.

And to Lucas, she was an abstraction: a victim. Did that make him less than human? He half-smiled at the introspective thought; he tried to stay away from introspection. Bad for the health.

But in truth he didn't feel much for Lisa LaCourt. He'd seen too many dead children. Babies in garbage cans, killed by their parents; toddlers beaten and maimed; thirteen-year-olds who shot each other with a zealous enthusiasm scraped right off the TV screen. Not that their elders were much better. Wives killed with fists, husbands killed with hammers, homosexuals slashed to pieces in frenzies of sexual jealousy. After a while it all ran together.

On the other hand, he thought, if it were *Sarah* . . . His mouth straightened into a thin line. He couldn't put his daughter together with the images of violent death that he'd collected over the years. They simply would not fit. But Sarah was almost ready for school now, she'd be moving out into the bigger world.

His knuckles were white on the steering wheel. He shook off the thought and looked out the window.

Grant's Main Street was a three-block row of slightly shabby storefronts, elbow to elbow, like a town in the old west. The combinations would have been strange in other places, were typical for the North Woods: a Laundromat-bookstore-bar, an Indian souvenir store–computer outlet, a satellite dish-plumber. There were two bakeries, a furniture store, a scattering of insurance agents and real estate dealers, a couple of lawyers. The county courthouse was a low rambling building of fieldstone and steel at the end of Main. A cluster of sheriff's trucks sat in a parking lot in back and Lucas wheeled in beside them. A Bronco with an unfamiliar EYE3 logo was parked in a visitor's slot by the door.

A deputy coming out nodded at him, said, "Mornin'," and politely held the door. The sheriff's outer office was behind a second door, decorated with curling DARE antidrug posters and the odors of aging nicotine and bad nerves. A reporter and a cameraman were slumped in green leatherette chairs scarred with cigarette burns and what looked like razor cuts. The reporter was working on her lipstick with a gold compact and a small red brush. She looked up when Lucas stepped in. He nodded and she nodded back. A steel door and a bullet-proof glass window were set in the wall opposite the reporter. Lucas went to the window, looked at the empty desk behind it, and pushed the call button next to the window.

"It'll just piss them off," the reporter said. She had a tapered fox-face with a tiny chin, big eyes and wide cheekbones, as though she'd been especially bred for television. She rubbed her lips together, then snapped the compact shut, dropped it in her purse, and gave him a reflexive smile. The cameraman was asleep.

"Yeah? Where're you guys from?" Lucas asked. The reporter was very pretty, with her mobile eyes and trained expressions, like a latter-day All-American geisha girl. Weather could never work for television, he thought. Her features were too distinctive. Could be a movie star, though.

"Milwaukee," she said. "Are you with the *Star-Tribune?*"

"Nope." He shook his head, giving her nothing.

"A cop?" The reporter perked up.

"An interested onlooker," Lucas said, grinning at her. "Lots of reporters around?"

"I guess so," she said, a frown flitting across her face. "I heard Eight talking on their radios, so they're up here somewhere, and I heard the *Strib* came in last night. Probably out at the lake. Are you one of the lab people from Madison?"

"No," Lucas said.

A harried middle-aged woman bustled up behind the glass, peered through, and said, "Davenport?"

"Yes." The reporter was wearing perfume. Something slightly fruity.

"I'll buzz you in," the woman said.

"FBI?" the reporter pressed.

"No," he said.

The woman inside pressed her entry button and as Lucas slipped through the door, the reporter called, "Tell Sheriff Carr we're gonna put something on the air whether he talks to us or not."

CARR HAD A CORNER office overlooking the parking lot, the county garage and a corroded bronze statue of a World War I doughboy. The beige walls were hung with a dozen photographs of Carr with other politicians, three plaques, a bachelor's degree certificate from the University of Wisconsin/River Falls, and two fish-stamp prints with the actual stamps mounted in the mats below the prints. A computer and laser printer sat on a side table, and an intricate thirty-button decorator-blue telephone occupied one corner of an expansive walnut desk. Carr was sitting behind the desk, looking gloomily across a tape recorder at Henry Lacey.

"You got reporters," Lucas said, propping himself in the office door.

"Like deer ticks," Carr said, looking up. "Morning. Come in."

"All you can get from deer ticks is Lyme's disease," said Lacey. "Reporters can get your ass *fired.*"

"Should I let them shoot pictures of the house?" Carr asked Lucas. "They're all over me to let them in."

"Why wouldn't you?" Lucas asked. He stepped into the office and dropped into a visitor's chair, slumped, got comfortable.

Carr scratched his head. "I dunno . . . it doesn't seem right."

"Look, it's all bullshit," Lucas said. "The outside of a burnt house doesn't mean anything to anybody, especially if they live in Milwaukee. Think about it."

"Yeah." Carr was still reluctant.

"If I were you, I'd draw up a little site map and pass it out—where the bodies were and so on," Lucas said. "That doesn't mean shit either, but they'll think you're a hell of a guy. They'll give you a break."

"I could use a break," Carr said. He scratched his head again, working at it.

"Did the guys from Madison get here?" Lucas asked.

"Two hours ago," said Lacey. "They're out at the house."

"Good." Lucas nodded. "How's it look out there?"

"Like last night. Uglier. There was a lump of frozen blood under Frank's head about the size of a milk jug. They're moving the bodies out in an hour or so, but they say it could take a couple of weeks to process the house."

"We gotta push them: there's something in there we need, or the guy wouldn't have burned the place," Lucas said irritably. Two weeks? Impossible. They needed information *now.* "Anything more new?"

"Yeah. We got a call," Carr said. He reached across his desk and pushed a button on the tape recorder. There was a burst of music, a woman country-western singer, then a man's voice: *You tell them goddamned flatheads down at FNR to stay away from white women or they'll get what LaCourt got.*

Lucas stuck out his bottom lip, shook his head: this was bullshit.

The music swelled, as if somebody had taken his mouth away from the phone, then a new voice said, *Give'm all a six-pack of Schlitz and send them down to Chicago with the niggers.*

The music came up, then there were a couple of indistinguishable words, a barking laugh, a click and a dead line.

"Called in on the 9-1-1 number, where we got an automatic trace. Went out to a pay phone at the Legion Hall. There were maybe fifty people out there," Lacey said. "Mostly drunk."

"That's what it sounded like, drunks," Lucas agreed. A waste of time. "What's the FNR? The Res?"

"Yeah. Forêt Noire," Carr said. He pronounced it For-A Nwa. "The thing is, most everybody in town'll know about the call before this afternoon. The girl on the message center talked it all over the courthouse. The guys from the tribe'll be up here. We're gonna have to tell the FBI. Possible civil rights whatcha-majigger."

"Aw, no," Lucas groaned, closing his eyes. "Not the feebs."

"Gonna have to," Carr said, shaking his head. "I'll try to keep them off, but I bet they're here by the weekend."

"Tell him about the windigo," Lacey said.

"There's rumors around the reservation that a windigo's been raised by the winter," Carr said, looking even gloomier.

"I've heard of them," Lucas said, "But I don't know . . ."

"Cannibal spirits, roaming the snowdrifts, eating people," Lacey said. "If you see one, bring him in for questioning."

He and Carr started to laugh, then Carr said, "We're getting hysterical." To Lucas he said, "Didn't get any sleep. I picked out some guys to work with you, six of them, smartest ones we got. They're down in the canteen. You ready?"

"Yup. Let's do it," Lucas said.

THE DEPUTIES ARRANGED themselves around a half-dozen rickety square tables, drinking coffee and chewing on candy bars, looking Lucas over. Carr poked his finger at them and called out their names. Five of the six wore uniforms. The sixth, an older man, wore jeans and a heavy sweater and carried an automatic pistol just to the left of his navel in a cross-draw position.

". . . Gene Climpt, investigator," Carr said, pointing at him. Climpt nodded. His face was deeply weathered, like a chunk of lake driftwood, his eyes careful, watchful. "You met him out at the house last night."

Lucas nodded at Climpt, then looked around the room. The best people in the department, Carr said. With two exceptions, they were all white and chunky. One was an Indian, and Climpt, the investigator, was lean as a lightning rod. "The sheriff and I worked out a few approaches last night," Lucas began. "What we're doing today is talking to people. I'll talk to the firefighters who were the first out at the house. We've also got to find the LaCourts' personal friends, their daughter's friends at school, and the people who took part in a religious group that Claudia LaCourt was a member of."

They talked for twenty minutes, dividing up the preliminaries. Climpt took two deputies to begin tracking the LaCourts' friends, and he'd talk to the tribal people about any job-related problems LaCourt might have had at the casino. Two more deputies—Russell Hinks and Dustin Bane, Rusty and Dusty—would take the school. The last man would canvass all the houses down the lake road, asking if anyone had seen anything unusual before the fire. The night before, Climpt had been looking for immediate possibilities.

"I'll be checking back during the day," Lucas said. "If anybody finds anything, call me. And I mean anything."

As the deputies shuffled out, pulling on coats, Carr turned to Lucas and said, "I've got some paperwork before you leave. I want to get you legal."

"Sure." He followed Carr into the hallway, and when they were away from the other deputies asked, "Is this Climpt guy . . . is he going to work with me? Or is he gonna be a problem?"

"Why should he be?" Carr asked.

"I'm doing a job that he might have expected to get."

Carr shook his head. "Gene's not that way. Not at all."

BERGEN STUMBLED INTO the hallway, looked around, spotted Carr. "Shelly . . ." he called.

Carr stopped, looked back. Bergen was wearing wind pants and a three-part parka, a Day-Glo orange hunter's hat, ski mitts and heavy-duty pac boots. He looked more like an out-of-shape lumberjack than a priest. "Phil, how'r you feeling?"

"You ought to know," Bergen said harshly, stripping his mitts off and slapping them against his leg as he came down the hall. "The talk all over town is, Bergen did it. Bergen killed the LaCourts. I had about half the usual congregation at Mass this morning. I'll be lucky to have that tomorrow."

"Phil, I don't know . . ." Carr started.

"Don't BS me, Shelly," Bergen said. "The word's coming out of this office. I'm the prime suspect."

"If the word's coming out of this office, I'll stop it—because you're not the prime suspect," Carr said. "We don't have any suspects."

Bergen looked at Lucas. His lower lip trembled and he shook his head, turned back to Carr: "You're a little late, Shelly; and I'll tell you, I won't put up with it. I have a reputation and you and your hired gun"—he looked at Lucas again, then back to Carr—"are ruining it. That's called slander or libel."

Carr took him by the arm, said, "C'mon down to my office, Phil." To Lucas he said, "Go down there to the end of the hall, ask for Helen Arris."

Helen Arris was a big-haired office manager, a woman who might have been in her forties or fifties or early sixties, who chewed gum and called him dear, and who did the paperwork in five minutes. When they finished with the paper, she took his photograph with a Polaroid camera, slipped the photo into a plastic form, stuck the form into a hot press, slammed the press, waited ten seconds, then handed him a mint-new identification card.

"Be careful out there," she said, sounding like somebody on a TV cop show.

LUCAS GOT A NOTEBOOK from the Explorer and decided to walk down to Grant Hardware, a block back toward the highway. This would be a long day. If they were going to break the killings, they'd do it in a week. And the more they could get early, the better their chances were.

A closet-sized book-and-newspaper store sat on the corner and he stopped for a *Wall Street Journal;* he passed a t-shirt store, a shoe repair shop, and one of the bakeries before he crossed in midblock to the hardware store. The store had a snowblower display in the front window, along with a stack of VCRs and pumpkin-colored plastic sleds. A bell rang over the door when Lucas walked in, and the odor of hot coffee hung in the air. A man sat on a wooden stool, behind the cashier's counter, reading a *People* magazine and drinking coffee from a deep china cup. Lucas walked down toward the counter, aging wooden floor creaking beneath him.

"Dick Westrom?"

"That's me." the counterman said.

"Lucas Davenport. I'm . . ."

"The detective, yeah." Westrom stood up and leaned across the counter to shake hands. He was big, fifty pounds too heavy for his height, with blond hair fading to white and large watery cow eyes that looked away from Lucas. He tipped his head at another chair at the other end of the counter. "My girl's out getting a bite, but there's nobody around . . . we could talk here, if that's all right."

"That's fine," Lucas said. He took off his jacket, walked around the counter and sat down. "I need to know exactly what happened last night, the whole sequence."

Westrom had found Frank LaCourt's body, nearly tripping over it as he hauled hose off the truck.

"You didn't see him right away, laying there?" Lucas asked.

"No. Most of the light was from the fire, it was flickering, you know, and Frank had a layer of snow on him," Westrom said. He had a confidential manner of talking, out of the side of his mouth, as though he were telling secrets in a prison yard. "He was easy to see when you got right on top of him, but from a few feet away . . . hell, you couldn't hardly see him at all."

"That was the first you knew there were dead people?"

"Well, I thought there might be somebody inside, there was a smell, you know. That hit us as soon as we got there, and I think Duane said something like, 'We got a dead one.' "

Westrom insisted that the priest had passed the fire station within seconds of the alarm.

"Look. I got nothing against Phil Bergen," Westrom said, shooting sideways glances at Lucas. "Shelly Carr was trying to get some extra time out of me last night, so I know where *he's* at. But I'll tell you this: I was nukin' a couple of ham sandwiches . . ."

"Yeah?" Lucas said, a neutral noise to keep Westrom rolling.

"And Duane said, 'There goes Father Phil. Hell of a night to be out.' Duane was standing by the front window and I saw Phil going by. Just then the buzzer went off on the microwave. I mean *right then,* when I was looking at the tail-lights. I says, 'Well, he's a big-shot priest with a big-shot Grand Cherokee, so he can go *where* he wants, *when* he wants.' "

"Sounds like you don't care for him," Lucas said. And Lucas didn't care for Westrom, the eyes always slipping and sliding.

"Well, personally, I don't. But that's neither here nor there, and he can go about his business," Westrom said. He pursed his lips in disapproval. His eyes touched Lucas' face and then skipped away. "Anyway, I was taking the sandwiches out, they're in these cellophane packets, you know, and I was just trying to grab them by the edges and not get burned. I said 'Come and get it,' and the phone rang. Duane picked it up and he said, 'Oh, shit,' and punched in the beeper code and said, 'It's LaCourts', let's go.' I was still standing there with the sandwiches. Never got to open them. Phil hadn't gone by more'n ten seconds before. Shelly was trying to get me to say it was a minute or two or three, but it wasn't. It wasn't more'n ten seconds and it might have been five."

"Huh." Lucas nodded.

"Check with Duane," Westrom said. "He'll tell you."

"Is Duane a friend of yours?"

"Duane? Well, no. I like him okay. We just don't, you know . . . relate."

"Do you know of anything that Father Bergen might have against the La-Courts?"

"Nope. But he was close to Claudia," Westrom said, with a distinct spin on the word *close.*

"How close?" Lucas asked, tilting his head.

Westrom's eyes wandered around Lucas without settling. "Claudia had a reputation before she married Frank. She got around. She was a pretty thing, too, she had the big . . ." Westrom cupped his hands at his chest and bounced them a couple of times. "And Phil . . . He *is* a man. Being a priest and all, it must be tough."

"You think he and Claudia could have been fooling around?" Lucas asked.

Westrom edged forward in his chair and said confidentially, "I don't know about that. We probably would have heard if she was. But it might go way back, something with Father Phil. Maybe Phil wanted to get it started again or something." Westrom's nose twitched.

"How many black Jeeps in Ojibway County?" Lucas asked. "There must be quite a few."

"Bet there aren't, not in the winter. Not Grand Cherokees—those are mostly summer-people cars. I can't think of any besides Phil's." He looked at Lucas curiously: "Are you a Catholic?"

"Why?"

" 'Cause you sound like you're trying to find an excuse for Phil Bergen."

LUCAS' NOTEBOOK COVER SAID, "Westrom, Helper." He drew a line through Westrom, started the Explorer, headed out Highway 77 to the fire station.

In the daytime, with sunlight and the roads freshly plowed, the half-hour trip of the night before was cut to ten minutes. From the high points of the road, he could see forever across the low-lying land, with the contrasting black pine forests cut by the silvery glint of the frozen lakes.

The firehouse was a tan pole barn built on a concrete slab, nestled in a stand of pine just off the highway. One end of the building was dominated by three oversized garage doors for the fire trucks. The office was at the other end, with a row of small windows. Lucas parked in one of four plowed-out spaces and walked into the office, found it empty. Another door led out of the office into the back and Lucas stuck his head through.

"Hello?"

"Yeah?" A heavyset blond man sat at a worktable, a fishing reel disassembled in the light of a high-intensity lamp. A thin, almost transparent beard covered his acne-pitted face. His eyes were blue, careful. A small kitchen area was laid out along one wall behind him. At the other end of the room, a broken-down couch, two aging easy chairs and two wooden kitchen chairs faced a color television. Lockers lined a third wall, each locker stenciled with a man's last name. Another door led back into the truck shed. A flight of stairs went up to a half-loft.

"I'm looking for Duane Helper," Lucas said.

"That's me. You must be Davenport," Helper said. He had a heavy, almost Germanic voice, and stood up to shake hands. He was wearing jeans with wide red suspenders over a blue work shirt. His hand was heavy, like his body, but crusted with calluses. "A whole caravan of TV people just came out of the lake road. The sheriff let them in to take pictures of the house."

"Yeah, he was going to do that," Lucas said.

"I heard Phil Bergen is the main suspect." Helper said it bluntly, as a challenge.

Lucas shook his head. "We don't have any suspects yet."

"That's not the way I heard it," Helper said. The television was playing a game show and Helper picked up a remote control and punched it off.

"Then what you heard is wrong," Lucas said sharply. Helper seemed to be looking for an edge. He was closed-faced, with small eyes; when he played his fingers through his beard, the fingers seemed too short for their thickness, like sausages. Lucas sat down across the round table from him and they started through the time sequence.

"I remember seeing the car, but I didn't remember it was right when the alarm came in," Helper said. "I thought maybe I'd walked up and looked out the window, saw the car, and then we'd talked about something else and I'd gone back to the window again and that's when the alarm came in. That's not the way Dick remembers it."

"How sure are you? Either way?"

Helper rubbed his forehead. "Dick's probably right. We talked about it and he was sure."

"If you went to the window twice, how much time would there have been between the two trips?" Lucas asked.

"Well, I don't know, it would have only been a minute or two, I suppose."

"So even if you went twice, it wasn't long."

"No, I guess not," Helper said.

"Did you actually see Bergen's Jeep come out of the lake road?"

"No, but that's the impression I got. He was moving slow when he went past, even with the snow, and he was accelerating. Like he'd just turned the corner onto 77."

"Okay." Lucas stood up, walked once around the room. Looked at the stairs. "What's up there?"

"There's a bunk room right at the top. I live in the back. I'm the only professional firefighter here."

"You're on duty twenty-four hours a day?"

"I have time off during the day and early evenings, when we can get volunteers to pick it up," Helper said. "But yeah, I'm here most of the time."

"Huh." Lucas took a turn around the room, thumbnail pressed against his upper teeth, thinking. The time problem was becoming difficult. He looked at Helper. "What about Father Bergen? Do you know him?"

"Not really. I don't believe I've spoken six words to him. He drinks, though. He's been busted for drunk driving, but . . ." He trailed off and looked away.

"But what?" Helper was holding something back, but he wanted Lucas to know it.

"Sheriff Carr's on the county fire board," Helper said.

"Yeah? So what?" Lucas made his response a little short, a little tough.

"He's thick with Bergen. I know you're from the outside, but if I talk, and if it gets back to Shelly, he could hurt me." Helper let the statement lie there, waiting.

Lucas thought it over. Helper might be trying to build an alliance or drive a wedge between himself and Carr. But for what? Most likely he was worried for exactly the reason he claimed: his job. Lucas shook his head. "It won't get back to him if it doesn't need to. Even if it needs to, I can keep the source to myself. If it seems reasonable."

Helper looked at him for a moment, judging him, then looked out the window toward the road. "Well. First off, about that drunk driving. Shelly fixed it. Fixed it a couple of times and maybe more."

He glanced at Lucas. There was more to come, Lucas thought. Helper mentioned the ticket-fixing as a test. "What else?" he pressed.

Helper let it go. "There're rumors that Father Bergen's . . . that if you're a careful dad, you wouldn't want your boy singing in his choir, so to speak."

"He's gay?" Gay would be interesting. Small-town gays felt all kinds of pressure, especially if they were in the closet. And a priest . . .

"That's what I've heard," Helper said. He added, carefully, "It's just gossip. I never gave it much thought. In fact, I don't think it's true. But I don't know. With this kind of thing, these killings, I figured you'd probably want to hear everything."

"Sure." Lucas made a note.

They talked for another five minutes, then three patrol deputies stomped in from duty at the LaCourt house. They were cold and went straight to the coffee. Helper got up to start another pot.

"Anything happening down at the house?" Lucas asked.

"Not much. Guys from Madison are crawling around the place," said one of the deputies. His face was red as a raw steak.

"Is the sheriff down there?"

"He went back to the office, he was gonna talk to some of the TV people."

"All right."

Lucas looked back at Helper, fussing with the coffee. Small-town fireman. He heard things, sitting around with twenty or thirty different firemen every week, nothing much to do.

"Thanks," he said. He nodded at Helper and headed for the door, the phone ringing as he went out. The wind bit at him again, and he hunched against it, hurried around the truck. He was fumbling for his keys when Helper stuck his head out the door and called after him: "It's a deputy looking for you."

Lucas went back inside and picked up the phone. "Yeah?"

"This is Rusty, at the school. You better get your ass up here."

GRANT JUNIOR HIGH WAS a red-brick rectangle with blue-spruce accents spotted around the lawn. A man in a snowmobile suit worked on the flat roof, pushing snow off. The harsh scraping sounds carried forever on the cold air. Lucas parked in front, zipped his parka, pulled on his ski gloves. Down the street, the bank time-and-temperature sign said −21. The sun was rolling across the southern sky, as pale as an old silver dime.

Bob Jones was waiting outside the principal's office when Lucas walked in. Jones was a round-faced man, balding, with rosy cheeks, a short black villain's mustache and professional-principal's placating smile. He wore a blue suit with a stiff-collared white shirt, and his necktie was patriotically striped with red, white, and blue diagonals.

"Glad to see you," he said as they shook hands. "I've heard about you. Heck of a record. Come on, I'll take you down to the conference room. The boy's name is John Mueller." The school had wide halls painted an institutional beige, with tan lockers spotted between cork bulletin boards. The air smelled of sweat socks, paper, and pencil-sharpener shavings.

Halfway down the hall, Jones said, "I'd like you to talk to John's father about this. When you're done with him. I don't think there's a legal problem, but if you could talk to him . . ."

"Sure," Lucas said.

Rusty and Dusty were sitting at the conference table drinking coffee, Rusty with his feet on the table. They were both large, beefy, square-faced, white-toothed, with elaborately casual hairdos, Rusty a Chippewa, Dusty with the transparent pallor of a pure Swede. Rusty hastily pulled his feet off the table when Lucas and Jones walked in, leaving a ring of dirty water on the tabletop.

"Where's the kid?" Lucas asked.

"Back in his math class," said Dusty.

"I'll get him," Jones volunteered. He promptly disappeared down the hall, his heels echoing off the terrazzo.

Dusty wiped the water off the tabletop with his elbow and pushed a file at Lucas. "Kid's name is John Mueller. We pulled his records. He's pretty much of an A-B student. Quiet. His father runs a taxidermy shop out on County N, his mother works at Grotek's Bakery."

Lucas sat down, opened the file, started paging through it. "What about this other kid? You said on the phone that another kid was murdered."

Rusty nodded, taking it from Dusty. "Jim Harper. He went to school here, seventh grade. He was killed around three months back," Rusty said.

"October 20th," said Dusty.

"What's the story?" Lucas asked.

"Strangled. First they thought it was an accident, but the doc had the body sent down to Milwaukee, and they figured he was strangled. Never caught anybody."

"First murder of a local resident in fourteen years," Rusty said.

"Jesus Christ, nobody told me," Lucas said. He looked up at them.

Dusty shrugged. "Well . . . I guess nobody thought about it. It's kind of embarrassing, really. We got nothing on the killing. Zero. Zilch. It's been three months now; I think people'd like to forget it."

"And he went to this school, and he was in classes with the LaCourt girl . . . I mean, Jesus. . . ."

Jones returned, ushering a young boy into the room. The kid was skinny and jug-eared, with hair the color of ripe wheat, big eyes, a thin nose and wide mouth. He wore a flannel shirt and faded jeans over off-brand gym shoes. He looked like an elf, Lucas thought.

"How are you? John? Is that right?" Lucas asked as Jones backed out of the room. "I understand you have some information about Lisa."

The kid nodded, slipped into the chair across the table from Lucas, turned a thumb to the other two deputies. "I already talked to these guys," he said.

"I know, but I'd like to hear it fresh, if that's okay," Lucas said. He said it serious, as though he were talking to an adult. John nodded just as seriously. "So: how'd you know Lisa?"

"We ride the bus together. I get off at County N and she goes on."

"And did she say something?" Lucas asked.

"She was really scared," John said intently. His ears reddened, sticking out from his head like small Frisbees. "She had this picture, from school."

"What was it?"

"It was from a newspaper," John said. "It was a picture of Jim Harper, the kid who got killed. You know about him?"

"I've heard."

"Yeah, it was really like . . ." John looked away and swallowed, then back. "He was naked on the bed and there was this naked man standing next to him with, you know, this, uh, I mean it was stickin' up."

Lucas looked at him, and the kid peered solemnly back. "He had an erection? The man?" Lucas asked.

"Yup," John said earnestly.

"Where's the picture?" Lucas felt a tingle: this was something.

"Lisa took it home," John said. "She was going to show it to her mom."

"When? What day?" Lucas asked. Rusty and Dusty watched the questioning, eyes shifting from Lucas to the kid and back.

"Last week. Thursday, 'cause that's store night and Mom works late, and when I got home Dad was cooking."

"Do you know where she got the picture?" Lucas asked.

"She said she got it from some other kid," John said, shrugging. "I don't know who. It was all crinkled up, like it had been passed around."

"What'd the man look like? Did you recognize him?"

"Nope. His head wasn't in the picture," the boy said. "I mean, it looked like the whole picture was there, but it cut off his head like somebody didn't aim the camera right."

Dammit. "So you could only see his body."

"Yeah. And some stuff around him. The bed and stuff," John said.

"Was the man big or small? His body?" Lucas asked.

"He was pretty big. Kind of fat."

"What color was his hair?" asked Lucas.

John cocked his head, his eyes narrowing. "I don't remember."

"You didn't notice a lot of chest hair or stomach hair or hair around his crotch?" Lucas fished for a word the kid could relate to: "I mean, like really kind of gross?"

"No. Nothing like that . . . but it was a black-and-white picture and it wasn't very good," John said. "You know those newspapers they have at the Super Valu . . . ?"

"*National Enquirer,*" Rusty said.

"Yeah. The picture was like from that. Not very good."

If the hair didn't strike him as gross, then the guy was probably a blond, Lucas thought. Black hair on cheap paper would blot. "If it wasn't very good, could you be sure it was Jim?" Lucas asked.

The boy nodded. "It was Jim, all right. You could see his face, smiling like Jim. And Jim lost a finger and you could see if you looked real close that the kid in the picture didn't have a finger. And he had an earring and Jim wore an earring. He was the first guy in the school to get one."

"Mph. You say Lisa was scared? How do you know she was scared?"

"Because she showed it to me," John said.

"What?" Lucas frowned, missing something.

"She's a girl. And the picture—you know . . ." John twisted in his chair. "She wouldn't show something like *that* to a boy if she wasn't scared about it."

"Okay." Lucas ran over the questions one more time, probed the contents of the picture the boy had seen, but got nothing more. "Is your dad out at his shop?"

"Sure—I guess," the kid said, nodding.

"Did you tell him about the picture?"

"No." John looked uncomfortable. "I mean . . . how could I tell him about that?"

"Okay," Lucas said. "Let's ride out there and I'll tell him about you talking to us. Just so everything's okay. And I think we ought to keep it between us."

"Sure. I'm not going to tell anybody else," John said. "Not about that," he said earnestly, eyes big.

"Good," Lucas said. He relaxed and smiled. "Go get your stuff, and let's go out to your place."

"Did we do good?" Rusty asked lazily when John had gone.

"Yeah, you did good," Lucas said.

The two deputies slapped hands and Lucas said, "You're all done with Lisa's friends?"

"Yeah, all done," Rusty said.

"Great. Now do this other kid's friends. The Harper kid. Look for connections between Lisa and Harper," Lucas said. "And if this picture was passed around, find out who passed it."

LUCAS USED A PAY PHONE in the teachers' lounge to call the sheriff's office. "You sound funny," he said when Carr came on.

"You're being relayed. What'd you need?"

"Are we scrambled?"

"Not really."

"I'll talk to you later. Something's come up."

"I'm on my way to the LaCourts'."

"I'm heading that way, so I'll see you there," Lucas said. He hung up momentarily, then redialed the sheriff's office, got Helen, the office manager, and asked her to start digging up the files on the Harper murder.

John Mueller had gone to put his books away and get his coat and boots. As Lucas waited for him at the front door, a bell rang and kids flooded into the hallways. Another, non-student head bobbed above the others in the stream, caught his eye. The doctor. He took a step toward her. He'd been a while without a woman friend; thought he could get away from the need by making a hermit of himself, by working out. He was wrong, judging from the tension in his chest . . . unless he was having a heart attack. Weather was pulling on her cap as she came toward him, and oversized mittens with leather palms. She nodded, stopped and said, "Anything good?"

"Not a thing," he said, shaking his head. *Not pretty*, he thought, *but very attractive. A little rough, like she might enjoy the occasional fistfight. Who is she dating? There must be someone. The guy is probably an asshole; probably has little tassels on his shoes and combs them straight in the morning, before he puts the mousse on his hair.*

"I was doing TB patches down there." She nodded back down the hall, toward a set of open double doors. A gymnasium. "And one kid was scared to death that somebody was going to come kill him in the night."

Lucas shrugged. "That's the way it goes." As soon as he said it, he knew it was wrong.

"Mr. Liberal," she said, her voice flat.

"Hey, nothing I can do about it except catch the asshole," Lucas said, irritated. "Look, I didn't really . . ." He was about to go on but she turned away.

"Do that," she said, and pushed through the door to the outside.

Annoyed, Lucas leaned against the entryway bulletin board, watching her walk to her car. Had a nice walk, he decided. When he turned back to the school, looking for John, he saw a yellow-haired girl watching *him*.

She stood in a classroom doorway, staring at him with a peculiar intensity, as though memorizing his face. She was tall, but slight, angular with just the first signs of an adolescent roundness. And she was pale as paper. The most curious thing was her hair, which was an opaque yellow, the color of a sunflower petal, and close-cropped. With her pointed chin, large tilted eyes and short hair, she had a waifish look, like she should be selling matches. She wore a homemade dress of thin print material, cotton, with short sleeves: summer wear. She held three books close to her chest. When he looked at her, she held his eyes for a moment, a gaze with a solid sexuality to it, speculative, but at the same time, hurt, then turned and walked away.

John arrived in a heavy parka with a fur-lined hood and mittens. "Do you have a cop car?" he asked.

"No. A four-by-four," Lucas said.

"How come?"

"I'm new here."

JOHN'S FATHER WAS a mild, round-faced man in a yellow wool sweater and corduroys. "How come you didn't tell me?" he asked his son. He sat on a high stool. On his bench, a fox skin was half-stretched over a wooden form. John shrugged, looked away.

"Embarrassed," Lucas said. "He did the right thing, today. We didn't want you to think we were grilling him. We'd of called you, to get you in, but I was right there and he was . . ."

"That's okay, as long as John's not in trouble," his father said. He patted John on the head.

"No, no. He did the right thing. He's a smart kid," Lucas said.

. . .

THE PICTURE WAS CRITICAL. He felt it, knew it. Whistled to himself as he drove out to the LaCourt house. Progress.

Helper was working in the fire station parking lot, rolling hose onto a reel, when Lucas passed on his way to the LaCourts'. A sheriff's car was parked in a cleared space to one side of the LaCourts' driveway, and a deputy waved him through. A half-dozen men were working around or simply standing around the house, which was tented with sheets of Army canvas, and looked like an olive-drab haystack. Power lines, mounted on makeshift poles, ran through gaps in the canvas. Lucas parked at the garage and hurried inside. Two sheriff's deputies were warming themselves at the stove, along with a crime tech from Madison.

"Seen the sheriff?" Lucas asked.

"He's in the house," one of the deputies said. To the tech he said, "That's Davenport."

"Been looking for you," the tech said, walking over. "I'm the lab chief here . . . Tod Crane." Crane looked like he might be starving. His fingers and wrists were thin, bony, and the skin on his balding head seemed to be stretched over his skull like a banjo covering. When they shook hands, an unexpected muscle showed up: he had a grip like a pair of channel-lock pliers.

"How's it going?" Lucas asked.

"It's a fuckin' mess," Crane said. He held up his hands, flexed them. They were bone-white and trembling with cold. "Whoever did it spread gas-oil pre-mix all over the house. When he touched it off, Boom. We're finding stuff blown right through some of the internal walls."

"Premix from the boats?"

"Yeah, that's what we think. Maybe some straight gas from the snowmobiles. We've found three six-gallon cans. The LaCourts had two boats, a pontoon and a fishing rig, and there aren't any gas cans with them. And premix, you put it in a bottle with a wick, it's called a Molotov cocktail."

"Any chance our man was hurt? Or burned?" Lucas asked.

"No way to tell, but he'd have to be careful," Crane said. "He spread around quite a bit of gas. We've got an arson guy coming up this afternoon to see if we can isolate where the fire started."

Lucas nodded. "I'm looking for a piece of paper," he said. "It was a picture, apparently torn from a magazine or a newspaper. It shows a naked man and a naked boy on the bed behind him. It might be in the house."

"Yeah? That's new?" Crane's eyebrows went up.

"Yup."

"Think he was trying to burn it up?" Crane asked.

"The thought crossed my mind."

"I'll tell you right now, there were a couple of filing cabinets that were dumped and doused with gas, and he shot some gas into a closet full of paper stuff, photographs, like that. He did the same thing on the chests of drawers in the parents' bedroom, after he dumped them."

"So maybe . . ."

"There ought to be some reason he torched the place. I mean, besides being nuts," Crane said. "If he'd just killed them and walked, it might of been a day or two before anybody found them. He'd have time to set up an alibi. This way he tipped his hand right away."

"So find the paper," Lucas said.

"We'll look," Crane said. "Hell, it's nice to have something specific to look for."

CARR CAME IN WHILE they were talking. He'd mellowed since morning, a small satisfied smile on his face. "They're gone, the reporters. Most of them, anyway," he said. "Poof."

"Probably found a better murder," Lucas said.

"I talked to Helen, back at the office," Carr said. "What's this about Jim Harper?"

"Rusty and Dusty found a kid at the junior high who says Jim Harper posed for sex photos with an adult male," Lucas said. "That'd be a long-term felony and might be worth killing somebody for. The picture came out of a pulp-paper magazine or newspaper. Some kids got hold of it and it may have been passed around the school. Lisa LaCourt had it last. She took it home on Thursday and showed it to this kid who talked to me."

"Who is it? The kid at the school?"

"John Mueller. His father's a taxidermist," Lucas said.

Carr nodded. "Sure, I know him. That's an okay family. Damn, these things could be tied."

Lucas shrugged. "It's a possibility. The Harper kid's parents, are they around?"

"One of them is, the old man, Russ. The wife left years ago, went out to California. She was back for the funeral, though."

"What does Harper do?" Lucas asked.

"Runs an Amoco station out at Knuckle Lake."

"Okay, I'll head out there."

"Whoa, whoa." Carr shook his head. "Better not go alone. Are you gonna be up late?"

"Sure."

"Harper's open till midnight. He'd never talk to us if he didn't have to: never to a cop. Why don't I pick up a search warrant for Jim Harper's stuff out at his house, and we'll get a couple deputies and go out there late? I got church."

"All right," Lucas said. "Harper's an asshole?"

"He is," Carr said, nodding. And he said, "Lord, if these two cases are tied together and we could nail them down in a day or two . . . that'd make me a very happy man."

"Will Father Bergen be at your service tonight?" Lucas asked.

"Probably not. He's pretty shook up. You heard him this morning."

"Yeah." Lucas crossed his arms, watching Carr. "The Mueller kid said the adult in the photo was a big guy. And probably blond or fair. The kid didn't re-member the guy as being hairy, which means he probably didn't have much."

"Like Father Phil," Carr said, flushing. "Well, it wasn't Phil. There are a thousand chunky blonds in this county. I'm one."

"I talked to the firemen. Westrom thinks Bergen did it. He says so. And he looks like someone who'd talk about it."

"Dick's the gossip-central for the whole town," Carr said. Then, his voice dropping almost to a whisper, "God damn him."

"Have you ever heard anything about Bergen being involved in sexual es-capades?"

Carr stepped back. "No. Absolutely not. Why?"

"Just bullshit, probably. There are rumors around that he's messed with both women and men."

"A homosexual?" Carr was flabbergasted. "That's ridiculous. Where'n the heck are you getting this stuff?"

"Just asking around. Anyway, we've gotta talk to him again," Lucas said. "After your service? Then we can hit Harper."

Carr looked worried. "All right. I'll see you at the church at nine o'clock. Are we still meeting with the other guys at five?"

"Yeah. But I don't think there's much, except for Rusty and Dusty coming up with the photo thing."

"You're not going to tear Phil up, are you?" Carr asked.

"There's something out of sync, here," Lucas said, avoiding a direct answer. "He's not telling us something, maybe. I gotta think about it."

THE YELLOW-HAIRED GIRL SAT ON a broken-legged couch, smok-ing an unfiltered Camel, working on her math problems; old man Schuler would be on her ass if she didn't finish all ten of them. She hated Schuler. He had a way of embarrassing her.

The couch cushions were stained with Coke and coffee spills, the cushions pulled out of shape by shrunken upholstery. The yellow-haired girl's brother had seen the couch sitting on the street late one rainy night, waiting for the annual spring trash pickup, and had hauled it away himself. Almost good as new, ex-cept for the cushions.

She exhaled, playing with the smoke with her mouth and nose. Snorted it.

Trying to think. Across the room, the letter-woman, what's-her-name, the blonde, was turning letters on "Wheel of Fortune." She turned two *t*'s and the audience applauded.

A train is traveling west at twenty-five miles an hour. Another train is traveling east at forty-five . . .

Bullshit.

The yellow-haired girl looked back at the television. The letter-woman wore a silky white dress with a deep neckline, some kind of an overlap on the material, with padding at the shoulders. She looked good in the dress; but she had the complexion and the body for it.

The yellow-haired girl checked herself every morning in the mirror on the back of her door, lifting her small breasts with her hands, squeezing them to make a cleavage, looking at herself sideways and straight-on, at her back over her shoulders. She tried all of Rosie's clothes and some of her brother Mark's. Mark's t-shirts were best. She'd wear them downtown next summer, to Juke's, without a bra. If she lightly brushed the tips of her nipples, they'd firm up and faintly indent the t-shirt material, if she arched her back. Very sexy.

If the trains start two hundred miles apart, how long will . . .

Doritos sacks littered the floor at her feet. A round cardboard tray, marked with scrapings of chocolate-cake frosting, sat on a spindly-legged TV-dinner table. An aluminum ashtray was piled with cigarette butts, and she'd just dropped another burning butt into the hole of a mostly empty Coke can. The butt guttered in the dampness at the bottom, and the stench of burning wet tobacco curdled the air; and beneath that, the smell of old coffee grounds, spoiled bananas, rotting hamburger.

On the "Wheel of Fortune," the contestants had found the letters *T - - - - n - t - - - - n - n -* . She stared at them, moving her lips. *Turn? No, it couldn't be "turn," you just thought that because you could see the* t's *and the* n's.

Huh. Could be two . . . ?

The truck rattled into the driveway and her heart skipped. The girl hopped to her feet, peered out the window, saw him climbing down, felt her breath thicken in her chest. His headlights were still on and he walked around to the front of the truck, peered at a tire. Sometimes, in her young-old eyes, he looked like a dork. He weighed too much, and had that turned-in look, like he wasn't really in touch with the world. He had temper tantrums, and did things he was sorry for. Hit her. Hit Mark. Always apologized . . .

At other times, when he was with her, or with Mark or Rosie or the others, when they were having a fuck-in . . . then he was different. The yellow-haired girl had seen a penned wolf once. The wolf sat behind a chain-link fence and looked her over with its yellow eyes. The eyes said, *If only I was out there . . .*

His eyes were like that, sometimes. She shivered: he was no dork when he looked like that. He was something else.

And he was good to her. Brought her gifts. Nobody had ever brought her gifts—not good ones, anyway—before him. Her mom might get her a dress that she bought at the secondhand, or some jeans at K-Mart. But he'd given her a Walkman and a bunch of tapes, probably twenty now. He bought her Chic jeans and a bustier and twice had brought her flowers. Carnations.

And he took her to dinner. First he got a book from the library that told about the different kinds of silverware—the narrow forks for meat, the wide forks for salad, the little knives for butter. After she knew them all, they talked about the different kinds of salads, and the entrées, and the soups and desserts. About scooping the soup spoon away from you, rather than toward you; about keeping your left hand in your lap.

When she was ready, they did it for real. She got a dress from Rosie, off-the-shoulder, and some black flats. He took her to Duluth, to the Holiday Inn. She'd been awed by the dining room, with the view of Superior. Two kinds of wine, red and white. She'd remember it forever.

She loved him.

Her old man had moved away two years before, driven out by Rosie and her mom, six months before the cancer had killed her mom. All her old man had ever given her were black eyes—and once he'd hit her in the side, just below her armpit, so hard that she almost couldn't breathe for a month and thought she was going to die.

He was worse with Rosie: he tried to fuck Rosie and everybody knew that wasn't right; and when Rosie wouldn't fuck him, he'd given her to Russ Harper for some tires.

When he'd started looking at the yellow-haired girl—started showing himself, started peeing with the bathroom door open when he knew she'd walk by, when he came busting in when she was in the shower—that's when Rosie and her mom had run him off.

Not that they'd had to.

Her old man had worn shapeless overalls, usually covered with dirt, and old-fashioned sleeveless undershirts that showed off his fat gut, hanging from his chest like a pig in a hammock. She couldn't talk to him, much less look at him. If he'd ever come into her bedroom after her, she'd kill him.

Had told him that.

And she would have.

THIS MAN WAS DIFFERENT. His voice was soft, and when he touched her face he did it with his fingertips or the backs of his fingers. He never hit her. Never. He was educated. Told her about things; told her about sophisticated women and the things they had to know. About sophisticated love.

He loved her and she loved him.

The yellow-haired girl tiptoed into the back of the double-wide and looked into the bedroom. Rosie was facedown on the bed, asleep, a triangle of light from the hallway crossing her back. One leg thrust straight down the bed and was wrapped from knee to ankle with a heavy white bandage. The yellow-haired girl eased the door shut, pulling the handle until she heard the bolt click.

He was climbing the stoop when she got to the door, a sack of groceries in his arms. There was a puddle of cold water on the floor and she stepped in it, said, "Shit," wiped her foot on a rag rug and opened the door. His heavy face was reddened with the cold.

"Hi," she said. She lifted herself on her tiptoes to kiss him on the cheek: she'd seen it done on television, in the old movies, and it seemed so . . . right. "Rosie's asleep."

"Cold," he said, as though answering a question. He pushed the door shut and she walked away from him into the front room, hips moving under her padded housecoat. "Is Rosie still hurting?"

"Yeah, she bitches all day. The doctor was back and took the drain out, but it'll be another week before she takes out the stitches . . . stunk up the whole house when she took the drain out. Bunch of gunk ran out of her leg."

"Nasty," he said. "How was the birthday party?"

"Okay, 'cept Rosie was so bitchy because of her leg." The yellow-haired girl had turned fourteen the day before. She looked at the cake ring on the floor. "Mark ate most of the cake. His friend had some weed and we got wrecked."

"Sounds like a good time." His cheeks were red like jolly old St. Nick's. "Get anything good? For your birthday?"

"The fifty bucks from you was the best," she said, taking his hand, smiling into his eyes. "Rosie gave me a Chili Peppers t-shirt and Mark gave me an album for the Walkman."

"Well, that sounds pretty good," he said. He dumped the groceries on the kitchen table.

"There was a cop at school today, one I never seen before," the yellow-haired girl said.

"Oh, yeah?" He took a six-pack of wine coolers out of the sack, but stopped and looked at her. "Guy looks like an asshole, a big guy?"

"He was kinda good-looking but he looked like he could be mean, yeah," she said.

"Did you talk to him?"

"No. But he had some kids in the office," she said. "Lisa's friends."

"What'd they tell 'em?" He was sharp, the questions rapping out.

"Well, everybody was talking about it in the cafeteria. Nobody knew anything. But the new cop took John Mueller home with him."

"The taxidermist's kid?" His thin eyebrows went up.

"Yeah. John rode on the bus with Lisa."

"Huh." He dug into the grocery sack, a thoughtful look on his face.

"The cop was talking to the doctor," she said. "The one who takes care of Rosie."

"What?" His head came around sharply.

"Yeah. They were talking in the hall. I saw them."

"Were they talking about Rose?" He glanced down the hall at the closed door.

"I don't know; I wasn't that close. I just saw them talking."

"Hmm." He unscrewed the top of one of the wine bottles, handed it to the yellow-haired girl. "Where's your brother?"

Jealousy scratched at her. He was fond of Mark and was helping him explore his development. "He's over at Ricky's, working on the car."

"The Pinto?"

"Yeah."

The man laughed quietly, but there was an unpleasant undertone in the sound. Was *he* jealous? Of Ricky, for being with Mark? She pushed the thought away.

"I wish them the best," he said. He was focusing on her, and she walked back to the couch and sat down, sipping the wine cooler. "How have you been?"

"Okay," she said, and wiggled. She tried to sound cool. *Okay.*

He knelt in front of her and began unbuttoning her blouse, and she felt the thickness in her chest again, as though she were breathing water. She put down the wine cooler, helped him pull the blouse off, let him reach around her and unsnap the brassiere; he'd showed her how he could do it with one hand.

She had solid breasts like cupcakes, and small stubby nipples.

"Wonderful," he whispered. He stroked one of her nipples, then stood up and his hand went to his fly. "Let's try this one."

She was aware of him watching, of his intent blue eyes following her; he pushed her hair out of her face.

Behind him the blonde woman on "Wheel of Fortune" was turning around the last of the letters.

Two Minute Warning, the sign said.

WHEN THE ICEMAN LEFT, he drove out to the county road, to the first stop sign, and sat there, smoking, thinking about John Mueller and Weather Karkinnen. So many troubling paths were opening. He tried to follow them in his mind, and failed: they tangled like a rats' nest.

If the photograph turned up, and if they identified him, they'd have him on the sex charge. That's all he'd wanted to stop. When Harper called and said Frank LaCourt had the photo but didn't know who was in it, all he'd wanted was to get it back. Get it before the sheriff got it.

Then he'd killed Claudia too quickly and hadn't gotten the photo. Now the photo would mean they'd look at him for the killings. More than that: when they saw the photo, they'd figure the whole thing out.

He was in a perfect position to monitor the investigation, anyway. He'd know when they found the photo. He'd probably have a little time: until Weather saw it, anyway.

He'd been crazy to let the kid take the picture. But there was something about seeing yourself, contemplating yourself at a distance. Now: had John Mueller seen? Did he have a copy or know where it came from?

If they found the photo, they'd have a place to start. And if they showed it to enough people, they'd get him. He had to have it. Maybe it had burned in the fire. Maybe not. Maybe the Mueller kid knew.

And Weather Karkinnen. If *she* saw the photo, she'd know him for sure. *Dammit.*

He rolled down the window a few inches, flipped the cigarette into the snow.

He'd once seen himself in a movie. A comedy, no less. *Ghostbusters.* Silly scene—a jerk, a nebbish, is possessed by an evil spirit, and talks to a horse. When the cabriolet driver yells at him, the nebbish growls and his eyes burn red, and the power flares out at the driver.

Good for a laugh—but the Iceman had seen himself there, just for an instant. He also had a force inside, but there was nothing funny about it. The force was powerful, unafraid, influential. Manipulating events from behind the screen of a bland, unprepossessing face.

Flaring out when it was needed.

He had a recurring dream in which a woman, a blonde, looked at him, her eyes flicking over him, unimpressed. And he let the force flare out of his eyes, just a flicker, catching her, and he could feel the erotic response from her.

He'd wondered about Weather. He'd stood there, naked under his hospital gown, she examined him. He'd let the fire out with her, trying to look her into a corner, but she'd seemed not to notice. He'd let it go.

He often thought about her after that encounter. Wondering how she saw him, standing there; she must've thought *something,* she *was* a woman.

The Iceman looked out at the frozen snowscape in his headlights.

The Mueller kid.

Weather Karkinnen.

A N HOUR AFTER DARK, the investigation group gathered in Carr's office. Climpt, the investigator, and two other men had worked the La-Courts' friends and found nothing of significance. No known feud, nothing criminal. The Storm Lake road had been run from one end to the other, and all but two or three people could account for themselves at the time of the killings; those two or three didn't seem to be likely prospects. Several people had seen Father Bergen loading his sled on his trailer.

"What about the casino?" Lucas asked Climpt.

"Nothing there," Climpt said, shaking his head. "Frank didn't have nothing to do with money; never touched it. There was no way he could rig anything, either. He was in charge of physical security for the place, mostly handling drunks. He just didn't have the access that could bring trouble."

"Do the tribe people think he's straight?"

"Yup. No money problems that they know of. Didn't gamble himself. Didn't use drugs. Used to drink years back, but he quit. Tell you the truth, it felt like a dead end."

"All right . . . Rusty, Dusty, how about that picture."

"Can't find anybody who admitted seeing it," Rusty said. "We're talking to Lisa LaCourt's friends, but there's been some flu around, and we didn't get to everybody yet."

"Keep pushing."

The next day would be more of the same, they decided. Another guy to help Rusty and Dusty check Lisa's friends. "And I'll want you to start interviewing Jim Harper's pals, if you can find any."

THE SHERIFF'S DEPARTMENT'S investigators shared a corner office. One did nothing but welfare investigations, worked seven-to-three, and was out of the murder case. A second had gotten mumps from his daughters and was on sick leave. The third was Gene Climpt. Climpt had said almost nothing during the meeting. He'd rolled an unlit cigarette in his fingers, watching Lucas, weighing him.

Lucas moved into the mumps-victim's desk and Helen Arris brought in a lockable two-drawer file cabinet for papers and personal belongings.

"I brought you the Harper boy's file," she said. She was a formidable woman with very tall hair and several layers of makeup.

"Thanks. Is there any coffee in the place? A vending machine?"

"Coffee in the squad room, I can show you."

"Great." He tagged along behind her, making small talk. He'd recognized her type as soon as Carr sent him to her for his ID. She knew everybody and tracked everything that went on in the department. She knew the forms and the legalities, the state regs and who was screwing who. She was not to be trifled with if you wanted your life to run smoothly and end with a pension.

She wouldn't be fooled by false charm either. Lucas didn't even try it: he got his coffee, thanked her, and carried it back to the office, left the door open. Deputies and a few civilian clerks wandered past, one or two at a time, looking him over. He ignored the desultory parade as he combed through the stack of paper on the county's first real homicide in six years.

Jim Harper had been found hanging from a pull-down towel rack in the men's room of a Unocal station in Bon Plaine, seventeen miles east of Grant. The boy was seated on the floor under the rack, a loop of the towel around his neck. His Levi's and Jockey shorts had been pulled down below his knees. The door had been locked, but it was a simple push-button that could be locked from the inside with the door open and remain locked when the door was pulled shut, so that meant nothing. The boy had been found by the station owner when he opened for business in the morning.

Harper's father had been questioned twice. The first time, the morning after the murder, was perfunctory. The sheriff's investigators were assuming accidental death during a masturbation ritual, which was not unheard of. The only interesting point on the preliminary investigation was a scrawled note to Carr: *Shelly, I don't like this one. We better get an autopsy. —Gene.*

Climpt. His desk was in the corner, and Lucas glanced at it. The desk was neatly kept, impersonal except for an aging photograph in a silver frame. He pushed the chair back and looked closer. A pretty woman, dressed in the styles of the late fifties or early sixties, with a baby in her arms. Lucas called Arris, asked her to find Climpt, and went back to the Harper file.

After an autopsy, a forensic pathologist from Milwaukee had declared the death a strangulation homicide. Russ Harper, the boy's father, was interviewed again, this time by a pair of Wisconsin state major-crime investigators. Harper didn't know anything about anything, he said. Jim had gone wild, had been drinking seriously and maybe smoking marijuana.

They were unhappy about it, but had to let it go. Russ Harper was not a suspect—he had been working at his gas station when the boy was murdered, and disinterested witnesses would swear to it. His presence was also backed by computer-time-stamped charge slips with his initials on them.

The state investigators interviewed a dozen other people, including some Jim's age. They'd all denied being his friend. One had said Jim didn't have any friends. Nobody had seen the boy at the crossroads gas station. On the day he was killed, nobody had seen him since school.

"HEAR YOU WANT to talk to me?"

Climpt was a big man in his middle fifties, deep blue eyes and a hint of rosiness about his cheeks. He was wearing a blue parka, open, brown pac boots with wool pants tucked inside, and carried a pair of deerhide gloves. A chrome pistol sat diagonally across his left hip bone, where it could be crossdrawn with his right hand, even when he was sitting behind a steering wheel. His voice was like a load of gravel.

Lucas looked up and said, "Yeah, just a second." He pawed through the file papers, looking for the note Climpt had sent to Carr. Climpt peeled off his parka, hung it on a hook next to Lucas', ambled over to his own desk and sat down, leaning back in his chair.

"How'd it go?" Lucas asked as he looked through the file.

"Mostly bullshit." The words came out slow and country. "What's up?"

Lucas found the note, handed it to him: "You sent this to Shelly after you handled that death report on the Harper kid. What was wrong out there? Why'd you want the autopsy?"

Climpt looked at the note, then handed it back to Lucas. "The boy was sittin' on the floor with his dick in his hand, for one thing. I never actually tried hanging myself, but I suspect that right near the end, you'd know something was going wrong and you'd start flapping. You wouldn't sit there pumpin' away until you died."

"Okay." Lucas nodded, grinned.

"Then there was the floor," Climpt continued. "There aren't many men's room floors *I'd* sit on, and this wasn't one of them. The gas station gets cleaned in the morning—maybe. There's a bar across the highway and guys'd come out of the bar at night, stop at the station for gas, the cold air'd hit 'em and they'd realize they had to take a whiz. Being half drunk, their aim wasn't always so good. They'd pee all over the place. I just couldn't see somebody sitting there voluntarily."

Lucas nodded.

"Another thing," Climpt said. "Those damn tiles were cold. You could frost-bite your ass on those tiles. I mean, it'd hurt."

"So you couldn't add it up."

"That's about it," Climpt said.

"Got any ideas about it?"

"I'd talk to Russ Harper if I was gonna go back into it," Climpt said.

"They talked to him," Lucas said, flipping through the stack of paper. "The state guys did."

"Well . . ." His eyes were on Lucas, judging: "What I mean was, I'd take him out back to my workshop, put his hand in the vise, close it about six turns and *then* ask him. And if that didn't work, I'd turn on the grinder." He wasn't smiling when he said it.

"You think he knows who killed his boy?" Lucas asked.

"If you asked me the most likely guy to commit a sneaky-type murder in this county, I'd say Russ Harper. Hands down. If his *son* gets killed, sneaky-like . . . that's no coincidence, to my way of thinkin'. Russ might not know who killed him, but I bet he'd have some ideas."

"I'm thinking of going out there tonight, talking to Harper," Lucas said. "Maybe take him out back to the shop."

"I'm not doin' nothing. Invite me along," Climpt said, stretching his legs out.

"You don't care for him?"

"If that son-a-bitch's heart caught on fire," Climpt said, "I wouldn't piss down his throat to put it out."

CLIMPT SAID HE'D GET dinner and hang around his house until Lucas was ready to go after Harper. Helen Arris had already gone, and much of the department was dark. Lucas tossed the Jim Harper file in his new file cabinet and banged the drawer shut. The drawer got off-track and jammed. When he tried to pull it back open, it wouldn't come. He knelt down, inspecting it, found that a thin metal rail had bent, and tried to pry it out with his fingernails. He got it out, but his hand slipped and he ripped the fingernail on his left ring finger.

"Mother—" He was dripping blood. He went down to the men's room, rinsed it, looked at it. The nail rip went deep and it'd have to be clipped. He wrapped a paper towel around it, got his coat, and walked out through the darkened hallways of the courthouse. He turned a corner and saw an elderly man pushing a broom, and then a woman's voice echoed down a side hallway: "Heck of a day, Odie," it said.

The doctor. Weather. Again. The old man nodded, looking down a hall at right angles to the one he and Lucas were in. "Cold day, miz."

She walked out of the intersecting corridor, still carrying her bag, a globe light shining down on her hair as she passed under it. Her hair looked like clover honey. She heard him in the hallway, glanced his way, recognized him, stopped. "Davenport," she said. "Killed anybody yet?"

Lucas had automatically smiled when he saw her, but he cut it off: "That's getting pretty fuckin' tiresome," he snapped.

"Sorry," she said. She straightened and smiled, tentatively. "I didn't mean . . . I don't know what I didn't mean. Whatever it was, I didn't mean it when I saw you at the school, either."

What? He didn't understand what she'd just said, but it sounded like an apology. He let it go. "You work for the county, too?"

She glanced around the building. "No, not really. The board cut out the public health nurse and I do some of her old route. Volunteer thing. I go around and see people out in the country."

"Pretty noble," Lucas said. The line came out sounding skeptical instead of wry. Before she could say anything, he put up a hand. "Sorry. That came out wrong."

She shrugged. "I owed you one." She looked at his hand. He was holding it at his side, waist height, clenching the towel in his fist. "What happened to your hand?"

"Broke a nail."

"You oughta use a good acrylic hardener," she said. And then quickly, "Sorry again. Let me see it."

"Aw . . ."

"Come on."

He unwrapped the towel and she held his finger in her hand, turned it in the weak light. "Nasty. Let me, uh . . . come more under the light." She opened her bag.

"Listen, why don't I . . . Is this gonna hurt?"

"Don't be a baby," she said. She used a pair of surgical scissors on the nail, trimming it away. No pain. She dabbed on a drop of an ointment and wrapped it with a Band-Aid. "I'll send you a bill."

"Send it to the sheriff, I got it on the job," he said. Then: "Thanks."

They stopped at the door, looked out at the snow. "Where're you going?" Lucas asked.

She glanced at her wristwatch. No rings. "Get something to eat."

"Could I buy you dinner?" he asked.

"All right," she said simply. She didn't look at him. She just pushed through the door and said *all right*.

"Where?" following her onto the porch.

"Well, we have six choices," she said.

"Is that a guess?"

"No." A grin flickered across her face and she counted the restaurants off on her fingertips. Lucas noticed that her fingers were long and slender, like a pianist's were supposed to be. Or a surgeon's. "There's Al's Pizza, there's a Hardee's, the Fisherman Inn, the Uncle Steve's American Style, Granddaddy's Cafe, and the Mill."

"What's the classiest joint?"

"Mmm." She tilted her head, thought about it, and said, "Do you prefer stuffed ducks or stuffed fish? On the wall, I mean, not the menu."

"That's a hard one. Fish, I guess."

"Then we'll go to the Inn," she said.

"Do you play piano?"

"What?" She stopped and looked up at him. "Have you been asking about me?"

"Huh?" He was puzzled.

"How did you know I play?"

"I didn't," he said. "I was just thinking your hands . . . they look like a pianist's."

"Oh." She looked at her hands. "Most of the pianists I've known have heavy hands."

"Like a surgeon's hands, then," he said.

"Most surgeons' hands are ordinary."

"Okay, okay." He started to laugh.

"Ordinary. They are."

"Why are you grumping at me?" Lucas asked.

She shrugged. "We're just getting over being awkward. It's always hard on a first date."

"What?" he asked, following down the sidewalk. He had the sense that something had just flown past him.

THE RESTAURANT HAD BEEN BUILT from two double-wide trailers set at right angles to each other, both covered with vinyl siding disguised as weathered wood. A neon Coors sign hung in the window. Lucas pulled into the parking lot and killed his light, trailed a few seconds later by Weather in her Jeep.

"Elegant," he said.

She pivoted her feet out of the Jeep, pulled off her pac boots. "I want to change shoes . . . elegant, what? The restaurant?"

"I think the vinyl siding combined with the sparkle of the Coors sign gives it a certain European ambiance. Swiss, I'd say, or possibly Old Amsterdam."

"Wait'll you find out that each table has its own red votive candle, personally lit by the maitre d', and a basket of cellophane-wrapped crackers and breadsticks," Weather said.

"Hey, it's a gourmet joint," Lucas said. "I expected nothing less. And a choice of wines, I bet."

"Yup."

And they both said, simultaneously, "Red or white," and laughed. Weather added, "If you ask for rosé, they say fine, and you see the bartender running into the back with a bottle of white and bottle of red."

"Where'd you get your name?" Lucas asked.

"My father was a sailboat freak. Homemade fourteen-foot dinghys and scows. He used to build them in the garage in the summer," she said. She pulled on the second loafer, tossed the pac boot onto the floor on the passenger side, stood up and slammed the car door with authority. And left it unlocked. "Anyway, Mom says he was always talking about the weather—'If the weather holds, if the weather turns.' Like that. So when I was born, they called me Weather."

"Does your mother live in town?"

"No, no. Dad died ten years ago, and then she went, three or four years later," Weather said, with just a color of sadness. "There was nothing particularly wrong with her. She just sorta died. I think she wanted to."

THE MAITRE D' WAS A chubby man with a neatly clipped black mustache and a Las Vegas manner. "Hello, Weather," he said. His eyes shifted to Lucas' throat and refused to lift any higher. "Two? No smoking?"

"Yeah, two," Lucas said.

"A booth," said Weather.

When he left them with the menus, Weather leaned forward and muttered, "I forgot about Arlen. The maitre d'. He'd like to get me in bed. Not actually leave Mother and the Kids, you understand, just do a little Mm-hmm with the lady doctor, preferably in some place like Hurley, where we might not get caught."

"What are his chances?" Lucas asked.

"Zero," she said. "There's something about the Alfred Hitchcock profile that turns me off."

The salad came with a French dressing redolent of catsup, sprinkled with a handful of croutons.

"I remember the news stories when you left Minneapolis. Very strange, all those stories about a cop. A lot of people at the ER knew you, I guess. They were all pissed. It made an impression on me."

"I used to come in there quite a bit," Lucas said. "I'd have these street guys working for me, and they'd get messed up and not have anybody to call. I'd go over and try to fix them up."

"Why'd you leave? Tired of the bullshit?"

"No . . ." He found himself opening up, told her about the internal games played in the department.

And the lure of money: "When you're a cop, you're always running into rich assholes who treat you like some kind of servant. Guys who oughta be in jail, but they're driving around in Lexuses and Cadillacs and Mercedes," he said, toy-ing with his wine. "People tell you, yeah, but you're doing a public service, blah blah blah, but after twenty years, you realize you wouldn't mind having a little money yourself. Nice house, nice car."

"You had a Porsche. You were famous for it."

"That was different. A rich guy has a Porsche, he does it because he's an asshole. A cop has a Porsche, it's like a comment on the assholes," he said. "Every cop in the department liked me driving a Porsche. It was like a fuck-you to the assholes."

"God, you have a rich ability to rationalize," she said, laughing at him. "Anyway, what're you doing now? Just consulting?"

"No, no. Actually, I write games. That's where I made my money. And I've started another little sideline that . . ."

"Games?"

"Yeah. I've done it for years, now I'm doing it full time."

"You mean like Monopoly?" she asked. She was interested.

"Like Dungeons and Dragons, and sometimes war games. They used to be mostly on paper, now it's mostly computers. I'm in a semipartnership with this college kid—he's a graduate student in computer science. I write the games and he programs them."

"And you can make a living at this?"

"Yeah. And now I've started writing simulation software for police crisis management, for training dispatch people. Most of that's computers, dispatch is. And you get in a crisis situation, the dispatchers are virtually running things for a while. This software lets them simulate it, and scores them. It's kind of taking off."

"If you're not careful, you could get rich," Weather said.

"I kind of am," Lucas said gloomily. "But goddamn, I'm bored. I don't miss the bullshit part of the PD, but I miss the *movement*."

AND LATER, OVER walleye in beer batter:

"You can't hold together a heavy-duty relationship when you're in medical school and working to pay for it," Weather said. He enjoyed watching her work with her knife, taking the walleye apart. *Like a surgeon.* "Then a surgical residency kills you. You've got no time for anything. You sit there and think about men, but it's impossible. You can fool around, but if you get serious about somebody, you can get torn apart between the work and the relationship. So you find it's easiest, if you meet somebody you might love, to turn away. Turning away isn't that hard if you do it right away, when you first meet."

"Sounds lonely," Lucas said.

"Yeah, but you can tolerate it if you're working all the time and you're convinced that you're right. You keep thinking, if I can just clear away this last thing, if I can just make it through next Wednesday or next month or through the winter, then I can get my life going. But time passes. Sneaks past. And all of a sudden your life is rushing up on you."

"Ah . . . the old biological clock," Lucas said.

"Yeah. And it's not just ticking for women. Men get it just as bad."

"I know."

She rolled on: "How many men do you know who decided that life was passing them by, and they jumped out of their jobs or their marriages and tried to . . . escape, or something?"

"A few. More felt trapped but hung on," said Lucas. "And got sadder and sadder."

"You're talking about me, I think," she said.

"I'm talking about everybody," Lucas said. "I'm talking about me."

AFTER A CARAFE OF WINE: "Do you worry about the people you've killed?" She wasn't joking. No smile this time.

"They were hairballs, every one of them."

"I asked that wrong," she said. "What I meant to ask was, has killing people screwed up your head?"

He considered the question for a moment. "I don't know. I don't brood about them, if that's what you mean. I had a problem with depression a couple of years ago. The chief at the time . . ."

"Quentin Daniel," she said.

"Yeah. You know him?"

"I met him a couple of times. You were saying . . ."

"He thought I needed a shrink. But I decided I didn't need a shrink, I needed a philosopher. Someone who knows how the world works."

"An interesting idea," she said. "The problem isn't you, the problem is Being."

"My God, that *does* make me sound like an asshole."

"CARR SEEMS LIKE a decent sort," Lucas said.

"He is. Very decent," Weather agreed.

"Religious."

"Very. You want pie? They have key lime."

"I'll take coffee; I'm bloated," Lucas said.

Weather waved at the waitress, said, *two coffees*, and turned back to Lucas. "Are you a Catholic?"

"Everybody asks me that. I am, but I'm seriously lapsed," he said.

"So you won't be going to the Tuesday meetings, huh?"

"No."

"But you're going over tonight, to talk to Phil." She made it a statement.

"I really don't . . ."

"It's all over town," Weather said. "He's the main suspect."

"He's not," Lucas said with a touch of asperity.

"That's not what I heard," she said. "Or everybody else hears, for that matter."

"Jesus, that's just wrong," Lucas said, shaking his head.

"If you say so," she said.

"You don't believe me."

"Why should I? You're going to question him again tonight after Shelly gets out of the Tuesday service."

The coffee came and Lucas waited until the waitress was gone before he picked up the conversation. "Is there anything that everybody in town doesn't know?"

"Not much," Weather admitted. "There are sixty people working for the sheriff and only about four thousand people in town, in winter. You figure it out. And have you wondered why Shelly's going to Tuesday service when he should be questioning Phil?"

"I'm afraid to ask," Lucas said.

"Because he wants to see Jeanine Perkins. He and Jeanine have been screwing at motels in Hayward and Park Falls."

"And everybody in town knows?" Lucas asked.

"Not yet. But they will."

"Carr's married."

"Yup. His wife is mad," Weather said.

"Uh . . ."

"She has a severe psychological affliction. She can't stop doing housework."

"What?" He started to laugh.

"It's true," Weather said solemnly. "It's not funny, buster. She washes the floors and the walls and the blinds and the toilets and sinks and pipes and the washer and drier and the furnace. And then she washes all the clothes over and over. Once she washed her own hands so many times that she rubbed a part of the skin off and we had to treat her for burns."

"My God." He still thought it was mildly funny.

"Nothing anybody can do about it. She's in therapy, but it doesn't help," Weather said. "A friend told me that she won't have sex with Shelly because it's dirty. I mean, not psychologically dirty, but you know—dirty. Physically dirty."

"So Carr solves his problem by having it off with a woman in his Pentecostal group."

"*Having it off* is such a romantic way to put it; British, isn't it?" she teased.

"YOU DON'T ACT LIKE a doctor," Lucas said.

"You mean because I gossip and flirt?"

"Mmmm."

"You have to live here a while," she said with a hint of tension in her voice. She looked around the room, at the people talking over the red votive candles. "There's nothing to do but work. Nothing."

"Then why stay?"

"I have to," she said. "My dad came here from Finland, and spent his life working in the woods, in the timber. And sailing on the lakes. Never had any money. But I maxed out in everything at school."

"You went to the high school here in Grant?"

"Yup. Anyway, I was trying to save money to go to college, but it looked tough. Then some of the teachers got together and chipped in, and this old fart county commissioner who I didn't know from Adam called down to Madison and pulled some strings and got me a full-load scholarship. And they kept the money coming all the way through medical school. I paid it all back. I even set up a little scholarship fund at the high school while I was working in Minneapolis, but that's not what everybody wanted."

"They wanted you back here," Lucas said.

"Yes." She nodded. She picked up her empty wineglass and turned it in her hands. "Everything around here is timber and tourism, with a little farming. The roads are not much good and there's a lot of drinking. The timber accidents are terrible—you ought to see somebody caught by a log when it's rolling down to a sawmill. And with tractor accidents and people run over with boat propellers . . . They had an old guy here who could do enough general surgery to get you on a helicopter to Duluth or down to the Cities, and as long as he was here I didn't feel like I had to come back."

"Then he retired."

"Kicked off," Weather said. "Heart attack. He was sixty-three. He ate six pancakes with butter and bacon every morning, cream in his coffee, cheeseburger for lunch, steak for dinner, drank a pint of Johnnie Walker every night and smoked like a chimney. It was amazing he made it as long as he did."

"They couldn't get anybody else?"

She laughed, not a pleasant laugh, looked out the window at the snow: "Are you kidding? Look outside. It's twenty-five below zero and still going down and the movie theater is closed in the winter."

"So what do you do for entertainment?"

"That's a little personal," she said, grinning, reaching across the table to touch the back of his hand, "for this stage of our relationship."

"What?"

THE DINNER LEFT LUCAS vaguely mystified but not unhappy. They said good-bye in the restaurant parking lot, awkwardly. He didn't want to leave. The talk ran on in the snow, the air so cold that it felt like after-shave. Finally they stepped apart and Weather got in her Jeep.

"See you," she said.

"Yeah." Definitely.

Lucas watched her go, pulled his hat on, and drove the six blocks to the church. Carr was waiting in the vestibule with two women, the three of them chatting brightly, nodding. One of the women was as large as Lucas and blond, and wore a red knitted hat with snowflakes and reindeer on it. Her coat carried a button that said *Free the Animals*. The other woman was small and dark, with gray streaks in her hair, lines at the corners of her eyes. Carr called the dark one *Jeanine* as Lucas came up.

"This is Lucas Davenport . . ." Carr was saying.

"Lieutenant Davenport," Jeanine said. She had soft, warm hands and a strong grip. "And our friend Mary . . ."

Mary fawned and Lucas retreated a couple of steps, said to Carr, "We better go."

"Yeah, sure," Carr said reluctantly. "Ladies, we gotta work."

They walked out together and Lucas asked Carr, "Did you talk to Bergen?"

"Not myself—Helen Arris got him. I had to go back out to the house. They're taking the place apart."

"How about the Harper warrant?"

"Got it." Carr patted his chest and then yawned. "It's getting to be a long day."

"How about the Harper place? What can we do?"

"We're allowed to go into the kid's room and the other principal rooms of the house, not including any office or Harper's own bedroom if that's separate from the kid's. We can look at anything we believe is the kid's, or that Harper says is the kid's."

"I'd like to poke around."

"So would I, but the judge didn't want to hear about it," Carr said. "He was gonna confine us to the boy's room, but I got him to include his other personal effects—we can look inside closets and cupboards and so on, in the main rooms. Of course, if we *see* anything that's clearly illegal . . ."

"Yeah. By the way, Gene Climpt . . ."

". . . invited himself along, which is fine with me. Gene's a tough old bird. And Lacey's coming; said he didn't want to miss it."

They'd walked around the church and started down the carefully shoveled sidewalk to the rectory.

"How many accidents has Bergen had? Car accidents?" Lucas asked.

Carr looked at him, frowning, and said, "Why?"

"I heard you fixed a couple of drunk-driving tickets for him," Lucas said. "I just wondered if he ever hit anything."

"Where'd you hear . . ."

"Rumors, Shelly. Has he ever hit anything?"

They'd stopped on the sidewalk and Carr stared at him for a moment and said, finally, "I got no leverage with you. You don't need the job."

"So . . ."

Carr started down the walk again. "He was in a one-car accident three years ago, hit a pylon at the end of a bridge, totaled out the car. He was drunk. He got caught two other times, drunk. One was pretty marginal. The other time he was on his butt."

"Gotta be careful about your relationship with him," Lucas said. "People are talking about this. The driving problems."

"Who?"

"Just people," Lucas said.

Carr sighed. "Darn it, Lucas."

"Bergen lied to me yesterday," Lucas said. "He told me he was a good driver . . . a small lie but it kind of throws some doubt on the rest of what he said."

"I don't understand it," Carr said. "I know in my soul that he's innocent. I just can't understand what he's hiding. If he's hiding anything. Maybe we just don't understand the sequence."

They were at the rectory door. Carr pushed the doorbell and they fell silent, hands in their pockets, breathing long gouts of steam out into the night air. After a moment Carr frowned, pushed the doorbell again. They could hear the chimes inside.

"I know he's here," Carr said. He stepped back from the porch, looked at the lighted windows, then pushed the doorbell a third time. There was a noise from inside, a thump, and Carr stood on his tiptoes to peer through the small window set in the door.

"Oh, no," he groaned. He pulled open the storm door and pushed through the inner door, Lucas trailing behind. The priest stood in the hallway, leaning on one wall, looking at them. He was wearing a white t-shirt, pulled out of his black pants, and gray wool socks. His hair stood almost straight up, as though he'd been electrocuted. He was holding a glass and the room smelled of bourbon.

"You idiot," Carr said quietly. He walked across the room and took the glass from the priest, who let it go, his hand slack. Carr turned back toward Lucas as though looking for a place to throw it.

"You know what they're saying," Bergen said at Carr's back. "They're saying I did it."

"Jesus, we've been trying . . ." Lucas started.

"Don't you blaspheme in this house!" the priest shouted.

"I'll kick your ass if you give me trouble," Lucas shouted back. He crossed the carpet, walking around Carr, who caught at his coat sleeve, and confronted the priest: "What happened out at the LaCourts'?"

"They were alive when I saw them!" Bergen shouted. "They were alive—every one of them!"

"Did you have a relationship with Claudia LaCourt? Now or ever?"

The priest seemed startled: "A relationship? You mean sexual?"

"That's what I mean," Lucas snapped. "Were you screwing her?"

"No. That's ridiculous." The wind went out of him, and he staggered to a La-Z-Boy and dropped into it, looking up at Lucas in wonder. "I mean, I've never . . . What are you asking?"

Carr had stepped into the kitchen, came back with an empty Jim Beam bottle, held it up to Lucas.

"I've heard rumors that the two of you might be involved."

"No, no," Bergen said, shaking his head. He seemed genuinely astonished. "When I was in the seminary, I slept with a woman from a neighboring college. I also got drunk and was talked into . . . having sex with a prostitute. One time. Just once. After I was ordained, never. I never broke my vows."

His face had gone opaque, either from whiskey or calculation.

"Have you ever had a homosexual involvement?"

"Davenport . . ." Carr said, a warning in his voice.

"*What?*" Bergen was back on his feet now, face flushed, furious.

"Yes or no," Lucas pressed.

"No. Never."

Lucas couldn't tell if Bergen was lying or telling the truth. He sounded right, but his eyes had cleared, and Lucas could see him calculating, weighing his responses. "How about the booze? Were you drinking that night, at the LaCourts'?"

The priest turned and let himself fall back into the chair. "No. Absolutely not. This is my first bottle in a year. More than a year."

"There's something wrong with the time," Lucas said. "Tell us what's wrong."

"I don't know," Bergen said. He dropped his head to his hands, then ran his hands halfway up to the top of his head and pulled out at the hair until it was again standing up in spikes. "I keep trying to find ways . . . I wasn't drinking."

"The firemen. Do you have any trouble with them?"

Bergen looked up, eyes narrowing. "Dick Westrom doesn't particularly care for me. I take my business to the other hardware store, it belongs to one of the parishioners. The other man, Duane . . . I hardly know him. I can't think what he'd have against me. Maybe something I don't know about."

"How about the people who reported the fire?" Lucas asked, looking across the room at Carr. Carr was still holding the bottle of Jim Beam as though he were presenting evidence to a jury.

"They're okay," Carr said. "They're out of it. They saw the fire, made the call. They're too old and have too many physical problems to be involved."

The three of them looked at each other, waiting for another question, but there were none. The time simply didn't work. Lucas searched Bergen's face. He found nothing but the waxy opacity.

"All right," he said finally. "Maybe there was another Jeep. Maybe Duane saw Father Bergen's Jeep earlier, going down the lake road, and it stuck in his mind and when he saw a car go by, he thought it was yours."

"He didn't see a Jeep earlier," Carr said, shaking his head. "I asked him that—if he'd seen Phil's Jeep go down the lake road."

"I don't know," Lucas said, still studying the priest. "Maybe . . . I don't know."

Carr looked at Bergen. "I'm dumping the bottle, Phil. And I'm calling Joe."

Bergen's head went down. "Okay."

"Who's Joe?" Lucas asked.

"His AA sponsor," Carr said. "We've had this problem before."

Bergen looked up at Carr, his voice rasping: "Shelly, I don't know if this guy believes me," he said, tipping his head at Lucas. "But I'll tell you: I'd swear on the Holy Eucharist that I had nothing to do with the LaCourts."

"Yeah," Carr said. He reached out and Bergen took his hand, and Carr pulled him to his feet. "Come on, let's call Joe, get him over here."

JOE WAS A DARK MAN, with a drooping black mustache and heavy eyebrows. He wore an old green Korean War–style olive-drab billed hat with earflaps. He glanced at Lucas, nodded at Carr and said, "How bad?"

"Drank at least a fifth," Carr said. "He's gone."

"Goddammit." Joe looked up at the house, then back to Carr. "He'd gone more'n a year. It's the rumors coming out of your office, Shelly."

"Yeah, I know. I'll try to stop it, but I don't know . . ."

"Better more'n try. Phil's got the thirst as bad as anyone I've ever seen." Joe stepped toward the door, turned, about to say something else, when Bergen pulled the door open behind him.

"Shelly!" he called. He was too loud. "Telephone—it's your office. They say it's an emergency."

Carr looked at Lucas and said, "Maybe something broke."

He hurried inside and Joe took Bergen by the shoulder and said, "Phil, we can handle this."

"Joe, I . . ." Bergen seemed overcome, looked glassily at Lucas, still on the sidewalk, and pulled Joe inside, closing the door.

Lucas waited, hands in his pockets, the warmth he'd accumulated in the house slowly dissipating. Bergen was a smart guy, and no stranger to manipulation. But he didn't have the sociopath edge, the just-below-the-surface glassiness of the real thing.

Thirty seconds after he'd gone inside, Carr burst out.

"Come on," he said shortly, striding past Lucas toward the trucks.

"What happened?"

"That kid you talked to, the one that told you about the picture?" Carr was talking over his shoulder.

"John Mueller." Jug-ears, off-brand shoes, embarrassed.

"He's missing. Can't be found."

"What?" Lucas grabbed Carr's arm. "Fuckin' tell me."

"His father was working late at his shop, out on the highway," Carr said. They were standing in the street. "He'd left the kid at home watching television. When his mother got home, and the kid wasn't there, she thought he was out at the shop. It wasn't until his parents got together that they realized he was gone. A neighbor kid's got a Nintendo and John's been going down there after school a couple nights a week, and sometimes stays for dinner. They called the neighbors but there wasn't anybody home, and they thought maybe they'd all gone down to the Arby's. So they drove around until they found the neighbors, but they hadn't seen him either."

"Sonofabitch," Lucas said, looking past Carr at nothing. "I might of put a finger on him."

"Don't even think that," Carr said, his voice grim.

THEY HEADED FOR THE Mueller house, riding together in the sheriff's truck, crimson flashers working on top.

"You were hard on him," Carr said abruptly. "On Phil."

"You've got four murder victims and now this," Lucas said. "What do you expect, violin music?"

"I don't know what I expected," Carr said.

The sheriff was pushing the truck, moving fast. Lucas caught the bank sign: minus twenty-eight.

He said it aloud: "Twenty-eight below."

"Yeah." The wind had picked up again, and was blowing thin streamers of snow off rooftops and drifts. The sheriff hunched over the steering wheel. "If the kid's been outside, he's dead. He doesn't need anybody to kill him."

A moment passed in silence. Lucas couldn't think about John Mueller: when he thought about him, he could feel a darkness creeping over his mind. Maybe the kid was at another friend's house, maybe . . .

"How long has Bergen had the drinking problem?" he asked.

"Since college. He told me he went to his first AA meeting before he was legal to drink," Carr said. His heavy face was a faint unhealthy green in the dashboard lights.

"How bad? DTs? Memory loss? Blackouts?"

"Like that," Carr said.

"But he's been dry? Lately?"

"I think so. Sometimes it's hard to tell, if a guy keeps his head down. He can drink at night, hold it together during the day. I used to do a little drinking myself."

"Lot of cops do."

Carr looked across the seat at him: "You too?"

"No, no. I've abused a few things, but not booze. I've always had a taste for uppers."

"Cocaine?"

Lucas laughed, a dry rattle: the kid's face kept popping up. Small kid, sweet-faced. "I can hear the beads of sweat popping out of your forehead, Shelly. No. I'm afraid of that shit. Might be too good, if you know what I mean."

"Any alcoholic'd know what you mean," Carr said.

"I've done a little speed from time to time," Lucas continued, looking out at the dark featureless forest that lined the road. "Not lately. Speed and alcohol, they're for different personalities."

"Either one of them'll kill you," Carr said.

They passed a video rental shop with three people standing outside; they all turned to watch the sheriff's truck go by. Lucas said, "People do weird things when they're drunk. And they forget things. If he was drunk, the time . . ."

"He says he wasn't," Carr said.

"Would he lie about it?"

"I don't think so," Carr said. "Under other circumstances, he might— drinkers lie to themselves when they're starting again. But with this, all these dead people, I don't think he'd lie. Like I told you, Phil Bergen's a moral man. That's why he drinks in the first place."

There were twenty people at the Muellers', mostly neighbors, with three deputies. A half-dozen men on snowmobiles were organizing a patrol of ditches and trails within two miles of the house.

Carr plunged into it while Lucas drifted around the edges, helpless. He didn't know anything about missing persons searches, not out here in the woods, and Carr seemed to know a lot about it.

A few moments after Carr and Lucas arrived, the boy's father hurried out into the yard, pulling on a snowmobile suit. A woman stood in the door in a white baker's dress, hands clasped to her face. The image stuck with Lucas: it was an effect of pure terror.

Mueller said something to Carr and they talked for a moment, then Carr shook his head. Lucas heard him say "Three of them up north. . . ."

The father had been looking around the yard, as though his son might walk out of the woods. Instead of the boy, he saw Lucas and stepped toward him. "You sonofabitch," he screamed, eyes rolling. A deputy caught him, jostled him, stayed between them. Faces in the yard turned toward Lucas. "Where's my boy, where's my boy?" Mueller screamed.

Carr came over and said, "You better leave. Take my truck. Call Lacey, tell him to get Gene, and the three of you go on out to Harper's place. There's nothing you can do here."

"Must be something," Lucas said. A deputy was talking to Mueller, Mueller's eyes still fixed on Lucas.

"There's nothing," Carr said. "Just get out. Go on down to Harper's like we planned."

LUCAS MET LACEY and Climpt at the 77 Tap, a bar ten miles east of Grant. The bar was an old one, a simple cube with shingle siding and a few dark windows up above, living rooms upstairs for the owner. An antique gas pump sat to one side of the place, with a set of rusting, unused bait tanks, all of it awash in snow. A Leinenkugel's sign provided most of the exterior lighting.

Inside, the bar smelled of fried fish and old beer; an Elton John song was playing on the jukebox. Lacey and Climpt were sitting in one of the three booths.

"No sign of the kid?" Lacey asked as he slid out of the booth. Climpt threw two dollars on the table and stood up behind him, chewing on a wooden matchstick.

"Not when I left," Lucas said.

Lacey and Climpt looked at each other and Climpt shook his head. "If he ain't at somebody's house . . ."

"Yeah."

"Ain't your fault," Climpt said, looking levelly at Lucas. "What're you supposed to do?"

"Yeah." Lucas shook his head and they started for the door. "So tell me about Harper."

Lacey was pulling on his gloves. "He's our local hood. He spent two years in prison over in Minnesota for ag assault—this was way back, must've been a couple of years after he got out of high school. He's been in jail since then, maybe three or four times."

"For?"

"Brawling, mostly. Fighting in bars. He'd pick out somebody, get on them, goad them into a fight and then hurt them. You know the type. He's beat up some women we know of, but they never wanted to do anything about it. Either because they were still hoping to get together with him or because they were scared. You know."

"Yeah."

"He's carried a gun off and on, smokes a little marijuana, maybe does a little coke, we've heard both," Lacey continued. "He says he needs the gun to protect himself when he's taking cash home from the station."

"He's a felon," Lucas said.

"Got his rights back," Lacey said. "Shouldn't of. There's been rumors that when he's been hard up for money, he'd go down to the Cities and knock over a liquor store or a 7-Eleven. Maybe that's just bar talk."

"Maybe," Climpt grunted. He looked at Lucas: "He's not like a TV bully. He's a bully, but he's not a coward. He's a mean sonofabitch."

CLIMPT AND LACEY RODE together, and Lucas followed them out, occasional muted cop chatter burbling out of the radio. The roads had cleared except for icy corners and intersections, and traffic was light because of the cold. They made good time.

Knuckle Lake popped up as a fuzzy ball of light far away down the highway, brightening and separating into business signs and streetlights as they got closer. There were a half dozen buildings scattered around the four corners: a motel, two bars, a general store, a cafe, and the Amoco station. The station was brightly lit, with snow piled twenty feet high along the back property lines. One car sat at a gas pump, engine off, the driver elsewhere. An old Chevy was visible through the windows of the single repair bay. They stopped in front of the big window, the other two trucks swinging in behind. A teenager in a ragged trench coat and tennis shoes peered through the glass at them: he was all by himself, like a guppie in a well-lit aquarium.

Lucas followed Climpt inside. Climpt nodded at the kid and said, "Hello, Tommy. How you doing?"

"Okay, just fine, Mr. Climpt," the kid said. He was nervous, and a shock of straw-colored hair fell out from under his watch cap, his Adam's apple bobbing spasmodically.

"How long you been out?" Climpt asked.

"Oh, two months now," the kid said.

"Tommy used to borrow cars, go for rides," Climpt said.

"Bad habit," Lucas said, crossing his arms, leaning against the candy machine. "Everybody gets pissed off at you."

"I quit," the kid said.

"He's a good mechanic," Climpt said. Then: "Where's Russ?"

"Down to the house, I guess."

"Okay."

"It'd be better if you didn't call him," Lucas said.

"Whatever," the kid said. "I'm, you know, whatever."

"Whatever," Climpt said. He pointed a finger at the kid's face, and the kid swallowed. "We won't be tellin' Russ we talked to you."

Back outside, Climpt said, "He won't call."

"How far is Harper's place?"

"Two minutes from here," Carr said.

"Think he'll be a problem?"

"Not if we get right on top of him," Climpt said. "He won't win no college scholarship, but he's not stupid enough to take on a whole . . . whatever we are."

"A posse," Lucas said.

Climpt laughed, a short bark. "Right. A posse."

JOHN MUELLER CAME BACK to Lucas' mind, like a nagging toothache, a pain that wouldn't go away but couldn't be fixed. Maybe he was at a friend's; maybe they'd already found him. . . .

Harper's house huddled in a copse of birch and red pine, alone on an unlit stretch of side road, a free-standing garage in back, a mercury-vapor yard-light overhead. Windows were lit in the back of the house. Climpt killed his lights and pulled into the end of the drive, and Lucas pulled in behind him.

Climpt and Lacey got out, pushed the truck doors shut instead of slamming them. "Are you carrying?" Climpt asked.

"Yeah."

"Might loosen it up. Russ's always got something around."

"All right." Lucas turned to Lacey, who had his hands in his pockets and was staring up at the house. "Henry, why don't you sit out here by the truck. Get the shotgun and just hang back."

Lacey nodded and walked back toward the Suburban.

"I'll try to get a little edge on him right away," Lucas told Climpt as they started up the driveway. "I won't pull any real shit, but you can act like you think I might."

Woodsmoke drifted down on them, an acrid odor that cut at the nose and throat. Two feet of pristine snow covered the front porch. "Looks like he doesn't use the front door at all," Climpt said.

As they walked around the side of the house, they heard the gun rack rattle as Lacey unlocked the shotgun and took it out, then the ratcheting sound of a twelve-gauge shell being pumped home. At the back door, Lucas could hear the sounds of a television—not the words but the rhythms.

"Stand down at the bottom where he can see you," Lucas told Climpt. He went to the top of the stoop and knocked on the door, then stepped to the side. A moment later the yellow porch light came on, and then a curtain pulled back. A man's head appeared behind the window glass. He looked at Climpt, hesitated, made a head gesture, and fumbled with the doorknob.

"We're okay," Lucas muttered.

Harper pulled open the inner door, saw Lucas, frowned. He was an oval-faced man, with a narrow chin, thick, short lips, and scar tissue on his forehead and under his eyes. His eyes were the size of dimes, and black, like a lizard's. He was unshaven. He pushed open the storm door, looked down at Climpt and said, "What do you want, Gene?"

"We need to talk to you about the death of your son, and we need to look through Jim's stuff again," Climpt said.

Harper's thick lips twisted. "You got a warrant?"

"Yeah, we got a warrant."

After another long moment Harper said, "Now what the fuck are you fuckin' with me for, Climpt?" The question came in a low voice, rough and guttural, angry but unafraid.

"We're not fuckin' with you," Lucas snapped back. He hooked the storm door handle with his left hand and jerked it open. Harper pulled back an inch, then settled in a fighting stance, ready to swing. He was round-shouldered but hard, with hands that looked granite-gray in the bad light. Lucas took his right hand out of his pocket, a bare hand with a .45. "Swing on me and I'll beat the shit out of you," he said. "And if I start to lose I'll blow your fuckin' nuts off."

"What?" Harper stepped back, dropping his right hand.

"You heard me, asshole."

"Oh, yeah," Harper said. He straightened, let the left hand drop. "You're the big city guy, uh? Big city guy, big city asshole gonna blow my nuts off." He took another step back, the anger spreading from his eyes over his face, ready to go again.

"Come on, motherfucker," Lucas said. He lifted the .45 out to the side. "You put your own boy out on the corner givin' blowjobs to fat guys, there's nobody in this county'd blame me if I spread your brains all over the house. So you wanna do it? Come on, come on . . ."

"You're fuckin' nuts," Harper said. But his voice had changed again, uncertainty near the surface, and his eyes shifted past Lucas to Climpt. "Why are you fuckin' with me, Gene?"

"The LaCourt girl, the one who was killed, had a picture of your boy, naked, with a grown-up male," Climpt said.

Lucas dropped the gun to his side, moved forward, one foot inside, shoulder against the door, forcing Harper back. "She showed it around and then the family was wiped out," he said. "We want to look at Jim's things, see if there's anything that might indicate who it was."

"Sure as shit wasn't me."

"We're looking for a guy who's blond and a little fat," Lucas said. He stepped through the storm door into a mudroom, crowding Harper, who backed through an inner door into the kitchen. Climpt was a step behind. "You don't have any friends that look like that, do you?"

Climpt called out to the truck, "Henry, c'mon."

"I want to see that warrant," Harper said, backing further into the kitchen. The kitchen smelled of onions and bad meat and old soured milk.

"Henry's got it," Climpt said. Harper looked past Lucas as Lacey walked up. Lacey pulled a paper out of his pocket and handed it to Lucas, who handed it to Harper. While Harper looked at it, Lucas decocked the .45. At the latching sound, Harper looked up and said, "Smith and Wesson. Is that the .40 or the .45?"

"The .45," Lucas said.

"I'd have gone with the .40," Harper said as the two deputies came in behind Carr. He'd gone into the asshole-cooperative mode, an almost imperceptible groveling learned in prisons.

"Right," said Lucas, ignoring the comment. He put the pistol back in his coat pocket. "Where's the kid's room?"

"You don't think I know about guns? I . . ."

"I don't give a fuck what you know," Lucas snapped. "Where's the kid's room?"

Harper muttered *shit*, crumbled the warrant in his hand and threw it on the floor, turned and led them through a narrow archway into the living room. The TV was tuned to professional wrestling, and a cardboard tray, stained orange from the sauce of an instant spaghetti dinner, sat on a round oak table with an empty crockery coffee cup. Harper brushed past it, into a hallway. The first door on the right was open, into a bathroom; the next door, to the left, was half-open, and Harper pulled it closed. "That's mine. Nothin' of Jim's in there."

At the last door, on the right, he stopped and gestured with his thumb: "That was Jim's."

Lucas pushed the door open. Jim Harper had been dead for more than two months, but his room was like he'd left it: a pair of dirty jeans, a t-shirt and pair of underpants tossed in a corner, now covered with dust. The bed was unmade, a discolored flat-sheet and an olive-drab Army blanket tangled on a yellowed fitted sheet. The pillow was small, gray, dotted with what might have been blood. Lucas looked closer: blood, all right, but only in small spots, as though the kid had acne and picked at the sores. Clothes were pinched in the drawers of the single bureau, and two of the drawers hung open.

"The cops already been through it, messed it up," Harper said over Lucas' shoulder. "Didn't find anything."

Lucas looked back down the hall at Lacey. "Henry, why don't you and Mr. Harper here go sit and watch some TV? Gene and I'll look around."

"Hey . . ." Harper said.

"Shut up," said Lucas.

. . .

"**THEY TURNED THE** room over and didn't find anything," Lucas said to Climpt. "If you were a kid, hiding something, where'd you put it?"

"What I've been thinking is, Russ's such an asshole, why would a kid hide anything from him? Nothing the kid could do would bother him much."

Lucas shrugged. "Maybe he'd hide something just so he could keep it."

"That's a point," Climpt said. After a moment: "I always hid stuff in the basement. Maybe in a closet if it was just overnight and small—dirty magazines, that sort of thing. I suppose the attic, if they got one."

"Let's do a quick run through this, then maybe look around a little."

The house was an old one, with hardwood planked floors covered with patches of linoleum, and lath-and-plaster walls. Lucas dug through the kid's closet, shaking out a stack of magazines and comic books, checking shoes and the few shirts hanging inside. There were no loose floorboards and the plaster wall was cracked but intact. Climpt tossed the bureau again, pulling out each drawer to turn it over, checked the heat register, found it solid. In ten minutes they'd decided the room was clean.

"Attic or basement?" asked Climpt.

"Let's see how much trouble the attic is."

The attic access was through a hatch in the bathroom. Standing on a chair, Lucas pushed up the hatch and was showered with dust and asbestos insulation. He pulled it shut again and climbed down, brushing the dirt out of his hair.

"Hasn't been open in a while," he said.

"Basement," said Climpt. They headed for the basement stairs, found Lacey digging through a freestanding wardrobe in the living room while Harper slumped in a chair.

"Anything?" Lucas asked.

"Nope."

"We'll be down the basement," Lucas said.

Harper watched them go, but said nothing. "I wish that fucker'd give me a reason to slam him up alongside the head," Climpt said.

The basement smelled of cobwebs, dust, engine oil, and coal. The walls' granite fieldstone was mortared with crumbling, sandy concrete. Two bare bulbs, dangling from ancient fraying wire, provided all the light. There were two small rooms, filled with the clutter of a rural half-century: racks of dusty Ball jars, broken crocks, an antique lawnmower, a lever-action .22 covered with rust. A dozen leg-hold jump traps hung from a nail, and hanging next to them, two dozen tiny feet tied together with twine.

"Gophers," Climpt said, touching them. They swayed like a grisly wind chime. "County used to pay a bounty on them, way back, nickel a pair on front feet."

A railroad-tie workbench was wedged into a corner with a rusting vise fitted at one end. A huge old coal furnace hunkered in the middle of the main room like a dead oak, stone cold. A diminutive propane burner stood in what had once been a coal room, galvanized ducts leading to the rooms above. The coal room was the cleanest place in the basement, apparently cleaned when the furnace was installed. At a glance, there was no place to hide anything.

Lucas wandered over to the coal furnace, pulled open the furnace door, looked at a pile of old ashes, closed it. "This could take a while," he said.

They took fifteen minutes, Climpt repeating, "Someplace where he could get it quick. . . ." They found nothing, and started up the steps, unsatisfied. The basement had too many nooks and crannies. "If one of those fieldstones pulled out . . ." Lucas started.

"We'd never find it: there must be two thousand of them," Climpt said.

And Lucas said, "Wait a minute," went back down the stairs and looked toward the propane burner.

"If that's the coal room, shouldn't there be a coal chute?" he asked.

"Yeah, there should," Climpt said.

They found the chute door set in the wall behind the propane burner, four feet above the floor and virtually invisible in the bad light. Lucas reached back, unlatched the door and felt inside. His hand fell on a stack of paper.

"Something," he said. "Paper." He pulled it out. Three glossy sex magazines and two sex comics. He handed them to Climpt, reached back inside for another quick check, came up with a small corner of notebook paper, blank, that might have been used as a bookmark. Lucas stuck the paper in his pocket.

"Porn," said Climpt, standing under one of the hanging light bulbs. They shook out the magazines, found nothing inside.

"Check 'em," Lucas said. "We're looking for a picture of a kid on a bed."

They flipped through the magazines, but all of the pictures were obviously commercial and involved women. The Mueller kid had described the photo he'd seen as rough, printed on newsprint.

"Nothing much," Climpt said. "I mean, a lot of pussy . . . Goddamn Shelly'd have a heart attack."

Lucas went back to the coal chute for a final check, reached far inside, felt just a corner of a piece of plastic. He had to stretch to fish it out.

A Polaroid.

Climpt came to look over his shoulder.

A young boy, slender, nude, standing in front of a crouched woman, pushing into her mouth. His hands were wrapped around her skull. All that was visible of the woman was her dark hair, the lower part of her face from her nose down, and part of her neck. She was obviously older, probably in her forties.

The boy's left hand was visible and a finger was gone.

"Don't know the woman, just from that," Climpt said. "But that's Jim doin' her."

"Hey, Lucas," Lacey called from upstairs.

"Yeah?"

"It's like . . . ah, Christ!" Lacey blurted.

Lucas looked at Climpt, who shrugged, and they headed up the stairs. Lacey was standing in the door to the living room, his face dead white. Harper sat in a chair, a half-amused look on his face. They were looking at the television. The video was cheap, clear enough: two men were lying on a bed, fondling each other.

"You sell this shit?" Climpt growled at Harper.

"I told Henry—it all belonged to Jim. I don't look at homo shit."

"Found it in the wardrobe," Lacey said. "There weren't any labels."

Lucas handed Lacey the Polaroid.

"Sonofagun," Lacey whispered.

"Yeah," Lucas said. "You want to look at this, Harper?" No more *Russ* or *Mr. Harper.* He held it out in front of Harper, who reached for it, but Lucas pulled it back. "Just look—don't touch."

Harper peered at the picture and drawled, "Looks like Jim, gettin' him some head. Damn, I wish I knew her—she looks like she knows what she's doing."

He still had the slightly amused look on his face. He was about to say something else when Climpt stepped past Lucas, grabbed Harper by the shirt, and hauled him out of the chair. "You motherfucker."

Harper covered his gut with his elbows, kept his hands up in front of his face. He didn't want to get hurt, but he wasn't scared, Lucas thought.

"Hey, hey," said Lacey, trying to intervene. "Let him . . ."

Climpt shoved Harper at Lucas, who caught him, still off-balance, said, "Fuck, I don't want him," and spun him into the wall. Climpt caught him on the rebound, dragged him backwards by the collar and as Lacey shouted, "Hey," banged the back of Harper's head against the opposite wall, then pulled him forward, letting go as Lucas put his hand in Harper's face and snapped him backwards into the chair.

"Knock it off," Lacey said.

"Set your own kid up for this shit, didn't you?" Climpt said, his face an inch from Harper's. Harper spit at him, a spray of spittle. Climpt caught him by the shirt collar and the skin under his neck and hoisted him a foot out of the chair. "Sold his ass to faggots and anybody else who wanted some young stuff. You know what they're gonna do to you in the joint? You know what they do to child fuckers? You're gonna wear out your kneecaps kneeling on the floors, blowing those guys."

Lacey, face red, had Climpt by the shoulder, pulling at him. Lucas put his arm between Harper and Climpt, said, "Gene, let him go. Gene . . ."

Climpt looked blindly at Lucas, then dropped Harper back in the chair, turned away, wiped his face with his forearm.

"Motherfucker," Harper said, pulling down his shirt.

Lucas turned to Lacey. "Could you get Shelly on the radio? Don't mention the Polaroid directly, but tell him we got something. And we need to see him."

Lacey stepped back, reluctantly. "You guys won't . . ."

"No, no," Lucas said. "And listen, ask him about the Mueller kid, if there's been any progress."

"What about the Mueller kid?" Harper asked.

"He's missing," Lucas said, turning back to him.

Lacey was walking out through the kitchen. When the back door banged shut, Lucas stepped up to Harper. "I believe you spit on deputy Climpt, and I feel kinda short-changed, you know. You didn't spit on me."

"Fuck you," Harper said. He looked from Lucas to Climpt and back. "I got my rights."

Lucas took him by the shirt as Climpt had, jerked him out of the chair, ran him straight back at the wall, slammed him against it. Harper covered, still not ready to resist. Climpt caught his right arm, twisted it. Both Lucas and Climpt were bigger than Harper, and pinned him on the wall.

"Remember what you said about your vise?" Lucas asked, face half-turned to Climpt. Climpt grunted. "Watch this—this is nasty."

He caught the flesh between Harper's nostrils by his thumb and middle fingers and squeezed, his fingernails digging into the soft flesh. Harper's mouth dropped as though he were going to scream, but Climpt's hand came up and squeezed his throat.

Lucas squeezed, squeezed, then said, "Who's the woman in the picture? *Who is it?*"

Harper, his body bucking, shook his head. "Better let go of his throat for a minute, Gene," Lucas said, and he let go of Harper's nose. Harper groaned, thrashed, sucked air, and Lucas asked, "Who is that, asshole? Who's the woman?"

"Don't know . . ."

"Let me try," Climpt said, and he caught Harper's nose as Lucas had, his thick yellow fingernails squeezing. . . .

The sound that came from Harper's throat might have been a scream if it had been pitched lower. As it was, it was a kind of blackboard scratching squeak, and he shuddered.

"Who is it?" Lucas asked.

"Don't . . ."

Climpt looked at Lucas, who shook his head, and they both released him at the same moment. Tears were running down Harper's face and he caught his head in his hands and dropped to his knees. Lucas squatted beside him.

"You know some stuff," Lucas said. "You know the woman or you know somebody who knows the woman."

Harper got one foot beneath him, then heaved himself up. His eyes were red, and tears still poured down his face. "Motherfuckers."

Climpt cuffed him on the side of the head. "You ain't listening. You know who this is, this woman. If you don't spit out the name . . ."

"You're gonna what? Beat me around?" Harper asked, defiant. "I been beat around before, so go ahead. I'll get my fuckin' lawyer."

"Yeah, you put a fuckin' lawyer out there and I'll pin this fuckin' picture on the bulletin board at the goddamn Super Valu with the note that you sold Jim's ass," Climpt said. "They'll find your fuckin' skin hanging from a tree out here, and you won't be in it."

"Go fuck yourself," Harper snarled. There was blood on his upper lip, trickling down from his nose.

Climpt pulled back his hand but Lucas blocked it. "Let it go," he said.

. . .

OUTSIDE, AS THEY WERE loading into the trucks, Lacey said, "Where's Harper?"

"Probably fixin' some dinner," Climpt said. Then, "He's okay, Henry, don't get your ass in an uproar."

Lacey shook his head doubtfully, then said, "Can I see that Polaroid again, just for a minute?"

Lucas handed it to him and Lacey turned on his truck's dome light and peered at the photo.

"Check this, right here," Lacey said. He touched the edge of the photograph with a fingernail. Lucas took it.

"It looks like a sleeve."

"Sure does," said Lacey, holding the photo four inches from his face. "Now, this here is a Spectra Polaroid. Spectras come with a remote control, a radio thing, so it might of been that there were only the two of them. But if that's a sleeve, and if there's somebody else behind the camera . . ."

"The camera angle's downward," Lucas said. "That'd be high for a tripod."

"So there must be a bunch of them," Lacey said.

"Yeah, probably," Lucas said, nodding. "We already know he was with a heavy white guy and here's a woman."

"Damn—if it's a bunch of people, it's gonna tear this county up," Climpt said.

"I'd say the county's already torn up," Lucas said.

Climpt shook his head: "This'd be worse'n the murders, a bunch of people screwing children. Believe me, around here, this'd be worse."

THEY HEADED BACK TO TOWN, Climpt riding with Lucas.

"Kind of liked your style back there," Climpt said.

"Thanks. I've worked on it," Lucas said.

The radio burped: Carr. *Need to see you guys at the courthouse.*

"Did you find the kid?" Lucas asked.

Nothing yet, Carr said.

Off the air, Lucas told Climpt, "I fucked up. The school principal was worried about cops talking to kids without the parents' permission. I took the kid out to his house so I could explain to his father. Goddammit."

"You didn't fuck up," Climpt said. He fumbled a cigarette out of a crumpled pack and lit it with a paper match. "That's not the kind of thing you can know. You're dealing with a crazy man. And you've got a reputation. People around here think you're Sherlock Holmes."

"I'm not. But I have dealt with psychos before. I should have known better than to show an interest in one witness," Lucas said. "I . . . Oh, shit."

"What?"

"Do you know where the doctor's house is? Weather Karkinnen?" Lucas asked, his voice urgent.

"Sure. Down on Lincoln Lake."

WEATHER LIVED IN A rambling, white-clapboard house with a steep, snow-covered roof. A fieldstone chimney, webbed with naked vines, climbed one end, a double garage anchored the other. A stand of red pines protected it from the north wind. Two huge white pines, one with a rope dangling from a lower branch, stood in back, along the edge of the frozen lake. The neighboring homes were as large or larger than Weather's, most of them with aging boathouses at the edge of the lake.

As Lucas and Climpt pulled into the driveway, a pod of snowmobiles whipped by on the lake, heading for a bar sign at the far end.

Weather's house was dark.

"Just be a minute or two," Lucas said, but a chilly anxiety plucked at his chest, growing heavier as he climbed out of the truck and hurried up to the house. He rang the doorbell, and when he didn't get a response, pounded on the front door and rattled the knob. The door was locked. He stepped back off the porch and started down the sidewalk, intending to try the garage doors, when a light came on inside.

He felt like a boulder had been lifted off his back. He turned and hurried back to the door, rang the doorbell again. And suddenly he was nervous again, afraid that she might think he was here to hustle her.

A moment later Weather opened the inner door, peered through the glass of the storm door, then pushed the storm door open. She was wearing a heavy throat-to-ankle terrycloth robe. She pulled the robe together at the neck as she leaned out and looked past him at the truck, still running in the driveway, and said, "Okay, what happened?"

Another boulder came off his back. She *didn't* think . . .

"There's a kid missing—after I talked to him at school today," Lucas blurted. "He might have wandered away from his house, but nobody really thinks so. He may have been taken by whoever did the LaCourts. Since we've spent some time together, you and I . . . You see . . ."

"Who's out in the truck?" Weather asked.

"Gene Climpt."

She waved at the truck, then said to Lucas, "Come on in for a moment and tell me about it."

Lucas kicked snow off his boots and stepped inside. The house smelled subtly of baking and herbs. A modern watercolor of a vase of flowers hung on an eggshell-white wall that faced the entry. Lucas knew almost nothing about modern art, but he liked it.

"Who's the kid?" Weather asked.

"John Mueller," Lucas said. "Do you know him?"

"Oh, God. His mom works at the bakery?"

"I guess . . ."

"Aw, jeez, I've seen him up there doing his homework. Aw, God . . ." She had her arms crossed over her chest, and was gripping the material on the sleeves of her robe, her knuckles white.

"If the killer took the kid, then he's out of control. Nuts," Lucas said. He felt large and awkward in the parka and boots and hat and gloves, looking down at her in her bathrobe. "It'd be best if you got out of here. At least until we can set up some security."

Weather shook her head: "Not tonight. I've got surgery in"—she looked at her watch—"seven hours. I've got to be up in five."

"Can you cancel?" Lucas asked.

"No." She shook her head. "My patient's already in the hospital, fasting and medicated. It wouldn't be right."

"I've got to go downtown," Lucas said. "I could come back and bag out on your couch."

"In other words, wake me up again," she said, but she smiled.

"Look, this is getting nasty." He was so serious that she tapped his chest, to hold him where he was standing, and said, "Wait a minute." She walked into the dark part of the house and a light came on. There was a moment of rattling, then she came back with a garage-door opener.

"C'mere . . . don't worry about the snow on your boots, it's only water." She led him through the living room to the hallway, opened the first door in the hall. "Guest room. The right bay in the garage is empty. You come through the garage door to the kitchen, then through here. I'll leave a couple of lights on."

Lucas took the garage-door opener, nodded, said, "I'll walk around your house, look in back. Keep your doors locked and stay inside. You've got dead bolts?"

"Yes."

"Then lock the doors," he said. "You've got a lock on your bedroom door?"

"Yes, but just a knob lock. It's not much."

"It'd slow somebody down," Lucas said. "Lock it. How about a gun. Do you have a gun?"

"A .22 rifle. My dad shot squirrels off the roof with it."

"Know how to use it? Got any shells?"

"Yes, and there's a box of shells with the gun."

"Load it and put it under your bed," Lucas said. "We'll talk tomorrow morning. Wake me up when you get up."

"Lucas, be careful."

"*You* be careful. Lock the doors."

He went to the entry, pulled open the inner door. As he was about to go out, she caught his sleeve, tugged him back, stood on her tiptoes and kissed him, and in almost the same movement, gave him a little shove that propelled him out through the storm door.

"See you in the morning," she said and closed the door. He waited until he heard the lock snap, then went back down the walk to the truck, still feeling the fleeting pressure of her lips on his.

"She okay?" Climpt asked.

"Yeah. Gimme the flashlight. In the glove compartment." Climpt grunted, dug around in the glove compartment, handed him the flash, and Lucas said, "I'll be right back."

The snow around the house was unbroken as far back as he could see. A low railed deck stuck out of the back, in front of a long sliding-glass door. A bird feeder showed hundreds of bird tracks and the comings and goings of a squirrel, but nothing larger. As he waded ponderously through the snow, returning to the truck, another pod of snowmobiles roared by on the lake, and Lucas thought about the sled used in the LaCourt attack.

Climpt was standing next to the truck, smoking an unfiltered Camel. When he saw Lucas coming, he dropped the cigarette on the driveway, stepped on it, and climbed back into the passenger seat.

"Find anything?" he asked as Lucas got in.

"No."

"We could get somebody down here, keep an eye on her."

"I'm gonna come back and bag out in her guest room," Lucas said. "Maybe we can figure something better tomorrow."

Lucas backed out of the drive and they rode in silence for a few minutes. Then Climpt, slouching against the passenger-side door, drawled, "That Weather's a fine-looking woman, uh-huh. Got a good ass on her." He was half-grinning. "She's single, I'm single. I'm quite a bit older, of course, but I get to feeling pretty frisky in the spring," Climpt continued. "I been thinking about calling her up. Do you think she'd go out with an old guy like me? I might still be able to show her a thing or two."

"I don't believe she would, Gene," Lucas said, looking straight out through the windshield.

Climpt, still smiling in the dark, said, "You don't think so, huh? That's a damn shame. I think she could probably show a fellow a pretty good time. And it's not like puttin' a little on me would leave her with any less of it, if you know what I mean."

"Stick a sock in it, Gene," Lucas said.

Climpt broke into a laugh that was half a cough, and after a minute, Lucas laughed with him. Climpt said, "Looking at you when you went up to her door, I'd say you're about half-caught, my friend. If you don't want to get all-caught, you better be careful. If you want to be careful."

CARR WAS GRAY-FACED, exhausted. Old.

"I've got to get back out there, on the search line," he said when Climpt and

Lucas walked into his office. Lacey was with him and four other deputies. "It's a mess. We got people who want to help who just aren't equipped for it. Not in this cold. They'll be dying out there, looking for the kid."

"The kid's dead if he's not inside," Climpt said bluntly. "And if he's inside somewhere, looking for him outside won't help."

"We thought of that, but you can't really quit, not when there's a chance," Carr said. "Where's this photograph Henry's been telling me about?"

Lucas took it out of his pocket and flipped it on Carr's desk. Carr looked at it for a moment and said, "Mother of God." To one of the deputies, he said, "Is Tony still down the hall?"

"Yeah, I think so."

Carr picked up the phone, poked in four numbers. They all heard a ringing far down the hall, then Carr said, "Tony? Come on down to my office, will you?"

When he'd hung up, Lucas said, "I had dinner with Weather Karkinnen and people have seen us talking. Gene and I stopped at her place. She's all right for now."

"I'll send somebody over," Carr suggested.

Lucas shook his head. "I'll cover it tonight. Tomorrow I'll try to push her into a safer place, maybe out of town, until this thing is settled. I just hope it doesn't start any talk in the town."

The sheriff shrugged. "It probably will, but so what? The truth'll get out and it'll be okay."

"There's another problem," Lucas said. "Everything we do seems to be all over town in a few minutes. You need to put the lid on, tight. If John Mueller's missing, and if he's missing because he talked to me, it's possible that our killer heard about it from a teacher or another kid. But it's also possible that it came out of the department here. Christ, everything that we've done . . ."

Carr nodded, pointed a finger at Lacey. "Henry, write up a memo. Anyone who talks out of place, to anyone, about this case, is gonna get terminated. The minute I hear about it. And I don't want anybody talking about substantive stuff on the radios, either. Okay? There must be a hundred police-band monitors in this town, and every word we say is out there."

Lacey nodded and opened his mouth to say something when a short dark-haired man stuck his head in the office and said, "Sheriff?"

Carr glanced up at him, nodded and said, "I need to talk to Tony for a minute. Could we get everybody out of here except Lucas and Henry? And Gene, you stay . . . Thanks."

When the others had gone, Carr said, "Shut the door." To Lucas: "Tony's my political guy." When the dark-haired man had closed the door, Carr handed him the Polaroid and said, "Take a look at this picture."

Tony took it, studied it, turned it, said "Huh," and nibbled on a thumbnail. Finally he looked up and said, "Sheriff?"

"You know that woman?"

"There're half-dozen people it could be," he said. "But something about her jaw . . ."

"Say the name."

"Judy Schoenecker."

"Damn," the sheriff said. "That's what I thought soon as I saw it. Gene?"

Gene took the photo, looked at it, shook his head. "Could be, but I don't know her that well."

"Let's check it out," Carr said. "Lucas, what're you going to do? It'd be best if you stayed away from the Mueller search, at least for a while."

Lucas looked at his watch. "I'm going back to Weather's. I'm about to drop dead anyway." He reached across the desk and tapped the photograph. "Why don't you call this a tentative identification and see if you can get a search warrant?"

"Boy, I'd hate to . . ." the sheriff started. Then: "Screw it. I'll get one as soon as the judge wakes up tomorrow."

"Have somebody call me," Lucas said.

"All right. And Lucas: You couldn't help it about the kid, John Mueller," Carr said. "I mean, if he's gone."

"You really couldn't," Lacey agreed.

"I appreciate your saying it," Lucas said bleakly. "But you're both full of shit."

SLEEP HAD ALWAYS BEEN DIFFICULT. The slights and insults of the day would keep him awake for hours, plotting revenge; and there were few days without slights and insults.

And night was the time that he worried. There was power in the Iceman—movement, focus, clarity—but at night, when he thought things over, the things he'd done during the day didn't always seem wise.

Lying awake in his restless bed, the Iceman heard the three vehicles arrive, one after another, bouncing off the roadway into the snow-packed parking lot. He listened for a moment, heard a car door slam. A clock radio sat on the bedstand: the luminous red numbers said it was two o'clock in the morning.

Who was out in the pit of night?

The Iceman got out of bed, turned on a bedside lamp, pulled on his jeans, and started downstairs. The floor was cold, and he stooped, picked up the docks he'd dropped on the floor, slipped them on, and went down the stairs.

A set of headlights still played across his side window, and he could hear—

or feel—an engine turning over, as if people were talking in the lot. As he reached the bottom of the stairs, the headlights and engine sounds died and a moment later someone began pounding on the door.

The Iceman went to the window, pulled back the gingham curtain, and peered out. Frost covered the center of the window in a shattered-paisley pattern, but through a clear spot he could see the roof-mounted auxiliary lights on Russ Harper's Toyota truck, sitting under the blue yard-light.

"Harper," he muttered. Bad news.

The pounding started again and the Iceman yelled "Just a minute" and went to the door and unlocked it. Harper was on the concrete stoop, stamping the snow off his boots. He looked up when the Iceman opened the door, and without a word, pushed inside, shoving the door back, his face like a chunk of wood. He wore a red-and-plaid wool hunting coat and leather gloves. Two other men were behind him, and a woman, all dressed in parkas with hoods and heavy ski gloves, corduroy or wool pants, and pac boots, faces pale with winter, harsh with stress.

"Russ," said the Iceman, as Harper brushed past. "Andy. Doug. How're you doin', Judy?"

"We gotta talk," Harper said, pulling off his gloves. The other three wouldn't directly meet the Iceman's inquiring eyes, but looked instead to Harper. Harper was the one the Iceman would have to deal with.

"What's going on?" he said. On the surface, his face was slack, sleepy. Inside, the beast began to stir, to unwind.

"Did you kill the LaCourts?" Harper asked, stepping close to him. The Iceman's heart jumped, and for just a moment he found it hard to breathe. But he was a good liar. He'd always been good.

"What? No—of course not. I was here." He put shock on his face and Harper said "Motherfucker," and turned away, shaking his head. He touched his lip and winced, and the Iceman saw what looked like a tiny rime of blood.

"What are you talking about, Russ?" he asked. "I didn't have a goddamned thing to do with it. I was here, there were witnesses," he complained. Public consumption: *I didn't mean to; they just fell down* . . .

As his voice rose, Harper was pulling off his coat. He tossed it on a card table, hitched his pants. "Motherfucker," he said again, and he turned and grabbed the Iceman by his pajama shirt, pulled him forward on his toes, off-balance.

"You motherfucker—you better not have," Harper breathed in his face. His breath smelled of sausage and bad teeth, and the Iceman nearly retched. "We don't want nothing to do with no goddamned half-assed killer."

The Iceman brought his hands up, shoulder height, shrugged, tried not to struggle against Harper's hold, tried not to breathe. *Kill him now* . . .

Of the people in their group, Harper was the only one who worried him. Harper might do anything. Harper had a craziness, a killer feel about him: scars on his shiny forehead, lumps. And when he was angry, there was nothing calculated about it. He was a nightmare you met in a biker bar, a man who liked to hurt, a man who never stopped to think that he might be the one to get damaged. He worried the Iceman, but didn't frighten him. He could deal with him, in his own time.

"Honest to God, Russ," he said, throwing his hands out to his sides. "I mean, calm down."

"I'm having a hard time calmin' down. The cops was out to my house tonight and they flat jacked me up," Harper said. "That fuckin' guy from Minneapolis and old Gene Climpt, they jacked my ass off the floor, you know what I'm telling you?" Spit was spraying out of his mouth, and the Iceman averted his face. "You know?"

"C'mon, Russ . . ."

Harper was inflexible, boosted him an inch higher, his work-hardened knuckles cutting into soft flesh under the Iceman's chin. "You know what we been doing? We been diddlin' kids. Fuckin' juveniles, that's what we been doin', all of us. All that fancy bullshit talk about teachin' 'em this or that—it don't mean squat to the cops. They'd put us all in the fuckin' penitentiary, sure as bears shit in the woods."

"There's no reason to think I did it," the Iceman said, forcing sincerity into his voice. And the beast whispered, *Let's kill him. Now now now . . .*

"Horseshit," Harper snarled. He snapped the Iceman away as though he were a bug. "You sure you didn't have nothing to do with it?" Harper looked straight into his eyes.

"I promise you," the Iceman said, his eyes turning away, down, then back up. He pushed the beast down, caught his breath. "Listen, this is a time to be calm."

The man called Doug was bearded, with the rims of old pock-scars showing above the beard and dimpling his purple nose. "The Indians think a windigo did it," he said.

"That's the most damn-fool thing I ever did hear," Harper said, turning his hostility toward Doug. "Fuckin' windigo."

Doug shrugged. "I'm just telling you what I hear. Everybody's talking about it, out at the Res."

"Jesus Christ."

"Judy and I are outa here," the man called Andy said abruptly, and they all turned to him. Judy nodded. "We're going to Florida."

"Wait—if you take off . . ." the Iceman began.

"No law against taking a vacation," Andy said. He glanced sideways at Harper. "And we're out of this. Out of the whole deal. I don't want to have nothing to do with you. Or any of the others, neither. We're taking the girls."

Harper stepped toward them, but Andy set his feet, unafraid, and Harper stopped.

"And I won't talk to the cops. You know I can't do that, so you're all safe. There's no percentage in any of you coming looking for us," Andy finished.

"That's a bullshit idea, running," Harper said. "Runnin'll only make people suspicious. If something does break, bein' in Florida won't help none. They'll just come and get you."

"Yeah, but if somebody just wants to come and talk, offhand, and we're not around . . . Well, then, maybe they'll just forget about it," Andy said. "Anyway, Judy and I decided: we're outa here. We already told the neighbors. Told them this weather was too much, that we're going away for a while. Nobody'll suspect nothing."

"I got a bad feeling about this," said Doug.

A car rolled by outside, the lights flashing through the window, then away. They all looked at the window.

"We gotta get going," Andy said finally, pulling on his gloves. To the Iceman he said, "I don't know whether to believe you or not. If I thought you did it . . ."

"What?"

"I don't know . . ." Andy said.

"Why did you people think . . ."

"Because of that goddamn picture Frank LaCourt had. As far as I know, the only person he talked to was me. And the only person I talked to was you."

"Russ . . . I . . ." The Iceman shook his head, put a sad look on his face. He turned to Andy. "When're you leaving?"

"Probably tomorrow night or the next day," Judy said. Her husband's eyes flicked toward her, and he nodded.

"Got a few things to wind up," he muttered.

ANDY AND JUDY LEFT FIRST, flipping up their hoods, stooping to look through the window for car lights before they went out into the parking lot. As Harper zipped his parka he said, "You better not be bullshitting us."

"I'm not." The Iceman stood with his heels together, fingertips in his pants pockets, the querulous, honest smile fixed on his face.

" 'Cause if you are, I'm going to get me a knife, and I'm gonna come over here and cut off your nuts, cook them up, and make you eat them," Harper said.

"C'mon, Russ . . ."

Doug was peering at him, and then turned to look at Harper. "I don't know if he did it or not. But I'll tell you one thing: Shelly Carr couldn't find his own asshole with both hands and a flashlight. No matter who did it, we'd be safe enough if Shelly is doing the investigation."

"So?"

"So if something happened to that cop from Minneapolis . . ."

Harper put the lizard look on him. "If something happened to him, it'd be too goddamned bad, but a man'd be a fool to talk about it to anyone else," he said. "Anyone else."

"Right," said Doug. "You're right."

WHEN THEY WERE GONE, the Iceman took a turn around the room, the beast rising in his throat. He ran a hand through his hair, kicked at a chair in frustration. "Stupid," he said. He shouted it: "STUPID."

And caught himself. Controlled himself, closed his eyes, let himself flow, regulated his breathing, felt his heartbeat slow. He locked the door, turned off the lights, waited until the last vehicle had left the parking lot, then climbed the stairs again.

He could go to Harper's tonight, with the .44. Take him off. Harper had handled him like he was a piece of junk, a piece of garbage. *Yes, said the beast, take him.*

No. He'd already taken too many risks. Besides, Harper might be useful. Harper might be a fall guy.

Doug and Judy and Andy . . . so many problems. So many branching pathways to trouble. If anybody cracked . . .

Judy's face came to mind. She was a plain woman, her face lined by forty-five winters in the North Woods. She worked in a video rental store, and she looked like . . . anybody. If you saw her in a K-Mart, you wouldn't notice her. But the Iceman had seen her having sex with the Harpers, father and son, simultaneously, one at each end, while her husband watched. Had watched her, watching the Iceman, as he taught her daughters to do proper blowjobs. She had seen her husband with their own daughters, had seen the Iceman with Rosie Harris and Mark Harris and Ginny Harris, the yellow-haired girl.

She'd seen all that, done all that, and yet she could lose herself in a K-Mart.

He again approached the problem of what to do. Fight or run? This time, though, the problem seemed less like an endless snaky ball of possibilities and more like a single intricate but manageable organism.

He was far from cornered. There were many things he might do. The image of John Mueller came to mind: red spots on white, like the eight of hearts, the red in the snow around the boy.

John Mueller was an example.

Action eliminated problems.

It was time for action again.

L UCAS STEPPED QUIETLY INTO the house, pulled off his boots, and stopped to listen. The furnace had apparently just come on: the heating ducts were clicking and snapping as they filled with hot air and expanded. Weather had left a small light on over the sink. He tiptoed through the kitchen and living room, down the hall to the guest room, and turned on the light.

The room felt unused, lonely. The bureau had been dusted, but there was nothing on top of it and the drawers were empty. A lamp and a small travel alarm sat on a bedstand, with a paper pad and a pen; the pad appeared to be untouched. The room was ready for guests, Lucas thought, but no guests ever came.

He peeled off his parka, shirt, pants, and thermal underwear and tossed them on the bureau. He'd stopped at the motel and picked up his shaving kit and fresh underwear. He put them on the bedstand with his watch, took his .45 from its holster, jacked a shell into the chamber, and laid it next to the clock. After listening for another moment at the open bedroom door, he turned off the light and crawled into bed. The bed was too solid, too springy, as though it had never been slept in. The pillow pushed his head up. He'd never get to sleep.

THE BED SAGGED.

Somebody there. Disoriented for a moment, he turned his head, opened his eyes. Saw a light in the hallway, remembered the weight. He half-sat, supporting himself with his elbows, and found Weather sitting on the end of the bed. She was dressed for work, carrying a cup of coffee, sipping from it.

"Jesus, what time is it?"

"A little after six. I'm outa here," she said. She was stone-cold awake. "Thanks for coming over."

"Let me get up."

"No, no. Shelly's sending a deputy over. I feel silly."

"Don't. There's nothing silly about it," he said sharply. "And you should go somewhere else at night. Pick someplace at random. A motel in Park Falls. Tell us you're leaving, and we'll have somebody run interference for you out the highway to make sure you're not followed."

"I'll think about it," she said. She patted his foot. "You look like a bear in the morning," she said. "And your long underwear is cute. I like the color."

Lucas looked down at the long underwear; it was vaguely pink. "Washed it with a red shirt," he mumbled. "And this is not the goddamn morning. Morning starts when the mailman arrives."

"He doesn't get here until one o'clock," Weather said.

"Then morning starts at one o'clock," he said. He dropped back on the pillow. "John Mueller?"

"They never found him," she said. "When the deputy called, I asked."

"Ah, God."

"I'm afraid he's gone," she said. She glanced at her watch. "And I've got to go. Make sure all the doors are locked, and go out through the garage when you leave. The garage door locks automatically."

"Sure. Would you . . ."

"What?"

"Have dinner with me tonight? Again?"

"God, you're rushing me," she said. "I like that in a man. Sure. But why don't we have it here? I'll cook."

"Terrific."

"Six o'clock," she said. She nodded at the bedstand as she went out the door. "That's a big gun."

He heard the door to the garage open and close, and after that the house was silent. Lucas drifted back to sleep, now comfortable in the strange bedroom. When he woke again, it was eight o'clock. He sat on the edge of the bed for a moment, then staggered down the hall to the bathroom, shaved, half-fell into the shower, got a dose of icy water for his trouble, huddled outside the plastic curtain until the water turned hot, then stood under it, letting the stinging jets of water beat on his neck.

Harper. They had to put the screws on Harper. So far, he was the only person who might know something. He stepped out of the shower, looked in the medicine cabinet for shampoo. There wasn't any, but there were two packs of birth control pills. He picked them up, turned them over, looked at the prescription label. More than two years old. Huh. He'd hoped he'd find that they'd been taken out the day before. Vanity. He dropped them back where he'd found them. Of course, if she hadn't been on the pill for two years, she probably didn't have much going.

He looked under the sink, found a bottle of Pert, got back in the shower and washed his hair.

Harper wasn't the only problem. There was still the time discrepancy. Something happened there. Something was going on with the priest. He didn't seem to fit with the child-sex angle. There'd been a notorious string of cases in Minnesota of priests abusing parish children, but in those cases, the men had invariably acted alone. The standing of a priest in a small community would almost seem automatically to preclude any kind of ring.

"Aw, no," Lucas sputtered.

He should have seen it. He stepped out of the shower, mopped his face and walked down the hall to the kitchen, found the telephone. He got Carr at his office.

"You get any sleep?" he asked.

"Couple hours on the office couch," Carr said. "We got a search warrant for Judy Schoenecker's place. You can take it out there."

"I'd like to take Gene along. He was pretty good with Harper."

"I understand Russ might have a sore nose this morning," Carr said.

"It's the cold weather," Lucas said. "Listen, how many people live down Storm Lake Road, beyond the LaCourts' house? How many other residences?"

"Hmp. Twenty or thirty, maybe. Plus a couple resorts, but those are closed, of course. Nobody there but the owners."

"Could you get a list for me?"

"Sure. The assessor'll know. We can get his plat books. What're you looking for?"

"I'll know it when I see it. I'll be there in twenty minutes," Lucas said.

When he hung up, he realized he was freezing, hustled back to the bathroom, and jumped into the shower. After two more minutes of hot water, he toweled off, dressed, and let himself out of the house.

CARR WAS MUNCHING on a powdered doughnut hole when Lucas got in. He pointed at a white paper bag and said, "Have one. Why do you want those names down the road?"

"Just to see what's down there," Lucas said, fishing a sweet roll out of the bag. "Did you get them?"

"I told George—he's the assessor—I told him we needed them ASAP, so they should be ready," Carr said. "I'll take you down."

George was tall and dark, balding, with fingers pointed like crow-quill pens. He pulled out a plat map of the lake area and used a sharp-nailed index finger to trace the road and tick off the inhabitants, right down to the infants. Three of the houses were lived in by single men.

"Do you know these guys?" Lucas asked Carr, touching the houses of the three single men.

"Yup," Carr said. "But the only one I know well is Donny Riley, he's in the Ojibway Rod and Gun Club. Pretty good guy. He's a retired mail carrier. The other two, Bob Dell works up in a sawmill and Darrell Anderson runs the Stone Hawk Resort."

"Are they married? Divorced, widowed? What?"

"Riley was married for years. His wife died. Darrell's gone off-and-on with one of the gals from the hospital, but I don't know much about him. Bob is pretty much a bachelor-farmer type."

"Any of them Catholics?" Lucas asked.

"Well . . ." Carr looked at the assessor, and then they both looked at Lucas. "I believe Bob goes to Sunday Mass."

"Does he come from here?"

"No, no, he comes from Milwaukee," Carr said. "What're we pushing toward here?"

"Nothing special," Lucas said. "Let's go back upstairs." And to the assessor he said, "Thanks."

Lacey was sitting in Carr's office, his feet on the corner of the sheriff's desk. When they came in, he quickly pulled his feet off, then crossed his legs.

"You're gonna ruin my desk and I'll take it out of your paycheck," Carr grumbled.

"Sorry," Lacey said.

"Now what the heck was all that about? Down there with George?" Carr asked Lucas as he settled into his swivel chair.

"There's a rumor around—just a rumor—that Phil Bergen's gay. That why I asked him last night if he'd ever had any homosexual contacts."

"That's the worst kind of bull," Carr blurted. "Where'd you hear that gay stuff?"

"Look: I keep trying to figure why he says he was at the LaCourts' when the LaCourts were dead," Lucas said. "Why he won't back off of it. And I got to thinking, what if he was somewhere else down the road, but can't say so?"

"Dammit," Carr said. He spun and looked out his window through the half-open venetian blinds. "You got a dirty mind, Davenport."

"Are you thinking about anybody in particular?" Lacey asked. Lucas repeated the three names. Lacey stared at him for a moment, then cleared his throat, edged forward in his chair, and looked at the sheriff. "Um, Shelly, listen. My wife knows Bob Dell. I once said something about he's a good-looking guy, just kidding her, and she said, 'Bob's not the sort that goes for women, I kinda think.' That's what she said."

"She was saying he's gay?" Carr asked, turning, pulling his head back, staring owlishly at his deputy.

"Well, not exactly," Lacey said. "Just that he wasn't the type who was interested in women."

"This is awful," Carr said, looking back to Lucas.

"It would explain a hell of a lot," Lucas said. "If people down there know that this Bob Dell is gay . . . maybe Bergen was down there, got caught in a lie, and then couldn't back off of it. Look at his drinking. If he's innocent, where's all the pressure coming from?"

"From this office for one thing," Carr said. He climbed out of his chair, took a meandering walk around the office, a knuckle pressed to his teeth. "We've got to check on Dell," he said finally.

"See if you can get his birthdate. Query the NCIC and Milwaukee, if that's where he's from," Lucas said. "And think about it: if this is Bergen's problem, then he's in the clear on the murder."

"Yeah." Carr spun and stared through his window, which looked out at a snowpile, a drifted-in fence and the backs of several houses on the next street. "But he wouldn't be clear on the gay thing. And that'd kill him."

They all thought about it for a minute, then Carr said, "Gene Climpt will meet you out at the Mill restaurant at noon." He passed Lucas a warrant.

Lucas glanced at it and stuck it in his coat pocket. "Nothing at all on John Mueller?"

Carr shook his head: "Nothing. We're looking for a body now."

LUCAS SPENT THE MORNING at the LaCourts'. An electric heater tried to keep the garage warm, but without insulation, and with the coming and going of the lab crew, couldn't keep up. Everybody inside wore their parkas, open, or sweaters; it was barely warm enough to dispense with gloves. A long makeshift table had been built out of two-by-fours and particle board, and was stacked with paper, electronic equipment, and a computer with a printer.

The crew had found a badly deformed slug in the kitchen wall. Judging from the base and the weight, allowing for some loss of jacketing material, the techs thought it was probably a .44 Magnum. Definitely not a .357. The gun Lucas found the night of the killings had not been fired.

"The girl was alive when her ear was cut off, and also some other parts of her face apparently were cut away while she was alive," a tech said, reading from a fax. "The autopsy's done, but there are a lot of tests still outstanding."

The tech began droning through a list of other findings. Lucas listened, but every few seconds his mind would drift from the job to Weather. He'd always been attracted to smart women, but few of his affairs had gone anywhere. He had a daughter with a woman he'd never loved, though he'd liked her a lot. She was a reporter, and they'd been held together by a common addiction to pressure and movement. He'd loved another woman, or might have, who was consumed by her career as a cop. Weather fit the mold of the cop. She was serious, and tough, but seemed to have an intact sense of humor.

Can't fuck this up with Weather, he thought, and again, *Can't fuck this thing up.*

Crane came in, blowing steam, stamping his feet, walked behind Lucas to a coffee urn. "He used the water heater to start the fire," he said to the back of Lucas' head.

"What?"

Lucas turned in his chair. Crane, still wrapped in his parka, was pouring himself a cup of coffee. "The hot water faucet was turned on over the laundry tub, and a lot of premix was splashed around the water heater. The heater's a mess, of course, but it looks like there might be traces of charred cotton coming out of the pilot port."

"Say it in English," Lucas suggested.

Crane grinned. "He splashed his premix around the house, soaked a rag in it and laid it across the burner in the water heater. He had to be careful to keep it away from the pilot light. Then he turned on the hot water faucet, let the water dribble out. Not too fast. Then he left. In a few minutes, the water level drops in the tank, cold water refills it . . ."

"And the burner lights up."

"Boom," said Crane.

"Why would he do that?"

"Probably to make sure he could get out. We figure there were fifteen gallons of premix spread around the place. He might've been afraid to toss a match into it. But it does mean he must've thought about burning the place. That's not something that would occur to you while you were standing there . . . if it happened at all."

"If it did happen, that means there'd be a delay between the time he left and the time the fire started, right?"

"Right."

"How much?"

"Don't know," Crane said. "We don't know the condition of the water tank before he turned the water on—how hot the water already was. He didn't turn the faucet on very far, just a steady dribble. Could have been anything from four or five minutes to twenty minutes."

More delay, Lucas thought. More time between the killings and the moment the Jeep passed the fire station. There was no hope for a minor error anymore, a time mixup. The priest *could not have been* at the LaCourts'.

"... through the surviving files ..." Crane was talking about the search for the missing photograph.

"It wouldn't be in a file," Lucas said abruptly. "They would have stuffed it someplace where they could get at it—someplace both casual and safe. Where if somebody needed to see it, they could just pick it up and say, 'Here it is.'"

"Okay. But where?" Crane asked.

"Cookie jar—like that."

"We've looked through most of the stuff in the kitchen and their bedroom, the stuff that survived. We haven't found anything like it."

"Okay."

"We'll take it apart inch-by-inch," Crane said. "But it's gonna take time."

LUCAS MADE TWO phone calls and took one. The first call went to a nun in the Twin Cities, an old friend, a college psychology professor. Elle Kruger: Sister Mary Joseph.

"Elle, this is Lucas. How're things?"

"Fine," she said promptly. "I got Winston's preproduction beta-copy of the new *Grove of Trees*. I ran it with Sister Louisa over the weekend, and we froze it up right away, some kind of stack-overflow error."

"Dammit, they said they fixed that." *Grove of Trees* was an intricate simulation of the battle of Gettysburg that he'd been working on for years. Elle Kruger was a games freak.

"Well, we were on Sister Louisa's Radio Shack compatible," she said. "There's something goofy about that machine, because I ran the same disk on my Compaq and it worked fine."

"All right, I'll talk to them. We ought to be compatible with everything, though," Lucas said. "Listen, I've got another problem and it involves the Church. I don't know if you can help me, but there are people being killed."

"There always are, aren't there?" she said. "Where are you? And how does it involve the Church?"

He sketched the problem out quickly: the priest, the missing time, the question about the man at the end of the road.

"Lucas, you should go through the archdiocese of Milwaukee," Elle said.

"Elle, I don't have time to fool around with Church bureaucracy, and you know what they're like when there's a possible scandal involved. It's like trying to get information out of a Swiss bank. This guy—priest—Bergen is about our age, and I bet you know people who know him. All I'm asking is that you make a couple of calls, see if you can find some friends of his. I understand he went to Marquette. Get a reading. Nothing formal, no big deal."

"Lucas, this could hurt me. With the Church. I have relationships."

"Elle ..." Lucas pressed.

"Let me pray over it."

"Do that. Try to get back to me tonight. Elle, there are people being killed, including at least one junior high boy and maybe two. Children abused. There are homosexual photos published in underground magazines."

"I get it," she snapped. "Leave me to pray. Just leave me."

A deputy came in as Lucas hung up. "Shelly was on the radio. He's on the way out, and he wants you to wait."

"Okay."

The second call went to the Minneapolis police department, to a burglary specialist named Carl Snyder.

"IF YOU WERE A woman casually hiding something in your house for a couple of days, a dirty picture, where drop-in neighbors wouldn't see it, but where you could get at it quickly, where'd you put it?"

"Mmm . . . got a pencil?" Snyder asked. Snyder knew so much about burglary that Lucas suspected that he might have done some field research. There had been a series of extremely elegant coin and jewel thefts in the Cities, stretching back twelve years. Nothing had ever been recovered.

"Don't talk to me," Lucas said. "There's a guy named Crane here, from the Wisconsin state crime labs. I'll put him on."

Crane talked to Snyder, saying *Yeah* a lot, his head nodding, and after hanging up, pulled on his parka and said, "Wanna come?"

"Might as well. Where're we going to look?" Lucas asked.

"Around the refrigerator. Then under boxes in the cupboard. Of course, there's not much left there."

The yard outside the house had been flattened by ice and the army of people working around it. They tramped across the frozen ground, pushed past a heavy canvas sheet, and went inside. Banks of tripod-mounted lights lit most of the interior; two refrigerator-sized electric heaters kept it vaguely warm. Most of the loose wreckage had been cleared away from the floors. Through the open door to the mudroom, Lucas could see a white chalk circle around the hole where they'd found the .44 slug.

"All right: around the refrigerator, on the kitchen counter," Crane muttered.

Wearing plastic gloves, he began sifting carefully through the wreckage on the kitchen counter top. The counter top had been yellowed by heat except where it had been covered. A bowl, a peanut butter jar, salt and pepper shakers left their bottom-shapes stenciled in white.

"No paper . . . how about the refrigerator?"

Crane found the remains of the photograph behind the magnetic message slate on the door of the refrigerator. He pried the message slate away from the door, was about to put it back and then said, "Whoa . . ."

"What is it?" Lucas felt a thump in his stomach.

Crane carried it to the window, held it to the light. A square of folded newsprint was stuck to the back of the slate, half of it charred black and imbedded in melted plastic. The other half was brown.

"I don't know; maybe we ought to send it down to Madison, have them separate it," Crane said. But as he said it, he slipped a finger under one edge of the newsprint and lifted. It broke at the burn line, and the browned part came free. Crane turned it over in his hand.

"It's kind of fucked up," he said. He looked at the paper melted into the plastic. "We might be able to recover part of that."

The browned portion of the paper was the left side of a photo, showing the back and buttocks of a nude man. The remaining caption under the photo said: LOOK AT THIS BIG BOY. DINNER.

Beneath the photo and caption was a series of jokes:

Guy walks into a bar, he's got a head the size of a baseball, says, "Gimme a beer." The bartender shoves a glass of Bud across the bar and says, "Listen, pal, it's none of my business, but a big guy like you—how'd you get a little teeny head like that?" The guy says, "Well, I was down in Jamaica, walking on the beach, when I see this bottle. I pull the top off, and holy shit, a genie pops out. I mean, she was gorgeous. She had a body that wouldn't quit, great ass, tits the size of watermelons. And she says I can have a wish. So I said, "Well look, you know, what I'd wish for, is to make love to you." And the genie says, "Sorry, that's one thing I'm not allowed to do." So then I say, "Okay, how about a little head?"

"Who does this kind of shit?" Lucas asked. He held the paper on the flat of his open hands, peering at the type. There was no indication of where it might have come from.

"Anybody and everybody who can afford a Macintosh computer, a laser printer, and a halftone scanner. You could set up a whole magazine with a few thousand bucks' worth of equipment. Not the printing, just the type."

"Is there any way to run it down?"

Crane shrugged. "We can try. Do the best possible copies, circulate it, see what happens."

"Do that," Lucas said. "We need to see the picture."

CRANE PUT THE PHOTO into an envelope and they carried it back to the garage. Carr was walking up from the car park, and they waited for him at the garage door. Inside, Crane showed him the remnants of the photo.

"Damn," Carr said. "That could have made us, if we'd got all of it."

"We'll try to trace it, but I can't promise anything," Crane said.

Carr looked at Lucas and said, "Come on outside a minute."

Lucas pulled his parka back on, zipped it, followed Carr through the door.

"We got Bob Dell's birthdate off his DMV records and ran those through the NCIC," Carr said. "He was arrested a few times in Madison, apparently when he was going to school there. Disturbing the peace and once for assault. The disturbing the peace things were for demonstrations, the assault was for a bar fight. The charge was dropped before it got to court and apparently didn't amount to much. I called Madison, and it was just an ordinary bar, not a gay bar or anything. The demonstrations involved some kind of political thing, but it wasn't gay rights, whatever it was."

"Nothing there," Lucas said.

"Well, you remember what Lacey's wife said about Dell not liking women? I called her up, and asked her what she meant, and she hemmed and hawed and finally said yeah, there were rumors among the eligible women in town that you'd be wasting your time chasing Dell."

"How solid were the rumors? Anything explicit?" Lucas asked.

"Nothing she knew about."

"Where's this place he works?"

"Sawmill, about ten minutes from here," Carr said.

"Let's go."

Carr led the way down to the sawmill, a yellow-steel pole barn on a concrete slab. A thirty-foot-high stack of oak logs was racked above a concrete ramp that led into the mill.

Inside the mill, the temperature hovered just above freezing. A half-dozen men worked around the saws. Lucas waited in the work bay while Carr poked his head into the office to talk to the owner. Lucas heard him say, "No, no, no, there's no problem, honest to God, we're just trying to run down every last . . ." And then a cut started, and he watched the saws until Carr came back out.

"That's Bob in the vest," Carr said. "I'll get him when they finish the cut."

Dell was a tall man, wearing jeans and a sleeveless down vest with heavy leather gloves and a yellow hard hat. He worked with the logs, jockeying them for the cut. When the cut was done, they took him outside, away from the noise of the mill. The tall man lit a cigarette and said, "What can I do for you, Sheriff?"

Lucas said, "Did you have any visitors, or see anybody out around your place the night the LaCourts were killed?"

Dell shook his head. "Nope. Didn't see anybody. I came home, watched TV, ate dinner, and then my beeper went off and I hauled my butt up there."

Carr snapped his fingers. "That's right: you're with the fire department."

Dell nodded. "Yeah. I figured you'd be around sooner or later, if you didn't catch somebody. I mean, me being a single guy and all, and just down that road."

"We don't want to cause you any trouble," Carr said.

"You already have," Dell said, looking back at the mill.

"So you saw nobody that night. From the time you left work until the time you went to the fire, you saw nobody," Lucas said.

"Nobody."

"Didn't Father Bergen stop by?" Lucas asked.

"No, no." Dell looked mystified. "Why would he?"

"Aren't you one of his parishioners?"

"Off and on, I guess," Dell said, "But he doesn't come around."

"So you're not close to him?"

"What's this about, Sheriff?" Dell asked, looking at Carr.

"I gotta ask you something here, Bob, and I swear it'll go no further than the three of us," Carr said. "I mean, I hate to ask . . ."

"Ask it," Dell said. He'd stiffened up; he knew what was coming.

"We've heard some rumors in town that you might be gay, is what I guess it is."

Dell turned away from them, looked up into the forest. "That's what it is, huh?" And after a minute, "What would that have to do with anything?"

The sheriff stared at him for a minute, then looked at Lucas and said, "Sonofabitch."

"I never saw Father Phil," Dell said. "Think whatever you want, I never saw him. I haven't laid eyes on him for three weeks, and that sure doesn't have anything to do with . . . my sex choices."

The sheriff wouldn't look at him. Instead, he looked at Lucas, but said to Dell, "If you're lying, you'll go to jail. This is critical information."

"I'm not lying. I'd swear in court," Dell said. "I'd swear in church, for that matter."

Now Carr looked at him, a level stare, and finally he said, "All right. Lucas, have you got anything more?"

"Not right now."

"Thanks, Bob."

"This is gonna ruin me here," Dell said quietly. "I'll have to leave."

"Bob, you don't . . ."

"Yeah, I will," Dell said. "But I hate to, because I liked it. A lot. Had friends, not gays, just friends. That's gone." He turned and walked away, down to the sawmill.

"WHAT DO YOU THINK?" Carr asked as he watched him go.

"It sounded like the truth," Lucas said. "But I've been lied to before and believed it."

"Want to go back to Phil?"

Lucas shook his head. "Not quite yet. We've got both of them denying it and nothing to show otherwise. Let's see what my Church friend has to say. I should hear from her tonight or tomorrow."

"We don't have time . . ." Carr started.

"If this is the answer to the time conflict, then it's not critical to the case," Lucas said. "Bergen would be out of it."

"It's a sad day," Carr said. He looked back at the mill as Dell disappeared inside. "Bob wasn't a bad guy."

"Well, he could hang on if he's got real friends."

"Naw, he's right," Carr said. "With his job and all, he's gonna have to leave, sooner or later."

LUCAS MET CLIMPT at the Mill, a restaurant-motel built on the banks of a frozen creek. The old mill pond, below the restaurant windows, had been finished with a Zamboni to make a skating rink. A dozen men sat on stools at a dining counter, and another dozen people were scattered in twos and threes at tables around the dining room. Climpt was standing by the windows with a mug of chicken broth, looking down at the mill pond, where a solitary old man in a Russian greatcoat turned circles on the ice.

"Been out there since I got here," Climpt said when Lucas stepped up beside him. "He's eighty-five this year."

"Every day now, for an hour, don't matter how cold it is," a waitress said, coming up to Lucas' elbow. The old man was turning eights, building off the circles, his hands clenched behind his back, his face turned up to the sky. He was smiling, not fiercely, or as a matter of focus, but with simple distracted pleasure, moving with a rhythm, a beat, that came from the past. The waitress watched with them for a moment, then said, "Are you going to eat, or . . ."

"I could take a cup of soup," Lucas said.

The waitress, still looking down at the old man on the rink, said, "He's trying to remember what it was like when he was a kid; that's what he says, anyway. I think he's getting ready to die."

She went away, and Climpt, voice pitched low, asked, "You got the warrant?"

"Yeah."

"I brought a crowbar and a short sledge in case we have trouble getting in."

"Good enough," Lucas said. The waitress came back with a mug of the chicken broth, and asked, "You're that detective Shelly brought in, aren't you?"

"Yes," Lucas said.

"We're praying for you," she said.

"That's right," said a man at the counter. He was heavyset, and a roll of fat on the back of his neck folded over the collar of his flannel shirt. Everybody in the place was looking at them. "You just find the sons of bitches," he said. "After that, you can leave them to us."

LUCAS AND CLIMPT rode to the Schoeneckers' house in Lucas' truck, hoping that it'd be less noticeable than a sheriff's van. "So what do you know about these people?" Lucas asked on the way over.

"They're private and quiet," Climpt said. "Andy's a bookkeeper, handles businesses in town. Judy stays home. They been here for twenty years, must be—come from over in Vilas County, I guess. You just never see them unless you see Andy going in or out of his office. They don't socialize that I know of. I don't know if they're church people, but I don't think so. Here, that's their driveway."

"Private house, too," Lucas said.

The Schoeneckers lived on an acreage at the north end of town, in a neat yellow rambler with blue trim. The lawn was heavily landscaped, dotted with clusters of blue spruce that effectively sheltered the house from both wind and eyesight. Lucas drove up to the garage and parked.

An inch of unbroken snow lay in the driveway.

"I got a bad feeling about this," Climpt said. "Nobody going in or out."

Lucas scuffed the snow with his boot. "They cleared it off after the last storm. This is all blown in."

"Yeah. Where are they?"

They went to the front door and Lucas rang the bell. He rang it twice more, but the house felt empty. "Got good locks," Climpt said, looking at the inner door through the glass of the storm door.

"Let's try the back, see if there's a door on the garage," Lucas suggested. "They're usually easier."

They followed a snow-blown sidewalk around to the back. The locks on the back door were the same as on the front. Climpt tried the knob, rattled it, put his weight against the door. It didn't budge. "Gonna have to break it," he said. "Let me get the bar."

"Hang on a second," Lucas said. A power outlet with a steel cover was set into the garage wall, just at light-switch height. Lucas lifted the cover, looked inside. Nothing. A post lantern with a yellow bug light sat at the corner of a back deck. He waded through thigh-deep snow to get to it, looked into the four-sided lantern, then lifted one of the glass elements, fished around, and came up with a key.

"Fuckin' rural-ass hayshakers," he said, grinning at Climpt.

The key worked on the door into the garage. The door between the garage and the house was unlocked. Lucas led the way in, found the inside of the Schoeneckers' house almost as cold as the outside. They walked through quickly, checking each room.

"Gone," Lucas said from the master bedroom. The closets and dressers were half-empty. A stack of wire hangers lay on the king-sized bed in the master bedroom. "Packed up."

"And not coming back in a hurry, either," Climpt said from down the hall. "Look at this."

Climpt was in the bathroom, staring into the toilet. Lucas looked. The bowl was empty, but stained purple with antifreeze. "They winterized."

"Yup. They'll be gone a while."

"So let's go through it," Lucas said.

They began with the parents' bedroom and found nothing at all. The second bedroom was shared by the Schoeneckers' daughters. Again, they came up empty. They worked through the bathroom, the living room, the dining room, took apart the kitchen, spent half an hour in the basement.

"Not a goddamned thing," Climpt growled, scratching his head. They were back in the living room. "I never seen a house so empty of anything."

"Not a single videotape," Lucas said. He walked back down the hall to the master bedroom, checked the television there. A tape player was built into the base. In the living room, a bigger television was hooked into a separate tape player. "They've got two videotape players and no tapes."

"Could rent 'em," Climpt said.

"Even then . . ."

"Did those boxes in the basement . . . just a minute," Climpt said suddenly, and disappeared down the basement steps.

Lucas wandered through the still, cold house, then went to the garage, opened the door, and looked in. Climpt came back up the stairs, carrying two boxes, and Lucas said, "They've got two cars. The garage is tracked on both sides."

"Yeah, I believe they do."

"How often do families go on vacations and take two cars when there are only four of them?" Lucas asked.

"Look at this," Climpt said. He held the boxes out to Lucas. One was the carton for a video camera. The other was a carton for a Polaroid Spectra camera. "A video camera and no videotapes. And last night Henry Lacey said that Polaroid was taken with a Spectra camera."

"Jesus." Lucas ran his hand through his hair. "Okay. Tell you what. You go through that file cabinet with the bills, get all the credit card numbers you can find. Especially gas card numbers, but get all of them. I'm going back to the girls' room. I can't believe teenagers wouldn't leave *something*."

He began going through the room inch by inch, pulling the drawers from all the dressers, looking under them, checking bottles and boxes, paging through piles of homework papers dating back to elementary school. He felt inside shoes, lifted the mattress.

Climpt came in and said, "I got all the numbers they had, I think. They had Sunoco and Amoco gas cards. They also bought quite a bit of gas from Russ Harper, which is pretty strange when you consider his station is fifteen miles from here."

"Keep those slips," Lucas said as he dropped the mattress back in place. "And check and see if there's any garbage outside."

"All right."

A half-dozen books sat upright on top of the bureau, pressed together by malachite bookends shaped like chess knights. Lucas looked at the books, turned them, held them page-down and flipped through them. An aluminum-foil gum wrapper fell from the Holy Bible. Lucas picked it up, unfolded it, found a phone number and the name *Betty* written in orange ink.

He put the book back, walked into the living room as Climpt came in from outside. "No garbage. They cleaned the place out, is what they did."

"Okay." Lucas picked up the phone, dialed the number on the gum wrapper.

The call was answered on the first ring. "This is the Ojibway Action Line. Can I help you?" The voice was female and professionally cheerful.

"What's the Ojibway Action Line?" Lucas asked.

"Who is this?" The voice lost a touch of its good cheer.

"A county sheriff's deputy," Lucas said.

"You're a deputy and don't know what the Ojibway Action Line is?"

"I'm new."

"What's your name?"

"Lucas Davenport. Gene Climpt is here if you want to talk to him."

"Oh, no, that's okay, I heard about you. Besides, it's not a secret—we're the crisis line for county human services. We're right in the front of the phone book."

"All right. Can I speak to Betty?"

There was a moment of silence, then the woman said, "There's not really a Betty here, Mr. Davenport. That's a code name for our sexual abuse counselor."

L UCAS PARKED IN Weather's driveway, climbed out of the truck, and trudged to the porch, carrying a bottle of wine. He was reaching for the bell when Weather pulled the door open.

"Fuck dinner," Lucas said, stepping inside. "Let's catch a plane to Australia. Lay on the beach for a couple of weeks."

"I'd be embarrassed. I'm so winter-white I'm transparent," Weather said. She took the bottle. "Come in."

She'd taken some trouble, he thought. A handmade rag rug stretched across the entry; that hadn't been there the night before. A fire crackled in the Volkswagen-sized fireplace. And there was a hint of Chanel in the air. "Pretty impressive, huh? With the fire and everything?"

"I like it," he said simply. He didn't smile. He'd been told that his smile sometimes frightened people.

She seemed both embarrassed and pleased. "Leave your coat in the closet and your boots by the door. I just started cooking. Steak and shrimp. We'll both need heart bypasses if we eat it all."

Lucas kicked off his boots and wandered through the living room in his stocking feet. He hadn't seen it in the dark, the night before, and in the morning he'd rushed out, thinking about Bergen. . . .

"How'd the operation go?" he called to her in the kitchen.

"Fine. I had to pin some leg bones back together. Nasty, but not too complicated. This woman went up on her roof to push the snow off, and *she* fell off instead. Right onto the driveway. She hobbled around for almost four days before she came in, the damn fool. She wouldn't believe the bone was broken until we showed her the X rays."

"Huh." Silver picture frames stood on a couch table, with hand-colored photos of a man and woman, still young. Sailboats figured in half the photographs. Her parents. A small ebony grand piano sat in an alcove, top propped up, sheet music for Erroll Garner's "Dreamy" on the music stand.

He went back into the kitchen. Weather was wearing a dress, the first he'd seen her in, simple, soft-shouldered; she had a long, slender neck with a scattering of freckles along her spine. She said, smiling, "I'm going to make stuff so good it'll hurt your mouth."

"Let me help," he said.

SHE HAD HIM HAUL a grill from the basement to the back deck, which she'd partially shoveled off. He stacked it with charcoal and started it. At the same time she put a pot of water on the stove. A bag of oversized, already-shelled shrimp went into a colander, which she set aside. Herbs and a carton of buttermilk became salad dressing; a lump of cheese joined a pile of mushrooms, celery, walnuts, watercress, and apples on the cutting board. She began slicing.

"I won't ask if you like mushrooms; you've got no choice," she said. "Oh— get the wine going. It's supposed to breathe for a while."

The outside temperature had been rising through the afternoon, and was now approaching zero. A breeze had sprung up and felt almost damp compared to the astringent dryness of the air at twenty below. Lucas put his boots back on and tended the charcoal; the cold felt good on his skin, taken only a few seconds at a time.

THE SALAD WAS TART and just right. The shrimp were killers. He ate a dozen of them, finally tearing himself away from the table long enough to put the steaks on.

"I haven't eaten like this since . . . I don't know when. You must like cooking," Lucas said as he stood inside the glass doors, looking out at the grill.

"I don't, really. I took a class at the high school called Five Good Things," she confessed. "That's what they taught me. How to make five good things. This is one of them."

"That's a class I need," Lucas said, slipping back outside with a plate. The steaks were perfect, she said. Red inside, a little char on the outside.

"No Mueller kid?" she asked.

He shook his head, and the feel of the evening suddenly warped. "I can't think about it right now," he said.

"Fine," she said hastily, picking up his mood. "It's a terrible business anyway."

"Let me tell you a couple of things," he said. "But it can't go any further."

"It won't."

He outlined what had happened. The priest and the time problem, the homosexual question and Harper, the Schoeneckers' search.

She listened solemnly and finally said, "I don't know Phil Bergen very well, but he never struck me as gay. The few times I've talked to him, he seemed almost shy. He was reacting to me."

"Well, we don't know for sure," Lucas said. "But it would explain a lot."

"So what's happening with the Schoeneckers?"

"Carr's meeting with the sexual therapist right now to see if they can match any calls with Schoeneckers' kids—the kids never actually came in, but they get a lot of anonymous calls that never develop into anything. The calls are taped, so there might be something. And we're checking credit cards, trying to find out where they are. They just took off, supposedly to Florida."

"If all this is true, the town'll be a mess," Weather said.

"The town'll handle it. I've seen this kind of thing happen before," Lucas said. "The big question is, how out-of-control is the killer? What is he doing?"

"Hey, you'll give me nightmares," she said. "Eat, eat."

Lucas gave up halfway through his steak and staggered off to an overstuffed couch in front of the fireplace. Weather put an ounce of cognac in each of two glasses, pulled open the drapes that covered the sliding glass doors to the deck, and dropped into an E-Z Boy that sat at right angles to the couch. They both put their feet on the scarred coffee table that ran the length of the couch.

"Blimp," Lucas said.

"Moi?" she said, raising an eyebrow.

"No, me. Christ, if somebody dropped a dictionary on my gut, I'd blow up. Look at that." Lucas pointed out the doors, where a crescent moon was just edging up over the trees across the lake.

"I feel like . . ." she started, looking out at the moon.

"Like what?"

"Like I'm starting out on an adventure."

"I wish I was," Lucas said. "All I do is lay around."

"Well, writing games . . . You said the money was pretty good."

"Yeah, like *you* came up here to make a lot of money."

"Not quite the same thing," she said.

"Maybe not," Lucas said. "But I'd like to do something useful. That's what I'm finding out. When I was a cop, I was doing something. Now I'm just making money."

"For now you're a cop again," she said.

"For a couple of weeks."

"How about going back to Minneapolis?"

"I've been thinking about it," Lucas said. He swirled his cognac in the glass, finished it. "I had a case last summer, in New York. Now this. I sometimes think I could make something out of it, just picking up work. But when I get real, I know it'll never happen. There's just not *enough* to do."

"Ah, well . . . nobody said life'd get easier."

"Yeah, but you always think it will," Lucas said. "The next thing you know, you're sixty-five and living in a rundown condo on Miami Beach, wondering how you're going to pay for your next set of false teeth."

Weather burst out laughing and Lucas grinned in the dark, listening to her, delighted that he'd made her laugh. "The man is an incorrigible optimist," she said.

THEY TALKED ABOUT PEOPLE they knew in common, both in Grant and in the Cities.

"Gene Climpt doesn't look like a tragedy, but he is," she told him. "He married his high school sweetheart right after he got in the Highway Patrol—he was in the patrol before Shelly, way back, this was when I was in junior high school. Anyway, they had a baby girl, a toddler. One day Gene's wife was running a bath for the baby, running just hot water and planning to cool it later, when the phone rang. She went to answer it, and the kid climbed on the toilet and leaned over the tub and fell in."

"My God."

"Yeah. She died from the scalding. Then, when Gene was at the funeral home, his wife shot herself. Killed herself. She couldn't stand the baby dying. They buried them both together."

"Jesus. He never remarried?"

She shook her head. "Nope. He's fooled around with a few women over the years, but nobody's ever got him. Quite a few tried."

Weather had worked nights at St. Paul-Ramsey General for seven years while she was doing her surgical residency at the University of Minnesota, and knew eight or ten St. Paul cops. Did she like them? "Cops are like everybody else, some of them are nice and some of them are assholes. They do have a tendency to hustle you," she said.

"A hospital's a good place to hang around if you're on patrol, and if the person you've brought in isn't a kid or your partner," Lucas said. "It's warm, you're safe, you can get free coffee. There are pretty women around. Most of the women you see, when you're working, are either victims or perpetrators. Nothing like having a good-looking woman tell you to stick your speeding ticket in your ass to chill off your day."

"They're right, cops should stick the tickets," Weather declared.

"Yeah?" He raised an eyebrow.

"Yes. It always used to amaze me, seeing cops writing tickets. The Cities are coming apart; people are getting killed every night and you can't walk downtown without a panhandler extorting money out of you. And half the time when you see a cop, he's giving a ticket to some poor jerk who was going sixty-five in a fifty-five zone. The whole world is going by at sixty-five even while he's writing the ticket. I don't know why cops do it, it just makes everybody mad at them."

"Sixty-five is breaking the law," Lucas said, tongue in cheek.

"Oh, bullshit."

"All right, it's bullshit."

"Don't they have quotas for tickets?" she asked. "I mean, really?"

"Well, yeah, but they don't call it that. They have *performance standards*. They say an on-the-ball patrolman should write about X number of tickets in a month. So a patrol guy gets to the end of the month and counts his tickets and says, 'Shit, I need ten more tickets.' So he goes out to a speed trap and spends an hour getting his ten tickets."

"That's a quota."

"Shhh. It's a hell of a lot more lucrative for the city than busting some dumb-ass junkie burglar."

". . . WOULDN'T TELL ME what the guy wanted, she was just too shy, and about fifteen minutes out of nursing school. It turned out he wanted his foreskin restored. He'd heard that sex felt better with a foreskin and he figured we could just take a stitch here and put a hem over there."

Weather had a cop's sense of humor, Lucas decided, laughing, probably developed in the emergency room; someplace where the world got bad enough, often enough, that you learned to separate yourself from the bad news.

"There's just a thimbleful of cognac left and I get it," Weather said, bouncing out of the chair.

"You can have it," Lucas said.

When she came back, she sat next to him on the couch, instead of in the chair, and put a hand behind his head, on his opposite shoulder.

"You didn't drink hardly any of the wine. I drank two-thirds of the bottle, and now I'm finishing the cognac."

"Fuck the cognac," Lucas said. "Wanna neck?"

"That's not very romantic," she said severely.

"I know, but I'm nervous."

"I still have a right to some romance," she said. "But yes, necking would be appropriate, I think."

A while later she said, "I'm not going to be coy about this; I go for the aging jock-cop image."

"Aging?"

"You've got more gray than I do—that's aging," she said.

"Mmmm."

"But I'm not going to sleep with you yet," she said. "I'm gonna make you sweat for a while."

"Whatever's right."

After a while she asked, "So how do you feel about kids?"

"We gotta talk," he said.

THE GUEST ROOM WAS COOL because of the northern exposure, and Lucas put on pajamas before he crawled into the bed. He lay awake for a few minutes, wondering if he should try her room, but he sensed that he should not. They'd ended the evening simply talking. When she left for her bedroom, she'd kissed him—he was sitting down—on the lips, and then the forehead, tousled his hair, and disappeared into the back of the house.

"See you in the morning," she'd said.

He was surprised when, almost asleep, he heard her voice beside the bed: "Lucas." Her hand touched his shoulder and she whispered, "There's someone outside."

"What?" He was instantly awake. She'd left a hallway light on in case he had to get up in the night to use the bathroom or get a drink of water, and he could see her squatting beside the bed. She was carrying the .22. He pushed back the blankets and swung his feet to the floor. The .45 was sitting on the nightstand and he picked it up. "How do you know?"

"I couldn't sleep right away."

"Neither could I."

"I've got a bath off my bedroom and I went for a glass of water. I saw a snowmobile headlight angling in toward the house from out on the lake. There's no trail that comes in like that. So I watched and the headlight went out—but I could see him in the moon, still coming. The neighbors have a roll-out dock and it's on their lawn. He stopped behind it, I think. They don't have a snowmobile. There's a windbreak down there, those pines. I didn't see him again."

She was calm, reporting almost matter-of-factly.

"How long ago?"

"Two or three minutes. I kept watching, thinking I was crazy. Then I heard something on the siding, scratching-like."

"Sounds like trouble," Lucas said. He jacked a shell into the .45.

"What'll we do?" Weather asked.

"Call in. Get some guys down here, on the lake and on the road. We don't want to scare him off before we can get things rolling."

"There's a phone in my bedroom—c'mon," she said. She padded down the hall, Lucas following. "What else?"

"He's got to find a place to get in, and that's gotta make *some* noise. I want you down by the kitchen, just listening. Stay behind the counter, on the floor. I'll be in the living room, by the couch. If you hear him, just sneak back and get me. Let's call."

They were at her room and she picked up the phone. "Uh-oh," she said, looking at him. "It's dead. That's never happened . . ."

"He took the wires out. Goddammit, he's here," Lucas said. "Get on the kitchen floor. I . . ."

"What?"

"I've got a handset in the truck." He looked at the garage door; it'd take him ten seconds.

A loud knocking from the front room turned him around.

"What?" whispered Weather. "That's the doors to the deck."

"Stay back." Lucas slipped down the hall, stopped at a corner, peeked around it, saw nothing. They'd left the curtains open so they could see the moon, but there was no visible movement on the deck outside the house, no face pressed against the glass. Nothing but a dark rectangle. The knocking started again, not as though someone were trying to force the door, but as if they were trying to wake up Weather.

"Hey . . ." A man's voice, muffled by the tri-pane glass.

"What?" Weather had stood up, and was walking through from the kitchen toward the living room.

"Get the fuck down," Lucas whispered urgently, waving the pistol at her. "Get down."

She hesitated, still standing, and Lucas scuttled across the room, caught her wrist in his left hand, pulled her down and toward a wall.

"Somebody needs help," she said.

"Bullshit: remember the phone," Lucas said. They both edged forward toward a corner.

Another call, as if from a distance. "Hey in there. Hey, we got a wreck, we got a wreck," and there were three more knocks. Lucas let go of Weather's wrist and did a quick peek around the corner.

"It can't be him—that's somebody looking for me," Weather said. She started past him, her white nightgown ghostly in the dim reflected light from the hall.

"Jesus," said Lucas. He was sitting on the floor at the corner and reached up to catch her arm, but she stepped into the sightline from the deck, eight feet from the glass.

The window exploded, showering the room with glass, and a finger of fire poked through at Weather. Lucas had already pulled her back and she came off her feet, sprawling, okay, and Lucas yelled, "Shotgun, shotgun . . ." and fired three quick shots through the door, pop-pop-pop and pulled back.

The shotgun roared again, sending more glass flying across the room, pellets ripping through the end of the leather couch, burying themselves in the far wall. Lucas did a quick peek, then another, fired a fourth shot.

Weather, on her hands and knees, lunged toward the kitchen, came up with the .22 rifle she'd left there, and started back.

"Fucker!" she screamed.

"Stay down, that's a twelve gauge," Lucas shouted. Another shotgun blast, then another, a long five seconds apart, the muzzle flash from the first lighting up the front of the room. The flash from the second seemed fainter, the pellets ricocheting around the stone fireplace.

Five seconds passed without another shot. "He's running," Lucas said. "I think he's running."

He got to his feet and dashed into Weather's bedroom, looked out on the lawn. He could see the man there, a hundred feet away, twenty feet from the shelter of the treeline, fifteen feet. "Goddammit." He stepped back and fired two quick shots through the window glass, shattering it, then one more at the fleeing figure, a hopeless shot.

The man disappeared into the trees. Lucas fired a final shot at the last spot he'd seen him, and the magazine was empty.

"Get him? Get him?" Weather was there with the rifle. He snatched it from her and ran down the hall to the living room, out through the deck and into the snow. He floundered across the yard, through snow thigh deep, following the tracks, through the treeline . . . and saw the red taillight of a snowmobile scudding across the lake, three or four hundred yards away. The rifle was useless at that range.

He was freezing. The cold caught at him, twisted him. He turned and began to run back toward the house, but the cold battered at him and he slowed, plodding in his bare feet, his pajamas hanging from him.

"Jesus, Lucas, Lucas . . ." Weather caught him under the arms, hauled him into the house. He was shaking uncontrollably.

"Handset in my truck. Get it," he grunted.

"You get in the goddamn shower—just get in it."

She turned and ran toward the garage, flipping on lights as she went. Lucas peeled off his sodden pajama top, so tired he could barely move, staggered back toward the bathroom. The temperature inside the house was plunging as the night air roared through the shattered windows, but the bathroom was still warm.

He got in the shower, turned on the hot water, let it run down his back, plastering his pajama pants to his legs. He was holding on to the shower head when Weather came back with the handset.

"Dispatch."

"This is Davenport down at Weather Karkinnen's place. We were just hit by a guy with a shotgun. Nobody hurt, but the house is a mess. The guy is headed west across Lincoln Lake on a snowmobile. He's about two minutes gone, maybe three."

"WEATHER, THAT'S THE DAMNEDEST stupidest thing . . ." Carr started, but Weather shook her head and looked at the blown-out window. "I won't leave," she said. "Not when it's like this. I'll figure out something."

Lucas was wrapped in a snowmobile suit. Carr shook his head and said, "All right, I'll get somebody from Hardware Hank out here."

The gunman had come in on snowshoes, as the LaCourt killer had. By the time an alert had been issued, he could have been any one of dozens of snowmobilers still out on the trails within two or three miles of Weather's house. The two on-duty deputies were told to stop sleds and take names. Nobody thought much would come of it.

"When I got the call about the shooting, I phoned Phil Bergen," Carr told Lucas.

"Yeah?"

"Nobody home," Carr said.

There was a moment of silence, then Lucas asked, "Does he have a shotgun?"

"I don't know. Anybody can get a gun, though."

"Why don't you have somebody check on the sled, see if it's at his house? See if he's out on it."

"That's being done," Carr said.

The Madison crime scene techs were taking pictures of the snowmobile tread tracks, the snowshoe tracks, and were digging shotgun shells out of the snow. Lucas, still shaking with cold, walked through the living room with Weather. A double-ought pellet had hit the frame on one of the photographs of her parents, but the photo was all right.

"Why did he do it that way, why . . . ?"

"I have to think about that," Lucas said.

"About . . . ?"

"He wanted you by those windows. If he'd gone to a door, you might not have let him in. And he'd need a hell of a gun to shoot through those oak doors and be sure about getting you. So the question is, did he know about the doors?"

"I think the glass was just the way he wanted to do it," Weather said after a minute. "He could get access up from the lake, nobody'd see him."

"That's possible, too. If you hadn't seen him, if we didn't know about the phones, you might've walked right up to the glass."

"I almost did anyway," she said.

Carr came back. "We can't find Phil, but his sled's in the garage. His car is gone."

"I don't know what that means," Lucas said.

"I don't either—but I've got dispatch calling Park Falls at Hayward. They're checking the bars for his car."

THE MAN FROM Hardware Hank brought three sheets of plywood and a Skil saw, broke the glass fragments out of the glass doors and the window in Weather's bedroom, fitted the openings with plywood, and set them in place with nails. "That'll hold you for tonight," he said as he left. "I'll check back to-morrow on something permanent."

By three o'clock that morning the crime scene techs were packing up and the phone company had come and gone. Bergen had still not been found.

"I'm going home," Carr said. "I'll leave somebody."

"No, we're okay," Weather said. "Lucas has his .45 and I have the rifle . . . and I seriously doubt that'd he'd be back again."

"All right," Carr said. He flushed slightly. Lucas realized that he assumed that he and Weather were in bed together. "Stay on the handset."

"Yeah," Lucas said. Then, glancing at Weather, said to Carr, "C'mere and talk a minute. Privately."

"What?" Weather asked, hands on her hips.

"Law enforcement talk," Lucas said.

Carr followed him into the guest bedroom. Lucas picked up his shoulder holster, took the pistol out. He'd reloaded after he got out of the shower, and now he punched out the chambered round and reseated it in the magazine.

"If we don't find Bergen tonight, he could get lynched tomorrow," he said.

"I know that," Carr said. "I'm praying he's drunk somewhere. First time for that."

"But the main thing I want to say is, we need to get Weather out of town. She's gonna fight it, but I've contaminated her. I can't quite think why, but I guess I have."

"So work on her," Carr said.

Lucas gestured to his bag on the floor, the rumpled bedclothes. "We're not quite as friendly as you think, Shelly."

Carr flushed again, then said, "I'll talk to her tomorrow, we'll work something out. I'll have a guy with her all day."

"Good."

When the last man left, Weather pushed the door shut, looked at Lucas.

"What was that little bull session about?" she asked suspiciously.

"I asked some routine questions and let Shelly get a good look at my clothes and my watch and the rumpled-up bed in the guest room," Lucas said. He shivered.

She looked at him for a moment, then said, "Huh. I appreciate that. I guess. Are you still cold?"

"Yeah. Freezing. But I'm okay."

"That was the stupidest goddamn thing I ever saw, you tearing through the snow like that in your bare feet. I honest to God thought you were in trouble when I got you back in here, I thought you were gonna have a heart attack."

"Seemed like the thing to do at the time," he said.

She walked back into the living room, looked at the damaged walls, and said, "I'm really cranked, Davenport. Pissed and cranked. I'm gonna have to reschedule the hysterectomy I had going this morning . . . maybe I can push it back into the afternoon. Jesus, I'm wound up."

"You've got about two quarts of adrenaline working their way through your body. You'll fall apart in an hour or so."

"You think so?" She was interested. "Hey, look at the holes in the walls—my God."

She called the hospital's night charge nurse, explained the problem, rescheduled the operation, unloaded then reloaded her .22, asked Davenport to demonstrate his .45, went repeatedly back to the buckshot holes, poking at them with an index finger, going outside to see if they'd gone through. She found three holes in her leather couch, and was outraged all over again. Lucas let her go. He went into the kitchen, made a bowl of chicken noodle soup, ate it all, went back into the living room, and fell on the couch.

"What about the shots you fired? Could you have hit somebody across the lake?" she demanded. She had the magazine out of his .45 and was pointing it at her own image in the mirror over the fireplace.

"No. Some people call a .45 slug a flying ashtray. It's fat, heavy, and slow. It'll knock the shit out of you close up, but it's not a long-range item. Fired from here, on the level, it wouldn't make it halfway across."

"Any chance you hit him?" she asked.

"No . . . I just didn't want him swarming through the door with the shotgun. I might of got him, but he would have got us, too."

"God, it was loud," she said. "The shots almost broke my eardrums."

"You lose a little high-frequency hearing every time you fire one without ear protection, and that's a fact," Lucas said.

She ran out of gas. Suddenly. She stopped talking, came over and slumped next to him on the couch.

"Snuggle up," he said, and pulled her down. She lay quietly for a moment, her back to him, then started to softly cry. "Goddamn him, he shot my house," she said.

Her body shook with the anger of it, and Lucas wrapped his arm around her and held on.

THE ICEMAN RODE WILDLY across the frozen lake, off the tracks, a plume of snow thrown high behind the sled when he banked through the long, sinuous turns that would take him to the Circle Lake intersection. He could see police flashers streaming down through the town, but couldn't hear them: and they certainly couldn't see him. He was running without lights, his sled as black as his snowmobile suit, invisible in the night.

The gunfight had surprised him, but not frightened him. He had simply seen the truth: not tonight. He couldn't get at her tonight, because if he stayed, if he fought it out with whoever was inside—and it was almost certainly the cop from Minneapolis—he could be hurt. And hurt was good as dead.

Time time time . . .

He was running out of it. He could feel it trickling through his fingers. Davenport and Crane had taken something out of the LaCourt house, and it was almost certainly the photograph. But they had sent it to the lab in Madison: maybe it had been ruined in the fire after all. He'd talked to the cops who'd been there when they were looking at it, but they had no precise details. Just a piece of paper, they said.

If Weather Karkinnen ever saw the photograph, they'd be on him.

Weather: why was Davenport at her house? Guarding her? Screwing her? Why would they be guarding her? Had she given them something? But the only thing she had to give them was the identification, and if she'd given them that, they'd be knocking on his door.

The intersection came up, marked by two distinctively pink sodium vapor lights. He was in luck: there were no other sleds at the crossing. If they saw him running a blacked-out sled, they'd be curious.

He bucked through the intersection, up the boat landing, down the landing road, onto the trail built in the ditch beside the road. A moment later he turned onto Circle Creek, ran under the road and two minutes later onto the lake. He turned on his lights in the creek bed but kept cranking. There were more snowmobiles on Circle Lake, and he crossed paths with them, moving south and west.

He worked through his options:

He could run. Get in the car, make some excuse for a couple days' absence, and never come back. By the time they started looking for him, he'd be buried in Alaska or the Northwest Territories. But if he was missing, it wouldn't take long for the cops to figure out what happened. And if he ran, he'd have to give up almost everything he had. Take only what would fit in the car, and he'd have to dump the car in a few days. And he still might get caught: they had his picture, his fingerprints.

He could go after the other members of the club, take them all out in one night. The problem was, some of them had already taken off. The Schoeneckers: how would he find them? No good.

He had to stay. He had to find out about the photograph. Had to go back for Weather. He'd missed her twice now, and he was uneasy about it. When he'd been a kid, working the schoolyard, there'd always been a few people he'd never been able to get at. They'd always outmaneuvered him, always foiled him, sometimes goading him into trouble. Weather was like that: he needed to get at her, but she turned him away.

He bucked up over another intersection, down a long bumpy lane cleared through the woods by the local snowmobile club, onto the next lake, and across. He came off the lake, took the boat landing road out to the highway, sat for a moment, then turned left.

THE YELLOW-HAIRED GIRL WAS waiting. So was her brother, Mark. Mark with the dark hair and the large brown eyes. The yellow-haired girl let him in, helped him take off his snowmobile suit. Mark was smiling nervously: he was like that, he needed to be calmed. The Iceman liked working with Mark *because* of the resistance. If the yellow-haired girl hadn't been there . . .

"Let's go back to my room," she said.

"Where's Rosie?"

"She went out drinking," the yellow-haired girl said.

"I gotta get going," said Mark.

"Where're you going?" Smiling, quiet. But the shooting still boiling in his blood. God, if he could get Weather someplace alone, if he could have her for a while . . .

"Out with Bob," said Mark.

"It's cold out there," he said.

"I'll be okay," Mark said. He wouldn't meet his eyes. "He's gonna pick me up."

"And I'll be here," said the yellow-haired girl. She was wearing a sweatsuit, old and pilled, wished it were something more elegant for him. She plucked at the pants leg, afraid of what he might say; of cruelty in his words.

But he said, "That's great." He touched her head and the warmth flowed through her.

. . .

LATER IN THE EVENING he was lying in her bed, smoking. He thought of Weather, of Davenport, of Carr, of the picture; of Weather, of Davenport, round and round . . .

The yellow-haired girl was breathing softly next to him, her hand on his stomach.

He needed time to find out about the photo. If he could just put them off for a few days, he could find out. He could get details. Without the photo, there wouldn't be a link, but he needed *time*.

THE TELEPHONE RANG in the kitchen.

Lucas let it ring, heard a voice talking into the answering machine. He should get it, he thought. He rolled over and looked at the green luminous numbers on the bedstand clock. Nine-fifteen.

Four hours lying awake, with a few sporadic minutes of sleep. The air in the house was cool, almost cold, and he pulled the blankets up over his ears. The phone rang again, two rings, then stopped as the answering machine came on. There was no talk this time. Whoever it was had hung up.

A minute later the phone rang twice again. Irritated, Lucas thought about getting up. The ringing stopped, and a moment later began again, two more rings. Angry now, he slipped out of bed, wrapped the comforter around his shoulders, stomped down the hall to the kitchen, and glared at the phone.

Ten seconds passed. It rang again, and he snatched it up. "What?" he snarled.

"Ah. I knew you were sleeping in," the nun said with satisfaction. "You've got a message on the answering machine, by the way."

Lucas looked down at the machine, saw the blinking red light. "I'm freezing my butt off. Couldn't . . ."

"The message isn't from me. I know you've got one because your phone's only ringing twice before the machine answers, instead of four or five times," she said, sounding even more pleased with herself.

"How'd you get the number?"

"Sheriff's secretary," Elle said. "She told me what happened last night, and you're guarding the body of some lady doctor who's quite attractive. Are you okay, by the way?"

"Elle . . ." Lucas said impatiently, "You sound too smug for this to be a gossip call."

"I'll be gone for the day and I wanted to talk to you," she said. "I found a couple of Phil Bergen's friends. I didn't want to put it on an answering machine."

"What'd they say?"

"They say he was awkward around women but that he was certainly oriented toward them. He was *not* interested in men."

"For sure?" Lucas thought, *Shit.*

"Yes. One of them laughed when I asked the question. Bergen's not a complete 'phobe, but he has a distaste for homosexuals and homosexuality. That attitude wasn't a cover for a secret interest, if you were about to ask me that."

Lucas chewed on his lower lip, then said, "Okay. I appreciate your help."

"Lucas, these are people who would know," Elle said. "One was Bergen's college confessor. He wouldn't have talked to me if homosexuality had ever been broached in confession, so it must not have been. And it would have been."

"All right," Lucas said. "Dammit. That makes things harder."

"Sorry," she said. "Will you be down next week?"

"If I get done up here."

"We'll see you then. We'll get a game. By the way, something serious was happening at the sheriff's office. Nobody had any time to speak to me, something about a lost kid . . ."

"Oh, my God," Lucas said. "Elle, I'll talk to you later."

He hung up, started to punch in the number for the sheriff's office, saw the blinking light on the answering machine and poked it.

Carr's voice rasped out of the speaker: "Davenport, where'n the heck are you? We found the Mueller kid. He's dead and it wasn't an accident. I'm going to send somebody over to wake you up."

Just before the phone hung up, Carr called to someone in the background, "Get Gene over to Weather Karkinnen's house."

There was a motor sound outside. Lucas used two fingers to separate the curtain over the kitchen sink and looked out. A sheriff's truck was pulling into the driveway. Lucas hurried to Weather's bedroom. The door was unlocked, and he opened it and stuck his head inside. She was curled under a down comforter, and looked small and innocent.

"Weather, wake up," he said.

"Huh?" She rolled, half-asleep, and looked up at him.

"They found the Mueller kid and he's dead," Lucas said. "I'm going."

She sat up, instantly awake, and threw off the bedcovers. She was wearing a long-sleeved white flannel nightgown. "I'm coming with you."

"You've got an operation."

"I'll be okay, a few hours is fine."

"You really don't . . ."

"I'm the county coroner, Lucas," she said, "I've got to go anyway." Her hair stuck out from her head in a corona and her face was still morning-slack. She had a red pillow-wrinkle on one cheek. Her cotton nightgown hid all of her figure except her hips, which shaped and moved the soft fabric. She started toward the bath that opened off her bedroom, felt him watching her, said, "What?"

"You look terrific."

"Jesus, I'm a wreck," she said. She stepped back to him, stood on her tip-toes for a kiss, and Climpt began banging on the door.

"That's Gene," Lucas said, stepping back toward the hall. "Five minutes."

"Ten," she said. "I mean, it won't make any difference to John Mueller."

She said it offhandedly, a surgeon and a coroner who dealt in death. But Lucas was stricken. She saw it in his face, a quick tightening, and said, "Oh, God, Lucas, I didn't mean it."

"You're right, though," he said, his voice gone hard. "Ten minutes. It won't make any difference to the kid."

Lucas let Climpt in, and while the deputy looked at the damage from the night's shooting, went back to the bathroom for a quick cleanup.

When he came back out, Weather was coming down the hall, dressed in insulated jeans and a wool shirt, carrying the bag she'd had at the LaCourts'. "Ready?"

"Yeah."

"You were lucky last night," Climpt said. He was standing in the living room, smoking a cigarette, looking at the damage from the firefight.

"I don't think there was anything lucky about it," Weather said. "Look what he did."

"If'd been me out there, you'd a been dead. He should of waited until you were right at the door."

"I'll tell him when I see him," Lucas said.

JOHN MUELLER'S BODY HAD BEEN dumped in an abandoned sand-pit off a blacktopped government road in the Chequamegon National Forest, fifteen miles from his home. A half-dozen sheriff's vehicles were jammed into the turnoff, and the snow had been beaten down by people walking into the pit.

"Shelly's freaked out," Climpt said, talking past a new cigarette. "Something happened at Mass today."

"They found Bergen?"

"Yeah, I guess. He was there."

They could see the sheriff standing alone, like a fat dark scarecrow, just inside the sandpit. "This is his worst nightmare," Weather said.

Climpt nodded. "All he wanted was a nice easy cruise up to retirement, taking care of people. Which he's pretty good at."

They parked and started up toward a cluster of cops at the edge of the sand-pit. A civilian in an orange parka stood off to the side, next to a snowmobile, talking to another deputy. Carr saw them coming and walked down the freshly trampled path to meet them.

"How are you?" Carr asked Weather. "Get any sleep?"

"Very little," Weather said. "Is the kid . . ."

"Right there. We haven't called his folks yet." Carr looked at Lucas. "How long will it take to catch this guy?"

"That's not a reasonable question," Weather snapped.

But Lucas looked up the rise to the cluster of cops around the body. "Three or four days," he said after a few seconds. "He's out of control. Unless we're missing some big connection on this kid, there wasn't any reason to kill him. He took a hell of risk for no gain."

"Will he kill more people?" Carr asked. His voice was a compound of anger, tension, and sorrow, as though he'd worked out the answer.

"He could." Lucas nodded, looking straight into Carr's dry, exhausted eyes. "Yeah, I'd say he could. You better find the Schoeneckers. If they're involved, and they're someplace where he could get at them . . ."

"We got bulletins out all over the south, from Florida to Arizona. We're interviewing their friends."

Weather was moving on toward the body, and Lucas trailed after her. Carr hooked his elbow. "You gotta figure a way to make something happen, Lucas."

"I know," Lucas said.

John Mueller's body had been found by the snowmobiler in the orange parka. He'd seen two coyotes working over the spot and assumed they'd killed a deer. He'd stopped to see if it was a buck and still had antlers. He chased off the dogs, saw the boy's coat, and called the sheriff's department. The first deputy at the scene had shot a coyote and covered the boy with a plastic tarp.

"Bad," Weather said when she lifted the tarp. Around them, the talking stopped as everybody looked at them crouched over the body. "Is that him?"

Lucas studied the child's half-eaten face, then nodded. "Yeah, that's him. I'm almost sure. Jesus Christ."

He walked away, unable to handle it. He hadn't had that problem since his third week on patrol: cops looked at dead people, end of story.

"You all right?" Climpt asked.

"Got on top of me," Lucas said.

He was halfway back to the cars when he saw Crane, the crime-scene tech from Madison, walking up the path.

"Anything for me?" Crane asked.

"I doubt it. The scene's pretty cut up and coyotes have been at the body. It'll take an ME to figure out how he was killed."

"I've got a metal detector, I'll check the site for shells. Listen, I got some news for you this morning. I tried to call and was told you were on the way out here. Remember that burnt-up page from the porno magazine that we sent down to Madison? The one with the picture you want?"

"Yeah?"

"We shipped it to all the major departments in Wisconsin, Illinois, and Minnesota, and we actually got a callback. A guy named . . ." Crane patted his pockets, pulled off a glove, dipped into one, and came up with a slender reporter's notebook. ". . . a guy named Curt Domeier with the Milwaukee PD. He says he might know the publisher. He says give him a call."

Lucas took the notebook page: something to do. He walked down to the truck, called the dispatcher, and was patched through to Milwaukee. Domeier worked with the sex unit. He wasn't in his office, but picked up a phone on a page. Lucas introduced himself and said, "The Madison guys say you might know who put out the paper."

"Yeah. I haven't seen this particular one, but he uses those little dingbats— that's what they call them, dingbats—at the ends of the stories. They look like playing-card suits. Hearts, diamonds, spades, and clubs. I've never seen that any-where else, but I've seen it with this guy." Domeier's voice was rusty but casual, the kind of cop who chewed gum while he drank coffee.

"Can we get our hands on him?" Lucas asked.

"No problem. He works out of his apartment, up on the north side off I-43. He's a crippled guy, does Macintosh services."

"Macintosh? Like the computer?"

"Exactly. He does magazine stuff, cheap," Domeier said. "Makeup, layout, that stuff."

"We got four dead up here," Lucas said.

"I been reading about it. I thought it was three."

"There'll be another in the paper tomorrow morning, a little kid."

"No shit?" Polite interest.

"We think the killer might have hit the family because of the picture on that page," Lucas said.

"I can talk to this guy right now or you could come down and we could both go see him," Domeier said. "Whatever you want."

"Why don't I come down?"

"Tomorrow?"

"How about this afternoon or tonight?" Lucas said.

"I'd have to talk to somebody here about overtime, but if your chief called down . . . I could use the bucks."

"I'll get him to call. Where'll we meet?" Lucas asked.

"There's a doughnut place, right off the interstate."

CARR WAS UNHAPPY about the trip: "We need pressure up here. I could send somebody else."

"I want to talk to this guy," Lucas said. "Think about it: he may have seen our man. He may *know* him."

"All right. But hurry, okay?" Carr said anxiously. "Have you heard about Phil?"

"Bergen? What?"

"He showed up for Mass. We'd been looking for him, couldn't find him, then he drove up a half hour before Mass, wouldn't talk to us. After his regular ser-mon at Mass this morning, he said he needed to talk to us as friends and neigh-bors. And he just let it out: he said he knew about the talk in town. He said he had nothing to do with the LaCourts or John Mueller, but that the suspicion was killing him. He said that he'd gotten drunk the night we found him, and said last night he'd gone to Hayward and started drinking again. Said he got right to the edge, right to the place where he couldn't get back, and he stopped. Said he talked to Jesus and stopped drinking. He asked us to pray for him."

"And you believe him?" Lucas asked.

"Absolutely. But you'd have to have been there to understand it. The man spoke to Jesus Christ, and while he was talking to us, the Holy Spirit was there in the church. You could feel it—it was like a . . . warmth. When Phil was walking away from the altar after the Mass, he broke down and began to cry, and you could feel the Spirit descending." Carr's eyes were glazing as he relived it. Lucas stepped away, spooked.

"I got a call from my nun friend," Lucas said. Carr wrenched himself back to the present. "She checked out some Church sources. They say Bergen's straight. Never had any sexual interest in men. That's not a hundred percent, of course."

Carr said, "Which leaves us the question of Bob Dell."

"We've got to talk to Bergen again. You can do it today or wait until I get back."

"We'll have to wait," Carr said. "After this morning, Phil's way beyond me."

"I'll try to get back tonight," Lucas said. "But I might not. If I don't, could you put somebody with Weather?"

"Yeah. I'll have Gene go on over," Carr said.

Weather declared John Mueller dead under suspicious circumstances and ordered the body shipped to a forensic pathologist in Milwaukee. Lucas told her he was leaving, explained, and said he would try to get back.

"That's a twelve-hour round trip," she said. "Take it easy."

"Gene'll take me into town. Could you catch a ride with Shelly?"

"Sure." They were standing next to Climpt's truck, a few feet from Climpt and Carr. When he turned to get in, she caught him and kissed him. "But hurry back."

On the way back, Climpt said, "You ever thought about having kids?"

"I've got one. A daughter," Lucas said. And then remembered Weather's story about Climpt's daughter.

Climpt nodded, said, "Lucky man. I had a daughter, but she was killed in an accident."

"Weather told me about it," Lucas said.

Climpt glanced at him and grinned. *He could have made a Marlboro commercial,* Lucas thought. "Everybody feels sorry for me. Sort of wears on you after a while, thirty years," Climpt said.

"Yeah."

"Anyway, what I was gonna say . . . I'm thinking I might kill this asshole for what he did to that LaCourt girl and now the Mueller kid. It we get him, and we get him in a place where we can do it, just sort of turn your head." His voice was mild, careful.

"I don't know," Lucas said, looking out the window.

"You don't have to do it—just don't stop me," Climpt said.

"Won't bring your daughter back, Gene."

"I know that," Climpt rasped. "Jesus Christ, Davenport."

"Sorry."

After a long silence, listening to the snow tires rumble over the rough roadway, Climpt said, "I just can't deal with people that kill kids. Can't even read about it in the newspaper or listen to it on TV. Killing a kid is the worst thing you can do. The absolute fuckin' worst."

THE DRIVE TO MILWAUKEE was long and complicated, a web of country roads and two-lane highways into Green Bay, and then the quick trip south along the lake on I-43. Domeier had given him a sequence of exits, and he got the right off-ramp the first time. The doughnut place was halfway down a flat-roofed shopping center that appeared to be in permanent recession. Lucas parked and walked inside.

The Milwaukee cop was a squat, red-faced man wearing a long wool coat and a longshoreman's watch cap. He sat at the counter, dunking a doughnut in a cup of coffee, charming an equally squat waitress who talked with a grin past a lipstick-smeared cigarette. When Lucas walked in she snatched the cigarette from her mouth and dropped her hand below counter level. Domeier looked over his shoulder, squinted, and said, "You gotta be Davenport."

"Yeah. You're telepathic?"

"You look like you been colder'n a well-digger's ass," Domeier said. "And I hear it's been colder'n a well-digger's ass up there."

"Got that right," Lucas said. They shook hands and Lucas scanned the menu above the counter. "Gimme two vanilla, one with coconut and one with peanuts, and a large coffee black," he said, dropping onto a stool next to Domeier. The coffee shop made him feel like a metropolitan cop again.

The waitress went off to get the coffee, the cigarette back in her mouth. "It's not so cold down here?" Lucas asked Domeier, picking up the conversation.

"Oh, it's cold, six or eight below, but nothing like what you got," Domeier said.

They talked while Lucas ate the doughnuts, feeling each other out. Lucas talked about Minneapolis, pension, and bennies.

"I'd like to go somewhere warmer if I could figure out some way to transfer pension and bennies," Domeier said. "You know, someplace out in the Southwest, not too hot, not too cold. Dry. Someplace that needs a sex guy and'd give me three weeks off the first year."

"A move sets you back," Lucas said. "You don't know the town, you don't know the cops or the assholes. A place isn't the same if you haven't been on patrol."

"I'd hate to go back in uniform," Domeier said with an exaggerated shudder. "Hated that shit, giving out speeding tickets, breaking up fights."

"And you got a great job right here," the waitress said. "What would you do if you didn't have Polaroid Peter?"

"Polaroid who?" asked Lucas.

"Peter," Domeier said, dropping his face into his hands. "A guy who's trying to kill me."

The waitress cackled and Domeier said, "He's like a flasher. He drops trow in the privacy of his own home, takes a Polaroid picture of his dick. Pretty average dick, I don't know what he's bragging about. Then he drops the picture around a high school or in a mall or someplace where there are bunches of teenage girls. A girl picks it up and zam—she's flashed. We think he's probably around somewhere, watching. Gettin' off on it."

Lucas had started laughing and nearly choked on a piece of doughnut. Domeier absently whacked him on the back. "What happens when a guy picks up the picture?" Lucas asked.

"Guys don't," Domeier said morosely. "Or if they do, they don't tell anybody. We've got two dozen calls about these things, and every time the picture's been picked up by a teenage girl. They see it laying there on the sidewalk, and they just gotta look. And if we got twenty-five calls, this guy must've struck a hundred times."

"Probably five hundred if you got twenty-five calls," Lucas said.

"Driving us nuts," Domeier said, finishing his coffee.

"Big deal," Lucas said. "Actually sounds kind of amusing."

"Yeah?" Domeier looked at him. "You wanna tell that to the mayor?"

"Uh-oh," Lucas said.

"He went on television and promised we'd get the guy soon," Domeier said. "The whole sex unit's having an argument about whether we oughta shit or go blind."

Lucas started laughing again and said, "You ready?"

"Let's go," Domeier said.

BOBBY McLAIN LIVED IN a two-story apartment complex built of concrete blocks painted beige and brown, in a neighborhood that alternated shabby old brown-brick apartments with shabby new concrete-block apartments. The streets were bleak, snow piled over the curbs, big rusting sedans from the seventies parked next to the snowpiles. Even the trees looked dark and crabbed. Domeier rode with Lucas, and pointed out the hand-painted Chevy van under a security light on the west side of the complex. "That's Bobby's. It's painted with a roller."

"What color is that?" Lucas asked as they pulled in beside it.

"Off-grape," Domeier said. "You don't see that many off-grape vans around. Not without Dead Head stickers, anyway."

They climbed out, looked up and down the street. Nobody in sight: not a soul other than themselves. At the door, they could hear a television going inside. Lucas knocked, and the television sound died.

"Who is it?" The voice squeaked like a new adolescent's.

"Domeier. Milwaukee PD." After a moment of silence, Domeier said, "Open the fuckin' door, Bobby."

"What do you want?"

Lucas stepped to the left, noticed Domeier edging to the right, out of the direct line of the door.

"I want you to open the fuckin' door," Domeier said.

He kicked it, and the voice on the other side said, "Okay, okay, okay. Just one goddamn minute."

A few seconds later the door opened. Bobby McLain was a fat young man with thick glasses and short blond hair. He wore loose khaki trousers and a white crew-neck t-shirt that had been laundered to a dirty yellow. He sat in an aging wheelchair, hand-powered.

"Come in and shut the door," he said, wheeling himself backwards.

They stepped inside, Domeier first. McLain's apartment smelled of old pizza and cat shit. The floor was covered with a stained shag carpet that might once have been apricot-colored. The living room, where they were standing, had been converted to a computer office, with two large Macintoshes sitting on library tables, surrounded by paper and other unidentifiable machines.

Domeier was focused on the kitchen. Lucas pushed the door shut with his foot. "Somebody just run out the back?" Domeier asked.

"No, no," McLain said, and he looked around toward the kitchen. "Really . . ."

Domeier relaxed, said, "Okay," and stepped toward the kitchen and looked in. Without looking back at McLain he said, "The guy there is named Davenport, he's a deputy sheriff from Ojibway County, up north, and he's investigating a multiple murder. He thinks you might be involved."

"Me?" McLain's eyes had gone round, and he stared up at Lucas. "What?"

"Some people were killed because of one of your porno magazines, Bobby," Lucas said. A chair next to one of the Macintoshes was stacked with computer paper. Lucas picked up the paper, tossed it on the table, and turned the chair around to sit on it. His face was only a foot from McLain's. "We only got a piece of one page. We need the rest of the magazine," he said.

Domeier stepped over to the crippled man and handed him a Xerox copy of the original page. At the same time he took one of the handles on the back of McLain's wheelchair and jiggled it. McLain glanced up nervously and then went back to the Xerox copy.

"I don't know," he said.

"C'mon, Bobby, we're talking heavy-duty shit here—like prison," Domeier said. He jiggled the chair handle again. "We all know where the goddamn thing came from."

McLain turned the page in his hand, glanced at the blank back side, then said, "Maybe." Domeier glanced at Lucas and then Bobby said, "I gotta know what's in it for me."

Domeier leaned close and said, "To start with, I won't dump you outa this chair on your fat physically challenged butt."

"And you get a lot of goodwill from the cops," Lucas said. "This stuff you print, kiddie porn, this shit could be a crime. And we can seize anything that's instrumental to a crime. If we get pissed, you could say good-bye to these computers."

Bobby looked nervously at the Xerox copy, then turned his head to Domeier and said irritably, "Quit fuckin' with my chair."

"Where's this magazine?"

McLain shook his head, then said, "Down the hall, goddammit."

He pivoted his chair and rolled down a short hallway past the bathroom to the door of the only bedroom, wheeled inside. The bedroom was chaotic; pieces of clothing were draped over chairs and the chest of drawers, the floor was littered with computer magazines and books on printing. A high-intensity reading light was screwed to the corner of a bed; the windows were covered with sheets of black paper thumbtacked in place. McLain pushed a jumble of old canvas gym shoes out of the way and jerked open a double-wide closet. The closet was piled chest-high with pulp black-and-white magazines. "You'll have to look through it, but this is all I got," he said. "There should be three or four copies of each issue."

Lucas picked up a stack of magazines, shuffled through them. Half were about sex or fetishism. Two were different white supremacist sheets, one was a computer hacker's publication, and another involved underground radio. They all looked about the same, neatly printed in black-and-white on the cheapest grade of newsprint, with amateurish layout and canned graphics. "Which issue was this stuff in?"

"I don't know offhand. What I do is, I go down to the bookstores and get these adult novels. I take stuff out of them, type it up in columns—sometimes I rewrite them a little—and I put in the pictures people send me. I've got a post office box."

"You've got a subscription list?" Lucas asked.

"No. This goes through adult stores," McLain said. He looked up at Lucas. "Let me see that copy again."

Lucas handed it to him and he glanced at the bottom of the page, then said, "Just a minute."

"What about this Nazi shit?" Domeier asked, looking through it. "Does that go through the bookstores?"

McLain had wheeled himself to a bookcase next to the bed, and was going through a stack of *Playboys*, glancing at the party jokes on the backs of the centerfolds. "No, that's all commissioned stuff. The Nazi magazines, the phreak and hacker stuff, the surplus military, that's all commission. I just do the sex and fetish."

He scanned the backside of a blonde with blow-dried pubic hair, then checked the cover. "Here . . . I crib jokes from *Playboy* when a column doesn't fill up. This is the August issue, and here's some of the jokes on the bottom of your page. So you're looking for something printed in the last six months, which would be maybe the top fifty or sixty magazines."

Domeier found the picture ten minutes later, halfway through a magazine called *Very Good Boys:* "Here it is."

Lucas took it, glanced at the caption and the little-head joke. They were right.

The photo at the top of the page had a nude man, turned half-sideways to display an erection. In the background, a boy sprawled across an unmade bed, smirking at the camera. His hair fell forward across his forehead, and his chest and legs were thin. He looked very young, younger than he must have been. His head was turned enough that an earring was visible at his earlobe. He held a cigarette in his left hand. His left wrist lay on his hip, the hand drooping slightly. He was missing a finger.

The photo was not good, but the boy was recognizable. The man in the foreground was not. He was visible from hips to knees and was slightly out of focus: the camera had concentrated on the boy, made a sexual prop out of the man.

"You said the kid's dead?" Domeier asked, looking over Lucas' shoulder.

"Yeah."

"There ain't much there, man," Domeier said.

"No."

There wasn't: the bed had no head or footboard, nor were there any other furnishings visible except what appeared to be a bland beige or tan carpet and a pair of gym shoes off to the left. Since the picture was black-and-white, none of the colors were apparent.

Lucas looked at McLain. "Where's the original?"

McLain shrugged, wheeled his chair back a few inches. "I shredded it and threw it. If I kept this shit around, I'd be buried in paper."

"Then how come you keep this?" Lucas asked, pointing at the stack of paper in the closet.

"That's references . . . for people who want to know what I do," McLain said.

Lucas turned his head to Domeier and said, "If we slapped this asshole around a little bit, maybe threw him in the bathtub, you think people'd get pissed off?"

Domeier looked at McLain, then at Lucas. "Who're they gonna believe, two cops or a fartbag like this? You wanna throw him?"

"Wait just a fuckin' minute," McLain complained. "I'm giving you what you asked for."

"I want the goddamn original," Lucas snapped.

McLain rolled back another foot. "Man, I don't fuckin' have it."

Lucas tracked him, leaning over him, face close. "And I don't fuckin' believe it."

McLain moved back another foot and said, "Wait. You come out in the kitchen."

They trailed him back down the hall, through the living room into the kitchen. McLain wheeled his chair up to a plastic garbage bag next to the back door, pulled the tie off, and started pulling out paper.

"See, these are the pasteups for the last one. I output the stuff on a laser printer, scan the picture, paste it up and ship it. I shred the originals. See, here's an original." He passed Lucas several strips of shiny plastic paper. A shredded Polaroid. "Here's some more."

Lucas looked at the strips of plastic, which showed the back half of a nude woman, sitting on an Oriental carpet. Then McLain passed him a few more strips, which showed the front half of her, doing oral sex on a man, who, as in the Jim Harper photos, was cut off at hips and knees. McLain dumped a torn-up pizza carton on the floor, found a few more pieces of originals.

"What about the laser printer copies?" Lucas asked.

"I get the pasteups back and I shred those, too," Bobby said.

"Why do you shred them?"

"I don't want garbagemen finding dirty pictures and calling Domeier," McLain said.

"You don't keep any?" Domeier asked.

McLain looked up from the garbage bag. "Listen, you see so much of this shit, after a while they're like 29-cent stamps. And some of the people who contribute this stuff aren't so nice, so I don't wanna leave around any envelopes with addresses or that kind of stuff. I wouldn't want to bring any shit down on them."

"All right," Lucas said. He tossed the strips of Polaroid back at McLain. "You're saying you never saw the guy who took the picture of the kid."

"That's right. People send me letters and some of them have pictures. I'll put in the letter and the picture if it can be reproduced. You'd be amazed at how bad most of the pictures are."

AFTER A FEW MORE QUESTIONS, they left McLain and walked back out to Lucas' four-by-four, taking McLain's four copies of the magazine.

"Did we do good?" Domeier asked.

"You did good, but *I* just shot myself in the foot," Lucas said. He turned on the dome light, opened a magazine again, and studied the picture. "The way things broke—the kid was murdered, then the LaCourts had gotten hold of the picture of him—I was sure there must be something in the picture. *Something.* But there's not a fuckin' thing here."

Just a blurry picture of a man in the foreground and the kid in the background.

"Maybe you could figure out how long his dick is, go around with a ruler," Domeier said straightfaced. "You know, hang out in the men's rooms."

"Not a bad idea. Why don't you come on up?"

Lucas tore the photo page out of the newspaper, threw the rest of the paper out of the truck into the parking lot, folded the page, and stuck it in his jacket pocket. "Goddammit. I thought we'd get more."

JUST SOUTH OF GREEN BAY, moving as fast as he could in the dark, Lucas ran into snow flurries, off-and-on squalls dropping wet, quarter-sized flakes. He paused at a McDonald's on the edge of Green Bay, got a cheeseburger and coffee, and pushed on. West of Park Falls on County F, he slowed for what he thought was a highway accident, two cars and a pickup on the road in the middle of nowhere.

A man in an arctic parka waved him through, but he stopped, rolled down his window.

"Got a problem?"

The man's face was a small oval surrounded by fur, only one eye visible at a time. He pointed toward a cluster of people gathered around a snowbank. "Got a deer down. She was walking down the road like she didn't know where she was, and she kept falling down. Starvin', I think."

"I'm a cop, I've got a pistol."

"Well, we're gonna try to tie her down, get her into town and feed her. She's just a young one."

"Good luck."

The snow grew heavier as he left Price County for Lincoln. Back in town, under the streetlights, the fat flakes turned the place into a corny advertisement for Christmas.

He found Weather and Climpt at her house, playing gin rummy in the living room.

"How'd it go?" Climpt asked. He dumped a hand without looking at it.

"We found the picture; not much in it," Lucas said. He took out the copy he'd ripped from the magazine, passed it to Climpt. Climpt opened it, looked at it, said, "That narrows it down to white guys."

Lucas shook his head and Weather reached for the photo, but Climpt held it away from her. "Not for ladies," he said.

"Kiss my ass, Gene," Weather said.

"Yes, ma'am, whatever you say," Climpt said with a dry chuckle. But he handed the photo back to Lucas. "Are you gonna bag out here again?"

"Yeah," Lucas said. "But I'd like to stick her somewhere that nobody knows about."

Weather put her hands on her hips. "That's right, talk around me—I'm a lamp," she said.

Climpt looked at her, sighed, said, "Goddamn feminists." And to Lucas: "You could put her at my place."

"Everybody in town would know about it in ten minutes," Weather said. "They know my car, they know your schedule . . . if there were lights in your place when you're supposed to be working, they'd be calling the cops."

"Yeah."

"I'm okay here as long as you guys are around," Weather said, looking from one of them to the other.

WHEN CLIMPT HAD GONE, Weather took Lucas by the collar, kissed him, and said, "Show me the picture."

He got his coat and handed it to her.

"Quite the display," she said, peering at it. She shook her head. "I've probably got thirty patients who look more or less like that—the belly and the fat butt. How do you identify them from that?" She shook her head. "You won't get any help from me."

"Bums me out," Lucas said, running a hand up through his hair. "We've got to find some way to crank up the pressure. I thought there'd be something in the picture. If it didn't ID the guy, there'd be *something.*"

"I'll tell you one thing," she said, poking the photograph at him. "If Jim Harper was involved in a sex ring, I can't believe that Russ wasn't aware of it. If blackmail ever occurred to anybody, it'd be Russ."

Lucas took the photo back, stared through it, thinking. Then: "You're right. We've gotta squeeze him. Squeeze him for public consumption. Maybe our asshole will come after him, or maybe Harper can put the finger on him." He wandered around the living room, touching her things: the photos of her parents, a Hummel doll, thinking. "If we play these Schoeneckers off against Harper . . . Huh . . ." He carefully folded the photograph, took his billfold out of his pocket, and stuck the photo in the fold, where he'd see it every time he paid for something. "How're you doing?"

She shrugged. "I'm tired but I can't sleep. I guess I'm a little scared."

"You should get out. Visit some friends in the Cities."

She shook her head. "Nope. He's not going to get on top of me."

"That's a little dumb."

"That's the way it is, though," she said. "How about you. Tired?"

"Stiff from the drive," Lucas said. He yawned and stretched.

"When I bought this place, the only big change I made was to fix up my bathroom. I've got a big whirlpool tub back there. Why don't you go in and lay in some hot water? I'll put together a snack."

"Terrific," he said.

The tub looked like it might be black marble, and was easily six feet long. He half-filled it, fooled with a control panel until he got the whirlpool jets working, then eased himself into it. He found he could rest his head on a back ledge and float free in the hot water. The heat smoothed him out, took him out of the truck.

The photograph had to be the key, and now he had the photograph. Why couldn't he see it? What was it?

The door opened and Weather walked in, wearing a robe, carrying a bottle of wine. Lucas, embarrassed, sat up, but she pulled off the robe. Naked, she tested the water with her foot. She had small, solid breasts, a smooth, supple back, and long legs.

"Hot," she said, stepping into the far end of the tub. She might have been blushing or it might have been the hot water.

"What about the snack?" Lucas asked.

"You're looking at it, honey," she said.

FOURTH FULL DAY OF the investigation: he felt like he'd been in Ojibway County forever. Felt like he'd known Weather forever.

Lucas made it into the sheriff's office a few minutes after eight. The day was warmer, above zero, with damp spots in the streets where ice-remover chemicals had cut through the snow. The sky was an impenetrable gray. Despite the clouds hanging overhead, Lucas felt . . . light.

Different. He could still smell Weather, although he wasn't sure if the smell was real or just something he'd memorized and was holding on to.

There was nothing light about Carr. He'd been heavy and pink, even at the LaCourt killing. Now he was gray-faced, drawn. He looked not hungry or starving, but desiccated, as though he were dying of thirst.

"Get it?" he asked when Lucas walked in.

Lucas handed him a copy of the porno magazine, folded open to the page with Jim Harper on it. "Is this it?" Carr asked, studying the photo.

"That's it. That's what the LaCourts had, anyway," Lucas said.

Carr held it to the window for extra light. Henry Lacey ambled in, nodded to Lucas, and Carr handed him the photo. "Who is it, Henry? Who's the fat guy?"

Lacey looked at it, then at Lucas. "I don't see anything. Am I missing something?"

"I don't think so," Lucas said. Carr put his thumb to his mouth, began nibbling his cuticles, then quickly put his hand back on his desk, his movements jerky, out of sync. Strung-out. "When was the last time you had any sleep?" Lucas asked.

"Can't remember," Carr said vaguely. "Somebody tell me what to do."

Lucas said, "How tight are you with the editor of the *Register*? And the radio station."

"Same thing," Carr said. He spun in his chair and looked out his window toward the city garage. "The answer is, pretty tight. Danny Jones is the brother to Bob Jones."

"The junior high principal?"

"Yup. We played poker most Wednesday nights. Before this happened, anyway," Carr said.

"If you just flat told him what you wanted in the paper, or on the radio, and explained that you needed it done to break this case, would he buy it?"

Carr, still staring out the window, thought it over, then said, "In this case—probably."

Lucas outlined his proposal: that they go to the county attorney with the photographs they'd found of Jim Harper and get an arrest warrant for Russ Harper. They would charge Harper with promoting child pornography, drop him in jail.

"He'll bail out in twenty minutes," Lacey objected.

"Not if we work it right," Lucas said. "We'll pick him up this afternoon, question him, charge him tonight. We won't have to take him to court until Monday. We tell the *Register* that he's been arrested in connection with a pornography ring that we uncovered during the investigation of the LaCourt murders. We also leak the word that Harper's dealing—that he's trying to make an immunity deal if he turns in other members of the ring. And we tell Harper that we'll give him immunity unless the Schoeneckers come in first. Anything about the Schoeneckers, by the way?"

"Nothing yet," Carr said, shaking his head. "What you're saying about Russ Harper is . . . we set him up. I mean, the charges wouldn't hold water."

"We're not setting him up. We're using him to make something happen," Lucas said. "And who knows? Maybe he has some ideas about the killer."

"If he doesn't, he'll sue our butts. He'll probably sue our butts anyway," Carr said.

"A good attorney would get him in court and stick those pictures of Jim right up his ass," Lucas said. Lucas leaned across the deck. "I'll tell you, Shelly, there's a possibility that the LaCourt murders and the Mueller kid and Jim Harper have nothing to do with this sex ring. Possible, but I don't believe it. There's a connection. We just haven't found it. And Weather said last night she can't believe a guy like Harper didn't have some idea of what his kid was up to."

"We've got to do it, Shelly," Lacey said somberly. "We've got nothing else going for us. Not a frigging thing."

"Let's do it then," Carr said. He looked up at Lucas, exhaustion in his eyes. "And you and me, we've got to go talk to Phil Bergen again."

BERGEN WAS WAITING for them. Like Carr, he'd changed. But Bergen looked rested, clear-faced. Sober.

"I know what you're here for," he said when he let them in to the rectory. "Bob Dell called me. I didn't know he was homosexual until he called."

"You've never . . ." Lucas began.

"Never." Bergen turned to Carr. "Shelly, I never would have believed that'd you'd think . . ."

"He didn't believe it," Lucas said. "I brought it up. I looked at a plat map of the lake road, saw Dell's house, made some inquiries, and maybe jumped to the wrong conclusion."

"You did."

Lucas shrugged. "I was trying to figure out why you might claim that you were at the LaCourts' when you weren't, and why you couldn't tell us." They were standing in the entry, coats, gloves, and hats still on. Bergen faced them on his feet, didn't invite them to sit.

"I was at the LaCourts'. I was there," Bergen said.

Lucas looked him over, then nodded. "Then we've still got a problem," he said. "The time."

"Forget the time," Bergen said. "I swear: I was there and they were alive. I believe the killer came just as I left—maybe even was there before I left, and waited until I'd gone—and killed them and spread the gas around, but accidently set it off too soon. If the firemen are wrong by a few minutes, then the times work out and you're barking up the wrong tree. And you've managed to severely . . . damage me in the process."

Carr looked at Lucas. Lucas looked at Bergen for a long beat, nodded, and said, "Maybe."

Bergen looked from Lucas to Carr, waiting, and Carr finally said, "Let's go." To Bergen: "Phil, I'm sorry about this. You know I am."

Bergen nodded, tight-mouthed, unforgiving.

Outside, Carr asked, "Do you believe him now?"

"I believe he's not gay."

"That's a start." They walked to the car in silence, then Carr said wearily, "And thanks for taking the rap on Bob Dell. Maybe when this is over, Phil and I can patch things up."

"I'm going to get Gene and take Harper. Why don't you catch a nap for a couple of hours?"

"Can't. My wife'd be cleaning," Carr said. "That's pretty noisy. I can't sleep worth a damn when she's working."

Lucas called Climpt on the radio, got him headed back toward the courthouse. While Carr returned to his office, Lucas found Henry Lacey talking to a deputy.

"I need to talk to you for a minute," he said.

Lacey nodded, said, "Check you later, Carl." And to Lucas, "What's going on?"

"There're rumors that Shelly's having an affair with a lady at the church. I think I met her the other night."

"So . . . ?" Lacey was defensive.

"Is she married or what?"

"Widowed," Lacey said reluctantly.

"You think you could get Shelly over to her house? On the sly? Get him a nap, get her to stroke him a little? The guy's on the edge of something bad."

Lacey showed the shadow of a smile and nodded. "I'll do it. I should have thought of it."

LUCAS, CLIMPT, AND THE young deputy Dusty, who'd first talked to John Mueller at the school, took Harper out of his gas station at 4:30, just before full dark.

Lucas and Climpt ate a long lunch, reviewed the newest information coming out of the Madison laboratory crew at the LaCourt house, stalled around until the county judge left the courthouse, then picked up Dusty and headed out to Knuckle Lake. When they pulled into the station in Climpt's Suburban, they could see Harper through the gas station window, counting change into a cash register. He came out snarling.

"If you ain't got a warrant I want you off my property," he said.

"You're under arrest," Climpt said.

Harper stopped so quickly he almost skidded. "Say what?"

"You're under arrest for the promotion of child pornography. Put your hands on the car."

Harper, dumbfounded, took the position on the truck. Dusty shook him down, then cuffed his hands. A kid who'd been working in the repair bay came out to watch, nervously wiping his hands with an oily rag. "You want him to stay open or you want to close down?" Climpt asked.

"You stay open until the regular quitting time, and there better be every last dime in the register," Harper shouted at the kid. He turned and looked at Lucas. "You motherfucker." And then back at the kid: "I'll call you. I should be out real quick."

"There's no bail hearing until Monday. Court's closed," Climpt told him.

"You fuckers," Harper snarled. "You're trying to do me." And he shouted at the kid: "You're in charge over the weekend. But I'm gonna count every dime."

On the way back to town, Lucas turned over to look at Harper, cuffed in the back. "I'll say two things to you, and you might talk them over with your attorney. The first is, the Schoeneckers. Think about them. The next thing is, *some-body* is gonna get immunity to testify. But only one somebody."

"You can kiss my ass."

Harper called an attorney from the jail's booking room. The attorney ran across the street from the bank building, spoke with Harper privately for ten minutes, then came out to discuss bail with the county attorney.

"We'll ask the judge to set it at a quarter million on Monday, in court," the county attorney said. He was a mildly fat man with light-brown eyes and pale brown hair, and he wore a medium-brown suit with buffed natural loafers.

"A quarter million? Eldon, my lord, Russ Harper runs a filling station," said Harper's attorney. He was a thin, weathered man with long yellow hair and weather-roughened hands. "Get real. And we figure this is important enough that we can get the judge out here tomorrow morning."

"I wouldn't want to call him on a Saturday. He goes fishing on Saturdays, and gets quite a little toot on, sittin' out there in that shack," the county attorney said. "And Russ's station could be worth a quarter million. Maybe."

"There's no way."

"We'll talk to the judge Monday," the county attorney said.

"I'm told that this gentleman"—Harper's attorney nodded at Lucas—"and Gene Climpt have already beat up my client on one occasion—and this is more harassment."

"Russ Harper's not the most reliable source, and we're talking about child pornography here," the county attorney said. But he looked at Lucas and Climpt. "And I'm prepared to guarantee that Mr. Harper will be perfectly safe in jail over the weekend. If he's not, somebody else will be sitting in there with him."

"He's safe enough," said Lacey, who'd joined them. "Nobody'll lay a finger on him."

Carr was in his office, looking perceptibly brighter.

"Get some sleep?" Lucas asked. "You're looking better."

"Three, four hours. Henry talked me into it," he said, a ribbon of guilt and pleasure running through his voice. "I need a week. All done with Harper?"

"He's inside," Lucas said.

"Good. Wanna call Dan?"

DAN JONES WAS THE perfect double of the junior high principal. "We're twin brothers," he said. "He went into education, I went into journalism."

"Dan was all-state baseball, Bob was all-state football. I remember when you boys were tearing the place up," Carr said, his face animated. And Lucas thought: *He does like it, the good-old-boy political schmoozing.*

"Glory days," said Dan. To Lucas: "Did you play?"

"Hockey," Lucas said.

"Yeah, typical Minnesota," Dan said, grinning. Then he turned to Carr and asked, "Exactly what is it you want, Shelly?"

Carr filled Jones in about Harper, and Jones took notes on a reporter's pad. "We don't want to mislead you," Carr said, just slightly formal. "We're not saying Russ killed the LaCourts—in fact, we know he didn't. But as background, so you won't go astray, we want you to know that we developed the information about the porno ring out of the murder investigation."

"So you think the two are related?"

"It's very possible . . . if you sort of leaned that way, you'd be okay," Carr said.

"To be frank—no bullshit—we want the story out to put pressure on the other members of this child-molester group, whoever they are. We need to break something open, but we don't want you to say that," Lucas said. "We think there's a chance that Harper'll try to deal. Go for immunity or reduced charges. That could be significant. But we'd like to have it reported as rumor," Lucas said.

Climpt was digging around on his desk, found the porno magazine from Milwaukee, said, "You can refer to this, but you can't say directly what's in it," and passed it across to the newspaper editor.

Jones recoiled. "Jesus H. Christ on a crutch," he said. Then he remembered, and glanced up at Carr: "Sorry, Shelly."

"Well, I know what you mean," Carr said lamely.

"Horseshit reproduction," Jones said, turning the paper in his hand. "This is like toilet paper."

"In more ways than one," Carr said. "What about the story? Can you do something with it?"

Jones was on his feet. "Oh, hell yes! The Russ Harper arrest is big. The AP'll want that, and I can string it down to Milwaukee and St. Paul. Sure. People are so freaked out I've been talking to old man Donohue . . ."

Climpt said to Lucas, "Donohue owns the paper."

". . . about putting out an extra. With Johnny Mueller and now this, I'll talk to him tonight, see if we can get it out Sunday morning. I'll need the arrest reports on Russ."

"Got them right here," Carr said, passing him some Xeroxed copies of the arrest log.

"Thanks. Whether or not Donohue goes with the extra, we'll have it on the radio in half an hour. It'll be all over town in an hour."

WHEN JONES HAD GONE, Carr leaned back in his chair, closed his eyes, and said, "Think we'll shake something loose?"

"Something," Lucas said.

WEATHER KARKINNEN THREW her scrub suit into the laundry rack and stepped into the shower. Her nipples felt sore and she scratched at them, wondering, then realized: beard burn. Davenport hadn't shaved for an entire day when she attacked him in the bathtub, and he had a beard like a porcupine.

She laughed at herself: she hadn't felt so alive in years. Lucas had been an energetic lover, but also, at times, strangely soft, as though he were afraid he might hurt her. The combination was irresistible. She thought about the tub again as she dried off with one of the rough hospital towels: that was the most contrived entrance she'd ever engineered. The bottle of wine, the robe slipping off . . .

She laughed aloud, her laughter echoing off the tiles of the surgeons' locker room.

SHE LEFT, HURRYING: almost six-thirty. Lucas said he'd be done with Harper by six or seven. Maybe they could drive over Hayward for dinner, or one of those places off Teal Lake or Lost Land Lake. Good restaurants over there.

As she left the locker, she stopped at the nurses' station to get the final list for the morning. Civilians sometimes thought surgeons worked every week or two, after an exhaustive study of the patient. More often, they worked every day, and sometimes two or three times a day, with little interaction with the patient at all. Weather was building a reputation in the North Woods, and now had referrals from all the adjoining counties. Sometimes she thought it was a conspiracy by the referring docs to keep her busy, to pin her down.

". . . Charlie Denning, fixing his toe," she said. "He can hardly walk, so you'll have to get a wheelchair out to his car. His wife is bringing him in."

As they went through it, she was aware that the charge nurse kept checking her, a small smile on her face. Everybody knew that Lucas was staying at her house in some capacity, and Weather suspected that a few of the nurses had, during the day, figured out the capacity. She didn't care.

". . . probably gonna have to clean her up, and I want the whole area shaved. I doubt that she did a very good job of it, she's pretty old and I'm not sure how clearly I was getting through to her."

The charge nurse's family had been a friend of her family, though the nurse was ten years older. Still, they were friends, and when Weather finished with the work list, she started for the door, then turned and said, "Is it that obvious?"

"Pretty obvious," the nurse said. "The other girls say he's a well set-up man, the ones who have seen him."

Weather laughed. "My God—small towns, I love 'em." She started away again. The nurse called, "Don't wear him out, Doctor," and as she went out the door, Weather was still laughing.

HER ESCORT WAS A surly, heavyset deputy named Arne Bruun. He'd been two years behind her in high school. He'd been president of the Young Republican Club and allegedly had now drifted so far to the right that the Republicans wouldn't have him. He stood up when she walked into the lobby, rolled a copy of *Guns and Ammo*, and stuck it in his coat pocket.

"Ready to roll?" He was pleasant enough but had the strong jaw-muscle complex of a marginal paranoid.

"Ready to roll," she said.

He went through the door first, looked around, waved her on, and they walked together to the parking lot. The days were beginning to lengthen, but it was fully dark, and the thermometer had crashed again. The Indians called it the Moon of the Falling Cold.

Bruun unlocked the passenger door of the Suburban, let her climb up, shut it behind her, and walked around the nose of the truck. The hospital was on the south edge of town; Weather lived on the north side. The quickest route to her home was down the frontage road along Highway 77 to Buhler's Road, and across the highway at the light, avoiding the traffic of Main Street.

"Gettin' cold again," Bruun said as he climbed into the truck cab. Following Carr's instructions, she'd called for a lift home. Bruun had been on patrol, and had waited in the lobby for only a few minutes: the truck was still warm inside. "If it gets much worse, there won't be any deer alive next year. Or anything else."

"I understand they're gonna truck in hay."

They were talking about the haylift when she saw the snowmobile on the side of the road. The rider was kneeling beside it, working on it, fifteen feet from the stop sign for Buhler's Road. There was a trail beside the road, and sleds broke down all the time. But something caught her attention; the man beside it looked down toward them while his hands continued working.

"Sled broke down," she said.

Bruun was already watching it. "Yup." He touched the brake to slow for the stop sign. They were almost on top of the sled. Weather watched it, watched it. The Suburban was rolling to a stop, just past the sled, the headlights reflecting off the snowbanks, back on the rider. She saw him stand up, saw the gun come out, saw him running toward her window.

"*Gun*," she screamed. "He's got . . ."

She dropped in the seat and Bruun hit the gas and the window six inches above her head exploded and Bruun shrieked with pain, jerked the steering wheel. The truck skidded, lurched, came around, and the rear window shattered over her, as though somebody had hit it with a hammer. Weather looked to her left; Bruun's head and face were covered with blood, and he crouched over the wheel, the truck still sliding in a circle, engine screaming, tires screeching . . .

The shotgun roared again: she heard it this time, the first time she'd heard it. And heard the shot pecking at the door by her elbow. Bruun grunted, stayed with the wheel . . . they were running now, the truck bumping . . .

"Gotta get back, gotta get . . ." Bruun groaned. Weather, sensing the speed, pushed herself up in the seat. The side window was gone, but the mirror was still there. The rider was on the sled, coming after them, and she flashed to the night of the murders, the sled running in the ditch . . .

They were passing a tree farm on the road back to the hospital parking lot, the straight, regimented rows of pine flashing by like a black picket fence.

"No, no," she said. Heart in her throat. Looked into the mirror, the sled closing, closing . . .

"Gun coming up!" she shouted at Bruun.

Bruun put his head down and Weather slid to the floor. Two quick shots, almost lost in the roar of the engine, pellets hammering through the shattered back window into the cab, another shot crashing through the back window into the windshield, ricocheting. Bruun groaned again and said, "Hit, I'm hit."

But he kept his foot on the pedal and the speed went up. The shotgun was silent. Weather sat higher, looking out the shattered side window, then out the back.

The road was empty. "He's gone," she said.

Bruun's chin was almost on the hub of the wheel. "Hold on," he grated. He hit the brake, but too late.

The entrance to the hospital parking lot was not straight in. The entry road went sharply right, specifically to slow incoming traffic. They were there—and they were going much too fast to make the turn. Weather braced herself, locking her arms against the dashboard. A small flower garden was buried under the snow where they'd hit. There was a foot-high wall around it . . .

The truck fishtailed when Bruun hit the brake, and then hit the flower-garden wall. The truck bounced, twisting, plowing through the snow, engine whining . . .

There were people in the parking lot.

She saw them clearly, sharply, frozen, like the face of the queen of hearts when somebody riffles a deck of cards.

Then the truck was in the parking lot, moving sideways. It hit a snowbank and rolled onto its side, almost as if it had been tripped. She felt it going, grabbed the door handle, tried to hold on, felt the door handle wrench away from her, fell, felt the softness of the deputy beneath her . . . Heard Bruun screaming . . .

And finally it stopped.

She'd lost track of anything but the sensations of impact. But she was alive, sitting on top of Bruun. She looked to her left, through the cracked windshield, saw legs . . .

Voices. "Stay there, stay there . . ."

And she thought: *Fire.*

She could smell it, feel it. She'd worked in a burn unit, wanted nothing to do with burns. She pulled herself up, carefully avoiding Bruun, who was alive, holding himself, moaning, "Oh boy, oh boy . . ."

She unlocked the passenger-side door, tried to push it open. It moved a few inches. More voices. Shouting.

Faces at the windshield, then somebody on top. A man looked in the side window: Robbie, the night-orderly body-builder, who she'd not-very-secretly made fun of because of his hobby. Now he pried the door open with sheer strength, and she'd never been so happy to see a muscleman. He was scared for her: "Are you all right, Doctor?"

"Snowmobile," she said. "Where's the man on the snowmobile?"

The body-builder looked up over into the group of people still gathering, and, puzzled, asked, "Who?"

WEATHER SAT ON the edge of the hospital bed in her scrub suit. Her left arm and leg were bruised, and she had three small cuts on the back of her left hand, none requiring stitches. No apparent internal injuries. Bruun was in the recovery room. She'd taken pellets out of his arm and chest cavity.

"You're gonna hurt like a sonofagun tomorrow," said Rice, the GP who'd come to look at her, and later assisted in the operation on Bruun. "You can bet on it. Take a bunch of ibuprofen before you go to bed. And don't do anything too strenuous tonight." His face was solemn, but his eyes flicked at Lucas.

"Yeah, yeah—take off," Weather said.

"DOES EVERYBODY KNOW?" Lucas asked when Rice had gone.

"I imagine there're a few Christian-school children that the secret's been kept from," Weather said.

"Mmmm."

"So what'd you find?" she asked.

"Just that you oughta be dead. Again. You would be if Bruun hadn't kept the truck rolling."

"And the asshole got away."

"Yeah. He waited in the trees by the stop sign until he saw you coming. After he fired the first shots, he followed you down the road to the spot where the power line cuts through the tree farm and then cut off through the trees. There was no chance of following him unless we'd been right there with a sled. He must've counted on that. He did a pretty good job setting it up. If Bruun had stuck the truck in the ditch, he'd of finished you off, no problem."

"Why didn't he shoot me through the door?"

"He tried," Lucas said. "Sometimes a double-ought pellet will make it through a car door, but most of the time it won't. Three went all the way through. One hit Bruun and the other two hit the dashboard. And we think Bruun got the arm hit through the broken window."

"Jesus," she said. She looked at Lucas. He was leaning against an exam table, his arms folded across his chest, his voice calm, almost sleepy. He might have been talking about a ball game. "You're not pissed enough," she said.

Lucas had come in just before she'd gone into the operating room, and waited. Hadn't touched her. Just watched her. She got down from the examination table, winced. Rice was right. She'd be sore.

"I was thinking all the way over here that I'm just too fuckin' vain and it almost caught up to me," Lucas said. He pushed away from the exam table and caught a fistful of hair at the back of her head, squeezed it, held her by the hair, head tipped up. "I want you the fuck out of here," he said angrily. "You're not gonna get hurt. You understand that? You're . . ."

"Why are you vain?" She'd grabbed his shirtfront with both hands, held on. Their faces were four inches apart, and they rocked back and forth.

He stopped, still holding her hair. "Because I thought he was coming after you because of me. I thought he went after the Mueller kid because of me."

"He didn't?"

"No. It's you he wants. You know him or you know something about him. Or he thinks you do. You don't know what it is, but he does."

She said, "Another snowmobile ran alongside my Jeep when I was coming back from the LaCourts' house, on the first night. I thought he was crazy."

"You didn't tell me."

"I didn't know."

He let go of her hair and put his arm around her shoulder, squeezed her, careful about her left arm. She squeezed with her right arm, then Lucas stepped back, took out his wallet, unfolded the photograph he'd stuck there.

"You know this fat man," he said. "He tried to kill you again. Who is he?"

"I don't know." She stared at the photo. "I don't have the foggiest."

17

THE PRIEST SAID, "I'm okay, Joe. Seriously."

He stood in the hall between the kitchen and the bedroom. He was grateful for the call and at the same time resented it: he should be doing the ministering.

"I had a decent day," he said, his head bobbing. "You know all the talk about me and the LaCourts—I was afraid to say anything that might make it worse. It was driving me crazy. But I found a way to handle it."

His tongue felt like sandpaper, from sucking on lemon drops. He'd gone through two dozen large sacks the last time he went off booze. He was now working his way through the first of what might be several more.

Joe was talking about *one day at a time,* and Bergen only half listened. When he'd gone off booze the year before, he hadn't really *wanted* to quit. He'd simply had to. He was losing his parish and he was dying. So he'd gone sober, he'd stopped dying, he'd gotten the parish back. That hadn't cured the problems for which bourbon was medication: the loneliness, the isolation, the troubles pressed upon him, for which he had no real answers. The drift in the faith.

This time he'd sat down to write an excuse for himself, a pitiful plea for understanding. Instead, he'd written the strongest lines of his life. From the reaction he'd gotten at the Mass that morning, he'd gotten through. He'd touched the parishioners and they'd touched him. He felt the isolation crumble; saw the possibility of an end to his loneliness.

He might, he thought, be cured. Dangerous thought. He'd suck the lemon drops anyway. Better safe . . .

". . . I won't be going out. I swear. Joe, things have changed. I've got something to do. Okay . . . And thanks."

The priest dropped the receiver back on the hook, sighed, and returned to his work chair. He wrote on a Zeos 386 computer, hammering down the words.

There's a devil among us. And somebody here in this church may know who it is.

(He would look around at this point, touching the eyes of each and every person in the church, exploiting the silence, allowing the stress to build.)

The murders of the LaCourt family must spring from deep in a man's tortured character, deep in a man's dirty heart. Ask yourself: Do I know this man? Do I suspect who he might be? Deep in my heart do I believe?

He worked for an hour, read through what he had. Excellent. He picked up the papers, carried them to his bedroom, and faced the full-length dressing mirror.

"There's a devil among us . . ." he began. No. He stopped. His voice should be slower, deeper, reflective of grief. He dropped it a half-octave, put some gravel into it: "There's a devil among us . . ."

Should he show some confusion, some bewilderment? Or would that be read as weakness?

". . . deep in a man's dirty heart," he said slowly, watching himself in the glass. He wagged his head, as though astonished that these things could take place here, in Ojibway County, and then, yet more slowly, but his voice rising urgently into something like anger: "Do I know this man? Do I suspect who he might be?"

He would rally the community, Philip Bergen would. And in turn the community would save him. He looked at the paper, relishing the flow of it.

But . . . he peered at it. Too many *hearts* there, too many *deeps*. He was repeating words, which set up a dissonance in the listener. Okay. Get rid of the last *deep* altogether and change the last *heart* to *soul*. ". . . DEEP in my soul do I believe . . ."

He worked in front of the mirror, watching himself through his steel-rimmed glasses, his jowls bouncing, trembling with anger and righteousness, his words booming around the small room.

Except for the sound of his own voice, the house was quiet: he could hear the Black Forest clock ticking behind him, the air ducts snapping as they expanded when the furnace came on, a scraping sound from outside—a snow shovel.

He went to the kitchen for a glass of water, caught sight of himself in a glass-fronted cabinet as he drank it. An older man now, permanent wrinkles in his forehead, hair thinning, paunch descending; a man coarsened by the work, a man whose best days were behind him. A man who would never leave Ojibway County . . . Ah, well.

He heard the ragged drag of a shovel again, went to the front window, parted the drapes with his fingertips, looked out. Across the street and three houses down, one of the McLaren kids scraping at a sidewalk with a snow shovel. Small kid, eleven o'clock at night. The McLarens were a family in distress: alcohol again, McLaren himself gone most of the time. Bergen turned back to his work chair, made a few more changes on the word processing screen, then saved the sermon to both the hard disk and a backup floppy, printed a new copy for himself.

There's a devil among us. And somebody here in this church may know who it is.

Maybe he should harden it:

Somebody here in this church knows who it is.

But that might suggest more than he wanted.

THE KNOCK AT THE door startled him.

He stopped in midsentence, turned, looked at the door, and muttered to himself, "Bless me." And then smiled at himself. Bless me? He *was* getting old. Must be Shelly Carr, coming to talk. Or Joe, making a check?

Stepping to the window, he parted the drapes again and looked out sideways at the porch. A man on the porch, a big man. Davenport, his interrogator, was a big man. With Lucas' face in his mind, Bergen went to the door, opened it, could see almost nothing through the frosted-over storm-door glass, pushed open the storm door and peered out.

"Yes?"

THE ICEMAN'S FACE WAS wrapped in a red-plaid scarf, the top of his head covered by a ski mask rolled up and worn like a watch cap. From the street, his face would be a furry unrecognizable cube, muffled and hatted, like everybody else. When he passed the time and temperature sign on the bank, it had been four below zero.

He was high from the attack on Weather, and angry. He'd missed again. Things didn't work like he thought they would. They just did not. He needed to plan better. He didn't foresee the possibility that the deputy would keep the truck rolling. Somehow, in his mind, the first shotgun blasts derailed the truck. But why would he think that? Too much TV?

Now the cops would focus on Weather. Who did she know that was involved in the case? He had to give them an answer, something that would hold them for a while.

And thinking about it, he became excited. This plan would work. This one would . . .

He stood on the rectory stoop, his left hand wrapped around the stock of the .44. Bergen was home, all right. The lights were on, and he'd seen a shadow on the drapes from where he'd been watching down the street. Facing the house, he reached up with his gloved right hand and pulled the ski mask down across his face. Then he knocked and half-turned to look back across the street, where some crazy kid was piling snow in a heap in his front yard. The kid paid no attention to him. He turned back to the house and gripped the storm-door handle with his right hand.

Bergen came to the door, pushed the storm door open two or three inches, leaned his head toward it. "Yes?"

The .44 was already coming up in the Iceman's left hand. With his right he jerked the door open, surged forward, the gun out, pointed at Bergen's forehead.

The priest reeled back, one hand up, as though to ward off the bullet.

"Get back," the Iceman snarled. "Get back, get back."

He thrust the oversized pistol at the priest, who was backing through his living room. "What?" he said. "What?"

The Iceman jerked the storm door shut, then backed against the inner door until he heard the latch snap.

"Sit down on the couch. Sit down."

"What?" Bergen's eyes were large, his face white. He made a broom-whisking motion with his hand, like he'd sweep the Iceman away. "Get out of here. Get out."

"Shut up or I'll blow your fuckin' brains out," the Iceman snapped.

"What?" Bergen seemed stuck on the word, uncomprehending. He dropped onto the couch, head tilted back, mouth open.

"I want the truth about the LaCourts," the Iceman rasped. "They were my friends."

Bergen stared at him, trying to penetrate the ski mask. He knew the voice, the bulk, but not well. Who was this? "I had nothing to do with it. I don't know myself what happened," Bergen said. "Are you going to kill me?"

"Maybe," the Iceman said. "Quite possibly. But that depends on what you have to say." He dipped into his parka pocket and took out a brown bag. "If you killed them."

"I tell you . . ."

"You're an alky, I know all about it," the Iceman said. He'd worked on this part of his speech. The priest must have confidence in him. "You were drinking again yesterday. You said so in Mass. And I asked myself, how do you get the truth out of a boozer?"

He stuck the brown paper bag in the armpit of the hand that held the gun, fumbled at the top of the bag with his gloved right hand, and pulled free a bottle of Jim Beam. "You give him some booze, that's how. A lot of booze. Then we'll get the truth out of him."

"I'm not drinking," Bergen said.

"Then I'll *know*, won't I?" the Iceman asked. "And if I know . . . I'll drop the hammer on you, priest. This is a .44 Magnum, and they'd find your brains in the next block." He'd moved around to the end of the couch, glanced down at the water glass on the end table. Excellent.

"Lean back on the couch," he ordered.

The priest settled back.

"If you try to get up, I'll kill you."

"Listen, Claudia LaCourt was one of my dearest friends."

"Shut up." The Iceman set the bottle on the table, turned the loosened top with his glove hand, took the top off and dropped it on the table. With his gun hand, he reached up, hooked his scarf with his thumb, pulled it down under his chin, then pushed his ski mask up until it was just over his upper lip.

With his glove hand, he picked up the bottle. He pointed the gun at the priest again, put the bottle to his lips, stuck his tongue into the neck of it to block the liquor, swallowed spit, took the bottle down, wiped his lips with the back of his gun hand. Bergen had to have confidence in the booze, too.

"I got you the good stuff, Father," he said, smacking his lips. He poured the water glass full almost to the top.

"Drink it down," he said. "Just slide across the couch, pick it up, and drink it down."

"I can't just drink it straight down."

"Bullshit. An alky like you could drink twice that much. Besides, you don't have much choice. If you don't drink it, I'm going to blow you up. Drink it."

Bergen edged across the couch, picked it up, looked at it, then slowly drank it; a quarter of it, then half.

"Drink the rest," the Iceman said, his voice rising. The gun waggled a foot from Bergen's head.

He drank the rest, the alcohol exploding in his stomach.

"Close your eyes," the Iceman said.

"What?"

"Close your eyes. You heard me. And keep them tight."

Bergen could feel the alcohol clawing its way into him, already spreading through his stomach into his lungs. *So good, so good* . . . But he didn't need it. He really didn't. He closed his eyes, clenched them. If he could get through this . . .

The Iceman picked up the bottle, poured another glass of bourbon, stepped back.

"Open your eyes. Pick up the glass."

"It'll kill me," Bergen protested feebly. He picked up the glass, looked at it.

"You don't have to drink this straight down. Just sip it. But I want it gone," he said. The gun barrel was three feet from Bergen's eyes, and unwavering. "Now—when was the last time you saw the LaCourts?"

"It was the night of the murder," Bergen said. "I was there, all right . . ." As he launched into the story he'd told the sheriff, the fear was still with him, but now it was joined by the certainty brought by alcohol. He was right, he was innocent, and he could convince this man. The intruder had kept his mask on: no point in doing that if he really planned to kill. *So he didn't plan to kill.* Bergen, pleased with himself for figuring it out, took another large swallow of bourbon when the Iceman prompted him, and another, and was surprised when the glass was suddenly empty.

"You're still sober enough to lie."

The glass was full again, and the man's voice seemed to be drifting away. Bergen sputtered, "Listen . . . you," and his head dropped on his shoulder and he nearly giggled. The impulse was smothered by what seemed to be a dark stain. The stain was spreading through his body, through his brain . . .

Took a drink, choking this time, dropped the glass, vaguely aware of the bourbon on him . . .

And now aware of something wrong. He'd never drunk this much alcohol this fast, but he'd come close a few times. It had never gotten on him like this; he'd never had this dark spreading stain in his mind.

Nothing was right; he could barely see; he looked up at the gunman, but his head wouldn't work right, couldn't turn. Tried to stand . . .

Couldn't breathe, couldn't breathe, felt the coldness at his lips, sputtered, alcohol running into him, a hand on his forehead . . . he swallowed, swallowed, swallowed. And at the last instant understood the Iceman: who he was, what he was doing. He tried, but he couldn't move . . . couldn't move.

THE ICEMAN PRESSED the priest's head back into the couch, emptied most of the rest of the bottle into him. When he was finished, he stepped back, looked down at his handiwork. The priest was almost gone. The Iceman took the priest's hand, wrapped it around the bottle, smeared it a bit, wrapped the other hand around it. The priest had sputtered alcohol all over himself, and that was fine.

The Iceman, moving quickly, put two prescription pill bottles on the table, the labels torn off. A single pill remained in one of the bottles to help the cops with identification. The priest, still sitting upright on the couch, his head back, mumbled something, then made a sound like a snore or a gargle. The Iceman had never been in the rectory before, but the office was just off the living room and he found it immediately. A yellow pad sat next to an IBM electric. He turned the typewriter on, inserted a sheet of paper with his gloved hand, pulled off his glove and typed the suicide note.

That done, he rolled the paper out without touching it, got the copy of the Sunday Bulletin from his pocket. Bergen signed all the bulletins.

When he got back to the living room, the priest was in deep sleep, his breathing shallow, long. He'd taken a combination of Seconal and alcohol, enough to kill a horse, along with Dramamine to keep him from vomiting it out.

The Iceman went to the window and peeked out. The kid who'd been shoveling snow had gone inside. He looked back at the priest. Bergen was slumped on the couch, his head rolled down on his chest. Still breathing. Barely.

Time to go.

18

L UCAS WOKE SUDDENLY, knew it was too early, but couldn't get back to sleep. He looked at the clock: 6:15. He slipped out of bed, walked slowly across the room to his right, hands out in front of him, and found the bathroom door. He shut the door, turned on the light, got a drink, and stared at himself in the mirror.

Why Weather?

If she was right about being chased on the night of the LaCourt murders, then the attacks had nothing at all to do with him.

He splashed water in his face, dried it, opened the door. The light from the bathroom fell across Weather and she rolled away from it, still asleep. Her arm was showing the bruises. She slept with it crooked under her chin, almost as though she were resting her head on her fists instead of the pillow. Lucas pulled the bathroom door most of the way shut, leaving just enough light to navigate. He tiptoed across the room and out into the hall, then went through the kitchen, turning on the lights, and, naked and cold, down into her basement. He got his clothing out of the dryer and carried it back up to the other bathroom to clean up and dress. When he went back to the bedroom for socks, she said, "Mmmm?"

"Are you awake?" he whispered.

"Mmm-hmm."

"I'm calling in. I'll get somebody down here until you're ready to leave."

As he said it, the phone rang, and she rolled and looked up at him, her voice morning-rough. "Every morning it rings and somebody's dead."

Lucas said "Just a moment" and padded into the kitchen. Carr was on the phone, ragged, nearly incoherent: "Phil's dead."

"What?"

"He killed himself. He left a note. He did it. He killed the LaCourts."

For a moment Lucas couldn't track it. "Where are you, Shelly?" Lucas asked. He could hear voices behind Carr.

"At the rectory. He's here."

"How many people are with you?" Lucas asked.

"Half-dozen."

"Get everybody the fuck out of there and seal the place off. Get the guys from Madison in there."

"They're on the way," Carr said. He sounded unsure of himself, his voice faltering.

"Get everybody out," Lucas said urgently. "Maybe Bergen killed himself, but I don't think he killed the LaCourts. If the note says he did, then he might have been murdered."

"But he did it with pills and booze—and the note's signed," Carr said. His voice was shrill: not a whine, but something nearer hysteria.

"Don't touch the note. We need to get it processed."

"It's already been picked up."

"For God's sake put it down!" Lucas said. "Don't pass it around."

Weather stepped into the hallway with the comforter wrapped around her, a question on her face. Lucas held up a just-a-moment finger. "How'd he do it? Exactly."

"Drank a fifth of whiskey with a couple bottles of sleeping pills."

"Yeah, that'd do it," Lucas said. "I'll be there as soon as I can. Look, it may be a suicide, but treat it like a homicide. Somebody almost got away with killing the Harper kid, making it look like an accident. He might be fucking with us again. Hold on for a minute."

Lucas took the phone down. "Do you know who Bergen's doctor is? GP?"

"Lou Davies had him, I think."

To Carr, Lucas said, "Bergen's doctor might have been a guy named Lou Davies. Call him, find out if Bergen had those prescriptions. And have somebody check the drugstore. Maybe all the drugstores around here."

"PHIL BERGEN'S DEAD?" Weather asked when Lucas hung up the phone.

"Yeah. Might be suicide—there's a note. And he confesses to killing the La-Courts."

"Oh, no." She wrapped her arms around herself. "Lucas . . . I'm getting scared now. Really scared."

He put an arm around her shoulder. "I keep telling you . . ."

"But I'm not getting out," she said.

"You could go down to my place in the Cities."

"I'm staying. But this guy . . ." She shook her head. Then she frowned. "That means . . . I don't see how . . ."

"What?"

"He would have been the guy who tried to shoot me last night. And the guy who was chasing me the first night."

"You were still at the LaCourts' when Shelly and I left, and we went into town to interview Bergen. Couldn't have been him," Lucas said.

"Maybe the guy wasn't chasing me—but after last night, I was sure that he was. I was sure, because it was so strange."

"Get dressed," Lucas said. "Let's go look at it."

SEVEN O'CLOCK IN THE MORNING, utterly dark, but Grant was awake, starting the day, people scurrying along the downtown sidewalks in front of a damp, cold wind. One city police car, two sheriff's cars, and the Madison techs' sedan were waiting at the rectory. Lucas nodded at the deputy on the door. Weather followed him inside. Carr was sitting on a couch, his face waxy. A lab tech from Madison was in the kitchen with a collection of glasses and bottles, dusting them. Carr wearily stood up when Lucas and Weather came in.

"Where is he?" Lucas asked.

"In here," Carr said, leading them down the hall.

Bergen was lying faceup on his bed, his head propped on a pillow, his eyes open, but filmed-over with death. His hands were crossed on his stomach. He wore a sweater and black trousers, undone at the waist. One shoe had come off and lay on the floor beside the bed; that foot dangled off the bed. His black sock had a hole at the little toe, and the little toe stuck through it. The other foot was on the bed.

"Who found him?" Lucas asked.

"One of the parishioners, when he didn't show up for early Mass," Carr said. "The front door was unlocked and a light was still on, but nobody answered the doorbell. They looked in the garage windows and they could see his car. Finally one of the guys went inside and found him on the bed. They knew he was dead—you could look at him and see it—so they called us."

"You or the town police?"

"We do the dispatching for both. And the Grant guys only patrol from seven in the morning until the bars close. We cover the overnight."

"So you got here and it was like this."

"Yeah, except Johnny—he's the deputy who responded—he picked up the note, then he handed it to one other guy, and then I picked it up. I was the last one to handle it, but we might of messed it up," Carr confessed.

"Where is it?"

"Out on the dining room table," Carr said. "But there's more than that. C'mon."

"I'll want to look at him," Weather said, bending over the body.

Lucas took a last look at Bergen, nodded to Weather, then followed Carr through the living room and kitchen to the mudroom, then out to the garage. The back gate of the Grand Cherokee was up. A pistol lay on the floor of the truck, along with a peculiar machete-like knife. The knife looked homemade, with wooden handles, taped, and a squared-off tip. Lucas bent over it, could see a dark encrustation that might be blood.

"That's a corn-knife," Carr said. "You don't see them much anymore."

"Was it just laying here like this?"

"Yeah. It's mentioned in the note. So's the gun. My God, who would've thought . . ."

"Let me see the note," Lucas said.

THE NOTE WAS TYPED on the parish's letterhead stationery.

"I assume he has an IBM typewriter," Lucas said.

"Yes. In his office."

"Okay . . ." Lucas read down through the note.

I have killed and I have lied. When I did it, I thought I did it for God; but I see now it was the Devil's hand. For what I've done, I will be punished; but I know the punishment will end and that I will see you all again, in heaven, cleansed of sin. For now, my friends, forgive me if you can, as the Father will.

He'd signed it with a ballpoint: *Rev. Philip Bergen.*

And under that: *Shelly—I'm sorry; I'm weak when I'm desperate: but you've known that since I kicked the ball out from under that pine. You'll find the implements in the back of my truck.*

"Is that his signature?"

"Yes. I knew it as soon as I looked at it. And there's the business about the pine."

Crane, the crime tech, stepped into the room, heard Lucas' question and Carr's answer, and said, "We're sending the note down to Madison. There might be a problem with it."

"What?" asked Lucas.

"When Sheriff Carr said you thought it could be a homicide, we got very careful. If you look at the note, at the signature . . ." He took a small magnifying glass from his breast pocket and handed it to Lucas. ". . . you can see what looks like little pen indentations, without ink, at a couple of places around the signature itself."

"So what?" Lucas bent over the note. The indentations were vague, but he could see them.

"Sometimes, when somebody wants to forge a note, he'll take a real signature, like from a check, lay it on top of the paper where he wants the new signature. Then he'll write over the real signature with something pointed, like a ballpoint pen, pushing down hard. That'll make an impression on the paper below it. Then he writes over the impression. It's hard to pick out if the forger's careful. The new signature will have all the little idiosyncrasies of an original."

"You think this is a fake?"

"Could be," Crane said. "And there are a couple of other things. Our fingerprint guy is gonna do the Super-Glue trick on the whiskey bottle and pill bottles, but he can see some prints sitting right on the glass. And except for the prints, the bottles are absolutely clean. Like somebody wiped them before Bergen picked them up—or printed Bergen's fingerprints on them after he was dead. Hardly any smears or partials or handling background, just a bunch of very clear prints. Too clear, too careful. They have to be deliberate."

"Sonofagun," Carr said, looking from the tech to Lucas.

"Could mean nothing at all," Crane said. "I'd say the odds are good that he killed himself. But . . ."

"But . . ." Carr repeated.

"Are you checking the neighborhood," Lucas asked Carr, "to see if anybody was hanging around last night?"

"I'll get it started," Carr said. A deputy had been standing, listening, and Carr pointed to him. He nodded and left.

Weather came in, shrugged. "There aren't any bruises that I can see, no signs of a struggle. His pants were undone."

"Yeah?"

"So what?" asked Carr.

"Lots of time suicides make themselves look nice. Women put on nice sleeping gowns and make up, men shave. It'd seem odd to be a priest, know you're killing yourself and undo your pants so you'd be found that way."

Carr looked back toward the bedroom and said, "Phil was kind of a formal guy."

"There's a knife out in his car," Lucas said to Weather. "Go have a look at it."

While she went out to the garage, Lucas walked back to the bedroom. Bergen, he thought, looked seriously disgruntled.

"We're checking the neighborhood now," Carr said, coming down the hall.

"Shelly, there's this Pentecostal thing," Lucas said. "I don't want to be insulting, but there are a lot of fruitcakes involved in religious controversies. You see it all the time in the Cities. You get enough fruitcakes in one place, working on each other, and one of them might turn out to be a killer. You've got to think about that."

"I'll think about it," Carr said. "You believe Phil was murdered?"

Lucas nodded. "It's a possibility. No signs of any kind of a struggle."

"Phil would have fought. And I guess the thing that sticks in my mind most of all is the business about the pine. We were out playing golf one time . . ."

"I know," Lucas said. "He kicked the ball out."

"How'd you know?"

"You told me," Lucas said, scratching his head. "I don't know when, but you did."

"Well, nobody else knew," Carr said.

They stood looking at the body for a moment, then Weather came up and said, "That's the knife."

"No question?"

"Not in my mind."

"It's all over town that he did it," Carr said mournfully. All three of them simultaneously turned away from the body and started down the hall toward the living room. They were passing Bergen's office, and Lucas glanced at the green IBM typewriter pulled out on a typing tray. A Zeos computer sat on a table to the other side, with a printer to its left.

"Wait a minute." He looked at the computer, then at the bookcase beside it. Instructional manuals for Windows, WordPerfect, MS-DOS, the Biblica RSV Bible-commentary and reference software, a CompuServe guide, and other miscellaneous computer books were stacked on the shelves, along with the boxes that the software came in. The computer had two floppy-disk drives. The 5.25 drive was empty, but a blue disk waited in the 3.5-inch drive. Lucas leaned into the hallway and yelled for Crane: "Hey, are you guys gonna dust the computer keys?"

"Um, if you want," Crane called back. "We haven't found any computer stuff, though."

"Okay. I'm going to bring it up," he said. To Carr: "I use WordPerfect."

With Carr and Weather looking over his shoulder, Lucas punched up the computer, typed WP to activate WordPerfect, then the F5 key to get a listing of files. He specified the B drive. The light went on over the occupied disk drive and a listing flashed onto the screen.

"Look at this," Lucas said. He tapped a line that said:

Ser1-9   .   5,213   01-08   12:38a

"What is it?"

"He was on the computer last night—this morning—at 12:38 A.M. That's when he closed the file. I wonder why he didn't compose his note on it? It's a lot easier and neater than a typewriter." He punched directional keys to select the last file and brought it up.

"It's a sermon . . . it looks like . . . Sermon 1-9. That would have been for to-morrow morning if that's the way he listed them." He reopened the index of files and ran his finger down the screen, "Yeah, see? Here's last Sunday, Ser1-2. Did you go to Mass?"

"Sure."

"Let's put it on Look." He called the second file up. "Is that Sunday's sermon?"

Carr read for a moment, then said, "Yeah, that's it. Right to the word, as far as I can tell."

"All right, so that's how he does it." Lucas tapped the Exit key twice to get back to the first file and began reading.

"Look at this," he said, pointing at the screen. "He's denying it. He's deny-ing he did it, at 12:38 A.M."

Carr read through the draft sermon, moving his lips, blood draining from his face. "Was he murdered? Or did this just trigger something, coming face-to-face with his own lies?"

"I'd say he was killed," Lucas said. Weather's hand was tight on his shoulder. "We have to go on that assumption. If we're wrong, no harm done. If we're right . . . our man's still out there."

19

THE ICEMAN LAY WITH his head on the pillow, the yellow-haired girl sprawled restlessly beside him. They were watching the tinny miniature television run through 1940s cartoons, Hekyll and Jekyll, Mighty Mouse.

Bergen was dead. The deputies the Iceman had talked to—a half-dozen of them, including the Madison people—had swallowed the note. They *wanted* to believe that the troubles were over, the case was solved. And just that morning he'd finally gotten something definitive about the magazine photo. The thing was worthless. The reproduction was so bad that nothing could be made of it.

At noon, he'd decided he was clear. At one o'clock, he'd heard the first rumors of dissent: that Carr was telling people Bergen had been murdered. And he'd heard about Harper. About a deal . . .

Harper would sell his own mother for a nickel. When his kid was killed, Harper treated it as an inconvenience. If Harper talked, if Harper said anything, the Iceman was done. Harper *knew* who was in the photograph.

The same applied to Doug Reston, the Schoeneckers, and the rest. But those problems were not immediate. Harper was the immediate problem.

Bergen's death made a difference, whether Carr liked it or not, whether he believed it or not. If the killings stopped, believing that Bergen was the killer would become increasingly convenient.

He sighed, and the yellow-haired girl looked at him, a worry wrinkle creasing the space between her eyes. "Penny for your thoughts," she said.

"Is that all, just a penny?" He stroked the back of her neck. Doug Reston had a particular fondness for her. She was so pale, so youthful. With Harper, she touched off an unusual violence: Harper wanted to bruise her, force her.

"I gotta ask you something," she said. She sat up, let the blanket drop down around her waist.

"Sure."

"Did you kill the LaCourts?" She asked it flatly, watching him, then continued in a rush: "I don't care if you did, I really don't, but maybe I could help."

"Why would you think that?" the Iceman asked calmly.

" 'Cause of that picture of you and Jim Harper and Lisa havin' it. I know Russ Harper thought you mighta done it, except he didn't think you were brave enough."

"You think I'm brave enough?"

"I know you are, 'cause I know the Iceman," she said.

. . .

THE YELLOW-HAIRED GIRL'S brother kept rabbits. Ten hutches were lined up along the back of the mobile home, up on stands, with a canvas awning that could be dropped over the front. Fed on Purina rabbit chow and garbage, the rabbits fattened up nicely; one made a meal for the three of them.

The Iceman pulled four of them out of their hutches, stuffed them into a garbage bag, and tied them to the carry-rack. The yellow-haired girl rode her brother's sled, a noisy wreck but operable. They powered down through the Miller tract and into the Chequamegon, the yellow-haired girl leading, the Iceman coming up behind.

The yellow-haired girl loved the freedom of the machine, the sense of speed, and pushed it, churning along the narrow trails, her breath freezing on her face mask, the motor rumbling in their helmets. They passed two other sleds, lifted a hand. The Iceman passed her at Parson's Corners, led her down a forest road and then into a trail used only a few times a day. In twenty minutes they'd reached the sandpit where John Mueller's body had been found. The snow had been cut up by the sheriff's four-by-fours and the crime scene people, but now snow was drifting into the holes they'd made. In two days even without much wind, there'd be no sign of the murder.

The Iceman pulled the sack of rabbits off the carry-rack, dropped it on the snow.

"Ready?"

"Sure." She looked down at the bag. "Where's the gun?"

"Here. He patted his pocket, then stooped, ripped a hole in the garbage bag, pulled out a struggling rabbit, and dropped it on the snow. The rabbit crouched, then started to snuffle around: a tame rabbit, it didn't try to run.

"Okay," he said. He took the pistol out of his pocket. "When it's this cold, you keep the pistol in your pocket as long as you can, 'cause your skin can stick to it if you don't." He pushed the cylinder release and flipped the cylinder out. "This is a .22 caliber revolver with a six-shot cylinder. Mind where you point it." He slapped the cylinder back in and handed it to her.

"Where's the safety?"

"No safety," said the Iceman.

"My brother's rifle has one."

"Won't find them on revolvers. Find them on long guns and automatics."

She pointed the pistol at the rabbit, which had taken a couple of tentative hops away. "I don't know what difference this makes. I kill them anyway."

"That's work—this is fun," the Iceman said.

"Fun?" She looked at him oddly, as though the thought had never occurred to her.

"Sort of. You're the most important thing that ever happened to this rabbit. You've got the power. All the power. You can do anything you want. You can snuff him out or not. Try to feel it."

She pointed the pistol at the rabbit. Tried to feel it. When she killed a rabbit for dinner, she just held it up by its back legs, whacked it on the back of the head with an aluminum t-ball bat, then pulled the head off to bleed it. Their heads came off easily. A squirrel, now, you needed an ax: a squirrel had neck muscles like oak limbs.

"Just squeeze," the Iceman coached.

And she did feel it. A tingle in her stomach; a small smile started at the corner of her mouth. She'd never had any power, not that she understood. She'd always been traded off and used, pushed and twisted. The rabbit took another tentative hop and the gun popped, almost without her willing it. The rabbit jumped once, then lay in the snow, its feet running.

"Again," said the Iceman.

But she stood and watched for a minute. Rabbits had always been like carrots or cabbages. She'd never really thought about them dying. This one was *hurting*.

The power was on her now, possibilities blossoming in her head. She wasn't just a piece of junk; she had a gun. Her jaw tightened. She put the barrel next to the rabbit's head and pulled the trigger.

"Excellent," said the Iceman. "Feel it?"

"Get another one," she said.

HARPER SAT ON THE jail bunk, scowling, shaking his head, his yellow teeth bared. His attorney, wearing a salt-and-pepper tweed suit that might have been made during the Roosevelt Administration, sat next to him, fidgeting.

"That ain't good enough," Harper said.

"Let me explain something to you, Russ," Carr said. Carr's double chin had collapsed into wattles, and the circles under his eyes were so black that he looked like he'd lost a bar fight. "Eldon Schaeffer has to get *elected* county attorney. If he cuts a deal with you, and it turns out you're a member of some sex ring, and that you know who the killer is but you didn't tell us, and Eldon gives you immunity and you walk out of here a free man . . . Well, Eldon ain't gonna win the next election. He's gonna be out of a job. So he isn't going to cut that deal. He's gonna want some jail time."

"Then he can stick it in his ass," Harper said. He nodded at his attorney. "If Dick here is right, I'll be out of here in an hour."

"You'll risk going to trial for multiple murder to save a couple years in jail? You could do two or three years standing on your head," Lucas said. He was leaning on the cell wall, looking down at Harper. "And I swear to Christ, if we tie you to the killer, if we even find a thread of evidence putting you two together, we'll slap your ass in jail so fast your head'll spin. For accessory to murder. You'll die in prison."

"If you're trying to cut me this kind of a deal, that means you ain't got shit on anybody," Harper said. His eyes flicked toward his attorney, then to Carr. "Take a fuckin' hike, Shelly."

AS THEY FILED OUT of the cell, Carr looked at Lucas and said, "Slap his ass in jail so fast his head'll spin? Some threat. I'm gonna send it in to *Reader's Digest.*"

"I'll sue," Lucas said, and Carr showed a bit of a smile. While they were waiting for the elevator, Harper's attorney came out and joined them. As they were waiting, Carr looked at the attorney and asked, "Why'd you have to go and do this, Dick? Why'd you call the judge? You coulda waited until Monday and everything would have been fine."

"Russ has the right . . ." The attorney's prominent Adam's apple bobbed up and down. A large Adam's apple, big hands, rough, porous skin, and the suit: he looked like a black-and-white photograph from the Depression.

The elevator doors opened and they stepped inside, faced the front. "Don't give me any 'rights,' Dick, I know all that," Carr said as they started down. "But we've got five dead and Russ knows who did it. Or he has some ideas. He's the only thing we've got. If he takes off, and we get more dead . . ."

"He's got a *right,*" the attorney said. But he didn't sound happy.

Carr looked at Lucas. "Phil's body must be on the way to Milwaukee."

"Yeah. I'm sorry about that, Shelly—I really am," Lucas said.

Tears started running down Harper's attorney's face, and he suddenly snuffled and wiped his coat sleeve across his eyes. "God, I can't believe Father Phil's dead," he said. "He was a good priest. He was the best."

"Yeah, he was," Carr said, patting the attorney on the shoulder.

Lacey was walking through the halls, hands in his pockets, peering in through open doors. When he saw Carr, he said, "There you are. Two FBI men just arrived. A couple more may be coming from Washington—a serial-killer team."

"Oh, boy." Carr hitched up his pants. "Where are they?"

"Down in your office."

Carr looked at Lucas. "Maybe they'll do some good."

"And maybe I'll get elected homecoming queen," Lucas said as they started down the hall.

Lacey looked at him. "Did you know your new girlfriend *was* the homecoming queen?"

"*What?*" There was no longer any point in being obtuse about his relationship with Weather.

"That's right," Lacey said enthusiastically. "Around homecoming time, people still talk about the dress she wore on the float. It was like one of those real warm days and she had this silver dress. Oh, boy. They called her . . ." He suddenly snapped his mouth shut and flushed.

"Called her what?"

Lacey looked at Carr and Carr shook his head. "You can't get your foot any deeper in your mouth than it already is, Henry. You might as well tell him," he said.

"Um—Miss Teen Tits of Ojibway County," Lacey said feebly.

"Glad you told me—gives me an edge on her," Lucas said.

"I hope you got an edge on the feebs," Lacey said gloomily. "About two minutes with them, I felt like I had big clods of horseshit on my shoes and straw sticking outa my ears."

"Dat's da feebs," Lucas said. "That's what they do best."

THEY TALKED FOR an hour with the two advance agents, Lansley and Tolsen. The two would have been hard to tell apart except that Lansley was the color of well-sanded birch plywood while Tolsen was polished ebony. They both wore gray suits with regimental neckties, long, dark winter coats with leather gloves, and rubbers on their wingtips.

". . . think there's some prospect that our man may be a traveler . . ."

Lucas, sitting behind Lansley, who was talking, looked past him at Carr and shook his head. No chance it was a traveler: none.

And after a while: ". . . name of the game is cooperation, and we'll do everything we can . . ."

Lucas broke in: "What we really need is computer support."

Tolsen was quick and interested. "Of what nature?"

"There are only about seven thousand permanent residents in this county. We can eliminate all women, all children, anyone with dark hair. Our man is obviously psychotic and may have a history of violence. If there's some way your computers could interface with the state driver's license bureau, process Ojibway County drivers and crosscheck the blond-male population with the NCIC records . . ."

Lansley and Tolsen took notes, Lansley using a hand-sized microcomputer. They came up with some ideas of their own and left in a hurry.

"What the heck was all that about?" Carr asked, scratching his head.

"They've got something to do," Lucas said. "It might even help if we need help three weeks from now."

A deputy knocked, stuck his head in the door. "Harper's out. Put up his gas station with Interstate Bond."

"That really frosts my butt," Carr said.

"Go home and get some sleep. Or check into a motel. You look so bad I'm seriously worried," Lucas said.

"That's a thought—the motel," Carr said distractedly. "What're you going to do?"

"Go someplace quiet and think," Lucas said.

·   ·   ·

WEATHER GOT HOME a few minutes after six, came in with a deputy, and found Lucas staring into a guttering fire. "This is Marge, my bodyguard," she said to Lucas. The deputy waved and said, "You got it from here," and left. Weather shed her coat and boots, came over to sit beside him. He put an arm around her shoulder. "You ought to throw another log on," she said.

"Yeah . . . goddammit, there are fewer people in this county than there are in some buildings in Minneapolis. We oughta be able to pick him out. There can't be that many candidates," Lucas said.

"Still think Phil Bergen was murdered?"

"Yeah. For sure. I don't know why he was killed, though. Did he know something? Was he supposed to distract us? What?"

"Schoeneckers'?"

"Not a goddamn thing," Lucas said.

"Could they be dead?"

"We've got to start considering the possibility," Lucas said. "We were lucky to find the Mueller kid. He could've laid out there until spring. Hell, if the killer had driven him two minutes back into the woods, we might not ever have found him."

"Are you watching Harper?"

"That's impossible. Where're you gonna watch him from? We'll check on him every couple of hours, though."

Weather shivered. "The man scares me. He's one of those people who just does what he wants and doesn't care who gets hurt. Sociopath. I don't think he even notices if somebody gets hurt."

They sat quietly for a moment, then Lucas smiled, remembering, and glanced at her. She was looking into the fire, her face serious. "We've been having a pretty good time in bed, haven't we?" he asked.

"Well, I hope so," she said, laughing. She patted his leg. "We fit pretty well."

"Um . . ." He pulled at his chin, looking into the fire. "There's something . . . I've always wanted to do, you know . . . sexually . . . and I haven't been able to find a woman who could do it."

Her smiled flickered. With an edge of uncertainty, she asked, "Well . . . ?"

"I always wanted to jump a homecoming queen wearing nothing but her white high heels and her crown. What do you think?" He pulled her closer.

"Those rotten jerks," she said, pushing him away. "I wasn't going to tell you until ten years from now."

"Miss Teen Tits of Ojibway County," he said.

"You should have seen me," she said, pleased. "The dress was cut fairly low in front, but *really* low in back. People said I had two cleavages."

"I like the image."

"Maybe we could work *something* out," she said, snuggling closer. "I don't know if I've still got the crown."

H ARPER WAS RELEASED at noon. He asked a deputy at the property window how he'd get back home, since the cops had brought him in. "Fuckin' hitchhike, Russ," the cop said, and slammed the window down. Harper called his station. No answer. He finally found a kid smoking a cigarette outside a game parlor and offered him five bucks to give him a ride. The kid said ten, Harper argued, the kid tossed his cigarette in the street and told him to go fuck himself. Harper paid the ten.

The gas station was closed and locked. Harper went inside, checked the register. There was money in the till and a note: "Russ, had to close. People are pissed at you they think your in on it."

"Motherfucker." Harper crumbled the note, threw it in the corner, locked up and walked out to his truck. The tires were flat, all four of them. Cursing, he checked them, found no sign that they'd been slashed. That was something. He pulled an air hose out of the lube bay and filled the tires. Worried about his house, he drove down to it, parked, checked the front and sides. No one had been there since he left it. Okay. Inside, he made a fried egg and onion sandwich, and wolfed it down. The anger was growing. The cops would get them all if they didn't hang together. He'd done his part.

He picked up the phone, thought about it, put it down, got in his truck, drove to the station, parked and walked across the highway to the Duck Inn. There was a wall phone between the men's and women's restrooms, and he dropped a quarter.

The Iceman answered.

"This is Russ. We gotta talk."

"I heard you were in jail," the Iceman said.

"I bailed out. Where can we get together?"

"I don't think that's a good idea, Russ. I think we better . . ."

"Fuck what you think," Harper snarled. His voice had gone up and he looked quickly back toward the bar and dropped his voice again. "We gotta make some contacts. If anybody talks to the cops, if anybody cracks, we're all going down. They know about the Schoeneckers. We gotta figure out a way to find them, tell them to stay lost. I'll call Doug."

"Doug's gone. I don't know where," said the Iceman.

"Ah, Jesus. Well, they don't know about him. Maybe that's best. But listen: the cops don't have shit on anybody at this point. But if just one of us talks . . ."

"Listen. Maybe . . . you know yellow-hair?" asked the Iceman. "You know who I mean?"

"Yeah?"

"She's alone at her place. Why don't you stop by around four o'clock? I can get away for a while."

"See you then," Harper said and hung up. He walked back out to the bar, climbed onto a barstool. The heavyset bartender was wiping the counter with a rag; he had slicked-down hair, a handlebar mustache, and rode with the Woods Runners M.C. The mustard stains on his apron were turning brown. "Gimme a Miller Lite, Roy," Harper said.

"Don't want your trade, Russ," the bartender said, concentrating on his rag. There were three other men in the bar, and they all went quiet.

"What?"

"I said I don't want your trade. I don't want you in here no more." Now the bartender looked up at him. He had small black eyes, underlined with scar tissue.

"You're telling me my money's no good?" Harper pulled a handful of dollar bills from his pocket, slapped them on the bar.

"Not in here it ain't," the bartender said.

"I HATE THE SONOFABITCH," the yellow-haired girl said. She sucked smoke from her mouth up her nostrils, looking cat-eyed sideways at the Iceman. "What're we going to do?"

"Well, the first thing is, he might of cut a deal with the county attorney," the Iceman said. He was sitting on the couch with a silver beer can in his hand. "He might be wearing a wire."

HARPER PULLED INTO the driveway at the yellow-haired girl's house at five minutes to four. The sky to the west was shiny-silver, but the sun was hidden behind the thin overcast. Cold. He shivered as he got out of the truck. The Iceman's truck was already there, with an empty snowmobile trailer behind it. Harper frowned, stopped to listen. He could hear the music coming from the broken-down double-wide. Jim used to listen to it. Heavy Metal. Thump-thump.

The Iceman's snowmobile was sitting next to the house. Harper walked around it, knocked on the door. A little tingle, now: the yellow-haired girl was a little skinny for his tastes, but she had all the right sockets. He waited a moment, irritated, and pounded on the door.

The yellow-haired girl answered. "Come on in," she said, pulling the door back. Harper nodded, stepped inside, and wiped his feet on the square of carpet next to the door. The house smelled of burnt cooking oil and French fries, fatty meat and onions. "He's in the can," she said.

Harper wiped his feet, and as the yellow-haired girl backed away, caught her by the arm. "I'm gonna want some pussy," he said.

"Whatever," she said, shrugging. She backed into the front room, pulling him along, smiling, tongue on her upper lip. Harper went along, caught by her . . .

And the Iceman was there with a shotgun, the muzzle only a foot from Harper's face.

"What?" Harper blurted.

The Iceman put his finger to his lips, said, "Do it," to the girl. She stepped closer to him, unzipped his parka, pulled it off his shoulders, patted it down. Harper watched for a moment, confused, then said, "Oh. You think . . ."

The Iceman waggled the shotgun at his head, and Harper shut up, but relaxed.

"Shirt," whispered the yellow-haired girl. She unbuttoned his shirt, pulled it off. Untied his boots, pulled them free, looked inside. Unzipped his pants, pulled them down, pulled them off.

"As long as you're down there," Harper joked.

The Iceman half-smiled. The yellow-haired girl pulled down his underpants, then pulled them back up. Lifted his t-shirt, pulled it down. "Don't see nothing," she said.

"Okay," the Iceman said. This had worked with the priest. People *want* to believe. He kept the shotgun on Harper's skull. "Now, Russ, we want to talk, but we're not sure you didn't cut a deal. We're just trying to be careful. We want you to sit down on that couch and Ginny's gonna put a little tape around your hands and ankles."

"Bullshit she is." Harper was wearing nothing but his underwear and socks.

"I got the gun and I'm scared," the Iceman said. He blurted it out—let his voice rise and break. "If anything cracks, I'll go to prison forever. You could handle prison, Russ, but I'd die there. Man, I'm scared shitless."

"You don't need no tape," Harper said. He went to the couch and sat down. The shotgun tracked him. "Anyway, gimme my pants."

"We need to tape you up," the Iceman insisted. "I gotta go outside and see if anybody came with you. You coulda made a deal."

"I didn't make no deal."

"Then the tape ain't gonna hurt, is it?"

Harper stared at the Iceman. The shotgun barrel never wavered. He finally shrugged. "All right, you motherfucker."

The yellow-haired girl was there with a roll of duct tape. "Cross your feet," she said.

"You're gettin' kinda bossy, ya little cunt," Harper said. But he crossed his feet. She taped them in a minute.

"Now your hands," she said. Harper looked at the gun, shrugged, and crossed his hands. "Behind you."

"Goddammit."

When he was taped, she stood up and looked at the Iceman. "Got him," she said.

"Go check," the Iceman said, tipping his head toward the door. "Go a half-mile up the road, both ways."

"What . . ." Harper began.

"Shut up," said the Iceman.

"Listen, motherfucker . . ."

The Iceman stepped close to him and hit him with the stock of the shotgun. The blow caught Harper on the ear and knocked him off the couch.

"You mother—" Harper groaned. He struggled to get up. The Iceman put a foot on his head and pressed. Harper thrashed, but the Iceman rode him, giggling. The girl pulled on a snowmobile suit, boots, ran out the door and started the snowmobile. She was back in five minutes.

"Nobody out there," she said.

"Is the tape strong enough to hold him?" the Iceman asked. He was sitting on Harper's head, Harper cursing weakly.

"That's all I got except for some of that paper tape," the yellow-haired girl said. Then brightened. "There's some wire that Rosie was gonna use for clothesline."

"Get it. And some pliers."

They wrapped the soft steel wire around Harper's wrists, and the yellow-haired girl turned it until Harper started to scream. "Fuckin' hurts, don't it," she said to him. She took three more turns, saw blood.

"Careful," the Iceman said. "Cops look for blood." Blood is evidence.

She nodded, and carefully wired his feet, wrapping it all the way to his knees. "That's got it," she said.

The Iceman stood up. Harper lay still for a moment, then tried to get to his knees. When he was halfway up, the Iceman kicked him in the middle of the back, and he pitched over on his face. "Motherfucker . . ."

"Hurts, don't it," the yellow-haired girl said, squatting next to him so she could look in his eyes. His eyelids flickered, showing the first sign of real fear. She reached down into his underpants. "You know what I think I'll do?" she asked playfully. "I think I'll get a knife and cut your dick off. How'd you like that?"

The Iceman, climbing into his snowmobile suit, said, "We don't have time to fuck around. You know how to get there?"

"Meet you in ten minutes," she said, intense, excited.

"Take it easy in the dark," the Iceman said.

Harper was thrashing on the floor again, managed to roll onto his back, tried to sit up. He was bleeding from his nose. The Iceman stooped, caught the wires between his ankles, and dragged him across the room, through the front door, down the porch. The yellow-haired girl was on the Iceman's snowmobile, waved, and pulled away. Harper's head banged off the stoop, and the Iceman pulled him through the snow to Harper's own truck, picked him up with some effort, and threw him in the back. Then he went back inside, gathered up Harper's clothes, got the truck keys, and went back out.

THE TRIP TO THE sandpit took seven or eight minutes. The Iceman took the right down to the pit, pulled off the road into the area beaten down by deputies' trucks when they'd found the Mueller kid. He climbed out, walked around in back, dropped the tailgate, and jerked Harper out of the back, letting him fall to the ground.

"You still alive?" he asked as Harper groaned. The temperature was below zero; in his underwear, Harper wouldn't last long. The Iceman dragged him around into the truck headlights as a snowmobile curved in from the trail. The yellow-haired girl stopped beside the truck and got down.

Harper, on his back, his face a mask of blood, spit once and then croaked, "You kill Jim?"

"Yup. Enjoyed it," the Iceman said. "Fucked him first."

"Thought you might of," Harper said. He thrashed for a moment, then began to weep, his body heaving. The Iceman walked back to the snowmobile, pulled his snowshoes off the rack, stepped into them and clipped them over his toes.

The yellow-haired girl was standing over Harper, watching him, her hand in her pocket.

"Got your gun?" the Iceman asked.

"Yup." She'd had it in her hand, and she pulled it out of her pocket.

"So shoot him."

"Me?" Harper tried to roll, but just managed to get facedown. She stared in fascination at the back of his head.

"Sure. It's a rush. Here." The Iceman stepped back from Harper, bent, grabbed his feet and rolled him in place until Harper was faceup again. Harper tried to sit up, but the Iceman stepped on his chest, pushing him flat.

"C'mon," Harper groaned. He saw the gun in the yellow-haired girl's hand. "C'mon—the cocksucker killed your school friends."

"Weren't no friends of mine. And besides, you're the one who just had to fuck me in the ass and hurt me. You remember that, Russ Harper? Me hurtin' and you laughin' ?" She looked at the Iceman. "Where should I shoot him?"

"In the head's best," the Iceman said.

She leaned forward with the gun, holding it two feet from Harper's forehead. He closed his eyes, squeezed them. When she didn't pull the trigger, he said, "Fuck you then. Fuck you."

She still didn't pull the trigger, and he opened his eyes. As they opened, she pulled it, and the bullet hit in the left side of the forehead. He groaned, started to thrash.

"Again," said the Iceman. "Do it again."

She fired twice more, one bullet going through Harper's left eye, the other through the bridge of his nose. The second bullet killed him. She fired the third because it felt good. The gun snapped in her hand, like a gun should. She could feel the power going out.

"How's that feel?" the Iceman asked. Harper was still in the snow, his head at an odd angle; the blood running down his face looked purely black in the headlight.

"God . . . that was intense," said the yellow-haired girl. She knelt to look at Harper's face, squeezed his nose, then looked up at the Iceman. "Now what?"

"Now I carry him into the woods where they won't find him right away, and then I drive his truck out onto Welsh Lake by the fish shacks and leave it there. You pick me up."

"If we get another one, can I . . . ?"

"We'll see," the Iceman said, looking down at Harper. There was very little blood. "If you're good, maybe," the Iceman said. And he started to giggle.

ON SUNDAY, LUCAS and Weather slept late. For Weather, that was nine o'clock. After that, she was up, humming around the house, and at ten o'clock he gave up and got out of bed.

"There won't be much to do," she said. "Let's rent some skis and get outside."

"Let me check downtown. If nothing's happening, we could go out this afternoon."

"Good. I can go down to the Super-Valu and do some shopping. See you back here for lunch."

CARR WAS SITTING IN his office, alone. When Lucas looked in, he said, "Harper's gone."

"Goddammit," Lucas said. "When?"

"We never even saw him once," Carr said. "Every time we check, nobody home. Nobody at the gas station. No truck. I put out a bulletin."

· "We should have found a way to keep him inside," Lucas said.

"Yeah. What're you going to do?"

"Read the paper on the case, hang around. Wait. See if I can figure out some other button to push. Nothing on the Schoeneckers?"

"I'd bet they're dead," Carr said. His voice was flat, as though he didn't care.

Climpt came by just before noon. "Not a damn thing going on," he said. "I was back out at the Schoeneckers', nothing there."

"Why'd he kill the priest?" Lucas asked half to himself.

"Don't know," Climpt said.

"There are about three or four knots in this thing," Lucas said. "If we could just unravel one of them, if we could find the Schoeneckers, or break Harper, figure out why Bergen was killed. If we could figure out that time problem when the LaCourts were killed."

"Or the picture," Climpt said. "You got that copy?"

"Yeah." Lucas dug his wallet out of his pants pocket, unfolded the picture, passed it to Climpt, who peered at it.

"Beats the shit out of me," he said after a minute. "There's nothing here."

Lucas took it back, looked at it, shook his head. The adult male in the picture might be anyone.

That afternoon Lucas and Weather rented cross-country skis and ran a ten-kilometer loop through the national forest. At the end of it, Weather, breathing hard, said, "You're in shape."

"You can get in shape if you don't have anything to do," he said.

On Monday, Weather got up before first light. A morning person, she said cheerfully, as Lucas tried to sleep. All surgeons are. "Then if you've got two or three surgeries in a day, the hospital can fit them on one nursing shift. One surgical tech, one anesthesiologist, one circulating nurse. Keeps the costs down."

"Yeah, surgeons are famous for that," Lucas mumbled. "Go the fuck away."

"You didn't say that last night," she said. But Lucas pulled the bed covers over his head. She bent over him, pulled the blanket down, kissed him on the temple, and pulled the cover back up and walked out, humming.

Five minutes later she was back. She whispered, "You awake?"

"Yes."

"Rusty's here to take me down to the hospital," she said. "I checked the TV weather. There's another storm coming up from the southwest and we could get hit. They say it should start late tonight or early tomorrow. I'm outa here."

Lucas made it down to the courthouse at nine o'clock, yawning, face braced by the cold. The sky overhead was sunny, but a finger of slate-colored cloud hung off to the southwest, like smoke from a distant volcano. Dan Jones, the newspaper editor, was just climbing out of his Bronco as Lucas got out of his truck and they walked up to the sheriff's department together.

"So Bergen's not the guy?" he asked.

"I don't think so. We should hear something from Milwaukee today."

"If he's not the guy, how long before you get him?" Jones asked.

"Something'll break," Lucas said. The words sounded hollow. "Something'll give. I'd be surprised if it was a week."

"Will the FBI help?"

"Sure. We can always use extra resources," Lucas said.

"I meant *really* . . . off the record."

Lucas looked at him and said, "If a reporter screws me one time, I never talk to him again."

"I wouldn't screw you," Jones said.

Lucas looked him in the eyes for a moment, then nodded. "All right. The goddamn FBI couldn't find a Coke can in a six-pack of Budweiser. They're not bad guys—well, some of them are—but most of them are basically bureaucrats, scared to death they'll fuck up and get a bad personnel report. So they don't do anything. They're frozen. I suggested some computer stuff they could do and they jumped at it. High-tech, nothing to foul up, don't have to go outdoors."

"What'll break it? What are you looking at?"

"Still off the record?" Lucas asked.

"Sure."

"I can't figure out why Bergen was killed. He was involved right from the first day, so there must be something about him. He was seen leaving the La-Courts', admitted it, but they couldn't have been alive when he left. Or if they were, something's seriously out of whack. We've gone back to the firemen who saw him, and they're both solid, and there's no reason to think that they're lying. Something's screwed up and we don't know what. If I can figure that out . . ." Lucas shook his head, thinking.

"What else?"

"That picture I showed you. We think the killer was looking for it, but there's nothing in it," Lucas said. "Maybe he just hasn't seen it and doesn't know the top of his body's cut off. But that's hard to believe, 'cause it was a Polaroid."

"You need a better print than the one you're looking at," Jones said.

"The original was destroyed. So was the what-cha-callit, not the stick-up . . ." Jones grinned. "The pasteup?"

"Yeah, the pasteup," Lucas said. "They were shoved into a shredder and sent out to the landfill, like six months ago."

"What about the offset negative?"

"The what?" Lucas asked.

CARR WAS UNHAPPY: ". . . I don't want you leaving. Too much is going on," he said. He hunched over his desk, head down. A man confused, perhaps desperate. Mourning.

"It's the only thing I've got," Lucas said. "What am I supposed to do, go interview more school kids?"

"Then fly," Carr said. "You can be there in an hour and a half."

"Man, I hate planes," Lucas said. He could feel his stomach muscles contract at the thought of flying.

"How about a helicopter?" Lacey asked.

"A helicopter? I can deal with a helicopter," Lucas said, nodding.

"We can have one at the airport in twenty minutes," Lacey said.

"Get it," said Lucas, stepping toward the door.

"I want you back here tonight, whatever happens," Carr called after him. "We got a storm coming in."

Climpt had been standing in the doorway, smoking. "Take care of Weather," Lucas said.

DOMEIER, THE MILWAUKEE COP, had the day off. Lucas left a message, and the Milwaukee watch commander said somebody would try to reach him.

The Grant Airport was a single Quonset-hut hangar at the west end of a short blacktopped runway. The hangar had a windsock on the roof, an office, and plane-sized double doors. The manager told him to pull his truck inside, where four small planes huddled together, smelling of engine oil and gasoline.

"Hoser'll be here in five minutes. I just talked to him on the radio," the manager said. The manager was named Bill, an older man with a thick shock of steel-gray hair and blue eyes so pale they were almost white. "He'll put down right outside the window there."

"He's a pretty good pilot?" Lucas could handle helicopters because they didn't need runways. You could get down in a helicopter.

"Oh, yeah. Learned to fly in Vietnam, been flying ever since." The manager sucked his false teeth, his hands in his overall pockets, staring out the window. "You want some coffee?"

"A cup'd be good," Lucas said.

"Help yourself, over by the microwave."

A Pyrex pot of acidic-looking coffee sat on a hot plate next to some paper cups. Lucas poured a cup, took a sip, thought *nasty*, and the manager said, "If you get back late, the place'll be locked up. I'll give you a key for the doors so you can get your truck out. Here he comes."

The chopper was white, with a rakish HOSER AIR scrawled on the side, and kicked up a hurricane of snow as it put down on the pad. Lucas got the door key from the manager, and then, ducking, scurried under the chopper blades and the pilot popped the door open. The pilot wore an olive-drab helmet, black glasses, and a brush-cut mustache. He shouted over the beat of the blades, "You got pac boots?"

"Back in the truck."

"Better go get 'em. The heater ain't working quite right."

They took off three minutes later, Lucas pulling on the pac boots. "What's wrong with the heater?" he shouted.

"Don't know yet," the pilot shouted back. "The whole goddamn chopper's a piece of shit."

"Glad to hear it."

The pilot smiled, his teeth improbably white and even. "Little pilot joke," he said.

A HALF HOUR AFTER takeoff, the pilot got a radio call, answered, and then said, "You'll have a guy waiting for you. Domeier?"

"Yeah, good."

They put down at a general aviation airport at the north end of the city. The pilot would wait until ten o'clock, he said. "Got that storm coming in. Ten o'clock shouldn't be a problem, but if you were as late as midnight, I might not get out at all."

"I'll call," Lucas promised, pulling off the pac boots and slipping on his shoes.

"I'll be around. Call the pilots' lounge. There's a guy waving at us, and I think he means you."

Domeier was waiting at the gate, hands in his pockets, chewing gum.

"Didn't expect to see you," Lucas said. "I was told you were off."

"Overtime," Domeier said. "I got a daughter down at Northwestern, exploring her potentialities, so I need the fuckin' work. What're we doing?"

"Talking to Bobby McLain again," Lucas said. "About a thing called an offset negative."

McLAIN WAS AT HOME, with a woman in a red party dress. The woman sat on a couch, eating popcorn from a microwave bag. She had dark hair and matched her hair color with too much eye liner.

". . . suppose he could have it," McLain said. "He'll kill me if I send you out there, though."

"Bobby, you know what we're dealing with," Lucas said. "You know what could happen."

"Jeez . . ."

"What could happen?" asked the woman on the couch.

"Some people have been killed. If Bobby doesn't help us out, you could say he's an accomplice," Domeier said. He shrugged, and looked sorry about it.

The woman's mouth hung open for a minute, then she looked at Bobby. "Jesus Christ, you're dragging your feet about Zeke? The guy would trade you in for a fifty-watt light bulb."

"Zeke?" said Lucas.

"Yeah. He's a teacher out at the vo-tech," the woman said. She tried a winning smile, unsuccessfully. "He does all our printing."

"At the vo-tech?"

"Sure. He's a teacher there. He's got all this great equipment. And if we're not using it, it just sits there all night, doing nothing."

"Who buys the paper?" Domeier asked.

McLain's eyes shifted. "Mmm, that's part of his price."

"Part of the price? You mean the vo-tech is buying your printing paper?"

McLain shrugged. "The price is right."

McLAIN DROVE THE grape-colored van; Lucas and Domeier followed him west through the suburbs. The vo-tech was a one-story orange-brick building surrounded by parking lots. A cluster of thirty or forty crows was settled around a heap of snow at one end of the building, like lost lumps of coal.

McLain parked and used an electric lift to get himself out the side door of the van. He was in a power chair this time, and rolled along in front of them, up a ramp, and down a long cold hallway lined with student lockers. Zeke was alone in his classroom. When McLain rolled through the door, he straightened, started a smile. When Lucas and Domeier followed McLain through the door, the smile vanished.

"Sorry," McLain said. "I hope we can maintain our business relationship."

Domeier said, "Milwaukee PD, Zeke."

. . .

"I just . . . I just . . . I needed . . ." Zeke waved his hand, unable to find the right word, and then said, "Money."

They were standing in his office, a cool cubicle of yellow-painted concrete block, with a plastic-laminated desk and two file cabinets. Zeke was short and balding, wore his hair long and combed it in oily strands over his bald spot. He wore a checked sport coat and his hands shook when he talked. "I just . . . I just . . . Should I get a lawyer?"

"You gotta right . . ." Domeier started.

Lucas broke in: "I don't care about your goddamn printing business. I just don't have time to fuck around. I want the goddamn negatives or I'll put some handcuffs on you and we'll drag you outa the school by your fuckin' hair, and then we'll get a search warrant and we'll tear this place apart and your house and any other goddamn thing we can find. You show me the fuckin' negatives and I'm gone. You and Domeier can make any kind of deal you want."

Zeke looked at Domeier, and when the Milwaukee cop rolled his eyes up to the ceiling, he said, "I keep the negatives at home."

"So let's go," Lucas said.

"How about me?" McLain asked.

"Take off," said Domeier.

Halfway to his house, Zeke, in the backseat of Domeier's Dodge, began to weep. "They're gonna fire me," he gasped. "You're gonna put me in jail. I'll get raped."

"Do you print for more than Bobby McLain or is he the only one?" Domeier asked, looking at him in the rearview mirror.

"He's the only one," Zeke said, his body shuddering.

"Shit. If there was more, you had some names, maybe we could work something out."

The weeping stopped and Zeke's voice cleared. "Like what?"

AN AGING BLACK LABRADOR with rheumy eyes met them at the door.

"If I went to jail, what'd happen to Dave?" Zeke asked Domeier.

The dog wagged his tail when his name was mentioned. Domeier shook his head and said, "Jesus Christ."

The dog watched as they went through a closet full of offset negatives. The negatives were filed in oversized brown envelopes, with the name of the publication scrawled in the corner. They found the right set and the right negative, and Zeke held it up to the light. "Yup, this is it. Looks pretty sharp."

They trooped back to the vo-tech. The printer was the size of a Volkswagen, but the first print was done in ten minutes. Zeke stripped it out and handed it to Domeier.

"That's as good as I can get it," he said. "It's still a halftone, so it won't be as sharp as a regular photograph."

Domeier glanced at it and handed it to Lucas, saying, "Same old shit. You wasted your time."

The print was still black-and-white, but considerably sharper. Lucas put it under a table light and peered at it. A man with an erection and a nude boy in the background. Nothing on the walls.

"The guy's leg looks weird." He took the folded newsprint version out of his pocket. The leg was so washed-out that no detail was visible. "Is this . . . whatever it is . . . is this the picture or is there something wrong with his leg?" Lucas asked.

Zeke brought a photo loupe over to the table, put it on the print, bent over it, moved it. "That's his leg, I think. It looks like it's stitched together or something, like a quilt."

"Goddamn," Lucas said. His throat tightened. "Goddamn. That's why he wants Weather. She must've fixed his leg."

"You got him?" asked Domeier.

"Got something," Lucas said. "Is there a doc around I can talk to?"

"Sure. We can stop at the medical examiner's on the way to the airport. There'll be somebody on duty."

"Can I go home now?" asked Zeke.

"Er, no," Domeier said. "Actually, we gotta go get a truck, the two of us."

"What for?"

"I'm gonna take every fuckin' envelope out of your house, and we're gonna find somebody to print them up for us. And I'm gonna want those names."

Lucas stopped on the way out of the house to call the airport, and got the pilot in the general aviation lounge. "It didn't take long. I'm on my way."

"Hurry. That storm's coming in fast, man," the pilot said. "I want to get out of here quick."

THE ASSISTANT MEDICAL examiner was sitting in his office, feet on his desk, reading a *National Enquirer*.

He nodded at Domeier, looked without interest at Lucas and Zeke. "Breaks my heart, what the younger women have done to the British Royal Family," he said. He balled up the paper and fired it at a wastebasket. "What the fuck do you want, Domeier? More pictures of naked dead women?"

"Actually, I want you to look at my friend's photograph," Domeier said.

Lucas handed the doc the print and said, "Can you tell what's wrong with his leg?"

Zeke asked, "You don't really have pictures of naked dead women, do you?"

The doctor, bent over the photo, muttered, "All the time. If you need some, maybe I can get you a rate." After a minute he straightened and said, "Burns."

"What?"

He flipped the photo across his desk to Lucas. "Your man's been burned. Those are skin grafts."

LUCAS TRIED TO GET Carr or Lacey from the airport; the dispatcher said they were out of touch. He called Weather at home, got a busy signal. The pilot was leaning against the back of a chair, impatiently waiting to go. Lucas waited two minutes, tried again: busy.

"We gotta go, man," the pilot said. Lucas looked out the lounge windows. He could see airplanes circling ten miles out. "It looks pretty clear."

"Man, that storm is coming like a fuckin' train. We're gonna get snowed on as it is."

"Once more . . ." Weather's line was still busy. He punched in the dispatcher's number again: "I'm on my way back. Got something. And if the chopper crashes, a guy named Domeier has the negative. He's with the Milwaukee sex unit."

"If the chopper crashes . . ." the pilot snorted as they walked out of the lounge.

"Got the heater fixed?" Lucas asked.

THEY LIFTED OUT OF Milwaukee at seven o'clock, six degrees above zero, clear skies, Domeier standing at the gate with Zeke until the chopper was off the ground. Zeke waved.

"Glad you called," the pilot said. He grinned but he didn't look happy. "I was getting nervous about waiting until ten. The storm's already through the Twin Cities. The weather service says they're getting three to four inches of snow an hour, and it's supposedly headed right up our way."

"You're not out of Grant, though," Lucas said.

"Nope, Park Falls. But we're both gonna get it."

The ground lights were sharp as diamonds in the dry cold air, a long sparkling sweep north and south along the Lake Michigan waterfront, fed by the long, living snakes of the interstates. They headed northwest, past the lesser glitter of Fond du Lac and Oshkosh, individual house lights defining the blankness of Lake Winnebago. Later, they could see the distant glow from Green Bay far off to the east; to the west, there was nothing, and Lucas realized that they'd lost the stars and were now under cloud cover.

"Do any good?" the pilot asked.

"Maybe."

"When you catch the sonofabitch, you oughta just blow him away. Do us all a favor."

They caught the first hint of snow twenty miles from Grant. "No sweat," said the pilot. "From here we're on cruise control."

They settled down five minutes later, Lucas ducking under the blades, fumbling for the key to the airport Quonset. As soon as he was inside, he could hear the chopper's rotors pick up, and a moment later it was gone.

He rolled out of the Quonset, locked the door, and started for town. The snow was light, tiny flakes spitting into his windshield, but with authority. This wasn't a flurry, this was the start of something.

Weather's house was lit up, a sheriff's Suburban in the drive. He used the remote to lift the garage door, drove in, parked.

Inside, the house was quiet. "Weather?" No answer. His stomach tightened and he walked through the front room. No sign of trouble. "Hey, Weather?"

Still no answer. He noticed that the curtain was caught in the sliding door, walked over to it, and turned on the porch light. There were fresh tracks across the snow-covered deck. He pushed the door open.

And heard her laughing, and felt something go loose in his knees. She was all right. He cupped his hands around his mouth. "Weather . . ."

"Yeah, yeah, we're coming."

She came up the lake bank on skis, out of the night; fifty feet behind her, floundering, lathered with sweat, Climpt followed.

"Gene's never been on skis before," she said, laughing. "I've been embarrassing him."

"Never fuckin' again," Climpt rasped as he toiled behind in her tracks. "I'm too old for this shit. My goddamn crotch feels like it's gonna fall off. Christ, I need a cigarette."

Weather's smile faded. "Henry Lacey called. He said you might have something."

"Yeah. Come on in and get your skis off," Lucas said. He started to turn back to the house, but first stooped and kissed her on the nose.

"Now, *that's* embarrassing," Climpt said. "On the nose?"

LUCAS SHOOK THE PHOTO out of the manila envelope onto the kitchen counter and Weather bent over it. "Better picture," she said. She looked at it, then up at Lucas, puzzled. "What?"

"Look at the guy's leg. It looks like a quilt. I'm told they might be skin grafts."

Weather peered at the photo, looked up at Lucas, stunned, looked at the photo again, then turned to Climpt. "Jesus, it's Duane."

"Duane?" asked Lucas. "The fireman?"

"Yeah—Duane Helper. The fireman who saw Father Phil. He was at the station . . . how'd he do that?"

CARR HAD SPENT THE afternoon at a motel, but still looked desperately weary. He was unshaven, his hair uncombed, his eyes swollen as though he'd been crying. He looked curiously at Weather and then back to Lucas. "What'd you get?"

Lacey came in just as Carr asked the question, and Lucas pushed the door shut behind him.

"Got a better picture," Lucas said, handing it to him across the desk. "If you look really close—you couldn't see it in the newsprint picture—you can see that his leg looks patched up. Those are skin grafts. Weather says it's Duane Helper."

"Duane? How could it be . . . ?"

"We've been talking, Gene and I, and we think the first thing we gotta do, tonight, is pick up Dick Westrom," Lucas said. "We don't know what he has to do with it, except that he backs up Helper's story. We put him on the grill. If we need to, we lock him up until we find out more about Helper."

"Why don't we just grab him? Helper?" Carr asked.

"We've been thinking about a trial," Lucas said, tipping his head toward Climpt. Climpt was rolling an unlit cigarette around his mouth. "Helper dropped the gun and knife on Bergen. A defense attorney will use that—he'll put Bergen on trial. All we've got is a bad picture, and the only witness we know for sure is Jim Harper, and he's dead. Nothing on the Schoeneckers?"

"No. Can't find Harper either," Lacey said. "They dropped off the earth."

"Or they're out in the goddamn snow somewhere, with coyotes chewing on them," Climpt said.

"Dammit." Lucas bit his thumbnail, thinking, then shook his head, looked at Carr. "Shelly, I really think we gotta get Westrom in here. We gotta figure out what happened."

Carr nodded. "Then let's do it. You want to go get him?"

"You should," Lucas said. "One way or another, we're gonna break this thing. Since you're an elected sheriff . . ."

"Right." Carr took a set of keys out of his pocket, opened his bottom desk drawer, and pulled out a patrol-style gun belt with a revolver. He stood up and strapped it on. "Haven't seen this thing in months. Let's go get him."

CARR, CLIMPT, AND LUCAS went after Westrom while Lacey and Weather waited at Carr's office. "We'll bring him in the front so we don't have to go by dispatch," Carr told Lacey as they left. "We want to keep this quiet. We'll call you before we start back so you can open the door for us."

"Okay. What about his wife?" Lacey asked.

Carr looked at Lucas. "We oughta ask her to come along," Lucas said. "I mean, if Westrom's in this with Helper, then his wife's probably involved at some level. If she tipped Helper off, we'd be screwed."

"What if she doesn't want to come?" Carr asked.

Lucas shrugged. "Then we bust her. You can always apologize later."

Westrom was wearing blue flannel pajamas when he came to the door. He first peeked out, saw Carr, frowned, opened the inner door and pushed open the storm door. "Shelly? What's going on? Nothing's happened to Tommy?"

"No, nothing happened to Tommy," Carr said. He stepped forward, into the house, and Lucas and Climpt pressed in behind them. "We need to talk to you, Dick," Carr said. "You better get dressed."

If Westrom was guilty of anything, Lucas decided, he deserved an Academy Award for acting. He was getting angry. "Why dressed? Shelly, what the hell is going on?"

Westrom's wife, a small woman with pink plastic curlers in her hair, stepped into the room, wearing a robe. "Shelly?"

"You better get dressed, too, Janice. We need you to come down to the courthouse. We'll talk about it there."

"Well, what's it about?" Westrom asked.

"About the LaCourt killings," Carr said. "We've got more questions."

WHILE THE WESTROMS WERE dressing, Carr asked, "What do you think?"

"They don't know what's happening," Lucas said. "Who's Tommy?"

"That's their boy," said Climpt. "He goes to college down in Eau Claire."

THE WESTROMS THOUGHT they wanted a lawyer. And they didn't want Weather in the room. "What's she here for?"

"She's another witness," Carr said, glancing at Weather.

"About a lawyer . . ."

"And we'll get you a lawyer if you really want one. But honestly, if you haven't done anything, you won't need one, and it'll be a big expense," Carr said. "You know me, Dick. I won't bust you just for show."

"We didn't do anything," Westrom protested. His wife, in jeans and a yellow sweatshirt, kept looking between Carr and her husband.

"What happened the night of the fire?" Lucas asked. "You were cooking and Duane was there, and he was looking out the window . . ."

"We've told you a hundred times," Westrom insisted. "Honest to God, that's what happened."

Lucas stared at him for a moment, then said, "Did you actually see Father Phil's Jeep? I mean . . ."

"Yeah, I saw it."

". . . could you have identified it from where you were standing if Helper hadn't been there? Could you have said, 'That's Father Bergen's Jeep'?"

Westrom stared down at the floor for a moment, thinking, then said, "Well, no. I mean, I saw the lights as it went by—and Father Phil admitted it was him."

"Like regular truck lights?" Lucas asked.

"Yeah."

"Bergen was pulling a trailer," Lucas said suddenly.

Westrom frowned. "I didn't see any trailer lights," he said.

Weather had been looking at Lucas and she picked up on him. "If you don't mind me asking, Dick, what were you doing before you were cooking? Just hanging out?"

Lucas glanced up at her and nodded, cracked a small smile. Westrom said,

"Well, kinda. I came on, took a nap, then Duane called and I went down . . ."

"How long were you sleeping?" Lucas asked intently.

"An hour maybe." Westrom said. He looked around at them. "What?"

"Do you usually take a nap when you go on duty at the fire station?"

"Well, yeah."

"How often? What percentage of times?"

"Well, it's just my routine. I get out there around five, take a nap for an hour or so. Nothing to do. Duane's not much company. Maybe we watch a little TV."

"Duane's got a snowmobile?"

"Arctic Cat," said Westrom.

Lucas nodded, glanced at Carr. "That's it. It took timing, but that's it."

Carr leaned across his desk. "Dick, Janice, I hate to inconvenience you, but we'd like you to stay here overnight—for your own protection. You don't have to stay in jail—we could find an empty office and put some bedding inside—but we want you safe until we can arrest him."

Westrom looked at Lucas, at Carr, and then at his wife. Janice Westrom spoke up for the first time since she arrived at the courthouse. "We'll do anything you want if you think he might come looking for us," she said. She shivered. "Anything you want."

WHEN THEY WERE GONE, Lucas said, "You want me to run it down?"

"Go ahead," said Carr, leaning back in his chair. He looked almost sleepy.

Lucas said, "Duane Helper finds out somehow that Lisa LaCourt has a picture of him with the Harper kid. He's seen the original, so he knows that his skin grafts are showing. But he doesn't know that the photo in the paper is so bad that his grafts are washed out of the picture. Or maybe he does know, but he's scared to death that once a cop sees the newsprint copy, we'll find a better one.

"Anyway, Westrom shows up for his shift at the firehouse and goes upstairs to bed. Helper climbs on his sled, goes on down to the LaCourts'. Someplace along the line, he sees Father Bergen, probably as Bergen leaves the LaCourts'.

"He kills the LaCourts, looks for the photo, doesn't find it, sets the place to burn—Crane tells me that he used the water heater to delay the fire—and he heads back to the firehouse. That's a three-minute trip on a snowmobile if you hurry."

"And dammit, we should have thought about that fire delay, about a fireman knowing that kind of stuff."

Climpt picked it up: "He gets back, parks the sled, pulls off his snowmobile suit, wakes up Westrom for dinner . . ."

Weather: ". . . He sees a car go by, any car, and says, 'There goes Father Bergen.' Westrom sees the lights, has no reason to think it's not Father Bergen, later has it confirmed that it was . . ."

"And it all gives Helper what he thought would be the perfect alibi," Lucas said. "He's in the firehouse, with a witness, when the alarm goes off. With the storm, he figures the priest won't know exactly how long it took him to get from one place to another, so that covers any little time problems. And he's right. He's only messed up because Shelly sees that the snow is too deep on Frank LaCourt's body, and then Crane finds the delay mechanism on the water heater."

Climpt: "He killed Phil because Phil kept insisting that the LaCourts were alive when he left, just like they were. And if they were alive, then the firemen had to be wrong . . . and if we looked at the firemen . . ."

"We still couldn't have resolved it," Lucas said. "We needed the picture."

"But we figured him out," Carr growled. "Now how're we gonna get the sonofabitch?"

DUANE HELPER—THE ICEMAN—sat at the picnic table with the two lab techs, halfheartedly playing three-handed stud poker for dimes.

"Goddamn Jerry's had four hands in a row, Duane, ya gotta *do* something." The older of the two crime-lab people dealt the cards. They had almost finished the LaCourt house, they said. They'd wrung it out. Two more days, or three, and they'd be done. When they were gone, and the possibility of more developments began to fade, and the killing stopped, interest in the case would dwindle. He had to reach the Schoeneckers, but he'd thought about it. Before they came back, they'd almost surely call to talk. Bergen dead, Harper dead.

He'd done it.

The Iceman listened and played his cards.

A truck pulled into the parking area, doors slammed. Climpt came in, stamping snow off his boots. The Minneapolis cop, Davenport, was behind him, shoulders hunched against the cold. He hadn't shaved, and looked big-eyed, too thin.

Outside, in the early-morning light, snow swirled around the fire building. The storm had begun in earnest just before dawn, thunder booming through the forest, the snow coming in waves. Almost nothing was moving on the highway except snowplows.

"Wicked out there," Climpt said. His face was wet with snow. He took off his gloves and wiped his eyebrows with the back of his hand. "Understand you got some coffee."

"Help yourself," said the Iceman. He pointed at an oversized coffee urn on a bench behind the lab people. "You out at the house?"

"Yeah. They're giving up for the day, tying everything down, getting back to town before the snow gets too bad," Lucas said. He looked at the techs. "Crane says to get your asses back there."

"Want to get my ass back to Madison," said the older of the two techs.

"Find a warm coed," said the younger one. "One more hand."

Davenport peeled off his parka and brushed off the snow. He nodded to the Iceman, took a cup of coffee from Climpt, and sat on the end of the picnic table bench.

"Anything new on the prints?" he asked.

"Nope. We're pretty much cleaned up," said the older tech. He dealt a round of three cards. "We've shipped in a few hundred sets, but hell, we printed Bergen after he croaked, and we can't even find a match to him. And we *know* he was there."

The younger tech chipped in: "The guy used a .44 and a corn-knife, took them with him. If it wasn't Bergen, he wiped the handles. And it was so cold, he had to have gloves with him. He probably just put them on after he chopped the kid."

Exactly, thought the Iceman. He sat and polished.

"Yeah. Goddammit." Lucas looked into the coffee cup, then sipped from it.

"You heard about the autopsy on Father Bergen?" Climpt asked. He was leaning against the cupboard by the coffeepot.

"There were some problems, I guess," the tech said. He flipped out another set of cards. "Duane's got ace 'n' shit, George's looking at shit 'n' shit, and I'm queen-jack. I'm in for a dime."

"They couldn't find any chemical traces of gelatin in his stomach. The sleeping pills he supposedly took with the booze came in gelatin capsules," Climpt said. "We didn't find any empty caps at the house, so he either flushed them or somebody dumped them in the booze and forced him to drink it . . . and forgot about the capsules."

The Iceman hadn't thought about the capsules. He'd flushed them, right here in the firehouse.

"So what does that mean?" the tech asked. "Sounds like it could go either way—either Bergen flushed them or somebody else did, but we don't know which."

"Yeah, that's right," Climpt said.

The tech ran out another round of cards: "Duane picks up an eight to give him a pair with his ace, George holds with his fours, and I'm looking at a possible straight. Another dime on the jack-queen-nine."

The second tech asked, "How about that picture? Do you any good?"

Lucas brightened. "Yeah. Maybe. Milwaukee found the guy who published the paper. He still had the page negative, and they made a better print. Should have been here today, but with this storm . . . should be here in the morning."

The Iceman sat and listened, as he had for a week, in the center of the only warm public place within miles of the LaCourt house. The cops had dropped in from the first night, looking for a place to sit and gossip.

"Anything in it?" the younger tech asked.

"Won't know until we see it," Lucas said.

"If you find time to look at it," Climpt snorted, burying his nose in his cup. His voice had a certain tone and the two crime techs and the Iceman all looked at Lucas.

Lucas laughed and said, "Yeah. Fuck you, Gene, you're jealous."

Climpt tipped his head at Lucas. "He's seeing—I'm choosing my words carefully—he's seeing one of our local doctors."

"Female, I hope," said the older of the techs.

"No doubt about that," said Climpt. "I wouldn't mind myself."

"Careful, Gene," Lucas said. He glanced at his watch. "We probably ought to get back to town."

The tech was still dealing the round of five-card stud, flipped another ace out to the Iceman. "Whoa, two pair, aces and eights," he said. He flipped over his own cards. "You can have it."

WHEN CLIMPT AND DAVENPORT LEFT, the Iceman stood up and drifted toward the window, watched them as they stopped at the nose of the truck, said a few words, then got in the truck. A moment later they were gone.

"I guess we oughta get back," the older tech said. "Goddamn, a couple more days of this shit and we're outa here."

"If anything can get out of here," said the other man. He went to the window, pulled back a curtain, and looked out. "Jesus, look at it come down."

AFTER THE TECHS HAD GONE, the Iceman sat alone, thinking. *Time to get out*, said a voice at the back of his head. He could start packing his trunk now, be ready to go by dark. With the storm, nobody would be stopping by the firehouse. He could be in Duluth in two hours, Canada in another four. Once across the border, he could lose himself, head north and west out to Alaska.

If he could take down Weather Karkinnen . . . But there'd still be the Schoeneckers and Doug and the others. But they were thousands of miles away. Nobody might ever find them. It could still work.

And besides, he wanted Weather. He could feel her out there, a hostile eminence. She *deserved* to die.

Get out, said the voice.

Kill her, thought the Iceman.

THE WISCONSIN STATE TROOPER had buried himself in a snowdrift across from the fire station. He wore an insulated winter camouflage suit that he'd bought for deer hunting, pac boots, and a camo face mask. He kept a pair of binoculars in a canvas bag with the radio, and a Thermos of hot chocolate in another bag. He'd been in place for two hours, reasonably warm, fairly comfortable.

He'd watched Davenport and Climpt go into the station to nail Helper down. After they'd been inside for a minute, the FBI man, the black guy, jogged up from the back, used a key to go through the access door into the truck bay. Two minutes later the FBI man slipped out and disappeared into the snow. Then Davenport and Climpt pulled out, followed by the crime techs from Madison. Since then, nothing. The trooper had expected immediate action. When it hadn't come, sitting in the drift out of the wind, he'd felt a bit sleepy; the winter storm muffled all sound, dimmed all color, eliminated odors. He unscrewed the top of the Thermos, took a hit of chocolate, screwed the top back on. He was pushing the jug back into his carry sack when he saw movement. The door on the far truck bay, where the FBI man had gone in, was rolling up.

The trooper pulled the radio from the bag, put it to his face: "We got movement," he said. "You hear me?" The radio was unfamiliar, provided by the FBI, all talk scrambled.

We hear you. How's he moving?

"Hang on," the patrolman said. He studied the open door through the binoculars. A moment later Helper bumped out through the door on his snow-mobile, looked right and left, then turned toward the highway.

"He's on the sled," the patrolman said into the radio. "He's moving, he's on the trail down 77. He's coming up toward your post . . . He's not moving too fast . . . wait a minute, he's moving now, he's really taking off."

Davenport, are you monitoring?

"Yes, I heard." Lucas was at the hospital, among the smells of alcohol and disinfectant and the stray whiffs of raw meat and urine. "Are you tracking him?"

We got him, and he's moving your way. The caller was the FBI man who'd provided them with the special handsets and the radio beacons now attached to Helper's sled and truck. *He's coming up on us. We'll let him pass and then try to hang on.*

"We're set here. Keep us posted," Lucas said. He looked at Weather. "He's coming." Lucas pulled the magazine from his .45, checked it. Climpt, who'd been sitting on an examination stool, picked up his Ithaca twelve-gauge and jacked a shell into the chamber. "He ought to be here in twenty minutes."

"If he's coming here," Carr said. The sheriff had buckled on his pistol again, but left it untouched in its holster.

"I got a buck that says he is," Lucas said. He slipped the magazine back into the .45 and slapped it tight with the heel of his hand.

"You're going to kill him, aren't you?" Weather asked.

"We're not trying to kill him," Lucas said levelly. "But he has to make his move."

"I don't see how you won't kill him," Weather said. "If he has a gun in his hand . . ."

"We'll warn him. If he opts to fight, what can we do?"

She thought for a moment, then shook her head. "If we had more time, I could think of something."

"Women shouldn't be involved in this sort of thing," Climpt said.

"Hey, fuck you, Gene," she said harshly.

"Take it easy," Lucas said mildly. He put the .45 up to his face and clicked the safety on and off, on and off, on. He saw the look on her face and said, "Sorry."

"I'm not being silly about this," she said. "Better he dies than anyone else. This ambush just seems so . . . cold."

"We ain't playing patty-cake," Climpt said.

The FBI came back: *He's passing us . . . Okay, he's past, he looked us over pretty good. No chance that we can keep up with him, Jesus, this snow is something else, it's like driving into a funnel . . . He must be doing forty down there in the ditch, he must be flying blind . . . we're doing thirty . . . Manny, he'll be coming up on you in five minutes.*

A second voice, the other FBI man: *Got him on the scope . . . Davenport, we're five minutes out, he's still coming, he's maybe two miles back.*

"Got that," Lucas said. To Climpt, Weather, and Carr: "Get ready. I'll talk to the twins." He ran down the hall, pushed open the double doors at the end of the corridor. Two cops were climbing onto snowmobiles, pistols strapped around their waists, one with a shotgun in a jury-rigged scabbard hung on the side of the sled.

"You been listening?"

"Got it," said one of the cops. Rusty and Dusty. In their helmets they were unidentifiable.

"All right. Stand off behind the lot, there. As soon as he gets off his sled, we'll bring you in. If something happens, be ready to roll. One way or another, we take him."

"Got it."

The two men took off and Lucas ran back down the corridor, clumping along in his boots, zipping his jacket over the body armor. Henry Lacey trotted down the hall toward him.

"Good luck," he called as he passed Lucas.

Carr was hanging up the phone when Lucas got back. "More stuff coming in on the sonofabitch. Lot of stuff from Duluth. He resigned there, just like he told us, but if he hadn't, the cops were gonna get him for ripping off homes after fires. A couple of arson guys think he might have set some of the fires himself."

"Good. The more we can pile up, the better, if there's a trial."

Davenport, you got it right. He's coming, he's past us, he's on the hospital road, he's on the hospital road, we're running parallel down the highway . . . Goddamn, it's hard to see anything out here.

"Shelly, you know where to go. Weather, get your coat on. Tighten up the straps, goddammit." He pulled the adjustments tight on the body armor, helped her with her mountain parka. She'd be cold without her regular jacket, but it'd only be for a minute or two. "You know what we're doing now."

"Pace it out, take it slow, stay with you. As soon as anybody yells, get down. Stay on the ground."

"Right. And everybody knows the panic drill if he decides to come inside." Lucas looked at Climpt and Carr, and they nodded, and Carr gulped and wiped his nose with the back of his hand.

"Nervous?" Lucas asked Weather, trying a smile.

"I'm okay." She swallowed. "Cottonmouth," she said.

EVEN ON A BLIZZARD DAY, there'd be twenty or thirty people in the hospital—nurses, orderlies, maintenance people. Unless Helper had freaked out, he wouldn't try a frontal assault on the building. And he knew that Weather had a deputy as a bodyguard. His only chance was to snipe her with a rifle or to get in close with a pistol or shotgun, shoot it out with her bodyguard, like he'd tried when he ambushed Weather and Bruun. They'd set up Weather's Jeep within a rough circle of cars, they'd given him places to hide, places they could reach with snipers on the roof. They'd show her to him, just long enough.

As soon as he flashed a gun, they'd have him.

He's thirty seconds out.

Anybody see a weapon?

Didn't see a thing when he went by. He didn't show a long gun on the machine.

He's ten seconds out. All right, he's slowing down, he's slowing down. He's stopped right at the entrance to the parking lot. Davenport, you got him?

Lucas put the radio to his mouth, stared through the waiting room window out to the parking lot. He was looking into a bowl of snowflakes. "We can't see a thing from in here, the goddamn snow."

He's still sitting there, can you guys on the roof see anything?

I can see him, he's not moving.

What's he doing?

He's just sitting there.

"Is he coming in?" Weather asked.

"Not yet."

Wait a minute, wait a minute, he's moving . . . He's moving past the lot, he's going past the lot down the hospital road. He's moving slow.

Where's he going?

He's going on past the hospital.

Lucas: "You guys on the sleds, he's coming your way, stay out of sight."

We're up in the woods, don't see him. Where is he?

Still coming your way.

Don't see him.

He's on the road by that gas thing, that natural-gas pump thing, he's just going by.

Wait a minute, we got him, he's moving slow. What do we do?

"Stay right there, let the FBI guys track him," Lucas said.

He's passing us. Boy, you can hardly see out here.

The FBI man's voice came in over the others: "He's stopped. He's stopped. He's two hundred yards behind the hospital, by that big woods."

"Janes' woodlot," Climpt said. "He's gonna come through the woods, sneak in through the back door by the dumpsters."

"That's always locked," Weather said.

"Maybe he's got some way to get in."

He's not moving. Somebody's got to take a look.

Carr, fifty feet away, by radio: *Lucas, if he doesn't move in the next minute or so, I think the guys on the sleds ought to cruise by. If he's just sitting there, they can keep going, like club riders. If he's back in the woods, we ought to know.*

Lucas put the radio to his mouth. "You guys on the sleds—cruise him. Stuff your weapons inside your suits, out of sight. And be careful. Don't stop, keep going. If you see him, just wave."

Lucas turned to Climpt. "We better get set up by the back door. If he comes through, we should be able to see if he's carrying."

You guys on the roof—we might have to turn you around, he may come in the back. One of you go out back right now, keep a lookout.

Got that.

"If we spot him coming in, we could have Weather just walk across the end of the t-corridor," Climpt said. "He'd be able to see her from the door, but he wouldn't have time to react. If he starts running down that way . . ."

They worked it out as they ran to the back of the hospital, Weather and Carr hurrying behind. Henry Lacey, pale-faced, stood by the reception desk with his .38. The nurses had been moved down to the emergency room, where they had concrete walls to huddle behind.

Rusty: *We just passed his sled. He's not here. It looks like he's gone up in the woods. Doesn't look like he's wearing snowshoes, Let's, uh . . .*

There was a moment of silence, then the same voice.

We'll cruise him again.

"What are they doing?" Lucas asked Climpt. "They're not going back . . . ?" He put the radio to his mouth: "What're you doing? Don't go back!"

Just coming back now.

There was a dark, abrupt sound on the radio, a sound like a cough or a bark, and a last syllable from the deputy that might have been . . .

He's . . .

Silence. One second, two. Lucas straining at the radio. Then an anonymous radio voice from the roof.

We got gunfire! We got gunfire from Janes' woodlot! Holy shit, somebody's shooting—somebody's shooting.

WEATHER WAS THE KEY, the Iceman had decided after Davenport and Climpt left, but he couldn't go running off yet. Had to wait for the cops to clear.

He opened the green Army footlocker, took out the top tray, full of cleaning equipment, ammunition, and spare magazines, and looked into the bottom.

Four pistols lay there, two revolvers, two automatics. After a moment's thought he selected the Browning Hi Power 9mm automatic and a double-action Colt Python in .357 Magnum.

The shells were cool but silky, like good machinery can be. He loaded both pistols with hollow points, stuffed thirteen more 9mm rounds into a spare magazine for the automatic, and added a speedloader with six more rounds for the .357.

Then he watched television, the guns in his lap, like steel puppies. He sat in his chair and stared at the game shows, letting the pressure build, working it out. He couldn't chase her down, he couldn't get at her in the house. Wasn't even sure she was still at the house. He'd have to go back to the hospital again.

Weather usually left the hospital at the end of the first shift. She'd stay to brief the new shift on her patients. The fire volunteers would be arriving a few minutes after five. If he were going to pull this off, he'd have to be back by then.

A two-hour window.

He looked down into his lap at the guns. If he put one in his mouth, he'd never feel a thing. All the complications would be history, the pressure.

And all the pleasure. He pushed the thought away. Let himself feel the anger: they'd ganged up on him. Bullied him. They were twenty-to-one, thirty-to-one.

The adrenaline started. He could feel the tension rise in his chest. He'd thought it was over. Now there was this thing. The anger made him squirm, pushed him into a fantasy: *Standing in the snow, gun in each hand, shooting at enemy shadows, the muzzle flashes like rays coming from his palms.*

His watch brought him back. The minute hand ticked, a tiny movement in the real world, catching his eye with the time.

Two-fourteen. He'd have to get moving. He heaved himself out of his chair, let the television ramble on in the empty room.

Weather would walk out to the parking lot. Through the swirling snow. With a bodyguard. On any other day, a rifle would be the thing. With the snow, a scope would be useless: it'd be like looking into a bedsheet.

He'd just have to get close, to make sure, this time. Nothing fancy. Just a quick hit and gone.

THE RIDE TO THE HOSPITAL was wild. He could feel himself moving like a blue light, a blue force, through the vortex of the storm, the snow pounding the Lexan faceplate, the sled throbbing beneath him, bucking over bumps, twisting, alive. At times he could barely see; other times, in protected areas or where he was forced to slow down, the field of vision opened out. He passed a four-by-four, looked up at the driver. A stranger. Didn't look at him, on his sled, ten feet away. Blind?

He pushed on, following the rats' maze of trails that paralleled the highway, along the edge of town. Past another four-by-four. Another stranger who didn't look at him.

A hell of a storm for so many strangers to be out on the road, not looking at snowmobiles . . .

Not looking at snowmobiles.

WHY DIDN'T THEY LOOK at him? He stopped at the entrance to the hospital parking lot, thought about it. He could see Weather's Jeep. Several other cars close by; he could put the sled around the corner of the building, slip out into the parking lot.

Why didn't they look at him? It wasn't like he was invisible. If you're riding in a truck and a sled goes tearing past, you look at it.

The Iceman turned off the approach to the hospital, cruised on past. Something to think about. Kept going, two hundred, three hundred yards. Janes' woodlot. He'd seen Dick Janes in here all fall, cutting oak. Not for this year, but for next.

The Iceman pulled off the trail, ran the sled up a short slope, sinking deep in the snow. He clambered off, moved fifteen feet, huddled next to a pile of cut branches.

Coyotes did this. He knew that from hunting them. He'd once seen a coyote moving slow, apparently unwary, some three or four hundred yards out. He'd followed its fresh tracks through the tangle of an alder swamp, then up a slope, then back around . . . and found himself looking down at his own tracks across the swamp and a cavity in the snow where the mutt had laid down, resting, while he fought the alders. Checking the back trail.

Behind the pile of cuttings, he was comfortable enough, hunkering down in the snow. He was out of the wind, and the temperature had begun climbing with the approach of the storm.

He waited two minutes and wondered why. Then another minute. He was about to stand up, go back to the sled, when he heard motors on the trail. He squatted again, watched. Two sleds went by, slowly. Much too slowly. They weren't getting anywhere if they were travelers, weren't having any fun if they were joyriders. And there was nothing down this trail but fifteen or twenty miles of trees until they hit the next town, a crossroads.

Not right.

The Iceman waited, watching.

Saw them come back. Heard them first, took the .357 from his pocket.

He could see them clearly enough, peering through the branches of the trim pile, but he probably was invisible, down in the snow, above them. They stopped.

They stopped. They knew. They knew who he was, what he was doing.

The lifelong anger surged. The Iceman didn't think. The Iceman acted, and nothing could stand against him.

The Iceman half-stood, caught the first man's chest over the blade of the .357.

Didn't hear the shot. Heard the music of a fine machine, felt the gun bump.

The first man toppled off his sled, the second man, black-Lexan-masked, turning. All of this in slow motion, the second man turning, the gun barrel popping up with the first shot, dropping back into the slot, the second man's body jumped, but he wavered, not falling, a hand coming up, fingers spread, to ward off the .357 JHPs; a third shot went through his hand, knocked him backwards off the sled. And the gun kept on, shots filing out, still no noise, a fourth, a fifth, and a sixth . . .

And in the soft snow, the bumping stopped and the Iceman heard the hammer falling on empty shells, three times, four, the cylinder turning.

Click, click, click, click.

Hᴇ'ꜱ ᴍᴏᴠɪɴɢ, ʜᴇ'ꜱ ᴍᴏᴠɪɴɢ, *he's moving fast, what happened what happened?*

The radio call bounced around the tile corridor, Carr echoing it, shouting, *What happened, what happened*—and knowing what had happened. Weather sprinted toward the emergency room, Lucas two steps behind, calling into the radio, *Stay with him stay with him, we might have some people down.*

The ambulance driver was talking to a nurse. Weather ran through the emergency room, screamed at him: "Go, go, go, I'll be there, get started."

"Where . . . ?" The driver stood up, mouth hanging.

Lucas, not knowing where the ambulance was, shouted, "Go," and the driver went, across the room, through double hardwood doors into a garage. The ambulance faced out, and the driver hit a palm-sized button and the outside door started up. He went left and Lucas right, climbed inside. The back doors opened, and a white-suited attendant scrambled aboard, carrying his parka, then Weather with her bag and Climpt with his shotgun.

"Where?" the driver shouted over his shoulder, already on the gas.

"Right down the frontage road, Janes' woodlot, right down the road."

"What happened?"

"Guys might be shot—deputies." And she chanted, staring at Lucas: "Oh, Jesus, Oh, Jesus God . . ."

The ambulance fishtailed out of the parking garage, headed across the parking lot to the hospital road. A deputy was running down the road ahead of them, hatless, gloveless, hair flying, a chrome revolver held almost in front of his face. Henry Lacey, running as hard as he could. They passed him, looking to the right, in the ditch and up the far bank, snow pelting the windshield, the wipers struggling against it.

"There." Lucas said. The snowmobiles sat together, side-by-side, what looked like logs beside them.

"Stay here," Lucas shouted back at Weather.

"What?"

"He might still be up there."

The ambulance slid to a full stop and Lucas bolted through the door, pistol in front of him, scanning the edge of the treeline for movement. The body armor pressed against him and he waited for the impact, waited, looking, Climpt out to his right, the muzzle of the shotgun probing the brush.

Nothing. Lucas wallowed across the ditch, Climpt covering. The deputies looked like the victims of some obscure third-world execution, rendered black-and-white by the snow and their snowmobile suits, like a grainy newsphoto. Their bodies were upside down, uncomfortable, untidy, torn, unmoving. Rusty's face mask was starred with a bullet hole. Lucas lifted the mask, carefully; the slug had gone through the deputy's left eye. He was dead. Dusty was crumbled beside him, facedown, helmet gone, the back of his head looking as though he'd been hit by an ax. Then Lucas saw the pucker in the back of his snowmobile suit, another hit, and then a third, lower, on the spine. He looked at Rusty: more hits in the chest, hard to see in the black nylon. Dusty's rifle was muzzledown in the snow. He'd cleared the scabbard, no more.

Climpt came up, weapon still on the timber. "Gone," he said. He meant the deputies.

"Yeah." Lucas lumbered into the woods, saw the ragged trail of a third machine, fading into the falling snow. He couldn't hear anything but the people behind him. No snowmobile sound. Nothing.

He turned back, and Weather was there. She dropped her bag. "Dead," she said. She spread her arms, looking at him. "They were children."

The ambulance driver and the attendant struggled through the snow with an aluminum basket-stretcher, saw the bodies, dropped the basket in the snow, stood with their hands in their pockets. Henry Lacey ran up, still holding the gun in front of his face.

"No, no no," he said. And he kept saying it, holding his head with one hand, as though he'd been wounded himself: "No, no . . ."

Carr pulled up in his Suburban, jumped out. Carr looked at them, his chief deputy wandering in circles chanting, "No, no," both hands to his head now, as though to keep it from exploding.

"Where is he?" Carr shouted.

"He's gone. The feds better have him, because it'd be hell trying to follow him," Lucas shouted back.

The feds called: *We still got him, he's way off-road and moving fast, what's going on?*

"We got two down and dead," Lucas called back. "We're heading back to the hospital, gearing up. You track him, we'll be with you in ten minutes."

Lucas and Climpt took Carr's Suburban, churned back to the hospital. Lucas stripped off the body armor, got into his parka and insulated pants.

"Rusty's truck is around back, right? With the trailer?"

"Yeah."

"We'll take the sleds," Lucas said. "Right now we need a decent map."

They found one in the ambulance dispatch room, a large-scale township map of Ojibway County. The feds were using tract maps from the assessor's office, even better. Lucas got on the radio:

"Still got him?" he asked.

Yeah. We got him. You better get out here, though, we can't see him and we got nothing but sidearms.

Helper was already eight miles away, heading south.

"He could pick a farmhouse, go in shooting, take a truck," Climpt said. "Nobody would know until somebody checked the house."

Lucas shook his head. "He's gone too far. He knows where he's going. I think he'll stay with the sled until he gets there."

"The firehouse is off in that direction."

"Better get somebody down there," Lucas said. "But I can't believe he'd go there." He touched the map with his finger, reading the web of roads. "In fact, if he was going there, he should have turned already. On the sled, if he knows the trails, he probably figures he's safe, at least for the time being."

"So let's go."

They stripped the map from the wall, hurried around back to Rusty's truck. The keys were gone, probably with the body. Lucas ran back through the hospital, past the gathering groups of nurses, ran outside and got the Suburban.

Climpt pulled the trailer off Rusty's truck, and when Lucas got back, hitched the trailer to the Suburban.

Ten deputies were at the shooting site now. The bodies still exposed, only one person looking at them; cars stopped on the highway, drivers' white faces peering through the side windows. Carr was angry, shouting into the radio, and Weather stood like a scarecrow looking down at the bodies.

Lucas and Climpt crossed the well-trampled ditch, climbed on the sleds, started them.

"Kill him," Carr said.

Weather caught Lucas by the arm as they loaded the snowmobiles onto the trailer. "Can I go?"

"No."

"I want to ride."

"No. You go back to the hospital."

"I want to go," she insisted.

"No, and that's it," Lucas said, pushing her away.

Climpt had traded his shotgun for an M-16, said, "I'll drive," and hustled around to the cab. Lucas climbed in the passenger side; when they pulled away, he saw Weather recrossing the ditch to the sheriff.

"Buckle up and hold on," Climpt said. "I'm gonna hurry."

THEY TOOK COUNTY ROAD AA south from the highway, a road of tight right-angle turns and a slippery, three-segment, two-lane bridge over the Menomin Flowage. Lucas would have taken the truck into a ditch a half-dozen times, but Climpt apparently knew the road foot-by-foot, knew when to slow down, when the turns were coming. But the snow was beating into the windshield, and the deputy had to wrestle the tailwagging truck through the tighter spots, one foot on the brake, the other on the gas, all four wheels grinding into the shoulders.

Lucas stayed on the handset with the feds.

He's either on the Menomin Branch East or the Morristown trail, still going south.

"We're coming up on you, we're on AA about to cross H," Lucas said.

Okay, we're about four miles further on. Jesus, we can't see shit.

Carr: *We're loading up, heading your way. If you get him, pin him down and we'll come in and finish it.*

Then the feds: *Hey, he's stopped. He's definitely stopped, he's up ahead, must be along County Y, two miles east of AA. We're about four or five minutes out.*

Lucas: *Find a good place to stop and wait. We're all coming in. We don't know what kind of weapons he's carrying.*

"THERE'S NOT MUCH down that road," Climpt said, thinking about it. His hands were tight, white on the steering wheel, holding on, his head pressed forward, searing the snowscape. "Not around there. I'm trying to think. Mostly timber."

Carr came up: *Weather thinks he's at the Harris place. Duane was supposedly seeing Rosie Harris. That's a mile or so off AA on Y. Should be on the tract maps.*

"Goddammit," said Lucas. "Weather's riding with Carr."

Climpt grunted. "Could of told you she wouldn't stay put."

"Gonna get her ass shot," Lucas said.

"Eight dead that we know of," Climpt said, his voice oddly soft. A red stop sign and a building loomed out of the snow, and Climpt jumped on the brake, slowing, then went on through. "Can't find Russ Harper or the Schoeneckers, and I wouldn't make any bets on them being alive, either. Goddamn, I thought it only happened in New York and Los Angeles and places like that."

"Happens all over," Lucas said as they went through the stop sign.

"But you don't believe that, living up here," Climpt said. He glanced out the window. A roadhouse showed a Coors sign in the window. Three people, uni-sex in their parkas, laughing, cross-country skis on their shoulders, walked toward the door. "You just don't believe it can happen."

THE FEDS HAD STOPPED at a farmhouse a half-mile from where their ranging equipment said the radio beacon was. Visibility was twenty feet and was falling. In little more than an hour it would be dark. Lucas and Climpt pulled in behind the federal truck, climbed down, and went to the house. Tolsen met them at the door. "I'm gonna go down and watch the end of the drive, make sure he doesn't tear out of there in a car."

"Okay. Don't go in."

Tolsen nodded. "I'll wait for the troops," he said grimly. "Those two boys are gone?"

Lucas nodded, grimacing. "Yes."

"Shit."

A farm couple sat in the kitchen with a grown son, three pale people in flannel while Lansley talked on the telephone. He hung up as Lucas and Climpt came in, said, "We've got a hostage negotiator standing by on the phone from Washington. He can call in if we need him. If there's a hostage deal going down." He looked worn.

"We've got to do something quick," Climpt said. "If there's another sled in there, or if he gets out in a truck, we'll never find him."

"So what's the plan?" asked Lansley. "Where's Carr?"

"They're ten or fifteen minutes back," Lucas said. "Why don't you go down and back up Tolsen. Just watch the drive, don't get close. Gene and I'll go in on the sleds until we're close, then go in on foot. He can't see us any better than we can see him, and if we catch him outside, we can ambush him."

"You got snowshoes?"

"No. We'll just have to make the best of it," Lucas said.

The farmer cleared his throat. "We got some snowshoes," he said. He looked at his son. "Frank, whyn't you get the shoes for these folks."

. . .

LUCAS AND CLIMPT UNLOADED the sleds and rode them through the farmyard. The farmer had given them a compass as well as the snowshoes. Fifty feet past the barn, they needed it. Lucas took them straight west, riding over what had been a soybean field, the stubble now three feet below the surface. The snow was riding on a growing wind, coming in long curving waves across the open fields. The world was dimming out.

Lucas had strung the radio around his neck, and turned it up loud enough to hear the occasional burp: *No movement . . . Nothing . . . Five minutes out . . . Get a couple more sleds down here, see if you can rent a couple at Lamey's.*

A darker shape shimmered through the snow. Pine tree. The farmer said there was one old white pine left in the field, two hundred feet from the Harris's property windbreak. Lucas pointed and Climpt lifted a hand in acknowledgment. A minute later the windbreak loomed like a curtain, the blue spruces so dark they looked black. Climpt moved off to the left, fifteen feet, as they closed on it. At the edge of the treeline, they stopped, then Climpt pointed and shouted over the storm. "We're back too far. We gotta go through that way, I think. Windbreak's only three or four trees deep, so take it easy."

They moved back toward the road, Climpt leading. After a hundred feet he waved and cut the engine on his sled. Lucas pulled up beside him and pulled the long trapper's snowshoes off the carry-rack.

"This is fuckin' awful," Climpt said.

Inside the windbreak, the wind lessened, but swirled among the trees, building drifts. They plodded through, and a light materialized from the screen of white. Window. Lucas pointed and Climpt nodded. They slid further to the right, moving down the lines of pine, coming up on the back of the double-wide mobile home. A snowmobile track crossed the backyard, curved around the side and out of sight.

"Let's get back a bit. I don't think they could see us."

Keeping the trees between themselves and the house, they moved around to the front. A snowmobile sat next to the door. A space had been cleared for a truck or a car, but the space was empty.

"I'll watch the back," Climpt said. He'd slung the M-16 over his shoulder and now slipped it off into his hands.

"Sit where we can see each other," Lucas said. "We gotta stay in touch."

Climpt moved back the way they came, stopped, beat out a platform with the snowshoes, and sat down. He lifted a hand to Lucas and put the rifle between his knees.

Lucas spoke into the radio. "We're here. We can see a snowmobile parked in front. No other vehicle. The windows are lit."

Any sign of life?

"Not yet. There're lots of lights on."

Carr: *We're here—we see you guys on the road.*

Feds: *Nothing's come out.*

Carr got with the agents. Deputies would block County Y in both directions.

Others would filter into the treeline and occupy the abandoned chicken house in back of the Harris home.

We're talking about how long we wait for him. What do you think? Carr asked.

"Not long," Lucas said into the radio. "There's no vehicle here. I don't see any fresh tracks, but I can't see the other side of the yard. It's possible that he dumped his sled and took off on another one before we got here."

The feds have some kind of shrink on the line. He could call. We got some tear gas coming.

"Talk it out, Shelly. Talk to the hostage guy. I'm not a hostage specialist. All I can do from here is ambush the guy."

Okay.

A moment later Carr came back: *We've got a pickup coming in. Stand by.*

Two minutes later, from Carr: *We've got Rosie and Mark Harris in the pickup. They say their sister's in there, Ginny Harris. They say Helper's seeing* her, *not Rosie. They say there weren't any other vehicles there. They've got only this pickup and a sled, and the sled's in the back of the pickup. So they must be inside.*

"So we wait?" Lucas asked.

Just a minute.

Lucas sat in the snow, watching the door, face wet with melting snow, snow clinging to his eyelashes. Climpt was thirty feet away, a dark blob in a drift, his rifle pointed up into the storm. He'd rolled a condom over the muzzle to keep the snow out. From the distance, Lucas couldn't see the color, but back at the farmhouse, where Climpt had rolled it on, it was a shocking blue.

"Got neon lights on it?" Lucas had asked as they got ready to go out.

"Don't need no lights," Climpt said. "If you look close, you'll notice that it's an extra large."

Lucas, we're gonna have Rosie call in. We can patch her through from here. If Helper answers, she'll ask for Ginny. That's the young one. She'll tell the girl to go to the door when Helper's doing something, and just run out the front and down the driveway. Once she's out, we'll take the place apart.

Lucas didn't answer immediately. He sat in the snow, thinking, and finally Carr came back: *What do you think? Think it'll work?*

"I don't know," Lucas said.

You got any better ideas?

"No."

There was an even longer pause, then Carr:

We're gonna try it.

28

THE ICEMAN SAT ON the couch, furious, the unfairness choking his mind. He'd never had a chance, not from when he was a child. They'd always picked on him, victimized him, tortured him. And now they'd hunt him down like a dog. Kill him or put him in a cage.

"Motherfuckers," he said, knuckles pressed into his teeth. "Motherfuckers." When he closed his eyes, he could see opalescent white curtains blowing away from huge open windows, overlooking a city somewhere, a city with yellow buildings covered with light.

When he opened his eyes, he saw a rotting shag rug on the floor of a double-wide with aluminum walls. The yellow-haired girl had put a prepackaged ham-and-cheese in the microwave, and he could smell the cheap cheddar bubbling.

They'd set him up. They knew he'd done the others. The knowledge had come on him when he saw the deputies coming back, the knowledge had blown up into rage, and the gun had come up and had gone off.

He had to run now. Alaska. The Yukon. Up in the mountains.

He worked it out. The cops would call on every outlying farm and house in Ojibway County. They'd be carrying automatic weapons, wearing flak jackets. If he holed up, he wouldn't have a chance: they would simply knock on every door, look in every room in every house, until they found him.

He wouldn't wait. The storm could work for him. He could cut cross-country on the sled, along the network of Menomin Flowage snowmobile trails. He knew a guy named Bloom down at Flambeau Crossing. Bloom was a recluse, lived alone, raised retrievers and trained cutting horses. He had an almost-new four-by-four. If he could make it that far—and it was a long ride, especially with the storm—he could take Bloom's truck and ID, head out Highway 8 to Minnesota, then take the interstate through the Dakotas into Canada. And if he stuck the horse trainer's body in a snowdrift behind the barn, and unloaded enough feed to keep the animals quiet, it'd be several days before the cops started looking for Bloom and his truck.

By then . . .

He jumped off the couch, fists in his pants pockets, working the road map through his head. He could dump the truck somewhere in the Canadian wilderness, somewhere it wouldn't be found until spring. Then catch a bus. He'd be gone.

"Where'n the fuck are they?" he shouted at the yellow-haired girl.

"Should be here," she said calmly.

He needed Rosie and Mark to get back. Needed the gas from the truck if he was going to make the run down to Flambeau Crossing.

The yellow-haired girl had put the ham-and-cheese in the microwave and then she'd gone back to her bedroom and started changing. Longjohns, thick socks, a sweater. Got out her snowmobile suit, her pac boots, began to go through her stuff. Took pictures. Pictures of her mom, her brother and sister, found a photo of her father, flipped it facedown on the floor without a second look. She took a small gold-filled cross on a gold chain, the chain broken. She put it all in her purse. She could stuff the purse inside her snowmobile suit.

Helper had told her about the cops. There had been nothing he could do about it. They were right on top of him. She could feel the sense of entrapment, the anger. She patted him on the shoulder, held his head, then offered him food and went to pack.

She heard the watch chiming, then the *ding* of the microwave. She carried her stuff to the kitchen, dumped it on a chair, took the ham-and-cheese out of the oven. The package was hot, and she juggled it onto a plate. She'd put a cup of coffee in with the ham and cheese, but it wasn't quite ready yet. She punched it for another minute and called, "Come and get it."

Her mom used to say that a long time ago. She sometimes couldn't quite remember her face. She could remember the voice, though, whining, as often as not, but sometimes cheerful: *Come and get it.*

The phone rang, and without thinking she reached over and picked it up. "Hello?"

The Iceman looked at her from the couch.

Rosie spoke, her voice a harsh, excited whisper. "Ginny—don't look at Duane, okay? Don't look at him. Just listen. Duane just killed two cops and all those other people. There are cops all around the house. You gotta get out so they can come in and get him. When Duane's in the bathroom or something, whenever you get a chance, just go right out the front door and run down the driveway. Don't put a coat on or anything, just run. Okay? Now say something like 'Where the heck are you?' "

"Where the heck are you?" the yellow-haired girl said automatically. She turned to look at Duane.

"Tell him we're still downtown and we wanted to know about the roads out there. Now say something about the roads."

"Well, they're a mess. It's snowing like crazy," the yellow-haired girl said. "The drive's filling up, and a plow came by a little while ago and plowed us in."

The Iceman was off the couch, whispering. "Tell her we need them to come out. I gotta have the gas. Don't tell them I'm here."

She put a finger to her lips, then went back to the phone. "I really kind of need you out here," she said.

Rosie caught on. "Is he listening?"

"Yes."

"Okay. Tell him we'll be out in a while. And when you get a chance, you run for it. Okay?"

"Okay."

"God bless you," Rosie said. "Run for it, honey."

The yellow-haired girl nodded. Duane was focused on her, fists in his pockets. "Sure, I will," she said.

THE SNOW WAS GETTING heavier and the thin daylight was fading fast. Climpt was a dark lump in the snow to his left, unmoving. Lucas had settled behind a tree, the pine scent a delicate accent on the wind. And they waited.

Five minutes gone since Carr had called on the radio: *Okay, the kid knows, she's gonna make a break for it. Everybody hold your fire.*

A man moved along the edge of the woods opposite Lucas, and then another man, behind him, both carrying long arms. They settled in, watching the door.

The radio kept burping in Lucas' ear:

John, you set?

I'm set.

I don't think there's any way he could get out this end—the storm windows got outside fasteners.

Can't see shit out back. Where's Gene and Lucas?

Lucas: "I'm in the trees about even with the front door. Gene's looking at the back." A shadow crossed the curtain over the glass viewport in the front door, stayed there. Lucas went back to the radio: "Heads up. Somebody's at the front door."

But nobody moving fast, he thought, heart sinking. The kid wasn't running. The porch light came on, throwing a circle of illumination across the dark yard. Climpt stood up, looked at him. Lucas said, "Watch the back, watch the back, could be a decoy."

Climpt lifted a hand and Lucas turned back to the trailer home. A crack of brilliant white light appeared at the door, then the large bulk of a man and a struggling child.

"Hold it, hold it!" Helper screamed. He pushed through the storm door to the concrete-block stoop, crouched behind the yellow-haired girl. He had one arm around her neck, another hand at her head. "I got a gun in her ear. Shoot me and she dies. She fuckin' dies. I got my thumb on the hammer."

Lucas waved Climpt over and Climpt half-walked, half-crawled through the snow, using the trees to screen himself from the mobile home. "What the fuck?" he grunted.

Helper and the girl were in the porch light, dressed in snowmobile suits. Helper was wearing a helmet. "I wanna talk to Carr," he screamed. "I want him up here."

Carr, on the radio: *Lucas? What do you think?*

Lucas ducked behind a tree, spoke as softly as he could. "Talk to him. But stay out of sight. Get one of the guys on the other side to yell back to him that you're on the way. He can't see us—we're only about thirty feet away."

"I wanna talk to Carr," Helper screamed. He jerked the girl to the left, toward his snowmobile, nearly pulling her off her feet.

A few seconds later a voice came from the forest on the other side: "Take it easy, Duane, Shelly's coming in. He's coming in from the road. Take it easy."

Helper swiveled toward the voice. "You motherfuckers, the hammer's back— you shoot me and the gun'll blow her brains all over the fuckin' lot!"

"Take it easy."

Carr, on the radio: *Lucas, I'm walking up the driveway. What do I tell him?*

"Ask him what he wants. He'll want a truck or something, some way to get out."

Then what?

"Basically, if we get up against it, let him have it. Try to trade it for the kid. If we can get him away from the kid for a second, Gene's got one of your M-16s and he'll take him out. We just need a second."

What if he wants to keep the girl?

"I'd say let them go. I don't think he's figured out the tracking beacon yet. If the feds have another one, we could stick it in the truck, if that's what he wants."

The feds: *We got another one.*

Carr: *I can see the light from the porch, I'm moving off to the side.*

Lucas turned to Climpt. "How good are you with that rifle?"

"Real good," Climpt said.

"If he didn't have the gun on the girl, could you hit him in the head?"

"Yeah."

"With pressure?"

"Fuck pressure. Without pressure, I could hit him in one eye or the other, your choice. This way you might have to settle for somewhere in the face. You think I oughta . . ."

"When Shelly starts talking to him, I'm going to stand up, let him see me. I'm going to talk. You put your sights on his head, and if he pokes that gun at me, you take it off."

Climpt stared at him, suddenly sounded less sure. "I don't know, man. What if the kid's still in the way or . . ."

"We're gonna have a problem if he takes her," Lucas said. "I'd say it's fifty-fifty that he kills her, but even if he just dumps her somewhere, in this storm, she could be in trouble. She'd have a better chance with you shooting."

Climpt stared at him for a moment, then gave a jerky nod. "Okay."

Lucas looked at him and grinned. "Don't hang fire, huh? Just do it. I don't want him shooting me in the nuts or something."

Climpt said nothing; stared at his gun.

LUCAS CALLED CARR: "Shelly, where are you?"

I'm fifty feet down the driveway, sitting in the snow. I'm gonna yell up there now.

"When you're talking to him, I'm gonna let him see me. I'll be talking to him, too."

What for?

"Gene and I are working on something. Don't worry about it, just . . ."

Helper bellowed down the driveway, "Where in the fuck is Carr?"

"Duane . . ." Carr called from the growing darkness. "This is Shelly Carr. Let the little girl go and I'll come get you personally. You won't be hurt, I guarantee."

"Hey, fuck that!" Helper shouted back. "I want a truck up here and I want it in five minutes. I want it parked right here, and I want the guy who drives it to walk away. I won't touch him. But I don't want anybody else around it. I'll be watching from the house. When I come back out with the kid, I'll have the gun in her ear, and if there's anybody around the truck, I'll drop the hammer."

As Helper was talking, Lucas slid away to his right, then stood up. Carr shouted, "Duane, if you hurt her, you'll die one second later."

Helper laughed, a wild sound, weirdly sharp in the driving snow. "You're gonna kill me anyway, don't shit me, Shelly. If you don't kill me, you'll be digging ditches next year instead of being sheriff. So get me the fuckin' truck."

Helper backed toward the house, dragging the girl with him. She hadn't said a word, and Lucas could see her hair shining oddly yellow in the porch light. He remembered her from the school, the little girl who'd watched him in the hallway, the one with the summer dress and thin shoulders.

"Duane . . ." Lucas called. He shuffled forward. He knew he must be almost invisible in the darkness, away from the light. "This is Davenport. We got feds out here, we got people from other agencies. We wouldn't hurt you, Duane, if you let the girl go."

Helper turned, peered at him. Lucas lifted his hands over his head, spread them, palms forward, took three more steps.

"Davenport?"

"We won't . . ."

"Get away from me, man, or I swear to Christ I'll blow her brains all over the fuckin' yard, I . . . *get away* . . ." His voice rose to a near-hysterical pitch, but the gun never left the yellow-haired girl's head. Lucas could feel her staring at him, passive, on the edge of death, helpless.

"All right, all right." Lucas backed away, backed away. "I'm going, but think about it."

"You'll get the truck," Carr shouted from the dark. "We got the truck coming in. Duane—for God's sake don't hurt the girl."

Helper and the girl backed up to the door. The girl reached behind him, found the doorknob, pushed it, and Helper backed through, the pistol shining weakly silver in the porch light.

The feds, on the radio: *Got a beacon on the truck.*

Carr: *Get it up here. Get it up here.*

The feds: *It's rolling now.*

Carr: *Davenport—what the hell were you doing?*

"I was trying to get him to point the gun at me," Lucas said. "Gene was holding on his head with the M-16. If he'd taken the muzzle away from the girl, we'd of had him."

Good Lord. Where's that truck?

On the way.

The Suburban turned up the driveway, stopped with its headlights reaching toward the mobile home. The truck door slammed, the sound muffled by the snow, then it rolled forward again, its high lights on. It stopped where Helper had indicated, and Shelly Carr crawled down from the driver's seat, squared his shoulders as if waiting for a bullet, and walked back down the driveway.

"Idiot," Climpt said just behind Lucas' ear.

"Takes some guts," Lucas said.

"And if we get Helper, it sure as shit wraps up the next election. Here they come."

THE DOOR OPENED AGAIN and Helper pushed through, his arm again wrapped around the squirming girl's neck. His free hand was bare, holding the revolver, his thumb arched as it would be if the hammer were cocked. The girl was carrying a gas can and what might have been aquarium tubing.

"What are they doing?" Climpt asked. He had the rifle up, following Helper's head through the sights.

The radio: *Girl's got a syphon.*

Helper was talking to her.

"Keep tracking him," Lucas said. They couldn't hear the words, but they could hear the rhythm of them. She unscrewed the gas cap on the truck, dropped it in the snow, stuck the tube in the gas tank, and pushed it down. She put the other end in the open top of the gas can, then squeezed a black bulb on the tube.

"Taking gas," Climpt said, and a moment later a vagrant wisp of gasoline odor mixed with the pine scent.

"He's going out on the snowmobile," Lucas said. "He's getting gas for it."

"Without that kid," Climpt muttered, tracking Helper with the rifle.

Lucas jabbed the radio: "He's taking gas out of the truck. I think he's going to refuel his snowmobile and take off. Gene and I left our sleds back a way, we better go get them."

Carr: *One of you better wait there until I get somebody up that side of the house.*

Lucas said to Climpt: "How're you doing? Gettin' shaky?"

"Just a bit," Climpt admitted. His eyebrows were clogged with snow, his face wet.

"You head back to the sled, let me take the rifle," Lucas said. "Where does it shoot?"

"Put it right over his ear," Climpt said. He held on Helper for another second, then said, "Ready?"

"Yeah."

Climpt handed him the rifle. Lucas put the front sight on Helper's helmet, right where his ear should be. He held it there, his cone of vision narrowing to nothing. He couldn't see the top of the girl's head, although it was only inches from Helper's ear. He could only infer its position.

"Come in as soon as you hear him start that machine. You can ride me back for the other," Lucas said, speaking around the black plastic stock. The stock was icy cold on his cheek, but he kept the sight on Helper's ear. "Can't be more than a couple hundred feet."

Climpt touched him on the shoulder and was gone in the snow.

The transfer of gasoline seemed to take forever, Helper leaning nervously against the truck while the girl stood passively in front of him, watching the syphon. Finally she pulled the tube out of the truck, dropped it on the ground, and she and Helper edged back to his snowmobile, the girl struggling with the can. Five gallons, Lucas thought, probably thirty-five pounds. And she wasn't a big kid. Next to Helper she looked positively frail.

The yellow-haired girl boosted the can up with her thigh, tilted it so the spout fit into the mouth of the gas tank. Again, it seemed to take forever to fill the tank, Lucas tracking, tracking, tired of looking at Helper over the sight.

The girl said something to Helper. Lucas caught one word, "Done." The girl tossed the can aside and Helper pushed her up on the driver's seat of the sled. A pair of snowshoes was strapped to the back, and Helper straddled them, sat down. His gun hand never wavered.

"Don't try to follow," Helper screamed, looking awkwardly over his shoulder as the girl started the snowmobile. They lurched forward, stopped, then started again. Helper screamed, "Don't try . . ." The rest of his words were lost as they started around the side of the house, heading toward the back. The forest was now almost perfectly dark, and silent except for the chain-saw roar of the sled. Lucas stood to watch them go, putting the rifle's muzzle up, clumping out into the yard, following the diminishing red taillight as long as he could.

The radio was running almost full time, voices . . .

He's going out the back.

Heading toward the flowage.

Can't see him.

And the feds: *We got the beacon, he's moving east.*

* · ·

CARR CAME RUNNING UP the driveway. "Lucas, where'n hell . . . ?"

"Over here." Lucas waded through the snow to the driveway. Three other deputies pushed out of the woods, heading for them. Carr was breathing hard, his eyes wide and wild.

"What . . ."

"Gene and I'll go after them on the sleds. You follow with the trucks," Lucas said.

"Remember what he did to the other two, hit 'em on the back trail," Carr said urgently. "If he's waiting for you, you'd never see him."

"The feds should know when he stops," Lucas said. He realized they were shouting at each other and dropped his voice. "Besides, we've got no choice. I don't think he'll keep the kid—she'll slow him down. If he doesn't kill her, we got to be out there to pick her up. If she starts wandering around on her own . . ."

Climpt had come up on a single sled, and Lucas swung his leg over the backseat, holding the rifle out to the side. "Okay, go, go," Carr shouted, and Climpt rolled the accelerator forward and they cut back through the trees to the second sled. Lucas handed Climpt the rifle. Climpt slung it over his shoulder as Lucas hopped on the second sled and fired it up.

"How do you want to do this?" Climpt shouted.

"You lead, stay on his trail. Look for the kid in case he's dumped her. If you see his taillight . . . shit, do what seems right. I'll hang on to the radio. If you see me blinking my lights, stop."

"Gotcha," Climpt said and powered away.

HELPER WAS RUNNING four or five minutes ahead of them. Lucas couldn't decide whether he would be moving faster or slower. He presumably knew where he was going, so that should help his speed. On the other hand, Lucas and Climpt were simply following his track, which was easy enough to do despite the snow. Helper had to navigate on his own. Even if he stayed on the trails, the snow had gotten so heavy that they'd be obscured, white-on-white, under the sled's headlights. And that would slow him down.

They started off, Climpt first, Lucas following, and lost the lights around the house within thirty seconds. After that, they were in the fishbowl of their own light. When Climpt dropped over the top of a rise or into a bowl, Lucas' span of vision would suddenly contract, and expand again when Climpt came back into view. When Climpt suddenly moved out, his taillight would dwindle to almost nothing. When he slowed, Lucas would nearly overrun him. After two or three minutes, Lucas found the optimum distance, about fifteen yards, and hung there, the feds feeding tracking updates through the radio.

The snow made the ride into a nightmare, his face unprotected, wet, freezing, snow clogging his eyebrows, water running down his neck.

He's just about crossing MacBride Road.

Lucas flashed his lights at Climpt, pulled up beside him, took off his glove, looked at his watch, marked the time.

"You know MacBride Road?" he shouted.

"Sure. It's up ahead somewhere."

"The feds think he crossed it about forty-five seconds ago. Let me know when we cross it and we can figure out how far behind we are."

"Sure."

They crossed it two minutes and ten seconds after Lucas marked the time, so they were less than three minutes behind. Closing, apparently.

"Still moving?" he asked the feds.

Still moving east.

Carr: *He'll be crossing Table Bay Road by Jack's Cafe. Maybe we can beat him down there, get a look at him, see if he's still got the kid.*

THEY WERE RIDING through low country, but generally following creek beds and road embankments, where they were protected from the snow. Two or three minutes after crossing MacBride Road, they broke out on a lake, and the snow beat at them with full force, coming in long curving lines into their headlights. Visibility closed to ten feet, and Climpt dropped his speed to a near-walking pace. Lucas wiped snow from his face, out of his eyes, drove, watching Climpt's taillight. Wiped, drove. Getting harder . . . Helper's track was filling more quickly, the edges obscured, harder to pick out. Four minutes later they were across and back into a sheltered run.

Carr: *We're setting up at Jack's. Where is he?*

He's four miles out and closing, but he's moving slower.

How's it going, Lucas?

Lucas, tight from the cold, lifting his brake hand to his face: "We're still on his track. No sign of the kid. It's getting worse, though. We might not be able to stay with him."

All right. I've been talking to Henry. We might have to make a stand here at Table Bay.

"I wonder if the kid's with him. I can't believe he'd still have her, but we haven't seen anything that might have been tracks."

No way to tell until we see him.

Climpt stopped, then broke to his right, then turned in a circle, stopped. "What?" Lucas shouted, pulling up behind him.

"Trail splits. Must've been another sled came through here. I don't know if he went left or right."

"Where's Table Bay Road?"

"Off to the right."

"That's where he's headed."

Climpt nodded and started out again, but the pace grew jagged, Climpt sawing back and forth, checking the track. Lucas nearly overran him a half-dozen times, swerving to avoid a collision. He was breathing through his mouth now, as though he'd been running.

THE ICEMAN POUNDED DOWN the trail, the yellow-haired girl behind him, on top the snowshoes. They'd stopped just long enough to trade places, and then went on through the thickening snow, along an almost invisible track, probing for the path through the woods.

They were safe enough for the moment, lost in the storm. If he could just get south . . . He might have to dump the girl, but she was certainly replaceable. Alaska, the Yukon, there were women out there for the asking; not nearly enough men. They'd do anything you wanted.

If he was going to make it south to the horse trainer's place, he'd have to get up on the north side of the highway, take Blueberry Lake across to the main stem of the flowage. He could take Whitetail Creek.

THE FEDS: *He's turning. He's turning. He's heading north, he's not heading to-ward Table Bay Road anymore, he's headed up toward the intersection of STH 70 and Meteor Drive.*

Carr: *We're moving, we're going that way.*

Lucas flashed Climpt, pulled alongside.

"They've just turned, heading north . . . wait a minute." He pushed the trans-mit button: "Do you know what trail that is? What snowmobile trail? Is it marked on the map?"

Feds: *There's a creek down there, Whitetail Run. We think that's it.*

"He's on a creek called Whitetail Run, heading up to Meteor Drive," Lucas said.

Climpt nodded. "That can't be far. This trail crosses it at right angles—we'll see the turn."

Carr: *We're coming up on the bridge at Whitetail. We'll nail down both sides.*

Another voice: *They'll see the lights.*

Carr: *Yeah. We'll let 'em. Henry and I been talking. We decided we gotta let him know that he can't get away. We gotta give him the choice of giving up the kid and quitting, or dying. The kid's gonna die if she stays with him. If he just leaves her out in the snow somewhere, she's gone. And if he stops someplace, gets a car, he can't leave her to tell anybody. Sooner or later he'll dump her.*

Feds: *If he realizes there's a beacon on him, he may look for it, then we'd lose him.*

Carr: *We're not going to let him go this time. And if he gets away somehow . . . heck, we gotta risk it.*

Feds: *Your call, Sheriff.*

Carr: *That's right. How far out is he?*

Feds: *Half-mile. Forty seconds, maybe.*

THE ICEMAN ROARED through the turn onto Whitetail, and he was al-most to the bridge when he saw the lights, shining down through the snow. He knew what they were. The cops, and especially Davenport, had some kind of karma edge on him. They kept finding him when finding him was impos-sible.

"No!" He shouted it out as he hit the brake. The lights were there, big hand-held million-candlepower jobs, probing the creek. He slid to a stop, turned to the yellow-haired girl:

"That's the cops up there. They're tracking us somehow. If I had time . . . I'll have to try it on foot. I want you to take the sled back down the creek here, just ride around for a while. When they find you, tell them I'm heading for Jack's Cafe down by the flowage. Tell them that you think I'm going after a car. They'll believe that."

"I want to go with you," she said. "You're my husband."

"Can't do it now," he said. He pulled his helmet back, leaned forward, and kissed her on the lips. Her lips were stiff with the cold, her face wet with snow— she hadn't had a helmet—and a few tears.

"I tried, but we can't get through," he said. "You'll have to put them off me. But I'll come back. I'll get you."

"You'll get me?" she asked.

"I swear I will. And I'm counting on you now. You're the only woman who can save me."

She stood in the deep snow beside the sled, watched him snap into the snowshoes. He had his pistol in his hand, his helmet back on. With the snow-mobile suit, he looked almost like a spaceman.

"Give me five minutes," he said. "Then take off. Just roll around for a while. When they find you, tell them I'm headed for Jack's."

"What'll you do?"

"I'll stop the first car coming down the road and take it," he said.

"Jesus." She looked up at the faint light, then cocked her head and frowned. "Somebody's coming."

"What?" The Iceman looked up at the bridge.

"Not that way . . . from behind us."

"Motherfucker," he said. "You go, go."

LUCAS AND CLIMPT WERE moving again, the track filling in front of them, nothing in their world but a few lights and the rumble of the sleds.

Climpt's taillight came up and he leaned to the left, taking the sled through the turn. Lucas followed, pressed the radio button, trying to talk through the bumps. "How long will it take him to get from Whitetail to the bridge?"

Feds: *About two minutes.*

Lucas flashed Climpt, pulled up alongside, shouted, "We're coming up on him in maybe a minute. They're gonna let him see them."

He's stopped.

Carr: *Where?*

"Two or three hundred yards out, maybe. Can't really tell that close.

Can he see our lights?

Maybe.

"I'll take the lead from here. I'll count it out. You get the rifle limbered up."

Climpt nodded, pulled the rifle down. Lucas started counting, rolled the accelerator forward with his right hand, touched the pocket on his left thigh where he kept the pistol. The pocket was sealed with Velcro, so he could get at it quickly enough once he'd shed his gloves . . . *one thousand six, one thousand seven, one thousand eight.* Seconds rolling away like a slow heartbeat.

Radio voice: *Don't see him, don't see him.*

Lucas slowed, Climpt closed from behind. *One thousand thirty-eight, one thousand thirty-nine . . .*

Lucas rolled forward, straining to see. His headlight beam was cupped, shortened by the snow. Looking into it was like peering into a foam plastic cup. They hit a hump, swooped down over the far side, Lucas absorbing up the lurch with his legs, beginning to feel the ride in his thighs. *One thousand sixty . . .* Lucas rolled the accelerator back, slowed, slowed . . .

There.

Red flash just ahead.

Lucas hit the brake, leaned left, dumped his speed in a skid, stayed with the sled, got it straight, headlight boring in on Helper's sled . . . and Helper himself.

Helper stood behind his snowmobile, caught in the headlight. Climpt had gone right when Lucas broke left, came back around, catching Helper in his lights, fixing him in the crossed beams. Lucas ripped his gloves off, had the pistol . . .

Helper was running. He was on snowshoes, running toward the treeline above the creek. Couldn't take a sled in there, too dense. Lucas hit the accelerator, pulled closer, closer. Helper looking back, still wearing his helmet, face mask a dark oval, blank.

THE ICEMAN LUMBERED toward the treeline, but the sound of the other snowmobiles was growing; then the lights popped up and suddenly they were there, careening through the deep snow. The lead sled swerved toward him while the other broke away.

He lifted his pistol, fired a shot, and the sled swerved and the passenger dumped off. The other sled broke hard the other way, spinning, trying to miss the fallen man, out of control.

The Iceman kept running, running, his breath beating in his throat, tearing his chest, running blindly with little hope, looking back.

THE MUZZLE BLAST WAS like lightning in the dark. Lucas cut left, came off the sled. Stunned, he thrashed for a moment, got upright, snow in his eyes and mouth, sputtering, put too much weight on one foot, crunched through to the next layer of snow, got to his knees, the .45 coming up, felt Climpt spinning past him.

Helper was at the treeline, barely visible, nothing more than a sense of motion a hundred feet away.

Lucas fired six shots at him, one after another, tracking the motion, firing through brush and brambles, through alder branches and small barren aspen. The muzzle flash blinded him after the first shot and he fired on instinct, where Helper should have been. And where was Climpt, why wasn't he . . . ?

And then the M-16 came in, two bursts at the treeline.

Radio: *Gunfire, we got gunfire.*

Carr: *What's happening, what's happening?*

SNOWSHOES. THEY'D need the snowshoes.

Lucas' sled had burrowed into a snowdrift. He started for it, then looked back at Helper's sled, saw the yellow-haired girl. She was on the snow, trying to get to her feet. Struggling. Hurt?

Lucas turned toward her, pushed the transmit button:

"He's on foot—heading up toward the road—he's in the woods—we got the kid. She's here—we're on the creek just below the bridge. Watch out for him. We shot up around him, he could be hit."

Ginny Harris was squatting next to Helper's snowmobile, her hair gold-yellow in the lights of the snowmobiles, focused on the woods where Helper had gone. As Lucas ran up, struggling with the knee-deep snow, she turned her head and looked up at him, eyes large and feral like a trapped fox's.

THE YELLOW-HAIRED GIRL crouched by the sled as the man on the first sled fired a series of shots into the wood. He looked menacing, a man all in black, the big pistol popping in his hand. Then there was a loud ratcheting noise from the man on the second sled, the stutter of flame reaching out toward her man like God's finger.

The first man said something to her, but she couldn't hear him. She could see his lips moving, and his hand came up. Reaching out? Pointing a gun? She rolled.

SHE ROLLED AWAY FROM him and he called, "You're okay, okay," but she kept rolling and her hand came up with what looked like a child's shiny chrome compact.

A .22, a fifty-dollar weapon, a silly thing that could do almost nothing but kill people who made mistakes. He was leaning forward, his hand toward her, reaching out. He saw the muzzle and just before the flash felt a split second of what might have been embarrassment, caught like this. He started to turn, to flinch away. Then the flash.

The slug hit him in the throat like a hard slap. He stopped, not knowing quite what had happened, heard the pop-pop of other guns around him, not the heavy bang-bang, but something softer, more distant. Very far away.

Lightning stuttered in the dark and flung the girl down, then Lucas hit the snow on his back, his legs folding under him. His head was downhill, and when he hit, the breath rushed out of his lungs. He tried to take a breath and sit up, but nothing happened. He felt as though a rubber stopper had been shoved into his windpipe. He strained, but nothing.

The snow felt like sand on his face; he could feel it clearly, the snow. And in his mouth, a coppery, cutting taste, the taste of blood. But the rest of the world, all the sounds, smells, and sights, were in a mental rectangle the size of a shoe box, and somebody was pushing in the sides.

He could hear somebody talking: "Oh, Jesus, in the neck, call the goddamn doctor, where's the doctor, is she still riding . . ."

And a few seconds later a shadow in his eyesight, somebody else: "Christ, he's dead, he's dead, look at his eyes."

But Lucas could see. He could see branches with snow on them, he could feel himself move, could feel his angle of vision shifting as someone sat him up, he could feel—no, hear—somebody shouting at him.

And all the time the rectangle grew smaller, smaller . . .

He fought the closing walls for a while, but a distant warmth attracted him, and he felt his mind turning toward it. When he let the concentration go, the walls of the square lurched in, and now he was holding mental territory no bigger than a postage stamp.

No more vision. No more sense of the snow on his face. No taste of blood.

Nothing but a single word, which seemed not so much a sound as a line of type, a word cut from a newspaper:

"Knife."

THE ICEMAN WAS THERE, almost in the treeline, when the shot ripped through his back, between his spine and his shoulder blade. He went down facefirst, and a burst of automatic weapons fire tore up the aspen overhead. His mind was clear as ice, but his body felt like a flame.

There was another burst, slashing through the trees, then another, but the last was directed somewhere else. The Iceman got to his feet, pain riding his back like a thousand-pound knapsack. He pushed deeper into the woods, deeper. Couldn't go far, had to sit down. With the sudden profusion of lights below, he could see the vague outlines of trees around him, and he fought through them, heading at an angle toward the road. Behind him, his tracks filled with snow almost as fast as he made holes in it.

Then he was out of the light. Caught in the darkness, he probed ahead with his hands. The pain in his back grew like a cancer, spreading through him, into his belly, his legs, turning his body to lead. A tree limb caught him in the face mask, snapped his head back. His breath came harder: he pulled off the helmet, threw it away. He needed to feel . . .

He was bleeding. He could feel the blood flowing down his belly and his back, warm, sticking between his shirt and his skin. He took another step, waving his hands like a blind man; another, waving his hands. A branch snapped him in the face, and he swore, twisted, tripped, went down. Swore, struggled to his feet, took another three steps, fell in a hole, tried to get up.

Failed this time.

Felt so quiet.

Lay there, resting; all he needed was a little rest, then he could get up.

Yukon. Alaska.

WEATHER, COMING UP, saw Lucas on the snow and the blood on his face, screamed, "No, God . . ."

"He's hit, he's hit," Climpt screamed.

He was cradling Lucas' head, Henry Lacey standing over both Lucas and Climpt, Carr beside the yellow-haired girl, other deputies milling through the snow.

Like a scene shot in slow motion, Weather saw Lacey's teeth flashing in the snowmobile headlights, saw the face of the little girl, serene, dead, her coat puckered with bullet holes, and she thought, *Gone to the angels*, as she dropped to her knees next to Lucas.

Lucas thrashed, his eyes half open, the whites showing, straining, straining. She grabbed his jaw, found blood, tipped his head back, saw the entry wound, a small puncture that might have been made with a ballpoint pen. He couldn't breathe. She pulled off her gloves, pried open his jaws, and pushed one of the gloves into the corner of his mouth to keep him from snapping his teeth on her fingers. With his mouth wedged open, she probed his throat with her fingers, found the blockage, a chunk of soft tissue where there shouldn't have been anything.

Her mind went cold, analytical.

"Knife," she said to Lacey.

"What?" Lacey shouted down at her, shocked. She realized that he had a gun in his hand.

"Give me your fuckin' knife—your knife!"

"Here, here." Climpt thrust a red jackknife at her, a Swiss Army knife, and she scratched open the larger of the two blades.

"Hold his head down," she said to Climpt. Lacey dropped to his knees to help as she straddled Lucas' chest. "Put your hand on his forehead. Push down."

She pushed the point of the blade into Lucas' throat below the Adam's apple and twisted it, prying . . . and there was a sudden frightening croak as air rushed into his lungs. "Keep his head down—keep his head down."

She thrust her index finger into the incision and crimped it, keeping the hole open.

"Let's get him out—let's get him out," she shouted, slipping off his chest. Lucas seemed to levitate, men at each thigh and two more at either shoulder. "Keep his head down."

They rushed him out of the woods, up to the sheriff's Suburban.

With each awkward, bloody breath, Lucas, eyes closed now, said, "Awwwk . . . awk" like a dying crow.

A SIREN SCREAMED AWAY down the road just above him. Helper was lying in the ditch below the road, he realized. All he had to do was crawl to the top, and when the cops were gone, flag a car.

A small piece of rationality bit back at him: the cops wouldn't be going. Not now. They knew he was here, now.

The Iceman laughed. They'd find him, they were coming.

He tried to roll, get up; he would crawl to the top, flag the cops. Quit. After he healed, he could try again. There was always the possibility of breaking out of jail, always possibilities.

But he couldn't get up. Couldn't move. His mind was still clear, working wonderfully. He analyzed the problem. He was stiff from the wound, he thought. Not a bad wound, not a killer, but he was stiffening up like a wounded deer.

When you shot a deer and failed to knock it down, you waited a half hour or so and invariably found it lying close by, unable to move.

If he was going to live, he had to get up.

But he couldn't.

Tried. Couldn't.

They'd come, he thought. Come and get him. The trail was only a couple of hundred yards long. They'd track him, they'd find him. All he had to do was wait.

"IF HE'S NOT HIT, then going in there'd be suicide. If he is hit, he's dead. Just set up the cordon and let it go until daylight," Carr said. Lacey nodded, stepped to another deputy to relay the word.

"I want three or four men together everywhere," Carr called after him. "I don't want anyone out there alone, okay? Just in case."

THEY FOUND HIM LYING in the ditch beside the road. Still alive, still alert.

The Iceman sensed them coming; not so much heard them, but simply knew. Cocked his head up; that was as far as he could move now. But still: if they got him right into town, they could save him. They could still save him.

"Help me," he groaned.

Something skittered away, then returned.

"Help."

Something touched his face; something colder than he was. He moved and they fell away. And came back. Nipped at him; there was a snarl, then a twisting flight, then they were back.

Coyotes. Brought by the scent of blood and the protection of the dark.

Hungry this year.

Hungry with the deep snow. Most of the deer dead and gone.

They came closer; he tried to move; failed. Tried to lift his hand, tried to roll, tried to cover his face. Failed.

Mind clear as water. Sharper teeth at his face, snapping, ripping, pulling him apart. He opened his mouth to scream; teeth at his lips.

NINE DEPUTIES WERE at the scene, four of them as pickets, guarding against the return of Helper. The rest worked over the scene, searching for blood sign and shells, or simply watched. The yellow-haired girl was a bump under a blue plastic tarp. Lacey and Carr stood to one side, Carr talking into the radio. When he signed off, Lacey was looking into the dark. "I still think if we went slow . . ."

"Forget it," Carr said. "If he's laying up, he'd just take out more of us. Keep the cordon along the road. Davenport got off a half-dozen shots at him, Gene chopped up the woods—I think there's a good chance that he's down. What we need . . ."

"Wait," Lacey snapped. He held up a gloved hand, turned, and looked northeast at an angle toward the road. He seemed to be straining into the dark.

"What?"

"Sounded like a scream," Lacey said.

They listened together for a moment, heard the chatter of the deputies around them, the distant muffled mutter of trucks idling on the road, and beneath it all the profoundly subtle rumble of the falling snow.

Nothing at all like the scream of a man being eaten alive.

Carr shook his head. "Probably just the wind," he said.

HE WAS ON SNOWSHOES, working along the ridges across the access road to his cabin. After the first mile, he was damp with sweat. He took his watch cap off, stuffed it in his pocket, unzipped his parka to cool down, and moved on.

The alders caught at his legs, tangled him. They were small, bushy trees with thumb-sized trunks marked with speckles, like wild cherries. In some places they'd been buried by the frequent snowfalls. When he stepped over a buried bush, his snowshoe would collapse beneath him as though he'd stepped in a hole, which, in fact, he had—a snow dome, held up by the flexible branches of a buried alder. Then he'd be up to his knee or even his crotch, struggling to get back on the level.

As he fought across the swamp, a rime of ice formed on his sunglasses, and his heart thumped like a drum in the silence of the North Woods. He climbed the side of a narrow finger ridge; when he reached its spine, he turned downhill and followed it back to the swamp. At the point where the ridge subsided into the swamp, a tangle of red cedars hugged the snow. Deer had bedded all through the cedars, shedding hair, discoloring the snow. There were pinkish urine holes everywhere, piles of scat like liver-colored .45 shells; but no deer. He would have been as obvious to them as a locomotive, and they'd be long gone. He felt a spasm of guilt. He shouldn't be running deer, not this winter. They'd be weak enough.

His legs twitched, twitched against the pristine white sheets, white like the snow. The winter faded.

"Wake up, you . . ."

Lucas opened his eyes, groaned. His back was stiff, his neck stretched and immobile in the plastic brace. "Goddamn, I was out of it," he said hoarsely. "What time is it?"

"Four o'clock," Weather said, smiling down at him. She was wearing her surgeon's scrub suit. "It'll be dark in an hour. How're you feeling?"

Lucas tested his throat, flexing. "Still hurts, but not so bad. Feels more like tight."

"It'll do that as it heals. If it gets worse, we'll go back in and release some of the scar tissue."

"I can live with the tight feeling," he said.

"What? You don't trust me?" The .22 slug had entered below his jawbone, penetrating upwards, parallel to his tongue, finally burying itself in the soft tissue at the back of his throat. When he'd tried to inhale, he'd sucked down a flap of loose tissue not much bigger than a nickel and had almost choked to death. Weather had fixed the damage with an hour of work on the table at Lincoln Memorial.

"Trust a woman, the next thing you know, they're cutting your throat," Lucas said.

"All right, so now I'm not going to tell you about the Schoeneckers."

"What?" He started to sit up, but she pushed him down. "They found them?"

"Camping in Baja. This morning. They used a gas credit card last night, and they found them about ten o'clock our time. Henry Lacey called and said the folks don't know nothin' about nothin', but one of the girls is giving them quite an earful. Henry may fly out there with a couple of other deputies to bring them back."

"Far out. They can squeeze them on the other people in the sex thing."

"They? You're not going to help?"

Lucas shook his head. "Not my territory anymore. I gotta figure out something to do. Maybe go back to Minneapolis."

"Hmph," she said.

"Well, Jesus Christ," Lucas said, picking up her change of mood, "I was hoping you'd help me figure it out. One way or another, you'll be around, right?"

"We gotta talk," she said. "When you get out of here."

"What does that mean? You don't want to be around?"

"I want to be around," she said. "But we gotta talk."

"All right."

Shelly Carr knocked on the door. "Visiting hours?" He had a wool-plaid hunting cap in his hands, with earflaps.

"Come on in," Lucas croaked. Carr asked, and Lucas said he felt fine. "What's the word on Harper? Weather says you found his truck."

"Yeah—out on a lake. There's a big collection of fishing shacks. Lot of people around there. We think he might have met somebody, got a ride so we couldn't put out a bulletin on his license. God knows where he is now, but we're looking."

"You look pretty good," Lucas said.

"Got some rest," Carr said.

"Have you talked to Gene again?"

"Yeah. He's still up at your cabin," Carr said. "He just sits up there and watches television and reads. I'm kind of worried."

"He needs professional help, but there's no chance he'd talk to a psychiatrist," Weather said. "Big macho guy like that, no chance."

"Yeah, well . . . I know where he's at," Lucas said. "It's like the Church. If you don't believe, it won't do you any good to go. He's gonna have to work it out himself."

"The whole thing was odd," Carr said. "He was okay until he went to her funeral. He shouldn't have gone. I told him that."

"He might of had to," Lucas said.

"Yeah, I know," Carr said reluctantly. "But as soon as he saw her face, that was that. I mean, she looked like an angel. You know about his daughter."

"Yeah."

They sat for a moment, not talking, then Carr said, "I gotta go." He whacked Lucas twice on the leg. "Get better."

WHEN HE WAS GONE, Weather said, "Shelly's doing all right politically. Lacey's made sure that everybody knows about him walking up the driveway to deal with Helper."

"Took some balls," Lucas said.

"And somehow all the dead people are just . . . dead. Seems like nobody really talks about it that much. It's been less than a week."

"That's the way it goes," Lucas said.

"Did you see the paper?" she asked.

"A nurse brought it in this morning, just after you left," he said.

"Great picture, Shelly with the FBI guys, taking credit," she said. "Kind of made me mad."

"Shelly's just taking care of business," Lucas said mildly. He was amused.

"I know. I had a little talk with him about his wife, by the way. I suggested that they both might be better off divorced."

"What'd he say?"

"He said, 'Divorce is a sin.' "

. . .

AFTER A FEW MINUTES he said, "Push the door shut."

She looked at the door, then stepped over, pushed it shut, sat on the bed next to him, kissed him. He couldn't turn his head much, but he could move his arm, and he held her to him as long and hard as he could.

She finally pulled away, laughing, straightened her hair.

"Jeez, it's hard not to take advantage of you, a man in your condition," she said.

"Hey. I don't hurt all that bad. So come back here." He tried to reach for her, but she danced away.

"I wasn't referring to your getting shot. I was referring to the fact that you're falling in love with me."

"I am?"

"Take my word for it," she said. She stepped closer, bent over, kissed him lightly on the forehead. He tried to reach for her again, but she danced away. "Try to get some rest. You're probably gonna need it when you get out."

"You've got a sense of humor like a cop," Lucas said. "Nasty. And you hide behind it. Like a cop."

She'd been smiling, but now the smile narrowed, turned uncertain. "I guess I do."

"Because you're right. I am falling in love with you. You don't have to be funny about it."

This time she touched him on the tip of the nose and said, "Get well." She was smiling, but seemed to have tears in her eyes, and she left in a hurry.

Lucas drifted for a while, punched up the TV, turned it off, used the bed-lift control to raise his head. He could see out the window, across the lawn toward the town, with the small houses and the smoke curling out of the chimneys. Not much to see: white snow, blue sky, small houses.

And it was bitterly cold, everybody said, the worst cold of the winter.

From inside it didn't look so bad. From inside, it looked pretty good. He smiled and closed his eyes.

For Esther Newberg

1

THE NIGHT WAS WARM, the twilight inviting: middle-aged couples in
pastel shirts, holding hands, strolled the old cracked sidewalks along the
Mississippi. A gaggle of college girls jogged down the bike path, wearing sweat-
suits and training shoes, talking as they ran, their uniformly blond ponytails
bouncing behind them. At eight, the streetlights came on, whole blocks at once,
with an audible pop. Overhead, above the new green of the elms, nighthawks
made their *skizzizk* cries, their wing-flashes like the silver bars on new first-
lieutenants.

Spring was shading into summer. The daffodils and tulips were gone, while
the petunias spread across their beds like Mennonite quilts.

Koop was on the hunt.

He rolled through the residential streets in his Chevy S–10, radio tuned to
Country-Lite, his elbow out the window, a bottle of Pig's Eye beer between his
thighs. The soft evening air felt like a woman's fingers, stroking his beard.

At Lexington and Grand, a woman in a scarlet jacket crossed in front of him.
She had a long, graceful neck, her dark hair up in a bun, her high heels rattling
on the blacktop. She was too confident, too lively, moving too quickly; she was
somebody who knew where she was going. Not Koop's type. He moved on.

Koop was thirty-one years old, but at any distance, looked ten or fifteen years
older. He was a short, wide man with a sharecropper's bitter face and small, suspicious gray eyes; he had a way of looking at people sideways. His strawberry-
blond hair was cut tight to his skull. His nose was pinched, leathery, and long,
and he wore a short, furry beard, notably redder than his hair. His heavy shoulders and thick chest tapered to narrow hips. His arms were thick and powerful,
ending in rocklike fists. He had once been a bar brawler, a man who could work
up a hate with three beers and a mistimed glance. He still felt the hate, but controlled it now, except on special occasions, when it burned through his belly like
a welding torch. . . .

Koop was an athlete, of a specialized kind. He could chin himself until he got bored, he could run forty yards as fast as a professional linebacker. He could climb eleven floors of fire stairs without breathing hard.

Koop was a cat burglar. A cat burglar and a killer.

KOOP KNEW ALL THE streets and most of the alleys in Minneapolis and St. Paul. He was learning the suburbs. He spent his days driving, wandering, looking for new places, tracking his progress through the spiderweb of roads, avenues, streets, lanes, courts, and boulevards that made up his working territory.

Now he drifted down Grand Avenue, over to Summit to the St. Paul Cathedral, past a crack dealer doing business outside the offices of the archdiocese of St. Paul and Minneapolis, and down the hill. He drove a couple of laps around United Hospitals, looking at the nurses on their way to their special protected lot—a joke, that. He looked in at antique stores along West Seventh, drove past the Civic Center, and then curled down Kellogg Boulevard to Robert Street, left on Robert, checking the dashboard clock. He was early. There were two or three bookstores downtown, but only one that interested him. The Saint had a reading scheduled. Some shit about Prairie Women.

The Saint was run by a graying graduate of St. John's University. Books new and used, trade your paperbacks two-for-one. Coffee was twenty cents a cup, get it yourself, pay on the honor system. A genteel meat-rack, where shy people went to get laid. Koop had been inside the place only once. There'd been a poetry reading, and the store had been populated by long-haired women with disappointed faces—Koop's kind of women—and men with bald spots, potbellies, and tentative gray ponytails tied with rubber bands.

A woman had come up to ask, "Have you read the *Rubaiyat*?"

"Uh . . . ?" What was she talking about?

"*The Rubaiyat of Omar Khayyam*? I just read it again," she babbled. She had a thin book in her hand, with a black poetical cover. "The Fitzgerald translation. I hadn't read it since college. It really touched me. In some ways it's analogous to the poems that James was reading tonight."

Koop didn't give a shit about James or his poems. But the question itself, *Have you read the* Rubaiyat? had a nice ring to it. Intellectual. A man who'd ask that question, *Have you read the* Rubaiyat?, would be . . . safe. Thoughtful. Considerate.

Koop hadn't been in the market for a woman that night, but he took the book and tried to read it. It was bullshit. Bullshit of such a high, unadulterated order that Koop eventually threw it out his truck window because it made him feel stupid to have it on the seat beside him.

He threw the book away, but kept the line: *Have you read the* Rubaiyat?

KOOP CROSSED I-94, then recrossed it, circling. He didn't want to arrive at the bookstore until the reading had begun: he wanted people looking at the reader, not at him; what he was doing tonight was out of his careful pattern. He couldn't help it—the drive was irresistible—but he would be as careful as he could.

Back across the interstate, he stopped at a red light and looked out the window at the St. Paul police station. The summer solstice was only two weeks away, and at eight-thirty, there was light enough to make out faces, even at a distance. A group of uniformed cops, three men, a couple of women, sat talking on the steps, laughing about something. He watched them, not a thing in his mind, just an eye. . . .

The car behind him honked.

Koop glanced in the left mirror, then the right, then up at the light: it had turned green. He glanced in the rearview mirror again and started forward, turning left. In front of him, a group of people started across the street, saw him coming, stopped.

Koop, looking up, saw them and jammed on his brakes, jerking to a halt. When he realized they'd stopped, he started through the turn again; and when they saw him stop, they started forward, into the path of the truck. In the end, they scattered, and Koop swerved to miss a barrel-shaped man in coveralls who was not quite agile enough to get out of the way. One of them shouted, an odd cawing sound, and Koop gave him the finger.

He instantly regretted it. Koop was the invisible man. He didn't give people the finger, not when he was hunting or working. He checked the cops, still a half block away. A face turned toward him, then away. He looked in the rearview mirror. The people in the street were laughing now, gesturing to each other, pointing at him.

Anger jumped up in his stomach. "Faggots," he muttered. "Fuckin'-A fags. . . ."

He controlled it, continued to the end of the block, and took a right. A car was easing out of a parking place across the street from the bookstore. Perfect. Koop did a U-turn, waited for the other car to get out, backed in, locked the truck.

As he started across the street, he heard the cawing sound again. The group he'd almost hit was crossing the end of the block, looking toward him. One of them gestured, and they made the odd cawing sound, laughed, then passed out of sight behind a building.

"Fuckin' assholes." People like that pissed him off, walking on the street. Ass-wipes, he oughta . . . He shook a Camel out of his pack, lit it, took a couple of angry drags, and walked hunch-shouldered down the sidewalk to the bookstore. Through the front window, he could see a cluster of people around a fat woman, who appeared to be smoking a cigar. He took a final drag on the Camel, spun it into the street, and went inside.

The place was crowded. The fat woman sat on a wooden chair on a podium, sucking on what turned out to be a stick of licorice, while two dozen people sat on folding chairs in a semicircle in front of her. Another fifteen or twenty stood behind the chairs; a few people glanced at Koop, then looked back at the fat woman. She said, "There's a shocking moment of recognition when you start dealing with shit—and call it what it is, good Anglo-Saxon words, horseshit and pig shit and cow shit; I'll tell you, on those days when you're forkin' manure, the first thing you do is rub a little in your hair and under your arms, really rub it in. That way, you don't have to worry about getting it on yourself, you can just go ahead and work. . . ."

At the back of the store, a sign said "Photography," and Koop drifted that way. He owned an old book called *Jungle Fever*, with pictures and drawings of naked black women. The book that still turned him on. Maybe he'd find something like that. . . .

Under the "Photography" sign, he pulled down a book and started flipping pages. Barns and fields. He looked around, taking stock. Several of the women had that "floating" look, the look of someone reaching for connections, of not really being tuned to the author, who was saying, ". . . certain human viability from hand-hoeing beans; oh, gets hot, sometimes so hot that you can't spit. . . ."

Koop was worried. He shouldn't be here. He shouldn't be hunting. He'd had a woman last winter, and that should have been enough, for a while. *Would* have been enough, if not for Sara Jensen.

He could close his eyes and see her. . . .

SEVENTEEN HOURS EARLIER, having never in his life seen Sara Jensen, Koop had gone into her apartment building, using a key. He'd worn a light coat and hat against the prying eyes of the video cameras in the lobby. Once past the cameras, he took the fire stairs to the top of the building. He moved quickly and silently, padding up the stairs on the rubber-soled loafers.

At three in the morning, the apartment hallways were empty, silent, smelling of rug cleaner, brass polish, and cigarettes. At the eleventh floor, he stopped a moment behind the fire door, listened, then went quietly through the door and down the hall to his left. At 1135, he stopped and pressed his eye to the peephole. Dark. He'd greased the apartment key with beeswax, which deadened metal-to-metal clicking and lubricated the lock mechanism. He held the key in his right hand, and his right hand in his left, and guided the key into the lock. It slipped in easily.

Koop had done this two hundred times, but it was a routine that clattered down his nerves like a runaway freight. What's behind door number three? A motion detector, a Doberman, a hundred thousand in cash? Koop would find out. . . . He turned the key and pushed: not quickly, but firmly, smoothly, his heart in his mouth. The door opened with a light *click*. He waited, listening, then stepped into the dark apartment, closed the door behind him, and simply stood there.

And smelled her.

That was the first thing.

Koop smoked unfiltered Camels, forty or fifty a day. He used cocaine almost every day. His nose was clogged with tobacco tars and scarred by the coke, but he *was* a creature of the night, sensitive to sounds, odors, and textures—and the perfume was dark, sensual, compelling, riding the sterile apartment air like a naked woman on a horse. It caught him, slowed him down. He lifted his head, ratlike, taking it in. He was unaware that he left his own scent behind, the brown scent of old tobacco smoke.

The woman's living room curtains were open, and low-level light filtered in from the street. As his eyes began to adjust, Koop picked out the major pieces of furniture, the rectangles of paintings and prints. Still he waited, standing quietly, his vision sharpening, smelling her, listening for movement, for a word, for anything—for a little red light from an alarm console. Nothing. The apartment was asleep.

Koop slipped out of his loafers and in surefooted silence crossed the apartment, down a darker hallway past a bathroom to his left, an office to his right. There were two doors at the end of the hall, the master bedroom to the left, a guest room to the right. He knew what they were, because an ex-con with Logan Van Lines had told him so. He'd moved Jensen's furniture in, he'd taken an impression of her key, he'd drawn the map. He'd told Koop the woman's name was Sara Jensen, some rich cunt who was, "like, in the stock market," and had a taste for gold.

Koop reached out and touched her bedroom door. It was open an inch, perhaps two. Good. Paranoids and restless sleepers usually shut the door. He waited another moment, listening. Then, using just his fingertips, he eased the door open a foot, moved his face to the opening, and peered inside. A window opened to the left, and as in the living room, the drapes were drawn back. A half-moon hung over the roof of an adjoining building, and beyond that, he could see the park and the lake, like a beer ad.

And he could see the woman clearly in the pale moonlight.

Sara Jensen had thrown off the light spring blanket. She was lying on her back, on a dark sheet. She wore a white cotton gown that covered her from her neck to her ankles. Her jet-black hair spread around her head in a dark halo, her face tipped slightly to one side. One hand, open, was folded back, to lie beside her ear, as if she were waving to him. The other hand folded over her lower belly just where it joined the top of her pelvic bone.

Just below her hand, Koop imagined that he could see a darker triangle; and at her breasts, a shading of her brown nipples. His vision of her could not have been caught on film. The darkening, the shading, was purely a piece of his imagination. The nightgown more substantial, less diaphanous than it seemed in Koop's mind, but Koop had fallen in love.

A love like a match firing in the night.

KOOP PAGED THROUGH the photo books, watching, waiting. He was looking at a picture of a dead movie star when his woman came around the corner, looking up at *Hobbies & Collectibles.*

He knew her immediately. She wore a loose brown jacket, a little too long, a bit out of fashion, but neat and well-tended. Her hair was short, careful, tidy. Her head was tipped back so she could look up at the top shelves, following a line of books on antiques. She was plain, without makeup, not thin or fat, not tall or short, wearing oversize glasses with tortoiseshell frames. A woman who wouldn't be noticed by the other person in an elevator. She stood looking up at the top shelf, and Koop said, "Can I reach something for you?"

"Oh . . . I don't know." She tried a small smile, but it seemed nervous. She had trouble adjusting it.

"Well, if I can," he said politely.

"Thanks." She didn't turn away. She was waiting for something. She didn't know how to make it happen herself.

"I missed the reading," Koop said. "I just finished the *Rubaiyat*. I thought there might be something, you know, analogous. . . ."

And a moment later, the woman was saying, ". . . it's Harriet. Harriet Wannemaker."

SARA JENSEN, SPREAD ON her bed, twitched once.

Koop, just about to step toward her dresser, froze. Sara had been a heavy smoker in college: her cigarette subconscious could smell the nicotine coming from Koop's lungs, but she was too far down to wake up. She twitched again, then relaxed. Koop, heart hammering, moved closer, reached out, and almost touched her foot.

And thought: *What am I doing?*

He backed a step away, transfixed, the moonlight playing over her body. *Gold.*

He let out his breath, turned again toward the dresser. Women keep every goddamned thing in the bedroom—or the kitchen—and Jensen was no different. The apartment had a double-locked door, had monitor cameras in the hall, had a private patrol that drove past a half-dozen times a night, occasionally stopping to snoop. She was safe, she thought. Her jewelry case, of polished black walnut, sat right there on the dressing table.

Koop picked it up carefully with both hands, pulled it against his stomach like a fullback protecting a football. He stepped back through the door and padded back down the hall to the living room, where he placed the case on the rug and knelt beside it. He carried a small flashlight in his breast pocket. The lens was covered with black tape, with a pinhole through the tape. He turned it on, held it between his teeth. He had a needle of light, just enough to illuminate a stone or show a color without ruining his night vision.

Sara Jensen's jewelry case held a half-dozen velvet-lined trays. He took the trays out one at a time, and found some good things. Earrings, several pair in gold, four with stones: two with diamonds, one with emeralds, one with rubies. The stones were fair—one set of diamonds were more like chips than cut stones. Total retail, maybe five thousand. He'd get two thousand, tops.

He found two brooches, one a circle of pearls, the other with diamonds, a gold wedding band, and an engagement ring. The diamond brooch was excellent, the best thing she owned. He would have come for that alone. The engagement stone was all right, but not great. There were two gold bracelets and a watch, a woman's Rolex, gold and stainless steel.

No belt.

He put everything into a small black bag, then stood, stepping carefully around the empty trays, and went back through the bedroom. Slowly, slowly, he began opening the dresser drawers. The most likely place was the upper left drawer of the chest. The next most likely was the bottom drawer, depending on whether or not she was trying to hide it. He knew this from experience.

He took the upper drawer first, easing it out, his hands kneading through the half-seen clothing. Nothing hard. . . .

The belt was in the bottom left-hand drawer, at the back, under some winter woolens. So she was a bit wary. He drew it out, hefting it, and turned back toward Sara Jensen. She had a firm chin, but her mouth had gone slightly slack. Her breasts were round and prominent, her hips substantial. She'd be a big woman. Not fat, just big.

Belt in his hands, Koop started to move away, stopped. He'd seen the bottle on the dressing table, and ignored it as he always ignored them. But this time . . . He reached back and picked it up. Her perfume. He started for the door again and almost stumbled: he wasn't watching the route, he was watching the woman, spread right there, an arm's length away, his breath coming hard.

Koop stopped. Fumbled for a moment, folding the belt, slipped it into his pocket. Took a step away, looked down again. White face, round cheek, dark eyebrows. Hair splayed back.

Without thinking, without even knowing what he was doing—shocking himself, recoiling inside—Koop stepped beside the bed, bent over her, and lightly, gently dragged his tongue over her forehead. . . .

HARRIET WANNEMAKER was frankly interested in a drink at McClellan's: she had color in her face, the warmth of excitement. She'd meet him there, the slightly dangerous man with the mossy red beard.

He left before she did. His nerves were up now. He hadn't made a move yet, he was still okay, nothing to worry about. Had anybody noticed them talking? He didn't think so. She was so colorless, who cared? In a few minutes . . .

The pressure was a physical thing, a heaviness in his gut, an inflated feeling in his chest, a pain in the back of his neck. He thought about heading home, ditching the woman. But he wouldn't. There was another pressure, a more demanding one. His hand trembled on the steering wheel. He parked the truck on Sixth, on the hill, opened the door. Took a nervous breath. Still time to leave . . .

He fished under the seat, found the can of ether and the plastic bag with the rag. He opened the can, poured it quickly into the bag, and capped the can. The smell of the ether was nauseating, but it dissipated in a second. In the sealed bag, it quickly soaked into the rag. Where was she?

She came a few seconds later, parked down the hill from him, behind the truck, spent a moment in the car, primping. A beer sign in McClellan's side window, flickering with a bad bulb, was the biggest light around, up at the top of the hill. He could still back out. . . .

No. Do it.

SARA JENSEN HAD TASTED of perspiration and perfume . . . tasted good. Sara moved when he licked her, and he stepped back, stepped away, toward the door . . . and stopped. She said something, a nonsense syllable, and he stepped quickly but silently out the door to his shoes: not quite running, but his heart was hammering. He slipped the shoes on, picked up his bag.

And stopped again. The key to cat burglary was simple: go slow. If it seems like you might be getting in trouble, go slower. And if things get really bad, run like hell. Koop collected himself. No point in running if she wasn't waking up, no sense in panic—but he was thinking *asshole asshole asshole.*

But she wasn't coming. She'd gone back down again, down into sleep; and though Koop couldn't see it—he was leaving the apartment, slowly closing the door behind himself—the line of saliva on her forehead glistened in the moonlight, cool on her skin as it evaporated.

KOOP SLIPPED THE PLASTIC bag in his coat pocket, stepped to the back of his truck, and popped the camper door.

Heart beating hard now. . . .

"Hi," she called. Fifteen feet away. Blushing? "I wasn't sure you could make it."

She was afraid he'd ditch her. He almost had. She was smiling, shy, maybe a little afraid but more afraid of loneliness. . . .

Nobody around. . . .

Now it had him. A darkness moved on him—literally a darkness, a kind of fog, an anger that seemed to spring up on its own, like a vagrant wind. He unrolled the plastic bag, slipped his hand inside; the ether-soaked rag was cold against his skin.

With a smile on his face, he said, "Hey, what's a drink. C'mon. And hey, look at this . . ."

He turned as if to point something out to her; that put him behind her, a little to the right, and he wrapped her up and smashed the rag over her nose and mouth, and lifted her off the ground; she kicked, like a strangling squirrel, though from a certain angle, they might have been lovers in a passionate clutch; in any case, she only struggled for a moment. . . .

SARA JENSEN HIT THE SNOOZE button on the alarm clock, rolled over, holding her pillow. She'd been smiling when the alarm went off. The smile faded only slowly: the peculiar nightmare hovered at the back of her mind. She couldn't quite recover it, but it was there, like a footstep in an attic, threatening. . . .

She took a deep breath, willing herself to get up, not quite wanting to. Just before she woke, she'd been dreaming of Evan Hart. Hart was an attorney in the bond department. He wasn't exactly a romantic hero, but he was attractive, steady, and had a nice wit—though she suspected that he suppressed it, afraid that he might put her off. He didn't know her well. Not yet.

He had nice hands. Solid, long fingers that looked both strong and sensitive. He'd touched her once, on the nose, and she could almost feel it, lying here in her bed, a little warm. Hart was a widower, with a young daughter. His wife had died in an auto accident four years earlier. Since the accident, he'd been preoccupied with grief and with raising the child. The office gossip had him in two quick, nasty affairs with the wrong women. He was ready for the right one.

And he was hanging around.

Sara Jensen was divorced; the marriage had been a one-year mistake, right after college. No kids. But the breakup had been a shock. She'd thrown herself into her work, had started moving up. But now . . .

She smiled to herself. *She* was ready, she thought. Something permanent; something for a lifetime. She dozed, just for five minutes, dreaming of Evan Hart and his hands, a little bit warm, a little bit in love. . . .

And the nightmare drifted back. A man with a cigarette at the corner of his mouth, watching her from the dark. She shrank away . . . and the alarm went off again. Sara touched her forehead, frowned, sat up, looked around the room, threw back the blankets with the sense that something was wrong.

"Hello?" she called out, but she knew she was alone. She went to use the bathroom, but paused in the doorway. Something . . . what?

The dream? She'd been sweating in the dream; she remembered wiping her forehead with the back of her hand. But that didn't seem right. . . .

She flushed the toilet and headed for the front room with the image still in her mind: sweating, wiping her forehead. . . .

Her jewelry box sat on the floor in the middle of the front room, the drawers dumped. She said aloud, "How'd that get there?"

For just a moment, she was confused. Had she taken it out last night, had she been sleepwalking? She took another step, saw a small mound of jewelry set to one side, all the cheap stuff.

And then she knew.

She stepped back, the shock climbing up through her chest, the adrenaline pouring into her bloodstream. Without thinking, she brought the back of her hand to her face, to her nose, and smelled the nicotine and the other . . .

The what?

Saliva.

"No." She screamed it, her mouth open, her eyes wide.

She convulsively wiped her hand on the robe, wiped it again, wiped her sleeve across her forehead, which felt as if it were crawling with ants. Then she stopped, looked up, expecting to see him—to see him materializing from the kitchen, from a closet, or even, like a golem, from the carpet or the wooden floors. She twisted this way, then that, and backed frantically toward the kitchen, groping for the telephone.

Screaming as she went.

Screaming.

2

⊠

LUCAS DAVENPORT HELD the badge case out the driver's-side window. The pimply-faced suburban cop lifted the yellow plastic crime-scene tape and waved him through the line. He rolled the Porsche past the fire trucks, bumped over a flattened canvas hose, and stopped on a charred patch of dirt that a few hours earlier had been a lawn. A couple of firemen, drinking coffee, turned to check out the car.

The phone beeped as he climbed out, and he bent down to pull it off the visor. When he stood up, the stink from the fire hit him: the burned plaster, insulation, paint, and old rotting wood.

"Yeah? Davenport."

Lucas was a tall man with heavy shoulders, dark-complected, square-faced, with the beginnings of crow's feet at the corners of his eyes. His dark hair was just touched with gray; his eyes were a startling blue. A thin white scar crossed his forehead and right eye socket, and trailed down to the corner of his mouth. He looked like a veteran athlete, a catcher or a hockey defenseman, recently retired.

A newer pink scar showed just above the knot of his necktie.

"This is Sloan. Dispatch said you were at the fire." Sloan sounded hoarse, as though he had a cold.

"Just got here," Lucas said, looking at the burned-out Quonset.

"Wait for me. I'm coming over."

"What's going on?"

"We've got another problem," Sloan said. "I'll talk to you when I get there."

Lucas hung the phone back on the visor, slammed the door, and turned to the burned-out building. The warehouse had been a big light-green World War II Quonset hut, mostly galvanized steel. The fire had been so hot that the steel sheets had twisted, buckled, and folded back on themselves, like giant metallic tacos.

With pork.

Lucas touched his throat, the pink scar where the child had shot him just before she had been chopped to pieces by the M-16. That case had started with a fire, with the same stink, with the same charred-pork smell that he now caught drifting from the torched-out hulk. Pork-not-pork.

He touched the scar again and started toward the blackened tangle of fallen struts. A cop was dead inside the tangle, the first call had said, his hands trussed behind his back. Then Del had called in, said the cop was one of his contacts. Lucas had better come out, although the scene was outside the Minneapolis jurisdiction. The suburban cops were walking around with grim one-of-us looks on their face. Enough cops had died around Lucas that he no longer made much distinction between them and civilians, as long as they weren't friends of his.

Del was stepping gingerly through the charred interior. He was unshaven, as usual, and wore a charcoal-gray sweatshirt over jeans and cowboy boots. He saw Lucas and waved him inside. "He was already dead," Del said. "Before the fire got to him."

Lucas nodded. "How?"

"They wired his wrists and shot him in the teeth, looks like three, four shots in the fuckin' teeth from all we can tell in that goddamned nightmare," Del said, unconsciously dry-washing his hands. "He saw it coming."

"Yeah, Jesus, man, I'm sorry," Lucas said. The dead cop was a Hennepin County deputy. Earlier in the year, he'd spent a month with Del, trying to learn the streets. He and Del had almost become friends.

"I warned him about the teeth: no goddamned street people got those great big white HMO teeth," Del said, sticking a cigarette into his face. Del's teeth were yellowed pegs. "I told him to pick some other front. Anything would have been better. He coulda been a car-parts salesman or a bartender, or anything. He had to be a fuckin' street guy."

"Yeah . . . so what'd you want?"

"Got a match?" Del asked.

"You wanted a match?"

Del grinned past the unlit cigarette and said, "C'mon inside. Look at something."

Lucas followed him through the warehouse, down a narrow pathway through holes in half-burned partitions, past stacks of charred wooden pallets. Toward the back, he could see the black plastic sheet where the body was, and the stench of burned pork grew sharper. Del took him to a fallen plasterboard interior wall, where the remnants of a narrow wooden box held three small-diameter pipes, each about five feet long.

"Are these what I think they are?" Del asked.

Lucas squatted next to the box, picked up one of the pipes, looked at the screw-threading at one end, tipped up the other end, and looked inside at the rifling. "Yeah, they are—if you think they're fifty-cal replacement barrels." He dropped the barrel back on the others, duckwalked a couple of feet to another flattened box, picked up a piece of machinery. "This is a lock," he said. "Bolt-action single-shot fifty-cal. Broken. Looks like a stress-line crack, bad piece of steel . . . What was in this place?"

"A machine shop, supposedly."

"Yeah, a machine shop," Lucas said. "They were turning out these locks, I bet. Gettin' the barrels from somewhere else—you wouldn't normally see them on single-shots, they're too heavy. We ought to have the identification guys look at them, see if we can figure out where they came from, and who got them at this end." He dropped the broken lock on the floor, stood up, and tipped his head toward the body. "What was this guy into?"

"The Seeds, is what his friends say."

Lucas, exasperated, shook his head. "All we need is those assholes hanging around."

"They're getting into politics," Del said. "Want to kill themselves some black folks."

"Yeah. You want to look into this?"

"That's why I got you out here," Del said, nodding. "You see the guns, you smell the pork, how can you say no?"

"All right. But you check with me every fuckin' fifteen minutes," Lucas said, tapping him on the chest. "I want to know everything you're doing. Every name you find, every face you see. Any sign of trouble, you back away and talk to me. They're dumb motherfuckers, but they'll kill you."

Del nodded, said, "You're sure you don't have a match?"

"I'm serious, Del," Lucas said. "You fuck me around, I'll put your ass back in a uniform. You'll be directing traffic outside a parking ramp. Your old lady's knocked up and I don't wanna be raising your kid."

"I really need a fuckin' match," Del said.

The Seeds: the Hayseed Mafia, the Bad Seed M.C. Fifty or sixty stickup men, car thieves, smugglers, truck hijackers, Harley freaks, mostly out of northwest Wisconsin, related by blood or marriage or simply shared jail cells. Straw-haired baby-faced country assholes: have guns, will travel. And they were lately infected by a virulent germ of apocalyptic anti-black weirdness, and were suspected of killing a minor black hood outside a pool hall in Minneapolis.

"Why would they have the fifty-cals?" Del asked.

"Maybe they're building a Waco up in the woods."

"The thought crossed my mind," Del said.

WHEN THEY GOT BACK outside, a Minneapolis squad was shifting through the lines of fire trucks, local cop cars, and sheriff's vehicles. The squad stopped almost on their feet, and Sloan climbed out, bent over to the driver, a uniformed sergeant, and said, "Keep the change."

"Blow me," the driver said genially, and eased away.

Sloan was a narrow man with a slatlike face. He wore a hundred-fifty-dollar tan summer suit, brown shoes a shade too yellow, and a fedora the color of beef gravy. "How do, Lucas," he said. His eyes shifted to Del. "Del, you look like shit, my man."

"Where'd you get the hat?" Lucas asked. "Is it too late to take it back?"

"My wife bought it for me," Sloan said, sliding his fingertips along the brim. "She says it complements my ebullient personality."

Del said, "Still got her head up her ass, huh?"

"Careful," Sloan said, offended. "You're talking about my hat." He looked at Lucas. "We gotta go for a ride."

"Where to?"

"Wisconsin." He rocked on the toes of the too-yellow shoes. "Hudson. Look at a body."

"Anybody I know?" Lucas asked.

Sloan shrugged. "You know a chick named Harriet Wannemaker?"

"I don't think so," Lucas said.

"That's who it probably is."

"Why would I go look at her?"

"Because I say so and you trust my judgment?" Sloan made it a question. Lucas grinned. "All right."

Sloan looked down the block at Lucas's Porsche. "Can I drive?"

"PRETTY BAD IN THERE?" Sloan asked. He threw his hat in the back and downshifted as they rolled up to a stop sign at Highway 280.

"They executed him. Shot him in the teeth," Lucas said. "Think it might be the Seeds."

"Miserable assholes," Sloan said without too much heat. He accelerated onto 280.

"What happened to what's-her-name?" Lucas asked. "Wannabe."

"Wannemaker. She dropped out of sight three days ago. Her friends say she was going out to some bookstore on Friday night, they don't know which one, and she didn't show up to get her hair done Saturday. We put out a missing persons note, and that's the last we know until this morning, when Hudson called. We shot a Polaroid over there; it wasn't too good, but they think it's her."

"Shot?"

"Stabbed. The basic technique is a rip—a stick in the lower belly, then an upward pull. Lots of power. That's why I'm looking into it."

"Does this have something to do with what's-her-name, the chick from the state?"

"Meagan Connell," Sloan said. "Yeah."

"I hear she's trouble."

"Yeah. She could use a personality transplant," Sloan said. He blew the doors off a Lexus SC, allowing himself a small smile. The guy in the Lexus wore shades and driving gloves. "But when you actually read her files, the stuff she's put to-gether—she's got something, Lucas. But Jesus, I hope this isn't one of his. It sounds like it, but it's too soon. If it's his, he's speeding up."

"Most of them do," Lucas said. "They get addicted to it."

Sloan paused at a stoplight, then ran the red and roared up the ramp onto Highway 36. Shifting up, he pushed the Porsche to seventy-five and kept it there, cutting through traffic like a shark. "This guy was real regular," he said. "I mean, if he exists. He did one killing every year or so. Now we're talking about four months. He did the last one just about the time you were gettin' shot. Picked her up in Duluth, dumped the body up at the Carlos Avery game reserve."

"Any leads?" Lucas touched the pink scar on his throat.

"Damn few. Meagan's got a file."

. . .

THEY TOOK TWENTY MINUTES getting to Wisconsin, out the web of interstates through the countryside east of St. Paul, the landscape green and heavy after a wet spring. "It's better out here in the county," Sloan said. "Christ, the media's gonna get crazy with this cop killed."

"Lotta shit coming down," Lucas said. "At least the cop's not ours."

"Four killed in five days," Sloan said. "Wannemaker will make five in a week. Actually, we might have six. We're looking into an old lady who croaked in her bed. A couple of the guys think she might've been helped along. They're calling it natural, for now."

"You cleared the domestic on Dupont," Lucas said.

"Yeah, with the hammer and chisel."

"Hurts to think about it." Lucas grinned.

"Got it right between the eyes," Sloan said, impressed. He'd never had a hammer-and-chisel job before, and novelty wasn't that common in murder. Most of it was a half-drunk guy scratching his ass and saying, *Jesus, she got me really pissed, you know?* Sloan went on: "She waited until he was asleep, and whack. Actually, whack, whack, whack. The chisel went all the way through to the mattress. She pulled it out, put it in the dishwasher, turned the dishwasher on, and called 911. Makes me think twice about going asleep at night. You catch your old lady staring at you . . ."

"Any defense? Long-term abuse?"

"Not so far. So far, she says it was hot inside, and she got tired of him laying there snoring and farting. You know Donovan up in the prosecutor's office?"

"Yeah."

"Says he'd of taken a plea to second if it'd been only one whack," Sloan said. "With whack-whack-whack, he's gotta go for first degree."

A truck moved in front of them suddenly, and Sloan swore, braked, swung behind it to the right and passed.

"The Louis Capp thing," Lucas said.

"We got him," Sloan said with satisfaction. "Two witnesses, one of them knew him. Shot the guy three times, got a hundred and fifty bucks."

"I chased Louis for ten years, and I never touched him," Lucas said. There was a note of regret in his voice, and Sloan glanced at him, grinned. "He got any defense?"

"Two-dude," Sloan said. *Some other dude done it.* "Ain't gonna work this time."

"He was always a dumb sonofabitch," Lucas said, remembering Louis Capp. Huge guy, arms like logs, with a big gut. Wore his pants down under his gut, so the crotch of his pants dropped almost to his knees. "The thing is, what he did was so simple, you had to be there to catch him. Sneak up behind a guy, hit him on the head, take his wallet. The guy must have fucked up to two hundred people in his career."

Sloan said, "He's as mean as he was dumb."

"At least," Lucas agreed. "So that leaves what? The Hmong gang-banger and the fell-jumped-pushed waitress."

"I don't think we'll get the Hmong; the waitress had skin under her finger-nails," Sloan said.

"Ah." Lucas nodded. He liked it. Skin was always good.

Lucas had left the department two years earlier, under some pressure, after a fight with a pimp. He'd gone full-time with his own company, originally set up to design games. The computer kids he worked with had pushed him in a new direction, writing simulations for police dispatch computers. He'd been making a fortune when the new Minneapolis chief asked him to come back.

He couldn't return under civil service; he'd taken political appointment as deputy chief. He'd work intelligence, as he had before, with two main objectives: put away the most dangerous and the most active criminals, and cover the department on the odd crimes likely to attract media attention.

"Try to keep us from getting ambushed by the fruitcakes out there," the chief said. Lucas played hard to get for a little while, but he was bored with business, and he finally hired a full-time administrator to run the company, and took the chief's offer.

He'd been back on the street for a month, trying to rebuild his network, but it had been harder than he'd expected. Things had changed in just two years. Changed a lot.

"I'm surprised Louis was carrying a gun," Lucas said. "He usually worked with a sap, or a pipe."

"Everybody's got guns now," Sloan said. "Everybody. And they don't give a shit about using them."

THE ST. CROIX WAS A steel-blue strip beneath the Hudson bridge. Boats, both sail and power, littered the river's surface like pieces of white confetti.

"You oughta buy a marina," Sloan said. "I could run the gas dock. I mean, don't it look fuckin' wonderful?"

"Are you getting off here, or are we going to Chicago?"

Sloan quit rubbernecking and hit the brakes, cut off a station wagon, slipped down the first exit on the Wisconsin side, and headed north into Hudson. Just ahead, a half-dozen emergency vehicles gathered around a boat ramp, and uniformed Hudson patrolmen directed traffic away from the ramp. Two cops were standing by a dumpster, their thumbs hooked in their gun belts. To one side, a broad-backed blond woman in a dark suit and sunglasses was facing a third cop. They appeared to be arguing. Sloan said, "Ah, shit," and as they came up to the scene, ran his window down and shouted, "Minneapolis police" at the cop directing traffic. The cop waved him into the parking area.

"What?" Lucas asked. The blonde was waving her arms.

"Trouble," Sloan said. He popped the door. "That's Connell."

A bony deputy sheriff with a dark, weathered face had been talking to a city cop at the dumpster, and when the Porsche pulled into the lot, the deputy grinned briefly, called something out to the cop who was arguing with the blond woman, and started over.

"Helstrom," said Lucas, digging for the name. "D. T. Helstrom. Remember that professor that Carlo Druze killed?"

"Yeah?"

"Helstrom found him," Lucas said. "He's a good guy."

They got out of the car as Helstrom came up to Lucas and stuck out his hand. "Davenport. Heard you were back. Deputy chief, huh? Congratulations."

"D. T. How are you?" Lucas said. "Haven't seen you since you dug up the professor."

"Yeah, well, this is sorta worse," Helstrom said, looking back at the dumpster. He rubbed his nose.

The blond woman called past the cop, "Hey. Sloan."

Sloan muttered something under his breath, and then, louder, "Hey, Meagan."

"This lady working with you?" Helstrom asked Sloan, jerking a thumb at the blonde.

Sloan nodded, said, "More or less," and Lucas tipped his head toward his friend. "This is Sloan," he said to Helstrom. "Minneapolis homicide."

"Sloan," the woman called. "Hey, Sloan. C'mere."

"Your friend's a pain in the ass," Helstrom said to Sloan.

"You'd be a hundred percent right, except she's not my friend," Sloan said, and started toward her. "I'll be right back."

THEY WERE STANDING ON a blacktopped boat ramp, with striped spaces for car and trailer parking, a lockbox for fees, and a dumpster for garbage. "What you got?" Lucas asked Helstrom as they started toward the dumpster.

"A freak . . . He did the killing on your side of the bridge, I think. There's no blood over here, except what's on her. She'd stopped bleeding before she went in the dumpster, no sign of anything on the ground. And there must've been a lot of blood . . . Jesus, look at that."

Up on the westbound span of the bridge, a van with yellow flashing roof lights had stopped next to the rail, and a man with a television camera was shooting down at them.

"That legal?" Lucas asked.

"Damned if I know," Helstrom said.

Sloan and the woman came up. The woman was young, large, in her late twenties or early thirties. Despite her anger, her face was as pale as a dinner candle; her blond hair was cropped so short that Lucas could see the white of her scalp. "I don't like the way I'm being treated," the woman said.

"You've got no jurisdiction here. You can either shut up or take yourself back across the bridge," Helstrom snapped. "I've had about enough of you."

Lucas looked at her curiously. "You're Meagan O'Connell?"

"Connell. No O. I'm an investigator with the BCA. Who are you?"

"Lucas Davenport."

"Huh," she grunted. "I've heard about you."

"Yeah?"

"Yeah. Some kind of macho asshole."

Lucas half-laughed, not sure she was serious, looked at Sloan, who shrugged. She was. Connell looked at Helstrom, who had allowed himself a small grin when Connell went after Lucas. "So can I see her, or what?"

"If you're working with Minneapolis homicide . . ." He looked at Sloan, and Sloan nodded. "Be my guest. Just don't touch anything."

"Christ," she muttered, and stalked down to the dumpster. The dumpster came to her collarbone, and she had to stand on her tiptoes to look in. She stood for a moment, looking down, then walked away, down toward the river, and began vomiting.

"Be my fuckin' guest," Helstrom muttered.

"What'd she do?" Lucas asked.

"Came over like her ass was on fire and started screaming at everyone. Like we forgot to scrape the horseshit off our shoes," Helstrom said.

Sloan, concerned, started after Connell, then stopped, scratched his head, walked down to the dumpster, and looked inside. "Whoa." He turned away, and said, "Goddamnit," and then to Lucas, "Hold your breath."

Lucas was breathing through his mouth when he looked in. The body was nude, and had been in a green garbage bag tied at the top. The bag had split open on impact when it hit the bottom of the dumpster, or someone had split it open.

The woman had been disemboweled, her intestines boiling out like an obscene corn smut. And Sloan's earlier description was right: she hadn't been stabbed, she'd been opened like a sardine can, a long slit running from her pelvic area to her sternum. He thought at first that maggots were already working on her, but then realized that the sprinkles of white on the body were grains of rice, apparently somebody's garbage.

The woman's head was in profile against the green garbage sack. The garbage sack had a red plastic tie, and it snuggled just above the woman's ear like a bow on a Christmas package. Flies crawled all over her, like tiny black MiGs . . . Above her breasts, two inches above the top of the slash, were two smaller cuts in what might be letters. Lucas looked at them for five seconds, then backed away, and waited until he was a half-dozen strides from the dumpster before he started breathing through his nose again.

"The guy who dumped her must be fairly strong," Lucas said to Helstrom. "He had to either throw her in there or carry her up pretty high, without spilling guts all over the place."

Connell, white-faced, tottered back up the ramp.

"What'd you just say?"

Lucas repeated it, and Helstrom nodded. "Yeah. And from the description we got, she wasn't a complete lightweight. She must've run around 135. If that's Wannemaker."

"It is," Sloan said. Sloan had walked around to the other side of the dumpster, and was peering into it again. From Lucas's perspective, eyes, nose, and ears over the edge of the dumpster, he looked like Kilroy. "And I'll tell you what: I've seen a videotape of the body they found up in Carlos Avery. If the same guy didn't do this one, then they both took cuttin' lessons at the same place."

"Exactly the same?" Lucas asked.

"Identical," Connell said.

"Not quite," Sloan said, backing away from the Dumpster. "The Carlos Avery didn't have the squiggles above her ti . . . breasts."

"The squiggles?" Connell asked.

"Yeah. Take a look."

She looked in again. After a moment, she said, "They look like a capital S and a capital J."

"That's what I thought," Lucas said.

"What does that mean?" Connell demanded.

"I'm not a mind reader," Lucas said, "Especially with the dead." He turned his head to Helstrom. "No way to get anything off the edge of this thing, is there? Off the dumpster?"

"I doubt it. It's rained a couple times since Friday, people been throwing stuff in there all weekend . . . Why?"

"Better not take a chance." Lucas went back to the Porsche, popped the trunk, took out a small emergency raincoat, a piece of plastic packed in a bag not much bigger than his hand. He stripped the coat out, carried it back to the dumpster, and said, "Hang on to my legs so I don't tip inside, will you, D.T.?"

"Sure. . . ."

Lucas draped the raincoat carefully over the edge of the dumpster and boosted himself up until he could lay his stomach over the top. His upper body hung down inside, his face not more than a foot from the dead woman's.

"She's got, uh . . ."

"What?"

"She's got something in her hand . . . Can't see it. Like maybe a cigarette."

"Don't touch."

"I'm not." He hung closer. "She's got something on her chest. I think it's to-bacco . . . stuck on."

"Garbage got tossed on her."

Lucas dropped back onto the blacktop and started breathing again. "Some of it's covered with blood. It's like she crumbled a cigarette on herself."

"What're you thinking?" Helstrom asked.

"That the guy was smoking when he killed her," Lucas said. "That she snatched it out of his mouth. I mean, she wouldn't have been smoking, not if she was being attacked."

"Unless it wasn't really an attack," Sloan said. "Maybe it was consensual, they were relaxing afterwards, and he did her."

"Bullshit," Connell said.

Lucas nodded at her. "Too much violence," he said. "You wouldn't get that much violence after orgasm. That's sexual excitement you're looking at."

Helstrom looked from Lucas to Connell to Sloan. Connell seemed oddly satisfied by Lucas's comment. "He was smoking when he did it?"

"Get them to make the cigarette, if that's what it is. I can see the paper," Lucas told Helstrom. "Check the lot, see if there's anything that matches."

"We've picked up everything in the parking lot that might mean anything—candy wrappers, cigarettes, bottle tops, all that."

"Maybe it's marijuana," Connell said hopefully. "That'd be a place to start."

"Potheads don't do this shit, not when they're smoking," Lucas said. He looked at Helstrom. "When was the dumpster last cleaned out?"

"Friday. They dump it every Tuesday and Friday."

"She went missing Friday night," Sloan said. "Probably killed, brought here at night. You can't see into the dumpster unless you stand on your tiptoes, so he probably just tossed her in and pulled a couple of garbage bags over her and let it go at that."

Helstrom nodded. "That's what we think. People started complaining about the smell this morning, and a guy from the marina came over and poked around. Saw a knee and called us."

"She's on top of that small white bag, like she landed on it. I'd see if there's anything in it to identify who threw it in," Lucas suggested. "If you can find the guy who dumped the garbage, you might nail down the time."

"We'll do that," Helstrom said.

Lucas went back for a last look, but there was nothing more to see, just the pale-gray skin, the flies, and the carefully colored hair with the streak of white frost. She'd taken care of her hair, Lucas thought; she'd liked herself for her hair, and now all that liking was gone like evaporating gasoline.

"Anything else?" Sloan asked.

"Nah, I'm ready."

"We gotta talk," Connell said to Sloan. She was squared off to him, fists on her hips.

"Sure," Sloan said, an unhappy note in his voice.

Lucas started toward the car, then stopped so quickly that Sloan walked into him. "Sorry," Lucas said as he turned and looked back at the dumpster.

"What?" Sloan asked. Connell was looking at him curiously.

"Do you remember Junky Doog?" Lucas asked Sloan.

Sloan looked to one side, groping for the name, then snapped his fingers, looked back at Lucas, a kernel of excitement in his eyes. "Junky," he said.

"Who's that?" Connell asked.

"Sexual psychopath who fixated on knives," Lucas said. "He grew up in a junkyard, didn't have any folks. Guys at the junkyard took care of him. He liked to carve on women. He'd go after fashion models. He'd do grapevine designs on them, and sign them." Lucas looked at the dumpster again. "This is almost too crude for Junky."

"Besides, Junky's at St. Peter," Sloan said. "Isn't he?"

Lucas shook his head. "We're getting older, Sloan. Junky was a long time ago, must've been ten or twelve years. . . ." His voice trailed off, and his eyes wan-

dered away to the river before he turned back to Sloan. "By God, he was seventeen years ago. The second year I was out of uniform. What's the average time
in St. Peter? Five or six years? And remember a few years ago, when they came
up with that new rehabilitation theory, and they swept everybody out of the state
hospitals? That must've been in the mid-eighties."

"First killing I found was in '84, in Minneapolis, and it's still open," Connell said.

"We need to run Junky," Sloan said.

Lucas said, "It'd be a long shot, but he was a crazy sonofabitch. Remember
what he did to that model he followed out of that Dayton's fashion show?"

"Yeah," Sloan said. He rubbed the side of his face, thinking. "Let's get Anderson to look him up."

"I'll look him up too," Connell said. "I'll see you back there, Sloan?"

Sloan was unhappy. "Yeah. See you, Meagan."

BACK IN THE CAR, Sloan fastened his seat belt, started the engine, and
said, "Uh, the chief wants to see you."

"Yeah? About what?" Lucas asked. "About this?"

"I think so." Sloan bumped the car out of the ramp and toward the bridge.

"Sloan, what did you do?" Lucas asked suspiciously.

Sloan laughed, a guilty rattle. "Lucas, there's two people in the department
who might get this guy. You and me. I got three major cases on my load right
now. People are yelling at me every five minutes. The fuckin' TV is camped out
in my front yard."

"This wasn't my deal when I came back," Lucas said.

"Don't be a prima donna," Sloan said. "This asshole is killing people."

"If he exists."

"He exists."

There was a moment of silence, then Lucas said, "Society of Jesus."

"What?"

"Society of Jesus. That's what Jesuits belong to. They put the initials after their
name, like, Father John Smith, SJ. Like the SJ on Wannemaker."

"Find another theory," Sloan said. "The Minneapolis homicide unit ain't
chasin' no fuckin' Jesuits."

AS THEY CROSSED the bridge, Lucas looked down at the dumpster and
saw Connell still talking to Helstrom. Lucas asked, "What's the story on Connell?"

"Chief'll tell you all about her," Sloan said. "She's a pain in the ass, but she
invented the case. I haven't seen her for a month or so. Goddamn, she got here
fast."

Lucas looked back toward the ramp. "She's got a major edge on her," he said.

"She's in a hurry to get this guy," Sloan said. "She needs to get him in the
next month or so."

"Yeah? What's the rush?"

"She's dying," Sloan said.

3

THE CHIEF'S SECRETARY WAS a bony woman with a small mole on her cheekbone and overgrown eyebrows. She saw Lucas coming, pushed a button on her intercom, and said, "Chief Davenport's here." To Lucas she said, "Go on in." She made her thumb and forefinger into a pistol and pointed at the chief's door.

ROSE MARIE ROUX SAT BEHIND a broad cherrywood desk stacked with reports and memos, rolling an unlit cigarette under her nose. When Lucas walked in, she nodded, fiddled with the cigarette for a moment, then sighed, opened a desk drawer, and tossed it inside.

"Lucas," she said. Her voice had a ragged nicotine edge to it, like a hangnail. "Sit down."

When Lucas had quit the force, Quentin Daniel's office had been neat, ordered, and dark. Roux's office was cluttered with books and reports, her desk a mass of loose paper, Rolodexes, calculators, and computer disks. Harsh blue light from the overhead fluorescent fixtures pried into every corner. Daniel had never bothered with computers; a late-model IBM sat on a stand next to Roux's desk, a memo button blinking at the top left corner of the screen. Roux had thrown out Daniel's leather men's-club furniture and replaced it with comfortable fabric chairs.

"I read Kupicek's report on the tomb burglaries," she said. "How is he, by the way?"

"Can't walk." Lucas had two associates, Del and Danny Kupicek. Kupicek's kid had run over his foot with a Dodge Caravan. "He's gone for a month."

"If we get a media question on the tombs, can you handle it? Or Kupicek?"

"Sure. But I doubt that it'll ever get out."

"I don't know—it's a good story." A persistent series of tomb break-ins had first been attributed to scroungers looking for wedding rings and other jewelry, though the departmental conspiracy freaks had suggested a ring of satanists, getting body parts for black Masses. Whatever, the relatives were getting upset. Roux had asked Lucas to look at it. About that time, polished finger and toe bones had started showing up in art jewelry. Kupicek had found the designer/saleswoman, squeezed her, and the burglaries stopped.

"Her stuff does go well with a simple black dress," Lucas said. " 'Course, you want to match the earrings."

Roux showed a thin smile. "You can talk that way because you don't give a shit," she said. "You're rich, you're in love, you buy your suits in New York. Why should you care?"

"I care," Lucas said mildly. "But it's hard to get too excited when the victims are already dead. . . . What'd you want?"

There was a long moment of silence. Lucas waited it out, and she sighed again and said, "I've got a problem."

"Connell."

She looked up, surprised. "You know her?"

"I met her about an hour ago, over in Wisconsin, running her mouth."

"That's her," Roux said. "Running her mouth. How'd she hear about it?"

Lucas shrugged. "I don't know."

"Goddamnit, she's working people inside the department." She nibbled at a fingernail, then said, "Goddamnit," again and heaved herself to her feet, walked to her window. She stuck two fingers between the blades of her venetian blinds, looked out at the street for a moment. She had a big butt, wide hips. She'd been a large young woman, a good cop in decent shape. The shape was going now, after too many years in well-padded government chairs.

"There's no secret about how I got this job," she said finally, turning back to him. "I solved a lot of political problems. There was always pressure from the blacks. Then the feminists started in, after those rapes at Christmas. I'm a woman, I'm a former cop, I've got a law degree, I was a prosecutor and a liberal state senator with a good reputation on race relations. . . ."

"Yeah, yeah, you were right for the job," Lucas said impatiently. "Cut to the chase."

She turned back to him. "Last winter some game wardens found a body up in the Carlos Avery reserve. You know where that's at?"

"Yeah. Lots of bodies up there."

"This one's name was Joan Smits. You probably saw the stories in the papers."

"Vaguely. From Duluth?"

"Right. An immigrant from South Africa. Walked out of a bookstore and that was it. Somebody stuck a blade in her just above the pelvic bone and ripped her all the way up to her neck. Dumped her in a snowdrift at Carlos Avery."

Lucas nodded. "Okay."

"Connell got the case, assisting the local authorities. She freaked. I mean, something snapped. She told me that Smits comes to her at night, to see how the investigation is going. Smits told her that there'd been other killings by the same man. Connell poked around, and came up with a theory."

"Of course," Lucas said dryly.

Roux took a pack of Winston Lights from her desk drawer, asked, "Do you mind?"

"No."

"This is illegal," she said. "I take great pleasure in it." She shook a cigarette out of the pack, lit it with a green plastic Bic lighter, and tossed the lighter back in the desk drawer with the cigarettes. "Connell thinks she's found the tracks of a serial sex-killer. She thinks he lives here in Minneapolis. Or St. Paul or whatever, the suburbs. Close by, anyway."

"Is there? A serial killer?" Lucas sounded skeptical, and Roux peered across her desk at him.

"You've got a problem with the idea?" she asked.

"Give me a few facts."

"There are several," Roux said, exhaling smoke at the ceiling. "But let me give you another minute of background. Connell's not just an investigator. She's big in the left-feminist wing of the state AFSCME—American Federation of State, County and Municipal Employees."

"I know what it is."

"That's an important piece of my constituency, Lucas. AFSCME put me in the state senate and kept me there. And maybe sixty percent of them are female." Roux flicked a cigarette ash toward her wastebasket. "They're my rock. Now. If I pull off this chief's job, if I go four, maybe six years, and get a little lucky, I'll go up to the U.S. Senate as a liberal law-and-order feminist."

"Okay," Lucas said. Everybody hustles.

"So Connell came down to talk to me about her serial-killer theory. The state doesn't have the resources for this kind of investigation, but we do. I make nice noises and say we'll get right on it. I'm thinking *Nut,* but she's got contacts all over the women's movements and she's AFSCME."

Lucas nodded, said nothing.

"She gives me her research . . ." Roux tapped a thick file-folder on her desk. "I carried it down to homicide and asked them to make some checks. Connell thinks there have been a half-dozen murders and maybe more. She thinks there have been two here in Minnesota, and others in Iowa, Wisconsin, South Dakota, just across the border in Canada."

"What'd homicide say?" Lucas asked.

"I got the eye-rolling routine, and I started hearing Dickless Tracy comments again. Two of the killings had already been cleared. The Madison cops got a conviction. There're local suspects in a couple other cases."

"Sounds like—"

He was about to say *bullshit,* but Roux tapped her desk with an index finger and rode her voice over his. "But your old pal Sloan dug through Connell's research and he decided there's something to it."

"He mentioned that," Lucas admitted. He looked at the file folder on Roux's desk. "He didn't seem too happy with Connell, though."

"She scares him. Anyway, what Connell had was not so much evidence as an . . ." She groped for the right word: ". . . argument."

"Mmmm."

The chief nodded. "I know. She could be wrong. But it's a legitimate argument. And I keep thinking, *What if I ditch it, and it turns out that I'm wrong?* A fellow feminist, one of the constituency, comes to me with a serial killer. We blow it off and somebody else gets murdered and it all comes out."

"I'm not sure . . ."

"Besides, I can feel myself getting in trouble here. We're gonna set a new record for murders this year, unless something strange happens. That doesn't have anything to do with me, but I'm the chief. I take the blame. You're starting to hear that 'We need somebody tough up there.' I'm getting it from both inside and outside the department. The union never misses a chance to kick my ass. You know they backed MacLemore for the job."

"MacLemore's a fuckin' Nazi."

"Yes, he is. . . ." Roux took a drag on the cigarette, blew smoke, coughed, laughing, and said, "There's even more. She thinks the killer might be a cop."

"Ah, man."

"It's just a theory," Roux said.

"But if you start chasing cops, the brotherhood's gonna be unhappy."

"Exactly. And that's what makes you perfect," Roux said. "You're one of the most experienced serial-killer investigators in the country, outside the FBI. Inside this department, politically, you're both old-line and hard-line. *You* could chase a cop."

"Why does she think it's a cop?"

"One of the victims, a woman in Des Moines, a real estate saleswoman, had a cellular phone in her car. She had a teenaged daughter at home, and called and said she was going out with a guy for a drink, that she might be getting home late. She said the guy was from out of town, and that he was a cop. That's all."

"Christ." Lucas ran his hand through his hair.

"Lucas, how long have you been back? A month?"

"Five weeks."

"Five weeks. All right. I know you like the intelligence thing. But I've got all kinds of guys running different pieces of intelligence. We got the division, and the intelligence unit, and the gang squad in that, and vice and narcotics and licensing . . . I brought you back, gave you a nice soft political job, because I knew I'd eventually run into shit like this and I'd need somebody to handle it. You're the guy. That was the deal."

"So you can run for the Senate."

"There've been worse senators," she said.

"I've got things—"

"Everybody's got things. Not everybody can stop insane killers," Roux said impatiently. She came and stood next to him, looking out the window, took another greedy drag on her cigarette. "I could give you some time if we hadn't had this Wannemaker thing. Now I gotta move, before the press catches on. And if we don't do something heavy, Connell might very well leak it herself."

"I—"

"If it gets out and you're already on it, it'd go easier for all of us."

Lucas finally nodded. "You saved my ass from the corporate life," he said. "I owe you."

"That's right," she said. "I did, and you do." Roux pushed her intercom button and leaned toward it. "Rocky? Round up the usual suspects. Get their asses in here."

. . .

ROUX TOOK FIVE MINUTES to put together a meeting: Lester, head of the Criminal Investigation Division, his deputy Swanson, and Curt Myer, the new head of intelligence. Anderson, the department's computer freak, was invited at Lucas's request.

"How're we doing?" Roux asked Lester.

"The bodies are piling up. I've honest to God never seen anything like it." He looked at Lucas. "Sloan tells me there's not much chance that Wannemaker got it in Hudson. She was probably transported there."

Lucas nodded. "Looks like."

"So we got another one."

Roux lit another cigarette and turned to Lucas. "What do you need?"

Lucas looked back at Lester. "Same deal as last time. Except I want Sloan."

"What's the same deal?" Roux asked.

Lester looked at Roux. "Lucas works by himself, parallel to my investigation. Everything he finds out, and everything from the up-front investigation, goes into a book on a daily basis. Anderson does the book. He essentially coordinates."

Lester hooked a thumb at Anderson, who nodded, then turned to Lucas. "You can't have Sloan."

Lucas opened his mouth, but Lester shook his head. "You can't, man. He's my best guy and we're fuckin' drowning out there."

"I've been off the street. . . ."

"Can't help it," Lester said. To Roux: "I'm telling you, pulling Sloan would kill us."

Roux nodded. "You'll have to live with it, at least for a while," she said to Lucas. "Can't you use Capslock?"

He shook his head. "He's got something going with this deputy that was killed. We need to stay on it."

"I could let you have one guy," Lester said. "He could run errands. Tell you the truth, you could help him out. Show him how it's done."

Lucas's eyebrows went up. "Greave?"

Lester nodded.

"I hear he's an idiot," Lucas said.

"He's just new," Lester said defensively. "You don't like him, give him back."

"All right," Lucas said. He looked at Anderson. "And I need to know where a guy is. A knife guy from years ago."

"Who's that?"

"His name was Junky Doog. . . ."

WHEN THE MEETING BROKE UP, Roux held Lucas back. "Meagan Connell is gonna want to work it," she said. "I'd appreciate it if you'd take her."

Lucas shook his head. "Rose Marie, damnit, she's got a state badge, she can do what she wants."

"As a favor to me," Roux said, pressing him. "There's no way homicide'll take her. She's really into this. She's smart. She'd help you. I'd appreciate it."

"All right, I'll find something for her to do," Lucas said. Then: "You know, you never told me she was dying."

"I figured you'd find out by yourself," Roux said.

ROUX'S SECRETARY HAD a dictation plug in her ear. When Lucas walked out of Roux's office, she pointed a finger at Lucas and held up her hand to stop him, typed another half-sentence, then pulled the plug out of her ear.

"Detective Sloan stopped by while you were talking," she said, her dark eyebrows arching. She took a manila file-folder from her desk and handed it to him. "He said fingerprints confirm that it's Wannemaker. She had a piece of an unfiltered cigarette in her hand, a Camel. They sent it to the lab in Madison. He said to look at the picture."

"Thanks." Lucas turned away and opened the folder.

"I already looked at it," she said. "Gross. But interesting."

"Umm." Inside the folder was an eight-by-ten color photograph of a body in a snowdrift. The faceup attitude was almost the same as that of the Wannemaker woman, with the same massive abdominal wound; pieces of a plastic garbage bag were scattered around in the snow. The secretary was looking over his shoulder, and Lucas half-turned. "There's a state investigator who's been in and out of here, name of Meagan Connell. Could you find her and ask her to call me?"

LUCAS'S OFFICE WAS fifteen feet square, no window, with a door that opened directly to a hallway. He had a wooden desk and chair, three visitor's chairs, two file cabinets, a bookcase, a computer, and a three-button phone. A map of the Twin Cities metro area covered most of one wall, a cork bulletin board another. He hung his jacket on a wooden hanger and the wooden hanger on a wall hook, sat down, pulled open the bottom desk drawer with his toe, put his feet on it, and picked up the telephone and dialed. A woman answered.

"Weather Karkinnen, please." He didn't recognize all the nurses' voices yet.

"Doctor Karkinnen is in the operating room. . . . Is this Lucas?"

"Yes. Could you tell her I called? I might be late getting home. I'll try her there later."

He punched in another number, got a secretary. "Lucas Davenport for Sister Mary Joseph."

"Lucas, she's in Rome. I thought you knew."

"Shit . . . Oh, jeez, excuse me." The secretary was a novice nun.

"Lucas. . . ." Feigned exasperation.

"I forgot. When is she back?"

"Two weeks yet. She's going on some kind of dig."

"Goddamnit . . . Oh, jeez, excuse me."

Sister Mary Joseph—Elle Kruger when they had gone to elementary school together—was an old friend and a shrink, with an interest in murder. She'd helped him out on other cases. Rome. Lucas shook his head and opened the file that Connell had put together.

The first page was a list of names and dates. The next eight pages were wound photos done during autopsies. Lucas worked through them. They were not identical, but there were inescapable similarities.

The wound photos were followed by crime-scene shots. The bodies had been dumped in a variety of locations, some urban, some rural. A couple were in roadside ditches, one in a doorway, one under a bridge. One had been simply rolled under a van in a residential neighborhood. There was little effort to hide them. In the background of several, he could see shreds of plastic garbage bags.

Going back and forth from each report to the relevant photographs, Lucas picked up a thread that seemed to tie them together in his mind. The women had been . . . littered. They'd been thrown away like used Kleenex. Not with desperation, or fear, or guilt, but with some discretion, as though the killer had been afraid of being caught littering.

The autopsy reports also showed up differences.

Ripped was a subjective description, and some of the wounds looked more like frantic knife strikes than deliberate ripping. Some of the women had been beaten, some had not. Still, taken together, there was a *feel* about the killings. The feel was generated almost as much by the absence of fact as by the presence of it.

Nobody saw the women when they were picked up. Nobody saw the man who picked them up, or his car, although he must have been among them. There were no fingerprints, vaginal smears turned up no semen, although signs of semen had been found on the clothing of one of the women. Not enough for a blood or DNA type, apparently: none was listed.

When he finished the first reading, he skipped through the reports again, quickly, looking at the small stuff. He'd have to read them again, several times. There were too many details for a single reading, or even two or three. But he'd learned when he looked back from other murders that the files often pointed at the killer way before he was brought down. Truth was in the details. . . .

His rummaging was interrupted by a knock. "Yeah. Come in."

Connell stepped through, flustered, but still pale as a ghost. "I was in town. I thought I'd come by, instead of calling."

"Come in. Sit down," Lucas said.

Connell's close-cropped hair was disconcerting: it lent a punkish air to a woman who was anything but a punk. She had a serious, square face, with a short, Irish nose and a square chin. She was still wearing the blue suit she'd worn that morning, with a darker stripe of what might have been garbage juice on the front of it. An incongruous black leather hip pack was buckled around her hips, the bag itself perched just below her navel: a rip-down holster for a large gun. She could take a big gun: she had large hands, and she stuck one of them out and Lucas half-rose to shake it.

She'd opted for peace, Lucas thought; but her hand was cold. "I read your file," he said. "That's nice work."

"The possession of a vagina doesn't necessarily indicate stupidity," Connell said. She was still standing.

"Take it easy," Lucas said, his forehead wrinkling as he sat down again. "That was a compliment."

"Just want things clear," Connell said crisply. She looked at the vacant chair, still didn't sit. "And you think there is something?"

Lucas stared at her for another moment, but she neither flinched nor sat down. Holding her eyes, he said, "I think so. They're all too . . . not alike, but they have the feeling of a single man."

"There's something else," Connell said. "It's hard to see it in the files, but you see it when you talk to the friends of these women."

"Which is?"

"They're all the same woman."

"Ah. Tell me. And sit down, for Christ's sakes."

She sat, reluctantly, as if she were giving up the high ground. "One here in the Cities, one in Duluth, now this one, if this latest one is his. One in Madison, one in Thunder Bay, one in Des Moines, one in Sioux Falls. They were all single, late twenties to early forties. They were all somewhat shy, somewhat lonely, somewhat intellectual, somewhat religious or at least involved in some kind of spirituality. They'd go out to bookstores or galleries or plays or concerts at night, like other people'd go out to bars. Anyway, they were all like that. And then these shy, quiet women turn up ripped. . . ."

"Nasty word," Lucas said casually. "Ripped."

Connell shuddered, and her naturally pale complexion went paper-white. "I dream about the woman up at Carlos Avery. I was worse up there than I was today. I went out, took a look, started puking. I got puke all over my radio."

"Well, first time," Lucas said.

"No. I've seen a lot of dead people," Connell said. She was pitched forward in her chair, hands clasped. "This is way different. Joan Smits wants vengeance. Or justice. I can hear her calling from the other side—I know that sounds like schizophrenia, but I can hear her, and I can feel the other ones. All of them. I've been to every one of those places, where the murders happened, on my own time. Talked to witnesses, talked to cops. It's one guy, and he's the devil."

There was a hard, crystalline conviction in her voice and eyes, the taste and bite of psychosis, that made Lucas turn his head away. "What about the sequence you've got here?" Lucas asked, trying to escape her intensity. "He was putting a year between most of them. But then he skipped a couple—once, twenty-one months, another time, twenty-three. You think you're missing a couple?"

"Only if he completely changed his MO," Connell said. "If he shot them. My data search concentrated on stabbings. Or maybe he took the time to bury them and they were never found. That wouldn't be typical of him, though. But there are so many missing people out there, it's impossible to tell for sure."

"Maybe he went someplace else—L.A. or Miami, or the bodies were just never found."

She shrugged. "I don't think so. He tends to stay close to home. I think he drives to the killing scene. He picks his ground ahead of time, and goes by car. I plotted all the places where these women were taken from, and except for the one in Thunder Bay, they all disappeared within ten minutes of an interstate that runs through the Cities. And the one in Thunder Bay was off Highway 61. So maybe he went out to L.A.—but it doesn't feel right."

"I understand that you think it could be a cop."

She leaned forward again, the intensity returning. "There are still a couple of things we need to look at. The cop thing is the only hard clue we have: that one woman talking to her daughter. . . ."

"I read your file on it," Lucas said.

"Okay. And you saw the thing about the PPP?"

"Mmm. No. I don't remember."

"It's in an early police interview with a guy named Price, who was convicted of killing the Madison woman."

"Oh, yeah, I saw the transcript. I haven't had time to read it."

"He says he didn't do it. I believe him. I'm planning to go over and talk to him if nothing else comes up. He was in the bookstore where the victim was picked up, and he says there was a bearded man with PPP tattooed on his hand. Right on the web between his index finger and thumb."

"So we're looking for a cop with PPP on his hand?"

"I don't know. Nobody else saw the tattoo, and they never found anybody with PPP on his hand. A computer search doesn't show PPP as an identifying mark anywhere. But the thing is, Price had been in jail, and he said the tattoo was a prison tattoo. You know, like they make with ballpoint ink and pins."

"Well," Lucas said. "It's something."

Connell was discouraged. "But not much."

"Not unless we find the killer—then it might help confirm the ID," Lucas said. He picked up the file and paged through it until he found the list of murders and dates. "Do you have any theories about why the killings are so scattered around?"

"I've been looking for patterns," she said. "I don't know. . . ."

"Until the body you found last winter, he never had two killings in the same state. And the last one here was almost nine years ago."

"Yes. That's right."

Lucas closed the file and tossed it back on his desk. "Yeah. That means different reporting jurisdictions. Iowa doesn't know what we're doing, and Wisconsin doesn't know what Iowa's doing, and nobody knows what South Dakota's doing. And Canada sure as hell is out of it."

"You're saying he's figured on that," Connell said. "So it *is* a cop."

"Maybe," said Lucas. "But maybe it's an ex-con. A smart guy. Maybe the reason for the two gaps is, he was inside. Some small-timer who gets slammed for drugs or burglary, and he's out of circulation."

Connell leaned back, regarding him gravely. "When you crawled into the dumpster this morning, you were cold. I couldn't be that cold; I never would have seen that tobacco on her."

"I'm used to it," Lucas said.

"No, no, it was . . . impressive," she said. "I need that kind of distance. When I said we only had one fact about him, the cop thing, I was wrong. You came up with a bunch of them: he was strong, he smokes—"

"Unfiltered Camels," Lucas said.

"Yeah? Well, it's interesting. And now these ideas . . . I haven't had anybody bouncing ideas off me. Are you gonna let me work with you?"

He nodded. "If you want."

"Will we get along?"

"Maybe. Maybe not," he said. "What does that have to do with anything?"

She regarded him without humor. "Exactly my attitude," she said. "So. What are we doing?"

"We're checking bookstores."

Connell looked down at herself. "I've got to change clothes. I've got them in my car. . . ."

WHILE CONNELL WENT to change, Lucas called Anderson for a reading on homicide's preliminary work on the Wannemaker killing. "We just got started," Anderson said. "Skoorag called in a few minutes ago. He said a friend of Wannemaker's definitely thinks she was going to a bookstore. But if you look at the file when she was reported missing, somebody else said she might have been going to the galleries over on First Avenue."

"We're hitting the bookstores. Maybe your guys could take the galleries."

"If we've got time. Lester's got people running around like rats," Anderson said. "Oh—that Junky Doog guy. I got lots of hits, but the last one was three years ago. He was living in a flop on Franklin Avenue. Chances of him being there are slim and none, and slim is outa town."

"Give me the address," Lucas said.

WHEN HE FINISHED WITH Anderson, Lucas carried his phone book down the hall, Xeroxed the Books section of the Yellow Pages, and went back to his office for his jacket. He *had* bought the jacket in New York; the thought was mildly embarrassing. He was pulling on the jacket when there was a knock at the door. "Yeah?"

A fleshy, pink-cheeked thirties-something man in a loose green suit and moussed blond hair poked his head inside, smiled like an encyclopedia salesman, and said, "Hey. Davenport. I'm Bob Greave. I'm supposed to report to you."

"I remember you," Lucas said as they shook hands.

"From my Officer Friendly stuff?" Greave was cheerful, unconsciously rumpled. But his green eyes matched his Italian-cut suit a little too perfectly, and he wore a fashionable two days' stubble on his chin.

"Yeah, there was a poster down at my kid's preschool," Lucas said.

Greave grinned. "Yup, that's me."

"Nice jump, up to homicide," Lucas said.

"Yeah, bullshit." Greave's smile fell away, and he dropped into the chair Connell had vacated, looked up. "I suppose you've heard about me."

"I haven't, uh . . ."

"Greave the fuckup?"

"Haven't heard anything like that," Lucas lied.

"Don't bullshit me, Davenport." Greave studied him for a minute, then said, "That's what they call me. Greave-the-fuckup, one word. The only goddamned reason I'm in homicide is that my wife is the mayor's niece. She got tired of me being Officer Friendly. Not enough drama. Didn't give her enough to gossip about."

"Well . . ."

"So now I'm doing something I can't fuckin' do and I'm stuck between my old lady and the other guys on the job."

"What do you want from me?"

"Advice."

Lucas spread his hands and shrugged. "If you liked being an Officer Friendly . . ."

Greave waved him off. "Not that kind of advice. I can't go back to Officer Friendly, my old lady'd nag my ears off. She doesn't like me being a cop in the first place. Homicide just makes it a little okay. And she makes me wear these fuckin' Italian fruit suits and only lets me shave on Wednesdays and Saturdays."

"Sounds like you gotta make a decision about her," Lucas said.

"I love her," Greave said.

Lucas grinned. "Then you've got a problem."

"Yeah." Greave rubbed the stubble on his chin. "Anyway, the guys in homicide don't do nothing but fuck with me. They figure I'm not pulling my load, and they're right. Whenever there's a really horseshit case, I get it. I got one right now. Everybody in homicide is laughing about it. That's what I need your advice on."

"What happened?"

"We don't know," Greave said. "We've got it pegged as a homicide and we know who did it, but we can't figure out how."

"Never heard of anything like that," Lucas admitted.

"Sure you have," Greave said. "All the time."

"What?" Lucas was puzzled.

454 ✖ JOHN SANDFORD

"It's a goddamned locked-room mystery, like one of them old-lady English things. It's driving me crazy."

Connell pushed through the door. She was wearing a navy suit with matching low heels, a white blouse with wine-colored tie, and carried a purse the size of a buffalo. She looked at Greave, then Lucas, and said, "Ready."

"Bob Greave, Meagan Connell," Lucas said.

"Yeah, we sorta met," Greave said. "A few weeks ago."

A little tension there. Lucas scooped Connell's file from his desk, handed it to Greave. "Meagan and I are going out to the bookstores. Read the file. We'll talk tomorrow morning."

"What time?"

"Not too early," Lucas said. "How about here, at eleven o'clock?"

"What about my case?" Greave asked.

"We'll talk tomorrow," Lucas said.

As Lucas and Connell walked out of the building, Connell said, "Greave's a jerk. He's got the Hollywood stubble and the *Miami Vice* suits, but he couldn't find his shoes in a goddamn clothes closet."

Lucas shook his head, irritated. "Cut him a little slack. You don't known him that well."

"Some people are an open book," Connell snorted. "He's a fuckin' comic."

CONNELL CONTINUED TO IRRITATE him: their styles were different. Lucas liked to drift into conversation, to schmooze a little, to remember common friends. Connell was an interrogator: just the facts, sir.

Not that it made much difference. Nobody in the half-dozen downtown bookstores knew Wannemaker. They picked up a taste of her at the suburban Smart Book. "She used to come to readings," the store owner said. He nibbled at his lip as he peered at the photograph. "She didn't buy much, but we'd have these wine-and-cheese things for authors coming through town, and she'd show up maybe half the time. Maybe more than that."

"Did you have a reading last Friday?"

"No, but there were some."

"Where?"

"Hell, I don't know." He threw up his hands. "Goddamn authors are like cockroaches. There're hundreds of them. There's always readings somewhere. Especially at the end of the week."

"How'd I find out where?"

"Call the *Star-Trib*. There'd be somebody who could tell you."

LUCAS CALLED FROM A corner phone, another number from memory. "I wondered if you'd call." The woman's voice was hushed. "Are you bringing up your net?"

"I'm doing that now. There're lots of holes."

"I'm in."

"Thanks, I appreciate it. How about the readings?"

"There was poetry at the Startled Crane, something called Prairie Woman at The Saint—I don't know how I missed that one—Gynostic at Wild Lily Press, and the Pillar of Manhood at Crosby's. The Pillar of Manhood was a male-only night. If you'd called last week, I probably could have gotten you in."

"Too late," Lucas said. "My drum's broke."

"Darn. You had a nice drum, too."

"Yeah, well, thanks, Shirlene." To Connell: "We can scratch Crosby's off the list."

THE OWNER OF THE Startled Crane grinned at Lucas and said, "Cheese it, the heat . . . How you been, Lucas?" They shook hands, and the store owner nodded at Connell, who stared at him like a snake at a bird.

"Not bad, Ned," Lucas said. "How's the old lady?"

Ned's eyebrows went up. "Pregnant again. You just wave it at her, and she's knocked up."

"Everybody's pregnant. I gotta friend, I just heard his wife's pregnant. How many is that for you? Six?"

"Seven . . . what's happening?"

Connell, who had been listening impatiently to the chitchat, thrust the photos at him. "Was this woman here Friday night?"

Lucas, softer, said, "We're trying to track down the last days of a woman who was killed last week. We thought she might've been at your poetry reading."

Ned shuffled through the photos. "Yeah, I know her. Harriet something, right? I don't think she was here. There were about twenty people, but I don't think she was with them."

"But you see her around?"

"Yeah. She's a semiregular. I saw the TV stuff on *Nooner.* I thought that might be her."

"Ask around, will you?"

"Sure."

"What's *Nooner?*" Connell asked.

"TV3's new noon news," Ned said. "But I didn't see her Friday. I wouldn't be surprised if she was somewhere else, though."

"Thanks, Ned."

"Sure. And stop in. I've been fleshing out the poetry section."

Back on the street, Connell said, "You've got a lot of bookstore friends?"

"A few," Lucas said. "Ned used to deal a little grass. I leaned on him and he quit."

"Huh," she said, thinking it over. Then, "Why'd he tell you about poetry?"

"I read poetry," Lucas said.

"Bullshit."

Lucas shrugged and started toward the car.

"Say a poem."

"Fuck you, Connell," Lucas said.

"No, c'mon," she said, catching him, facing him. "Say a poem."

Lucas thought for a second then said, "The heart asks pleasure first/And then excuse from pain/and then those little anodynes/that deaden suffering. And then to go to sleep/and then if it should be/the will of its inquisitor/the privilege to die."

Connell, already pale, seemed to go a shade paler, and Lucas, remembering, thought, *Oh, shit.*

"Who wrote that?"

"Emily Dickinson."

"Roux told you I have cancer?"

"Yes, but I wasn't thinking about that. . . ."

Connell, studying him, suddenly showed a tiny smile. "I was kind of hoping you were. I was thinking, *Jesus Christ, what a shot in the mouth.*"

"Well . . . ?"

She stepped toward the car. "Where's next?"

"The Wild Lily Press over on the West Bank."

She shook her head. "I doubt it. That's a feminist store. He'd be pretty noticeable."

"Then The Saint, over in St. Paul."

ON THE WAY TO ST. PAUL, Connell said, "I'm in a hurry on this, Davenport. I'm gonna die in three or four months, six at the outside. Right now I'm in remission, and I don't feel too bad. I'm out of chemo for the time being, I'm getting my strength back. But it won't last. A couple weeks, three, and it'll come creeping up on me again. I want to get him before I go."

"We can try."

"We gotta do better than that," she said. "I owe some people."

"All right."

"I don't mean to scare you," she said.

"You're doing it."

THE OWNER AT THE SAINT recognized Wannemaker immediately. "Yes, she was here," he said. His voice was cool, soft. He looked at Lucas over the top of his gold-rimmed John Lennon specs. "Killed? My God, she wasn't the kind to get killed."

"What kind was she?" Lucas asked.

"Well, you know." He gestured. "Meek. A wallflower. She did ask a question when Margaret finished the reading, but I think it was because nobody was asking questions and she was embarrassed. That kind of person."

"Did she leave with anyone?"

"Nope. She left alone. I remember, 'cause it was abrupt. Most readings, she'd hang around; she'd be the last to leave, like she had nothing else to do. But I remember, she headed out maybe fifteen minutes after we broke things up. There were still quite a few people in the store. I thought maybe she didn't like Margaret."

"Was she in a hurry?"

The store owner scratched his head, looked out his window at the street. "Yeah. Now that you mention it, she did sort of seem like she was going somewhere."

Lucas looked at Connell, who was showing just the faintest color.

The store owner, frowning, said, "You know, when I think about it, the question she asked was made up, like maybe she was dragging things out. I was sort of rolling my eyes, mentally, anyway. Then she leaves in a hurry. . . ."

"Like something happened while she was in the store?" Connell prompted.

"I hate to say it, but yes."

"That's interesting," Lucas said. "We'll need a list of everybody you know was here."

The store owner looked away, embarrassed. "Hmm. I think, uh, a lot of my clients would see that as an invasion of privacy," he said.

"Would you like to see the pictures of Wannemaker?" Lucas asked gently. "The guy ripped her stomach open and all her intestines came out. And we think he might be hanging around bookstores."

The store owner looked at him for a moment, then nodded. "I'll get a list going," he said.

Lucas used the store phone to call Anderson, and told him about the identification. "She left here at nine o'clock."

"We got her car fifteen minutes ago," Anderson said. "It was in the impound lot, towed out of downtown St. Paul. Hang on a minute. . . ." Anderson spoke to somebody else, then came back. "It was towed off a hill on Sixth. I'm told that's next to Dayton's."

"So she must have been headed somewhere."

"Unless she already was somewhere, and walked back to the store."

"I don't think so. That'd be eight or ten blocks. There's a lot of parking around here. She would have driven."

"Is there anything around Dayton's at nine? Was the store open?"

"There's a bar up there—Harp's. On the corner. Connell and I'll stop in."

"Okay. St. Paul'll process the car," Anderson said. "I'll pass on what you found out at this bookstore. You're getting a list of names?"

"Yeah. But it might not be much."

"Get me the names and I'll run 'em."

Lucas hung up and turned around. Connell was marching toward him from the back of the store, where the owner had gone to talk with one of his clerks about people at the reading.

"One of the men here was a cop," she said fiercely. "A St. Paul patrolman named Carl Erdrich."

"Damnit," Lucas said. He picked up the phone and called Anderson back, gave him the name.

"What?" Connell wanted to know when he got off the phone.

"We'll check the bar," Lucas said. "There'll have to be some negotiations before we can get a mug of Erdrich."

Connell spun around and planted herself in front of him. "What the fuck is this?" she asked.

"It's called the Usual Bullshit," he said. "And calm down. We're talking about an hour or two, not forever."

But she was angry, heels pounding as they walked back to Lucas's Porsche. "Why do you drive this piece of crap? You ought to buy something decent," she snapped.

Lucas said, "Shut the fuck up."

"What?" She goggled at him.

"I said shut the fuck up. You don't shut the fuck up, you can take the bus back to Minneapolis."

CONNELL, STILL ANGRY, trailed him into Harp's and muttered, "Oh, Lord" when she saw the bartender. The bartender was a dark-haired pixieish woman with large black eyes, two much makeup, and a bee-stung lower lip. She wore a slippery low-cut silk pullover without a bra, and a black string tie with a turquoise clasp at her throat. "Cops?" she asked, but she was smiling.

"Yeah." Lucas nodded, grinned, and tried to meet her eyes. "We need to talk to somebody who was here Friday night."

"I was," she said, dropping her elbows on the bar and leaning toward Lucas, glancing at Connell. The bartender smelled lightly of cinnamon, like a dream; she had a soft freckled cleavage. "What do you need?"

Lucas rolled out the photo of Wannemaker. "Was she here?"

The bartender watched his eyes, and, satisfied with her effect, picked up the photo and studied it. "She look like this?"

"Pretty much," Lucas said, steadfastly holding her eyes.

"What'd she do?" the bartender asked.

"Was she here?" Lucas asked again.

"Meanie," she said. "You don't want to tell me." The bartender frowned, pushed out her lower lip, studied the picture, and slowly shook her head. "No, I don't think she was. In fact, I'm sure she wasn't, if she dressed like this. Our crowd's into black. Black shirts, black pants, black dresses, black hats, black combat boots. I'd have noticed her."

"Big crowd?"

"In St. Paul?" She picked up her bar rag and scrubbed at a spot on the bar.

"Okay. . . ."

As they started out, the bartender called after them, "What'd she do?"

"It was done to her," Connell said, speaking for the first time. She made it sound like a punishment.

"Yeah?"

"She was killed."

The bartender recoiled. "Like, murdered? How?"

"Let's go," said Lucas, touching Connell's coat sleeve.

"Stabbed," said Connell.

"Let's go," Lucas repeated.

" 'Do not wait for the last judgment. It takes place every day,' " the bartender said solemnly, in a quotation voice.

Now Lucas stopped. "Who was that?" he asked.

"Some dead French dude," the bartender said.

"THAT WAS DISGUSTING," Connell fumed.

"What?"

"The way she was throwing it at you."

"What?"

"You knew."

Lucas looked back at the bar, then at Connell, a look of utter astonishment on his face. "You think she was coming on to me?"

"Kiss my ass, Davenport," she said, and stalked off toward the car.

Lucas called Anderson again. "Roux's still talking to St. Paul," Anderson said. "She wants you back here, ASAP."

"What for?"

"I don't know. But she wants you back."

CONNELL COMPLAINED MOST of the way back. They had something, she said. They should stay with it. Lucas, tired of it, offered to drop her at the St. Paul police headquarters. She declined. Roux was up to something, she said. When they walked into the chief's outer office, the bony secretary flipped a thumb toward the chief's door and they went through.

Roux was smoking furiously. She glanced at Connell, then nodded. "I guess you better stay and hear this."

"What's going on?" Lucas asked.

Roux shrugged. "We're outa here, is what's going on. No crime committed in Minneapolis. You just proved it. Wannemaker goes to that bookstore in St. Paul, gets dumped in Hudson. Let them fight about it."

"Wait a minute," said Connell.

Roux shook her head. "Meagan, I promised to help you and I did. But we've got lots of trouble right now, and this is St. Paul's killing. Your killing, up in Carlos Avery, is either Anoka County's or Duluth's. Not ours. We're putting out a press release that says our investigation concludes the murder was not committed here, that we'll cooperate with the investigating authorities, and so on."

"WAIT A FUCKING MINUTE!" Connell shouted. "Are you telling me we're done?"

"*We're* done," Roux said, still friendly, but her voice sharpening. "*You've* still got some options. We'll get your research to St. Paul, and I'll ask that they let you assist their investigation. Or you could continue with the Smits case. I don't know what Duluth is doing with that anymore."

Connell turned to Lucas, her voice harsh. "What do you think?"

Lucas stepped back. "It's an interesting case, but she's right. It's St. Paul's."

Connell's face was like a stone. She stared at Lucas for a heartbeat, then at

Roux, and then, without another word, spun and stalked out, slamming the office door behind her.

"You might have found a better way to handle that," Lucas said.

"Probably," Roux said, looking after Connell. "But I didn't know she was coming, and I was so damn happy to be out from under. Christ, Davenport, you saved my ass in four hours, finding that bookstore."

"So now what?"

Roux waved her hand expansively. "Do what you want." She took a drag on her cigarette, then took it out of her mouth and looked at it. "Jesus, sometimes I wish I was a man."

"Why?" Lucas was amused by her excitement.

" 'Cause then I could take out a big fuckin' Cuban cigar and smoke its ass off."

"You could still do that."

"Yeah, but then people who don't already think I'm a bull dyke would start thinking I'm a bull dyke. Besides, I'd barf."

LUCAS TALKED BRIEFLY to Anderson and Lester about wrapping up the paper on the case. "St. Paul will probably want to talk to you," Lester said.

"That's fine. Give them my home phone number if they call. I'll be around," Lucas said.

"Connell thinks it's a cheap shot, doesn't she? Dumping the case."

"It *is* cheap," Lucas said.

"Man, we're hurting," Lester said. "We've never hurt this bad. And if you're looking for something to do, we've still got bodies coming out of our ears. Did Greave tell you about his?"

"He mentioned something, but it didn't sound very interesting."

Sloan wandered in, hands in his pockets. He nodded to them, yawned, stretched, and to Lester said, "You gotta Coke or something? I'm a little dry."

"Do I look like a fuckin' vending machine?" Lester asked.

"What happened, Sloan?" Lucas asked, picking up the signs.

Sloan yawned again, then said, "A little pissant student named Lanny Bryson threw Heather Tatten off the bridge."

"What?" A smile broke across Lester's face, like the sun coming up.

"Got him on tape," Sloan said, ostentatiously studying his fingernails. "She was hooking, part-time. She fucked him once, but wouldn't do it twice, not even for money. They were arguing, walking across the bridge, and he tried to smooch her but she hit him with her fist, in the nose. It hurt and he got mad and when she walked away, he hit her on the back of the head with an economics textbook—big fat motherfucker—and knocked her down. She was stunned and he just picked her and pushed her over the railing. She tried to hang on at the last minute, scratched him all the way down his forearms."

"Did you use the cattle prods?" Lucas asked.

"Told us the whole fuckin' thing in one long sentence," Sloan said. "We Miranda-ed him twice on the tape. Got Polaroids of his arms; we'll get a

DNA match later. He's over in the lockup now, waiting for the public defender."

Lucas, Anderson, and Lester looked at each other, then back at Sloan. Lester stepped close, took him by the arm, and said, "Can I kiss you on the lips?"

"Better not," Sloan said. "People might think you favor me at promotion time."

A pizza arrived, too much for somebody's lunch, so they cut it up, got Cokes from the machine in the basement, had a little party, giving Sloan a hard time.

Lucas left smiling. Sloan was a friend, maybe his best friend. But at the same time, he felt . . . He looked for a word. Disgruntled? Yes. Sloan had his victory. But somewhere out there, a monster was roaming around. . . .

KOOP WAS SLICK WITH sweat, eyes shut, counting: *eleven, twelve, thirteen.* His triceps were burning, his toes reaching for the floor, his mind holding them off. *Fourteen, fifteen . . . sixteen?* No.

He was done. He dropped to the floor between the parallel bars and opened his eyes, the sweat running from his eyebrows. The burn in his arms began to even out, and he stumbled over to the toe-raise rack where he'd left the towel, mopped his face, picked up a pair of light dumbbells, and headed back to the posing room.

TWO GUY'S BODY SHOP, with a misplaced apostrophe, was the end unit of a dying shopping center on Highway 100, a shopping center marked by knee-high weeds growing out of cracked blacktop, and peeling hand-painted signs for failing tax services and obscure martial arts. Koop had parked the truck in a litter of crumbling blacktop, locked it, and gone inside.

To the right, one of the Two Guys sat behind the front desk, reading an old *Heavy Metal* magazine. To the left, a woman and two men were working around a variety of free-weight racks. The Guy looked up when Koop came in, grunted, and went back to the magazine. Koop walked past him, down a hallway where fifty musclemen stared down from curling Polaroids thumbtacked to the paneling, into the men's locker room. He changed into a jock, cutoff sweatpants, and a sleeveless T-shirt, strapped on a lifting belt, pulled on goatskin gloves stiff with dried sweat, and went back out into the main room.

Koop had a system: He divided his body into thirds, and worked a different third each day for three days. Then he took a day off, and the day after that, started over.

Shoulders and arms, first day; chest and back, second day; and then lower body. This was shoulders and arms: he worked the delts, triceps, biceps. Unlike a lot of people, he worked his forearms hard, squeezing rubber rings until the muscles screamed with acid.

And he worked his neck, both on the neck machine and with bridges. He'd never seen anyone else at Two Guy's doing bridges, but that didn't bother Koop. He'd once gone to a University of Minnesota–University of Iowa wrestling meet, and the Hawks were doing bridges. They'd kicked ass.

Koop liked bench presses. Hell, everybody liked bench presses. He did pyramids, ten reps at 350, two or three at 370, one or two at 390. He did seated behind-the-neck presses; he did curls, topping out at eighty pounds on the dumbbells, working his biceps.

At the very end, soaked with sweat, he got on a stair climber and ran up a hundred stories, then, breathing hard, he went back to the posing room.

A woman in a sweat-stained orange bikini was working in the mirrors on the west wall, moving from a frontal pose, arms over head, to a side pose, biceps flexed against her stomach. Koop dropped the dumbbells on a pad and stripped down to his jock. He picked up the dumbbells, did ten quick pumps, tossed them back on the pad, and began his routine. In the back of his mind, he could hear the woman grunting as she posed, could hear the exhaust fan overhead, but all he could see was himself . . . And sometimes, through the mist of sweat, the gossamer-wrapped body of Sara Jensen, spread-eagled on the bed, the dark pubic mound and . . .

Slam it, slam it, slam it, go, go. . . .

The woman stopped, picked up her towel. He was vaguely aware that she was standing in a corner, watching.

When he finally quit, she tossed him his towel. "Gettin' the pecs," she said.

"Need more work," he mumbled, wiping himself down. "Need more work." He carried his workout clothes back to the locker room, soaked them under a shower, wrung them by hand, threw them into a dryer and turned the dryer on. Then he showered, toweled off, dressed, went out to the main room, bought a Coke, drank it, went back and took his clothes out of the dryer, hung them in his locker, and left.

He hadn't said a word to anyone, except, "Need more work. . . ."

JOHN CARLSON WAS ALREADY in summer mode, black Raiders jacket over knee-length rapper shorts and black Nikes with red laces.

"What's happening, dude?" John was black and far too heavy. Koop handed him a small roll. John didn't check it, just stuffed it in his pocket.

"Gotta date," Koop said.

"Far out, man . . ." John rapped the car with his knuckles, as if for luck. "Get you some latex, man, you don't want to get no fuckin' AIDS."

"Do that," Koop said.

John backed away, took off his cap, and scratched his head. Koop started down the block, turned the corner. Another black kid was walking down the sidewalk. He swerved across the dirt parking strip to the curb, and when Koop slowed next to him, tossed a plastic twist through the passenger window and turned away. Koop kept going. Three blocks later, with nothing in his rearview, Koop stopped for a taste. Just a taste to wake him up.

KOOP DIDN'T UNDERSTAND his fascination with Jensen. Didn't understand why he was compelled to watch her, to get close to her. To hurry his daily rounds to meet her after work . . .

He finished liquidating the jewelry he'd taken from Jensen's apartment in a bar on the I-494 strip in Bloomington, selling the engagement ring and the wedding band to a guy who dressed and talked like an actor playing a pro athlete: a tan, a golf shirt, capped teeth, and a gold chain around his thick neck. But he knew stones, and the smile was gone from his eyes when he looked at them. He gave Koop $1,300. The total take from the apartment pushed $6,000, not counting the belt. It never occurred to Koop to feel a connection between the jewelry and the woman who'd caught his heart. The jewelry was his, not hers.

He left the Bloomington strip and idled back into Minneapolis, killing time behind the wheel, eventually turning east, to an Arby's on St. Paul's east side. He'd called the moving man who'd given him the map of Jensen's apartment, and arranged to meet. Koop was both early and late for the meetings, arriving a half hour early, watching the meeting spot from a distance. When his man arrived, alone, on time, he'd watch for another ten minutes before going in. He'd never had a contact turn on him. He didn't want it to happen, either.

The moving man arrived a few minutes early, hurried straight into the Arby's. The way he moved gave Koop some confidence that everything was okay: there was no tentativeness, no looking around. He carried a notebook in his hand. Koop waited five more minutes, watching, then went in. The guy was sitting in a booth with a cup of coffee, a young guy, looked like a college kid. Koop nodded at him, stopped for a cup of coffee himself, paid the girl behind the counter, and slid into the booth. "How're you doing?"

"It's been a while," the guy said.

"Yeah, well . . ." Koop handed him a Holiday Inn brochure. The guy took it and looked inside.

"Thanks," he said. "You must've done okay."

Koop shrugged. He wasn't much for chitchat. "Got anything else?"

"Yeah. A good one." The guy pushed the notebook at him. "I was pissing my pants waiting for you to call. We was moving some stuff into this house on Upper St. Dennis in St. Paul, you know where that is?"

"Up the hill off West Seventh," Koop said, pulling in the notebook. "Some nice houses up there. A little riffraff, too."

"This a nice house, man." The guy's head was bobbing. "*Nice.* There was a guy from a safe company there. They'd just set a big fuckin' safe in concrete, down in the basement, in a corner of a closet. I seen it myself."

"I don't do safes. . . ." The notebook was too thick. Koop opened it and found a key impression in dried putty. He'd shown the guy how to do it. The impression was crisp, clean.

"Wait a minute, for Christ's sakes," the guy said, holding up his hands. "So when he was talking to the safe guy, he was walking around with this piece of paper in his hand. When they finished, he came up and asked how long we were gonna be, 'cause he wanted to take a shower and shave, 'cause he was going out. We said we'd be a while yet, and he went up and took a shower in the bathroom. The bathroom off his bedroom. We were working right down the hall, my buddy was settin' up a guest bed. So I stepped down the hall and looked into his bedroom. I could hear the shower going, and I saw this paper laying on the dresser with his billfold and watch, and I just took the chance, man. I zipped over and looked at it, and it was the fuckin' combination. How about that, huh? I wrote it down. And listen, you know what this guy does? This guy runs half the automatic car washes in the Twin Cities. And he was braggin' to us about going out to Vegas all the time. I bet that fuckin' safe is stuffed."

"How about his family?" This sounded better; Koop would rather steal money than anything.

"He's divorced. Kids live with his old lady."

"The key's good?"

"Yeah, but, uh . . . There's a security system on the door. I don't know nothing about that."

Koop looked at the man for a minute, then nodded. "I'll think about it."

"I could use some cash, get out of this fuckin' place," the guy said. "My parole's up in September. Maybe go to Vegas myself."

"I'll get back," Koop said.

He finished his drink, picked up the notebook, nodded to the guy, and walked out. As he pulled out of the parking lot, he glanced at his watch. Sara should be getting off. . . .

KOOP HAD KILLED HIS MOTHER.

He'd killed her with a long, slender switchblade he'd found in a pawnshop in Seoul, Korea, where he'd been with the Army. When he'd gotten back to the States, he'd spent a long weekend hitchhiking from Fort Polk to Hannibal, Missouri, for the sole purpose of ripping her.

And he'd done that. He'd banged on the door and she'd opened it, a Camel glued to her lip. She'd asked, "What the fuck do you want?" and he'd said, "This." Then he'd stepped up into the trailer and she'd stepped back, and he'd stuck the knife in just about her belly button, and ripped up, right up through her breastbone. She'd opened her mouth to scream. Nothing came out but blood.

Koop had touched nothing, seen nobody. He'd grown up in Hannibal, just like Huck Finn, but he hadn't been any kind of Huck. He'd just been a dumbshit kid who never knew his father, and whose mother gave blow jobs for money after she got off work at the bar. On a busy night she might have four or five drunks stop by, banging on the aluminum door, sucking them, spitting in the sink next to his bedroom, spitting and gargling salt-and-soda, half the night gone. She'd drag him downtown, respectable eyes tearing at them, women in thigh-length skirts and tweedy jackets, pitying, disdaining. "Bitches; bitches ain't no better'n me, you better believe it," his mother said. But she was lying, and Koop knew *that* for sure. They *were* better than his mother, these women in their suits and hats and clack-clack high heels. . . .

He'd been back at Fort Polk, sitting on his bunk reading *Black Belt* magazine, when the battalion sergeant-major came by. He'd said, "Koop, I got some bad news. Your mother was found dead."

And Koop had said, "Yeah?" and turned the page.

WHEN KOOP HAD BEEN in Korea, he'd learned from the hookers outside the base that he had a problem with sex. Nothing worked right. He'd get turned on thinking about it, but then the time would come . . . and nothing would happen.

Until, in his anger, he smacked one of the women. Hit her in the forehead with a fist, knocked her flat. Things started to work.

He'd killed a woman in New Orleans. He thought of the murder as an accident: he was pounding on her, getting worked up, and suddenly she wasn't fighting back, and her head was flopping a little too loosely. That'd scared him. They had the death penalty in Louisiana, and no qualms about using it. He'd run back to Fort Polk, and was astonished when nothing happened. Nothing. Not even a story in the newspaper, not that he could find.

That's when he'd gotten the idea about killing his mother. Nothing complicated. Just do it.

AFTER THE ARMY, he'd spent a year working on the Mississippi, a barge hand. He'd eventually gotten off in St. Paul, drifted through a series of crappy jobs, finally got smart and used his veteran's preference for something a little better. A year after that, he'd picked up a woman at a Minneapolis bookstore. He'd gone for a lifter's calendar and the woman had come to him. He'd recognized her immediately: she had the wool suit and the clack-clack high heels. She'd asked him something about exercise; he couldn't remember what, it'd obviously been a pickup. . . .

He hadn't thought to take her off, but he had, and that had been better than pounding on hookers. There had been a quality to the woman, the nylons and the careful makeup, the well-rounded sentences. She was one of those women so distinctly better than his mother.

And they were everywhere. Some were too smart and tough to be taken. He stayed away from that kind. But there were also the tentative ones, awkward, afraid: not of death or pain or anything else so dramatic, but of simple loneliness. He found them in a Des Moines art gallery and in a Madison bookstore and a Thunder Bay record shop, a little older, drinking white wine, dressed carefully in cheerful colors, their hair done to hide the gray, their smiles constant, flitting, as though they were sparrows looking for a place to perch.

Koop gave them a place to perch. They were never so much wary as anxious to do the right thing. . . .

. . .

KOOP PICKED UP JENSEN when she left her office, escorted her to a Cub supermarket. Followed her inside, watching her move, her breasts shifting under her blouse, her legs, so well-muscled; the way she brushed the hair out of her eyes.

Her progress through the produce section was a sensual lesson in itself. Jensen prowled through it like a hunting cat, squeezing this, sniffing at those, poking at the others. She bought bing cherries and oranges and lemons, fat white mushrooms and celery, apples and English walnuts, grapes both green and red, and garlic. She made a brilliant salad.

Koop was in the cereals. He kept poking his head around the corner, looking at her. She never saw him, but he was so intent that he didn't see the stock kid until the kid was right on top of him.

"Can I help you?" The kid used a tone he might have used on a ten-year-old shoplifter.

Koop jumped. "What?" He was flustered. He had a cart with a package of beef jerky and a jar of dill pickles.

"What're you looking for?" The kid had a junior-cop attitude; and he was burly, too-white, with pimples, crew cut, and small pig-eyes.

"I'm not looking. I'm thinking," Koop said.

"Okay. Just asking," the kid said. But when he moved away, he went only ten feet and began rearranging boxes of cornflakes, ostentatiously watching Koop.

Sara, at the very moment that the kid asked his first question, decided she'd gotten enough produce. A moment later, as the kid went to work in the cornflakes, she came around the corner. Koop turned away from her, but she glanced up at his face. Did he see the smallest of wrinkles? He turned his back and pushed his cart out of the aisle. The fact is, she might have seen him twenty times, if she'd ever scanned the third layer of people around her, if she'd noticed the guy on the bench on the next sidewalk over as she jogged. Had she remembered him? Was that why her forehead had wrinkled? The kid had seen him watching her. Would he say anything?

Koop thought about abandoning his cart, but decided that would be worse than hanging on. He pushed it to the express lane, bought a newspaper, paid, and went on to the parking lot. While he was waiting to pay, he saw the kid step out of an aisle, his fists on his hips, watching. A wave of hate washed over him. He'd get the little fucker, get him in the parking lot, rip his fucking face off . . . Koop closed his eyes, controlling it, controlling himself. When he fantasized, the adrenaline started rolling through his blood, and he almost *had* to break something.

But the kid just wasn't worth it. Asshole. . . .

He left the supermarket parking lot, looking for the kid in his rearview mirror, but the kid had apparently gone back to work. Good enough—but he wouldn't be going back there. Out of the lot, he pulled into a street-side parking space and waited. Twenty minutes later, Jensen came by.

His true love. . . .

Koop loved to watch her when she was moving. He loved her on the streets, where he could see her legs and ass, liked to see her body contorting as she leaned or bent or stooped; liked to watch her tits bobbling when she went for a run around the lake. Really liked that.

He was aflame.

MONDAY WAS A WARM NIGHT, moths batting against the park lights. Jensen finished her run and disappeared inside. Koop was stricken with what might have been grief, to see her go like that. He stood outside, watching the door. Would she be back out? His eyes rolled up the building. He knew her window, had known from the first night. . . . The light came on.

He sighed and turned away. Across the street, a man fumbled for keys, opened the lobby door to his apartment building, walked through, then used his key to unlock the inner door. Koop's eyes drifted upward. The top floor was just about even with Jensen's.

With a growing tingle of excitement, he counted floors. And crashed. The roof would be below her window, he thought. He wouldn't be able to see inside. But it was worth checking. He crossed the street, moving quickly, stepped into the apartment lobby. Two hundred apartments, each with a call button. He slapped a hundred of them: somebody would be expecting a visitor. The intercom scratched at him, but at the same moment the door lock buzzed, and he pushed through, leaving behind the voice on the intercom: "Who's there? Who's there?"

This would work twice, but he couldn't count on it more often than that. He turned the corner to the elevators, rode to the top. Nobody in the hall. The Exit sign was far down to the left. He walked down to the Exit sign, opened the door, stepped through it. A flight of steps went down to the left, and two more went up to the right, to a gray metal door. A small black-and-white sign on the door said, "Roof Access—Room Key Necessary to Unlock and to Re-enter."

"Shit." He pulled at the door. Nothing. Good lock.

He turned to the steps, thinking to start back down. Then thought: *Wait.* Did the window at the end of the hall look out at Jensen's building?

It did.

Koop stood in the window, looking up, and a bare two stories above, Sara Jensen came to the window in a robe and looked down. Koop stepped back, but she was looking at the street and hadn't noticed him in the semidark window. She had a drink in her hand. She took a sip and stepped away, out of sight.

Jesus. A little higher, and he'd be virtually in her living room. She never pulled the drapes. Never. . . .

KOOP WAS AFLAME. A match; a killer.

He needed a key. Not sometime. He needed one now.

He'd picked up his philosophy at Stillwater: power comes out of the barrel of a gun; or from a club, or a fist. Take care of number one. The tough live, the weak die. When you die, you go into a hole: end of story. No harps, no heavenly choir. No hellfire. Koop resonated with this line of thought. It fit so well with everything he'd experienced in life.

He went back to his truck for equipment, not thinking very much, not on the surface. When he needed something—anything—that thing became his: the people who had it were keeping it from him. He had the *right* to take it.

Koop was proud of his truck. It might have belonged to anyone. But it didn't. It belonged to him, and it was special.

He didn't carry much in the back, in the topper: a toolbox, a couple of bags of Salt 'N Sand left over from winter, a spade, a set of snow tires, a tow rope that had been in the truck when he bought it. And a few lengths of rusty concrete reinforcement rod—the kind of thing you might find lying in the dirt around a construction site, which was, in fact, where he had found it. The kind of thing a workingman would have back there.

Most of the stuff was simply a disguise for the big Sears toolbox. That's where the action was. The top tray contained a few light screwdrivers, pliers, a ratchet set, a half-dozen Sucrets cans full of a variety of wood screws, and other small items. The bottom compartment held a two-pound hammer, a cold chisel, two files, a hacksaw, a short pry-bar, a pair of work gloves, and a can of glazier's putty. What looked like an ordinary toolbox was, in fact, a decent set of burglary tools.

He put the gloves in his jacket pocket, took out the glazier's putty, dumped the screws from one of the Sucrets cans into an empty compartment in the top tray, and scooped a gob of putty into the Sucrets tin. He smoothed the putty with his thumb, closed the tin, and dropped it into his pocket.

Then he selected a piece of re-rod. A nice eighteen-inch length, easy to hide and long enough to swing.

He still wasn't thinking much: the room key was his. This asshole—some asshole—was keeping it from him. *That* made him angry. Really angry. Righteously angry. Koop began to fume, thinking about—*his fuckin' key*—and headed back to the apartment building, driving the truck.

He parked half a block away, walked down to the apartment entrance, pulling on the work gloves, the re-rod up his jacket sleeve. Nobody around. He stepped into the lobby, pushed up the glass panel on the inset ceiling light, and used the re-rod to crack both fluorescent tubes. Now in the dark, he dropped the panel back in place and returned to the truck. He left the driver's-side door open an inch and waited.

And waited some more. Not much happening.

The passenger seat was what made the truck special. He'd gotten some work done in an Iowa machine shop: a steel box, slightly shallower but a bit longer and wider than a cigar box, had been welded under the seat. The original floor was the lid of the box, and from below, the bottom of the box looked like the floor of the passenger compartment. To open the box, you turned the right front seat support once to the right, and the lid popped up. There was enough room for any amount of jewelry or cash. . . . Or cocaine.

Half the people in Stillwater were there because they'd been caught in a traffic stop and had the cocaine/stolen stereo/gun on the backseat. Not Koop.

He watched the door for a while longer, then popped the lid on the box, pulled out the eight-ball, pinched it, put it back. Just a little nose, just enough to sharpen him up.

Two mature arborvitae stood on either side of the apartment's concrete stoop, like sentinels. Koop liked that: the trees cut the vision lines from either side. To see into the outer lobby, you had to be standing almost straight out from the building.

A couple came down the walk, the man jingling his keys. They went inside, and Koop waited. A woman was next, alone, and Koop perked up. But she was walking straight down the sidewalk, distracted, and not until the last minute did she swerve in toward the building. She would have been perfect, but she hadn't given him time to move. She disappeared inside.

Two men, holding hands, came down the walk. No. Two or three minutes later, they were followed by a guy so big that Koop decided not to risk it.

Then Jim Flory turned the corner, his keys already in his hand. Flory scratched himself at his left sideburn and mumbled something, talking to himself, distracted. He was five-ten and slender. Koop pushed open the car door and slipped out, started down the sidewalk. Flory turned in at the building, took his keys out of his pocket, fumbled through them, pulled open the outer door, went inside.

Koop was angry: he could feel the heat in his bowels. *Fucker has my key. Fucker.* . . .

Koop followed Flory up the walk; Koop was whistling softly, an unconscious, disguising tactic, but he was pissed. *Has my key* . . . Koop was wearing a baseball cap, jeans, a golf shirt, and large white athletic shoes, like a guy just back from a Twins game. He kept the hat bill tipped down. The steel re-rod was in his right pocket, sticking out a full foot but hidden by his naturally swinging arm.

Goddamned asshole, got my key . . . *Zip-a-dee-doo-dah*, he whistled, *Zip-a-dee-ay*, and he was getting angrier by the second. *My key.* . . .

Through the glass outer door, he could see Flory fumbling in the dark at the inner lock. Key must be in his hand. Koop pulled open the outer door, and Flory, turning the key on the inner door, glanced back and said, "Hi."

Koop nodded and said, "Hey," kept the bill of his hat down. Flory turned back to the door and pulled on it, and as he did, Koop, the cocaine right there, slipped the re-rod out of his pocket.

Flory might have felt something, sensed the suddenness of the movement: he stopped with the key, his head coming up, but too late.

Motherfucker has my key/key/key. . . .

Koop slashed him with the re-rod, smashed him behind the ear. The re-rod hit, *pak!*, metal on meat, the sound of a butcher's cleaver cutting through a rib roast.

Flory's mouth opened and a single syllable came out: "Unk." His head bounced off the glass door and he fell, dragging his hands down the glass.

Koop, moving fast now, nothing casual now, bent, glancing ferretlike outside, then stripped Flory of his wallet: *a robbery*. He stashed the wallet in his pocket, pulled Flory's key from the lock, opened the Sucrets tin, and quickly pressed one side and then the other into the glazier's putty. The putty was just firm, and took perfect impressions. He shut the tin, wiped the key on his pants leg, and pushed it back into the lock.

Done.

He turned, still half crouching, reached for the outer door—and saw the legs.

A woman stumbled on the other side of the door, trying to backpedal, already turning.

She wore tennis shoes and a jogging suit. He'd never seen her coming. He exploded through the door, batting the glass out of his way with one hand, the other pulling the re-rod from his pocket.

"No." She shouted it. Her face was frozen, mouth open. In the dim light, she could see the body on the floor behind him, and she was stumbling back, trying to make her legs move, to run, shocked. . . .

Koop hit her like a leopard, already swinging the re-rod.

"No," she screamed again, eyes widening, teeth flashing in fear. She put up her arm and the re-rod crashed through it, breaking it, missing her head. "No," she screamed again, turning, and Koop, above her and coming down, hit her on the back of the neck just where it joined her skull, a blow that would have decapitated her if he'd been swinging a sword.

Blood spattered the sidewalk and she went down to the stoop, and Koop hit her again, this time across the top of her undefended skull, a full, merciless swing, ending with a *crunch*, like a heavy man stepping on gravel.

Her head flattened, and Koop, maddened by the interference, by the trouble, by the crisis, kicked her body off the step behind the arborvitae.

"Motherfucker," he said. "Motherfucker." He hadn't intended this. He had to *move*.

Less than a minute had passed since he'd hit Flory. No one else was on the walk. He looked across the street, for motion in the windows of Sara Jensen's apartment building, for a face looking down at him. Nothing that he could see.

He started away at a fast walk, sticking the re-rod in his pocket. Jesus, what was this: there was blood on his jacket. He wiped at it with a hand, smeared it. If a cop came . . .

The anger boiled up: the goddamned bitch, coming up like that.

He swallowed it, fighting it, kept moving. *Gotta keep moving* . . . He glanced back, crossed the street, almost scurrying, now with the smell of warm human blood in his nose, in his mouth. Didn't mind that, but not here, not now. . . .

Maybe, he thought, he should walk out. He was tempted to walk out and return later for the company car: if somebody saw him hit the woman and followed him to the car, they'd see the badge on the side and that'd be it. On the other hand, the cops would probably be taking the license numbers of cars in the neighborhood, looking for witnesses.

No. He would take it.

He popped the driver's-side door, caught a glimpse of himself in the dark glass, face twisted under the ball cap, dark scratches across it.

He fired up the truck and wiped his face at the same time: more blood on his gloves. Christ, it was all over him. He could taste it, it was in his mouth. . . .

He eased out of the parking space. Watched in the rearview mirror for somebody running, somebody pointing. He saw nothing but empty street.

Nothing.

The stress tightened him. He could feel the muscles pumping, his body filling out. Taste the blood . . . And suddenly, there was a flush of pleasure with a rash of pain, like being hand-stroked while ants crawled across you. . . .

More good than bad. Much more.

6

WEATHER WASN'T HOME. Lucas suppressed a thump of worry: she should have been home an hour earlier. He picked up the phone, but there was nothing on voice mail, and he hung up.

He walked back to the bedroom, pulling off his tie. The bedroom smelled almost subliminally of her Chanel No. 5; and on top of that, very faintly of wood polish. She'd bought a new bedroom set, simple wooden furniture with an elegant line, slightly Craftsman-Mission. He grumbled. His old stuff was good enough, he'd had it for years. She didn't want to hear it.

"You've got a twenty-year-old queen-sized bed that looks like it's been pounded to death by strange women—I won't ask—and you don't have a headboard, so the bed just sits there like a launching pad. Don't you read in bed? Don't you know about headboard lights? Wouldn't you like some nice pillows?"

Maybe, if somebody else bought them.

And his old dresser, she said, looked like it had come from the Salvation Army.

He didn't tell her, but she was precisely correct.

She said nothing at all about his chair. His chair was older than the bed, bought at a rummage sale after a St. Thomas professor had died and left it behind. It was massive, comfortable, and the leather was fake. She did throw out a mostly unused second chair with a stain on one arm—Lucas couldn't remember what it was, but it got there during a Vikings-Packers game—and replaced it with a comfortable love seat.

"If we're going to watch television in our old age, we should sit next to each other," she said. "The first goddamn thing men do when they get a television is put two E-Z Boys in front of it and a table between them for beer cans and pizzas. I swear to God I won't allow it."

"Yeah, yeah, just don't fuck with my chair," Lucas had said. He'd said it lightly, but he was worried.

She understood that. "The chair's safe. Ugly, but safe."

"Ugly? That's genuine glove . . . material."

"Really? They make gloves out of garbage bags?"

WEATHER KARKINNEN WAS a surgeon. She was a small woman in her late thirties, her blondish hair beginning to show streaks of white. She had dark-blue eyes, high cheekbones, and a wide mouth. She looked vaguely Russian, Lucas thought. She had broad shoulders for her size, and wiry muscles; she played a vicious game of squash and could sail anything. He liked to watch her move, he liked to watch her in repose, when she was working over a problem. He even liked to watch her when she slept, because she did it so thoroughly, like a kitten.

When Lucas thought of her, which he might do at any moment, the same image always popped up in his mind's eye: Weather turning to look at him over her shoulder, smiling, a simple pearl dangling just over her shoulder.

They would be married, he thought. She'd said, "Don't ask yet."

"Why? Would you say no?"

She'd poked him in the navel with her forefinger. "No. I'd say yes. But don't ask yet. Wait a while."

"Until when?"

"You'll know."

So he hadn't asked; and somewhere, deep inside, he was afraid, he was relieved. Did he want out? He'd never experienced this closeness. It was different. It could be . . . frightening.

LUCAS WAS DOWN TO his underpants when the phone rang in the kitchen. He picked up the silent bedroom extension and said, "Yeah?"

"Chief Davenport?" Connell. She sounded tight.

"Meagan, you can start calling me Lucas," he said.

"Okay. I just wanted to say, uh, don't throw away your files. On the case." There was an odd thumping sound behind her. He'd heard it before, but he couldn't place it.

"What?"

"I said, don't throw away your files."

"Meagan, what're you talking about?"

"I'll see you tomorrow. Okay?"

"Meagan . . . ?" But she was gone.

Lucas looked at the telephone, frowned, shook his head, and hung it up. He dug through the new dresser, got running shorts, picked up a sleeveless sweatshirt that he'd thrown on top of a hamper, pulled it on, and stopped with one arm through a sleeve. The thumping sound he'd heard behind Connell—keyboards. Wherever she was, there were three or four people keyboarding a few feet away. Could be her office, though it was late.

Could be a newspaper.

Could be a television station.

His line of thought was broken by the sound of the garage door going up. Weather. A small rock rolled off his chest. He pulled the sweatshirt over his head, picked up his socks and running shoes, and walked barefoot back through the house.

"Hey." She'd stopped in the kitchen, was taking a Sprite out of the refrigerator. He kissed her on the cheek. "Do anything good?"

"I watched Harrison and MacRinney do a free flap on a kid with Bell's palsy," she said, popping the top on the can.

"Interesting?" She put her purse on the kitchen counter and turned her face up to him: her face was a little lopsided, as though she'd had a ring career before turning to medicine. He loved the face; he could remember reacting the first time he'd talked with her, in a horror of a burned-out murder scene in northern Wisconsin: she wasn't very pretty, he'd thought, but she was *very* attractive. And a little while later, she'd cut his throat with a jackknife. . . .

Now she nodded. "Couldn't see some of the critical stuff—mostly clearing away a lot of fat, which is pretty picky. They had a double operating microscope, so I could watch Harrison work part of the time. He put five square knots around the edge of an artery that wasn't a heck of a lot bigger than a broom straw."

"Could you do that?"

"Maybe," she said, her voice serious. He'd learned about surgeons and their competitive instincts. He knew how to push her buttons. "Eventually, but . . . You're pushing my buttons."

"Maybe."

She stopped, stood back and looked at him, picking something up from his voice. "Did something happen?"

He shrugged. "I had a fairly interesting case for about fifteen minutes this afternoon. It's gone now, but . . . I don't know."

"Interesting?" She worried.

"Yeah, there's a woman from the BCA who thinks we've got a serial killer around. She's a little crazy, but she might be right."

Now she was worried. She stepped back toward him. "I don't want you to get hurt again, messing with some maniac."

"It's over, I think. We're off the case."

"Off?"

Lucas explained, including the strange call from Connell. Weather listened intently, finishing the Sprite. "You think she's up to something," she said when he finished.

"It sounded like it. I hope she doesn't get burned. C'mon. Let's run."

"Can we go down to Grand and get ice cream afterwards?"

"We'll have to do four miles."

"God, you're hard."

AFTER DARK, AFTER THE run and the ice cream, Weather began review-ing notes for the next morning's operation. Lucas was amazed by how often she operated. His knowledge of surgery came from television, where every opera-tion was a crisis, undertaken only with great study and some peril. With Weather, it was routine. She operated almost every day, and some days, two or three times. "You've got to do it a lot, if you're going to do it at all," she said. She'd be in bed by ten and up by five-thirty.

Lucas did business for a while, then prowled the house, finally went down the basement for a small off-duty gun, clipped it under his waistband and pulled his golf shirt over it. "I'm going out for a while," he said.

Weather looked up from the bed. "I thought the case was over."

"Ehh. I'm looking for a guy."

"So take it easy," she said. She had a yellow pencil clenched between her teeth, and spoke around it; she looked cute, but he picked up the tiny spark of fear in her eyes.

He grinned and said, "No sweat. I'll tell you straight out when there might be a problem."

"Sure."

Lucas's house was on the east bank of the Mississippi, in a quiet neighbor-hood of tall dying elms and a few oaks, with the new maples and ginkgoes and ash trees replacing the disappearing elm. At night, the streets were alive with middle-class joggers working off the office flab, and couples strolling hand in hand along the dimly lit walkways. When Lucas stopped in the street to shift gears, he heard a woman laugh somewhere not too far away; he almost went back inside to Weather.

Instead, he headed to the Randolph Lake Bridge, crossed the Mississippi, and a mile farther on was deep into the Lake Street strip. He cruised the cocktail lounges, porno stores, junk shops, rental-furniture places, check-cashing joints, and low-end fast-food franchises that ran through a brutally ugly landscape of cheap lighted signs. Children wandered around at all times of day and night, mixing with the suburban coke-seekers, dealers, drunks, raggedy-hip insurance salesmen, and a few lost souls from St. Paul, desperately seeking the shortcut home. A pair of cops pulled up alongside the Porsche at a stoplight and looked him over, thinking *Dope dealer*. He rolled down his window and the driver grinned and said something, and the passenger-side cop rolled down his win-dow and said, "Davenport?"

"Yeah."

"Great car, man."

The driver called across his partner, "Hey, dude, you got a little rock? I could use a taste, mon."

. . .

FRANKLIN AVENUE WAS AS rugged as Lake Street, but darker. Lucas pulled a slip of paper from his pocket, turned on a reading light, checked the address he had for Junky Doog, and went looking for it. Half the buildings were missing their numbers. When he found the right place, there was a light in the window and a half-dozen people sitting on the porch outside.

Lucas parked, climbed out, and the talk on the porch stopped. He walked halfway up the broken front sidewalk and stopped. "There a guy named Junky Doog who lives here?"

A heavyset Indian woman heaved herself out of a lawn chair. "Not now. All my family live here now."

"Do you know him?"

"No, I don't, Mr. Police." She was polite. "We've been here almost four months and never heard the name."

Lucas nodded. "Okay." He believed her.

LUCAS STARTED CRAWLING BARS, talking to bartenders and customers. He'd lost time on the street, and the players had changed. Here and there, somebody picked him out, said his name, held up a hand: the faces and names came back, but the information was sparse.

He started back home, saw the Blue Bull on a side street, and decided to make a last stop.

A half-dozen cars were parked at odd attitudes around the bar's tiny parking lot, as though they'd been abandoned to avoid a bombing run. The Blue Bull's windows were tinted, so that patrons could see who was coming in from the lot without being seen themselves. Lucas left the Porsche at a fire hydrant on the street, sniffed the night air—creosote and tar—and went inside.

The Blue Bull could sell cheap drinks, the owner said, because he avoided high overhead. He avoided it by never fixing anything. The pool table had grooves that would roll a ball though a thirty-degree arc into a corner pocket. The overhead fans hadn't moved since the sixties. The jukebox had broken halfway through a Guy Lombardo record, and hadn't moved since.

Nor did the decor change: red-flocked whorehouse wallpaper with a patina of beer and tobacco smoke. The obese bartender, however, was new. Lucas dropped on a stool and the bartender wiped his way over. "Yeah?"

"Carl Stupella still work here?" Lucas asked.

The bartender coughed before answering, turning his head away, not bothering to cover his mouth. Spit flew down the bar. "Carl's dead," he said, recovering.

"Dead?"

"Yeah. Choked on a bratwurst at a Twins game."

"You gotta be kidding me."

The bartender shrugged, started a smile, thought better of it, and shrugged again. Coughed. "His time was up," he said piously, running his rag in a circle. "You a friend of his?"

"Jesus Christ, no. I'm looking for another guy. Carl knew him."

"Carl *was* an asshole," the bartender said philosophically. He leaned one elbow on the bar. "You a cop?"

"Yup."

The bartender looked around. There were seven other people in the bar, five sitting alone, looking at nothing at all, the other two with their heads hunched together so they could whisper. "Who're you looking for?"

"Randolph Leski? He used to hang out here."

The bartender's eye shifted down the bar, then back to Lucas. He leaned forward, dropping his voice. "Does this shit bring in money?"

"Sometimes. You get on the list. . . ."

"Randy's about eight stools down," he muttered. "On the other side of the next two guys."

Lucas nodded, and a moment later, leaned back a few inches and glanced to his right. Looking at the bartender again, he said quietly, "The guy I'm looking for is big as you."

"You mean fat," the bartender said.

"Hefty."

The bartender tilted his head. "Randy had a tumor. They took out most of his gut. He can't keep the weight on no more. They say he eats a pork chop, he shits sausages. They don't digest."

Lucas looked down the bar again, said, "Give me a draw, whatever."

The bartender nodded, stepped away. Lucas took a business card out of his pocket, rolled out a twenty and the business card. "Thanks. What's your name?"

"Earl. Stupella."

"Carl's . . ."

"Brother."

"Maybe you hear something serious sometime, you call me," Lucas said. "Keep the change."

LUCAS PICKED UP THE glass of beer and wandered down the bar. Stopped, did a double take. The thin man on the stool turned his head: loose skin hung around his face and neck like a basset hound's, but Randy Leski's mean little pig-eyes peered out of it.

"Randy," Lucas said. "As I live and breathe."

Leski shook his head once, as though annoyed by a fly in a kitchen. Leski ran repair scams, specializing in the elderly. Lucas had made him a hobby. "Go away. Please."

"Jesus. Old friends," Lucas said, spreading his arms. The other talk in the bar died. "You're looking great, man. You been on a diet?"

"Kiss my ass, Davenport. Whatever you want, I don't got it."

"I'm looking for Junky Doog."

Leski sat a little straighter. "Junky? He cut on somebody?"

"I just need to talk to him."

Leski suddenly giggled. "Christ, old Junky." He made a gesture as if wiping a tear away from his eyes. "I tell you, the last I heard of him, he was working out at a landfill in Dakota County."

"Landfill?"

"Yeah. The dump. I don't know which one, I just hear this from some guys. Christ, born in a junkyard, the guy gets sent to the nuthouse. When they kick him out of there, he winds up in a dump. Some people got all the luck, huh?" Leski started laughing, great phlegm-sucking wheezes.

Lucas looked at him for a while, waiting for the wheezing to subside, then nodded.

Leski said, "I hear you're back."

"Yeah."

Leski took a sip of his beer, grimaced, looked down at it, and said, "I heard when you got shot last winter. First time I been in a Catholic church since we were kids."

"A church?"

"I was praying my ass off that you'd fuckin' croak," Leski said. "After a lot of pain."

"Thanks for thinking of me," Lucas said. "You still run deals on old people?"

"Go hump yourself."

"You're a breath of fresh air, Randy . . . Hey." Leski's old sport coat had an odd crinkle, a lump. Lucas touched his side. "Are you carrying?"

"C'mon, leave me alone, Davenport."

Randy Leski never carried: it was like an article of his religion. "What the hell happened?"

Leski was a felon. Carrying could put him inside. He looked down at his beer. "You seen my neighborhood?"

"Not lately."

"Bad news. Bad news, Davenport. Glad my mother didn't live to see it. These kids, Davenport, they'll kill you for bumping into them," Leski said, tilting his head sideways to look at Lucas. His eyes were the color of water. "I swear to God, I was in Pansy's the other night, and this asshole kid starts giving some shit to this girl, and her boyfriend stands up—Bill McGuane's boy—and says to her, 'C'mon, let's go.' And they go. And I sees Bill, and I mention it, and he says, 'I told that kid, don't fight, ever. He's no chickenshit, but it's worth your life to fight.' And he's right, Davenport. You can't walk down the street without worrying that somebody's gonna knock you in the head. For nothin'. For not a fuckin' thing. It used to be, if somebody was looking for you, they had a reason you could understand. Now? For nothing."

"Well, take it easy with the piece, huh?"

"Yeah." Leski turned back to the bar and Lucas stepped away and turned. Then Leski suddenly giggled, his flaps of facial flesh trembling with the effort, and said, "Junky Doog." And giggled some more.

Outside, Lucas looked around, couldn't think of anything else to do. Far away, he could hear sirens—lots of them. Something going on, but he didn't know where. He thought about calling in, finding out where the action was; but that many sirens, it was probably a fire or an auto accident. He sighed, a little tired now, and headed back to the car.

WEATHER WAS ASLEEP. She'd be up at six, moving quietly not to wake him; by seven, she'd be in the OR; Lucas would sleep for three hours after that. Now, he undressed in the main bath down the hall from the bedroom, took a quick shower to get the bar smoke off his skin, and then slipped in beside her. He let himself roll against her, her leg smooth against his. Weather slept in an old-fashioned man's T-shirt and bikini pants, which left something—not much—to the imagination.

He lay on his back and got a quick mental snapshot of her in the shirt and underpants, bouncing around the bedroom. Sometimes, when she wasn't operating the next morning, he'd get the same snapshot, couldn't escape it, and his hand would creep up under the T-shirt. . . .

Not tonight. Too late. He turned his head, kissed her goodnight. He should always do that, she'd told him: her subconscious would know.

What seemed like a long time later, Lucas felt her hand on him and opened his eyes. The room was dimly lit, daylight filtering around the curtains. Weather, sitting fully dressed on the bed beside him, gave him another tantalizing twitch. "It's nice that men have handles," she said. "It makes them easy to wake up."

"Huh?" He was barely conscious.

"You better come out and look at the TV," she said, letting go of him. "The *Openers* program is talking about you."

"Me?" He struggled to sit up.

"What's that quaint phrase you police officers use? 'The fuckin' shit has hit the fan?' I think that's it."

ANDERSON WAS WAITING IN the corridor outside Lucas's office, reading through a handful of computer printouts. He pushed away from the wall when he saw Lucas.

"Chief wants to see us *now*."

"I know, I got a call. I saw TV3," Lucas said.

"Paper for you," Anderson said, handing Lucas a manila file. "The overnights on Wannemaker. Nothing in the galleries. The Camel's confirmed, the tobacco on her body matched the tobacco in the cigarette. There were ligature marks on her wrists, but no ties; her ankles were tied with a piece of yellow polypropylene rope. The rope was old, partially degraded by exposure to sunlight, so if we can find any more of it, they could probably make a match."

"Anything else? Any skin, semen, anything?"

"Not so far . . . And here's the Bey file."

"Jesus." Lucas took the file, flipped it open. Most of the paper inside had been Xeroxed for Connell's report; a few minor things he hadn't seen before. Mercedes Bey, thirty-seven, killed in 1984, file still open. The first of Connell's list, the centerpiece of the TV3 story.

"Have you heard about the lakes?" Anderson asked, his voice pitching lower, as though he were about to tell a particularly dirty joke.

"What happened?" Lucas looked up from the Bey file.

"We've got a bad one over by the lakes. Too late to make morning TV. Guy and his girlfriend, maybe his girlfriend. Guy's in a coma, could be a veggie. The woman's dead. Her head was crushed, probably by a pipe or a steel bar. Or a rifle barrel or a long-barreled pistol, maybe a Redhawk. Small-time robbery, looks like. Really ugly. *Really* ugly."

"They're freaking out in homicide?"

"Everybody's freaking out," Anderson said. "Everybody went over there. Roux just got back. And then this TV3 thing—the chief is hot. Really hot."

Roux was furious. She jabbed her cigarette at Lucas. "Tell me you didn't have anything to do with it."

Lucas shrugged, looked at the others, and sat down. "I didn't have anything to do with it."

Roux nodded, took a long drag on her cigarette; her office smelled like a bowling alley on league night. Lester sat in a corner with his legs crossed, unhappy. Anderson perched on a chair, peering owlishly at Roux through his thick-lensed glasses. "I didn't think so," Roux said. "But we all know who did."

"Mmm." Lucas didn't want to say it.

"Don't want to say it?" Roux asked. "I'll say it. That fuckin' Connell."

"Twelve minutes," Anderson said. "Longest story TV3's ever run. They *must* have had Connell's file. They had every name and date nailed down. They dug up some file video on the Mercedes Bey killing. They used stuff they'd have never used back then, when they made it. And the stuff on Wannemaker, Jesus Christ, they had video of the body being hoisted out of the Dumpster, no bag, no nothing, just this big fuckin' lump of guts with a face hanging off it."

"Shot it from the bridge," Lucas said. "We saw them up there. I didn't know the lenses were that good, though."

"Bey's still an open file, of course," Lester said, recrossing his legs from one side to the other. "No statute of limitations on murder."

"Should have thought of that yesterday," Roux said, getting up to pace the carpet, flicking ashes with every other step. Her hair, never particularly chic, was standing up in spots, like small horns. "They had Bey's mother on. She's this fragile old lady in a nursing-home housecoat, a face like parchment. She said we abandoned her daughter to her killers. She looked like shit, she looked like she was dying. They must've dumped her out of bed at three in the morning to get the tape."

"That video of Connell was pretty weird, if she's the one who tipped them," Anderson suggested.

"Aw, they phonied it up," Roux said, waving her cigarette hand dismissively. "I did the same goddamned thing when I was sourcing off the appropriations committee. They take you out on the street and have you walk into some building so it looks like surveillance film or file stuff. She did it, all right." Roux looked at Davenport. "I've got the press ten minutes from now."

"Good luck." He smiled, a very thin, unpleasant smile.

"You were never taken off the case, right?" Her left eyebrow went up and down.

"Of course not," Lucas said. "Their source was misinformed. I spent the evening working the case and even developed a lead on a new suspect."

"Is that right?" The eyebrow again.

"More or less," Lucas said. "Junky Doog may be working at a landfill out in Dakota County."

"Huh. I'd call that a critical development," Roux said, showing an inch of satisfaction. "If you can bring him in today, I'll personally feed it directly and exclusively to the *Strib*. And anything else you get. Fuck TV3."

"If Connell's their source, they'll know you're lying about not calling off the case," Lester said.

"Yeah? So what?" Roux said. "What're they gonna do, argue? Reveal their source? Fuck 'em."

"Is Connell still working with me?" Lucas asked.

"We've got no choice," Roux snapped. "If we didn't call off the investigation, then she must still be on it, right? I'll take care of her later."

"She's got no later," Lucas said.

"Jesus," Roux said, stopping in midpace. "Jesus, I wish you hadn't said that."

THE TV3 STORY HAD BEEN a mélange of file video, with commentary by a stunning blond reporter with a distinctly erotic overbite. The reporter, street-dressed in expensive grunge, rapped out long, intense accusations based on Connell's file; behind her, floodlit in the best Addams Family style, was the redbrick slum building where Mercedes Bey had been found slashed to death. She recounted Bey's and each of the subsequent murders, reading details from the autopsy reports. She said, "With Chief Roux's controversial decision to sweep the investigation under the rug . . ." and "With the Minneapolis police abandoning the murder investigation for what appear to be political reasons . . ." and "Will Mercedes Bey's cry for justice be crushed by the Minneapolis Police Department's logrolling? Will other innocent Minneapolis-area women be forced to pay the killer's brutal toll because of this decision? We shall have to wait and see...."

"Nobody fucks with me like this," Roux was shouting at her press aide when Lucas left her office with Anderson. "Nobody fucks with me...."

Anderson grinned at Lucas and said, "Connell does."

GREAVE CAUGHT LUCAS in the hall. "I read the file, but it was a waste of time. I could have gotten the executive summary on TV this morning." He was wearing a loose lavender suit with a blue silk tie.

"Yeah," Lucas grunted. He unlocked his office door and Greave followed him inside. Lucas checked his phone for voice mail, found a message, and poked in the retrieval code. Meagan Connell's voice, humble: "I saw the stories on TV this morning. Does this change anything?" Lucas grinned at the impertinence, and scribbled down the number she left.

"What're we doing?" Greave asked.

"Gonna see if we can find a guy down in Dakota County. Former sex psycho who liked knives." He'd been punching in Connell's number as he spoke. The phone rang once, and Connell picked up. "This is Davenport."

"Jeez," Connell said, "I've been watching TV...."

"Yeah, yeah. There're three guys in town don't know who the source is, and none of them are Roux. You better lay low today. She's smokin'. In the meantime, we're back on the case."

"Back on." She made it a statement, with an overtone of satisfaction. No denials. "Is there anything new?"

He told her about Anderson's information from the Wisconsin forensic lab.

"Ligatures? If he tied her up, he must've taken her somewhere. That's a first. I bet he took her to his home. He lives here—he didn't at the other crime scenes, so he couldn't take them.... Hey, and if you read the Mercedes Bey file, I think she was missing awhile, too, before they found her."

"Could be something," Lucas agreed. "Greave and I are going after Junky Doog. I've got a line on him."

"I'd like to go."

"No. I don't want you around today," Lucas said. "It's best, believe me."

"How about if I make some calls?" she asked.

"To who?"

"The people on the bookstore list."

"St. Paul should be doing that," Lucas said.

"Not yet, they aren't. I'll get going right now."

"Talk to Lester first," Lucas said. "Get them to clear it with St. Paul. That part of the investigation really does belong to them."

"ARE YOU GONNA LISTEN to my story?" Greave asked as they walked out to the Porsche.

"Do I gotta?"

"Unless you want to listen to me whine for a couple hours."

"Talk," Lucas said.

A schoolteacher named Charmagne Carter had been found dead in her bed, Greave said. Her apartment was locked from the inside. The apartment was covered by a security system that used motion and infrared detectors with direct dial-out to an alarm-monitoring company.

"Completely locked?"

"Sealed tight."

"Why do you think she was murdered?"

"Her death was very convenient for some bad people."

"Say a name."

"The Joyce brothers, John and George," Greave said. "Know them?"

Lucas smiled. "Excellent," he said.

"What?"

"I played hockey against them when I was a kid," he said. "They were assholes then, they're assholes now."

The Joyces had almost been rich, Greave said. They'd started by leasing slum housing from the owners—mostly defense attorneys, it seemed—and renting out the apartments. When they'd accumulated enough cash, they bought a couple of flophouses. When housing the homeless became fashionable, they brought the flops up to minimum standards and unloaded them on a charitable foundation.

"The foundation director came into a large BMW shortly thereafter," Greave said.

"Skipped his lunches and saved the money," Lucas said.

"No doubt," Greave said. "So the Joyces took the money and started pyramiding apartments. I'm told they controlled like five to six million bucks at one point. Then the economy fell on its ass. Especially apartments."

"Aww."

"Anyway, the Joyces saved what they could from the pyramid, and put every buck into this old apartment building on the Southeast Side. Forty units. Wide hallways."

"Wide hallways?"

"Yeah. Wide. The idea was, they'd throw in some new drywall and a bunch of spackling compound and paint, cut down the cupboards, stick in some new low-rider stoves and refrigerators, and sell the place to the city as public housing for the handicapped. They had somebody juiced: the city council was hot to go. The Joyces figured to turn a million and a half on the deal. But there was a fly in the ointment."

The teacher, Charmagne Carter, and a dozen other older tenants had been given long-term leases on their apartments by the last manager of the building before the Joyces bought it, Greave said. The manager knew he'd lose his job in the sale, and apparently made the leases as a quirky kind of revenge. The city wouldn't take the building with the long-term leases in effect. The Joyces bought out a few of the leases, and sued the people who wouldn't sell. The district court upheld the leases.

"The leases are $500 a month for fifteen years plus a two-percent rent increase per year, and that's that. They're great apartments for the price, and the price doesn't even keep up with inflation," Greave said. "That's why these people didn't want to leave. But they might've anyway, because the Joyces gave them a lot of shit. But this old lady wasn't intimidated, and she held them all together. Then she turned up dead."

"Ah."

"Last week, she doesn't make it to school," Greave continued. "The principal calls, no answer. A cop goes by for a look, can't get the door open—it's locked from the inside and there's no answer on the phone. They finally take the door down, the alarms go off, and there she is, dead in her bed. George Joyce is dabbing the tears out of his eyes and looking like the cat that ate the canary. We figured they killed her."

"Autopsy?"

"Yup. Not a mark on her. The toxicology reports showed just enough sedative for a couple of sleeping pills, which she had a prescription for. There was a beer bottle and a glass on her nightstand, but she'd apparently metabolized the alcohol because there wasn't any in her blood. Her daughter said she had long-term insomnia, and she'd wash down a couple of sleeping pills with a beer, read until she got sleepy, and then take a leak and go to bed. And that's exactly what it looks like she did. The docs say her heart stopped. Period. End of story."

Lucas shrugged. "It happens."

"No history of heart problems in her family. Cleared a physical in February, no problems except the insomnia and she's too thin—but being underweight goes against the heart thing."

"Still, it happens," Lucas said. "People drop dead."

Grave shook his head. "When the Joyces were running the flops, they had a guy whose job it was to keep things orderly. They brought him over to run the apartments. Old friend of yours; you busted him three or four times, according to the NCIC. Remember Ray Cherry?"

"Cherry? Jesus. He *is* an asshole. Used to box Golden Gloves when he was a kid. . . ." Lucas scratched the side of his jaw, thinking. "That's a nasty bunch you got there. Jeez."

"So what do I do? I got nothing."

"Get a cattle prod and a dark basement. Cherry'd talk after a while." Lucas grinned through his teeth, and Greave almost visibly shrank from him.

"You're not serious."

"Mmm. I guess not," Lucas said. Then, brightening: "Maybe she was stabbed with an icicle."

"What?"

"Let me think about it," Lucas said.

THERE WERE TWO LANDFILLS in Dakota County. Adhering to Murphy's Law, they went to the wrong one first, then shifted down a series of blacktopped back roads to the correct one. For the last half-mile, they were pinched between two lumbering garbage trucks, gone overripe in the freshening summer.

"Office," Greave said, pointing off to the left. He dabbed at the front of his lavender suit, as though he were trying to whisk away the smell of rotten fruit.

The dump office was a tiny brick building with a large plate-glass window, overlooking a set of truck scales and the lines of garbage haulers rumbling out to the edge of the raw yellow earth of the landfill. Lucas swung that way, dumped the Porsche in a corner of the lot.

Inside the building, a Formica-topped counter separated the front of the office from the back. A fat guy in a green T-shirt sat at metal desk behind the counter, an unlit cigar in his mouth. He was complaining into a telephone and picking penny-sized flakes of dead skin off his elbows; the heartbreak of psoriasis. A door behind the fat man led to a phone booth–size room with a sink and a toilet. The door was open, and the stool was gurgling. A half-used roll of toilet paper sat on the toilet tank, and another one lay on the floor, where it had soaked full of rusty water.

"So he says it'll cost a hunnert just to come out here and look at it," the fat guy said to the telephone, looking into the bathroom. "I tell you, I run up to Fleet-Farm and I get the parts . . . Well, I know that, Al, but this is drivin' me fuckin crazy."

The fat guy put his hand over the mouthpiece and said, "Be with you in a minute." Then to the phone, "Al, I gotta go, there's a couple guys here in suits. Yeah." He looked up at Lucas and asked, "You EPA?"

"No."

The fat man said, "No," to the phone, listened, then looked up again. "OSHA?"

"No. Minneapolis cops."

"Minneapolis cops," the fat man said. He listened for a minute, then looked up. "He sent the check."

"What?"

"He sent the check to his old lady. Put it in the mail this morning, the whole thing."

"Terrific," Lucas said. "I really hope he did, or we'll have to arrest him for misfeasance to a police officer on official business, a Class Three felony."

Greave turned away to smile, while the fat man repeated what Lucas said into the phone, then after a pause said, "That's what the man said," and hung up. "He says he really mailed it."

"Okay," said Lucas. "Now, we're also looking for a guy who supposedly hangs around here. Junky Doog. . . ." The fat man's eyes slid away, and Lucas said, "So he's out here?"

"Junky's, uh, kind of . . ." The fat man tapped his head.

"I know. I've dealt with him a few times."

"Like, recently?"

"Not since he got out of St. Peter."

"I think he got Alzheimer's," the fat man said. "Some days, he's just not here. He forgets to eat, he shits in his pants."

"So where is he?" Lucas asked.

"Christ, I feel bad about the guy. He's a guy who never caught a break," the fat man said. "Not one fuckin' day of his life."

"Used to cut people up. You can't do that."

"Yeah, I know. Beautiful women. And I ain't no softy on crime, but you talk to Junky, and you *know* he didn't know any better. He's like a kid. I mean, he's not like a kid, because a normal kid wouldn't do what he did . . . I mean, he just doesn't know. He's like a . . . pit bull, or something. It just ain't his fault."

"We take that into account," said Greave, his voice soft. "Really, we're concerned about these things."

The fat man sighed, struggled to his feet, walked around the counter to a window. He pointed out across the landfill. "See that willow tree? He's got a place in the woods over there. We ain't supposed to let him, but whatcha gonna do?"

LUCAS AND GREAVE scuffed across the yellow-dirt landfill, trying to stay clear of the contrails of dust thrown up by the garbage trucks rumbling by. The landfill looked more like a highway construction site than a dump, with big D-9 Cats laboring around the edges of the raw dirt; and only at the edges did it look like a dump: a jumble of green plastic garbage bags, throwaway diapers, cereal boxes, cardboard, scraps of sheet plastic and metal, all rolled under the yellow dirt, and all surrounded by second-growth forest. Seagulls, crows, and pigeons hung over the litter, looking for food; a bony gray dog, moving jackal-like, slipped around the edges.

The willow tree was an old one, yellow, with great weeping branches bright green with new growth. Beneath it, two blue plastic tarps had been draped tent-like over tree limbs. Under one of the tarps was a salvaged charcoal grill; under the other was a mattress. A man lay on the mattress, faceup, eyes open, un-moving.

"Jesus, he's fuckin' dead," Greave said, his voice hushed.

Lucas stepped off the raw earth, Greave tagging reluctantly behind, followed a narrow trail around a clump of bushes, and was hit by the stink of human waste. The odor was thick, and came from no particular direction. He started breathing through his mouth, and unconsciously reached across to his hipbone and pulled his pistol a quarter inch out of the holster, loosening it, then patted it back. He moved in close before he called out, "Hello. Hey."

The man on the mattress twitched, then subsided again. He lay with one arm outstretched, the other over his pelvis. There was something wrong with the outstretched arm, Lucas saw, moving closer. Just off the mattress, a flat-topped stump was apparently being used as a table. A group of small brown cylinders sat on the stump, like chunks of beef jerky. Beside the stump was a one-gallon aluminum can of paint thinner, top off, lying on its side.

"Hey. . . ."

The man rolled up farther, tried to sit up. Junky Doog. He was barefoot. And he had a knife, a long curved pearl-handled number, open, the blade protrud-ing five inches from the handle. Doog held it delicately, like a straight razor, and said, "Gothefuckaway," one word. Doog's eyes were a hazy white, as though covered with cataracts, and his face was burned brown. He had no teeth and hadn't shaved in weeks. Graying hair fell down on his shoulders, knotted with grime. He looked worse than Lucas had ever seen him: looked worse than Lucas had ever seen a human being look.

"There's shit all over the place," Greave said. Then: "Watch it, watch the blade. . . ."

Junky whirled the knife in his fingers with the dexterity of a cheerleader twirling a baton, the steel twinkling in the weak sunlight. "Gothefuckaway," he screamed. He took a step toward Lucas, fell, tried to catch himself with his free hand, the hand without the knife, screamed again, and rolled onto his back, cradling the free hand. The hand had no fingers. Lucas looked at the stump: the brown things were pieces of finger and several toes.

"Jesus Christ," he muttered. He glanced at Greave, whose mouth was hanging open. Junky was weeping, trying to get up, still with the knife flickering in his good hand. Lucas stepped behind him, and when Junky made it to his knees, put a foot between his shoulder blades and pushed him facedown on the worn dirt just off the mattress. Pinning him, he caught the bad arm, and as Junky squirmed, crying, caught the other arm, shook the knife out of his hand. Junky was too weak to resist; weaker than a child.

"Can you walk?" Lucas asked, trying to pull Junky up. He looked at Greave. "Give me a hand."

Junky, caught in a crying jag, nodded, and with a boost from Lucas and Greave, got to his feet.

"We gotta go, man. We gotta go, Junky," Lucas said. "We're cops, you gotta come with us."

They led him back through the shit-stink, through the weeds, Junky stumbling, still weeping; halfway up the path, something happened, and he pulled around, looked at Lucas, his eyes clearing. "Get my blade. Get my blade, please. It'll get all rusted up."

Lucas looked at him a minute, looked back. "Hold him," he said to Greave. Junky had nothing to do with the killings; no way. But Lucas should take the knife.

"Get the blade."

Lucas jogged back to the campsite, picked up the knife, closed it, and walked back to where Greave held Junky's arm, Junky swaying in the path. Junky's mind had slipped away again, and he mutely followed Lucas and Greave across the yellow dirt, walking stiffly, as though his legs were posts. Only the big toes remained on his feet. His thumb and the lowest finger knuckles remained on his left hand; the hand was fiery with infection.

Back at the shed, the fat man came out and Lucas said, "Call 911. Tell them a police officer needs an ambulance. My name is Lucas Davenport and I'm a deputy chief with the City of Minneapolis."

"What happened, did you . . . ?" the fat man started, then saw first Junky's hand, and then his feet. "Oh my sweet Blessed Virgin Mary," he said, and he went back into the shed.

Lucas looked at Junky, dug into his pocket, handed him the knife. "Let him go," he said to Greave.

"What're you gonna do?" Greave asked.

"Just let him go."

Reluctantly, Greave released him, and the knife, still closed, twinkled in his hand. Lucas stepped sideways from him, a knife fighter's move, and said, "I'm gonna cut you, Junky," he said, his voice low, challenging.

Junky turned toward him, a smile at the corner of his ravaged face. The knife turned in his hand, and suddenly the blade snapped out. Junky stumbled toward Lucas.

"I cut you; you not cut me," he said.

"I cut you, man," Lucas said, beginning to circle to his right, away from the blade.

"You not cut me."

The fat man came out and said, "Hey. What're you doin'?"

Lucas glanced at him. "Take it easy. Is the ambulance coming?"

"They're on the way," the fat man said. He took a step toward Junky. "Junky, man, give me the knife."

"Gonna cut him," Junky said, stepping toward Lucas. He stumbled, and Lucas moved in, caught his bad arm, turned him, caught his shabby knife-arm sleeve from behind, turned him more, grabbed the good hand and shook the knife out.

"You're under arrest for assault on a police officer," Lucas said. He pushed the fat man away, picked up the knife, folded it and dropped it in his pocket. "You understand that? You're under arrest."

Junky looked at him, then nodded.

"Sit down," Lucas said. Junky shambled over and sat on the flat concrete stoop outside the shack. Lucas turned to the fat man. "You saw that. Remember what you saw."

The fat man looked at him doubtfully and said, "I don't think he would have hurt you."

"Arresting him is the best I can do for him," Lucas said quietly. "They'll put him inside, clean him up, take care of him."

The fat man thought about it, nodded. The phone rang, and he went back inside. Lucas, Greave, and Junky waited in silence until Junky looked up suddenly and said, "Davenport. What do you want?"

His voice was clear, controlled, his eyes focused.

"Somebody's cuttin' women," Lucas said. "I wanted to make sure it wasn't you."

"I cut some women, long time ago," Junky said. "There was this one, she had beautiful . . . you know. I made a grapevine on them."

"Yeah, I know."

"Long time ago; they liked it," he said.

Lucas shook his head.

"Somebody cuttin' on women?" Junky asked.

"Yeah, somebody's cuttin' on women."

After another moment of silence, Greave asked Junky, "Why would they do that? Why would he be cuttin' women?" In the distance, over the sound of the trucks moving toward the working edge of the fill, they could hear a siren. The fat man must have made it an emergency.

"You got to," Junky said solemnly to Greave. "If you don't cut them, especially the pretty ones, they get out of hand. You can't have women getting outa hand."

"Yeah?"

"Yeah. You cut 'em, they stay put, that's for sure. They stay put."

"So why would you go a long time and not cut any women, then start cuttin' a lot of women?"

"I didn't do that," Junky said. He cast a defensive eye at Greave.

"No. The guy we're looking for did that."

Lucas looked on curiously as the man in the lavender Italian suit chatted with the man with no toes, like they were sharing a cappuccino outside a café.

"He just started up?" Junky asked.

"Yup."

Junky thought about that, pawing his face with his good hand, then his head bobbed, as though he'd worked it out. " 'Cause a woman turns you on, that's why. Maybe you see a woman and she turns you on. Gets you by the pecker. You go around with your pecker up for a few days, and you *gotta* do *something.* You know, you gotta cut some women."

"Some woman turns you on?"

"Yup."

"So then you cut her."

"Well." Junky seemed to look inside himself. "Maybe not her, exactly. Sometimes you can't cut her. There was this one. . . ." He seemed to drift away, lost in the past. Then: "But you gotta cut somebody, see? If you don't cut somebody, your pecker stays up."

"So what?"

"So what? You can't go around with your pecker up all the time. You can't."

"I wish I could," Greave cracked.

Junky got angry, intent, his face quivering. "You can't. You can't go around like that."

"Okay. . . ."

The ambulance bumped into the landfill, followed a few seconds later by a sheriff's car.

"Come on, Junky, we're gonna put you in the hospital," Lucas said.

Junky said to Greave, pulling at Greave's pant leg with his good hand, "But you got to get her, sooner or later. Sooner or later, you got to get the one that put your pecker up. See, if she goes around putting your pecker up, anytime she wants, she's outa hand. She's just outa hand, and you gotta cut her."

"Okay. . . ."

Lucas filed a complaint with the sheriff's deputy who followed the ambulance in, and Junky was hauled away.

"I'M GLAD I CAME WITH YOU," Greave said. "Got to see a dump, and a guy cutting himself up like a provolone."

Lucas shook his head and said, "You did pretty good back there. You've got a nice line of bullshit."

"Yeah?"

"Yeah. Talking to people, you know, that's half of homicide."

"I got the bullshit. It's the other part I ain't got," Greave said gloomily. "Listen, you wanna stop at my mystery apartment on the way back?"

"No."

"C'mon, man."

"We've got too much going on," Lucas said. "Maybe we'll catch some time later."

"They're wearing me out in homicide," Greave said. "I get these notes. They say, 'Any progress?' Fuck 'em."

GREAVE WENT ON TO homicide to check in, while Lucas walked down to Roux's office and stuck his head in.

"We picked up Junky Doog. He's clear, almost for sure."

He explained, and told her how Junky had mutilated himself. Roux, nibbling her lip, said, "What happens if I feed him to the *Strib*?"

"Depends on how you do it," Lucas said, leaning against the door, crossing his arms. "If you did it deep off-the-record, gave them just the bare information . . . it might take some heat off. Or at least get them running in a different direction. In either case, it'd be sorta cynical."

"Fuck cynical. His prior arrests were here in Hennepin, right?"

"Most of them, I think. He was committed from here. If you tipped them early enough, they could get across the street and pull his files."

"Even if it's bullshit, it's an exclusive. It's a lead story," Roux said. She rubbed her eyes. "Lucas, I hate to do it. But I'm taking some serious damage now. I figure I've got a couple of weeks of grace. After that, I might not be able to save myself."

BACK AT HIS OFFICE, a message was waiting on voice mail: "This is Connell. I got something. Beep me."

Lucas dialed her beeper number, let it beep, and hung up. Junky had been a waste of time, although he might be a bone they could throw the media. Not much of a bone. . . .

With nothing else to do, he began paging through Connell's report again, trying to absorb as much of the detail as he could.

There were several threads that tied all the killings together, but the thread that worried him most was the simplicity of them. The killer picked up a woman, killed her, dumped her. They weren't all found right away—Connell suggested he might have kept one or two of them for several hours, or even overnight—but in one case, in South Dakota, the body was found forty-five minutes after the woman had been seen alive. He wasn't pressing his luck by keeping the woman around; they wouldn't get a break that way.

He didn't leave anything behind, either. The actual death scenes might have been in his vehicle—Connell suggested that it was probably a van or a truck, although he might have used a motel if he'd been careful in his choices.

In one case, in Thunder Bay, there may have been some semen on a dress, but the stain, whatever it was, had been destroyed in a failed effort to extract a blood type. A note from a cop said that it might have been salad dressing. DNA testing had not yet been available.

Vaginal and anal examinations had come up negative, but there was oral bruising that suggested that some of the women had been orally raped. Stomach contents were negative, which meant that he didn't ejaculate, ejaculated outside their mouth, or they lived long enough for stomach fluids to destroy the evidence.

Hair was a different problem. Foreign-hair samples had been collected from several of the bodies, but in most cases where hair was collected, several varieties were found. There was no way to tell that any particular hair came from the killer—or, indeed, that any of the hair was his. Connell had tried to get the existing hair samples cross-matched, but some of it had been either destroyed or lost, or the bureaucratic tangles were so intense that nothing had yet been done. Lucas made a note to search for hair crosses on Wannemaker and Joan Smits. All were relatively recent, with autopsies done by first-rate medical examiners.

Closing the file, Lucas got out of his chair and wandered around to stare sightlessly out the window, working it through his head. The man never left anything unique. Hair, so far, was the only possibility: they needed a match, and needed it badly. They had nothing else that would tie a specific man to a specific body. Nothing at all.

The phone rang. "This is Meagan. I've got somebody who remembers the killer. . . ."

LATE IN THE AFTERNOON, sun warm on the city sidewalks. Greave didn't want to go. "Look, I'm not gonna be much help to you. I don't know what you and Connell are into, where your heads are at—but I really want to do my own thing. And I already been to a fuckin' dump today."

"We need somebody else current with the case," Lucas said. "You're the guy. I want somebody else seeing these people, talking to them."

Greave rubbed his hair with both hands, then said, "All right, all right, I'll go along. But—if we've got time, we stop at my apartments, right?"

Lucas shrugged. "If we've got time."

CONNELL WAS WAITING on a street corner in Woodbury, under a Quick Wash sign, wearing Puritan black-and-white, still carrying the huge purse. An automotive diagnostic center sprawled down the block.

"Been here long?" Greave asked. He was still pouting.

"One minute," she said. She was strung out, hard energy overlying a deep weariness. She'd been up all night, Lucas thought. Talking to the TV. Dying.

"Have you talked to St. Paul?" he asked.

"They're dead in the water," Connell said, impatience harsh in her voice. "The cop at the bookstore was one of theirs. He drinks too much, plays around on his wife. A guy over there told me that he and his wife have gotten physical. I guess one of their brawls is pretty famous inside the department—his wife knocked out two of his teeth with an iron, and he was naked chasing her around the backyard with a mop handle, drunk, bleeding all over himself. The neighbors called the cops. They thought she'd shot him. That's what I hear."

"So what do you think?"

"He's an asshole, but he's unlikely," she said. "He's an older guy, too heavy, out of shape. He used to smoke Marlboros, but quit ten years ago. The main thing is, St. Paul is covering like mad. They've been called out to his house a half-dozen times, but there's never been a charge."

Lucas shook his head, looked at the diagnosis center. "What about this woman?"

"Mae Heinz. Told me on the phone that she'd seen a guy with a beard. Short. Strong-looking."

Lucas led the way inside, a long office full of parts books, tires, cutaway muffler displays, and the usual odor of antifreeze and transmission fluid. Heinz was a cheerful, round-faced woman with pink skin and freckles. She sat wide-eyed behind the counter as Connell sketched in the murder. "I was talking to that woman," Heinz said. "I remember her asking the question. . . ."

"But you didn't see her go out with a man?"

"She didn't," Heinz said. "She went out alone. I remember."

"Were there a lot of men there?"

"Yeah, there were quite a few. There was a guy with a ponytail and a beard and his name was Carl, he asked a lot of questions about pigs and he had dirty fingernails, so I wasn't too interested. Everybody seemed to know him. There was a computer guy, kind of heavyset blond, I heard him talking to somebody.

"Meyer," Connell said to Lucas. "Talked to him this morning. He's out."

"Kind of cute," Heinz said, looking at Connell and winking. "If you like the intellectual types."

"What about . . . ?"

"There was a guy who was a cop," Heinz said.

"Got him," Lucas said.

"Then there were two guys there together, and I thought they might be gay. They stood too close to each other."

"Know their names?"

"No idea," she said. "But they were very well-dressed. I think they were in architecture or landscaping or something like that, because they were talking to the author about sustainable land use."

"And the guy with the beard," Connell said, prompting her.

"Yeah. He came in during the talk. And he must've left right away, because I didn't see him later. I sorta looked. Jesus—I could of been dead. I mean, if I'd found him."

"Was he tall, short, fat, skinny?"

"Big guy. Not tall, but thick. Big shoulders. Beard. I don't like beards, but I liked the shoulders." She winked at Connell again, and Lucas covered a grin by scratching his face. "But the thing is," she said to Connell, "you asked about smoking, and he snapped a cigarette into the street. I saw him do it. Snapped a cigarette and then came in the door."

Lucas looked at Connell and nodded. Heinz caught it. "Was that him?" she asked excitedly.

"Would you know him if we showed you a picture of him?" Lucas asked.

She cocked her head and looked to one side, as though she were running a video through her head. "I don't know," she said after a minute. "Maybe, if I saw an actual picture. I can remember the beard and the shoulders. His beard looked sort of funny. Short, but really dense, like fur . . . Kind of unpleasant, I thought. Maybe fake. I can't remember much about his face. Knobby, I think."

"Dark beard? Light?"

"Mmm . . . dark. Kind of medium, really. Pretty average hair, I think . . . brown."

"All right," Lucas said. "Let's nail this down. And let's get you with an artist. Do you have time to come to Minneapolis?"

"Sure. Right now? Let me tell my boss."

As the woman went to talk to her boss about leaving, Connell caught Lucas's sleeve. "Gotta be him. Smokes, arrives after the talk, then leaves right away. Wannemaker is lingering after the talk, but suddenly leaves, like somebody showed up."

"Wouldn't count on it," Lucas said. But he was counting on it. He felt it, just a sniff of the killer, just a whiff of the track. "We got to put her through the sex files."

The woman came back, animated. "How do you want to do this? Want me to follow you over?"

"Why don't I take you?" Connell offered. "We can talk on the way over."

. . .

GREAVE WANTED TO STOP at the apartment complex so Lucas could look at the locked-room mystery. "C'mon, man, it's twenty fuckin' minutes. We'll be back before she's done with the artist," he said. A pleading note entered his voice. "C'mon, man, this is killing me."

Lucas glanced at him, hands clutched, the too-hip suit. He sighed and said, "All right. Twenty minutes."

They took I-94 back to Minneapolis, but turned south instead of north toward City Hall. Greave directed him through a web of streets to a fifties-era midrise concrete building with a hand-carved natural-wood sign on the narrow front lawn that had a loon on top and the name "Eisenhower Docks" beneath the bird. A fat man pushed a mower down the lawn away from them, leaving behind the smell of gas and cheap cigar.

"Eisenhower Docks?" Lucas said as they got out.

"If you stand on the roof you can see the river," Greave said. "And they figured 'Eisenhower' makes old people feel good."

The man pushing the lawn mower made a turn at the end of the lawn and started back; Lucas recognized Ray Cherry, forty pounds heavier than he'd been when he'd fought in Golden Gloves tournaments in the sixties. Most of the weight had gone to his gut, which hung over beltless Oshkosh jeans. His face had gone from square to blocky, and a half-dozen folds of fat rolled down the back of his neck to his shoulders. His T-shirt was soaked with sweat. He saw Davenport and Greave, pushed the lawn mower up to their feet, and killed the engine.

"What're you doing, Davenport?"

"Lookin' around, Ray," Lucas said, smiling. "How've you been? You got fat."

"Y'ain't a cop no more, so get the fuck off my property."

"I'm back on the force, Ray," Lucas said, still smiling. Seeing Ray made him happy. "You oughta read the papers. Deputy chief in charge of finding out how you killed this old lady."

A look crossed Cherry's face, a quick shadow, and Lucas recognized it, had seen it six or seven hundred or a thousand times: Cherry had done it. Cherry wiped the expression away, tried a look of confusion, took a soiled rag out of his pocket, and blew his nose. "Bullshit," he said finally.

"Gonna get you, Ray," Lucas said; the smile stayed but his voice had gone cold. "Gonna get the Joyces, too. Gonna put you in Stillwater Prison. You must be close to fifty, Ray. First-degree murder'll get you . . . shit, they just changed the law. Tough luck. You'll be better'n eighty before you get out."

"Fuck you, Davenport," Cherry said. He fired up the mower.

"Come and talk to me, Ray," Lucas said over the engine noise. "The Joyces'll sell you out the minute they think it'll get them a break. You know that. Come and talk, and maybe we can do a deal."

"Fuck you," Cherry said, and he mowed on down the yard.

"Lovely fellow," Greave said in a fake English accent.

"He did it," Lucas said. He turned to Greave and Greave took a step back: Lucas's face was like a block of stone.

"Huh?"

"He killed her. Let's see her apartment."

Lucas started for the apartment door, and Greave trotted after him. "Hey, wait a minute, wait a minute. . . ."

THERE WERE A THOUSAND books in the apartment, along with a rolled-up Oriental carpet tied with brown twine, and fifteen cardboard cartons from U-Haul, still flat. A harried middle-aged woman sat on a piano bench, a handkerchief around her head; her face was wind- and sunburned, like a gardener's, and was touched with grief. Charmagne Carter's daughter, Emily.

". . . Soon as they said we could take it out. If we don't, we have to keep paying rent," she told Greave. She looked around. "I don't know what to do with the books. I'd like to keep them, but there're so many."

Lucas had been looking at the books: American literature, poetry, essays, history. Works on feminism, arranged in a way that suggested they were a conscious collection rather than a reading selection. "I could take some of them off your hands," he said. "I mean, if you'd like to name a price. I'd take the poetry."

"Well, what do you think?" Carter asked, as Greave watched him curiously.

"There are . . ." He counted quickly. ". . . thirty-seven volumes, mostly paper. I don't think any of them are particularly rare. How about a hundred bucks?"

"Let me look through them. I'll give you a call."

"Sure." He turned away from the books, more fully toward her. "Was your mother depressed or anything?"

"If you're asking if she committed suicide, she didn't. She wouldn't give the Joyces the pleasure, for one thing. But basically, she liked her life," Carter said. She became more animated as she remembered. "We had dinner the night before and she was talking about this kid in her class, black kid, she thinks he'll be a novelist but he needs encouragement . . . No way'd she kill herself. Besides, even if she wanted to, how'd she do it?"

"Yeah. That's a question," Lucas said.

"The only thing wrong with Mom was her thyroid. She had a little thyroid problem; it was overactive and she had trouble keeping her weight up," Carter said. "And her insomnia. That might have been part of the thyroid problem."

"She was actually ill, then?" Lucas glanced sideways at Greave.

"No. No, she really wasn't. Not even bad enough to take pills. She was just way too thin. She weighed ninety-nine pounds and she was five-six. That's below her ideal weight, but it's not emaciated or anything."

"Okay."

"Now that kid isn't gonna get help, the novelist," Emily said, and a tear started down her cheek.

Greave patted her on the shoulder—Officer Friendly—and Lucas turned away, hands in pockets, stepping toward the door. Nothing here.

"You ought to talk to Bob, next apartment down the hall," Emily said. She picked up a roll of packaging tape and a box, punched it into a cube. She stripped off a length of tape, and it sounded as if she were tearing a sheet. "He came in just before you got here."

"Bob was a friend of Charmagne's," Greave explained to Lucas. "He was here the night she died."

Lucas nodded. "All right. I'm sorry about your mother."

"Thanks. I hope you get those . . . those fuckers," Emily said, her voice dropping into a hiss.

"You think she was murdered?"

"Something happened," she said.

BOB WOOD WAS ANOTHER TEACHER, general science at Central in St. Paul. He was thin, balding, worried.

"We'll all go, now that Charmagne's gone. The city's going to give us some moving money, but I don't know. Prices are terrible."

"Did you hear anything that night? Anything?"

"Nope. I saw her about ten o'clock; we were taking our aluminum cans down for recycling and we came up in the elevator together. She was going off to bed right then."

"Wasn't depressed. . . ."

"No, no, she was pretty upbeat," Wood said. "I'll tell you something I told the other policemen: when she closed the door, I heard the lock snap shut. You could only throw the bolt from inside, and you had to do it with a key. I know, because when she got it, she was worried about being trapped inside by a fire. But then Cherry scared her one day—just looked at her, I guess, and scared her—and she started locking the door. I was here when they beat it down. They had to take a piece of the wall with it. They painted, but you can kind of see the outline there."

The wall showed the faint dishing of a plaster patch. Lucas touched it and shook his head.

"If anything had happened in there, I would have heard it," Wood said. "We share a bedroom wall, and the air-conditioning had been out for a couple of days. There was no noise. It was hot and spooky-quiet. I didn't hear a thing."

"So you think she just died?"

Wood swallowed twice, his Adam's apple bobbing. "Jeez. I don't know. If you know Cherry, you gotta think . . . Jeez."

IN THE STREET, LUCAS and Greave watched a small girl ride down the sidewalk on a tiny bicycle, fall down, pick it up, start over, and fall down again. "She needs somebody to run behind her," Greave said.

Lucas grunted. "Doesn't everybody?"

"Big philosopher, huh?

Lucas said, "Wood and Carter shared a wall."

"Yes."

"Have you looked at Wood?"

"Yeah. He thinks newspaper comics are too violent."

"But there might be something there. What can you do with a shared wall? Stick a needle through it, pump in some gas or something?"

"Hey. Davenport. There's no toxicology," Greave said with asperity. *"There's no fuckin' toxicology.* You look up *toxicology* in the dictionary, and there's a pic-ture of the old lady and it says, 'Not Her.' "

"Yeah, yeah. . . ."

"She wasn't poisoned, gassed, stabbed, shot, strangled, beaten to death . . . what else is there?"

"How about electrocuted?" Lucas suggested.

"Hmph. How'd they do it?"

"I don't know. Hook some wires up to her bed, lead them out under a door, and when she gets in bed, zap, and then they pull the wires out."

"Pardon me while I snicker," Greave said.

Lucas looked back at the apartment building. "Let me think about it some more."

"But Cherry did it?"

"Yup." They looked down the lawn. Cherry was at the other end, kneeling over a quiet lawn mower, fiddling, watching them. "You can take it to the bank."

LUCAS GLANCED AT HIS watch as they got back to the car: they'd been at the apartments for almost an hour. "Connell's gonna tear me up," he said.

"Ah, she's a bite in the ass," Greave said.

They bumped into Mae Heinz in the parking ramp, getting into her car. Lucas beeped the horn, called out, "How'd it go?"

Heinz came over. "That woman, Officer Connell . . . she's pretty intense."

"Yes. She is."

"We got one of those drawings, but . . ."

"What?"

Heinz shook her head. "I don't know whether it's my drawing or hers. The thing is, it's too specific. I can mostly remember the guy with the beard, but now we've got this whole picture, and I don't know if it's right or not. I mean, it seems right, but I'm not sure I'm really remembering it, or if it's just because we tried out so many different pictures."

"Did you look at our picture files, the mugs . . . ?"

"No, not yet. I've got to get my kid at day care. But I'm coming back tonight. Officer Connell is going to meet me."

CONNELL WAS WAITING IN Lucas's office. "God, where've you been?"

"Detour," Lucas said. "Different case."

Connell's eyes narrowed. "Greave, huh? Told you." She gave Lucas a sheet of paper. "This is him. This is the guy."

Lucas unfolded the paper and looked at it. The face that looked back was generally square, with a dark, tight beard, small eyes, and hard, triangular nose. The hair was medium length and dark.

"We gotta feed it to the TV. We don't have to say we're looking for a serial killer, just that we're looking for this guy on the Wannemaker case," Connell said.

"Let's hold off on that for a bit," Lucas said. "Why don't we take this around to the other people who were in the store and get it confirmed. Maybe ship it out to Madison, and anywhere else the guy might have been seen."

"We gotta get it out," Connell objected. "People gotta be warned."

"Take it easy," Lucas said. "Make the checks first."

"Give me one good reason."

"Because we haven't gotten anything unique to this guy," Lucas said. "If we wind up in court with a long circumstantial case, I don't want the defense to pull out this picture, hold it up by our guy, and say, 'See—he doesn't look anything like this.' That's why."

Connell pulled at her lip, then nodded. "I'll check with people tonight. I'll get every one of them."

KOOP WAS AT TWO GUY'S, working his quads. The only other patron was a woman who'd worked herself to exhaustion, and now sat, legs apart, on a bent-up folding chair by the Coke machine, drinking Gatorade, head down, her sweat-soaked hair dangling almost to the floor.

Muscle chicks didn't interest Koop: they just weren't right. He left them alone, and after a couple of tentative feelers, they left him alone.

Koop said to himself, *Five*, and felt the muscle failing.

A TV was screwed to the wall in front of the empty stair climbers, tuned to the midday news program, *Nooner*. A stunning auburn-haired anchorwoman said through a suggestive overbite that Cheryl Young was dead of massive head wounds.

Koop strained, got the last inch, and dropped his feet again, came back up, the muscle trembling with fatigue. He closed his eyes, willed his legs up; they came up a half inch, another quarter inch, to the top. *Six*. He dropped them, started up again. The burn was massive, as though somebody had poured alcohol on his legs and lit it off. He shook with the burn, eyes clenched, sweat popping. He needed an inch, one inch . . . and failed. He always worked to failure. Satisfied, he let the bar drop and pivoted on the bench to look at the television.

". . . believed to be the work of young drug addicts." And a cop saying, ". . . the attack was incredibly violent for so little gain. We believe Mr. Flory had less than thirty dollars in his wallet—that we believe it was probably the work of younger gang members who build their status with this kind of meaningless killing. . . ."

Good. They put it on the gangs. Little motherfuckers deserved anything they got. And Koop couldn't wait any longer. He knew he should wait. The people in the building would be in an uproar. If he was seen, and recognized as an outsider, there could be trouble.

But he just couldn't wait. He picked up his towel and headed for the locker room.

KOOP WENT INTO the lakes neighborhood on foot, a few minutes before nine, in the dying twilight. There were other walkers in the neighborhood, but nothing in particular around the building where he'd killed the woman: the blood had been washed away, the medical garbage picked up. Just another door in another apartment building.

"Stupid," he said aloud. He looked around to see if anyone had heard. Nobody close enough. Stupid, but the pressure was terrific. And different. When he went after a woman, that was sex. The impulse came from his testicles; he could literally feel it.

This impulse seemed to come from somewhere else; well, not entirely, but it was different. It drove him, like a child looking for candy. . . .

Koop carried his newly minted key and a briefcase. Inside the briefcase was a Kowa TSN-2 spotting scope with a lightweight aluminum tripod, a setup recommended for professional birders and voyeurs. He swung the briefcase casually, letting it dangle, keeping himself loose, as he started up the apartment walk. Feelers out: nothing. Up close, the arborvitae beside the apartment door looked beaten, ragged; there were footprints in the mud around the shrubs.

Inside, the lobby light was brighter, harsher. The management's response to murder: put in a brighter bulb. Maybe they'd changed locks? Koop slipped the key into the door, turned it, and it worked just fine.

He took the stairs to the top, no problem. At the top, he checked the hallway, nervous, but not nearly as tense as he was during an entry. He really shouldn't be here . . . Nobody in the hall. He walked down it, to the Exit sign, and up the stairs to the roof access. He used the new key again, pushed through the door, climbed another short flight to the roof, and pushed through the roof door.

He was alone on the roof. The night was pleasant, but the roof was not a particularly inviting place, asphalt and pea-rock, and the lingering odor of sun-warmed tar. He walked as quietly as he could to the edge of the roof, and looked across the street. Damn. He was just below Sara Jensen's window. Not much, but enough that he wouldn't be able to see her unless she came and stood near the window.

An air-conditioner housing squatted on the rooftop, a large gray-metal cube, projecting up another eight feet. Koop walked around to the back of it, reached up, pushed the briefcase onto the edge of it, then grabbed the edge, chinned and pressed himself up on top, never breaking a sweat or even holding his breath.

A three-foot-wide venting stack poked up above the housing. Koop squatted behind the stack and looked across the street.

Jensen's apartment was a fishbowl. To the right, there was a balcony with a wrought-iron railing in front of sliding glass doors, and through the doors, the living room. To the left, he looked through the knee-high windows into her bedroom. He was now a few feet higher than her floor, he thought, giving him just a small down-angle. Perfect.

And Jensen was home.

Ten seconds after Koop boosted himself onto the air-conditioner housing, she walked through the living room wearing a slip, carrying a cup of coffee and a paper. She was as clear as a goldfish in an illuminated aquarium.

"Goddamn," Koop said, happy. This was better than anything he'd hoped for. He fumbled with the briefcase, pulled out the spotting scope. "Come on, Sara," he said. "Let's see some puss."

Koop had two eyepieces for the Kowa, a twenty-power and a sixty. The sixty-power put him virtually inside her room, but was sensitive to the slightest touch, and the field of view was tiny: with the sixty, her face filled the field. He switched to the twenty-power, fumbling the eyepiece in his haste, cursing, screwing it down. Jensen walked back through the living room and in and out of the kitchen, which he couldn't see. He settled down to wait: he'd begun carrying a kerchief with him, with just a dab of her Opium. As he watched her windows, he held the kerchief beside his nose so he could smell her.

While she was out of sight, he scanned the living room. Huh. New lock. Something really tough. He'd expected that. She also had a new door. It was flat gray, as though awaiting a coat of paint. Metal, probably. Jensen had bought herself a steel-sheathed door after his visit.

Jensen showed up again in the bedroom and pulled the slip over her head, then stripped off her panty hose. She disappeared into the bathroom, came back out without her bra. Koop sucked air like a teenager at a carnival strip show.

Jensen had large, rounded breasts, the left one a bit larger than the right, he thought. She went back to the bathroom, came back a moment later without underpants. Koop was sweating, watched her digging something out of a dresser drawer—a towel? He couldn't quite tell. She disappeared again.

This time she didn't come back right away. Koop, feverish, heart pounding, kept his eye to the scope so long that his neck began to hurt, while running through his mind the sight of her body. She was solid, and jiggled a little when she walked, not quite a roll at her waist, but a certain fullness; she had an excellent ass, again the way he liked them, solid, sizable. With a little jiggle.

He took his face away from the eyepiece, dropped well below the level of the vent, lit a Camel in his carefully cupped hand, and looked down at the metal surface under his arm. He was not introspective, but now he thought: *What's going on?* He was breathing hard, as though he'd been on the stair climber. He was beginning to feel some kind of burn . . . Goddamn. He squeezed his eyes shut, imagined catching her on the street, getting her in the truck.

But then he'd have to do her. He frowned at the thought. And then he wouldn't have this. He peered over the top of the vent; she was still out of sight, and he dropped back on his elbow. He liked this. He needed this time with her. Eventually, he'd have to get with her. He could see that. But for now . . .

He peeked back over the edge. She was still out of sight, and he took two more hurried drags on the cigarette and ground it out. Another peek, and he lit another Camel.

When Sara Jensen finally emerged from the bathroom, she was nude except for a white terry-cloth towel wrapped around her head; she looked like a dark angel. She wasn't hurried, but she was moving with deliberation. Going somewhere, Koop thought, his heart pounding, his mouth dry. She was bouncing, her nipples large and dark, pubic hair black as coal. She took something from the same dressing table where he'd found the jewelry box—the box wasn't there anymore, and he wondered briefly where she'd put it—then sat on the bed and began trimming her toenails.

He groped in his pocket for the sixty-power eyepiece, made the switch. The new lens put him within a foot of her face: she was trimming her nails with a fierce concentration, wrinkles in her forehead and in the flesh along her sides, foot pulled within a few inches of her nose. She carefully put each clipping aside, on the bedspread. He let the scope drop to her legs; she was sitting sideways to him, her far leg pulled up; her navel was an "innie"; her pubic hair seemed artificially low. She probably wore a bikini in the summer. She had a small white scar on her near knee. On her hip, a tattoo? What? No, a birthmark, he thought. Or a bruise.

She finished with the far foot, and lifted the near one. From his angle on the roof, he could see just the curve of her vulva, with a bit of hair. He closed his eyes and swallowed, opened them again. He went back to her hip: definitely a birthmark. To her breasts, back to the pubic hair, to her face: she was so close, he could almost feel the heat from her.

When she finished with her foot, she gathered the trimmed nails in the palm of her hand and carried them out of sight into the bathroom. Again she was gone for a while, and when she came back, the towel was no longer wrapped around her head and her hair fell on her shoulders, frizzy, coiled, still damp.

She took her time finding a nightgown; walked around nude for a while, apparently enjoying it. When she finally pulled a nightgown out of her dresser, Koop *willed* her naked for just another second. But she pulled the nightgown over her head, facing him, and her body disappeared in a slow white erotic tumble of cotton. He closed his eyes: he simply couldn't take it. When he opened them, she was buttoning the gown at the neck; so virginal now, when just a moment before . . .

"No . . ." A single dry word, almost a moan. Go back, start over . . . Koop needed something. He needed a woman, was what he needed.

Koop put Sara Jensen to bed before he left, developing the same sense of loss he always felt when he left her; but this time he closed his eyes, saw her again. He waited a half hour, looking at nothing but darkness; when he finally dropped off the air conditioner and took the stairs, he could barely remember doing it. He just suddenly found himself in the street, walking toward the truck.

And the pressure was intense. The pressure was always there, but sometimes it was irresistible, even though it put his life in jeopardy.

Koop climbed into the truck, took Hennepin Avenue back toward the loop, then slid into the side streets, wandering aimlessly around downtown. He ran Sara Jensen behind his eyes like a movie. The curve of her leg, the little pink there . . . Thought about buying a bottle. He could use a drink. He could use several. Maybe find John, pick up another eight-ball. Get an eight-ball and a bottle of Canadian Club and a six-pack of 7-Up, have a party. . . .

Maybe he should go back. Maybe she'd get up and he could see her again. Maybe he could call her number on a cellular phone, get her up . . . but he didn't have a cellular phone. Could he get one? Maybe she'd undress again . . . He shook himself. Stupid. She was asleep.

KOOP SAW THE GIRL as he passed the bus station. She had a red nylon duffel bag by her feet and she was peering down the street. Waiting for a bus? Koop went by, looked her over. She was dark-haired, a little heavy, with a round, smooth, unblemished face. If you squinted, she might be Jensen; and she had the look he always sought in the bookstores, the passivity. . . .

Impulsively, he did a quick around-the-block, dumped the truck behind the station, started into the station, turned, ran back to the truck, opened the back, pulled out the toolbox, closed up the truck, and went through the station.

The girl was still standing at the corner, looking down Hennepin. She turned when she sensed him coming, gave him the half-smile and the shifting eyes that he saw from women at night, the smile that said, "I'm nice, don't hurt me," the eyes that said, "I'm not really looking at you. . . ."

He toted the heavy toolbox past her, and she looked away. A few feet farther down, he stopped, put a frown on his face, turned and looked at her.

"Are you waiting for a bus?"

"Yes." She bobbed her head and smiled. "I'm going to a friend's in Upper Town."

"Uptown," he said. She wasn't from Minneapolis. "Uh, there aren't many buses at this time of night. I don't even know if they run to Uptown . . . Can your friend come and get you?"

"He doesn't have a phone. I've only got his address."

Koop started away. "You oughta catch a cab," he said. "This is kind of a tough street. There're hookers around here, you don't want the cops thinking. . . ."

"Oh, no . . ." Her mouth was an O, eyes large.

Koop hesitated. "Are you from Minnesota?"

She really wasn't sure about talking to him. "I'm from Worthington."

"Sure, I've been there," Koop said, trying a smile. "Stayed at a Holiday Inn on the way to Sioux Falls."

"I go to Sioux all the time," she said. Something in common. She'd held her arms crossed over her stomach as they talked; now she dropped them to her sides. Opening up.

Koop put the toolbox on the sidewalk. "Look, I'm a maintenance guy with Greyhound. You don't know me, but I'm an okay guy, really. I'm on my way to South Minneapolis, I could drop you in Uptown. . . ."

She looked at him closely now, afraid but tempted. He didn't look that bad: tall, strong. Older. Had to be thirty.

"I was told that the bus . . ."

"Sure." He grinned again. "Don't take rides from strangers. That's a good policy. If you stick close to the bus stop and the station, you should be okay," he said. "I wouldn't go down that way, you can see the porno stores. There're weirdos going in and out."

"Porno stores?" She looked down the street. A black guy was looking in the window of a camera store.

"Anyway, I gotta go," Koop said, picking up his toolbox. "Take it easy. . . ."

"Wait," she said, her face open, fearful but hoping. She picked up the duffel. "I'll take the ride, if it's okay."

"Sure. I'm parked right behind the station," Koop said. "Let me get my tools stowed away . . . You'll be there in five minutes."

"This is my first time in Minneapolis," the girl said, now chatty. "But I used to go up to Sioux every weekend, just about."

"What's your name?" Koop asked.

"Marcy Lane," she said. "What's yours?"

"Ben," he said. "Ben Cooper."

Ben was a nice name. Like Gentle Ben, the bear, on television. "Nice to meet you, Ben," she said, and tried a smile, a kind of bohemian, woman-of-the-road smile.

She looked like a child.

A pie-faced kid from the country.

WEATHER HEARD THE PHONE at the far end of the house, woke up, poked him.

"Phone," she mumbled. "It much be for you."

Lucas fumbled around in the dark, found the bedroom phone, picked it up. Dispatch patched him through to North Minneapolis. Another one.

". . . recovered her purse and a duffel bag with some clothes. We got a license, says she's Marcy Lane with an address in Worthington," Carrigan said. His voice sounded like a file being run over sheet metal. "We're trying to run her folks down now. You better get your ass over here."

"Did you call Lester?" Lucas was sitting on the bed, hunched in the light from the bedside lamp, bare feet on the floor. Weather was still awake, unmoving, listening to the conversation over her shoulder.

"Not yet. Should I?"

"I'll call him," Lucas said. "Freeze every fuckin' thing. Freeze it. The shit's gonna hit the fan, and you don't want any mistakes. And don't talk to the uniforms, for Christ's sakes."

"It's froze hard," Carrigan said.

"Keep it that way." Lucas poked the phone's Cancel button, then redialed.

"Who's dead?" Weather asked, rolling onto her back.

"Some kid. Looks like our asshole did it," Lucas said. The dispatcher came on and he said, "This is Davenport. I need a number for a Meagan Connell. And I need to talk to Frank Lester. Now."

They found a number for Connell and he scribbled it down. As they put him through to Lester, he grinned at Weather, sleepy-eyed, looking up at him. "How often do they call you in the middle of the night?" she asked. "When you're working?"

"Maybe twenty times in twenty years," he said.

She rolled toward her nightstand, looked at the clock. "I get up in three hours."

"Sorry," he said.

She propped herself up on one elbow and said, "I never thought of it until now, but you've got very little hair on your ass."

"Hair?" The phone was ringing at the other end, and he looked down at his ass, confused. A sleepy Lester grunted, "Hello?"

"This is Davenport," Lucas said, going back to the phone, trying to get his mind off hair. "Carrigan just called. A young girl from Worthington got gutted and dumped in a vacant lot up on the north side. If it ain't the one that did Wannemaker, it's his twin brother."

After a moment of silence, Lester said, "Shit."

"Yeah. So now we got a new one. You better get with Roux and figure out what you're gonna do, publicity-wise."

"I'll call her. Are you going up there? Wherever?"

"I'm on my way," Lucas said.

LUCAS HUNG UP, THEN dialed the number for Connell. She picked it up, her voice a weak croak: "Hello?"

"This is Davenport," he said. "A girl from out in the country just got killed and dumped up on the north side. It looks like it's our guy."

"Where?" Wide-awake now. Lucas gave her the address. "I'll see you there."

Lucas hung up, hopped out of bed, and headed for the bathroom. "You were going to observe tomorrow," Weather said.

Lucas stopped, turned back. "Oh, jeez, that's right. Listen. If I finish up out there, I'll come over to the hospital. You're starting at seven-thirty?"

"Yes. That's when the kid's coming in."

"I can make that," he said. "Where do I go?"

"Ask at the front desk. Tell them the operating suite, and when you get up there, ask for me. They'll be expecting you."

"I'll try," he said. "Seven-thirty."

CARRIGAN'S SECOND CLAIM to fame was that he had small, fine feet, with which he danced. He had once appeared on stage at the Guthrie, in a modern interpretation of *Othello*, wearing nothing but a gold lamé jock and a headband.

His third claim to fame was that when a rookie had referred to him as a fag dancer, he'd held the rookie's head in a locker-room toilet for so long that homicide submitted the kid's name to the *Guinness Book of Records* for the longest free dive. The claim was noted, but rejected.

Carrigan's first claim to fame was that a decade earlier, he'd twice won the NCAA wrestling title at 198 pounds. Nobody fucked with him.

"Couldn't have been too long ago," he told Lucas, looking back at the crowd gathering on the corner. Carrigan was black, as was most of the crowd gathered across the street. "There was some people up here playing ball until dark, and there was no body then. Some kids cuttin' across the park found her a little after one o'clock."

"Anybody see any vehicles?"

"We've got people going door to door across the park there, but I don't think we'll get much. There's an interstate entrance just down the block and it's easy to miss it: people come in here to turn around and go back, so there's cars in and out all the time. Nobody pays any attention. Come on, take a look."

The body was still uncovered, lying on bare ground between a couple of large bushes. The bushes lined a bank that ran parallel to the third-base line on a softball field. Whoever had killed her didn't care if she was found; he must have realized that she'd be found almost immediately. Portable lights illuminated the area around the body, and a crime-scene crew was working it over. "Look for cigarettes," Lucas told Carrigan. "Unfiltered Camels."

"Okay. . . ."

Lucas squatted next to the dead girl. She was lying on her side, twisted, her head and shoulders facing down, her hips half-turned toward the sky. Lucas could see enough of the wound to tell that it was identical to Wannemaker's: a stab and a disemboweling rip. He could smell the body cavity. . . . "Nasty," Lucas said.

"Yeah," Carrigan said sourly.

"Can I move her?"

"What for?"

"I want to roll her back and look at her chest," Lucas said.

"If you want to—we got photos and all," Carrigan said. "But there's blood all over her, you better use gloves. Hang on. . . ." He came back a moment later with a pair of thin yellow plastic gloves and handed them to Lucas. Lucas pulled them on, took the woman by the arm, and rolled her back.

"Look at this," Lucas said. He pointed at two bloody squiggles on her breast. "What do they look like?"

"Letters. An S and a J," Carrigan said, shining a penlight on the girl's body. "Kiss my rosy red rectum. What is this shit, Davenport?"

"Insanity," Lucas said as he studied the body.

A moment later, Carrigan said, "Who's this?"

Lucas looked over his shoulder and saw Connell striding toward them, wrapped in a raincoat. "My aide," he said.

"Your fuckin' what?"

"Is it him?" Connell asked, coming up. Lucas stood up and stripped off the gloves.

"Yeah. Cut the *SJ* into her," Lucas said. He crooked his head back and looked up at the night sky, the faint stars behind the city lights. The guy had pissed him off. Somehow, Wannemaker didn't reach him so personally; this kid did. Maybe because he could still feel the life in her. She hadn't been dead long.

"He's out of his pattern," Connell said.

"Fuck pattern. We know he did Wannemaker," Lucas said. "The girl up north didn't have the letters cut into her."

"But she was on schedule," Connell said. "Wannemaker and this one, these are two that are out of order. I hope we don't have two guys."

"Nah." Lucas shook his head. "The knife in the stomach, man, it's a signature. More than the letters, even."

"I better look at her," Connell said. She crept under the bushes for a better look, squatted next to the body, turned the light on it. She studied it for a minute, then two, then walked away to spit. Came back. "I'm getting used to it," she said.

"God help you," said Carrigan.

A patrolman and a tall black kid were walking fast up the block, the kid a half-step ahead of the patrolman. The kid wore knee shorts, an oversize shirt, Sox hat, and an expression of eye-rolling exasperation.

Carrigan took a step toward them. "What you got, Bill?"

"Kid saw the guy," the patrolman said. "Sure enough."

Lucas, Connell, and Carrigan gathered around the kid. "You see him?"

"Man . . ." The kid looked up the block, where more people were wandering in, attracted by word of a murder.

"What's your name?" Connell asked.

"Dex?" The answer sounded like a question, and the kid's eyes rolled up to the sky.

"How long ago?" Lucas asked.

The kid shrugged. "Do I look like a large fuckin' clock?"

"You're gonna look like a large fuckin' scab if you don't watch your mouth," Carrigan said.

Lucas held up a hand, got close to the kid. "This is a farm girl, Dex. Just came up to the city, somebody let the air out of her."

"Ain't got nothin' to do with me," Dex said, looking at the crowd again.

"Come over here," Lucas said, his voice friendly. He took the kid's arm. "Look at the body."

"What?"

"Come on. . . ." He waved the kid over, then said to the patrolman, "Loan me your flashlight, will you, pal?"

Lucas took Dex around the bush, then duckwalked with him toward the woman on the wound side. He went willingly enough; hell, he'd seen six thousand bodies on TV, and once had walked by a place where some ambulance guys were taking a body out of a house. This'd be cool.

A foot from the body, Lucas turned the light on the stomach wound.

"Fuck," said Dex. He stood up, straight through the bush, and started thrashing his way out.

Lucas caught his web pocket, hauled him back down, rough. "Come on, man, you can tell people about this. How the cops let you check her out." He put the flashlight on the girl's face. "Look at her eyes, man, they're still open, they look like eggs. You can smell her guts if you get closer, kind of soapy smelling."

Dex's eyes moved toward the corpse's, and he shuddered and stood and tried to run. Lucas let him go: Carrigan was waiting when the kid fought free of the bush.

"Never saw nothin' like that before," Dex said. A line of saliva dribbled from one edge of his mouth, and he wiped it with his hand.

"So who was it?" Carrigan asked.

"White dude. Driving a pickup."

"What kind of pickup?"

"White with dark on it, maybe red, I don't know; I know the white part for sure," Dex said. He kept moving away from the body, around the bushes back toward the curb. Carrigan held one arm and Dex babbled on. "There was a camper on the back. People come up here to throw garbage sometimes. I thought that's what he was doin', throwing garbage."

"How close were you?" Connell asked.

"Down to the corner," Dex said, pointing. A hundred yards.

"What'd he look like, far as you could tell?" Connell pressed. "Big guy? Small guy? Skinny?"

"Pretty big. Big as me. And I think maybe he plays basketball, the way he got in the truck. He like hopped up there, you know. Just real quick, like he's got some speed. Quick."

Connell fumbled in her purse and took out a folded square of paper. She started to unfold it when Lucas realized what it was, reached out and caught her hand, shook his head. "Don't do that," he said. He looked at Dex and asked, "How long ago?"

"Hour? I don't know. 'Bout an hour." That meant nothing. For most witnesses, an hour was more than fifteen minutes and less than three hours.

"What else?"

"Man, I don't think there's anything else. I mean, let me think about it. . . ." He looked past Lucas. "Here comes my mom."

A woman rolled right through the police line, and when a cop reached out toward her, she turned around and snapped something that stopped him short, and she came on.

"What're you doing here?" she demanded.

"Talking to your son," Carrigan said, facing her. "He's a witness to a crime."

"He's never been in no trouble," the woman said.

"He's not in any trouble now," Connell said. "He might've seen a killer—a white man. He's just trying to remember what else he might've seen."

"He's not in no trouble?" She was suspicious.

Connell shook her head. "He's helping out."

"Momma, you oughta see that girl," Dex said, swallowing. He looked back toward the bush. The girl's hip was just visible from where they were standing. He looked back at Carrigan. "The truck had those steps on the sides, you know, what do they call them?"

"Running boards?" Lucas suggested.

Dex nodded. "That's it. Silver running boards."

"Chevy, Ford?"

"Shoot, man, they all look the same to me. Wouldn't have one, myself. . . ."

"What color was the camper?"

The kid had to think about it. "Dark," he said finally.

"What else?"

He scratched behind one ear, looked at his mother, then shook his head. "Just some white dude dumping garbage, is what I thought."

"Were you alone when you saw him?" Lucas asked.

He swallowed again and glanced at his mother. His mother saw it and slapped his back, hard. "You tell."

"I saw a guy named Lawrence, was up here," he said.

His mother put her hands on her hips. "You with Lawrence?"

"I wasn't with Lawrence, Momma. I just saw him up here, is all. I wasn't with him."

"You goddamn better not be with him or I throw your butt outa the house. You know what I told you," his mother said, angry. She looked at Carrigan and said, "Lawrence a pusher."

"Lawrence his first name or his last name?" Carrigan asked.

"Lawrence Wright."

"Lawrence Wright? I know him," Carrigan said. " 'Bout twenty-two or -three, tall skinny guy, used to wear a sailor hat all the time?"

"That's him," the woman said. "Trash. He comes from a long line of trash. Got a trashy mother and all his brothers are trash," she said. She smacked the kid on the back again. "You hanging around with that trash?"

"Where'd he go?" Lucas asked. "Lawrence?"

"He was around here until they found the body," Dex said, looking around as if he might see the missing man. "Then he left."

"Did he see the white guy?" Connell asked.

Dex shrugged. "I wasn't with him. But he was closer than me. He was walking up this way when the white dude went out of the park. I saw the white dude lookin' at him."

Lucas looked at Carrigan. "We need to get to this Lawrence right now."

"Does he smoke?" Carrigan asked Dex.

Dex shrugged, but his mother said, "He smokes. He's all the time walking around with his head up in the sky with that crack shit."

"We gotta get him," Lucas said again.

"I don't know where he hangs out, I just knew him from the neighborhood when I was working dope five years ago," Carrigan said uncertainly. "I could call a guy, Alex Drucker, works dope up here."

"Get him," Lucas said.

Carrigan glanced at his watch and chuckled. "Four-thirty. Drucker's been in bed about two hours now. He'll like this."

As Carrigan went back to his car, one of the crime-scene crew came over and said, "No cigarettes from tonight, just old bits and pieces."

"Forget it," Lucas said. "We're told she was dumped an hour ago. Might check the street from here back to . . . Nah, fuck it. We know who did it."

"We'll check," the crime-scene guy said. "Camels. . . ."

"Unfiltered," Lucas said. He turned to the mother. "We need to send Dex downtown with an officer to make a statement, and maybe get him to describe this guy for an artist. We'll bring him back. Or, if you want, you can ride along."

"Ride along?"

"If you want."

"I better do that," she said. "He's not in trouble?"

"He's not in trouble."

CARRIGAN CAME BACK. "Nobody at Drucker's place. No answer."

"The guy's known around here—why don't we walk down to the corner and ask?"

Carrigan looked down to the corner, then back to Lucas and Connell. "You two are pretty white to be askin' favors from them."

Lucas shrugged. "I'm not going to sweat them; I'm just gonna ask. Come on."

They walked down toward the corner, and Connell asked, "Why can't I show him the picture? He could give us a confirmation."

"I don't want to contaminate his memory. If we get a sketch out of him, I'd rather have it be what he remembers, not what he saw when you showed him a picture."

"Oh." She thought about it for a minute, then nodded.

As they reached the corner, the crowd went quiet, and Carrigan pushed right up to it. "Some white dude just cut open a little girl and dumped her body in the bushes back there," Carrigan said conversationally, without preamble. "A guy named Lawrence Wright saw him. We don't want to hassle Lawrence, we just want a statement: if anybody's seen him, or if he's here?"

"That girl, black or white?" a woman asked.

"White," Lucas said.

"Why you need to talk to Lawrence? Maybe he didn't see nothin'."

"He saw something," Carrigan said. "He was right next to this white dude."

"The guy is nuts," Lucas said. "He's like that guy over in Milwaukee, killed all those boys. This has got nothing to do with nothing, he's just killing people."

A ripple of talk ran through the crowd, and then a woman's voice said, "Lawrence went to Porter's." Somebody else said, "Shush," and the woman's voice said, "Shush, your ass, he's killing little girls, somebody is."

"White girls . . . that don't make no difference . . . still white . . . What'd Lawrence do . . . ?"

"We better get going," Carrigan said quietly. "Before somebody runs down to Porter's and tells Lawrence we're coming."

LUCAS AND CONNELL RODE with Carrigan. "Porter's is an after-hours place down on Twenty-ninth," Carrigan said. "We oughta get a squad to do some blocking for us."

"Wouldn't hurt," Lucas said. "The place'd still be open?"

"Another fifteen minutes or so. He usually closes about five in the summertime."

They met the squad four minutes later at a Perkins restaurant parking lot. One patrolman was black, the other white, and Lucas talked to them through the car windows, told them who they were looking for. "Just hold anybody coming out . . . You guys know where it is?"

"Yeah. We'll slide right down the alley. As soon as you see us going in, though, you better get in the front."

"Let's do it," Carrigan said.

"How bad might this get?" Connell asked.

Carrigan glanced at her. "Shouldn't be bad at all. Porter's is an okay place; Porter goes along. But you know . . ."

"Yeah. Lucas and I are white."

"Better let me go first. Don't yell at anybody."

THEY HESITATED AT the corner, just long enough for the squad to cut behind them, go halfway down the block, then duck into the mouth of the alley.

Carrigan rolled up to the front of a 1920s-style four-square house with a wide porch. The porch was empty, but when they climbed out of the car, Lucas could hear a Charles Brown tune floating out through an open window.

Carrigan led the way up the walk, across the porch. When he went through the door, Lucas and Connell paused a moment, making just a little space, then followed him through.

The living room of the old house had been turned into a bar; the old parlor had a half-dozen chairs in it, three of them filled. Two men and two women sat around a table in the living room to the left. Everything stopped when Lucas and Connell walked in. The air was layered with tobacco smoke and the smell of whiskey.

"Mr. Porter," Carrigan was saying to a bald man behind the bar.

"What can I do for you gentlemen?" Porter asked, both hands poised on the bar. Porter didn't have a license, but it wasn't usually a problem. One of the men at the table moved his chair back an inch, and Lucas looked at him. He stopped moving.

"One of your patrons saw a suspect in a murder—a white man who killed a white girl and dumped her body up in the park," Carrigan said, his voice formal, polite. "Guy's a maniac, and we need to talk to Lawrence Wright about it. Have you seen Lawrence?"

"I really can't recall. The name's not familiar," Porter said, but his eyes drifted deliberately toward the hall. A door had a hand-lettered sign that said Men.

"Well, we'll get out of your way, then," Carrigan said. "I'll just take a leak, if you don't mind."

Lucas had moved until his back was to a Grain Belt clock and where he could still block the door. His pistol was clipped to his back belt line, and he put one hand on his hip, as if impatient about waiting for Carrigan. A voice said, "Cops out back," and another voice asked, "What's that mean?"

Carrigan stepped down the hall, went past the door, then stepped back and pulled it open.

And smiled. "Hey," he called to Lucas, smiling, surprised. "Guess what? Lawrence is right here. Sittin' on the potty."

A whine came out of the room: "Shut that door, man. I'm doing my business. Please?"

The voice sounded like something from a bad sitcom. After a moment of silence, somebody in the living room laughed, a single, throaty, feminine laugh, and suddenly the entire bar fell out, the patrons roaring. Even Porter put his forehead down on his bar, laughing. Lucas laughed a little, not too much, and relaxed.

LAWRENCE WAS THIN, almost emaciated. At twenty, he'd lost his front teeth, both upper and lower, and he made wet slurping sounds when he spoke: ". . . I don't know, *slurp*, it was dark. Blue and white, I think, *slurp*. And he had a beard. Shitkicker wheels on the truck."

"Real big?"

"Yeah, real big. Somebody say he had running boards? *Slurp.* I don't think he had running boards. Maybe he did, but I didn't see any. He was a white guy, but he had a beard. Dark beard."

"Beard," Connell said.

"How come you're sure he was a white guy?"

Lawrence frowned, as if working out a puzzle, then brightened. "Because I saw his hands. He was takin' a pinch, man. He was tootin', that's why I looked at him."

"Coke?"

"Gotta be," Lawrence said. "Ain't nothing else looks like that, you know, when you're trying to toot while you're walkin' or doin' something else. *Slurp.* You just get a pinch and you put it up there. That's what he was doin'. And I saw his hands."

"Long hair, short?" Connell asked.

"Couldn't tell."

"Bumper stickers, license plates, anything?" asked Lucas.

Lawrence cocked his head, lips pursed. "Nooo, didn't notice anything like that, *slurp.*"

"Didn't see much, did you?" said Carrigan.

"I told you he was tootin'," Lawrence said defensively. "I told you he was white."

"Big fuckin' deal. That's Minneapolis outside, if you ain't noticed," Carrigan said. "There are approximately two point five million white people walking around."

"Ain't my fault," Lawrence said.

Red-and-white truck, or maybe blue-and-white, maybe with silver running boards, but then again, maybe not. Cokehead. White. A beard.

"Let's send him downtown and take him through the whole thing," Lucas said to Carrigan. "Get him on tape."

THEY WENT BACK TO the scene, but nothing had changed except that the sun had come up and the world had a pale, frosted look. Crime scene was videotaping the area, and trucks from TV3 and Channel 8 hung down the block.

"Your pals from TV3," Lucas said, poking Connell with an elbow.

"Cockroaches," she said.

"C'mon." He looked back at the truck. A dark-haired woman waved. He waved back.

"They make entertainment out of murder, rape, pornography, pain, disease," Connell said. "There's nothing bad that happens to humans that they can't make a cartoon out of."

"You didn't hesitate to go to them."

"Of course not," she said calmly. "They're cockroaches, but they're a fact of life, and they *do* have their uses."

CONNELL WANTED TO HEAR the interview with Lawrence, and to press the medical examiner on the Marcy Lane autopsy. Lucas let her go, looked at his watch. Weather would be leaving home in fifteen minutes; he couldn't make it before she left. He drove back to the Perkins where they'd met the squad, bought a paper, and ordered pancakes and coffee.

Junky Doog dominated the *Strib*'s front page: two stories, a feature and a harder piece. The hard story began, "A leading suspect in a series of midwestern sex slayings was arrested in Dakota County yesterday. . . ." The feature said, "Junky Doog lived under a tree at a Dakota County landfill, and one by one cut off the fingers of his left hand, and the toes. . . ."

"Good story." A pair of legs—nice legs—stopped by the table. Lucas looked up. A celebrity smiled down at him. He recognized her but couldn't immediately place her. "Jan Reed," she said. "With TV3? Could I join you for a cup?"

"Sure. . . ." He waved at the seat opposite. "I can't tell you much."

"The camera guys said you were pretty good about us," Reed said.

Reed was older than most TV reporters, probably in her middle thirties, Lucas thought. Like all of the latest crop of on-camera newswomen, she was strikingly attractive, with large dark eyes, auburn hair falling to her shoulders, and just a hint of the fashionable overbite. Lucas had suggested to Weather that a surgeon was making a fortune somewhere, turning out TV anchors with bee-stung lips and overbites. Weather told him that would be unethical; the next day, though, she said she'd been watching, and there were far too many overbites on local television to be accounted for by simple jaw problems.

"Why is that?" she'd asked. She seemed really interested.

Lucas said, "You don't know?"

"No. I don't," she said. She looked at him skeptically. "You're gonna tell me it's something dirty?"

"It's because it makes guys think about blow jobs," Lucas said.

"You're lying to me," Weather said, one hand on her hip.

"Honest to God," Lucas said. "That's what it is."

"This society is out of luck," Weather said. "I'm sorry, but we're going down the tubes. Blow jobs."

JAN REED SIPPED HER coffee and said, "One of our sources says it's the serial killer. We saw Officer Connell there, of course, so it's a reasonable presumption. Will you confirm it?"

Lucas thought about it, then said, "Listen, I hate talking on the record. It gets me in trouble. I'll give you a little information, if you just lay it off on an unnamed source."

"Done," she said, and she stuck her hand out. Lucas shook it: her hand was soft, warm. She smiled, and that made him feel even warmer. She *was* attractive.

Lucas gave her two pieces of information: that the victim was female and white, and that investigators believed it was the work of the same man who killed Wannemaker.

"We already had most of that," she said gently. She was working him, trying to make him show off.

He didn't bite. "Well, what can I tell you," he said. "Another day in the life of a TV reporter, fruitlessly chasing down every possible scrap."

She laughed, a nice laugh, musical, and she said, "I understand you used to date a reporter."

"Yes. We have a daughter," Lucas said.

"That's serious."

"Well. It was," Lucas said. He took a sip of coffee. "Some time ago."

"I'm divorced myself," she said. "I never thought it would happen." She looked at her hands.

Lucas thought he ought to mention Weather, but he didn't. "You know, I recognized you right away—I thought you were anchoring."

"Yes—I will be. I've done a little already, but I only got here three months ago. They're rotating me through the shifts so I can see how things work, while I anchor on a fill-in basis. In another month, I'll start getting more anchor time."

"Smart. Get to know the place."

They chatted for a few more minutes, then Lucas glanced at his watch and said, "Damn. I've got to go," and slid out of the booth.

"Got a date?" She looked up at him, and he almost fell into her eyes.

"Sort of," Lucas said, trying to look somewhere else. "Listen, uh . . . see you around, huh?"

"No doubt," she said, sending him off with a bee-stung smile.

WEATHER HAD SEEN Lucas working at close range, as he broke a murder case in her small northern Wisconsin town. Lucas had seen Weather working as a coroner—doctors were scarce up north, and they took turns at the county coroner's job—but the only time he'd been around when she was working on a live patient, he'd been unconscious: he'd been the patient.

He had promised her he'd come and watch what she did, not thinking about it much. She'd become insistent, and they'd set the visit up a week earlier, before the Wannemaker killing. He could just squeeze it in, he thought.

He touched the scar on his throat, thinking about Weather. Most of the scar had been caused by a Swiss Army knife that she'd used to open him up; the rest came from a .22 slug, fired by a little girl. . . .

· · ·

LUCAS LEFT HIS CAR in a parking ramp three blocks from University Hospitals and walked down through the cool morning, among the medical students in their short white coats, the staff doctors in their longer coats. A nurse named Jim showed Lucas the men's locker room, gave him a lock and key for a locker, and told him how to dress: "There're scrub suits in the bins, three different sizes. The shoe covers are down there in the bottom bin. The caps and masks are in those boxes. Take one of the shower cap types, and take a mask, but don't put it on yet. We'll show you how to tie it when you're ready. . . . Take your billfold and watch and any valuables with you. Dr. Karkinnen'll be out in a minute."

Weather's eyes smiled at him when he stepped out of the locker room. He felt like an idiot in the scrub suit, like an impostor.

"How does it feel?" Weather asked.

"Strange. Cool," Lucas said.

"The girl who was killed . . . was it him?"

"Yes. Didn't get much out of it. A kid saw him, though. He's white, he probably snorts coke, he drives a truck."

"That's something."

"Not much," he said. He looked down the hall toward the double doors that led to the operating rooms. "Is your patient already doped up?"

"She's right there," Weather said, nodding.

Lucas looked to his left. A thin, carefully groomed blond woman and a tiny redheaded girl sat in a waiting area, the little girl looking up at the woman, talking intently. The girl's arms were bandaged to the shoulder. The woman's head was nodding, as if she were explaining something; the little girl's legs twisted and retwisted as they dangled off the chair. "I need to talk to them for a minute," Weather said.

Weather went down the hall. Lucas, still self-conscious about the scrub suit, hung back, drifting along behind her. He saw the girl when she spotted Weather; her face contorted with fear. Lucas, even more uncomfortable, slowed even more. Weather said something to the mother, then squatted and started talking to the girl. Lucas stepped closer, and the little girl looked up at him. He realized that she was weeping, soundlessly, but almost without control. She looked back at Weather. "You're going to hurt me again," she wailed.

"It'll be fine," Weather said quickly.

"Hurts bad," the girl said, tears running down. "I don't want to get fixed anymore."

"Well, you've got to get better," Weather said, and as she reached out a finger to touch the girl's cheek, the dam burst, and the girl began to cry, clutching at her mother's dress with her bandaged arms like tree stumps.

"This won't hurt so bad today. Just a little pinch for the IV and that's all," Weather said, patting her. "And when you wake up, we'll give you a pill, and you'll be sleepy for a while."

"That's what you said last time," the girl wailed.

"You've got to get better, and we're almost done," Weather said. "Today, and one more day, and we should be finished." Weather stood and looked at the mother. "She hasn't eaten anything?"

"Not since nine o'clock," the woman said. Tears were running down her cheeks. "I've got to get out of here," she said desperately. "I can't stand this. Can we get going?"

"Sure," Weather said. "Come on, Lucy, take my hand."

Lucy slipped slowly out of the chair, took one of Weather's fingers. "Don't hurt me."

"We're gonna try really hard," Weather said. "You'll see."

WEATHER LEFT THE GIRL with the nurses and took Lucas along to an office where she started going through an inch-high stack of papers, checking them and signing. "Preop stuff," she said. "Who was the girl last night?"

"A teenager from out of state. From Worthington."

Weather looked up. "Pretty bad?"

"You'd have to see it to believe it."

"You sound a little pissed," she said.

"On this one, I am," he said. "This girl looked like . . . she looked like some-body who did her first communion last week."

THE ROUTINE OF THE operation caught him: precise, but informal. Everybody in the room except Lucas and the anesthesiologist was female, and the anesthesiologist left for another operation as soon as the girl was down, leav-ing the job in the hands of a female anesthetist. The surgical team put him in a rectangular area along a wall and suggested that he stay there.

Weather and the surgical assistant worked well together, the assistant ready with the instruments almost before Weather asked for them. There was less blood than Lucas expected, but the smell of the cautery bothered him; burning blood . . .

Weather explained quickly what she was doing, expanding and spreading skin to cover the burns on the girl's arms. Weather ran the show with quick, tight directions, and there were no questions.

And she spoke to Lucas from time to time, distractedly, focusing on the work. "Her father was running a power line from a 220 outlet to a pump down by the lake using an extension cord. The connection where the two cords came to-gether . . . started to pull apart. That's what they think. Lucy grabbed them to put them back together. They don't know exactly what she was doing, but there was a flash and she'd gotten hit on both arms, and around her back on her shoul-der blades. . . . We'll show you. We're doing skin grafts where we can, and in some places we're expanding the skin to cover."

After a while, talk around the table turned to a book about a love affair that was dominating the best-seller lists. About whether the lovers should have gone off together, destroying a marriage and a family.

"She was living a lie afterwards; she was hurting everyone," one of the nurses declared. "She should have gone."

"Right. And the family is wrecked and just because she has a fling doesn't mean she still doesn't love them."

"This was not exactly a fling."

In the background, music oozed from a portable radio tuned to an easy-listening station; on the table, under Weather's gloved hands and knife, Lucy bled.

They harvested skin from Lucy's thigh to cover a part of the wound. The skin harvester looked like a cross between an electric sander and a sod cutter.

"This looks like it's going to hurt," Lucas said finally. "Hurt a lot."

"Can't help it," Weather grunted, not looking up. "These are the worst, burns are. Skin won't regenerate, but you've got to cover the wounds to prevent infection. That means grafts and expansions. . . . We put the temporary skin on because we couldn't get enough off her the first couple of times, but you can't leave the temporary stuff, she'll reject it."

"Maybe you should have told her it was going to hurt," Lucas said. "When you were talking to her outside."

Weather glanced up briefly, as though considering it, but shook her head as she continued to tack down the advanced skin on one of the expansions. "I didn't tell her it wouldn't hurt. The idea was to get her in here, quiet, with a minimum of resistance. Next time, I can tell it's the last time."

"Will it be?"

"I hope so," Weather said. "We might need a touch-up if we get some rough scar development. Might have to release scar tissue. But the next one should be the last one for a while."

"Huh."

She looked at him, grave, quiet, over the top of her mask, her pink-stained fingers held in front of her, away from the girl's open wounds; the nurses were looking at him as well. "I don't do therapy," she said. "I do surgery. Sometimes you can't get around the pain. All you can do is fix them, and eventually the pain stops. That's the best I can do."

AND LATER, WHEN she was finished, they sat together in the surgeon's lounge for a few minutes and she asked, "What do you think?"

"Interesting. Impressive."

"Is that all?" There was a tone in her voice.

"I've never seen you before as the commander in chief," he said. "You do it pretty well."

"Any objections?"

"Of course not."

She stood up. "You seemed disturbed. When you were watching me."

He looked down, shook his head. "It's pretty strong stuff. And it wasn't what I'd expected, the blood and the smell of the cautery and that skin harvester thing . . . It's kind of brutal."

"Sometimes it is," she said. "But you were most bothered about my *attitude* toward Lucy."

"I don't know. . . ."

"I can't get involved," she said. "I have to turn off that part of me. I can like patients, and I like Lucy, but I can't afford to go into the operating room worrying that I'll hurt them, or wondering if I'm doing the right thing. I've worked that out in advance. If I didn't, I'd screw up in there."

"It did seem a little cold," he admitted.

"I wanted you to see that," she said. "Lucas, as part of my . . . surgeon persona, I guess you'd call it, I'm different. I have to make brutal decisions, and I do. And I run things. I run them very well."

"Well . . ."

"Let me finish. Since I moved down here, we've had some very good times in bed. We've had nice runs at night, and some fun going out and fooling around. *But this is what I am, right here.* What you saw."

Lucas sighed, and nodded. "I know that. And I admire you for it. Honest to God."

She smiled then, just a little. "Really?"

"Really. It's just that what you do . . . is so much harder than I thought."

Much harder, he thought again as he left the hospital.

In his world, or in Jan Reed's world, for that matter, very few thing were perfectly clear: the best players were always figuring odds. Mistakes, stupidity, oversights, lies, and accidents were part of the routine. In Weather's world, those things were not routine; they were, in fact, virtually unforgivable.

The surgery was another thing. The blood hadn't bothered him, but he *was* bothered by that moment where the knife hovered above the uncut skin, as Weather made her last-minute decisions on how she would proceed. Cutting in hot blood was one thing; doing it in cold blood—doing it on a child, even for the child's own good—was something else. It took an intellectual toughness of an order that Lucas hadn't encountered on the street. Not outside a psychopath.

That was what she'd wanted him to see.

Was she trying to tell him something?

LUCAS'S HEAD FELT large and fuzzy as he walked through the doors of City Hall and up to the chief's office. Lack of sleep. Getting older. Roux's secretary thumbed him through the door, but Lucas stopped for a second. "Check around and see if Meagan Connell's in the building, will you? Tell her where I am."

"Sure. Do you want me to send her in?"

"Yeah, why not?"

"Because she and the chief might get in a fistfight?"

Lester and Anderson were in visitor's chairs. Lonnie Shantz, Roux's press aide, leaned on the windowsill, arms crossed, an accusation on his jowly ward heeler's face. Roux nodded when Lucas arrived. "They're pissed over at the *Strib*," she said. "Have you seen the paper?"

"Yeah. The big thing on Junky."

"With this killing last night, they think we sandbagged them," Shantz said.

Lucas sat down. "What can you do? The guy's flipped out. Any other time, it might've held them for a few days."

"We're not looking good, Lucas," Roux said.

"What about the St. Paul cop?" Shantz asked. "Anything there?"

"I'm told that St. Paul had a shrink talk to him," Lester said. "They don't think he's capable of it."

"Beat up his wife," Shantz suggested.

"The charges were dropped. More like a brawl. His old lady got her licks in," Anderson said. "Hit him in the face with a Mr. Coffee."

"I heard it was an iron," Lucas said. "Where was he last night, by the way?"

"Bad news," Lester said. "His old lady moved out after the last big fight, and he was home. Alone. Watching TV."

"Shit," Lucas said.

"St. Paul's talking to him again, pinning down the shows he saw."

"Yeah, yeah, but with VCR time delays, he could have been anywhere," Shantz said.

"Bullshit," said Anderson.

Shantz was talking to Roux. "All we'd have to do is leak a name and the spousal-abuse charge. We could do it a long way from here—I could have one of my pals at the DFL do it for me. Hell, they like doing favors for media, for the paybacks. TV3'd pee their pants with that kind of tip. And it really *does* smell like a cover-up."

"They'd crucify him," Lester said. "They'd make it look like the charges were dropped because he's a cop."

"Who's to say they weren't?" Shantz asked. "And it would take some of the heat off us. Christ, this killing over at the lakes, that's a goddamn disaster. The woman's dead and the guy's a cabbage. Now we get this serial asshole again, knocking off some country milkmaid, we're talking firestorm."

"If you feed the St. Paul guy to the press, you'll regret it. It'd kill the Senate for you," Lucas said to Roux.

"Why is that?" Shantz demanded. "I don't see how. . . ."

Lucas ignored him, spoke to Roux. "Word would get out. When everybody figured out what happened—that you threw an innocent cop to the wolves to turn the attention away from you—they'd never forget and never forgive you."

Roux looked at him for a moment, then shifted her gaze to Shantz. "Forget it."

"Chief . . ."

"Forget it," she snapped. "Davenport is right. The risk is too big." Her eyes moved to her left, past Lucas, hardened. Lucas turned and saw Connell standing in the doorway.

"Come on in, Meagan," he said. "Do you have the picture?"

"Yeah." Connell dug in her purse, took out the folded paper, and handed it to Lucas. Lucas unfolded it, smoothed it, and passed it to Roux.

"This is not bullshit; this could be our man. More or less. I'm not sure you should release it."

Roux looked at the picture for a moment, then at Connell, then at Lucas. "Where'd you get this?" she asked.

"Meagan found a woman yesterday who remembers a guy at the St. Paul store who was there the same time Wannemaker was there. He's not on our list of names and this fits some of the other descriptions we've had. A guy last night who definitely saw him says he has a beard."

"And drives a truck," said Connell.

"Everybody who drives a truck has a beard," Lester said.

"Not quite," Lucas said. "This is actually . . . something. A taste of the guy."

"Why wouldn't I release it?" Roux asked.

"Because we're not getting enough hard evidence. Nothing that can tie him directly to a killing—a hair or a fingerprint. If this isn't a good picture of him, and we do finally track him down, and we're scraping little bits and pieces together to make a case . . . a defense attorney will take this and stick it up our ass. You know: *Here's the guy they were looking for—until they decided to pin it on my client.*"

"Is there anything working today? Anything that'd give us a break?"

"Not unless it comes out of the autopsy on Lane. That'll be a while yet."

"Um, Bob Greave got a call from TV3—a tip on a suspect," Connell said. "It's nothing."

"What do you mean, nothing? What is this, Lucas?" Roux asked.

"Beats me. First I heard of it," he said.

"Get his ass down here," Roux said.

GREAVE CAME DOWN carrying a slip of yellow paper, leaned in the doorway.

"Well?" Roux said.

He looked at the paper. "A woman out in Edina says she knows who the killer is."

Lucas: "And the bad news is. . . ."

"She called TV3 first. They're the ones who called us. They want to know if we're going to make an arrest based on their information."

"You should have come and told us," Roux said. "We've been sitting here beating our heads against the wall."

Greave held up a hand. "You have to understand, the woman doesn't have any actual proof."

Roux said, "Keep talking."

"She remembers the killer coming back from each of the murders, washing the blood off the knife and his clothes, and then raping her. She repressed all this until yesterday, when the memories were liberated with the help of her therapist."

"Oh, no," Lucas groaned.

"It could be," Shantz said, looking around.

"Did I mention that the killer is her father?" Greave asked. "Sixty-six years old, the former owner of a drive-in theater? A guy with arteriosclerosis so bad that he can't walk up a flight of stairs?"

"We gotta check it," Shantz said. "Especially with the TV all over it."

"It's bullshit," Lucas said.

"We gotta check," Roux said.

"We'll check," Lucas said, "But we really need to catch this guy, and talking to old heart-attack victims isn't gonna do it."

"This one time, Lucas, goddamnit," Roux said, adamant. "I want you out there interviewing the guy, and I want you giving the statement to TV3."

"When the fuck did the TV start running our investigations?" Lucas asked.

"Jesus, Lucas—we're entertainment now. We're cheap film footage. We sell deodorant and get votes. Or lose votes. It's all a big loop; I've been told you were the first guy to realize that."

"Christ, it wasn't like this," Lucas said. "It was more like one hand washing the other. Now it's . . ."

"Entertainment for the unwashed."

As Lucas walked out the door, Roux called, "Lucas. Hey—don't kill this old guy, huh? When you talk to him?"

THEY TOOK A COMPANY CAR, all three of them, Greave sprawled in the back.

"Let me do the TV interview," he suggested to Lucas. "I did them all the time when I was Officer Friendly. I'm good at that shit. I got the right suits."

"*You* were Officer Friendly?" Connell snorted, looking over the seat at him. Then, "You know, it fits."

She said it as an insult. Lucas glanced at her and almost said something, but Greave was rambling on. "Really? I thought so. Go into all those classrooms, tell all the little boys that they'd grow up to be firemen and policemen, all the little girls that they'd be housewives and hookers."

Lucas, moderately surprised, shut his mouth and looked straight out over the wheel, and Connell said, "Fuck you, Greave."

Greave, still cheerful, said, "Say, did I tell you about the deaf people?"

"Huh?"

"Some deaf people went into the St. Paul cops. They saw the thing on TV, you know, that Connell fed them? They think they saw the guy at the bookstore the night Wannemaker was taken off. Bearded guy with a truck. They even got part of his license tag."

Connell turned to look over the seat. "Why didn't you say something?"

"Unfortunately, they didn't get any numbers. Only the letters."

"Well, that'd get it down to a thousand—"

"Uh-uh," Greave said. "The letters they got were *ASS*."

"ASS?"

"Yeah."

"Damnit," Connell said, turning back front. The state banned license plates with potentially offensive letter combinations: there were no *FUK, SUK, LIK,* or *DIK*. No *CNT* or *TWT*. There was no *ASS*.

"Did we check?"

"Yup," Greave said. "There's nary a one. I personally think this old guy did it, then comes home and gives the daughter a little tickle."

"Kiss my ass," Connell said.

"Any time, any place," said Greave.

A TV3 TRUCK WAS PARKED on the street in front of the Weston house, a reporter combing her strawberry-blond hair in the wing mirror, a cameraman in a travel vest sitting on the curb, eating an egg-salad sandwich. The cameraman said something to the reporter as Lucas stopped at the house, and the reporter turned, saw him, and started across the street. She had long smooth legs on top of black high heels. Her dress clung to her like a new paint job on a '55 Chevy.

"I think she's in my *Playboy*," Greave said, his face pressed to the window. "Her name is Pamela Stern. She's a piranha."

Lucas got out and Stern came up, thrust out her hand, and said, "I think we've got him bottled up inside."

"Yeah, well . . ." Lucas looked up at the house. The curtains twitched in an old-fashioned picture window. The reporter reached out and turned over his necktie. Lucas looked down and found her reading the orange label.

"Hermes," she said. "I thought so. Very nice."

"His shoes are from Payless," Connell said from across the car.

"His shorts are from Fruit of the Loom," said Greave, chipping in. "He's one of the fruits."

"I *love* your sunglasses," Stern said, ignoring them, her perfect white teeth catching her lower lip for just an instant. "They make you look mean. Mean is *so* sexy."

"Jesus," Lucas said. He started up the walk with Greave and Connell, and found the woman right at his elbow. Behind her, the cameraman had the camera on his shoulder, and rolling. Lucas said, "When we get to the steps, I'm going to ask the guy if he wants me to arrest you for trespassing. If he does, I will. And I suspect he does."

She stopped in her tracks, eyes like chips of flint. "It's not nice to fuck with Mother Nature," she said. And then, "I don't know what Jan Reed sees in you."

Connell said, "Who? Jan Reed?" and Greave said, "Whoa," and Lucas, irritated, said, "Bullshit," and rang the doorbell. Ray Weston opened the door and peeked out like a mouse. "I'm Lucas Davenport, deputy chief of police, City of Minneapolis. I'd like to speak to you."

"My daughter's nuts," Weston said, opening the door another inch.

"We need to talk," Lucas said. He took off the sunglasses.

"Let them in, Ray," a woman's voice said. The voice was shaky with fear. Weston opened the door and let them in.

Neither Ray nor Myrna Weston knew anything about the killings; Lucas, Connell, and Greave agreed on that in the first five minutes. They spent another half hour pinning down times on the Wannemaker and Lane killings. The Westons were in bed when Lane was taken, and were watching *The Wild Ones* with friends when Wannemaker was picked up.

"Do you think you can get these bums off our back?" Ray Weston asked when they were ready to leave.

"I don't know," he said honestly. "That stuff your daughter's giving them— it's pretty heavy."

"She's nuts," Weston said again. "How can they believe that stuff?"

"They don't," Lucas said.

Outside, Stern was waiting, microphone in hand, the camera rolling, when Lucas, Connell, and Greave left the house. "Chief Davenport," she said. "What have you learned? Will you arrest Ray Weston, father of Elaine Louise Weston-Brown?"

Lucas shook his head. "Nope. Your whole irresponsible story is a crock of shit and a disgrace to journalism."

GREAVE WAS LAUGHING about Stern's reaction on the way back, and even Connell seemed a little looser. "I liked the double take she did. She was already rolling with the next question," Greave said.

"It won't seem so funny if they put it on the air," Connell said.

"They won't do that," Lucas said.

"The whole thing is like some weird feminist joke," Greave said. "If there was such a thing as a feminist joke."

"There are lots of feminist jokes," Connell said.

"Oh. Okay, I'm sorry. You're right," Grave admitted. "What I meant to say is, there are no *funny* feminist jokes."

Connell turned to him, a tiny light in her eye. "You know why women are no good at math?" she asked.

"No. Why?"

She held her thumb and forefinger two inches apart. "Because all their lives they're told this is eight inches."

Lucas grinned, and Greave let a smile slip. "One fuckin' funny joke after thirty years of feminism."

"You know why men give names to their penises?"

"I'm holding my breath," Greave said.

" 'Cause they don't want a complete stranger making all their important decisions for them."

Greave looked into his lap. "You hear that, Godzilla? She's making fun of you."

Just before they got back, Connell asked, "Now what?"

"I don't know," Lucas said. "Think about it. Read your files some more. Dredge something up. Wait."

"Wait for him to kill somebody else?"

"Something," Lucas said.

"I think we ought to push him. I think we ought to publish the artist's drawing. I couldn't find anybody to confirm it, but I'd bet there's some resemblance."

Lucas sighed. "Yeah, maybe we should. I'll talk to Roux."

ROUX AGREED. "It'll give us a bone to throw them," she said. "If they believe us."

Lucas went back to his office, stared at the phone, nibbling at his lower lip, trying to find a hold on the case. The easy possibilities, like Junky, were fading.

The door opened without a knock, and Jan Reed stuck her head in. "Whoops. Was I supposed to knock? I thought this was an outer office."

"I'm not a big enough deal to have an outer office," Lucas said. "Come on in. You guys are killing us."

"Not me," she said, sitting down, her legs crossed to one side. She'd changed since he saw her in the morning, and must've gotten some sleep. She looked fresh and wide awake, in a simple skirt with a white silk blouse.

"I wanted to apologize for Pam Stern. She's been out there a little too long."

"Who turned up the original story?"

"I really don't know—it was phoned in," she said.

"The therapist."

"I really don't know," she said, smiling. "And I wouldn't tell you if I did."

"Ah. Ethics raise their ugly head."

"Is there anything new?" she asked. She took a short reporter's notebook out of her purse.

"No."

"What should I look for next?"

"The autopsy. Evidence of the killer's semen or blood. If we get that, we've got something. There's a good chance that he's a prior sexual offender, and the state's got a DNA bank on prior offenders. That's next."

"All right," she said. She made a few notes. "I'll look for that. Anything else?"

Lucas shrugged. "That's about it."

"Okay. Well, that's it, then." And she left, leaving behind her scent. There's been just the tiniest, microscopic pause after she'd said "Okay." An opportunity to get personal? He wasn't sure.

CONNELL CAME BY LATE in the afternoon. "Nothing from the autopsy yet. There's a bruise on her face where it looks like somebody pinched her, and they're bringing in a specialist to see if they can lift a fingerprint. No great hopes."

"Nothing else?"

"Not yet. And I'm drawing blanks," she said.

"How about the PPP guy, the convict who saw the tattoo? What was his name—Price? If nothing comes up, why don't we drive over to Waupun tomorrow and talk to him?"

"Okay. What about Greave?"

"I'll tell him to work his own case for the day. That's all he wants to do anyway."

"Good. How far is Waupun?"

"Five or six hours."

"Why don't we fly?"

"Ah . . ."

"I can get a state patrol plane, I think."

WEATHER'S HEAD WAS snuggled in under Lucas's jaw, and she said, "You should have driven. You don't need the stress."

"Yeah, but I sound like such a chicken."

"Lots of people don't like to fly."

"But they do," he said.

She patted his stomach. "You'll be okay. I could get you something that'd mellow you out a little, if you want."

"That'd mess up my head. I'll fly." He sighed and said, "My main problem is, I'm not running this investigation. Connell's done everything, and I can't see beyond what she's done. I'm not thinking: the gears aren't moving like they used to."

"What's wrong?"

"I don't know, exactly—I can't get anything to start with. If I could get the smallest bite of personal information on the guy, I'd have something—we just can't get it. All I have to work with is paper."

"You said he might do cocaine. . . ."

"Maybe fifty thousand people in the Twin Cities do cocaine on a more or less regular basis," Lucas said. "I could jump a few dealers, but the chances of getting anywhere are nil."

"It's something."

"I need something else, and soon. He's gone crazy—less than a week between kills. He'll be doing another one. He'll be thinking about it already."

13 ✖

LUCAS HATED AIRPLANES, feared them. Helicopters, for reasons he didn't understand, were not so bad. They flew to Waupun in a small four-seater fixed-wing plane, Lucas in the back.

"I've never seen anything like that," Connell said, an undercurrent of satisfaction in her voice.

"You're exaggerating it," Lucas said, his face grim. The airport was open, windy, a patch on the countryside. A brown state car waited by the Waupun sign, and they walked that way.

"I thought you were going to throw the pilot out the window when we hit those bumps. I thought you were gonna explode. It was like your head was blowing up, like one of those Zodiac boats where the pressure builds up."

"Yeah, yeah."

"I hope you and the pilot can kiss and make up before we fly back," Connell said. "I don't want him flying scared."

Lucas turned to her and she stepped away, half smiling, half frightened. With the fish-white stone face behind the black glasses, he looked like a maniac; Lucas did not like airplanes.

A Waupun guard tossed a newspaper in the backseat of the state car and got out as they came up. "Ms. Connell?"

"Yes."

"Tom Davis." He was a mild-looking, fleshy man with rosy cheeks and vague blue eyes under a smooth, baby-clear forehead. He had a small graying mustache, just a bit wider than Hitler's. He smiled and shook her hand, then to Lucas, "And you're her assistant?"

"That was a joke," Connell said hastily. "This is, uh, Deputy Chief Lucas Davenport from Minneapolis."

"Whoops, sorry, Chief," Davis said. He winked at Connell. "Well, hop in. We got a little ride."

DAVIS KNEW D. WAYNE PRICE. "He's not a bad fella," he said. He drove with one foot on the gas and the other on the brake. The constant surging and slowing reminded Lucas of the airplane's motion.

"He was convicted of murdering a woman by slicing her open with a knife," Connell said. "They had to remove her intestines from the street with a bucket." Her voice was conversational.

"That wouldn't put him in the top ten percent of his class," the guard said, just as conversationally. "We got guys in here who raped and killed little boys before they ate them."

"*That's* bad," Lucas said.

"That *is* bad," said Davis.

"Is there any talk about Price?" Lucas asked. "He says he's innocent."

"So do fifty percent of the others, though most of them don't actually claim to be innocent. They say the law wasn't followed, or the trial wasn't fair. I mean, they did it, whatever it was, but they say the state didn't dot every single *i* and cross every single *t* before puttin' them away—and they say that's just not fair. There's nobody finickier about the law than a con," Davis said.

"How about Price?"

"I don't know D. Wayne that good, but some of the guys believe him," Davis said. "He's been pretty noisy about it, filing all kinds of appeals. He's never stopped; he's still doing it."

. . .

"DON'T LIKE PRISONS," Connell said. The interview room had the feel of a dungeon.

"Like the doors might not open again after you're inside," Lucas said.

"That's exactly it. I could stand it for about a week, and then they'd come to put me back in the cell, and I'd freak. I don't think I'd make a full month. I'd kill myself," Connell said.

"People do," Lucas said. "The saddest ones are the people they put on a suicide watch. They can't get out, and they can't get it over with. They just sit and suffer."

"Some of them deserve it."

Lucas disagreed. "I don't know if anybody deserves that."

D. WAYNE PRICE WAS a large man in his early forties; his face looked as if it had been slowly and incompetently formed with a ballpeen hammer. His forehead was shiny and pitted, with scars running up into his hairline. He had rough poreless skin under his eyes, scar tissue from being punched. His small round ears seem to be fitted into slots in his head. When the escort brought him to the interview room, he smiled a convict's obsequious smile, and his teeth were small and chipped. He was wearing jeans and a white T-shirt with "Harley-Davidson" on the front.

Lucas and Connell were sitting on a couple of slightly damaged green office chairs, facing a couch whose only notable quality was its brownness. The escort was a horse-faced older man with a buzz cut; he was carrying a yellow-backed book, said, "Sit," to Price, as though he were a Labrador retriever, said, "How do" to Lucas and Connell, then dropped onto the other end of the couch with his book.

"You smoke?" Connell asked Price.

"Sure." She fished in a pocket, handed him an open pack of Marlboros and a butane lighter. Price knocked a cigarette out of the pack, lit it, and Connell said, voice soft, "So, this woman in Madison. You kill her?"

"Never touched the bitch," Price said, testing, his eyes lingering on her.

"But you knew her," Connell said.

"I knew who she was," Price said.

"Sleep with her?" Lucas asked.

"Nope. Never got that close," Price said, looking at Lucas. "Had a nice ass on her, though."

"Where were you when she was killed?" asked Connell.

"Drunk. My buddies dropped me off at my house, but I knew if I went inside I'd start barfin', so I walked down to this convenience store for coffee. That's what got me."

"Tell me," said Connell.

Price looked up at the ceiling, stuck the cigarette in his mouth, looked down at it long enough to light it, blew some smoke and closed his eyes, remembering. "I was out drinking with some buddies. Shit, we were drinking all afternoon and shootin' pool. And so about eight o'clock my buddies brought me home 'cause I was too fuckin' drunk to drink."

"That's pretty drunk," Lucas said.

"Yeah, pretty," Price said. "Anyway, they dumped me off on my porch, and I sat there for a while, and when I could get going, I decided to go up to the corner and get some coffee. There was a 7-Eleven in one of them side-street shopping centers. There was like a drugstore and a cleaners and this bookstore. I was in the 7-Eleven, and she came down from the bookstore to get something. I was drunker'n shit, but I remembered her from some welding I done for her."

"Welding?"

"Yeah." Price laughed, the laugh trailing off into a cough. "She had this piece-of-shit '79 Cadillac, cream over key-lime green, and the bumper fell off. Just fuckin' fell off one day. The Cadillac place wanted like four hundred bucks to fix it, so she brought it over to my place and asked me what I could do. I welded the sonofabitch back on for twenty-two dollars. If that bumper hadn't fell off, I'd be a free man today."

"So you remembered her," Connell prompted. "In the store."

"Yeah. I said hello and come on to her a little bit, but she wasn't having it, and she left. I sort of followed along." Price's voice was slow and dreamy, pulling details out of his memory. "She went down to this bookstore. I was so fuckin' drunk, I kept thinking, *Hell, I'm gonna get lucky with this chick.* There was no chance. Even if she'd said, 'Hell, yes,' I was in no shape to . . . you know. Anyway, I went into the bookstore."

"How long did you stay?"

"About five minutes. There was a crowd in there, and I didn't fit so good. For one thing, I smelled like a Budweiser truck had peed on me."

"So?" Connell prompted.

"So I left." His voice hardened, and he sat up. "There was this pimply-faced asshole kid in there, a clerk. He said I stayed, and that later, when this book thing was over, I followed her out of the store. That's what he said. The lawyer asked him on the witness stand, he said, 'Can you point to the man who followed her out?' And this kid said, 'Yessir. That's the man right there.' He pointed to me. I was a gone motherfucker."

"But it wasn't you."

"Hell no. The kid remembered me because I bumped into him. Sorta pushed him."

"What's this tattoo business?" Lucas asked.

Price's eyes slid toward the escort, back to Lucas, back to the escort, back to Lucas, and his chin moved quickly right and left, no more than a quarter inch. "Tattoo? Kid didn't have no tattoo."

Connell, jotting down notes, missed it. She looked up. "According to my notes," she said, but Lucas rode over her.

"We gotta talk," he said to her. "I'd rather Mr. Price didn't hear this. . . . C'mon."

The escort had been browsing *The Encyclopedia of Pop, Rock and Soul.* He looked up and said, "I could take him. . . ."

"The corner is fine," Lucas said, pulling Connell along.

"What?" she asked, low-voiced.

Lucas got his back to Price and the escort. "D. Wayne doesn't want to talk about tattoos in front of the guard," Lucas said. "Talk to him for another five minutes, then ask the guard where the ladies' room is. Get him to take you—it's back through one set of doors."

"I can do that," she said.

The escort was back in his book when they sat down again. "So where'd you go when you left the store?" Lucas asked.

"Home."

"You didn't stay with her? You didn't try again?"

"Fuck, no. I was too drunk to follow her anywhere. I went back to the convenience store and got a couple more beers—never even got my coffee. I barely made it back home. I sat on my steps for a while, drank the beers, then I went inside and passed out. I didn't wake up until the cops came to get me."

"Must've been more to it than that," Lucas said.

Price shrugged. "There wasn't. The guy across the street even saw me sittin' on the steps, and said so. They found the fuckin' beer cans next to the step. Said it didn't prove nothing."

"Must've had a horseshit attorney," Lucas said.

"Public defender. He was all right. But you know . . ."

"Yeah?"

Price leaned back and looked at the ceiling again, as though weary of the story. "The cops wanted me. I was stealing stuff. I admit that. Tools. I specialized in tools. Most people steal, like, stereos. Shit, you can't get nothing for a stereo compared to what you can get for a good set of mechanic's tools, you know? Anyway, the cops were trying to get me forever, but they never could. I'd steal something, and before anybody knew it was gone, there was three niggers down in Chicago with a new welding rig, or something. I go into a shop, take out the tools, drive two hours and a half down to Chicago, unload them, drive back, and be drunk on my butt with the money in my pocket before anybody knows anything happened. I thought I was pretty smart. The cops *knew,* and I knew that they knew, but I never thought they'd just *get* me. But that's what they did."

"I read a file that said you might have done a couple of liquor stores, that some people got hurt. Old man got beat with a pistol," Connell said.

"Not me," Price said, but his eyes slid away.

"Took some booze with the cash," Connell said. "You *are* a booze hound."

"Look, I admitted the stealing," Price said. He licked his lips. "But I didn't kill the bitch."

"When you were in the store, did you see anybody else that might have been with her?"

"Man, I was *drunk,*" Price said. "When the cops come for me, I couldn't even remember seeing this gal, until they reminded me a lot."

"So you don't know shit about shit," Lucas said.

A little coal sparked in Price's eye that said he'd like to be alone with Lucas. "That's about it," Price said. Lucas held his eyes, and the coal died. "There were people down in the bookstore that night that nobody ever found. They were reading poems down there, and there was a whole bunch of people. It could have been any of them, more'n me."

Connell sighed, then looked at the escort. "Excuse me—is there a ladies' room back there?"

"Noooo . . ." He had to think about it. "Closest one is out."

"I wonder, do you mind? Could you?"

"Sure." The escort looked at Price. "You sit still, okay?"

Price spread his hands. "Hey, these guys are trying to help me out."

"Sure," the guard said. And to Connell: "Come along, girl."

Lucas winced, but Connell went. As soon as the door closed, Price leaned forward, voice low. "You think they're listening in?"

"I doubt it," Lucas said, shaking his head. "This is a defendant's interview room. If they got caught, they'd be in deep shit."

Price looked around at the pale walls, as though trying to spot a microphone. "I gotta take the chance," he said.

"On what?" Lucas asked, letting the skepticism ride in his voice.

Price leaned toward him again, talking in a harsh whisper. "At my trial I said I saw another con in the bookstore. A guy with a beard and PPP on his hand. Prison tattoo, ballpoint ink and straight pin. Nobody ever found him."

"That's why we're here," Lucas said. "We're trying to track the guy."

"Yeah, well, it wasn't PPP," Price said. He looked around at the walls again, then back to Lucas. He was literally sweating, his hammered forehead glistening in the lights. "Jesus Christ. You can't tell anybody."

"What?"

"I've seen the tattoo again. It wasn't PPP. I was looking at it upside down, and got it backwards. It was 666."

"Yeah? What is it—some kind of cult?"

"No, no," Price whispered. "It's the goddamn Seeds."

Now Lucas dropped his voice. "You sure?"

"Sure I'm sure. There are four or five of them in here right now. That's what's got me nervous. If they knew I was talking about them, I'd be a dead motherfucker. The 666 comes from Bad Seeds; that used to be the bikers."

"Can you describe him?"

"I can do better than that. His name is Joe Hillerod."

"How'd you get that?" They were both talking in whispers now, and Lucas had picked up Price's habit of scanning the walls.

"They brought me up here, and after I got through orientation and went into the population, one of the first guys I see, shit, *I thought it was him.* They looked just fuckin' exactly alike. The guy even had the same tattoo."

"This is the Joe guy?"

"No, no, this is Bob. The guy in here was Bob Hillerod, Joe's brother."

"What?"

"See, I started lifting weights, just to get close to this guy. Bob. I find out he's been in for a while—from way before this chick gets killed. And I see he's older than the guy in the store. I couldn't figure it out. But then I hear, Bob's got a brother, six or seven years younger. It's got to be him. Got to be."

Lucas leaned back, his voice rising. "Sounds like bullshit."

"No, no, I swear to Christ. It's him. Joe Hillerod. And this Joe—he's been inside. For sex." Price reached out and touched Lucas's hand. His eyes were wide, frightened.

"Sex?"

"Rape."

"Did you ask Bob . . . is it Bob in here?"

"Yeah, Bob was here, Joe was out. Joe is the guy. Bob is out now, but Joe is the guy."

"Did you ask Bob if Joe has the tattoo?"

Price leaned back. "Fuck no. One thing you learn in here is, you don't ask about those fuckin' tattoos. You just pretend they're not there," he said. "But Joe was inside. He was one of the Seeds. He's got it, I bet. I bet anything."

WHEN CONNELL AND THE escort returned, Lucas was taking notes. "Harry Roy Wayne and Gerry Gay Wayne," Price was saying, "They're brothers and they work at the Caterpillar place down there. They'll tell you."

"But that's all you got?" Lucas asked.

"You got everything else." D. Wayne slumped on the couch, smoking a second cigarette. He picked up the pack and put them in his pocket.

"I won't bullshit you," Lucas said. "I don't think that's enough."

"It will be if you catch the right guy," Price said.

"Yeah. If there is one," Lucas said. He stood up and said to Connell, "Unless you've got some more questions, we're outta here."

"WHAT DO WE HAVE?" Connell asked as they waited for the car. She was digging into a pack of chive-flavored potato chips, sixty cents from a machine.

"A hell of a coincidence," Lucas said. He told her briefly about Price's nervous statement, and about Del's investigation at the fire, the dead deputy, and the .50-caliber tubes. "So the Seeds are in the Cities."

"And this Joe Hillerod was convicted of rape?"

"Price said sex, so I don't know exactly what it was. If our guy is a member of the Seeds, it'd explain a lot," Lucas said. "Gimme a couple of chips."

She passed the pack. "What does it explain?"

Lucas crunched: starch and fat. Excellent. "They've had years of hassles with the law, they've even got a lawyer on retainer. They know how we operate. They move around all the time, but mostly in the Midwest, the states we're talking about. The gaps in the killings—this Joe guy might have been inside."

"Huh." Connell took the chips back, finished them. "That sounds *very* good. God knows, they're crazy enough."

CONNELL MADE A LONG phone call from the airport, talked to a woman at her office, took some notes. Lucas stood around, looking at nothing, while the pilot avoided him.

"Hillerod lives up near Superior," Connell said when she got off the phone. "He was convicted of aggravated assault in Chippewa County in March of '86 and served thirteen months. He got out in April of '87. There was a killing in August of '87."

"That's neat. He didn't do any other time?"

"Yeah. A couple of short jail terms, and then in January of '90, he was convicted for sexual assault and served twenty-three months, and got out a month before Gina Hoff was assaulted in Thunder Bay."

"But wasn't the South Dakota case—"

"Yeah," she said. "It was in '91, while he was inside. But that was the weirdest of all the cases I found. That's where the woman was stabbed as much as ripped. Maybe that *was* somebody else."

"What's he done since he got out?" Lucas asked.

Connell flipped through her notes. "He was charged with a DWI in '92, but he beat it. And a speeding ticket this year. His last known address was somewhere up around Superior, a town called Two Horse. Current driver's license shows an address in a town called Stedman. My friend couldn't find it on a map, but she called the Carren County sheriff's department, and they say Stedman is a crossroads a couple of miles out of Two Horse."

"Did your friend ask them about the Hillerods?"

"No. I thought we ought to do that in person."

"Good. Let's get our ass back to the Cities. I want to talk to Del before we start messing with the Seeds," Lucas said. He looked across the lounge at the pilot, who was sipping a cup of coffee. "Assuming that we make it back."

HALFWAY BACK, LUCAS, with his eyes closed and one hand tight around an overhead grip, said, "Twenty-three months. Couldn't have been much of a rape."

"A rape is a rape," Connell said, an edge in her voice.

"You know what I mean," Lucas said, opening his eyes.

"I know what *men* mean when they say that," Connell said.

"Kiss my ass," Lucas said. The pilot winced—almost ducked—and Lucas closed his eyes again.

"I'm not interested in putting up with certain kinds of bullshit," Connell said levelly. "A male commentary on rape is one of them. I don't care if the guy back at Waupun calls me a girl, because he's stupid and out of touch. But you're not stupid, and when you imply—"

"I didn't imply jackshit," Lucas said. "But I've known women who were raped who had to think about it before they realized what happened. On the other hand, you get some woman who's been beaten with a bat, her teeth are broken out, her nose is smashed, her ribs are broken, she's gotta have surgery because her vagina is ripped open. She doesn't have to think about it. If it's gonna happen, which way would you want it?"

"I don't want it at all," Connell said.

"You don't want death and taxes, either," Lucas said.

"Rape isn't death and taxes."

"All of the big ones are death and taxes," Lucas said. "Murder, rape, robbery, assault. Death and taxes."

"I don't want to argue," Connell said. "We have to work together."

"No, we don't."

"What, you're gonna dump me because I argue with you?"

Lucas shook his head. "Meagan, I just don't like getting jumped when I say something like, 'It must not have been much of a rape,' and you know what I'm talking about. I mean, there must not have been a lot of obvious violence with the rape, or they would have given him more time. Our killer is ripping these women. He might be smoking a cigarette while he's doing it. He's a fuckin' monster. If he rapes somebody, he's not gonna be subtle about it. I don't know the details of this rape, but twenty-three months doesn't sound like our man."

"You just don't want it to be that easy," Connell said.

"Bullshit."

"I'm serious. I keep getting the feeling you're playing some kind of weird game, looking for this guy. I'm not. I want to nail the asshole any way I can. If it's easy, that's good. If it's hard, that's okay too, as long as we put him in a cage."

"Fine. But stay out of my face, huh?"

DEL WAS SITTING ON the City Hall steps, elbows on his knees, smoking a Lucky Strike. He was watching red ants crawl out of a crack in the sidewalk. His hair was too long and plastered down with something that might have been lard. He wore an olive-drab army shirt with faded spots on the sleeves where sergeant's stripes had been removed, and a fading name tag over the right pocket that said "Halprin," which wasn't his name. The army shirt was missing its buttons, and was worn open, showing a giveaway rock-station T-shirt that said "KQ Sucks." Tattered khaki pants with dirt on the knees and black canvas sneakers completed his outfit. The sneaks had a hole near the base of his right big toe, and through the hole, the visible skin was as grimy as the shoes.

"Dude," he said, his head bobbing as Lucas and Connell came up. He had the nervous submissiveness of somebody who has eaten out of garbage cans for too many years.

Connell walked past him with a glance. When Lucas stopped, she said, "C'mon."

Lucas, hands in his pockets, nodded at Del. "What're you doing?"

"Watchin' ants," Del said.

"What else?"

Connell, who'd gotten as far as the door, drifted back toward them.

"Asshole's getting out in a few minutes. I want to see who picks him up." Del snapped the cigarette into the street and looked up at Lucas. "Who's the chick?"

"Meagan Connell. Investigator with the state," Lucas said.

Connell said, "Lucas, we're in a hurry, remember?"

Lucas said, "Meagan. Meet Del Capslock."

She looked down, and Del looked up and said, "How do."

"You're a . . ." She couldn't find the right word.

"A police officer, yes, ma'am, but there's been some bureaucratic foul-up and I ain't been paid the last few years."

"You *gotta* see this asshole?" Lucas asked him.

"Don't gotta."

"Then come on inside. We're doing this thing. . . ."

"Yeah?"

"The Seeds came up."

DEL HAD A DATABASE on the Seeds known to Wisconsin, Minnesota, Iowa, and Illinois police agencies. Joe Hillerod came in for twenty lines. "His brother Bob is heavily involved," Del said, scanning a computer file. "He transported drugs out of the port, down here and over to Chicago and maybe St. Louis, for some medium-time dealers. He didn't retail himself, not at the time, although he might be now. Then he had some hookers working all the big truck stops around Wisconsin and northern Illinois. Joe . . . the information says he mostly drove for his older brother but wasn't much of a businessman. Apparently he's a wild one; likes women and good times. And he seems to be the enforcer when they need one."

"What're they doing now?" Connell asked.

"Small-time retailing coke and crank through the roadhouses up there. And they've got a salvage yard outside of Two Horse."

"Any chance that they were involved with those fifty-cals you found?" Lucas asked.

Del shook his head doubtfully. "The Seeds have a bunch of little splinter groups. The fifty-cal guys are into this weird right-wing white-supremacy

Christian-Nazi shit. And they're mostly holdup guys and armored car guys. The Hillerods are a different splinter, mostly based around the old biker gang the Bad Seeds. They're dope and women. A couple of them supply women to the massage parlors over in Milwaukee and here in the Cities. One of them has a porno store in Milwaukee."

Lucas scratched his head and looked at Connell, who'd been peering over Del's shoulder. "I guess the only way we're gonna find out is go up there and roust them."

"Be a little careful," Del said.

"When?" Connell asked.

"Tomorrow," Lucas said. "I'll call the sheriff tonight, and we'll go first thing in the morning."

"Driving?"

Lucas showed a sickly grin. "Driving."

LUCAS AND CONNELL AGREED to meet at eight o'clock for the drive up north. "I'll check the medical examiner on Marcy Lane and see if anything's come up," she said. "I'll get everything I can on the Hillerods. The whole file."

Lucas stopped at homicide to check with Greave, but was told he was out. Another cop said, "He's down with that thing at Eisenhower Docks. He should be back by now."

From his office, Lucas called Lincoln County Sheriff Sheldon Carr at Grant, Wisconsin; touched the scar on his neck as Carr picked up the phone. Carr had been there when Lucas was shot by the child.

"Lucas, how are things?" Carr was hardy and country and smart. "You comin' up to fish? Is Weather pregnant yet?"

"Not yet, Shelly. We'll let you know . . . Listen, I gotta talk to George Beneteau over in Carren County. Do you know him?"

"George? Sure. He's okay. Should I give him a call?"

"If you would. I'll call him later on and talk. I'm going up there tomorrow to look at a guy involved with the Seeds."

"Ah, those assholes," Carr said with disgust. "They used to be around here, you know. We ran them off."

"Yeah, well, we're bumping into them down here now. I would appreciate an introduction, though."

"I'll call him right now. I'll tell him to expect to hear from you," Carr said. "You take it easy with those bad boys."

GREAVE CAME IN with a kid. The kid was wearing a black-and-white-striped French fisherman's T-shirt, dirty jeans, and stepped-on white sneakers. He had a pound of dirty-blond hair stuck up under a long-billed red Woody Wood-pecker cap.

"This is Greg," Greave said, throwing a thumb at the kid. "He does handy-man work around the apartments."

Lucas nodded.

"Don't tell nobody you talked to me or they'll fire my ass," Greg said to Lucas. "I need the job."

"Greg says that the day before the old lady died, the air-conditioning went out and it got really hot in the apartments. He and Cherry spent the whole day down the basement, taking things apart. He says it was so hot, almost everybody left their windows and even their doors open."

"Yeah?"

"Yeah." Greave prodded the kid. "Tell him."

"They did," the kid said. "It was the first real hot day of the year."

"So maybe they could have gotten in the old lady's apartment," Greave said. "Come in with a ladder and figured out some way to drop the window, locked. We know it couldn't be the door."

"What'd they do to her after they came in the window?"

"They smothered her."

"The medical examiner could determine that. And how do you drop a window, locked? Did you try it?"

"I haven't got it figured out yet," Greave said.

"We tried it a lot," the kid said to Lucas; Greave looked at him in exasperation. "Ain't no way."

"Maybe there's some way," Greave said defensively. "Remember, Cherry's the maintenance man, he'd know tricks."

"Woodworking tricks? Listen, Cherry's no smarter than you are," Lucas said. "If he could figure out a way to do it, you could. Whatever it was, must've been quiet. The neighbor didn't hear a thing. He said it was spooky-quiet."

"I thought maybe you could come down and take a look," Greave said. "Figure something out."

"I don't have the time," Lucas said, shaking his head. "But if you can figure a way to get them in and out . . . but even then, you'd have to figure out what killed her. It wasn't smothering."

"They must've poisoned her," Greave said. "You know how jockeys dope up horses and still pass the drug tests? That must be what they did—they went out and got some undetectable poison, put it in her booze, and she croaked."

"No toxicology," Lucas said.

"I *know* that. That's the whole *point.* It's undetectable, see?"

"No," said Lucas.

"That's gotta be it," Greave said.

Lucas grinned at him. "If they did, then you should lie down, put a cold rag on your forehead, and relax, 'cause you're never gonna convict anybody on the vanishing-drug theory."

"Maybe," Greave said. "But I'll tell you something else I figured out: it's gotta have something to do with the booze. The old lady takes booze and a couple of sleeping pills. That's the most noticeable thing she did, far as we know. Then she's murdered. That shit *had* to be poisoned. Somehow."

"Maybe she masturbated at night, and it put a heavy strain on her heart and she croaked," Lucas said.

"I thought of that," Greave said.

"You did?" Lucas started to laugh.

"But how does that explain the fact that Cherry did it?"

Lucas stopped laughing. Cherry *had* done it. "You got me there," he said. He looked at the kid. "Do you think Cherry did it?"

"He *could* do it," the kid said. "He's a mean sonofabitch. There was a little dog from across the street, belonged to this old couple, and he'd come over and poop on the lawn, and Ray caught it with a rope and strangled it. I seen him do it."

Greave said, "See?"

"I know he's mean," Lucas said. Then, to Greave: "Connell and I are headed up north tomorrow, checking on a guy."

"Hey, I'm sorry, man," Greave said. "I know I'm not helping you much. I'll do whatever you want."

"Anderson's doing a computer run: known sex offenders against trucks. Why don't you start pulling records, looking for any similarities in old charges, anything that refers to the motorcycle gang called the Bad Seeds. Or any motorcycle gang, for that matter. Flag anything that's even a remote possibility."

THE PHONE WAS RINGING when Lucas got home: Weather. "I'll be a while," she said.

"What happened?" He was annoyed. No. He was jealous.

"A kid chopped his thumb off in a paper cutter at school. We're trying to stick it back on." She was both excited and tired, the words stumbling over each other.

"A tough one?"

"Lucas, we took two hours trying to find a decent artery and get it hooked up, and George is dissecting out a vein right now. Christ, they're so small, they're like tissue paper, but if we get it back on, we'll give the kid his hand back . . . I gotta go."

"You'll be really late?"

"I'm here for another two hours, if the vein works," she said. "If it doesn't, we'll have to go for another one. That'd be late."

"See you then," he said.

LUCAS HAD BEEN IN love before, but with Weather, it was different. Everything was tilted, a little out of control. He might be overcommitting himself, he thought. On the other hand, there was a passion that he hadn't experienced before. . . .

And she made him happy.

Lucas sometimes found himself laughing aloud just at the thought of her. That hadn't happened before. And the house in the evening felt empty without her.

He sat at his desk, writing checks for household bills. When he finished, he dropped the stamped envelopes in a basket on an antique table by the front door. The antique was the first thing they'd bought together.

"Jesus." He rubbed his nose. He was in deep. But the idea of one single woman, for the rest of time . . .

15

S ARA JENSEN WORKED AT Raider-Garrote, a stockbrokerage in the Exchange Building. The office entry was glass, and on the other side of the glass was a seating area where investors could sit and watch the numbers from the New York Stock Exchange and NASDAQ scroll across a scoreboard. Few people actually went inside. Most of them—thin white guys with glasses, briefcases, gray suits, glasses, and thinning hair—stood mouth-open in the skyway until their number came up, then scurried away, muttering.

Koop loitered with them, hands in pockets, his look changing daily. One day it was jeans, white T-shirt, sneakers, and a ball cap; the next day it was long-sleeved shirt, khakis, and loafers.

Through the window, over the heads of the few people in the display area, past the rows of white-shirted men and well-dressed women who sat peering at computer terminals and talking on telephones, in a separate large office, Jensen worked alone.

Her office door was usually open, but few people went in. She wore a telephone headset most of the day. She often talked and read a newspaper at the same time. A half-dozen different computer terminals lined a shelf behind her desk, and every once in a while she'd poke one, watch the screen; occasionally, she'd rip paper out of a computer printer, look at it, or stuff it in her briefcase.

Koop had no idea what she was doing. At first, he thought she might be some kind of super secretary. But she never fetched anything, nobody ever gave her what appeared to be an order. Then he noticed that when one of the white shirts wanted to talk to her, the shirt was distinctly deferential. Not a secretary.

As he watched, he began to suspect that she was involved in something very complicated, something that wore her down. By the end of the day, she was haggard. When the white shirts and conservative dresses were standing up, stretching, laughing, talking, she was still working her headset. When she finally left, her leather briefcase was always stuffed with paper.

On this day, she left a bit earlier than usual. He followed her through the skyway to the parking ramp, walked past her, face averted, in a crowd. At the elevator, he joined the short queue, feeling the tension in the back of his neck. He'd not done this before. He'd never been this close. . . .

He felt her arrive behind him, kept his back to her, his face turned away. She'd ride up to the sixth floor, if she remembered where she left her car. Sometimes she forgot, and wandered through the ramp, lugging the briefcase, looking for it. He'd seen her do it. Today her car was on six, just across from the doors.

The elevator arrived and he stepped inside, turned left, pushed seven, stepped to the back. A half-dozen other people got on with her, and he maneuvered until he was directly behind her, not eight inches away. The smell of her perfume staggered him. A small tuft of hair hung down on the back of her neck; she had a mole behind her ear—but he'd seen that before.

The smell was the thing. The Opium . . .

The elevator started up and a guy at the front lost his balance, took a half-step back into her. She tried to back up, her butt bumping Koop in the groin. He stood his ground and the guy in front muttered "Sorry," and she half-turned to Koop at the same time, not looking at him, and said, "Sorry," and then they were at six.

Koop's eyes were closed, holding on. He could still feel her. She'd *pressed*, he thought.

She'd apparently noticed him, noticed his body under the chameleon's shirt, and had been attracted. She'd *pressed*. He could still feel her ass.

Koop got off at seven, stunned, realized he was sweating, had a ferocious hard-on. She'd done it on purpose. *She knew* . . . Or did she?

Koop hurried to his truck. If he came up beside her, maybe she'd give him a signal. She was a high-class woman, she wouldn't just come on to him. She'd do something different, none of this "Wanna fuck?" stuff. Koop fired up the truck, rolled down the ramp, around and around, making himself dizzy, the truck's wheels screeching down the spiral. Had to stay with her.

At the exit, there were three cars ahead of him. Jensen hadn't come down yet . . . The first and second cars went quickly. The third was driven by an older woman, who said something to the ticket taker. The ticket taker stuck his head out the window and pointed left, then right. The woman said something else.

A car came up from behind Koop, stopped. Not her. Then another car, lights on, down the last ramp, breaking left into the monthly-parker exit line. Jensen had an exit card. He caught a glimpse of her face as she punched the card into the automatic gate. The gate rose and she rolled past him on the left.

"Motherfucker, what's wrong? What're you doing?" Koop poked his horn.

The woman in the car ahead of him took ten seconds to turn and look behind her, then shrugged and started digging into her purse. She took forever, then finally passed a bill to the ticket taker. The ticket taker said something, and she dug into the purse again, finally producing the parking ticket. He took the ticket, gave her change, and then she said something else. . . .

Koop beeped again, and the woman looked into her rearview mirror, finally started forward, stopped at the curb, took a slow left. Koop thrust his money and ticket at the ticket taker.

"Keep the change," he said.

"Can't do that." The ticket taker was an idiot, some kind of goddamned faggot. Koop felt the anger crawling up his neck. In another minute . . .

"I'm in a fuckin' hurry," Koop said.

"Only take a second," the ticket man said. He screwed around with the cash register and held out two quarters. "Here you go, in-a-fuckin'-hurry."

The gate went up and Koop, cursing, pushed into the street. Jensen usually took the same route home. He started after her, pushing hard, making lights.

"C'mon, Sara," he said to his steering wheel. "C'mon, where are you?" He caught her a mile out. Fell in behind.

Should he pull up beside her? Would she give him a signal?

She might.

He was thinking about it when she slowed, took a right into a drugstore parking lot. Koop followed, parked at the edge of the lot. She sat inside her car for a minute, then two, looking for something in her purse. Then she swung her legs out, disappeared into the store. He thought about following, but the last time, he'd run into that kid. It was hard to watch somebody in a store unobtrusively, with all the anti-shoplifting mirrors around.

So he waited. She was ten minutes, came out with a small bag. At her car, she fumbled in her purse, fumbled some more. Koop sat up. What?

She couldn't find her keys. She started back toward the store, stopped, turned and looked thoughtfully at the car, and walked slowly back. She stooped, looked inside, then straightened, angry, talking to herself.

Keys. She'd locked her keys in the car.

He could talk to her: "What's the problem, little lady?"

But as he watched, she looked quickly around, walked to the rear of the car, bent, and ran her hand under the bumper. After a moment of groping, she came up with a black box. Spare key.

Koop stiffened. When people put spare keys on their car, they usually put in a spare house key, just in case. And if she had—and if she'd changed them since she changed her locks. . . .

He'd have to look.

KOOP WENT TO THE ROOF as soon as it was dark. Jensen had changed to a robe, and he watched as she read, listened to a stereo, and checked the cable movies. He was becoming familiar with her personal patterns: she never watched talk shows, never watched sitcoms. She sometimes watched game shows. She watched the news rerun on public television, late at night.

She liked ice cream, and ate it slowly, with a lot of tongue-on-the-spoon action. When she was puzzled about something, trying to make up her mind, she'd reach back and scratch the top of her ass. Sometimes she'd lie in bed with her feet straight up in the air, apparently looking past them for no reason. She'd do the same thing when she put on panty hose—she'd drop onto her back in bed, get her toes into the feet of the hose, then lift her legs over her head and pull them on. Sometimes she'd wander around the apartment while she was flossing.

Once, she apparently caught sight of her reflection in the glass of her balcony's sliding doors, and dropped into a series of poses, as though she were posing for the cover of *Cosmo*. She was so close, so clear, that Koop felt she was posing for him.

She went to bed at midnight, every working night. Two women friends had come around, and once, before Koop began following her home, she hadn't shown up at all until midnight. A date? The idea pissed him off, and he pushed it away.

When she went to bed—a minute of near nakedness, large breasts bobbling in the fishbowl—Koop left her, bought a bottle of Jim Beam at a liquor store, and drove home.

He barely lived in his house, a suburban ranch-style nonentity he'd rented furnished. A garden service mowed the lawn. Koop didn't cook, didn't clean, didn't do much except sleep there, watch some television, and wash his clothes. The place smelled like dust with a little bourbon on top of it. Oh, yes, he'd brought in Wannemaker. But only for an hour or two, in the basement; you could hardly smell that anymore. . . .

THE NEXT MORNING, Koop was downtown before ten o'clock. He didn't like the daylight hours, but this was important. He called her at her office.

"This is Sara Jensen. . . . Hello? Hello?"

Her voice was pitched higher than he'd expected, with an edge to it. When he didn't answer her second hello, she promptly hung up, and he was left listening to a dial tone. So she was working.

He headed for the parking ramp, spiraled up through the floors. She was usually on five, six, or seven, depending on how early she got in. Today, it was six again. He had to go to eight to find a parking place. He walked back down, checked under the bumper of her car, found the key box. He opened it as he walked away. Inside was a car key and a newly minted door key.

Shazam.

HE FELT LIKE VICTORY, going back in. Like a conqueror. Like he was home, with his woman.

Koop spent half the day at her apartment.

As soon as he got in, he opened a tool chest in front of the television. If somebody showed up, a cleaning woman, he could say he'd just finished fixing it . . . but nobody showed up.

He ate cereal from one of her bowls, washed the bowl, and put it back. He lounged in her front room with his shoes off, watching television. He stripped off his clothes, pulled back the bedcovers, and rolled in her slick cool sheets. Masturbated into her Kleenex.

Sat on her toilet. Took a shower with her soap. Dabbed some of her perfume on his chest, where he could smell it. Posed in her mirror, his blond, nearly hairless body corded with muscle.

This, he thought, she'd love: he threw the mirror a quarter-profile, arms flexed, butt tight, chin down.

He went through her chest of drawers, found some letters from a man. He read them, but the content was disappointing: had a good time, hope you had a good time. He checked a file cabinet in a small second bedroom-office, found a file labeled "Divorce." Nothing much in it. Jensen was her married name—her maiden name was Rose.

He went back to the bedroom, lay down, rubbed his body with the sheets, turned himself on again. . . .

By five, he was exhausted and exhilarated. He saw the time on her dresser clock, and got up to dress and make the bed: she'd just about be leaving her office.

SARA JENSEN GOT HOME a few minutes before six, carrying a sack full of vegetables under one arm, a bottle of wine and her purse in the opposite hand. The wet smell of radishes and carrots covered Koop's scent for the first few steps inside the door, to the kitchen counter, but when she'd dropped her sacks and stepped back to shut the door, she stopped, frowned, looked around.

Something wasn't right. She could smell him, but only faintly, subconsciously. A finger of fear poked into her heart.

"Hello?" she called.

Not a peep. *Paranoid.*

She tilted her head back, sniffing. There was something . . . She shook her head. Nothing identifiable. Nervous, she left the hallway door open, walked quickly to the bedroom door, and poked her head inside. Called out: "Hello?" Silence.

Still leaving the door open, she checked the second bedroom-office, then ventured into the bathroom, even jerking open the door to the shower stall. The apartment was empty except for her.

She went to the outer door and closed it, still spooked. Nothing she could put her finger on. She started unpacking her grocery sacks, stowing the vegetables in the refrigerator.

And stopped again. She tiptoed back to the bedroom. Looked to her right. A closet door was open just a crack. A closet she didn't use. She turned away, hurried to the hall door, opened it, stopped. Turned back. "Hello?"

The silence spoke of emptiness. She edged toward the bedroom, looked in. The closet door was just as it had been. She took a breath, walked to the closet. "Hello?" Her voice quieter. She took the knob in her hand, and feeling the fright of a child opening the basement door for the first time, jerked the closet door open.

Nobody there, Sara.

"You're nuttier'n a fruitcake," she said aloud. Her voice sounded good, broke the tension. She smiled and pushed the closet door shut with her foot, and started back to the living room. Stopped and looked at the bed.

There was just the vaguest body-shape there, as though somebody had dropped back on the bedspread. Had she done that? She sometimes did that in the morning when she was putting on her panty hose.

But had she gotten dressed first that morning, or made the bed first?

Had her head hit the pillow like that?

Spooked again, she patted the bed. The thought crossed her mind that she should look under it.

But if there were a monster under there . . .

"I'm going out to dinner," she said aloud. "If there's a monster under the bed, you better get out while I'm gone."

Silence and more silence.

"I'm going," she said, leaving the room, looking back. Did the bed tremble? She went.

THE CARREN COUNTY COURTHOUSE was a turn-of-the-century sand-stone building, set in the middle of the town square. A decaying band-stand stood on the east side of the building, facing a street of weary clapboard buildings. A bronze statue of a Union soldier, covered with pigeon droppings, guarded the west side with a trapdoor rifle. On the front lawn, three old men, all wearing jackets and hats, sat alone on separate wooden benches.

A squirrel ignored them, and Lucas and Connell walked past them, the old men as unmoving, unblinking as the Union soldier.

George Beneteau's office was in the back, off a parking lot sheltered by tall, spreading oaks. Lucas and Connell were passed through a steel security door and led by a secretary through a warren of fabric partitions to Beneteau's corner office.

Beneteau was a lanky man in his middle thirties, wearing a gray suit with a string tie under a large Adam's apple, and a pair of steel-rimmed aviator sunglasses. He had a prominent nose and small hairline scars under his eyes: old sparring cuts. A tan Stetson sat on his desk in-basket. He showed even, white teeth in a formal smile.

"Miz Connell, Chief Davenport," he said. He stood to shake hands with Lucas. "That was a mess over in Lincoln County last winter."

The observation sounded like a question. "We're not looking for trouble," Lucas said. He touched the scar on his throat. "We just want to talk to Joe Hillerod."

Beneteau sat down and steepled his fingers. Connell was wearing sunglasses that matched his. "We know that Joe Hillerod crossed paths with our killer. *At least* crossed paths."

Beneteau peered at her from behind the steeple. "You're saying that he might be the guy?"

"That's a possibility."

"Huh." He sat forward, picked up a pencil, tapped the pointed end on his desk pad. "He's a mean sonofagun, Joe is. He might kill a woman if he thought he had reason . . . but he might need a reason."

Lucas said, "You don't think he's nuts."

"Oh, he's nuts all right," Beneteau said, tapping the pencil. "Maybe not nuts like your man is. But who knows? There might be something in him that likes to do it."

"You're sure he's around?" Lucas asked.

"Yes. But we're not sure exactly where," Beneteau said. His eyes drifted up to a county road map pinned to one wall. "His truck's been sitting in the same slot since you called yesterday, down at his brother's place. We've been doing some drive-bys."

Lucas groaned inwardly. If they'd been seen . . .

Beneteau picked up his thought and shook his head, did his thin dry smile. "The boys did it in their private cars, only two of them, a couple of hours apart. Their handsets are scrambled. We're okay."

Lucas nodded, relieved. "Good."

"On the phone last night, you mentioned those .50-caliber barrels you found in that fire. The Hillerods have some machine tools down in that junk-yard," Beneteau said.

"Yeah?"

"Yeah." Beneteau stood up, looked at a poster for a missing girl, then turned back to Lucas. "I thought we oughta take along a little artillery. Just in case."

THEY WENT IN A CARAVAN, two sheriff's cars and an unmarked panel truck, snaking along a series of blacktop and gravel roads, past rough back-woods farms. Mangy cud-chewing cows, standing in patchy pastures marked by weather-bleached tree stumps, turned their white faces to watch the caravan pass.

"They call it a salvage yard, but the local rednecks say it's really a distribution center for stolen Harley-Davidson parts," Beneteau said. He was driving, his wrist draped casually over the top of the steering wheel. "Supposedly, a guy rips off a good clean bike down in the Cities or over in Milwaukee or even Chicago, rides it up here overnight. They strip it down in an hour or so, get rid of anything identifiable, and drop the biker up at the Duluth bus station. Proving that would be a lot of trouble. But you hear about midnight bikers coming through here, and the bikes never going back out."

"Where do they sell the parts?" Connell asked from the backseat.

"Biker rallies, I guess," Beneteau said, looking at her in the rearview mirror. "Specialty shops. There's a strong market in old Harleys, and the older parts go for heavy cash, if they're clean." They topped a rise and looked down at a series of rambling sheds facing the road, with a pile of junk behind a gray board fence. Three cars, two bikes, and two trucks faced the line of buildings. None of the vehicles were new. "That's it," Beneteau said, leaning on the accelerator. "Let's try to get inside quick."

Lucas glanced back at Connell. She had one hand in her purse. Gun. He slipped a hand under his jacket and touched the butt of his .45. "Let's take it easy in there," he said casually. "They're not really suspects."

"Yet," said Connell.

Beneteau's eyes flicked up to the rearview mirror again. "Got your game face on," he said to Connell in his casual drawl.

They clattered across a small board bridge over a drainage ditch and Lucas hooked the door handle with the fingers of his right hand as Beneteau drove them into the junkyard's parking lot. The other car went a hundred feet down the road, to the end of the lot, while the panel truck hooked in short. There were four deputies in the van, armed with M-16s. If somebody starting pecking at them with a fifty, the M-16s would hose them down.

The gravel parking lot was stained with oil and they slid the last few feet, raising a cloud of dust. "Go," Beneteau grunted.

Lucas was out a half second before Connell, headed toward the front door. He went straight through, not quite running, his hand on his belt buckle. Two men were standing at the counter, one in front of it, one in back, looking at a fat, greasy parts catalog. Startled, the man behind the counter backed up, said, "Hey," and Lucas pushed through the swinging counter gate and flashed his badge with his left hand and said, "Police."

"Cops," the counterman shouted. He wore a white T-shirt covered with oil stains, and jeans with a heavy leather wallet sticking out of his back pocket, attached to his belt with a brass chain. The man at the front of the counter, bearded, wearing a railway engineer's hat, backed away, hands in front of him. Connell was behind him.

"You Joe?" Lucas asked, crowding the counterman. The counterman stood his ground, and Lucas shoved his chest, backing him up. An open doorway led away to Lucas's right, into the bowels of the buildings.

"That's Bob," Beneteau said, coming in. "How you doing, Bob?"

"What the fuck do you want, George?" Bob asked.

A cop out front yelled, "We got runners . . ." and Beneteau ran back out the door.

"Where's Joe?" Lucas asked, pushing Bob.

"Who the fuck are you?"

"Keep them," Lucas said to Connell.

Connell pulled her pistol from her purse, a big stainless-steel Ruger wheel-gun, held with both hands, the muzzle up.

"And for Christ's sake, don't shoot anybody this time, unless you absolutely have to," Lucas said hastily.

"You're no fun," Connell said. She dropped the muzzle of the gun toward

Bob, who had taken a step back toward Lucas, and said, "Stand still or I'll punch a fuckin' hole right through your nose." Her voice was as cold as sleet, and Bob stopped.

Lucas freed his gun and went through the door into the back, pausing a second to let his eyes adjust to the gloom. The walls were lined with shelves, and a dozen freestanding metal parts racks stood between the door and the back wall. The racks were loaded with bike parts, fenders and tanks, wheels, stacks of Quaker State oil cans, coffee cans full of rusty nails, screws, and bolts. Two open cans of grease sat on the floor, and two open-topped fifty-five-gallon drums full of trash were at his elbow. A metal extrusion that might have been a go-cart chassis was propped against them. The only light came from small dirty windows on the back wall, and through a door at the back right. The whole place smelled of dust and oil.

Lucas started toward the door, gun barrel up, finger off the trigger. Then to the left, between a row of metal racks, he saw a scattering of white. Beyond it, an open door led into a phone booth–size bathroom, the brown-stained toilet directly in front of the door. He stepped toward the smear of white, which had broken out of a small plastic bag. Powder. Cocaine? He bent down, touched it, lifted his finger to his nose, sniffed it. Not coke. He thought about tasting it: for all he knew it was some kind of powdered bike cleaner, something like Drano. Put a tiny taste on his tongue anyway, got the instant acrid cut: speed.

"Shit." The word was spoken almost next to his ear, and Lucas jumped. The rack beside him lurched and toppled toward him, boxes of odd metal parts sliding off the shelf. Something heavy and sharp sliced into his scalp as he put an arm out to brace the rack. He pushed the rack back, staggering, and a man bolted out from behind the next row, ran down to the right toward the door, and out.

Lucas, struggling with the rack, aware of a dampness in his hair, fought free and went after him. As he burst through the door into the light, he heard somebody yell and looked right, saw Beneteau standing in an open field, pointing. Lucas looked left, saw the man cutting toward the junkyard, and ran after him.

Lost him in the piles of trash. Old cars, mostly from the sixties; he spotted the front end of a '66 bottle-green Pontiac LeMans, just like the one he'd owned when he'd first been in uniform. Lucas stalked through the piles, taking his time: the guy couldn't have gone over the fence, he'd have made some noise. He moved farther in: wrecks with hand-painted numbers on their doors, victims of forgotten county-fair enduro races.

Heard a clank to his left, felt a wetness in his eyebrow. Reached up and touched it: blood. Whatever had fallen off the shelf had cut him, and he was bleeding fairly heavily. Didn't hurt much, he thought. He moved farther left, around a pile, around another pile. . . .

A thin biker in jeans, a smudged black T-shirt, and heavy boots looked up at the board fence around the yard. He was dark-complected, with a tan on top of that.

The man goggled at Lucas's bloody head. "Jesus, what happened to you?"

"You knocked some shit on me," Lucas said.

The man showed a pleased smile, then looked at the top of the fence. "I'd never make it," he said finally. He stepped back toward Lucas. "You gonna shoot me?"

"No, we just want to talk." Lucas slipped the pistol back in its holster.

"Yeah, right," the man said, showing his yellow teeth. Suddenly he was moving fast. "But I'm gonna kick your ass first."

Lucas touched the butt of his pistol as the man's long wild swing came in. He lifted his left hand, batted the fist over his shoulder, hooked a short punch into the biker's gut. The man had a stomach like an oak board. He grunted, took a step back, circled. "You can hit me all day in the fuckin' gut," he said. He'd made no attempt at Lucas's pistol.

Lucas shook his head, circling to his right. "No point. I'm gonna hit you in the fuckin' head."

"Good luck." The biker came in again, quick but inept, three fast roundhouse swings. Lucas stepped back once, twice, took the third shot on his left shoulder, then hooked a fast right to the man's nose, felt the septum snap under the impact. The man dropped, one hand to his face, rolled onto his stomach, got shakily back to his feet, blood running out from under his hands. Lucas touched his own forehead.

"You broke my nose," the man said, looking at the blood on his fingers.

"What'd you expect?" Lucas asked, probing his scalp with his fingertips. "You cut my head open."

"Not on purpose. You broke my fuckin' nose on purpose," he complained. Beneteau ran into the junkyard, looked at them. The man said, "I give up."

BENETEAU STOOD IN THE parking lot and said quietly, "Earl says Joe is down at the house." Earl was the man who'd fought Lucas. "He's scared to death Bob'll find out he told us."

"Okay," Lucas said. He held a first-aid pad against his scalp. He'd already soaked one of them through, and was on his second.

"We're gonna head down there," Beneteau said. "Do you want to come? Or do you want to go into town and get that cut fixed up?"

"I'm coming," Lucas said. "How about the search warrants?"

"We got them, both for this place and Joe's and Bob's. That's a fine amount of speed back there, if that's what it is," Beneteau said.

"That's what it is," Lucas said. "There's probably six or eight ounces there on the floor."

"Biggest drug bust we've ever had," Beneteau said with satisfaction. He looked at the porch, where Bob Hillerod and Earl sat on a bench, in handcuffs. They'd cut the customer loose; Beneteau was satisfied that he'd been there for cycle parts. "I'm kind of surprised Earl was involved with it."

"It'd be hard to prove that he was," Lucas said. "I didn't see him with the stuff. He says he was back there getting an alternator when everybody started running. He said one of the guys who went into the woods panicked, and threw the bag toward the toilet as they ran out the back. He might be telling the truth."

Beneteau looked at the woods and laughed a little. "We got those guys pinned in the marsh over there. Can't see them, but I give them about fifteen minutes after the bugs come out tonight. If they last that long—they were wearing short-sleeved shirts."

"So let's get Joe," Lucas said.

BENETEAU TURNED THE JUNKYARD over to a half-dozen arriving deputies, including his crime-scene specialists. They took the same two sheriff's cars and the panel truck to Hillerod's house.

Joe Hillerod lived ten miles from the junkyard, in a rambling place built of three or four old lake cabins shoved together into one big tar-paper shack. A dozen cords of firewood were dumped in the overgrown back, in a tepee-shaped pile. Three cars were parked in the front.

"I love this backwoods shit," Lucas said to Beneteau as they closed on the house. "In the city, we'd call in the Emergency Response Unit . . ."

"That's a Minnesota liberal's euphemism for SWAT team," Connell said to Beneteau, who nodded and showed his teeth.

". . . and we'd stage up, and everybody'd get a job, and we'd put on vests and radios, and we'd sneak down to the area, and clear it," Lucas continued. "Then we'd sneak up to the house and the entry team'd go in . . . Up here, it's jump in the fuckin' cars, arrive in a cloud of hayseed, and arrest everybody in sight. Fuckin' wonderful."

"The biggest difference is, we arrive in a cloud of hayseed. Down in the Cities, you arrive in a cloud of bullshit," Beneteau said. "You ready?"

THEY HIT HILLEROD'S HOUSE just before noon. A yellow dog with a red collar was sitting on the blacktop in front of the place, and got up and walked off the road into a cattail ditch when he saw the traffic coming.

A young man with a large belly and a Civil War beard sat on the porch steps, drinking a beer and smoking a cigarette, looking as though he'd just got up. A Harley was parked next to the porch, and a scarred white helmet lay on the grass beside it like a fiberglass Easter egg produced by a condor.

When they slowed, he stood, and when they stopped, he ran in through the door. "That's trouble," Beneteau yelled.

"Go," Connell said, and she jumped out and headed for the door.

Lucas said, "Wait, wait," but she kept going, and he was two steps behind her.

Connell went through the screen door like a cornerback through a wide receiver, in time to see the fat man running up a flight of stairs in the back of the house. Connell ran that way, Lucas yelling, "Wait a minute."

In a back room, a naked couple was crawling off a fold-out couch. Connell pointed the pistol at the man and yelled, "Freeze," and Lucas went by her and took the stairs. As he went, he heard Connell say to someone else, "Take 'em, I'm going up."

The fat man was in the bathroom, door locked, working the toilet. Lucas kicked the door in, and the fat man looked at him and went straight out a window, through the glass, onto the roof beyond. He heard cops yelling outside and ran on down the hall, Connell now a step behind him.

The door at the end of the hall was closed and Lucas kicked it just below the lock, and it exploded inward. Behind it, another couple were crawling around in their underpants, looking for clothes. The man had something in his hand and Lucas yelled, "Police, drop it," and tracked his body with the front sight of the pistol. The man, looking up, dazed with sleep, dropped a gun. The woman sat back on the bed and pulled a bedspread over her breasts.

Beneteau and two deputies came up behind them, pistols drawn. "Got 'em?" He looked past Lucas. "That's Joe."

"What the fuck are you doing, George?" Joe asked.

Beneteau didn't answer. Instead, he looked at the woman and said, "Ellie Rae, does Tom know about this?"

"No," she said, hanging her head.

"Aw, God," Beneteau said, shaking his head. "Let's get everybody downstairs."

A DEPUTY WAS WAITING for them on the stairs. "Did you look in the dining room, Sheriff?"

"No, what'd we get?"

"C'mon, take a look," the deputy said. He led the way back through a small kitchen, then through a side arch to the dining room. Two hundred semiautomatic rifles were stacked against the walls. A hundred and fifty handguns, glistening with WD-40, were slotted into cardboard boxes on the floor.

Lucas whistled. "The gunstore burglaries. Out in the 'burbs around the cities."

"This is good stuff," Beneteau said, squatting to look at the long guns. "This is gun-store stuff all the way." Springfield M-1s, Ruger Mini-14s and Mini-30s, three odd-looking Navy Arms, a bunch of Marlins, a couple of elegant Brownings, an exotic Heckler and Koch SR9.

Beneteau picked up the H&K and looked at it. "This is a fifteen-hundred-dollar gun, I bet," he said, aiming it out the window at a Folger's coffee can in the side yard.

"What's the story on the woman up there?" Connell asked.

"Ellie Rae? She and her husband run the best diner in town. Rather, she runs it and he cooks. Great cook, but when he gets depressed, he drinks. If they break up, he'll get steady drunk, and she'll quit, and that'll be the end of the diner."

"Oh," Connell said. She looked at him to see if he was joking.

"Hey, that's a big deal," Beneteau said defensively. "There are only two of them, and the other one's a grease pit."

Joe Hillerod looked a lot like his brother, with the same blunt, tough German features. "I got fifteen hundred bucks in my wallet, cash, and I want witnesses to that. I don't want the money going away," he said sullenly.

Ellie Rae said, "I'm a witness."

"You shut up, Ellie Rae," Beneteau said. "What the hell are you doing here, anyway?"

"I love him," she said. "I can't help myself."

A deputy helped the fat man into the room. He was bleeding all over his head, shoulders, and arms from the window, and was dragging one leg.

"Dumb bunny jumped off the roof," the deputy said. "After he crashed through the window."

"He was flushing shit upstairs," Lucas said. *Dumb bunny? The guy looks like a mastodon.* "He got some of it on the toilet seat, though."

"Check that," Beneteau said to one of the deputies.

Connell had put away her gun, and now she stepped up behind Hillerod and pulled at his hand, immobilized by the cuffs.

"What the fuck?" Hillerod said, trying to turn to see what she was doing.

"See?"

Lucas looked. Hillerod had the 666 on the web between his thumb and forefinger. "Yeah."

The woman who'd been on the fold-out couch had been watching Connell, taking in Connell's inch-long hair. "I was sexually abused," she said finally. "By the cops."

Connell said, "Yeah?"

Lucas was climbing the stairs, and Connell hurried after him. In the bedroom, a decrepit water bed was pushed against one wall, with a bedstand and light to one side and a chest of drawers against the wall at the foot of the bed. Magazines and newspapers were scattered around the room. An ironing board sat in a corner, buried in wrinkled clothing, the iron lying on its side at the pointed end of the board.

A long stag-handled folding knife sat in a jumble of junk on the chest of drawers. Connell bent over next to it, carefully not touching it, looked at it, and said, "Goddamn, Davenport. The autopsies say it's a knife like this. The blade's just right."

She picked up a matchbook and used it to rotate the knife. The excitement rose in her voice. "There's some gunky stuff in the hinge or whatever you call it, where it folds; it could be blood."

"But look at the cigarettes," Lucas said.

A pack of Marlboros sat on the nightstand. There wasn't a Camel in the house.

17

THE HILLERODS CALLED A Duluth lawyer named Aaron Capella. The lawyer arrived at midafternoon in a dusty Ford Escort, talked to the county attorney, then to his clients. Lucas went to the local emergency room, had four stitches taken in his scalp, then met Connell for a late lunch. Afterward, they hung out in Beneteau's office or wandered around the courthouse, waiting for Capella to finish with the Hillerods.

The crime-scene crew called from the junkyard to say they'd found three half-kilo bags of cocaine behind a false panel in the junkyard bathroom. Beneteau was more than pleased: he was on television with each of the Duluth-Superior stations.

"Gonna get my ass reelected, Davenport," he said to Lucas.

"I'll send you a bill," Lucas said.

They were talking in his office, and they saw Connell coming up the walk outside. She'd been down at a coffee shop, and carried a china cup with her.

"That's a fine-looking woman," Beneteau said, his eyes lingering on her. "I like the way she sticks her face into trouble. If you don't mind my asking, have you two . . . got something going?"

Lucas shook his head. "No."

"Huh. Is she with anybody else?"

"Not as far as I know," Lucas said. He started to say something about her being sick, hesitated.

"I mean, she's not a lesbian or anything," Beneteau said.

"No, she's not. Look, George . . ." He still couldn't think of exactly what he wanted to say. What he said was, "Look, do you want her phone number, or what?"

Beneteau's eyebrows went up. "Well, I get down to the Cities every now and then. You got it?"

AARON CAPELLA WAS A PRO. Beneteau knew him, and they shook hands when Capella walked into the sheriff's office. Beneteau introduced Lucas and Connell.

"I've spoken to my clients. Another unconscionable violation of their civil rights," Capella said mildly to Beneteau.

"I know, it's a shame," Beneteau said, tongue in cheek. "The right of felons to bear stolen assault weapons while distributing cocaine and speed."

"That's what I keep telling people, and you're the only guy who under-stands," Capella said. "C'mon, Bich is waiting."

They walked through the courthouse, Beneteau and Capella talking about Capella's sailboat, which he kept on Lake Superior. ". . . guy from Maryland was telling me, 'A lake just isn't the ocean.' So I say, 'Where do you sail?' and he says, 'The Chesapeake.' And I say, 'You could put six Chesapeakes in Superior, and still have a Long Island Sound around the edges.'"

Bich was the county attorney, a serious, red-faced man in a charcoal suit. "They're bringing your client up now, Aaron," he said to Capella. They all fol-lowed the prosecutor into his office, settling into chairs, Bich joining the sailing talk until a deputy brought Joe Hillerod down from the lockup.

Hillerod's lip lifted in an uncontrollable sneer when he saw Beneteau. He dropped into a chair next to Capella and said, "How're we doing?"

BICH SPOKE TO CAPELLA as if Hillerod weren't there, but everything he said was aimed at Hillerod: Capella and Bich had already been over the ground.

"Tell you what, Aaron, your client's in bad shape," Bich said professorially. "He's got two years left on his parole. Possession of a gun'll put him back in-side. There won't be any trial, none of that bullshit. All it takes is a hearing."

"We'd contest."

Bich rolled past him. "We found him with a house full of stolen guns. We could try him for possessing firearms as a felon and possession of stolen firearms. Then we could send him to Minnesota, to be tried for burglary. He'd go back to Waupun, serve out the rest of his parole, start his new Wisconsin time after that, and then go to Minnesota to serve out his time over there. That's a lot of time."

The lawyer spread his hands. "Joe had nothing to do with the guns. He thought they were legit. A friend left them there, the same guy you grabbed up in the bathroom."

"Right." Bich rolled his eyes.

"But we're not discussing the guns; that's another issue," Capella said. "We can talk, right? That's why Lucas and Ms. Connell are here, right? A little friendly extortion?"

"If he'll ride along with us," Bich said, poking a finger at Hillerod's chest, "we might be inclined to forget the parole violation, the possession of a gun. That we got him on already."

"So what are we talking about?" Capella asked.

Bich looked at Lucas. "Do you want to explain to Mr. Hillerod?"

Lucas looked at him and said, "I won't bullshit you. There are some good reasons to think that you've been slicing up women. Ripping their guts out. Six or more times now. We need to ask you some questions and get some answers."

Hillerod had known what was coming, having spoken to Capella. He started shaking his head before Lucas was finished talking. "Nah, nah, never did it, that's bullshit, man."

"We're running your knife through the crime lab," Connell said. "It looks like it might have some blood gummed up in the hinges."

"Well, shit," Hillerod said, and he looked uncomfortable for a moment as he thought about what she'd said. "If there's blood, it's animal blood. That's a hunting knife."

"This ain't exactly deer season," Lucas said.

"If there's any goddamned blood on that knife, it's deer blood—or you put it there just to get me," Hillerod said heatedly. "You fuckin' cops think you can get away with anything."

Capella's voice rode over his client's. "My client remembers the bookstore in Madison."

"That's a long time to remember," Bich marveled. "Several years, if I've got it right."

"I remember 'cause it's the only bookstore I ever been in," Hillerod snarled.

Capella kept talking. ". . . and he's got a witness of good reputation who spent that whole night with him down in Madison, and he's sure she'll remember it independently of anything we talk about here. Without any prompting from me or Joe. I will state that we have not been in touch with her, and that Joe's confident that she'll remember."

"You've got a name?" Lucas asked.

"You can have the name and the circumstances in which they met," the lawyer said. "The fact is, he picked her up at the bookstore."

"I didn't have nothing to do with the guns," Hillerod said sullenly.

"We're not talking about that," his lawyer said quickly. He patted Hillerod on the knee. "That's not part of the deal."

"We know the killer smokes Marlboros," Lucas said, leaning toward Hillerod. "You smoke Marlboros, right?"

"No, no, I usually smoke Merits, I'm trying to quit," Hillerod said. "I just got the Marlboros that once."

"Your man is lying to us," Lucas said to Capella. "We know he's smoked Marlboros for years."

Capella said, "He says Merits . . . I gotta believe him."

"Merits taste like shit," Bich said. "Why'd you smoke Merits? Is that all you smoke?"

"Well, I'm trying to quit," Hillerod said, not meeting their eyes. "I smoke some Marlboros, but I didn't kill anybody. I smoke some Ventures, too."

The Marlboro bluff hadn't worked. "We want to know about the bookstore," Connell said.

"In Madison?" Hillerod's eyes defocused for a moment, and then he said, "How'd you know about that, anyway?"

"We've got a witness," Connell said. "You left with a woman."

"That's right," Hillerod said. Then he said, "She's gotta be the one who told you."

"She's not," Lucas said. "Our witness . . . well, it's a woman, but it's not your friend. If you've *got* a friend. But we want to know about the other woman. The one who turned up dead the next day."

"Wasn't me," Hillerod said. "The woman I left with, she's still alive. And she must've told you that I couldn't have done it, 'cause I was with her."

"What's her name?" asked Connell.

Hillerod scratched his face, glaring at her, but Connell looked levelly back, as though she were an entomologist examining a not-particularly-interesting beetle. "Abby Weed," he said finally.

"Where does she live?"

Hillerod shrugged. "I don't know the address, just how to get there. But you can get her at the university."

"She works at the university?" Lucas asked.

"She's a professor," he said. "In fine art. She's a painter."

Lucas looked at Connell, who rolled her eyes. "Who were you there with? At the bookstore?"

"Wasn't there with nobody," Hillerod said. "I went in to get a book on my bike, if they had one, which they didn't."

"How long were you in there?"

Hillerod shrugged. "Hour."

"That's a long time to look for a book that they didn't have," Lucas said.

"I only spent five minutes looking for the book. Then I saw Abby giving me the eye, and I hung around to bullshit her a little bit. She had the big . . ." He glanced at Connell. "Headlights."

"She went home with you?" Connell said.

"We went to her place."

"You spent the night?"

"Shit, I spent about four nights," Hillerod said with a small smile, talking to Connell. "Every time I tried to get out of bed, I'd find her hanging on to my dick. . . ." The smile went flat, and he looked at Lucas. "The fuckin' cop," he said. "That fuckin' cop picked me out, didn't he?"

"What cop?"

"The cop at the store."

Lucas looked at him for a long beat, then said, "You have a 666 on your hand."

Hillerod looked at the tattoo, shook his head. "Goddamnit, I knew that was stupid, the fuckin' 666. Everybody was getting them. I told people, the cops'll use them against us."

"Did you see anybody in the store that looked like this?" Connell asked. She handed him the composite.

Hillerod looked it over, then looked curiously from Connell to Lucas to Bich to Capella. "Well. Not anyone else. Not that I remember."

"What? What'd you mean, anyone else?" Lucas asked.

He shrugged. "You should know. It looks like your cop."

"The cop?" Connell looked at Lucas again. "How did you know he was a cop?"

"The way he looked at me. He was a cop, all right. He looked at my hand, then at me, and then my hand. He knew what it was."

"Could have been a con," Lucas said.

Hillerod thought about it, then said, "Yeah. Could have been, I guess. But I felt like he was a cop."

"And he looked like this picture," Connell said.

"Yeah. It's not quite right, I don't think. I can't remember that well, but his beard's wrong," he said, studying the drawing. "And there's something wrong about the mouth. And the guy's hair was flatter . . . But that's who it mostly looks like."

"The cop," Lucas said.

"Yeah. The cop."

"SONOFAGUN," CONNELL said bitterly. They stood next to a water fountain, the office lawyers and secretaries flowing around them. "The cop shows up again. Davenport—I believe him." She gestured down the hall at Bich's office, where Hillerod waited. "I can't believe he just pulled that out of his ass. He's not smart enough."

"Don't panic yet," Lucas said. "We've still got some lab work to do. We've got the knife."

"You know as well as I do . . . Are we sure the St. Paul cop is out of it?"

"St. Paul says he is."

"There's no way they'd cover for a guy on something like this," she said, not quite making it a question.

"No way," Lucas agreed. "I talked to one of their guys, and they worked him over pretty good."

"Goddamnit," Connell said. She shook her head. "We're going back to the beginning."

CONNELL DROVE: she wanted to handle the Porsche. On the way out to the interstate, the sun dropping toward the horizon, windshield greased by a million bugs from the roadside ditches, she said, "George Beneteau was surprisingly professional. I mean, for a county sheriff."

Lucas rode along for a minute, then said, "He asked about you. Marital status, that kind of thing."

"What?"

Lucas grinned at her and she flushed. "He said . . ." Lucas dropped into a cornball accent, which Beneteau didn't have, "that's a fine-lookin' woman."

"You are lying to me, Davenport."

"Honest to God," Lucas said. After a minute, he said, "He wanted your phone number."

"Did you give it to him?"

Lucas said, "I didn't know what to do, Meagan. I didn't know whether to tell him you were sick, or what. So I . . . yeah, I gave it to him."

"You didn't tell him I was sick?"

"No. I didn't."

They drove on for another minute, in silence, and then Connell began to weep. Eyes open, head up, big hands square on the wheel, she began sobbing, breath tearing from her chest, tears streaming down her face. Lucas started to say something, looking for words, but she just shook her head and drove on.

18

Evan Hart stood with one hand in his pocket, his voice low, concerned. His back was to the balcony, so he was framed in the dark square; he wore a blue suit with a conservative striped shirt, and carried a square Scotch glass in his left hand. He'd taken his necktie off and thrust it in his pocket. Sara could see just the point of it sticking out from under the flap of his coat pocket. "Have you talked to the police?"

She shook her head. "I don't know what I'd tell them." She crossed her arms over her chest, rubbed her triceps with her hands, as though she were cold. "It's like having a ghost," she said. "I *feel* somebody, but I've never *seen* anything. I had the burglary, and since then . . . nothing. They'd say it's paranoia—paranoia brought on by the burglary. And I hate being patronized."

"They'd be right about the paranoia. You can't be a good trader if you're not paranoid," Hart said. He sipped the Johnnie Walker Black.

" 'Cause somebody *is* out to get you," she said, finishing the old Wall Street joke. She drifted across the front room toward him. She also had a glass, vodka martini, three olives. She looked out across the balcony, over the building across the street, toward the park. "To tell the truth, I am a little scared. A woman was killed just across the street, and the guy with her is still in a coma. This was just a few days ago, a couple of days after my burglary. They haven't caught anybody yet—they say it was gang kids. I've never seen any gang kids here. It was supposed to be safe. I used to walk around the lake in the evenings, but I've stopped."

Hart's face was serious again. He reached out and brushed her arm with two fingertips, just a light touch. "Maybe you should think about moving out of here."

"I've got a lease," Sara said, away from the balcony, toward him. "And the apartment is really handy to work. And it should be safe. It *is* safe. I've changed the locks, I've got a steel door. I don't know. . . ."

Hart stepped over to the balcony, looked out, his back toward her. She wondered if she made him nervous. "It's a pretty neighborhood. And I guess no place is really perfectly safe. Not anymore."

There was a moment of silence, and then she asked, "Do I make you nervous?"

He turned, a weak, slowly dying smile on his face. "Yeah, a little."

"Why?"

He shrugged. "I like you too much. You're very attractive . . . I don't know, I'm just not very good at this."

"It is awkward," she said. "Look, why don't you come over and sit down, and I'll put my head on your shoulder, and we'll go from there."

He shrugged again. "All right." He put down his glass, crossed the room, sat quickly, put his arm around her shoulder, and she let her head sink onto his chest.

"Now, is this bad?" she asked, and suddenly broke into a giggle.

"No, this isn't bad at all," Evan said. He sounded nervous, but he felt committed, and when she lifted her head to smile at him, he kissed her.

She felt good. She made a hundred and thirty thousand dollars a year, took vacations in Paris and Mexico and Monaco; she was the toughest woman she knew.

But a chest felt . . . excellent. She snuggled into it.

KOOP GRABBED THE EDGE of the air-conditioner housing, pulled himself up, and saw Jensen on the couch with a man, saw her turn her face up and the man kiss her.

"Oh, fuck me," he said aloud. "Oh, fuck me," and he felt his world shake.

The guy across the street put his hand on Jensen's waist, then moved it up a few inches, under her breast. Koop thought he recognized the guy, then realized he'd seen somebody like him on television, an old movie. Henry Fonda, that was it; Henry Fonda, when he was young. "Motherfucker. . . ."

Koop stood up without thinking, hand holding the scope, the living room couch jumping toward him. Their faces were locked together and the guy was definitely copping a feel. Remembering himself, Koop dropped to a crouch, felt the heat climbing into his face. He looked down and hammered his fist into the steel housing; and for the first time since—when? never?—felt something that might have been emotional pain. How could she do this? This wasn't right, she was *his*. . . .

He looked back toward Sara's apartment. They were talking now, backed off a little. Then she tipped her head onto his shoulder, and that was almost worse than the kiss. Koop put the scope on them, and watched so hard that his head began to hurt. Christ, he hoped they didn't fuck. Please, don't do it. Please.

They kissed again, and this time the guy's hand cupped Jensen's breast, held it. Koop, in agony, rolled over on his shoulder and looked away, decided not to look back until he counted to a hundred. Maybe it would go away. He counted one, two, three, four, five and got to thirty-eight before he couldn't stand it, and flipped over.

The guy was standing.

She'd said something to him; a pulse of elation streaked through his soul. She must've. She was getting ready to throw him out, by God. Why else would he have stopped; Christ, he had her on the couch. He had her in hand, for Christ's sake. Then the guy picked up a glass and looked at her, said something, and she threw back her head and laughed.

No. That didn't look good.

Then she was on her feet, walking toward him. Slipped two fingers between the buttons of his shirt, said something—Koop would have mortgaged his life for the ability to lip-read—then stood on tiptoe and kissed him again, quickly this time, and walked away, picked up a newspaper, and waved it at him, said something else.

They talked for another five minutes, both standing now, circling each other. Sara Jensen kept touching him. Her touch was like fire to Koop. When she touched the guy, Koop could feel it on his arm, in his chest.

Then the guy moved toward the door. He was leaving. Both still smiling.

At the door she stepped into him, her face up, and Koop rolled over again, refusing to watch, counting: one, two, three, four, five. Only got to fifteen, counting fast, before he turned back.

She was still in his arms, and he'd pressed her to the door. Jesus.

Gotta take him. Gotta take him now.

The impulse was like a hammer. He'd gut the cocksucker right in the driveway. He was messing with Koop's woman. . . .

But Koop lingered, unwilling to leave until the guy was out the door. They finally broke apart, and Koop, in a half-crouch, waited for him to go. Jensen was holding his hand. Didn't want him to go. Tugged at him.

"Cocksucker . . ." he thought, and realized he'd spoken aloud. Said it again: "Cocksucker, cut your fuckin' heart out, man, cut your fuckin' . . ."

AND THE ROOF ACCESS door opened. A shaft of light, shocking, blinding, snapped across the roof and climbed the airconditioner housing. Koop went flat, tense, ready to fight, ready to run.

Voices crossed each other, ten feet away. There was a sharp rattle and a bang as the door was pushed open, then closed of its own weight.

Cops.

"Gotta be quick." Not cops. A woman's voice.

Man's voice. "It's gonna be quick, I can promise that, you got me so hot I can't hold it."

Woman's voice: "What if Kari looks for the pad?"

"She won't, she's got no interest in camping . . . c'mon, let's go behind the air-conditioner thing. C'mon."

The woman giggled and Koop heard them rattling across the graveled roof, and the sound of a plastic mat being unrolled on the gravel. Koop looked sideways, past the duct toward Jensen's building. She was kissing the guy good-bye again, standing on her tiptoes in the open door, his hand below her waist, almost on her ass.

Below him, eight feet away, the man was saying, "Let me get these, let me get these . . . Oh, Jesus, these look great. . . ."

And the woman: "Boy, what if Kari and Bob could see us now . . . Oh, God . . ."

Across the street, Jensen was pushing the door shut. She leaned back against it, her head cocked back, an odd, loose look on her face, not quite a smile.

The woman: "Don't rip it, don't rip it. . . ."

The man: "God, you're wet, you're a hot little bitch. . . ."

Koop, blind with fury, his heart pounding like a triphammer, lay quiet as a mouse, but getting angrier and angrier. He thought about jumping down, of taking the two of them.

He rejected the idea as quickly as it had come. A woman had already died at this building, and a man was in a coma. If another two died, the cops would know *something* was happening here. He'd never get back up.

Besides, all he had was his knife. He might not get them both—and he couldn't see the guy. If the guy was big, tough, it might take a while, make a lot of noise.

Koop bit his lip, listening to the lovemaking. The woman tended to screech, but the screeching sounded fake. The guy said, "Don't scratch," and she said, "I can't help myself," and Koop thought, *Jesus. . . .*

And Sara Jensen's lover was getting away. Better to let him go . . . goddamnit.

He turned his head back to Jensen's apartment. Jensen went into the bathroom and shut the door. He knew from watching her that when she did that, she'd be inside for a while. Koop eased himself over onto his back and looked up at the stars, listened to the couple on the roof below him. Goddamnit.

Man's voice: "Let me do it this way, c'mon. . . ."

The woman: "God, if Bob knew what I was doing . . ."

19 ✖

GREAVE HAD HIS FEET up on his desk, talking on the phone, when Lucas arrived in the morning. Anderson drifted over and said, "A homicide guy in Madison interviewed somebody named Abby Weed. He says she confirmed that she met Joe Hillerod in a bookstore. She doesn't remember the date, but she remembered the discussion, and it was the right one. She said she spent the night with him, and she was unhappy about being questioned."

"Damnit," Lucas said. He said it without heat. Hillerod hadn't felt right, and he hadn't expected much. "Have you seen Meagan Connell?"

Anderson shook his head, but Greave, still on the phone, held up a finger, said a few more words, then covered the mouthpiece with his palm. "She called in, said she was sick. She'll be in later," he said. He went back to the phone.

Sick. Connell had been plummeting into depression when Lucas left her the night before. He hadn't wanted to leave—he'd suggested that she come home with him, spend the night in a guest room, but she'd said she was fine.

"I shouldn't have mentioned Beneteau asking about you," Lucas said.

She caught his arm. "Lucas, you did right. It's one of the nicer things that's happened to me in the last year." But her eyes had been ineffably sad, and he'd had to turn away.

GREAVE DROPPED THE RECEIVER on the hook and sighed. "How far did you get on the sex histories?" Lucas asked.

"Not very far." Greave looked away. "To tell you the truth, I hardly got started. I thought I might have something on my apartment."

"Goddamnit, Bob, forget the fuckin' apartment," Lucas said, his voice harsh. "We need these histories—and we need as many people thinking about the case as we can get."

Greave stood up, shook himself like a dog. He was a little shorter than Lucas, his features a little finer. "Lucas, I can't. I try, but I just can't. It's like a nightmare. I swear to God, I was eating an ice cream cone last night and I started wondering if they poisoned her ice cream." Lucas just looked at him, and Greave shook his head after a minute and said, "They didn't, of course."

And they both said, simultaneously, "No toxicology."

JAN REED FOUND LUCAS in his office. She had great eyes, he thought. Italian eyes. You could fall into them, no problem. He had a quick male mini-vision: Reed on the bed, pillow under her shoulders, head back, a half inch from orgasm. She looks up at the final instant, eyes opening, her awareness of him the sexiest thing in the universe . . .

"Nothing," he said, flustered. "Not a thing."

"But what about the people you grabbed in that raid over in Wisconsin?" There was a pinprick of amusement in her eyes. She knew the effect she had on him.

And she knew about the raid. "An unrelated case, but a good story," Lucas lied. He babbled: "It's a group of people called the Seeds—there used to be a motorcycle gang called the Bad Seeds, from up in northwest Wisconsin, and they evolved into a criminal organization. Cops call it the Hayseed Mafia. Anyway, these are the guys who were hitting the suburban gun stores. We got a lot of the guns back."

"That *is* interesting," she said. She made a note in her notebook, then put the eraser end of her pencil against her teeth, pensively, erotically. He was starting to fixate on the idea of television anchorwomen and oral sex, Lucas thought. "The gun issue's so hot . . . right now." She would pause every so often, leaving a gap in the conversation, almost as though she were inviting him to fill it in.

She paused now, and Lucas said, "Reed's an English name, right?"

"Yes. I'd be English on my father's side," she said. "Why?"

"I was thinking," Lucas said. "You've got great Italian eyes, you know?"

She smiled and caught her bottom lip with an upper tooth, and said, "Well, thank you. . . ."

When she left, Lucas went to the door with her. She moved along a little more slowly than he did, and he found himself almost on top of her, ushering her out. She smelled fine, he thought. He watched her down the hall. She wouldn't be an athlete. She was soft, smooth. She turned at the corner to see if he was watching, and just at that moment, when she turned, and though they resembled each other not at all, she reminded him of Weather.

THE REST OF THE DAY WAS a wasteland of paper, old reports, and conjectures. Connell wandered in after two, even paler than usual, said she'd been working on the computers. Lucas told her about the interview with Abby Weed. Connell nodded: "I'd already written them off. Hitting the Hillerods was just our good deed for the day."

"How're you feeling?"

"Sick," she said. Then quickly: "Not from last night. From . . . the big thing. It's coming back."

"Jesus, Meagan. . . ."

"I knew it would," she said. "Listen, I'm going to talk to Anderson, and start helping Greave on those histories. I can't think of anything else."

She left, but came back ten seconds later. "We've got to get him, Lucas. This week or next."

"I don't know. . . ."

"That's all the time I've got this round . . . and the next round will be even shorter."

LUCAS GOT HOME EARLY, found Weather on the couch reading *The Robber Bride*, her legs curled beneath her.

"A dead end?"

"Looks like it," Lucas said. "The woman in Madison confirmed Joe Hillerod's story. We're back to looking at paper."

"Too bad. He sounds like a major jerk."

"We've got him on the guns, anyway," Lucas said. "He handled most of the rifles, and their ID guys got good prints. And they found bolt cutters and a crowbar in his truck, and the tool-marks guy matched them to the marks on a gunshop door out in Wayzata."

"So what's left? On the murder case?"

"God, I don't know. But I feel like things are moving."

Lucas spent the late evening in the study, going through Anderson's book on the case—all the paper that anybody had brought in, with the histories that Greave had completed. Weather came to the door in her cotton nightgown and said, "Be extra quiet when you come to bed. I've got a heavy one tomorrow."

"Yeah." He looked up from the paper, his hair in disarray, discouraged. "Christ, you know, there's so much stuff in here, and so much of it's bullshit. The stuff in this file, you could spend four years investigating and never learn a fuckin' thing."

She smiled and came over and patted his hair back into place, and he wrapped an arm around her back and pulled her close, so he could lean his head between her breasts. There was something animal about this: it felt so good, and so natural. Like momma. "You'll get him," she said.

AN HOUR LATER, HE WAS puzzling over Anderson's note on the deaf people. Everything sounded right: a guy with a beard, going to the bookstore, in a truck. How in the hell did they screw up the license so bad? He glanced at his watch: one o'clock, too late to call anybody at St. Paul. He leaned back in his chair and closed his eyes. Maybe something would bubble to the surface of his mind. . . .

KOOP BROUGHT A SACK of Taco Bell soft tacos to the rooftop, tossed the sack on top of the air-conditioner housing, and pulled himself up after them. There was still enough light that Sara Jensen might see him if she looked out her window, so he duckwalked across the housing until he was behind the exhaust vent.

Putting the tacos aside, he shook the Kowa scope out of its canvas case and surveyed the apartment. Where was the blond guy? Had he come back? His heart was chilly with the fear. . . .

The drapes from both rooms were open, as usual. Sara Jensen was nowhere in sight. The bathroom door was closed.

Satisfied for the moment, Koop settled in behind the vent, opening the tacos, gulping them down. He dripped sour cream on his jacket: Shit. He brushed the sour cream with a napkin, but there would be a grease stain. He tossed the napkin off the edge off the housing, then thought, *I shouldn't do that,* and made a mental note to pick it up before he left.

Ten minutes after he arrived, Sara Jensen walked—hurried—out of the bathroom. She was nude, and the thrill of her body ran through him like an electric current, like a hit of speed. He put the scope on her as she sat at her dressing table and began to work on her makeup. He enjoyed seeing this, the careful work under the eyes, the touch-up of the lashes, the sensuous painting of her full lips. He dreamed about her lips. . . .

And he loved to watch her naked back. She had smoothly molded shoulders, the ripple of her spine from the top of her round ass straight to the nape of her neck. Her skin was fine, clear—one small dark mole on her left shoulder blade, the long, pale neck . . .

She stood, turned toward him, face intent, her breasts bobbing, the gorgeous pubic patch . . . She dug through her dresser, looking at what? Underwear? She pulled on a pair of underpants, took them off, threw them back, pulled on a much briefer pair, looked at herself in the mirror. Looked again, backed away, pulled the bottom elastic of her pants away from her thighs, let it snap back, turned to look at her butt.

And Koop began to worry.

She found a bra to go with the pants, an underwired bra, perhaps: it seemed to push her up. She didn't really need it, he thought, but it did look good. She turned again, looking at her self, snapped the elastic on her pants leg again.

Posed.

She was pleased with herself.

"What are you doing, Sara?" Koop asked. He tracked her with the scope. "What the fuck are you doing?"

She disappeared into a closet and came back out with a simple dark dress, either very dark blue or black. She held it to her breasts, looked into the mirror, shook her head at herself, and went back into the closet. She came back out with blue jeans and a white blouse, held them up, put them on, tucked in the shirt. Looked at herself, made a face in the mirror, shook her head, went back into the closet, emerged with the dress. She took off the jeans, stripping for him again, exciting him. She picked up the dress, pulled it over her head, smoothed it down.

"Are you going out, Sara?"

She looked in the mirror again, one hand on her ass, then took the dress off, tossed it on the bed, and looked thoughtfully at her chest of drawers. Walked to the chest, opened the bottom drawer, and took out a pale-blue cotton sweat suit. She pulled it on, pushed up the sleeves on the sweatshirt, went back to the mirror. Pulled off the sweatshirt, took off the bra, pulled the sweatshirt back on.

Koop frowned. Sweat suit?

The dress had been simple but elegant. The jeans casual but passable at most places in the Cities. But the sweat suit? Maybe she'd just been trying on stuff. But if so, why all the time in the bathroom? Why the sense of urgency?

Koop turned away, dropped behind the duct, lit a Camel, then rolled onto his knees and looked back through her window. She was standing in front of her mirror, flipping her hair with her hands. Brushing it back: breaking down its daytime structure.

Huh.

She stopped suddenly, then ducked back at the mirror, gave her hair a last flip, then hurried—skipped once—going out of the bedroom, into the front room, to the door. Said something, a smile on her face, then opened the door.

Goddamn it.

The blond guy was there. He had a chin on him, a butt-chin, with a dimple in it. He was wearing jeans and a canvas shirt, looking as tousled as she did. She stepped back from him, pulled a piece of her sweat suit out from her leg, almost as if she were about to curtsy.

Butt-chin laughed and stepped inside and leaned forward as if he were about to peck her on the cheek, and then the peck ignited and they stood there in each other's arms, the hallway door still open behind them. Koop rose to a half-stoop, looking across the fifty feet of air at his true love in another man's arms. He groaned aloud and hurled his cigarette toward them, at the window. They never saw it. They were too busy.

"Motherfuckers. . . ."

They didn't go out. Koop watched in pain as they moved to the couch. He realized, suddenly, why she had rejected the jeans and vacillated between the dress and the sweat suit: access.

A guy can't get his hands in a tight pair of jeans, boyo. Not without a lot of preliminaries. With a sweatsuit, there were no barriers. No problems getting your hands in. And that's where Blondy's were—in Sara's loose sweatpants, under her loose sweatshirt, Sara writhing beneath his touch—before they went to the bedroom.

BLONDY STAYED THE NIGHT.

So did Koop, huddled behind the vent on the air-conditioner housing, fading from consciousness to unconsciousness—not exactly sleep, but something else, something like a coma. Toward dawn, with just the light jacket, he got very cold. When he moved, he hurt. About four-thirty, the stars began to fade. The sun rose into a flawless blue sky and shone down on Koop, whose heart had turned to stone.

He felt it: a rock in his chest. And no mercy at all.

HE HAD TO WAIT more than an hour in the light before there was any movement in Sara Jensen's apartment. She woke first, rolled over, said something to the lump on the other side. Then he said something—Koop thought he did, anyway—and she moved up behind him, both of them on their sides, talking.

Two or three minutes later, Blondy got up, yawning, stretching. He sat naked on the bed, his back to Koop, then suddenly snatched the blankets down. Sara was there, as naked as he was, and he flopped on top of her, his head between her breasts. Koop turned away, squeezed his eyes shut. He just couldn't watch.

And he just couldn't *not* watch. He turned back. Blondy was nibbling on one of Sara Jensen's nipples, and Sara, back arched, her hands in his hair, was enjoying every second of it. The stone in Koop's heart began to fragment, to be replaced by a cold, unquenchable anger. The fucking whore was taking on another man. The fucking whore . . .

But he loved her anyway.

He couldn't help himself.

And couldn't help watching when she pushed him flat on the bed, and trailed her tongue from his chest down across his navel. . . .

THE BLOND GUY FINALLY left at seven o'clock.

Koop had stopped thinking long before that. For an hour, he'd simply been waiting, his knife in his hand. He occasionally ran it down his face, over his beard, as if he were shaving. He was actually getting in tune with it, the steel in the blade. . . .

When the door closed behind Blondy, Koop barely gave Sara Jensen a thought. There'd be time for her later. She turned away, hurrying back to the bedroom to get ready for work.

Koop, wearing his glasses and snap-brimmed hat, flew off the air-conditioner housing. He had just enough control to check the apartment hallway before bursting into it from the roof access; a man stood in it, facing the elevator. Koop cursed, but the man suddenly stepped forward and was gone. Koop ran the length of the hall and took the stairs.

Took the stairs as though he were falling, a long circular dash, with no awareness of steps or landings, just a continuous drop, his legs flashing, shoes slapping like a machine gun on the concrete.

At the bottom, he checked the lobby through the window in the stairway door. Three or four people, and the elevator bell dinged: more coming. Frustrated, he looked around, then went down another flight, into the basement. And found a fire exit, leading out through the back. Just before he hit the back door, he saw a sign and read the first words, DO NOT, and then he was through. Somewhere behind him, an alarm went off, a shrill ringing like King Kong's telephone.

Were there pictures? The possibility flashed through his brain and then disappeared. He'd worry about that later. That he hadn't been seen in the building—that was important. That he catch Blondy in the street—that was even more important.

Koop ran down the alley at the back of the building, around the building. There were a dozen people up and down the street, in business clothes, some coming toward him, some walking away, briefcases, purses. A cane.

He groped in his pocket, wrapping his fist around the knife again. Checked faces, checked again. Blondy was not among them. Where in the hell . . . ?

Koop pulled the hat farther down on his head, looked both ways, then started walking toward the entrance of Sara Jensen's apartment. Had he already gotten down? Or was he slow getting down? Or maybe she'd given him a parking card and he'd left his car in her ramp. He swerved toward the ramp exit, although if the guy was in a Mercedes or a Lexus what was he gonna do, stab it? He thought he might.

A car came out of the ramp, with a woman driver. Koop looked back at the door—and saw him.

Blondy had just come out. His hair was wet, his face soft, sated. His necktie, a conservative swath of silk, was looped untied around his shirt collar. He carried a raincoat.

Koop charged him. Started way back at the entrance to the parking ramp and hurtled down the sidewalk. He wasn't thinking, wasn't hearing, wasn't anything: wasn't aware of anyone other than Blondy.

Wasn't aware of the noise that came out of his mouth, not quite a scream, more of a screech, the sound of bad brakes . . .

Wasn't aware of other people turning . . .

Blondy saw him coming.

The soft look fell off his face, to be replaced by a puzzled frown, then alarm as Koop closed.

Koop screamed, "Motherfucker," and went in, the blade flicking out of his fist, his long arm arcing in a powerful, upward rip. But quicker than Koop could believe, Blondy stepped right, swung his arm and raincoat, caught Koop in the wrist, and Koop's hand went past Blondy's left side. They collided and they both staggered: the guy was heavier than he looked, and in better shape. Koop's mind began working again, touched by a sudden spark of fear. Here he was, on the street, circling a guy he didn't know. . . .

Koop screamed again, and went in. He could hear the guy screaming "Wait. Wait.", but it sounded distant, as though it came from the opposite shore of a lake. The knife seemed to work on its own, and this time he caught the blond, caught his hand, and blood spattered across Koop's face. He went in again, and then staggered: he'd been hit. He was astonished. The man had hit him.

He went in again, and Blondy kept backing, swinging. Koop was ready this time, blocked him.

And got him.

Really got him.

Felt the knife point go in, felt it coming up . . .

Then he was hit again, this time on the back of the head. He spun, and another man was there, and a third one coming, swinging a briefcase like a club. Koop felt Blondy go down behind him, with a long ripping groan; almost tripped over his body, avoiding the briefcase, swung the blade at the new attacker, missed, slashed at the second one, the one who'd hit him in the head, missed again.

His attackers both had dark hair. One had glasses, both had bared teeth, and that was all he saw: hair, glasses, teeth. And the briefcase.

Blondy was down and Koop stumbled and looked down at him, saw the scarlet blood on his shirt and a fourth man yelled at him, and Koop ran.

He could hear them screaming, "Stop him, stop him . . ." He ran sideways across the street, between parked cars. A woman on the sidewalk jumped out of the way. Her face was white, frightened; she had a red necktie and matching hat and large horsy teeth, and then he was past her.

One of the men chased him for two hundred feet, alone. Koop suddenly stopped and started back at him, and the man turned and started to run away. Koop ran back toward the park, into it, down the grassy tree-shaded walks.

Ran, blood gushing from his nose, the knife folding in his hand, as if by magic, disappearing into his pocket. He wiped his face, pulled off the hat and glasses, slowed to a walk.

And was gone.

THE CURB OUTSIDE City Hall was lined with TV vans. Something had happened.

Lucas dumped the Porsche in a ramp and hurried back. A *Star-Tribune* reporter, a young guy with a buzz cut, carrying a notebook, was coming up from the opposite direction. He nodded at Lucas and held the door. "Anything happening with your case?" he asked.

"Nothing serious," Lucas said. "What's going on?"

"You haven't heard?" Buzz Cut did a mock double take.

"I'm just coming in," Lucas said.

"You remember that couple that was jumped up by the lakes, the woman was killed?"

"Yeah?"

"Somebody else got hit, right across the street. Four hours ago. Thirty feet away from the first scene," Buzz Cut said. "I ain't bullshitting you, Lucas: I been out there. Thirty feet. This guy came out of nowhere like a maniac, broad daylight. Big fucking switchblade. He sounded like somebody from a horror movie, had a hat over his face, he was screaming. But it wasn't any gang. It was white-on-white. The guy who got stabbed is a lawyer."

"Dead?" Lucas asked. He'd relaxed a notch: not his case.

"Not yet. He's cut to shit. Got a knife in the guts. He's still in the operating room. He spent the night with his girlfriend, and the next morning, he walks out the door and this asshole jumps him."

"Has she got a husband or ex-husband?"

"I don't know," the reporter said.

"If I were you, I'd ask," Lucas said.

The reporter held up his notebook, which was turned over to a page with a list of indecipherable scrawls. "First question on the list," he said. Then he said, "Whoa."

Jan Reed was lounging in the hall, apparently waiting for the press conference to start. She saw Lucas and lifted her chin and smiled and started toward them, and the reporter, without moving his lips, said, "You dog."

"Not me," Lucas muttered.

"Lucas," she said, walking up. Big eyes. Pools. She touched him on the back of his hand and said, "Are you in on this?"

Lucas despised himself for it, but he could feel the pleasure of her company unwinding in his chest. "Hi. No, but it sounds like a good one." He bounced on his toes, like a basketball player about to be sent into a game.

She looked back toward the briefing room. "Pretty spectacular right now. It could wind up as a domestic."

"It's right across the street from that other one."

She nodded. "That's the angle. That's what makes it good. Besides which, the people are white."

"Is that a requirement now?" Buzz Cut asked.

"Of course not," she said, laughing. Then her voice dropped to the confidential level, including him in the conspiracy. "But you know how it goes."

The reporter's scalp flushed pink and he said, "I better get inside."

"What's wrong with him?" she asked, watching him go. Lucas shrugged, and she said, "So, do you have time for a cup of coffee? After the press conference?"

"Uhhmm," Lucas said, peering down at her. She definitely wound his clock. "Why don't you stop by my office," he said.

"Okay . . . but, your tie, your collar's messed up. Here. . . ."

She fixed his collar and tie, and though he was fairly certain that there'd been nothing wrong with them, he liked it, and carried her touch down the hall.

CONNELL WAS THE PERFECT contrast to Jan Reed: a big solid blonde who carried a gun the size of a toaster and considered lipstick a manifestation of Original Sin. She was waiting for him, dark circles under her eyes.

"How're you feeling?"

"Better. Still a little morning sickness," she said dismissively, brushing the illness away. "Did you read the histories?"

"Yeah. Not much."

She looked angry: not at Lucas or Greave, but maybe at herself, or the world. "We're not gonna get him this time, are we? He's gonna have to kill somebody else before we get him."

"Unless we get a big fuckin' break," Lucas said. "And I don't see a break coming."

JAN REED CAME BY Lucas's office after the press conference, and they ambled through the Skyways to a restaurant in the Pillsbury Building. Since she was new to Minnesota, they chatted about the weather, about the lakes, about the Guthrie Theater, and about the other places she'd worked: Detroit, Miami, Cleveland. They found a table not too close to anyone else, Reed with her back to the door—"I get pestered sometimes"—and ordered coffee and croissants.

"How was the press conference?" Lucas asked, peeling open one of the croissants.

Reed opened her notebook and looked at it. "Maybe not domestic," she said. "The guy's name is Evan Hart. His girlfriend's been divorced for seven years. Her ex lives out on the West Coast and he was there this morning. Besides, she says he's a nice guy. That they broke up because he was too mellow. No alimony or anything. No kids. Sort of a hippie mistake. And she hasn't gone out with anybody else, seriously, for a couple of years."

"How about this Hart?" Lucas asked. "Has he got an ex? Is he bisexual? What does he do?"

"He's a widower," Reed said. She put the yellow pencil in her mouth and turned pages. A little clump of hair fell over her eyes and she brushed it back; Weather did that. "His wife was killed in a traffic accident. He's a lawyer for a stockbrokerage company, he has something to do with municipal bonds. He doesn't sell anything, so it's not that. He didn't ruin anybody."

"Doesn't sound like a fruitcake, though," Lucas said. "It sounds like the guy was mad about something."

"That's what it sounds like," she said. "But Jensen's really freaked out. That other attack happened right down below her apartment window."

"That's what I heard. Jensen's his girlfriend? She was actually there at the press conference?"

"Yeah. She was. Sara Jensen. Sharp. Good-looking, runs her own mutual fund, probably makes two hundred thousand a year," Reed said. "Dresses like it. She has just gorgeous clothes—she must go to New York. She was really angry. She wants the guy caught. Actually, it sounded like she wants the guy killed, like she was there to ask the cops to find him and kill him."

"Very strange," Lucas said. "The guys in homicide are having a hard time right now. . . ."

The conversation rambled along, through new subjects, Lucas enjoying it, laughing. Reed was nice-looking, amusing, and had spent a little time on the streets. They had that in common. Then she said something about gangs. Gangs was a code word for blacks, and as she talked, the code word pecked away at the back of Lucas's mind. Reed, he thought after a bit, might have a fine ass and great eyes, but she was also a bit of a racist. Racism was becoming fashionable in the smart set, if done in a suitably subtle way. Was it immoral to jump a racist? How about if she didn't have a good time, but you did?

He was smiling and nodding and Reed was rambling on about something sexual but safe, the rumored affair between an anchorman and a cameraman, carried out in what she said was a TV van with bad springs.

". . . So there they were on Summit Avenue outside the governor's mansion, and everybody's going in for the ball and this giant van with TV3 on the side is practically jumping up and down, and her husband is out on the sidewalk, pacing back and forth, looking for her." Reed was playing with her butter knife as she talked, and she twirled it in her fingers, a cheerleader's baton twirl.

Like Junky Doog, Lucas thought. What had Junky said when Greave had asked him why a man might start cutting on women? *'Cause a woman turns you on, that's why. Maybe you see a woman and she turns you on. Gets you by the pecker . . .*

The Society of Jesus, SJ.

Or . . .

Lucas said, suddenly, sitting up, "What was the guy's wound like?"

"What?" She'd been in midsentence.

"This guy who was attacked this morning," Lucas said impatiently.

"Uh . . . well, he was stabbed in the stomach," Reed said, startled by the sudden roughness in his voice. "Two or three times. He was really messed up. I guess they're still trying to put him together in the operating room."

"With a switchblade. The kid from the *Strib* said it was a switchblade."

"A witness said that," Reed said. "Why?"

"I gotta go," Lucas said, looking at his watch. He threw a handful of dollars on the table. "I'm sorry, but I really got to run. I'm sorry. . . ."

Now she looked distinctly startled, but he did run, once he was out of sight. His office was locked, nobody around. He went down the hall to homicide and found Anderson eating an egg-salad sandwich at his desk. "Have you seen Connell?"

"Uh, yeah, she just went into the women's can." He had a fleck of egg white on his lip.

Lucas went down to the women's can and pushed the door open. "Connell?" he shouted. "Meagan?"

After a moment, a reluctant, hollow, tile-walled "Yeah?"

"Come out here."

"Christ . . ." She took two minutes, Lucas walking up and down the hall, cooling off. Very unlikely, he thought. But the wound sounded right. . . .

Connell came out, tucking her shirt into her skirt. "What?"

"The guy that was attacked this morning," Lucas said. "He was ripped in the stomach by a guy with a switchbladelike knife."

"Lucas, it was a guy, it was daylight, he doesn't fit anything . . ." She was puzzled.

"He'd spent the night with his girlfriend, Sara Jensen."

Still she looked puzzled.

Lucas said, "SJ."

22

✖

THEY FOUND SARA JENSEN at Hennepin General, distraught, pacing the surgical waiting room. A uniformed cop sat in a plastic chair reading *Road & Track*. They took Jensen to an examination room, shut the door, and sat her down.

"It's about goddamn time somebody started taking this seriously," Jensen said. "You had to wait until Evan got stabbed. . . ." Her voice was contained, but with a thread of fear that suggested she was at the edge of her self-control. "It's the goddamn burglar. If you'd find him . . ."

"What burglar?" Lucas asked. The place smelled like medical alcohol and skin and adhesive tape.

"What burglar?" Her voice rose in anger, until she was nearly shouting. "What burglar? What burglar? The burglar at my place."

"We don't know anything about that," Connell said quickly. "We work homicide. We're looking for a man who has been killing women for years. The last two he's marked with the initials *SJ*—your initials. We're not sure it's you, but it might be. The attack on Mr. Hart resembles the technique he has used to kill the women. The weapon appears to be similar. He fits the descriptions we've had. . . ."

"Oh, God," Jensen said, her hand going to her mouth. "I saw it on TV3, the man with the beard. The man who attacked Evan had a beard."

Lucas nodded. "That's him. Do you know anybody who looks like that? Somebody you've dated, somebody you have a relationship with? Maybe with some frustration? Or maybe somebody who just watches you, somebody you can feel in your office?"

"No." She thought about it again. "No. I know a couple of guys with beards, but I haven't dated them. And they seem to be ordinary enough . . . Besides, it's not them. It's the goddamn burglar. I think he's been coming back to my apartment."

"Tell us about the burglar," Lucas said.

She told them: the initial burglary, the loss of her jewelry and belt, the smell of saliva on her forehead. And she told them about the sense she had, that somebody had been in and out of her apartment since the burglary—and the feeling that it was the same man. "But I'm not sure," she said. "I thought I was going crazy. My friends thought it was stress from the burglary, that I was imagining it. But I don't think so: the place just didn't feel right, like there was something in the air. I think he sleeps in my bed." Then she laughed, a short, barely amused bark. "I sound like the Three Bears. Somebody's been eating my porridge. Somebody's been sleeping in my bed."

"So you say that when he came in the first time, he must've touched you—kissed you on the forehead."

"More like a lick," she said, shuddering. "I can remember it, like a dream."

"What about the actual entry?" Lucas asked. "Did he break the door?"

There hadn't been a sound, she said, and the door had been untouched, so he must have had a key. But she was the only one with a key—and the building manager, of course.

"What's he like? The manager?"

"Older man. . . ."

They went through the list: who had the key, who could get it, who could copy it. More people than she'd realized. Building employees, a cleaning woman. How about valet-parking places? A few valets—"But I changed the locks again after the burglary. He'd have to get my key twice."

"Gotta be somebody in the building," Connell said to Lucas. She'd grabbed his wrist to get his attention. She was sick, but she was a strong woman, and her grip had the strength of desperation.

"If somebody's actually coming back," Lucas said. "But whoever it was is a pro. He knew what he wanted and where it was. He didn't rip the place apart. A cat burglar."

"A cat burglar?" Jensen said doubtfully.

"I'll tell you something: movies romanticize cat burglars, but real cat burglars are cracked," Lucas said. "They get off on creeping apartments while the residents are home. Most burglars, the last thing they want is to run into a home owner. Cat burglars get off on the thrill. Every one of them does dope, cocaine, speed, PCP. Quite a few of them have rape records. A lot of them eventually kill somebody. I'm not trying to scare you, but that's the truth."

"Oh, God. . . ."

"The way the attack happened would suggest that the guy knows about you and Mr. Hart," Connell said. "Do you talk to anybody in your building about him?"

"No, I really don't have any close friends in the building, other than just to say hello to," Jensen said. Then, "Last night was the first time Evan stayed over. It was actually the first time we'd slept together. Ever. It's like whoever it is, knew about us."

"Did you tell anybody at work that he was coming over?"

"I have a couple of friends who knew we were getting close. . . ."

"We'll need their names," Lucas said. And to Connell: "Somebody at the office might have occasional access to her purse; they could get the keys that way. We should check all the apartments that adjoin hers, too. People in her hallway." To Jensen: "Do you feel any attention from anybody in your apartment? Just a little creepy feeling? Somebody who seems sort of anxious to meet you, or talk to you, or just looks you over?"

"No, no, I don't. The manager is a heck of a nice guy. Really straight. I don't mean, you know, repressed, or weird, or a Boy Scout leader or anything. He's like my dad. God, it gives me the shakes, thinking about somebody watching me," she said.

"How about an outsider?" Lucas asked. "Is there a building across the street where you could be watched from? A Peeping Tom?"

She shook her head. "No. There's a building across the street—that's the building where that woman was killed last week—but I'm on the top floor, which is higher even than their roof," Jensen said. "I look right across their roof into the park, and the other side of the park is residential. There's nothing as high as me on the other side of the park. Besides, that's a mile away."

"Okay . . ." Lucas studied her for a moment. She was very different than the other victims. Watching her, Lucas felt a small chord of doubt. She was fashionable, she was smart, she was tough. There was no hint of deference, no air of wistfulness, no feeling of time and years slipping away.

"I've got to get out of the apartment," Jensen said. "Could a policeman come with me while I get some things?"

"You can have a cop with you until we get the guy," Lucas said. He reached forward to touch her arm. "But I hope you won't leave. We could move you to another apartment inside the building, and give you escorts: armed policewomen in plain clothes. We'd like to trap the guy, not scare him off."

Connell joined in: "We don't really have any leads, Ms. Jensen. We're almost reduced to waiting until he kills somebody else, and hoping we find something then. This is the first break we've had."

Jensen stood up and turned away, shivered, looked down at Lucas, and said, "How much chance is there that he'd . . . get to me?"

Lucas said, "I won't lie to you: there's always a chance. But it's small. And if we don't get him, he might outwait our ability to escort you and then come after you. We had a case a few years ago where a guy in his middle twenties went after a woman who'd been his ninth-grade teacher. He'd brooded about her all that time."

"Oh, Jesus. . . ." Then, suddenly: "All right. Let's do it. Let's get him."

The uniformed cop who'd been in the waiting room rapped on the door, stuck his head inside, and said to Jensen, "Dr. Ramihat is looking for you."

Jensen took Lucas's forearm, her fingers digging in, as they went back down the hall to the waiting area. They found the surgeon greedily sucking on a cigarette and eating a Twinkie. "There's an awful lot of damage," he said, in light Indian accents. "There aren't any guarantees, but we've got him more or less stable and we've stopped the bleeding. Unless we get something unexpected, his chances are good. There'll be an infection problem, but he's in good physical shape and we should be able to handle it."

Jensen collapsed in a chair, face in her hands, began to blubber. Ramihat patted her on the shoulder with one hand, ate the second Twinkie with his cigarette hand, and winked at Lucas. Connell pulled Lucas aside and said quietly, "If we can keep her in line, we got him."

. . .

THEY SPENT THE REST of the morning setting it up: Sloan came in to work with Lucas, Connell, and Greave in checking people with access to Jensen's keys. Five women from intelligence, narcotics, and homicide would rotate as close escorts.

After some discussion, Jensen decided that she could stay in the apartment as long as an escort was always with her. That way, she wouldn't have to move anything out, and open the possibility that if the killer was in the building, she'd be seen doing it.

Hart came out of surgery at three o'clock in the afternoon, hanging on.

23

KOOP WAS STILL IN a rage as he fled the lakes. He couldn't think of the guy in bed with Jensen without hyperventilating, without choking the truck's steering wheel, gripping it, screaming at the windshield. . . .

In calmer moments, he could still close his eyes and see her as she was that first night, lying on the sheets, her body pressing up through the nightgown. . . .

Then he'd see her on Hart again, and he'd begin screaming, strangling the steering wheel. Crazy. But not entirely gone. He was sane enough to know that the cops might be coming for him. Somebody might have seen him getting in the truck, might have his license number.

Koop had done his research in his years at Stillwater: he knew how men were caught and convicted. Most of them talked to the cops when they shouldn't. Many of them kept scraps and pieces of past crimes around them—television sets, stereos, watches, guns, things with serial numbers.

Some of them kept clothing with blood on it. Some of them left blood behind, or semen.

Koop had thought about it. If he was taken, he swore to himself that he would say nothing at all. Nothing. And he would get rid of everything he wore or used in any crime: he would not give the cops a scrap to hang on to. He would try to build an alibi—anything that a defense attorney could use.

HE WAS STILL IN psychological flight from the attack on Hart when he dumped the coat and hat. The coat was smeared with Hart's blood, a great liverish-black stain. He wrapped it, with the hat, in a garbage bag and dumped it with a pile of garbage bags on a residential street in Edina. The garbage truck was three blocks away. The bag would be at the landfill before noon. He threw the plain-pane glasses out the car window into the high grass of a road-side ditch.

Turned on the radio, found an all-news station. Bullshit, bullshit, and more bullshit. Nothing about him.

In his T-shirt, he stopped at a convenience store, bought a six-pack of spring-water, a bar of soap, a laundry bucket, and a pack of Bic razors. He continued south to Braemar Park, climbed into the back of the truck, and shaved in the bucket. His face felt raw afterward; when he looked in the truck mirror, he barely recognized himself. He'd picked up a few wrinkles since he'd last been bare-faced, and his upper lip seemed to have disappeared into a thin, stern line.

He couldn't bring himself to throw away the knife or the apartment keys. He washed the knife as well as he could, using the last of the springwater, sprayed both the knife and the keys with WD-40, wrapped them in another garbage bag, knotted the mouth of the bag, walked up a hill near the park entrance, and buried the bag near a prominent oak. He felt almost lonely when he walked away from it. He'd recover it in a week or so . . . if he was still free.

Cleansed of the immediate evidence of the crime, Koop headed east out of St. Paul.

As he passed White Bear Avenue:

Police are on the scene of a brutal murder attempt in south Minneapolis that took place about an hour and fifteen minutes ago. The site is less than a block from the building where a woman was murdered and a man was badly beaten last week; the man is still in a coma from that attack, and may not recover. In this latest attack, witnesses say a tall, bearded man wearing steel-rimmed glasses and a brown snap-brimmed hat attacked attorney Evan Hart as he left a friend's apartment this morning. Hart is currently in surgery at Hennepin General, where his condition is listed as critical. The attacker fled and may be driving a mint-green late-model Taurus sedan. Witnesses say that the attacker repeatedly slashed Hart with a knife. . . .

Green Taurus sedan? What was that? Tall? He was five-eight.

Was either white or a light-skinned black man . . .

What? They thought he was black. Koop stared at the radio in amazement. Maybe he didn't have to run at all.

Still: He drove for an hour and a half, losing the Twin Cities radio stations sixty miles out. He stopped at a big sporting goods outlet off I-94, bought a shirt, a sleeping bag, a cheap spinning rod with a reel, a tackle box, and some lures. He stripped them of bags and receipts, threw the paper in a trash can, and turned north, plotting the roads in his head. At Cornell, he bought some bread, lunch meat, and a six-pack of Miller's, and carefully kept the receipt with its hour-and-day stamp, crumbled in the grocery sack, thrust under the seat. Before he left the store parking lot, he looked carefully around the lot for any discarded receipts, but didn't see any.

North of Cornell, he turned into the Brunet Island State Park and parked at a vacant campsite away from the boat launching ramp. Two boat trailers were parked at the ramp, hooked onto pickups. When he had the ramp to himself, he dug around in a trash can for a moment. There were two grocery bags crumpled inside; he opened the first, found it empty, but in the second, he found another grocery receipt. There was no time on it, but the date and the store name were, and the date was from the day before.

He carried it back to the truck and threw it in the back.

He could see only one boat on the water, so far away that he could barely make out the occupants. Koop was not much of a fisherman, but he got the rod and reel, tied on a spinner bait, and walked back toward the ramp. Nobody around. Ducking through the brush, he moved up to one of the trailers, unscrewed a tire cap, and pushed the valve stem with his fingernails. When the tire was flat, he carefully backed away and tossed the cap into weeds.

After that, he waited; wandered down the shoreline, casting. Thinking about Jensen's treachery. How could a woman do that? It wasn't right. . . .

Deep in thought, he was annoyed, five minutes later, when he got a hit. He ripped a small northern off the hook and tossed the fish back up in the weeds. Fuck it.

An hour after he'd let the air out of the trailer tire, an aluminum fishing boat cut in toward the ramp. Two men in farm coveralls climbed out of the boat and walked back to the trailer with the flat. The older of the two backed the trailer into the water while the other stood on the side opposite the flat and helped the boat up to the ramp. After the boat was loaded and pulled out, the man on the ramp yelled something, and after some talk back and forth, the man in the car got out to look at the trailer tire. Koop drifted toward them, casting.

"Got a problem?" he called.

"Flat tire."

"Huh." Koop reeled in his last cast and walked over toward them. The driver was talking to his friend about taking the boat off, pulling the wheel, and driving it into town to get it fixed.

"I got a pump up in my truck," Koop said. "Maybe it'd hold long enough to get you into town."

"Well." The farmers looked at each other, and the driver said, "Where's your truck?"

"Right over there, you can see it. . . ."

"We could give 'er a try," the driver said.

Koop retrieved the pump. "Hell of a nice boat," he said as they pumped up the tire. "Always wanted a Lund. Had it long?"

"Two years," the driver said. "Saved for that sucker for ten years; got it set up perfect." When the tire was up, they watched it for a moment, then the driver said, "Seems to hold."

"Could be a real slow leak," Koop said. "Check it this morning before you went out?"

"Can't say as I did," the driver said, scratching his head. "Listen, thank you much, and I think I'll get our butts into town before it goes flat again."

So he had receipts and he'd been seen fishing on the ramp; and he took the boat registration number. He'd have to think about that: maybe he shouldn't be able to remember all of it, just that it was a red Lund and the last two registration letters were *LS* . . . Or maybe that the first number on it was 7. He'd have to think about it.

On his way through town, he stopped at the store that issued the register receipt he'd found in the trash can, bought a Slim Jim and a can of beer, and stuffed the receipt and the sack under the seat. Maybe they'd remember his face in the store, maybe not—but he'd been there, he could describe the place, and he could even describe the young woman who'd waited on him. Too heavy. Wore dark-green fashion overalls.

A little before five, he started back to the Cities. He wanted to be within radio range, to pick up the news. To see if they were looking for him. . . .

THEY WERE NOT, as far as he could tell. One of the evening talk shows was devoted to the attack, and the attack the week before, but it was all a bunch of crazies calling in.

Huh.

They were looking for the wrong guy. . . .

He went back to the park, got the knife and keys. Felt better for it.

At one o'clock in the morning, Koop wasn't quite drunk, but he was close. Driving around, driving around, up and down the Cities, Jensen was more and more on his mind.

At one, he drove past her apartment. A light shone behind her window. A man was walking down the street, walking a small silvery dog. At one-fifteen, Koop cruised it again. Still the light. She was up late; couldn't sleep, after the fight—Koop thought about it as a fight. Blondy'd asked for it, fucking Koop's woman; what was a guy supposed to do?

Koop's mind was like a brick, not working right. He knew it wasn't working right. He could not pull it away from Jensen. He had other things to think about—he'd been cruising his next target, he was ready to make an entry. He couldn't think about it.

At one-thirty, the light was still on in Jensen's apartment, and Koop decided to go up to his spy roost. He knew he shouldn't risk it; but he would. He could feel himself being pulled in, like a nail to a magnet.

At one thirty-five, he went into the apartment across the street from Jensen's climbed the stairs. Physically, he was fine, moving as smoothly and quietly as ever. It was his mind that was troubling. . . .

He checked the hall. Empty. Had to be quiet: everybody would be spooked. He went to the roof entry, climbed the last flight, pushed through the door, and quickly closed it behind himself. He stood there for a moment, the doorknob still in his hand, listening. Nothing. He stepped to the edge of the door hutch and looked up at Jensen's window. The light was on, but at the angle, he couldn't see anything.

He crossed to the air-conditioner housing, grabbed the edge, and pulled himself up. He crawled to the vent and looked around the corner. Nobody in sight. He leaned back behind the vent, put his back to it. Looked up at the stars.

He thought about what he'd become, caught by this passion. He would have to stop. He knew he would have to stop, or he was doomed. He could think of only one way to stop it—and that way touched him. But he would like to have her first, if he could.

Before he killed her.

Koop looked around the corner past the vent, and, shocked, almost snatched his head back. Almost, but not quite. He had the reflexes and training of a cat burglar, and had taught himself not to move too quickly. Across the street, in Jensen's window, a man was looking out. He was six feet back from the glass, as though he were taking care not to be seen from the street. He wore dark slacks and a white dress shirt, without a jacket.

He wore a shoulder holster.

A cop. They knew. They were waiting for him.

WEATHER CURLED UP on the couch. The television was tuned to CNN, and Lucas watched it without seeing it, brooding. "Nothing at all?" she asked.

"Not a thing," he said. He didn't look at her, just pulled at his lip and stared at the tube. He was tired, his face gray. "Three days. The media's killing us."

"I wouldn't worry so much about the media, if I were you."

Now he turned his head. "That's because you don't have to worry. You guys bury your mistakes," Lucas said. He grinned when he said it, but it wasn't a pleasant smile.

"I'm serious. I don't understand. . . ."

"The media's like a fever," Lucas explained. "Heat starts to build up. The people out in the neighborhoods get scared, and they start calling their city councilmen. The councilmen panic—that's what politicians, do, basically, is panic—and they start calling the mayor. The mayor calls the chief. The chief is a politician who is appointed by the mayor, so she panics. And the shit flows downhill."

"I don't understand all the panic. You're doing everything you can."

"You have to look at Davenport's first rule of how the world really works," Lucas said.

"I don't think I've heard that one," Weather said.

"It's simple," he said. *"A politician will never, ever, get a better job when he's out of office."*

"That's it?"

"That's it. That explains everything. They're desperate to hang on to their jobs. That's why they panic. They lose the election, it's back to the car wash."

After a moment of silence, Weather asked, "How's Connell?"

"Not good," Lucas said.

CONNELL'S FACIAL SKIN WAS stretched, taut; dark smudges hung under her eyes, her hair was perpetually disarranged, as though she'd been sticking her fingers into an electric outlet.

"Something's wrong," she said. "Maybe the guy knows we're here. Maybe Jensen was imagining it."

"Maybe," Lucas said. They waited in Jensen's living room, stacks of newspapers and magazines by their feet. A Walkman sat on a coffee table. A television was set up in the second bedroom, but they couldn't listen to the stereo for fear that it would be heard in the hallway. "It sure felt good, though."

"I know . . . but you know what maybe it could be?" Connell had a foot-high stack of paper next to her hand, profiles and interviews with apartment employees, residents of Jensen's floor, and everyone else in the building with a criminal record. She had been pawing through it compulsively. "It could be, like, a relative of somebody who works here. And whoever works here goes home and lets it slip that we're in here."

Lucas said, "The keys are a big question. There are any number of ways that a cat burglar could get one key, but two keys—that's a problem."

"Gotta be an employee."

"Could be a valet service at a restaurant," he said. "I've known valets who worked with cat burglars. You see the car come in, you get the plate number, and from that, you can get an address and you've got the key."

"She said she hadn't used a valet since she got the new key," Connell said.

"Maybe she forgot. Maybe it's something so routine that she doesn't remember it."

"I bet it's somebody at her office—somebody with access to her purse. You know, like one of the messenger kids, somebody who can go in and out of her office without being noticed. Grab the key, copy it. . . ."

"But that's another problem," Lucas said. "You've got to have some knowledge to copy it, and a source of blanks."

"So it's a guy working with a cat burglar. The burglar supplies the knowledge, the kid supplies the access."

"That's one way that it works," Lucas admitted. "But nobody in her office seems like a good bet."

"A boyfriend of somebody in the office; a secretary picks up the key, lays it off. . . ."

Lucas stood up, yawned, wandered around the apartment, stopped to look at a framed black-and-white photograph. It wasn't much, a flower in a roundish pot, a stairway in the background. Lucas didn't know much about art, but this felt like it. A tiny penciled signature said Andre something, something with a K.

He yawned again and rubbed the back of his neck and looked at Connell going through the paper.

"How'd you feel this morning?"

She looked up. "Hollow. Empty."

"I don't understand how it works, the whole chemotherapy thing," Lucas said.

She put down the paper. "Basically, the kind of chemo I get is poisonous. It knocks down the cancer, but it also knocks down my body," she said. Her voice was neutral, informed, like a medical commentator on public television. "They can only use it so long before the chemotherapy starts doing too much damage. Then they take me off it, and my body starts recovering from the chemo, but so does the cancer. The cancer gains a little every time. I've been on it for two years. I'm down to seven weeks between treatments. I've been five. I'm feeling it again."

"Lots of pain?"

She shook her head. "Not yet. I can't really describe it. It's a hollow feeling, and a weakness, and then a sickness, like the worst flu in the world. I understand, toward the end, it'll get painful, when it gets into my bone marrow . . . I expect to opt for other measures before then."

"Jesus," he said. Then: "What are the chances that the chemo will knock it down completely?"

"It happens," she said with a brief, ghostly smile. "But not for me."

"I don't think I could handle it," Lucas said.

The balcony door was closed, and Lucas moved over toward it, staying six feet back from the glass, and looked out at the park. Nice day. The rain had quit, and the light-blue sky was dappled with fair-weather clouds, cloud shadows skipping across the lake. A woman dying.

"But the other problem," Connell said, almost to herself, "besides the key, I mean, is why he hasn't come up here. Four days. Nothing."

Lucas was still thinking about cancer, had to wrench himself back. "You're talking to yourself," Lucas said.

"That's because I'm going crazy."

"You want a pizza?" Lucas asked.

"I don't eat pizza. It clogs up your arteries and makes you fat."

"What kind don't you eat?"

"Pepperoni and mushroom," Connell said.

"I'll get one delivered to the manager. I can run down and get it when it comes in," he said, yawning again. "This is driving me nuts."

"Why doesn't he come?" Connell asked rhetorically. "Because he knows we're here."

"Maybe we just haven't waited long enough," Lucas said.

Connell continued: "How does he know we're here? One: he sees us. Two: he hears about us. Okay, if he sees us, how does he know we're cops? He doesn't—unless he's a cop, and he recognizes people coming and going. If he hears about us, how does he hear about us? We've been over that."

"Pepperoni and mushroom?"

"No fuckin' anchovies."

"No way." Lucas picked up the phone, frowned, hung it up, and walked back to the glass door. "Did somebody check the roof on the other side of the street?"

Connell looked up. "Yeah, but Jensen was right. It's below the level of her window. She doesn't even bother to pull the drapes."

"It's not below the level of the air-conditioner housing," Lucas said. "C'mere. Look at this."

Connell stood up and looked. "There's no way to get up on it."

"He's a cat burglar," Lucas said. "And if he got up on it, he'd be looking right into the apartment. Who went over the roof?"

"Skoorag—but he just strolled around the roof. I saw him do it. Said there wasn't anything up there."

"We ought to take a look," Lucas said.

Connell looked at her watch. "Greave and O'Brien'll be here in an hour. We could go over then."

O'BRIEN CARRIED A BROWN paper sack with a magazine inside, and tried to hide it from Connell. Greave said, "I've been thinking: how about if we picked up all three of them, the brothers and Cherry, separate them, tell them we've got a break, and tell them the first one who talks gets immunity."

Lucas grinned but shook his head. "You're thinking right, but you've got to have *something*. If you don't, they'll either tell you to go fuck yourself, or, which is worse, the guy who actually did the killing is the one who talks. He walks, and Roux hangs you out the window by your nuts. So, you gotta get something."

"I've gotten something," Greave said.

"What?"

"I've gotten desperate."

"O'BRIEN HAD A *Penthouse*," Connell said.

"It's a very boring job," Lucas said mildly.

"Think about this," Connell said. "What if women brought porno magazines to work, pictures of men with huge penises? And the women sat there and looked at the pictures, then looked at you, then looked at the picture. Wouldn't you find that just a little demeaning?"

"Not me, personally," Lucas said, face straight. "I'd just see it as another career opportunity."

"Goddamn you, Davenport, you always weasel away."

"Not always," Lucas said. "But I do have a well-developed sense of *when* to weasel." Then, as they crossed the street, "This is where the woman was killed and the guy fucked up."

They climbed the steps and buzzed the manager. A moment later, a door opened in the lobby and a middle-aged woman looked out. Her hair was not quite blue. Lucas held up his badge, and she let him in.

"I'll get somebody to let you up on the roof," the woman said when Lucas explained what they wanted. "That was awful, that poor guy stabbed."

"Were you here when those two people were attacked outside?"

"No, nobody was here. Except tenants, I mean," she said.

"I understand the guy was between the inner and outer doors when he was attacked."

The woman nodded. "One more second and he would have been inside. His key was in the lock."

"Sonofabitch," Lucas said. To Connell: "If somebody wanted to get a key and cover what they were doing . . . The whole attack didn't make sense, so they said gang kids did it. Trouble is, the gang unit hasn't heard a thing from the gangs. And they should have heard."

THE JANITOR'S NAME WAS CLARK, and he opened the door to the roof and blocked it with an empty Liquid Plumber bottle. Lucas walked across the gravel-and-tar-paper roof. Greave and O'Brien were standing in Jensen's apartment, visible from the shoulders up.

"Can't see much from here," Lucas said. He turned to the air-conditioner housing.

"It looks high enough," Connell said. They walked around it: it was a gray cube, with three featureless metal faces. A locked steel service hatch, and a warranty sticker with a service number, were the only items on the fourth side. There was no access to the top of the cube.

"I can get a stepladder," Clark offered.

"Why don't you just give me a boost," Lucas said. He slipped out of his shoes and jacket, and Clark webbed his fingers together. Lucas put his foot in the other man's hands and stepped up. When his shoulders were over the edge of the housing, he pushed himself up with his hands.

The first thing he saw were the cigarette butts, forty or fifty of them, water-stained, filterless. "Oh, Christ." One butt was fresh, and he duckwalked over to it, peered at it.

"What?" Connell called.

"About a million cigarette butts."

"Are you serious? What kind?"

Lucas duckwalked back to the edge, peered down, and said, "Unfiltered Camels, each and every one."

Connell looked across the street. "Can you see in the apartment?"

"I can see O'Brien's shoes," Lucas said.

"The sonofabitch *knew*," Connell cried. "He was up here, he looked in, he saw us. *We were this fuckin' close.*"

THE CRIME-SCENE TECH LIFTED the single fresh Camel with a pair of tweezers, put it in a bag, and passed it down. "We can try," he said to Lucas, "but I wouldn't count on much. Sometimes you get a little skin stuck to the butts, sometimes enough to do a DNA or at least get a blood type, but these have been out here a while." He shrugged. "We'll try, but I wouldn't hold my breath."

"What're the chances of DNA?" Connell demanded.

He shrugged. "Like I said, we'll try."

Connell looked at Lucas. "We've had cold matches on DNA."

"Yeah—two," Lucas said.

"We gotta make a run at it," she said.

"Sure." He looked across the street. Sloan waved. "We'll put a night-vision scope over there, in case he comes back. Goddamnit. I hope we haven't scared him completely."

"If we haven't, he's nuts," Connell said.

"We *know* he's nuts," Lucas answered. "But I'm afraid that if he has seen us, we're frustrating the hell out of him. I hope he doesn't go for another. I hope he comes in first. . . ."

25

JOHN POSEY'S HOUSE WAS a three-level affair, like a white-brick-and-cedar layer cake, overlooking a backyard duck pond rimmed by weeping willows. From a street that ran at a ninety-degree angle to Posey's street, Koop could see the back of the house. Two separate balconies overlooked the pond, one above the other, slightly offset.

A security-system warning sign was stuck in the front yard, by the door. Koop knew the system: typically magneto-offset doors, usually with motion detectors sweeping the first floor.

If the detectors were tripped, they'd automatically dial out to an alarm service after a delay of a minute to two minutes. The alarm service would make a phone check, and if not satisfied, would call the cops. If the phone wires were cut, an alarm would go off at the monitoring service. If other phones in the neighborhood weren't out, the cops would be on their way.

Which didn't make the place impossible. Not at all. For one thing, Posey had a dog, an old Irish setter. The setter was often in the front window, even when Posey wasn't home. If there was a motion detector, it was either turned off or it only guarded the parts of the house that the dog couldn't get to.

He would wait until Posey left and then go straight in, Koop decided. No hiding, nothing subtle. Smash and grab.

Koop was in no condition for subtlety. He thought about Sara Jensen all the time. Reran his mental tapes. He would see her in another woman—with a gesture or a certain step, a turn of the head.

Jensen was a sliver under the skin. He could try to ignore her, but she wouldn't go away. Sooner or later, he'd have to deal with her. Bodyguards or no bodyguards.

But Koop knew something about the ways of cops. They'd watch her for a while, and then, when nothing happened, they'd be off chasing something else.

The only question was, could he wait?

AT EIGHT-THIRTY, KOOP stopped at a downtown parking garage. He followed a Nissan Maxima up the ramp, parked a few slots away from it, got slowly out of the truck. The Maxima's owners took the elevator; Koop took the plates off the Maxima.

He carried them back to the truck, stepped out of sight for a moment when another car came up the ramp, then clipped the stolen plates on top of his own with steel snap-fasteners. A matter of two minutes.

Posey had an active social life and went out almost every night, mostly to sports bars. Koop checked by calling, calling again, calling a third time, never getting an answer, before heading back to the house.

The night was warm, humid, and smelled like cut grass. The whole neighborhood hummed with the air conditioners tucked in at the sides of the houses. Windows and doors would be closed, and he could get away with a little more noise, if he had to.

Four blocks from Posey's, a group of teenagers, three girls, two boys, stood on a street corner smoking, long hair, long shirts hung out over their jeans, looking at him with narrowed eyes as he passed in the truck.

A few porch lights were still on, yellow and white, and the sound of easy-listening music seeped from an open, lit garage. There were cars—not many—parked on the street; the neighborhood was too affluent for that.

He cruised the house. It looked right—Posey usually left two lights on when he was out. Koop had an eight-ball with him: he did a hit, then another, got his tools from under the passenger seat, and drove back to the house. Pulled into the driveway. Waited a second, watching the curtains, checking the street, picked up his tools and got out, walked up to the front door, and rang the doorbell.

The dog barked; the bark was loud, audible in the street. Nobody came to the door. The dog kept barking. Koop walked back down the front of the house, checked the neighborhood one last time, then walked down the side of the garage.

The side of the garage was windowless, and faced the windowless garage next door. Between them, he couldn't be seen. The backyard, though, was different, potentially dangerous. He stopped at the corner of the garage and scanned the houses on the next street, facing Posey's. There were lights, and a man reading a newspaper behind a picture window two houses down. Okay. . . .

KOOP WORE A JOGGING SUIT, the jacket open over a white T-shirt. In the hand-warmer pocket he carried a pair of driving gloves. A sailing compass, called a "hockey puck," was stuffed in one glove, a small plastic flashlight in the other. He carried an eighteen-inch crowbar down his pants' leg, the hook over the waistline of the pants.

He waited two minutes, three, his heartbeat holding up, then zipped the jacket and pulled on the gloves. Nearly invisible, he edged around the corner of the house until he was standing behind a dwarf spruce, looking up at the first balcony.

The bottom of the balcony was eight feet overhead. He bent the spruce, found a branch two feet above the ground that would bear his weight. He stepped up, feeling the spruce sag, but hooked the lower bar of the railing with one hand, then the other. He swarmed up like a monkey, scuffing his kneecap on the concrete edge of the balcony. He waited a few seconds, ignoring the pain in his knee, listening, hearing nothing, then tested the balcony railing for rigidity.

Solid. He stood on it, balancing carefully, reached around the edge of the upper balcony, grabbed the railing, and let himself swing free. When his swinging motion slowed, he pulled himself up and clambered over the railing onto the higher balcony.

Again he stopped to listen. The dog had stopped barking. Good. He was now on the third floor, outside a room he believed was unused. He'd spotted Posey's bedroom in a second-floor corner. This should be a guest room, if the moving man's map was correct. And it wouldn't be rigged for an alarm, unless Posey was truly paranoid.

Hearing nothing, he stood up and looked at the sliding glass doors. The track was not blocked: that made things easier. He tried the door itself, on the chance that it was unlocked. It was not. He took the crowbar out of his pants, pressed the point of it against the glass, and slowly, carefully put his weight against it. The glass cracked, almost silently. He started again, just above the first point, bearing down . . . and got another crack.

The third time, the glass suddenly collapsed, leaving a hole the size of his palm. He hadn't made a sound louder than a careful cough. He reached through the hole, flipped up the lock and pulled the latch, and slid the door back. Stopped. Listened. Inside, he turned on the flashlight. Yes. A bedroom, with a feel of disuse.

He crossed the room to the bedroom door, which was closed, took out the compass, waited until the needle settled, then ran it along the edge of the door. The needle remained steady, except at the handle, where it deflected. The door was not protected; he hadn't expected it to be, but it took only a moment to check.

He opened the door, half expecting the dog to be there, but found an empty hall, dimly lit from the lights downstairs.

Down the stairs, slowly, listening. Nothing. Through the hall.

Then: the dog's nails on the kitchen's vinyl floor, with a tentative *woof*. A few woofs were okay, but if the dog got out of hand . . . He reversed his grip on the crowbar, holding it by the flat end.

The dog came around the corner of the kitchen, saw him standing there, barked. Old dog, his legs stiff, his muzzle hair going white . . .

"Here, boy, c'mere," Koop said, his voice soft. "C'mere, boy . . ." He walked toward the dog, his left hand out, cupped, right hand behind him. The dog backed away, upright, barking, but let Koop get closer. . . .

"Here, boy." One more step, one more.

"Woof." Sensing danger, trying to back away . . .

Koop swatted the dog like a fly. The crowbar caught it in the center of the skull, and the dog went down without a whimper, just a final *woof*. Dead when it hit the floor, its legs jerked, running spasmodically on the vinyl.

Koop turned away. No need to be quiet anymore. He checked the front door. There was a keypad next to it showing an alarm light: the system was armed, but he wasn't sure what that meant. At the basement door, he again checked with the compass. Again, nothing. Must only be the outer doors.

He eased the door open, took a step. Okay. Walked down to the bottom of the stairs, into the basement—and the moment he stepped into the basement, heard the rapid *beep-beep-beep* of the alarm system's warning, a bit louder than an alarm clock.

"Shit," he said.

One minute. He started a running count at the back of his head. *Sixty, fifty-nine . . .*

The safe was there, just as the moving man said. He worked the combination the first time and looked inside. Two sacks, two jewelry boxes. He took them out. One sack was cash. The other was as heavy as a car battery. Gold, probably. No time to think.

Thirty. Twenty-nine, twenty-eight . . .

He ran back up the stairs, to the front door, the alarm making its urgent *beep-beep-beep* warning. He hit it with the crowbar, silencing it. The call would be made anyway, but if someone was passing in the street, he wouldn't hear the beeping.

Koop walked out the front door, back to the truck. Tossed the tools and the money bags on the front seat, started the truck, backed into the street.

Thinking: *Fourteen, thirteen, twelve . . .*

At *zero*, he'd turned the corner and was heading down the hill to West Seventh Street. Fifteen seconds later, he was in heavy traffic. He never did see a cop.

KOOP CHECKED THE BAGS in a Burger King parking lot. The first contained forty-five hundred dollars in cash: twenties, fifties, and hundreds. The second bag held fifty gold coins, Krugerrands. Already, one of the best scores he'd ever had. The first box held a gold chain with a ten-diamond cross. The diamonds were small but not tiny. He had no idea what they were worth. A lot, he thought, if they were real. In the second box, earrings to go with the necklace.

A wave of pleasure ran through him. The best score; the best he'd ever done. Then he thought of Jensen, and the pleasure began to fade.

Shit. He looked at the gold in his lap. He really didn't want this. He could get money anytime.

He knew what he wanted.

He saw her every time he closed his eyes.

KOOP CRUISED JENSEN'S APARTMENT. The apartment was lit up. He slowed, and thought he might have seen a shadow on the window. Was she naked? Or was the place full of cops?

He couldn't loiter. The cops might be watching.

He thought about the dog, the feet scratching on the vinyl floor. He wondered why they did that. . . .

The night had pushed him into a frenzy: exhilaration over the take at Posey's, frustration over the lights at Jensen's. He drove down to Lake Street, locked up the truck, and started drinking. He hit Flower's Bar, Lippy's Lounge, the Bank Shot, and Skeeter's. Shot some pool with a biker at Skeeter's. Scored another eight-ball at Lippy's and snorted most of it sitting on the toilet in the Lippy's men's room.

The coke gave him a ferocious headache after a while, tightening up his neck muscles until they felt like a suspension spring. He bought a pint of bourbon, went out to his truck and drank it, and started doing exercises: bridges, marine push-ups.

At one o'clock, Koop started back downtown, drunk. At five after one, drunk, he saw the woman walking back toward the hotel off Lyndale. A little tentative, a little scared. Her high heels going clackety-clack on the street. . . .

"Fuck her," he said aloud. He didn't have his ether, but had muscle and his knife. He passed the woman, going in the same direction, pulled the truck to the curb, put it in neutral. He popped the passenger seat, groped beneath it until he found the bag, stripped out the knife, and threw the keys back in the box. Did a quick pinch of cocaine, then another. Groped behind the seat until he found his baseball hat, put it on.

"Fuck her," he said. She was walking up to the back of the truck, on the sidewalk. The night was warm for Minnesota, but she wore a light three-quarters trench coat. Koop wore a T-shirt that said "Coors."

Out of the truck, around the nose, a gorilla, running.

The woman saw him coming. Screamed, "Don't!"

Dropped her purse.

Everything cocaine sharp, cocaine powerful.

Plenty of fuel, plenty of hate: "FUCK YOU."

Koop screamed it, and the knife blade snicked out, and she backed frantically away. He grabbed her, got the shoulder of her coat. "Get in the fuckin' truck."

He could see the whites of her eyes, turning up in terror, pulled at her. The coat came away, the woman thrashing, slipping out of it, trying to run. She went through a sidewalk flower garden, crushing pink petunias, lost one of her shoes, backed against the building and began to scream; the odor of urine rode out on the night air.

And she screamed. A high, piercing, loud scream, a scream that seemed to echo down the sidewalks.

Koop, drunk, stoned, teeth as large as tombstones, on top of her: "Shut the fuck up." He hit her backhanded, knocked her off her feet. The woman sobbing, trying to crawl.

Koop caught her by the foot, dragged her out of the flower garden, the woman trying to hold on to petunias. Petunias . . .

She began screaming again; no more words, screaming, and Koop, angrier and angrier, dragged her toward the truck.

Then, from above:

"You stop that." A woman's voice, shrill, as angry as Koop was. "You stop that, you asshole, I'm calling the police."

Then a man's voice: "Get away from her. . . ."

From the apartment across the street, two people yelling down at him, one two or three floors up, the other five or six. Koop looked up, and the woman began to sob.

"Fuck you!" Koop screamed back.

Then a flash: the woman had taken a picture of him. Koop panicked, turned to run. The woman on the sidewalk looked at him, still screaming, pulling away.

Christ: she'd seen him close, from two inches.

Another flash.

Man's voice: "Get away from that woman, police are coming, get away."

And another light, steady this time: somebody was making movies.

The rage roared out of him, like fire; the knife with a mind of its own.

Koop grabbed the woman by the throat, lifted her off the sidewalk, the woman kicking like a chicken.

And the knife took her. She slipped away from him, onto the sidewalk, almost as though she had fainted.

Koop looked down. His hands were covered with blood; blood ran down the sidewalk, black in the streetlight. . . .

"Get away from that woman, get away. . . ."

No need to be told. Panic was on him, and he ran to the truck, climbed in, gunned it.

Around the corner, around another.

Two minutes, up the interstate ramp. Cop cars everywhere, down below lights flashing, sirens screeching. Koop took the truck off the interstate, back into the neighborhoods, and pushed south. Side streets and alleys all the way.

He stayed inside for ten minutes, then jumped on the Crosstown Expressway for a quick dash to the airport. Took a ticket, went up the ramp, parked. Crawled in the back.

"Motherfucker," he breathed. Safe for the moment. He laughed, drank the last mouthful from the pint bottle.

He got out of the truck, hitched his pants, walked around behind, and climbed in.

Safe, for the time being.

He rolled up his jogging jacket to use as a pillow, lay down, and went to sleep.

Eloise Miller was dead in a pool of black blood before the cops got there.

In St. Paul, a patrol cop looked at Ivanhoe the dog and wondered who in the fuck would do that. . . .

"**W**E GOT PICTURES OF HIM," Connell said. Lucas found her on the sixth floor, in the doorway of a small apartment, walking away from a gray-haired woman. Connell was as cranked as Lucas had ever seen her, a cassette of thirty-five-millimeter film in her fist. "Pictures of him and his truck."

"I heard we got movies," Lucas said.

"Aw, man, come on . . ." Connell led him down the stairs. "You gotta see this."

On four, two cops were talking to a thin man in a bathrobe. "Could you run the tape?" Connell asked.

One of the cops glanced at Lucas and shrugged. "How's it going, chief?"

"Okay. What've we got?"

"Mr. Hanes here took a videotape of the attack," the older of the two cops said, pointing a pencil at the man in the bathrobe.

"I didn't think," the man said. "There wasn't any time."

The younger cop pushed the button on the VCR. The picture came up, clear and steady: a picture of a bright light shining into a window. At the bottom of it, what appeared to be two sets of legs doing a dance.

They all stood and watched silently as the tape rolled on: they could see nothing on the other side of the window except the legs. They saw the legs only for a few seconds.

"If we get that downtown, we should be able to get a height estimate on the guy," Lucas said.

The bathrobe man said, mournful as a bloodhound, "I'm sorry."

The older cop tried to explain. "See, the light reflected almost exactly back at the lens, so whatever he pointed it at is behind the light."

"I was so freaked out. . . ."

In the hallway, Lucas said, "How do we know we don't have the same thing on the film?"

" 'Cause she went out on her terrace and shot it," Connell said. "There was no window to reflect back at her . . . There's a one-hour development place at Midway, open all night."

"Isn't there a better—"

She was shaking her head. "No. I've been told that the automated processes are the most reliable for this Kodak stuff. One is about as good as another."

"Did you see enough of the woman on the street?" Lucas asked.

"I saw too much," Connell said. She looked up at Lucas. "He's flipped out. He started out as this sneaky, creepy killer, really careful. Now he's Jack the Ripper."

"How about you?"

"I flipped out a long time ago," she said.

"I mean . . . are you hanging in there?"

"I'm hanging in," she said.

THE QUICK-SHOT OPERATOR was by himself, processing film. He could stop everything else, he said, and have prints in fifteen minutes, no charge.

"There's no way they can get messed up?" Lucas asked.

The operator, a bony college kid in a Stone Temple Pilots T-shirt, shrugged. "One in a thousand—maybe less than that. The best odds you're going to get."

Lucas handed him the cassette. "Do it."

SEVENTEEN MINUTES LATER, the kid said, "The problem is, she was trying to take a picture from a hundred and fifty or two hundred feet away, at night, with this little teeny flash. The flash is supposed to light up somebody's face at ten feet."

"There's nothing fuckin' there," Connell shouted at him, spit flying.

"Yeah, there is—you can see it," the kid said, indignant, peering at one of the almost-black prints. That particular print had a yellow smudge in the middle of it, what might have been a streetlight, above what might have been the roof of a truck. "That's exactly what you get when you take pictures in the dark with one of those little fuckin' cameras."

There was something going on in the prints, but they couldn't tell what. Just a lot of smudges that might have been a woman being stabbed to death.

"I DON'T BELIEVE IT," Connell said. She slumped in the car seat, sick.

"I don't believe in eyewitnesses or cameras," Lucas said.

Another three blocks and Connell said suddenly, urgently, "Pull over, will you? Right there, at the corner."

"What?" Lucas pulled over.

Connell got out and vomited. Lucas climbed out, walked around to her. She looked up weakly, tried to smile. "Getting worse," she said. "We gotta hurry, Lucas."

. . .

"WE'RE TALKING FIRESTORM," Roux said. She had two cigarettes lit at the same time, the one on the window ledge burning futilely by itself.

"We'll get him," Lucas said. "We've still got the surveillance at Sara Jensen's. There's a good chance he'll come in."

"This week," Roux said. "Gotta be this week."

"Very soon," Lucas said.

"Promise?"

"No."

LUCAS SPENT THE DAY following the Eloise Miller routine, reading histories, calling cops. Connell did the same, and so did Greave. Results from the street investigation began coming in. The guy was big and powerful, batted the woman like a rag doll.

There were three eyewitnesses: one said the killer had a beard, the other two said he did not. Two said he wore a hat, the other said he had black hair. All three said he drove a truck, but they didn't know what color. Something and white. There wasn't much dirt in the street to pick up tire tracks, even if two cop cars and an ambulance hadn't driven over them.

The autopsy came in. Nothing good. No DNA source. No prints. Still checking for hair.

AT FOUR O'CLOCK, he gave up. He went home, took a nap. Weather got home at six.

At seven, they lay on top of the bedsheet, sweat cooling on their skin. Outside the window, which was cracked just an inch or two, they could hear the cars passing in the street a hundred feet away, and sometimes, quietly, the muttering of voices.

Weather rolled up on her elbow. "I'm amazed at the way you can separate yourself from what you're doing," she said. She traced a circle on his chest. "If I was as stuck on a problem as you are, I couldn't think of anything else. I couldn't do this."

"Waiting is part of the deal," Lucas said. "It has always been that way. You can't eat until the cake is baked."

"People get killed while you're waiting," she said.

"People die for bad reasons all the time," Lucas said. "When we were running around in the woods last winter, I begged you to stay away. You refused to stay away, so I'm alive. If you hadn't been out there . . ." He touched the scar on his throat.

"Not the same thing," she objected. She touched the scar. Most of it, she'd made herself. "People die all the time because of happenstance. Two cars run into each other, and somebody dies. If the driver of one of them had hesitated five seconds at the last stoplight, they wouldn't have collided, and nobody would die. That's just life. Chance. But what you do . . . somebody might die because you can't solve a problem that's solvable. Or like last winter, you seemed to reach out and solve a problem that was unsolvable, and so people who probably would have died, lived."

He opened his mouth to reply, but she patted him on the chest to stop him. "This isn't criticism. Just observation. What you do is really . . . bizarre. It's more like magic, or palm reading, than science. I do science. Everybody I work with does science. That's routine. What you do . . . it's fascinating."

Lucas giggled, a startling sound, high-pitched, unlike anything she'd ever heard from him. Not a chuckle. A giggle. She peered down at him.

"Goddamn, I'm glad you moved in with me, Karkinnen," he said. "Conversations like this could keep me awake for weeks at a time. You're better than speed."

"I'm sorry. . . ."

"No, no." He pushed up on his elbow to face her. "I need this. Nobody ever looked into me before. I think a guy could get old and rusty if nobody ever looked into him."

WHEN WEATHER WENT INTO the bathroom, Lucas got up and wandered around, naked, hunting from room to room, not knowing exactly what. A picture of the dead Eloise Miller hung in his mind's eye: a woman on the way to feed a friend's dog while the friend was out of town. She'd made that walk, late at night, just once in her life. Once too often.

Lucas could hear Weather running water in the bathroom, and thought guiltily about the attractions of Jan Reed. He sighed, and pushed the reporter out of his mind. That's not what he was supposed to be thinking about.

They knew so much about the killer, he thought. Generally what he looked like, his size, his strength, what he did, the kinds of vehicles he drove, if indeed he drove that Taurus sedan in addition to the truck. Anderson was now cross-indexing joint ownerships, green Taurus sedans against pickups.

But so much of what they knew was conflicting, and conflicts were devastating in a trial.

Depending on who you believed, the killer was a white, short or tall police officer (or maybe a convict), a cocaine user who drove either a blue-and-white or red-and-white pickup truck, or a green Taurus sedan, and he either wore glasses or he didn't, and while he probably wore a beard at one time, he might have shaved it off by now. Or maybe not.

Terrific.

And even if that could be sorted out, they had not a single convicting fact. Maybe the lab would come through, he thought. Maybe they'd pull some DNA out of a cigarette, and maybe they'd find the matching DNA signature in the state's DNA bank. It had been done.

And maybe pigs would fly.

Lucas wandered into the dining room, tinkled a few keys on the piano. Weather had offered to teach him how to play—she'd taught piano in college, as an undergraduate—but he said he was too old.

"You're never too old," she'd said. "Here, have some more wine."

"I am too old. I can't learn that kind of stuff anymore. My brain doesn't ab-sorb it," Lucas said, taking the wine. "But I can sing."

"You can sing?" She was amazed. "Like what?"

"I sang 'I Love Paris' in the senior concert in high school," he said, some-what defensively.

"Do I believe you?" she asked.

"Well, I did." He sipped.

And she sipped, then put the glass on a side table and rummaged, some-what tipsily, through the piano bench and finally said, "Ah-ha, she calls his bluff. I have here the music to 'I Love Paris.' "

She played and he sang; remarkably well, she said. "You have a really nice baritone."

"I know. My music teacher said I had a large, vibrant instrument."

"Ah. Was she attractive?"

"It was a he," Lucas said. "Here. Have some more wine."

LUCAS STRUCK A FEW more notes, then wandered back toward the bed-room, thinking again about his eyewitnesses. They had more than a dozen of them now. Several had been too far away to see much; a couple of them had been so scared that they were more confusing than helpful; two men had seen the killer's face during the attack on Evan Hart. One said he was white, the other said he was a light-skinned black.

And some had seen the killer too long ago, and remembered nothing about him at all. . . .

WEATHER WAS NAKED, bent over the sink, her hair full of shampoo. "If you touch my butt, I'll wait until you're asleep and I'll disfigure you," she said.

"Cut off your nose to spite your face, huh?"

"We're not talking noses," Weather said, scrubbing.

He leaned in the doorway. "There's something women don't understand about good asses," he said. "A really good ass is an object of such sublime beauty, that it's almost *impossible* to keep your hands off."

"Try to think of a way," she said.

Lucas watched for a moment, then said, "Speaking of asses, some deaf peo-ple thought they saw the killer's truck. They were sure of it. But they gave us an impossible license plate number. A number that's not issued—ass, as in *A-S-S*." He touched her ass.

"I swear to God, Lucas, just 'cause you've got me helpless. . . ."

"Why would they be so sure, and then have such a bad number?"

Weather stopped scrubbing for a moment and said, "A lot of deaf people don't read English."

"What?"

She looked at him from under her armpit, her head still in the sink. "They don't read English. It's very difficult to learn English if you're nonhearing. A lot of them don't bother. Or they learn just enough to read menus and bus signs."

"Then what do they do? To communicate?"

"They sign," she said.

"I mean, communicate with the rest of us."

"A lot of them aren't interested in communicating with the rest of us. Deaf people have a complete culture: they don't need us."

"They can't read or write?" Lucas was astonished.

"Not English. A lot of them can't, anyway. Is that important?"

"I don't know," Lucas said. "But I'll find out."

"Tonight?"

"Did you have other plans?" He touched her ass again.

She said, "Not really. I've got to get to bed."

"Maybe I'll make a call," he said. "It's not even ten o'clock."

ANNALISE JONES WAS A sergeant with the St. Paul Police Department. Lucas got her at home.

"We had an intern do the translating. A student at St. Thomas. He seemed to know what he was doing," she said.

"Don't you have a regular guy?" Lucas asked.

"Yeah, but he was out."

"How do I get the names of these people? The deaf people?"

"Jeez, at this time of night? I'd have to call around," Jones said.

"Could you?"

AT ELEVEN O'CLOCK HE HAD a name and address off St. Paul Avenue. Maybe two miles away. He got his jacket. Weather, in bed, called sleepily, "Are you going out?"

"Just for a while. I gotta nail this down."

"Be careful. . . ."

The houses along St. Paul Avenue were modest postwar cottages, added-to, modified, with small, well-kept yards and garages out back. Lucas ran down the house numbers until he found the right one. There were lights in the window. He walked up the sidewalk and rang the bell. After a moment, he heard voices and then a shadow crossed the picture-window drapes, and the front door opened a foot, a chain across the gap. A small, elderly man peered out. "Yes?"

"I'm Lucas Davenport of the Minneapolis Police Department." Lucas showed his ID card and the door opened wider. "Does Paul Johnston live here?"

"Yes. Is he all right?"

"There's no problem," Lucas said. "But he went in and talked to the St. Paul police about a case we're working on, and I need to talk to him about it."

"At this time of night?"

"I'm sorry, but it's pretty urgent," Lucas said.

"Well, I suppose he's down at the Warrens'." He turned and called back into the house, "Shirley? Is Paul at the Warrens'?"

"I think so." A woman in a pink housecoat walked into the front room, clutching the housecoat closed. "What happened?"

"This is a policeman, he's looking for Paul. . . ."

THE WARRENS WERE A FAMILY of deaf people in Minneapolis, and their home was an informal gathering spot for the deaf. Lucas parked two houses away, at the end of a line of cars centered on the Warrens's house. A man and a woman were sitting on the front stoop, drinking beer, watching him. He walked up the sidewalk and said, "I'm looking for Paul Johnston?"

The two looked at each other, and then the man signed at him, but Lucas shook his head. The man shrugged and made a croaking sound, and Lucas took out his ID, showed them, pointed toward the house and said, louder, "Paul Johnston?"

The woman sighed, held up a finger, and disappeared inside. A moment later she came back, followed by a stringy blond teenage girl with a narrow face and small gray eyes. The first woman sat down again, while the blonde said, "Can I help you?"

"I'm a Minneapolis police officer and I'm looking for a Paul Johnston who contacted the St. Paul police about a case we're working on."

"The killings," the girl said. "We've been talking about that. Nothing ever happened."

"I understand St. Paul took a statement."

"Yeah, but we never heard any more . . . Wait, I'll get Paul."

She went back inside and Lucas waited, avoiding eye contact with the two people on the porch. They knew it, and seemed to think he was amusing. Every once in a while he'd accidentally make eye contact and either nod or lift his eyebrows, which made him feel stupid.

A moment later, the stringy teenager came back with a stocky dark-haired man, who looked closely at Lucas and then croaked once, querulously. Heavy oversize glasses with thick lenses made his eyes seem moonlike. He stood under the porch light, and the light made a halo of his long hair.

"I don't sign," Lucas said.

The blonde said, "No shit. So what do you want to know?"

"Just what he saw. We got a report with a license number, but the number was an impossible one. The state doesn't allow vulgarities or anything that might be a vulgarity, so there is no plate that says ASS on it."

The girl opened her mouth to say something, then turned to Johnston, her hands flying. A second later, Johnston shook his head in exasperation and began signing back.

"He says the guy at the police station is a jerk," the blonde said.

"I don't know him," Lucas said.

The blonde signed something, and Johnston signed back. "He was afraid that they might have messed up, but that jerk they had at the police station just couldn't sign," she said, watching his hands.

"It wasn't ASS?"

"Oh, yeah. That's why they remembered it. This guy almost ran over them, and Paul saw the plate, and started laughing, because it said ASS, and the guy was an ass."

"There aren't any plates that say ASS."

"How about ass backwards?"

"Backwards?"

She nodded. "To Paul, it doesn't make much difference, frontwards or backwards. He just recognizes a few words, and this ASS popped right out at him. That's why he remembered it. He knew it was backwards. He tried to explain all this, but I guess not everything got through. Paul said the guy at the police station was an illiterate jerk."

"Jesus. So the plate was SSA?"

"That's what Paul says."

Lucas looked at Paul, and the deaf man nodded.

Lucas, on the phone, heard Connell running down the hall and smiled. She literally skidded into the office. Her face was ashen, bare of any makeup; tired, drawn.

"What happened?"

Lucas put his hand over the receiver. "We maybe got a break. Remember those deaf people? St. Paul got the license number wrong."

"Wrong? How could they be wrong?" she demanded, fist on her hips. "That's stupid."

"Just a minute," Lucas said, and into the phone, "Can you shoot that over? Fax it? Yeah. I've got a number. And listen, I appreciate your coming in. I'll talk to your boss in the morning, and I'll tell him that."

"What?" Connell demanded when he hung up.

Lucas turned in the chair to face her. "The deaf guy who saw the plate—the translation got screwed up. The translator couldn't sign, or something. I looked at that report a half-dozen times, and I kept thinking, how could they screw that up? And I never went back and asked until tonight. The plate was SSA—ass backwards."

"I don't believe it."

"Believe it."

"It can't be that simple."

"Maybe not. But there are a thousand SSA plates out there, and two hundred and seventy-two of them are pickups. And what I got from the deaf guy sounded pretty good."

Anderson came in with two Styrofoam cups full of coffee. He sat down and started drinking alternately from the two cups. "You get the stuff?"

"They're faxing it to you."

"There oughta be a better way to do this," Anderson said. "Tie everything together. You oughta get your company to write some software."

"Yeah, yeah, let's go get it."

Greave, wearing jeans and T-shirt, caught up with them as they walked through the darkened hallways to Anderson's cubicle in homicide. Lucas explained to him as they walked along the hall. "So we'll look at everything Anderson can pump out of his databases. Looking for a cop, or anybody with a prison record, particularly for sex crimes or anything that resembles cat burglary."

AT FOUR O'CLOCK IN the morning, having found nothing at all, Lucas and Connell walked down to the coffee machine together.

"How're you feeling?"

"A little better today. Yesterday wasn't so good."

"Huh." They watched the coffee dribble into a cup, and Lucas didn't know quite what to say. So he said, "There's a lot more paper than I thought there'd be. I hope we can get through it."

"We will," Connell said. She sipped her coffee and watched Lucas's dribble into the second cup. "I can't believe you figured that out. I can't see how it occurred to you to check."

Lucas thought of Weather's ass, grinned, and said, "It sorta came to me."

"You know, when I first saw you, I thought you were a suit. You know, a *suit*," she said. "Big guy, kind of neat-looking in a jockstrap way, buys good suits, gets along with the ladies, backslaps the good old boys, and he cruises to the top."

"Change your mind?"

"Partially," she said. She said it pensively, as though it were an academic question. "I still think there might be some of that—but now I think that, in some ways, you're smarter than I am. Not a suit."

Lucas was embarrassed. "I don't think I'm smarter than you are," he mumbled.

"Don't take the compliment too seriously," Connell said dryly. "I said *in some ways*. In other ways, you're still a suit."

AT SIX O'CLOCK IN the morning, with the flat early light cutting sharp through the window like summer icicles, Greave looked up from a stack of paper, rubbed his reddened eyes, and said, "Here's something pretty interesting."

"Yeah?" Lucas looked up. They had seven possibilities, none particularly inspiring. One cop, one security guard.

"Guy named Robert Koop. He was a prison guard until six years ago. Drives a '92 Chevy S-10, red over white, no security agreement, net purchase price of $17,340."

"Sounds like a possibility," Connell said.

"If he was a prison guard, he probably doesn't have the big bucks," Greave said, as though he were thinking aloud. "He says he works at a gym called Two Guy's. . . ."

"I know the place," Lucas said.

"And he declares income of fifteen thousand a year since he left the prison. Where does he get off driving a new seventeen-thousand-dollar truck? And he paid cash, over a seven-thousand-dollar trade-in."

"Huh." Lucas came over to look at the printout, and Connell heaved herself out of her chair. "Lives in Apple Valley. Houses out there probably average what, one-fifty?"

"One-fifty for a house and a twenty-three-thousand-dollar truck is pretty good, on fifteen thousand a year."

"Probably skips lunch," Greave said.

"Several times a day," Lucas said. "Where's his license information?"

"Right here . . ." Greave folded over several sheets, found it.

"Five-ten, one-ninety," Lucas said. "Short and heavy."

"Maybe short and strong," Connell said. "Like our guy."

"What's his plate number?" Anderson called. His hands were playing across his keyboard. They had limited access to intelligence division's raw data files. Lucas read it off the title application, and Anderson punched it into the computer.

A second later he said, surprise in his voice, "Jesus, we got a hit."

"What?" This was the first they'd had. Lucas and Connell drifted over to Anderson to look over his shoulder. When the file came up, they found a long list of license plates picked up outside Steve's Fireside City. Intelligence believed that the stove and fireplace store was a front for a fence, but never got enough to make an arrest.

"High-level fence," Lucas said, reading between the lines of the intelligence report. "Somebody who would be moving jewelry, Rolexes, that kind of thing. No stereos or VCRs."

"Maybe he was buying a fireplace," Greave said.

"Couldn't afford one, after the truck," Lucas said. He took his phone book out of his coat pocket, thumbed through it. "Tommy Smythe, Tommy . . ." He picked up a telephone and dialed, and a moment later said, "Mrs. Smythe? This is Lucas Davenport, Minneapolis Police. Sorry to bother you, but I need to talk to Tommy . . . Oh, jeez, I'm sorry . . . Yeah, thanks." He scribbled a new number in the notebook.

"Divorced," he said to Connell.

"Who is he?"

"Deputy warden at Stillwater. We went to school together . . . He's another suit." He dialed again, waited. "Tommy? Lucas Davenport. Yeah, I know what time it is, I've been up all night. Do you remember a guard out at Stillwater, six years ago, named Robert Koop? Resigned?"

Smythe, his voice rusty with sleep, remembered. ". . . never caught him, but there wasn't any doubt. He was snitched out by two different guys who didn't know each other. We told him we were ready to bring him up on charges; either that, or get out. He got. Our case wasn't strong enough to just to go ahead."

"Okay. Any rumors about sex problems?"

"Nothing that I know of."

"Any connection with burglars?"

"Jeez, I can't remember all the details, but yeah. I think the main guy he was dealing to was Art McClatchey, who was a big-time burglar years ago. He fucked up and killed an old lady in one of his burglaries, got caught. That was down in Afton."

"Cat burglar?" Lucas asked.

"Yeah. Why?"

"Look, anything you can get from records, connecting the two of them, we'd appreciate. Don't go out in the population, though. Don't ask any questions. We're trying to keep all this tight."

"Do I want to know why you're asking?" Smythe asked.

"Not yet."

"We're not gonna get burned, are we?"

"I don't see how," Lucas said. "If there's any chance, I'll give you a ring."

Lucas hung up and said to the others, "He was selling dope to the inmates. Cocaine and speed. One of his main contacts was an old cat burglar named McClatchey."

"Better and better," Connell said. "Now what?"

"We finish the records, just in case we find another candidate. Then we talk to Roux. We want to take a close look at this Koop. But do it real easy."

THEY FINISHED WITH eleven possibilities, but Robert Koop was the good one. They put together a file of information from the various state licensing bureaus—car registration, driver's license, an old Washington County carry permit—with what they could get from Department of Revenue and the personnel section of the Department of Revenue.

When he'd worked at Stillwater, Koop had lived in Lakeland. A check with the property tax department in Washington County showed the house where Koop lived was owned by a Lakeland couple; Koop was apparently a renter. A check on the Apple Valley house, through the Dakota County tax collector, suggested that the Apple Valley house was also rented. The current owner showed an address in California, and tax stamps showed a 1980 mortgage of $115,000.

"If the owner's carrying a mortgage of $115,000 . . . let's see, I'm carrying $80,000. Jeez, I can't see that he could be renting it for less than fifteen hundred a month," Greave said. "Koop's income is coming up short."

"Nothing much from the NCIC," Anderson said. "He shows prints from Stillwater, and another set from the Army. I'm working on getting his Army records."

The phone rang and Lucas picked it up, listened, said, "Thanks," and put it back down.

"Roux," he said to Connell. "She's in. Let's go talk."

THEY GOT SLOAN AND DEL to help out, and a panel truck with one-way windows, equipped with a set of scrambled radios from intelligence. Lucas and Connell rode together in her car; Sloan and Del took their own cars. Greave and O'Brien drove the truck. They met at a Target store parking lot and picked out a restaurant where they could wait.

"Connell and I'll take the first shift," Lucas said. "We can rotate out every couple of hours; somebody can cruise it while we're moving the truck to make the change . . . Let's give him a call now, see if he's around."

Connell called, got an answer, and asked for Mr. Clark in the paint department. "He's home," she said when she'd rung off the cellular phone. "He sounded sleepy."

"Let's go," Lucas said.

THEY CRUISED PAST Koop's house, a notably unexceptional place in a subdivision of carefully differentiated houses. They parked two blocks away and slightly above it. The lawn was neat but not perfect, with an artificially green look that suggested a lawn service. There was a single-door, two-car garage. The windows were covered with wooden blinds. There was no newspaper, either on the lawn or porch.

Lucas parked the truck and crawled between seats into the back, where there were two captain's chairs, an empty cooler, and a radio they wouldn't use. Connell was examining the house with binoculars.

"It looks awful normal," she said.

"He's not gonna have a billboard out front," Lucas said. "I had a guy, a few years ago, lived in a quadruplex. Everybody said he was a great neighbor. He probably was, except when he was out killing women."

"I remember that," Connell said. "The mad dog. You killed him."

"He needed it," Lucas said.

"How do you think you would've done in court? I mean, if he hadn't gotten shot?"

Lucas grinned slightly. "You mean, if I hadn't shot him to death . . . Actually, we had him cold. It was his second attack on the woman."

"Was he obsessed by her?"

"No, I think he was just pissed off. At me, actually. We were watching him, and somehow he figured it out, slipped the surveillance and went after her. It was almost . . . sarcastic. He was crazier than a shithouse mouse."

"We don't have that good a case on Koop."

"That's an understatement," Lucas said. "I've been worried about it."

. . .

THEY TALKED FOR A WHILE, slowly ran down. Nothing happened. After two hours, they drove around the block, traded vehicles with Sloan and O'Brien, and walked up to the restaurant and sat with Del and Greave.

"We're talking about going to the movies," Del said. "We all got beepers."

"I think we should stay put," Connell said anxiously.

"Say that after you've had fifteen cups of coffee," Greave said. "I'm getting tired of peeing."

Del and Greave took the next shift, then Lucas and Connell again. O'Brien had brought his *Penthouse* with him again, forgot it in the truck. Halfway through the shift, Connell fell to reading it and looking at the pictures, occasionally laughing. Lucas nervously looked elsewhere.

Del and Greave were back on when Koop started to move. Their beepers went off simultaneously, and everybody in the restaurant looked at them. "Doctors' convention," Sloan said to an openmouthed suburbanite as they left.

"What do you got, Del?" Lucas called.

"We got the garage door up," Del said. "Okay, we got the truck, a red-and-white Chevy. . . ."

THEY FIRST SAW KOOP when he got out of his truck at a Denny's restaurant.

"No beard," Connell said, examining him with the binoculars.

"There's been a lot of publicity since Hart," Lucas said. "He would've shaved. Two of the Miller witnesses said he was clean-shaven."

Koop parked in the lot behind the restaurant and walked inside. He walked with a spring, as though he were coiled. He was wearing jeans and T-shirt. He had a body like a rock.

"He's a lifter," Lucas said. "He's a goddamned gorilla."

"I can see him, he's in a front booth," Sloan said. "You want me inside?"

"Let me go in," Connell said.

"Hang on a minute," Lucas said. He called back to Sloan. "Is he by himself?"

"Yeah."

"Don't go in unless somebody hooks up with him. Otherwise, stand off." To Connell: "You better stay out of sight. If this drags out and we need to keep you close to Jensen, you gotta be a fresh face."

"Okay." She nodded.

Lucas went back to the radio. "Sloan, can he see his truck from where he's at?"

"No."

"We're gonna take a look," Lucas said. They'd pulled into a car wash. "Let's go," he said to Connell.

Connell crossed the street, pulled in next to Koop's truck. Lucas got out, looked across the roof of the car toward the truck, then got back inside.

"Jesus," he said.

"What?" She was puzzled. "Aren't you gonna look?"

"There's a pack of Camels on the dashboard."

"What?" Like she didn't understand.

"Unfiltered Camels," he said.

Connell looked at Lucas, eyes wide. "Oh my God," she breathed. "It's him."

Lucas went to the radio. "Sloan, everybody, listen up. We sorta have a confirmation on this guy. Stay cool but stay back. We're gonna need some technical support. . . ."

THEY TRACKED KOOP while they talked at police headquarters, laying out the case. Thomas Troy, of the county attorney's criminal division, declared that there wasn't enough, yet, to pick him up.

He and Connell, sitting in Roux's office with Roux and Lucas and Mickey Green, another assistant county attorney, ran down the evidence:

—The woman killed in Iowa told a friend that her date was a cop. But Koop never was, said Troy.

—Hillerod saw him in Madison, said Koop recognized his prison tattoo, Connell said. Sounds like ESP, Troy said, and ESP doesn't work on the witness stand. Besides, Hillerod can't remember what he looked like, Green said, and Hillerod's just been arrested for a whole series of heavy felonies, along with a parole violation, and has a long criminal record. The defense will claim he'll tell us anything we want to get a deal. And, in fact, we've already negotiated a deal.

—He was seen dumping a body by two witnesses, Connell said, who described both him and his truck. The witnesses' descriptions conflict, even on the matter of the truck, Troy said. They saw the guy at night at a distance. One of them is an admitted crack dealer, and the other guy hangs around with a crack dealer.

—Camels, said Connell. There are probably fifty thousand Camel smokers in the Cities. And probably most of them drive trucks, Troy said.

—Shape was right for the man who attacked Evan Hart—big and muscular. *Tall*, big, and muscular, is what the witnesses said, Troy replied. Koop is distinctly short. Besides, the attack on Hart isn't necessarily related to the attacks on the women. The man who attacked Hart had a beard and wore glasses. Koop is clean-shaven, shows no glasses requirement on his driver's license, and wasn't wearing glasses that morning. The witnesses hadn't been able to pick his photo out of a display.

"You're working against us," Connell fumed.

"Bullshit," said Troy. "I'm just outlining an elementary defense. A good defense attorney will tear up everything you've got. We need one hard thing. Just one. Just get me one, and we'll take him down."

KOOP SPENT THE FIRST DAY of surveillance in his truck, driving long complicated routes around the Cities, apparently aimlessly. He stopped at Two Guy's gym, was inside for two hours, then moved on, stopping only to eat at fast-food joints, and once to get gas.

"I think he must've made us," Del called on one of the scrambled radios as they sat stalled in traffic on I-94 between Minneapolis and St. Paul. "Unless he's nuts."

"We know he's nuts," Connell said. "The question is, what's he doing?"

"He's not scouting," Lucas said from a third car. "He's moving too fast to be scouting. And he never goes back. He just drives. He doesn't seem to know where he's going—he's always getting caught in those circles and dead ends."

"Well, we gotta do something," Del said. " 'Cause if he hasn't made us yet, he will. He'll get us up in some of those suburban switchbacks and we'll bump into him one too many times. Where in the hell is tech support?"

"We're here," the tech-support guy said on the radio. "You stop the sono-fabitch, and we'll tag him."

At three o'clock, Koop stopped at a Perkins restaurant and took a booth. While Lucas and Connell watched from outside, Henry Ramirez from intelligence slipped under Koop's truck and hooked up a remote-controlled battery-powered transmitter, and placed a flat, battery-powered infrared flasher in the center of the topper. If Koop climbed on top of the truck, he'd see it. Otherwise, it was invisible, and the truck could be unmistakably tracked at night, from the air.

AT NINE O'CLOCK, in the last dying light of the day, Koop wandered out of the web of roads around Lake Minnetonka and headed east toward Minneapolis. They no longer had a lead car. Leading had proven impossible. The trailing cars were all well back. The radio truck followed silently, with the tracking plane doing all the work. From the air, the spotter, using infrared glasses, said Koop was clear all the way, and tracked him street by street into the Cities.

"He's going for Jensen," Lucas said to Connell as he followed the track on a map.

"I don't know where I am anymore."

"We're coming up on the lakes." Lucas called out to the others: "We're breaking off, we'll be at Jensen's."

He called ahead to Jensen's, but there was no answer at her phone. He called dispatch and got the number for the resident manager: "We've got a problem and we need a little help. . . ."

THE MANAGER WAS WAITING by the open door of the parking garage, the door open. Lucas pulled inside and dumped the car in a handicapped space.

"What do you want me to do?" the manager asked, handing him a key to Jensen's apartment.

"Nothing," Lucas said. "Go on back to your apartment. We'd like you near a telephone. Just wait. Please don't go out in the hallway."

To Connell: "If he comes up, we've got him. If we get him inside Jensen's place, that ties him to the stalking and the Camels on the air conditioner across the street. And the knife attack ties him to the other killings and the Camel we found on Wannemaker."

"You think he'll come up?" She asked as they hurried to the elevators.

"I hope so. Jesus, I hope so. That'd be it." At Jensen's apartment, they let themselves in, and Lucas turned on one light, slipped his .45 out of his shoulder holster and checked it.

"WHAT'S HE DOING?" Lucas asked.

"Moving very slowly, but he's moving," the spotter called. "Now, now, we've lost him, he's under some trees or some shit, wait, I got a flash, I see him again, now he's gone. . . ."

"I see him," Del called. "I'm parked in the bike shop lot, and he's coming this way. He's moving faster, but he's under trees, he'll be out in a sec. . . ."

"Got him," the spotter said. "He's going around the block again. Slowing down . . ."

"Real slow," Del called. "I'm on the street, walking, he's right in front of the apartment, real slow, almost stopped. No, there he goes. . . ."

"He's outa here," the spotter called a minute later. "He's heading into the loop."

"Did he see you, Del?"

"No way."

Connell said, "Well, shit. . . ."

"Yeah." Lucas felt like a deflated balloon. He walked twice around the room. "Goddamnit," he said. "Goddamnit. What's wrong with the guy? Why didn't he come up?"

Koop continued through downtown to a bar near the airport, where he drank three solitary beers, paid, bought a bottle at the liquor store down the street, and drove back to his house. The last light went off a few minutes after two o'clock.

Lucas went home. Weather was asleep. He patted her affectionately on the ass before he went down himself.

KOOP RESUMED THE DRIVING the next day, trailing through the suburbs east and south of St. Paul. They tracked him until one o'clock in the afternoon, when he stopped at a Wendy's. Lucas went on down the block to a McDonald's. Feeling dried out, older, bored, he got a double cheeseburger, a sack of fries, and a malt, and ambled back to the car, where Connell was eating carrot sticks out of a Tupperware box.

"George Beneteau called yesterday, while we were out," Connell said when they'd run out of everything else to talk about.

"Oh, yeah?" She had a talent for leaving him short of words.

"He left a message on my machine. He wants to go out and get a steak, or something."

"What'd you do?"

"Nothing." She said it flatly. "I can't deal with it. I guess tomorrow I'll give him a call and explain."

Lucas shook his head and pushed fries into his face, hoping that she wouldn't start crying again.

She didn't. But a while later, as they escorted Koop across the Lake Street bridge, Connell said, "That TV person, Jan Reed. You guys seem pretty friendly."

"I'm friendly with a lot of media," Lucas said uncomfortably.

"I mean friendly-friendly," she said.

"Oh, not really."

"Mmm," she said.

"Mmm, what?" Lucas asked.

"I'd think a very long time. This is one of those things where, you know— I suspect you're just a suit."

"Not quite bright," he said.

"Took the words out of my mouth," Connell said.

KOOP STOPPED AT A Firestone store but just sat in the truck. The surveillance van, watching him from a Best Buy store parking lot, said he seemed to be looking at a Denny's restaurant across the street.

"He ate less than an hour ago," Lucas said. They were a block away, parked in front of a used-car lot, a bit conspicuous. "Let's go look at some cars."

They got out and walked into the lot, where they could watch Koop through the windows of a used Buick. After ten minutes in the Firestone lot, Koop started the truck, rolled it across the street to the Denny's and went inside.

"He's looking for surveillance," Lucas said. On the radio: "Del, could you get in there?"

"On my way . . ." Then, a few seconds later, "Shit, he's coming back out. I'm turning around."

Koop walked out with a cup of coffee. Lucas caught Connell's arm as she started toward the car, and brought the radio to his face. "We're gonna stay here a minute; you guys tag him. Hey, Harvey?"

Harvey ran the surveillance van. "Yeah?"

"Could you put a video on the front of that Denny's see who else comes out?"

"You got it."

"He wasn't in there long enough," Lucas said to Connell. "He talked to somebody. Not long enough for a friend, so it must have been business."

"Unless his friend wasn't there," Connell said.

"He was *too* long for that. . . ." A moment later he said, "Here we go. Oh, shit, Harvey, cover that guy, you remember him?"

"I don't . . ."

"Just Plain Schultz," Lucas said.

Del, on the radio, from tracking Koop: *"Our* Just Plain Schultz?"

"Absolutely," Lucas said.

Schultz got in a red Camaro and carefully backed out of his parking slot. "C'mon," Lucas said to Connell, hustling her down to the car.

"Who is he?"

"Fence. Very careful."

In the car, Lucas tagged a half-block behind Schultz and called in a squad. "Just pull him over to the curb," he told the squad. "And stand by."

The squad picked Schultz up at the corner, stopped him halfway down the block, under a bright-green maple. Lucas and Connell passed them, pulled to the curb. A kid on a tricycle watched from the sidewalk, the flashing lights, the cop standing inside his open door. Schultz was watching the cop in his rearview mirror and didn't see Lucas coming from the front, until Lucas was right on top of him.

"Schultzie," Lucas said, leaning over the window, his hands on the roof. "How you been, my man?"

"Aw, fuck, what do you want, Davenport?" Schultz, shocked, tried to cover.

"Whatever you just bought from Koop," Lucas said.

Schultz was a small man with a round, blemished face. He had dark whiskers a razor couldn't quite control. His eyes were slightly protuberant, and when Lucas said "Koop," they seemed to bug out a bit farther.

"I can't believe *that* crazy motherfucker belongs to you," Schultz said after a moment, popping the door to get out of the car.

"He doesn't, actually," Lucas said. Connell was standing on the other side of the car, her hand in her purse.

"Who's the puss?" Schultz asked, tipping his head toward her.

"State cop," Lucas said. "And is that any way to talk about the government?"

"Fuck you, Davenport," Schultz said, leaning back against the car's front fender. "So what're we doing? Do I call a lawyer, or what?"

"Schultzie. . . ." Lucas said, spreading his arms wide.

"That's just plain Schultz," Schultz said.

THOMAS TROY WORE A blue military sweater over jeans. He looked neat but tough, like a lieutenant colonel in the paratroops. He was shaking his head.

"We don't have enough on the killings, by themselves, even with him cruising Jensen's place. We could fake it, though, and put him away."

"Like how?" Roux asked. "What do you suggest?"

"We take him on the burglary charges. We've got enough from Schultz to get a conviction on those. And we've got enough on the burglary charges to get search warrants for the truck and the house. If we don't find anything on the murders or his stalking Jensen, well—we got him on the burglaries, and in the pre-sentencing report, we let the judge know we think he's tied in to the murders. If we get the right judge, we can get an upward departure on the sentence and keep him inside for five or six years."

"Five or six years?" Connell came up out of her chair.

"Sit down," Troy snapped. She sat down. "If you get anything in the search, then there're more possibilities. If we find evidence of more burglaries, we'll get a couple of more years. If we get evidence that he's stalking Jensen, then we get another trial and go for a few more. And if there's anything that would suggest the murders—any tiny little thing more than what you've got—we could set up the murder trials to go at the end of the sequence, and maybe the publicity from the first two will put him away on the others."

"We're really betting on the come," Lucas said.

"All you need is a few hairs from Wannemaker or Marcy Lane, and with the circumstantial stuff you've got, that'd be enough," Troy said. "If you can give me *anything*—a weapon, a hair, a couple drops of blood, a print—we'd go with it."

Connell looked at Lucas, then Roux. "If we stay with him, we might see him approach somebody."

"What if he kills her the second they're in the truck?" Roux asked.

Lucas shook his head. "He doesn't always do that. Wannemaker had ligature marks on her wrists. He kept her a while, maybe a day, and messed with her."

"Didn't mess with Marcy Lane. He couldn't have had her more than an hour," Connell said grimly.

"We can't take that chance," Roux said. "We'd be crazy to take that chance."

"I don't know," Troy said. "If he even showed a knife—that'd be the ball-game."

"So we should wait?"

Lucas looked at Connell, then shook his head. "I think we should take him."

"Why?" Connell asked. "Getting him for five or six years, if we're lucky?"

"We've only been watching him for two days and a night. What if he's got somebody down his basement right now? What if he goes in the house and kills her while we're sitting outside? We know that he kept at least one of them for a while."

Connell swallowed, and Roux straightened and said, "If that's a possibility . . ."

"It's a very remote possibility," Lucas said.

"I don't care how remote," Roux said. "Take him now."

KOOP WAS IN MODIGLIANI'S Wine & Spirits off Lyndale Avenue when the cops got him. His arm was actually in the cold box, pulling out a six-pack of Budweiser, when a red-faced man in a cheap gray suit said, "Mr. Koop?" Koop realized a large black man had stepped to his elbow, and a uniformed cop was standing by the door. They'd appeared as if by magic; as if they had a talent for it, popping out of nowhere.

Koop said, "Yeah?" And straightened up. His heart beat a little faster.

"Mr. Koop, we're Minneapolis police officers," the red-faced man said. "We're placing you under arrest."

"What for?"

Koop stood flat-footed, hands in front of him, forcing himself to be still. But his back and arm muscles were twitching, ready to go. He'd thought about this possibility, at night, when he was waiting to go to sleep, or watching television. He'd thought about it a lot, a favorite nightmare.

Resisting a cop could bring a heavier charge than anything else they might have on you. In the joint, they warned you that if the cops really wanted you, and you gave them a chance, they just might blow you away. Of course, it was mostly the spooks that said that. White guys didn't see it the same way. But everybody agreed on one thing: your best shot was a decent defense attorney.

The red-faced cop said, "I think you know."

"I don't know," Koop protested. "You're making a mistake. You've got the wrong guy." He glanced toward the door. Maybe he *should* make a run for it. The red-faced guy didn't look like that much. The black guy he could outrun, and he'd take the guy at the door like a bowling pin. He had the power . . . but he didn't know what was outside. And these guys were armed. He sensed the cops were waiting for something, were looking at him for a decision. Everything in the store was needle-sharp, the rows of brown liquor bottles and green plastic jugs of mix, stacks of beer cans, the tops of potato chip bags, the black-and-white checkered tiles on the floor. Koop tensed, felt the cops pull into themselves. They were ready for him, and not particularly scared.

"Turn around, please, and place your hands on the top of the cooler," Redface said. Koop heard him as though from a distance. But there was a hardness in the guy's voice. Maybe he couldn't take them. Maybe they'd beat the shit out of him. And he didn't know yet what he was being arrested for. If it wasn't too serious, if it was buying cocaine, then resisting would bring him more trouble than the charge.

"Turn around. . . ." Peremptory this time. Koop gave the door a last look, then let out a breath and turned.

The cop patted him down, quickly but thoroughly. Koop had done it often enough at Stillwater to appreciate the professionalism.

"Drop your hands behind you, please. We're going to put handcuffs on, Mr. Koop, just as a precaution." The red-faced man was crisp and polite, the prefight tension gone now.

The black cop said, "You have the right to see an attorney. . . ."

"I want a lawyer," Koop said, interrupting the Miranda. The cuffs closed over his wrists and he instinctively flexed against them, pushing down a spasm of what felt like claustrophobia, not being able to move. The red-faced cop took him by the elbow and pivoted him, while the other finished the Miranda.

"I want a lawyer," Koop said. "Right now. You're making a mistake, and I'm gonna sue your butts."

"Sure. Step over this way, we'll go out to the car," the red-faced cop said.

They walked down a row of potato chips and bean dip and the black cop said, "Jesus, you sound like some kind of parrot. Polly want a lawyer?" but he grinned, friendly. His hand was hard on Koop's triceps.

"I want a lawyer." In the joint they said that after they warn you, the cops'll get friendly, try to get you talking about anything. After they get you rolling, when you're trying to make them happy— because you're a little scared, you don't want to get whacked around—then you'll start talking. Don't talk, they said in the joint. Don't say shit except "I want a lawyer."

They went out the door, a customer and the counterman gawking at them, and the red-faced man said, "My name is Detective Kershaw and the man behind you is Detective Carrigan, the famous Irish dancer. We'll need your keys to tow your truck, or we could just pop the tranny and tow it."

Two squad cars were nosed into the parking lot, one blocking the truck, four more cops standing by. Too many for a routine coke bust, Koop thought. "Keys are in my right side pocket," Koop said. He desperately wanted to know why he'd been arrested. Burglary? Murder? Something to do with Jensen?

"Hey, he can talk," the black cop said.

He slapped Koop on the shoulder in a comradely way, and they stopped while the red-faced cop took his keys out and tossed them to a patrolman and said, "Tow truck is on its way." To Koop, Kershaw said, "That black car over there."

While they opened the back door of the car, Koop said, "I don't know why I'm arrested." He couldn't help it, couldn't keep his mouth shut. The open back door of the car looked like a hungry mouth. "Why?"

Carrigan said, "Watch your head," and he put a hand on top of Koop's head and eased him into the car, and then said, "Why do you think?" and shut the door.

The two detectives spent a few minutes talking to the uniformed cops, letting Koop stew in the backseat of the car. The back doors had no inside handles, no way to get out. With his hands pinned behind him, he couldn't sit easily, had to sit upright on the too-soft seats. And the backseat smelled faintly of disinfectant and urine. Koop felt another spasm of claustrophobic panic, something he hadn't expected. The damn cuffs: he twisted against them, hard, gritting his teeth; no chance. The cops outside were still not looking at him. He was an insect. Why in the hell. . . .

And then Koop thought, *Softening me up.*

He'd done the same thing when there was a prison squabble that they had to look into. When the cops got back into the car, one of them would look at him, friendly-like, and ask, "Well, what do you think?"

The plainclothes cops spent another minute talking to the uniforms, then drifted back to the car, talking to each other, as if Koop were the last thing on their minds. A screen divided the front seat from the back. The black guy drove, and after he started the engine he looked at his partner in the passenger seat and said, "Let's stop at a Taco Bell."

"Oooh, good call." When they got going, the red-faced guy turned and grinned and said, "Well, what do you think?"

"I want a lawyer," Koop said. The red-faced guy pulled back a quarter inch on the other side of the screen, his eyes going dark. He couldn't help it, and Koop almost smiled. He could play this game, he thought.

LUCAS AND CONNELL WATCHED the arrest from a Super America station across the street, leaning on Connell's car, eating ice cream sandwiches. Koop came out, Kershaw a step behind, with one hand on Koop's right elbow. "I wanted to take him," Connell said between bites.

"Not for burglary," Lucas said.

"No." She looked at her watch. "The search warrants should be ready."

Carrigan and Kershaw were pushing Koop into the car. Koop's arms were flexed, and his muscles stood out like ropes. Lucas balled up the ice cream sandwich wrapper and fired it at a trash can; it bounced off onto the pavement.

"I want to get down to the house," Connell said. "See you there?"

"Yeah. I'll wait until they open the truck—I'll let you know if there's anything good."

LUCAS WANTED CRIME-SCENE PEOPLE to open the truck. "We might be talking about a couple of hairs," he told the patrolman with the keys. "Let's wait."

"Okay. Who was that guy?" the patrolman asked.

"Cat burglar," Lucas said. "He sure went nice and easy."

"He scared the shit out of me," the patrolman confessed, his eyes drifting back toward the store. "I was in the door and he looked over toward me, like he was gonna run. He had crazy eyes, man. He was right on the edge of flipping out. Did you see his arms? I wouldn't have wanted to fight the sonofabitch."

Crime scene arrived five minutes later. A half-carton of unfiltered Camels sat on the front seat. A bag of mixed salt and sand, jumper cables, a toolbox, and other junk occupied the back.

Lucas poked carefully through it but found nothing. He pulled the keys Koop had produced. There were two truck keys, what looked like two house keys, and a fifth one. Jensen's maybe. But it didn't look new enough. They'd have to check.

"Got a nice set of burglary tools back here," one of the crime-scene guys said. Lucas walked around to the back of the truck, where they'd carefully opened the toolbox. Unfortunately, burglary tools were nothing more than a slightly unusual selection of ordinary tools. You had to prove the burglary first. The crime-scene guy picked up a small metal-file and looked at it with a magnifying glass, just like Sherlock Holmes.

"Got some brass," he said.

"That'll help," Lucas said. Koop was cutting his own keys, by hand. "Anything like a knife? Any rope?"

"No."

"Goddamnit. Well, close it up and take it down," Lucas said, disappointed. "We want everything—prints, hair, skin, fluid. Everything."

LUCAS DROPPED THE PORSCHE at the curb and started up the driveway to Koop's house. The front and side doors were open, and two unmarked vans sat in the driveway, along with Connell's anonymous gray Chevy. Lucas was almost to the front steps when he saw two neighborhood women walking down the street, one of them pushing a baby buggy. Lucas walked back toward them.

"Hello," he said.

The woman pushing the buggy had her hair in curlers, covered with a rayon scarf. The other one had dishwater-blonde hair with streaks of copper through it. They stopped. "Are you police?" Neighbors always knew.

"Yes. Have you seen Mr. Koop recently?"

"What'd he do?" asked the copper-streaked one. The kid in the buggy was sucking on a blue pacifier, looking fixedly at Lucas with pale-blue eyes.

"He's been arrested in connection with a burglary," Lucas said.

"Told you," Copper Streak said to Hair Curler. To Lucas, she said, "We always knew he was a criminal."

"Why? What'd he do?"

"Never got up in the morning," she said. "You'd hardly ever see him at all. Sometimes, when he put his garbage out. That was it. He was never in his yard. His garage door would go up, always in the afternoon, and he'd drive away. Then he'd come back in the middle of the night, like three o'clock in the morning, and the garage door would go up, and he'd be inside. You *never* saw him. The only time I ever saw him, except for garbage, was that Halloween snowstorm a couple of years ago. He came out and shoveled his driveway. After that, he always had a service do it."

"Did he have a beard?"

Copper Streak looked at Hair Curler, and they both looked back at Lucas. "Sure. He's always had one."

One more thing, Lucas thought. They talked for another minute, then Lucas broke away and went inside.

Connell was in the kitchen, scribbling notes on a yellow pad.

"Anything?" Lucas asked.

"Not much. How about the truck?"

"Nothing so far. No weapon?"

"Kitchen knives. But this guy isn't using a kitchen knife. I'd be willing to bet on it."

"I just talked to a couple of neighbors," Lucas said. "They say he's always had a beard."

"Huh." Connell pursed her lips. "That's interesting . . . C'mere, down the basement." Lucas followed her down a short flight of stairs off the kitchen. The basement was finished. To the left, through an open door, Lucas could see a washer, dryer, laundry sink, and a water heater, sitting on a tiled floor. The furnace would be back here too, out of sight. The larger end of the basement was carpeted with a seventies-era two-tone shag. A couch, a chair, and a coffee table with a lamp pressed against the walls. The center of the rug was dominated by a plastic painter's drop cloth, ten feet by about thirteen or fourteen, laid flat on the rug. A technician was vacuuming around the edges of the drop cloth.

"Was that plastic sheet like that?" Lucas asked.

"No. I put it there," Connell said. "C'mere and look at the windows."

The windows were blacked out with sheets of quarter-inch plywood. "I went outside and looked," Connell said. "He's painted the outside of them black, so unless you get down on your knees and look into the window wells, it just looks like the basement is dark. He went to a lot of trouble with it: the edges are caulked."

"Yeah?"

"Yeah." She looked down the sheet. "I think this is where he killed Wannemaker. On a piece of plastic. There're a couple of three-packs of drop cloths in the utility room. One of them is unopened. The other one only had one cloth in it. I was walking around down here, and it looked to me like the rug was matted in a rectangle. Then I noticed the furniture: it's set up to look at something in the middle of the rug. When I saw the drop cloths . . ." She shrugged. "I laid it out, and it fit perfectly."

"Jesus . . ." Lucas looked at the tech. "Anything?"

The tech nodded and said, "A ton of shit: I don't think the rug's ever been cleaned, and it must've been installed fifteen years ago. It's gonna be a goddamned nightmare, sorting everything out."

"Well, it's something, anyway," Lucas said.

"There's one other thing," Connell said. "Up in the bedroom."

Lucas followed her back up the stairs. Koop's bedroom was spare, almost military, though the bed was unmade and smelled of sweat. Lucas saw it right away: on the chest of drawers, a bottle of Opium.

Lucas: "You didn't touch it?"

"Not yet. But it wouldn't make any difference."

"Jensen said he took it from her place. If her fingerprints are on it . . ."

"I called her. Her bottle was a half-ounce. She always gets herself a half-ounce at Christmas because it lasts almost exactly a year."

Lucas peered at the perfume bottle: a quarter-ounce. "She's sure?"

"She's sure. Damnit, I thought we had him."

"We should check it anyway," Lucas said. "Maybe she's wrong."

"Yeah, we'll check—but she was sure. Which brings up the question, why Opium? Does he obsess on the perfume? Does the perfume attract him somehow? Or did he go out and buy some of his own, to remind him of Jensen?"

"Huh," Lucas said.

"Well? Is it the perfume or the woman?" She looked at him, expecting to pull a rabbit out of a hat. Maybe he could. Lucas closed his eyes. After a moment, he said, "It's because Jensen uses it. He's creeping into her apartment in the dark, goes into her bedroom, and something sets him off. The perfume. Or maybe seeing her there. But the perfume really brings it back to him. It's possible, if he's really freaked out, that he used everything in the bottle he stole from her."

"Do you think it's enough? The beard being shaved, and the perfume bottle?"

He shook his head. "No. We've got to find something. One thing."

Connell moved around until she was looking straight into Lucas's eyes from no more than two feet. Her face was waxy, pale, like a dinner candle. "I was sick again this morning. In two weeks, I won't be able to walk. I'll be back in chemo, I'll start shedding hair. I won't be able to think straight."

"Jesus, Meagan. . . ."

"I want the sonofabitch, Lucas," she said. "I don't want to be dead in a hole and have him walking around laughing. You know he's the one, I know he's the one."

"So?"

"So we gotta talk. We gotta figure something out."

31

KOOP GOT OUT OF JAIL a few minutes after noon, blinking in the bright sunshine, his lawyer walking behind, a sport coat over his shoulder, talking.

Koop was very close to the edge. He felt as though he had a large crack in his head, that it was about to split in half, that a wet gray worm would spill out, a worm the size of a vacuum-cleaner hose.

He didn't like jail. He didn't like it at all.

"Remember, not a thing to anybody, okay?" the lawyer said, shaking his finger into the air. He'd learned not to shake it at his clients: one had almost pulled it off. He was repeating the warning for at least the twentieth time, and Koop nodded for the twentieth time, not hearing him. He was looking around at the outdoors, feeling the tension falling away, as though he were coming unwrapped, like a mummy getting its sheet pulled.

Jesus. His head was really out of control. "Okay."

"There's nothing you can say to the cops that would help you. Nothing. If you want to talk to somebody, talk to me, and if it's important, I'll talk to them. Okay?"

"No deals," Koop said. "I don't want to hear about no fuckin' deals."

"Is there any chance you can find the guy who sold you the stuff?" The lawyer looked like a mailman on PCP. Ordinary enough, but everything in his face too tight, too stretched. And though each of his words was enunciated clearly, there were far too many of them, spoken too quickly, a torrent of "I thinks" and "Maybe we'd bests." Koop couldn't keep up with them all, and had begun ignoring them. "What do you think, huh? Any chance you could find him? Any chance?"

Koop finally heard him, and shrugged, and said, "Maybe. But what should I do if I find him? Call the cops?"

"No-no. Nuh-nuh-no. No. No. You call me. You don't talk to the cops." The lawyer's eyes were absolutely flat, like old pasteboard poker chips. Koop suspected he didn't believe a word of his story.

Koop had told him that he bought the diamond cross and the matching earrings from a white boy—literally a boy, a teenager—wearing a Minnesota National Guard fatigue shirt, who hung around the Duck Inn, in Hopkins. The kid had a big bunch of dark hair and an earring, Koop had said. He said he bought the brooch and earrings for $200. The kid knew he was getting ripped off, but didn't know what else to do with them.

"How do we explain that you sold them to Schultz?" the attorney had asked.

Koop had said, "Hell, everybody knows Schultz. The cops call him Just Plain Schultz. If you've got something you want to sell, and you're not quite sure where it came from, you talk to Schultz. If I was really a smart burglar like the cops said, I sure as shit would never have gone to him. He's practically on their payroll."

The attorney had looked at him for a long time, and then said, "Okay. Okay. Okay. So you've been out of steady work since the recession started, except for this gig at the gym, and you saw a chance to pick up a few bucks, took it, and now you're sorry. Okay?"

That had been fine with Koop.

Now, with the lawyer following him out of the jail, babbling, Koop put his hands over his ears, pushed his head together. The lawyer stepped back, asked, "Are you all right?"

"Don't like that place," Koop said, looking back over his shoulder.

KOOP HURT. ALMOST EVERY muscle in his body hurt. He could handle the first part of the detention. He could handle the bend-over-and-spread-'em. But he could feel his blood draining away the closer he got to a cell. They'd had to urge him inside the cell, prod him, and once inside, the door locked, he'd sat for a moment, the fear climbing up into his throat.

"Motherfucker," he'd said aloud, looking at the corners of the cells. Everything was so close. And pushing in.

He could have gone over the edge at that moment. Instead, he started doing sit-ups, push-ups, bridges, deep knee bends, toe-raises, push-offs, leg lifts. He did step-ups onto the bunk until his legs quit. He'd never worked so hard in his life; he didn't stop until his muscles simply quit on him. Then he slept; he dreamed of boxes with hands and holes with teeth. He dreamed of bars. When he woke up, he started working again.

Halfway through the next morning, they'd taken him down to his lawyer. The lawyer'd said the cops had his truck, had searched his house. "Is this charge the only thing you see coming? The only thing, the only thing?" he'd asked. He seemed a bit puzzled. "The cops are all over you. All over you. This charge—this is minor shit. Minor shit."

"Nothing else I know of," Koop said. But he thought, *Shit.* Maybe they knew something else.

The lawyer met him again at the courthouse, for the arraignment. He waived a preliminary hearing at the advice of the lawyer. The arraignment was quick, routine: five thousand dollars bail, the bail bondsman right there to take the assignment of his truck.

"Don't fuck with the truck," Koop said to the bail bondsman. "I'll be coming to you with the cash, as soon as I get it."

"Yeah, sure," the bondsman said. He said it negligently. He'd heard all this too many times.

"Don't fuck with it," Koop snarled.

The bondsman didn't like Koop's tone, and opened his mouth to say something smart, but then he saw Koop's eyes and understood that he was a very short distance from death. He said, "We won't touch it," and he meant it. Koop turned away, and the bondsman swallowed and wondered why they'd let an animal like that out of jail once they had him in.

KOOP HAD NOT DECIDED what to do. Not exactly. But he knew for sure that he wouldn't be going back to jail. He couldn't handle that. Jail was death. There would be no deals, nothing that would put him inside.

There was an excellent chance he'd be acquitted, his attorney said: the state's case seemed to be based entirely on Schultz's testimony. "In fact, I'm surprised they bothered to arrest you. Surprised," the attorney said.

If he was convicted, though, Koop'd have to do some small amount of time—certainly not a year, although technically he could get six years. After the conviction, the state would continue bail through a presentencing investigation. He'd be free for at least another month. . . .

But if he was convicted, Koop knew, he'd be gone. Mexico. Canada. Alaska. Somewhere. No more jail. . . .

THE ATTORNEY HAD TOLD HIM where he could get the truck. "I checked, and they're finished with it." He needed the truck. The truck was *his*, gave him security. But what if the cops had him on some kind of watch list? What if they tagged him to the bank, where he had his stash? He needed to get at the stash, for the money to pay the bondsman.

Wait, wait, wait. . . .

The trial wasn't even going to be for a month. He didn't have to do anything in the next fifteen minutes. If they were watching him, he'd spot it. Unless they'd bugged the truck. Koop put his hands to his head and pushed: holding it together.

HE GOT THE TRUCK BACK—it was all routine, clerical, the bureaucrats didn't give a shit, as long as you had the paper—and drove to his house. Two of the neighborhood cunts were walking on the street and stepped up on a lawn when they saw him coming, wrenching a baby buggy up on the grass with them.

Bitches, he mouthed at them.

He pushed the button on the garage-door opener when he was still a half-block away, and rolled straight into the garage stall, the door dropping behind him. He took ten minutes to walk around the house. The cops had been all over the place. Things were moved, and hadn't been put back quite right. Nothing was trashed. Nothing was missing, as far as he could tell. The basement looked untouched.

He walked through the front room. An armchair sat facing the television. "Cocksucker," he screamed. He kicked the side of it, and the fabric caved in. Koop, breathing hard, looked around the room, at the long wall reaching down toward the bedrooms. Sheetrock. A slightly dirty, inoffensive beige. "Cocksucker," he screamed at it. He hit the wall with his fist; the sheetrock caved in, a hole like a crater on the moon. "Cocksucker." Struck again, another hole. "Cocksucker . . ."

Screaming, punching, he moved sideways down the hall, stopped only when he was at the end of it, looked back. Nine holes, fist-size, shoulder height. And pain. Dazed, he looked at his hand: the knuckles were a pulp of blood. He put the knuckles to his mouth, licked them off, sucked on them. Tasted good, the blood.

Breathing hard, blowing like a horse, Koop staggered back to the bedroom, sucking his knuckles as he went.

In the bedroom, the first thing he saw was the bottle of Opium, sitting on the chest. He unscrewed the top, sniffed it, closed his eyes, saw her.

White nightgown, black triangle, full lips . . .

Koop put some Opium on his fingertips, dabbed it under his nose, stood swaying with his eyes closed, just visiting. . . .

Finally, with the dreamlike odor of Sara Jensen playing with his mind, and the pain in his hand helping to reorder it, he got a flashlight and went back out to the garage. He began working through the truck, inch by inch, bolt by bolt, sucking his knuckles when the blood got too thick. . . .

32

LUCAS HOVERED IN THE men's accessories, next to the cologne, behind a rotating rack of wallets, keeping the top of Koop's head in sight. He carried a fat leather briefcase. Koop loitered in the men's sportswear, his hands in his pockets, touching nothing, not really looking.

Connell beeped. "What's he doing?"

"Killing time," Lucas said. A short elderly lady stopped to look at him, and he turned away. "Can you see him?"

"He's two aisles over."

"Careful. You're too close. Sloan?"

"Yeah, I got him. I'm going over to the north exit. That's the closest way out now. I'll go on through the skyway if he moves that way."

"Good. Del?"

"Just coming up to sportswear. I can't see him, but I'm right across from Connell. I can see Connell."

"You're real close to him. He's behind the shirt rack," Connell chirped.

"Excuse me, could you tell me where men's bathrobes are?" Lucas turned around, and looked down at the short elderly lady. She had ear curls like a lamb, and small thick glasses.

"Down by that post where you see the Exit sign," Lucas said.

"Thank you," she said, and tottered away.

Lucas angled through Ralph Lauren into Guess. A blond woman in a black dress stepped up to him and said, "Escape?"

"What?" He stepped toward her, and she stepped back and held up a cylindrical bottle as though she were defending herself.

"Just a spritz?"

Men's perfume. "Oh, no, I'm sorry," Lucas said, moving on. The woman looked after him.

Koop was moving, and Connell beeped. "He's headed toward the north door. Still moving slow."

"I've got him," Lucas said.

Sloan said, "I'm going through the skyway."

"I'll move into Sloan's spot," Del said. "Meagan, you've been the most exposed, you either oughta go through way ahead or stay back."

"It's too soon to go through ahead of him," Connell said. "I'll hang back."

"I'll catch up to you," Lucas said.

Lucas moved up to a glass case of Coach briefcases and looked down the store at Koop's back. Koop had stopped again, no more than thirty feet away, poking a finger through a rack of leather jackets. Lucas stepped back, focused on Koop, when a hand hooked his elbow. A youngish man in a suit was behind him, another to his left. The perfume woman was behind them.

"May I ask you what you're doing?" the man in the suit asked. Store security, a tough guy, with capped teeth. Lucas stepped hard behind the counter, out of sight of Koop, the two men lurching along with him. The security man's grip tightened.

"I'm a Minneapolis homicide cop on surveillance," Lucas said, his voice low and mean, like a hatchet. He reached into his pocket, pulled his badge case, flipped it open. "If you give me away, I'll pull your fucking testicles off and stuff them in your ears."

"Jesus." The security man looked at the bug in Lucas's ear, then at his face, at what looked like rage. He went pale. "Sorry."

"Get the fuck out of this end of the store, all of you," Lucas said. He pointed the other way. "Go that way. Go separately. Don't walk in the aisles and don't look back."

"I'm . . ." the man was stuttering. "I'm sorry, I used to be a cop."

"Yeah, right." Lucas turned away and sidled out from behind the case. Koop was gone. "Shit."

Connell beeped. "He's moving."

ROUX WAS SCARED TO DEATH. Connell's idea had scared her so badly that she thought about switching back to Gauloises.

But Jensen had come to see her the day before, wearing a power suit and carrying a power briefcase, and she'd laid it out: a sucker game might be the only way to take him.

Roux, stuck between a rock and a hard place, had gone for the hard place.

"Thanks," Connell had said to Jensen when they were in the hall outside of Roux's office. "Takes guts."

"I want to get him so bad that my teeth hurt," Jensen had said. "When will he get out?"

"Tomorrow morning," Connell had said. Her eyes defocused, as though she were looking into the future.

"And you," Jensen said to Lucas. "Did I tell you, you remind me of my older brother?"

"He must be a good-looking guy," Lucas said.

"God, I'm sick, and he's trying to push me under," Connell groaned. "The nausea is overwhelming. . . ."

They'd tracked him from the moment Koop had left the jail. Took him home, put him to bed. Everything was visual: all the tracking devices had temporarily been taken off the truck. If he thought about his arrest, he might wonder how they'd picked him up at a liquor store.

The next day, he'd left the house a little earlier than usual. He'd gone to his gym, worked out. Then he drove to a park, and ran. That had been a nightmare. They weren't ready for it, they were all in street shoes. They'd lost him a half-dozen times, but never for more than a minute or two, when he was running hills.

"This guy," Lucas said when they watched him run back to the truck, "is not somebody to fuck with. He just did three miles at a dead run. There are pro fighters in worse shape than he is."

"I'd take him on," Connell said.

Lucas looked at her. "Bullshit."

The Ruger was in a mufflike opening of her handbag, and she slipped it out in one motion. Big hands. She spun the cylinder. "I would," she said.

After the park, Koop went home. Stayed for an hour. Started out again, and wound up pulling the team through the skyways, right up to Jensen.

"WHERE'S HE GOING?" Connell asked as Lucas caught up. She took his arm, made them into a couple, a different look. "Is he going after her?"

"He's headed in her direction," Lucas said. They were closing a bit, and Lucas turned her around, spoke into the radio. "Sloan, Del, you got him. He's coming through."

"It's ten minutes to five," Connell said. "She gets off about now."

Sloan beeped. "Where is he?"

Del: "He's stopped halfway across, he's looking down at the street."

Lucas pulled Connell to one side. "Walk across the entrance sideways, glance down there. Don't come back if he's looking this way."

She nodded, walked across the aisle that led to the skyway, glanced to her left, continued across, looked back, and said, "He's just looking out." She waited a moment, then crossed back to Lucas, again glancing down the skyway.

"He's moving," she said to her radio.

"Got him," said Del. "He's out of the skyway."

"Coming through," Lucas said. "Raider-Garrote's in the Exchange Building."

Another department store separated them from the Exchange Building, but Koop didn't linger. He was moving quickly now, glancing at his watch. He went through the next skyway, Sloan out in front of him, Del breaking off to the side, then dashing down half a block and recrossing in a parallel skyway, turning back toward the surveillance team.

Lucas and Connell split up, single again, Connell now carrying her huge purse in one hand, like a briefcase. Lucas put the hat on.

"Sloan?"

"It's going down, man," Sloan said, sounding like he might be out of breath. "Something's gonna happen. I'm going past Raider-Garrote right now. I'm gonna stop here, in case he goes in, pulls some shit."

"Christ, Del, move up. . . ."

"I'm coming, I'm coming. . . ."

Connell moved back to him. "What're we doing?" she asked.

"Get close, but not too close. I'm gonna call Sara." Connell strode away, her gun hand resting on top of her purse. Lucas fumbled in his breast pocket, pulled out the cellular phone, pushed the memory-dial and the number 7. A moment later, the phone rang and Jensen picked it up.

"It's happening," Lucas said. "He's right outside your door. Don't look directly at him if you can avoid it. He'll see the trap in your eyes."

"Okay. I'm just leaving," Jensen said. She sounded calm enough; he felt like there might be a small smile in her voice.

"You'll take the elevator up?"

"Like always," she said.

LUCAS CALLED THE OTHER THREE, explained. Del came up and they started off together, Sloan interrupting: "Here he comes. And Connell's right behind him."

"We're coming in," Lucas said. "Del's coming first. You better move out of sight, Sloan. What's he doing?"

"He's looking through the windows . . . I see Connell."

DEL TOTTERED ON AHEAD, perfect as a skyway wanderer, a little drunk, nowhere to go, staying inside until the stores closed, and moving out on the streets for the night. People looked away from him—even through him—but not at him.

"I just went by him," he called back to Lucas. "He's looking through the window, like he's reading the numbers off their boards. Jensen's on the way out."

"I just walked back past him," Sloan said. "Del, you better get out of sight for a minute."

"I'm coming," Lucas said.

There was a moment of silence. Lucas was conspicuous, loitering in the skyway, and he crossed to a newsstand cut as a notch into the skyway wall. Sloan came on. "Jensen's out. He's walking away, same way I am, coming at you, Lucas."

"I'm going into the newsstand," Lucas said. "I'll pick him up."

A moment later Sloan said, "Christ, Lucas, put your radio away. I think he's coming in there."

Lucas turned it off, slipped it into his pocket, grabbed a copy of *The Economist* from the newsstand, opened it, turned his back to the entrance. A second later, Koop came in and looked around. Lucas glanced at him from the corner of his eye. The store was just big enough for the two of them plus the gum counter with a bored teenager behind it. Koop took down a magazine, opened it. Lucas felt him turn toward the skyway, glanced at him again. Koop's back was turned, and he was looking over the top of the magazine. Waiting for Jensen.

Sloan walked by, kept going. Koop was close enough that Lucas could smell him, a light scent of aging jock-sweat. People were streaming by the doorway as offices closed throughout the building, mostly women, a few of them still wearing the old eighties uniform of blue suit and after-work running shoes. Koop never looked at Lucas: he was completely focused on the skyway.

A man came in and said, "Give me a pack of Marlboros and a box of Clorets." The girl gave them to him, and he paid, opened the cigarettes, and threw all but two of them in a trash can and walked away.

"Doesn't want his wife to know," the girl said to Lucas.

"I guess." Shit. Koop would look at him.

Koop didn't. He tossed the magazine back on the rack and hurried out. Lucas looked after him. Just down the skyway, he saw Connell's blond hair and Jensen's black. He put the magazine back, and started after Koop, using the radio again.

"They're coming at you, Sloan. Del, where are you?"

"Coming up from behind. Sloan said you were pinned, and I stayed back in case he came that way. I'm coming up."

"Elevators," Connell grunted.

"I'm coming," Lucas said. "Del, Sloan, you better get your rides."

Sloan and Del acknowledged and Lucas said, "Greave, you guys ready?"

"We're ready." They were in the van, on the street.

"Elevator," Lucas said. He took the bug out of his ear, put it in his pocket.

Koop was facing the elevator door, waiting for it to return. He'd be the first on. Four other people waited, including Jensen and Connell. Jensen stood directly behind Koop's broad back, staring at the seam at his neck. Connell was beside her. Lucas edged in, just in front of Connell.

The elevator light went white, and the doors opened. Koop stepped in, pushed a button. Lucas stepped in beside him, turned the other way, pushed the button for Jensen's floor. Connell moved in on the other side of Lucas, in the corner, where Koop couldn't see her face. Lucas stood a half-step from the back of the elevator, quarter-turned toward Connell. Koop had never gotten a straight-on look at them, but they couldn't do this again, not for a couple of days. Jensen and another woman got on last, Jensen stepping immediately in front of Koop. The doors closed and they started up. Lucas couldn't see Koop, couldn't look at him. He said, "Long day," to Connell, who said, "Aren't they all . . . I think Del's coming down with a cold."

Elevator talk. The woman beside Jensen turned to look at Lucas, and Jensen stepped back a bit, her butt bumping the front of Koop's pants. "Sorry," she mumbled, flashing a glance back at him.

When they got off, Lucas and Connell got off behind her. The doors closed and Koop went on up. He was parked on seven.

"I saw that," Connell said to Jensen, grinning. "You're the bitch from hell."

"Thank you," Jensen said.

"Don't do it again," Lucas said as they walked toward the cars. "Right now, we're golden. A little too much, and we're screwed."

KOOP FOLLOWED JENSEN OUT to a small strip shopping center; waited outside while she bought groceries.

"He's gonna do it," Connell said. She was watching him with the binoculars. She sounded elated and grim at the same time, like a burned survivor of a plane crash.

"He hasn't looked away from the door since she went in. He's totally focused. He's gonna do it."

Koop tracked Jensen back to her apartment, the pod of cops all around him, running the parallel streets, ahead and behind, switching off. Jensen rolled into the parking ramp. Koop stopped, watched for a few minutes from his truck, then began wandering, out on the interstates. He did a complete loop of the Cities, driving I-494 and I-694.

"Go on back, you fucker," Connell hissed at him. "Get back there."

At nine o'clock, they sat at a stoplight and watched two middle-aged men on a par-three golf course, one with white hair and the other with a crew cut, trying to play in the quickly closing darkness. The crew cut missed a two-foot putt, Lucas shook his head, and Koop moved on.

Ten minutes later, he was on I-35, heading north. Through the Minneapolis loop—and then, like a satellite in a degrading orbit, watched as he was slowly pulled back toward Jensen's apartment.

"He's headed in," Lucas said. "I'm breaking off, I'll beat him there. If he changes direction, let me know."

He ran the backstreets, Connell calling Jensen on the cellular phone. A minute later they rolled into Jensen's parking garage, dumped the car.

"Where is he?" Lucas asked the radio.

"He's coming," Greave answered. Greave was riding the van. "I think he's looking for a parking place."

"Let's get set up, gang," Lucas said. Then the elevator came, and he and Connell rode up.

Jensen met them at the door. "He's coming?"

"Maybe," Lucas said, stepping past her. "He's just outside."

"He's coming," Connell said. "I can feel him. He's coming."

33

FROM THE MOMENT he'd left the jail, Koop had been consumed by his hunger for the woman.

Couldn't think of anything else.

Worked out, muscles still sore from jail, until he was loose again. Took a shower, thought about Jensen.

Went for a run in Braemar Park, up and over the hills. Went to an Arby's, ordered a sandwich, wandered away without it. The counter girl had to catch him in the parking lot. Thinking about Sara Jensen.

Then, in the elevator, he was crowded against the back of some big dude in an expensive suit, and Sara stood just in front of him. Halfway up, she stepped back and gave him another butt-rub. Yes.

She knew about him, all right.

This was the second time.

No mistake.

Koop drove the Cities, barely aware of the road, and found himself, just after dark, coming up to Sara Jensen's apartment house. He walked across the street and looked up. Frowned. The light wasn't quite right. She'd pulled one of the drapes in the bedroom at least partway.

Koop felt a pulse of danger: had they figured out the roof? Were they waiting up there? But if they had, she'd never have pulled the drapes. They'd leave everything alone.

No matter.

He'd go up anyway. . . .

"HE'S INSIDE," Greave called. "He had a key." Greave was still on the street, with the van. Del and Sloan had taken the elevators up as soon as it appeared that Koop was looking for parking. Sloan would wait at another apartment. Del was on his way to the roof.

"He did that couple, the woman across the street. To get the guy's keys," Connell said. "For sure."

Lucas said, "Yes."

Connell was sitting on the kitchen floor, below the counter. Lucas was in the hallway between the living room and Jensen's bedroom. Jensen was sitting on her bed. She'd partially pulled the drapes in her bedroom, so there was a two-foot-wide slit in them. Lucas had objected: "We should leave things the way they were."

"Wrong," she'd said. "I know what I'm doing."

She sounded so sure of herself that he let it go. Now he stood up and stepped toward her room. "Cameras," he said. "Action."

She stood up. She was wearing a white terry-cloth bathrobe, and showed bare legs and feet. "I'm set," she said. "Tell me what he's doing when you get it from Del."

"Sure. Don't look at me when I'm talking. Just keep reading."

They'd decided that she'd be reading in bed. Koop would be able to see most of her through the slot in the drapes. She picked up copies of the *Wall Street Journal* and *Investor's Daily*, spread them around, and dropped on the bed. "I'm a little jumpy."

"Remember: when I say get out, you don't do a thing but get," Lucas said.

They had an apartment down the hall, an older woman recommended by the manager. She'd agreed to let them use her apartment as long as she could be around for the action. Lucas had been unhappy, but she'd been firm, and he had finally given in. The woman was there now, opening the door for Sloan. Greave and the van waited on the street, with two more guys from intelligence.

When Koop entered Jensen's building—if he did—Greave and his partners would turn off the elevators from the main-floor control box, and seal the stairs. At the same time, Jensen would go to the woman's apartment, with Sloan, for safekeeping. Del would come off the roof, down the stairs, step into a maintenance closet at the other end of the hall.

When Koop arrived at Jensen's, they'd wait until he'd made a move at the door—tried to unlock it, tried to break it. Lucas would give the word, and Sloan would take him from one end of the hall, Del from the other. Lucas and Connell would come out of the apartment. Four-on-one.

Connell had her pistol out, checking it. She'd fed it with safety slugs. They'd rip massive holes in a slab of meat, but would pretty much fall apart when they hit a wall. She held the gun with the barrel up, her finger alongside the trigger guard, her cheek against the cylinder.

"On the roof. He's on the roof," Del called from Jensen's roof. He was breathing hard: he'd beaten Koop up to the top by thirty seconds. A moment later: "He's on the air conditioner."

KOOP PULLED HIMSELF UP, crawled to his protective vent, looked across the street. Sara was there, on the bed, reading. He'd seen her doing this twenty times, prowling through her papers. He put the Kowa scope on her and saw that she was looking through long lists of tables. Her concentration was intense. She turned a page.

She was wearing a white terry-cloth robe, the first time he'd seen it. He approved. It set off her dark, dramatic looks like nothing else would. If her hair had only been wet, she'd have looked like a movie star, on stage. . . .

. . .

"HE'S ON THE AIR CONDITIONER," Lucas said quietly to Jensen. She showed no sign that she'd heard, although she had.

"He's got a scope, and he's watching her," Del said. "Christ, he must feel like he's inside the room with her."

"I'm sure he does," Connell murmured into her headset. Lucas looked across at her: the gun was still against her cheek.

Jensen put down her newspaper and rolled off the bed, wandered toward the bathroom. This was not part of the script. "What?" Lucas asked.

She didn't answer, just ran water in the bathroom for a moment, then walked back out. The bathrobe had fallen open. Lucas was looking at her back, but he had a feeling . . .

JENSEN CAME OUT OF the bathroom. The bathrobe had fallen open, and she was wearing only underpants beneath it. Her breasts looked wonderful against the terry cloth, alternately exposed and hidden. She was apparently upset by something. She spent a few minutes pacing, back and forth across the gap in the curtains, sometimes exposed, sometimes not. All told, it was the best strip show Koop had ever seen. His heart caught in his throat each time she passed the window.

Then she dropped on the bed again, on one elbow, facing him, one breast showing, and began going through the papers. Then she rolled onto her back, bare legs folded, feet flat on the bed, knees up, head up on a pillow, the robe open again, breasts flattening of their own weight. . . .

Koop groaned with the heat of it. He nearly couldn't bear to watch it. *Absolutely* couldn't bear to take his eyes away.

LUCAS SWALLOWED, glanced back at Connell. She wasn't getting any of this. She simply sat, staring sightlessly at a cupboard. He looked back at Jensen, on the bed. Jensen's eyes had flicked toward him once, and he thought he saw the thinnest crease of a smile. Jesus. He began to feel what Koop did, the physical pull of the woman. She gave off some kind of weird Italianate hormone-cooking vibrations. Where'd she'd get the name Jensen? Had to be a married name; whatever was bubbling out of the woman on the bed, it wasn't Scandinavian.

Lucas swallowed again.

If there was such a thing as a politically correct cop manual, this would be specifically outlawed. But Lucas had no objection: if this didn't do it to Koop, nothing would.

SARA GOT OUT OF BED again, robe open, went into the bathroom, closed the door. When she did this, she usually stayed awhile.

Koop dropped back behind the ventilator duct, tried to light a cigarette. Found that the cigarette was damp, realized that he was soaked with sweat.

He couldn't do this. He had the hard-on of a lifetime. He found his knife, pushed the button. The blade sprang out like a serpent's tongue.

Time to go.

"HE'S DOWN," DEL SAID. "Holy shit, he's down. He's walking across the roof, he's through the door. . . ."

"Greave, you hear that? It's on you, man," Lucas said.

"We got it," Greave said.

Lucas stepped into the bedroom. "Sara. Time to go."

Jensen came out of the bathroom, the robe tied tight. "He's coming?"

"Maybe. He's off the roof, anyway," Lucas said. She felt vulnerable, intimate; he'd seen the show too. "Get your slippers."

Jensen got her slippers, a bundle of clothes, and her purse, and then they waited, waited, Jensen standing next to Lucas. He felt protective, sort of big-brotherly. Sort of . . .

"He's out the door," Greave called. "He's crossing the street."

"I'm coming down," Del said.

Greave: "He's got a key for that one, too, he's coming in, he's in the building. . . ."

"He's coming," Lucas said to Jensen. "Go."

Jensen left, running down the hall in her robe, with her purse and clothes, like a kid on her way to a slumber party. Connell, on her feet, moved back to the living room, still with the dreamy look in her eyes, the gun in her hand.

Lucas went with her, caught her arm. "I don't want any dumb-shit stuff. You've got a weird look about you. If you pull the trigger on the guy, you're just as likely to hit Del or Sloan. They'll be coming in a hurry."

She looked up at him and said, " 'Kay."

"Look, I fuckin' mean it," he said harshly. "This is no time . . ."

"I'm fine," she said. "It's just that I've been waiting a long time for this. Now we got him. I'm still alive for it."

Worried, Lucas left her and moved into the kitchen.

As soon as Koop opened the door, Lucas would hit it with his body weight. The unexpected impact should blow Koop back into the hallway. Del and Sloan would be coming, and Lucas would jerk the door open, be right on top of the guy. Greave and the other two would be on the stairs, coming up. . . .

They had him sewn up. They might already have enough for a trial, just with the entry across the street and the peeping.

But if he cracked Jensen's door, they had him for everything. If he just cracked it . . .

KOOP WENT QUICKLY through the building straight to the stairs, pulled open the door and into the stairwell. Before the door shut completely, he thought he heard a *flap-click*.

What? He froze, listening. Nothing. Nothing at all. He started up, silently, listening at each landing, then padding up another.

"HE'S TAKING THE STAIRS," Greave called. "He's not in the elevators. He's on the stairs."

"Got it," said Lucas. "Del?"

"I'm set."

"Sloan?"

"Ready."

KOOP WOUND AROUND the concrete stairs. What had that been, the *flap-click*? Like somebody running in the stairwell, a footfall and a door closing. Whatever it was, it had come from high in the building. Maybe even Jensen's floor. Koop got to the top, reached toward the door to the hall. And stopped. *Flap-click?*

There was one more flight of stairs above him, going to the roof of Jensen's building. Was he in a hurry? Not that much, he thought. Cat burglar: move slow . . .

He climbed the last flight, used his key—Sara's key—to let himself out on the roof. Nice night. Soft stars, high humidity, a little residual warmth from the day. He walked silently to the edge of the roof. Jensen's apartment would be the third balcony from the end.

At the edge of the roof, he looked over. Jensen's balcony was twelve feet below him. A four-foot drop, if he hung from the edge. Nothing at all. Unless he missed—then it was a forever and a day down to the street. But he couldn't miss. The balcony was six feet wide and fifteen feet long.

He looked across the street, at the apartment building where'd he'd spent some many good nights. There were lights, but only a few windows with the drapes undrawn, and nobody in those.

Twelve feet. *Flap-click.*

"WHERE'N THE FUCK IS HE?" Del asked from his closet. "Greave? You see him?"

"Must be on the stairs," Greave said. "You want me to go up?"

"No-no, stay put," Lucas said.

Connell was listening to the conversation through her earplug, and almost missed the light-footed *whop* fifteen feet away. With Lucas's "No-no," in her ear, she didn't even know where it came from, didn't think about it much, looked to her right. . . .

KOOP LANDED IN FRONT of the open balcony door, softly, both feet at once, absorbing the shock with his knees. The first thing he saw, there in the fish-bowl, was the blonde with the pistol beside her face, one hand to her head, pressed against the wall, waiting for the hallway door to open.

Koop didn't need to think about it. *He knew.* And he had no way out. The rage was there, ready, and it blew out.

Koop screamed and charged the woman on the wall. . . .

CONNELL SAW HIM COMING when he was ten feet away, had less than a half second to react. The scream froze her, the words in her ear scrambled her, and then Koop hit her, an open-handed blow to the side of her head. The blow knocked her down, stunned her, and then he was on top of her and there was blood in her mouth and the pistol was gone.

LUCAS HEARD THE SCREAM and turned and saw Koop hurtle past the archway to the living room wall, and he screamed "He's here he's here" into the headset and he ran toward the living room, where Koop and Connell were in a pile. Her pistol skittered across the rug and disappeared half under a couch. Koop's back was toward him, rolling over on Connell. Lucas couldn't use the pistol, not with Connell there; instead he raised it over his head and swung it at the back of Koop's head. Koop felt it coming: he cranked his body half around, one eye finding Lucas, the blow already on the way. Koop had time to bunch his shoulder and flinch, and the barrel hit him on the big muscle of his shoulder and Koop somehow found his feet and was coming at Lucas.

This was no boxing match. Koop launched himself straight up, came straight in, and Lucas hit him hard with a roundhouse left, but Koop blew through it as though he'd been hit with a marshmallow and his arms wrapped around Lucas's ribs.

Lucas and Koop staggered backward, together, wrapped up like drunken dancers, banging around inside the small kitchen, the pressure from Koop's arms like a machine-press around Lucas's chest, crushing him. Lucas slapped him on the side of the head with the pistol, but couldn't get a good swing. Feeling as though his spine might break, he finally pressed the pistol to Koop's ear and pulled the trigger, the slug going up through the ceiling.

The noise of the explosion an inch from his ear blew Koop's head back, stunned him like the blows hadn't. Lucas caught a breath, but a bad one: pain lanced through his chest, as though a bone were being pulled loose. Broken ribs. He caught the breath and hammered Koop once in the face, and then Koop stepped back and caught Lucas in the ribs with a short roundhouse. Lucas felt the ribs go, felt himself bounced by the blow, helplessly pulled his elbows in. He took one blow there, slapped the pistol weakly at Koop's face, cutting him, not breaking him, and Koop was crushing him again, Lucas wiggling, trying to hit, both of them crashing back and forth across the kitchen. Lucas could hear the beating on the outer door, people shouting, strained to look that way, Koop crushing him, crushing . . .

CONNELL LANDED ON Koop's back. She had short square nails but big hands and powerful fingers, and she dug them into Koop's small eyes, not more than two inches from Lucas's face. He saw her fingers dig in, way in, pulling at Koop's eye sockets, and thought, deep at the back of his mind, *Christ, she's blinded him.* . . . And she sunk her teeth into Koop's neck, her face contorted with hate, like a rabid animal's.

Koop screamed and let go of Lucas, and Lucas hit him again in the face, cutting him more, still not putting him down. Connell's fingers went deeper in his eyes and Koop bucked, tried to throw her. Her feet came off the floor and wrapped around his waist, her middle fingers digging into his skull, Koop screaming, twisting, dancing, reeling, Lucas hitting him, closing on him.

Then Koop, with a wild, blind, backhanded spin and swing, caught Lucas on the side of the head, coming in. Lucas lost everything for a moment, like a blown switch knocking out the lights in a house. Everything went dim for a moment, and he lost his feet, rolled back against a cupboard, scrambled up, headed back toward the twisting pair of them, Koop trying to wrench the woman free.

Still she rode him, and she was screeching now, like a madwoman. . . .

The door popped open and Sloan was there with his pistol, aiming at them, starting across, Lucas a stumbling step in front of him as Koop staggered backward, onto the balcony.

Connell felt him bump the railing just below his hips. She looked down. She was actually over. She unwrapped her legs, stood on the metal rail, saw Lucas coming. . . .

AND LUCAS SCREAMED at her: MEAGAN . . .

Connell, wrapped into Koop, pumped her powerful legs once, backward, and they both flipped together over the railing and out into the night.

LUCAS, TWO STEPS AWAY, dove then, actually touched Koop's foot, lost it, smashed into the railing, felt himself caught by Sloan. He leaned over the rail and saw them go.

Connell's eyes were open. She loosened her grip on Koop's head during the fall, and at the end, they were in a splayed-out star shape, like sky divers.

All the way to sidewalk.

And forever.

"JESUS CHRIST," SLOAN SAID. He looked from Lucas to the railing to Lucas again. Blood was pouring from Lucas's nose, down his shirt, and he was standing with one shoulder a foot lower than the other, crippled, hung over the balcony.

"Jesus H. Christ, Lucas. . . ."

34

LUCAS SAT IN HIS vinyl chair, staring at the television. A movie was playing, something about an average American family that was actually a bunch of giant bugs trying to blow up an atomic power plant and one of the kid-bugs smoked dope. He couldn't follow it, didn't care.

He couldn't think about Connell. He'd thought about her all he could, had considered all the different moves he might have made. He made himself believe, for a while, that she was ready to die. That she wanted it. That this was better than cancer.

Then he stopped believing it. She was dead. He didn't want her to be dead. He still had things to say to her. Too late.

Now he'd stopped thinking about her. She'd come back, in a few hours, and over the next days, and the next few weeks. And he'd never forget her eyes, looking back up at him. . . .

Ghost eyes. He'd be seeing them for a while.

But not now.

A door opened in the back of the house. Weather wasn't due for three hours. Lucas stood, painfully, stepped toward the door.

"Lucas?" Weather's voice, worried, inquiring. Her high heels snapped on the kitchen's tile floor.

Lucas stepped into the hallway. "Yeah?"

"Why are you standing up?" she asked. She was angry with him.

"I thought you were operating."

"Put it off," she said. She regarded him gravely from six feet away, a small woman, tough. "How do you feel?"

"I hurt when I breathe . . . Is the TV truck still out there?"

"No. They've gone." She was carrying a big box.

"Good. What's that?"

"One of those TV dinner trays," she said. "I'll set it up in the den so you don't have to move."

"Thanks . . ." He nodded and hobbled back to the vinyl chair, where he sat down very carefully.

Weather looked at the television. "What in God's name are you watching?

"I don't know," he said.

.   .   .

THE DOCTORS IN THE emergency room had held him overnight, watching his blood pressure. Blunt trauma was a possibility, they'd said. He had four cracked ribs. One of the doctors, who looked like he was about seventeen, said Lucas wouldn't be able to sneeze without pain until the middle of the summer. He sounded pleased by his prognosis.

WEATHER TOSSED HER PURSE onto another chair, waved her arms. "I don't know what to do," she said finally, looking down at him.

"What do you mean?"

"I'm afraid to touch you. With the ribs." She had tears in her eyes. "I need to touch you, and I don't know what to do."

"Come over and sit on my lap," he said. "Just sit very carefully."

"Lucas, I can't. I'd push on you," she said. She stepped closer.

"It'll be okay, as long as I don't move quick. It's quick that hurts. If you sort of snuggle onto my lap. . . ."

"If you're sure it won't hurt," she said.

The snuggling hurt only a little, and made everything feel better. He closed his eyes after a while and went to sleep, with her head on his chest.

AT SIX O'CLOCK, they watched the news together.

Roux triumphant.

And generous, and sorrowful, all at once. She paraded the detectives who worked on the case, all except Del, who hated his face to be seen. She mentioned Lucas a half-dozen times as the mastermind of the investigation. She painted a mournful portrait of Connell struggling for women's rights, dedicating herself to the destruction of the monster.

The mayor spoke. The head of the Bureau of Criminal Apprehension took a large slice of the credit. The president of the AFSCME said she could never be replaced. Connell's mother flew in from Bimidji, and cried.

Wonderful television, much of it anchored by Jan Reed.

"I was so scared," Weather said. "When they called . . ."

"Poor Connell," Lucas said. Reed had great eyes.

"Fuck Connell," Weather said. "And fuck you too. I was scared for myself. I didn't know what I'd do if you'd been killed."

"You want me to quit the cops?"

She looked at him, smiled, and said, "No."

Another television report showed the front of Lucas's house. Why, he didn't know. Another was shot from the roof of the apartment across the street from Jensen's, looking right into Jensen's place. The word *fishbowl* was used.

"Makes my blood run cold," Weather said. She shivered.

"Hard to believe," Lucas said. "A hot-blooded Finn."

"Well, it does. It's absolutely chilling."

Lucas looked at her, thought about her ass, that day in the bathroom. The aesthetic ass that led to all of this . . .

Lucas urged her off his lap, stood up, creaking, hurting. He stretched carefully, like an old arthritic tomcat, one piece at a time, and suddenly his smile flicked on and he looked happy.

The change was so sudden that Weather actually stepped away from him. "What?" she asked. Maybe the pain had flipped him out. "You better sit down."

"You're a beautiful woman, with a good mind and a better-than-average ass," he said.

"What?" Really perplexed.

"I gotta run into town," he said.

"Lucas, you can't." Angry now.

"I'm stoned on Advil," he said. "I'll be all right. Besides, the docs said I'm not that badly injured, I'm just gonna have a little pain."

"Lucas, I've had a broken rib," she said. "I know what it feels like. What could be important enough . . . ?"

"It's important," he said. "And it won't take long. When I get back, you can kiss the hurt for me."

He walked very carefully down toward the garage, feeling each and every bruise. Weather tagged behind. "Maybe I should drive you."

"No, I'm okay, really," he said. In the kitchen, he picked up the phone, dialed, got homicide and asked for Greave. Greave picked up.

"Man, I thought you were incommunicado," Greave said.

"You know that kid that does chores over at the Eisenhower Docks?" Lucas asked.

"Yeah?"

"Get him. Hold him there. I'll meet you in the lobby. And bring one of the cellulars, I'm gonna want to make a phone call."

GREAVE WAS WAITING IN the lobby when Lucas arrived. He was wearing jeans and a T-shirt under a light wool sports jacket, with his pistol clipped over his left front pelvic point, like Lucas. The kid was sitting in a plastic chair, looking scared. "What's going on, sir?" he asked.

"Let's go up on the roof," Lucas said, leading them toward the elevator. Inside, he pushed the button for the top floor.

"What're we doing up there?" Greave asked. "You've got something?"

"Well, Koop's gone, so we oughta solve this case," Lucas said. "Since the kid here won't talk, I thought we'd hold him off the roof by his ankles until he gave us something we could use."

"Sir?" The kid squeezed back against the elevator wall.

"Just kidding," Lucas said. He grinned, painfully, but the kid still pressed against the wall of the elevator. From the top floor, they walked up the short flight of stairs to the roof, wedged the door open, and Lucas asked, "Did you bring the phone?"

"Yeah." Greave fumbled in his pocket and pulled it out. "Tell me, goddamnit."

Lucas walked to the air-conditioner housing. The housing was new, no sign of rust on its freshly painted metal. "When did they put this in?" he asked the kid.

"When they were remodeling the building. A year ago, maybe."

High up on the edge of it was the manufacturer's tag with a service phone number, just like the tag he'd seen on the air conditioner across from Sara Jensen's building. Lucas opened the portable and dialed the number.

"Lucas Davenport, deputy chief, Minneapolis Police Department," he told the woman who answered. "I need to talk to the service manager. Yeah, it has to do with repair work on one of your installations."

Greave and the kid watched him as he waited, then: "Yes, Davenport, D-a-v-e-n-p-o-r-t. We're conducting a homicide investigation. We need to know if you repaired an air conditioner at the Eisenhower Docks apartment complex last month. You installed it about a year ago. Huh? Uh, well, you could call the department and ask. Then you could call me back . . . Okay." Lucas looked at Greave, his ear to the phone. To Greave he said, grinning, "He's got to call up a listing on his computer, but he doesn't remember it."

"What?" Greave was as perplexed as Weather. He looked at the air conditioner, then at the kid. The kid shrugged.

Lucas said into the phone, "You didn't? Isn't it under warranty? Un-huh. And that would cover all repairs, right? Okay. Listen, a detective named Greave will be coming over to take a statement from you later today. We'll try to make it before five o'clock."

Lucas rang off, folded the phone, handed it back to Greave, and looked at the kid. "When I talked to you, you said you were helping Ray with the air-conditioning."

"Yeah. It was broke."

"But nobody came from the air-conditioner company?"

"Not that I saw." The kid swallowed.

"What'd you do to it?" Lucas asked.

"Well, I don't know. I just handed him screwdrivers and helped him take shit apart. Sir."

"The ducts."

"Those big tubes," the kid said. *Ducts* wasn't solid in his vocabulary.

"You didn't mess with the motor or anything."

"No, sir, not me. Not anybody. Just the tubes."

"What?" asked Greave. "What? What?"

"They froze her," Lucas said.

GREAVE HALF-SMILED. "You're fuckin' joking."

"Well. Not exactly froze. They killed her with hypothermia," Lucas said. "She was an older woman, underweight because of her thyroid condition. She took sleeping pills every night with a beer, or maybe two. Cherry knew about the pills and the booze. She apparently joked about her medicine. So he watched her window until her lights went out, waited a half hour, and turned on the air-conditioning. They pumped cold air meant for the entire building into that one apartment. I bet it was colder in her apartment than the inside of a refrigerator."

"Jesus," Greave said, scratching his chin. "Would that do it?"

Lucas nodded. "Everybody says it was hot inside, because the air-conditioning was broken. The pictures of the body showed her curled up on a sheet, no blanket, because it *was* hot when she lay down. By age and body weight, she was the kind of person most susceptible to hypothermia," Lucas said. "The only thing that would make somebody *even more* susceptible is booze."

Greave said, "Huh."

"The thing that cinches it," Lucas said, "is that the cheapest goddamn real estate hustlers in town never called for warranty service. The air conditioner is covered. The service guy just told me that they'll fix anything that goes wrong for five years. He said if a screw falls out of the housing, they'd come out and put it back in."

"I don't see . . ." Greave said, still not believing.

"Think about the body shots again, the photographs," Lucas said. "She was on her side, curled, fetal position, as if she might have been cold, and unconsciously trying to protect herself. But the drugs knocked her down and out. She couldn't get back up. And it worked: they killed her. Not only did it work, there was no sign of what they did. No toxicology. The doors were bolted, the windows were locked, the motion sensors were armed. They killed her with cold."

Greave looked at the kid. The kid said, "Jeez. I helped Ray disconnect all them tubes and put them back together, but I didn't know what he was doing."

"They ran the air conditioner after he pulled the tubes, I bet," Lucas said.

"Yeah. They said they was testing it," the kid said.

"Kiss my ass," said Greave, a sudden light in his eye. "They froze the old bat. A batsicle."

"I think so," Lucas said.

"Can I bust them?" Greave asked. "Let me bust 'em, huh?"

"It's your case," Lucas said. "But if I were you, I'd think about playing them off against each other. Offer one of them a plea. They're all assholes, every one of them. Now that you know how they did it, one of them'll turn on the others."

"Froze her," Greave said, marveling.

"Yeah," Lucas said, looking around off the roof at the city. He could see just a sliver of the Mississippi in the distance. "It makes your blood run cold, doesn't it?"

LUCAS STOPPED TO TALK to Roux, and told her about the batsicle. "Is your butt saved?"

"For the time being," she said. She sounded unhappy. "But you know . . ."

"What?"

She had a half-inch-thick sheaf of paper in her hands. "We've had seven bank robberies in the last two months, by the same people. There were two here in town, one in St. Paul, four in various suburbs. I'm starting to get some heat from the banking community."

"That's supposed to be the Feds," Lucas said. "The Feds do banks."

"The Feds don't want to run for the Senate," Roux said.

"Oh, my achin' ass . . ." Lucas groaned.

AS HE WAS LEAVING, he ran into Jan Reed, looking very good. "Oh, my God, I was was worried," she said, and she looked worried. She touched his chest with an open hand. "I heard you got banged around pretty badly."

"Not that bad," he said. He tried to chuckle in a manly way, but winced.

"You *look* beat up," she said. She glanced at her watch. "I've got an hour before I've got to be back at the station. . . . Would you have time to finish that croissant and coffee we started last time?"

Jesus, she was pretty.

"God, I'd like to," Lucas said. "But, you know . . . I gotta go home."